ALL CLEAR

Connie Willis

Copyright © Connie Willis 2010

The right of Connie Willis to be identified as the author
of this work has been asserted by her in accordance with the
Copyright, Designs and Patents Act 1988.

First published in Great Britain in 2011 by Gollancz
An imprint of the Orion Publishing Group
Orion House, 5 Upper St Martin's Lane,
London WC2H 9EA
An Hachette UK Company

This edition published in Great Britain in 2012 by Gollancz

1 3 5 7 9 10 8 6 4 2

A CIP catalogue record for this book
is available from the British Library

ISBN 978 0 575 09932 6

Typeset by Deltatype Ltd, Birkenhead, Merseyside

Printed in Great Britain by Clays Ltd, St Ives plc

The Orion Publishing Group's policy is to use papers that
are natural, renewable and recyclable products and made
from wood grown in sustainable forests. The logging and
manufacturing processes are expected to conform to the
environmental regulations of the country of origin.

To all the

ambulance drivers
firewatchers
air raid wardens
nurses
canteen workers
planespotters
rescue workers
mathematicians
vicars
vergers
shopgirls
chorus girls
librarians
debutantes
spinsters
fishermen
retired sailors
servants
evacuees
Shakespearean actors
and mystery novelists
who won the war.

LONDON – 26 OCTOBER 1940

By noon Michael and Merope still hadn't returned from Stepney, and Polly was beginning to get really worried. Stepney was less than an hour away by tube. There was no way it could take Merope and Michael – correction, *Eileen* and *Mike*; she *had* to remember to call them by their cover names – no way it could take them six hours to go and fetch Eileen's belongings from Mrs Willett's and come back to Oxford Street. What if there'd been a raid and something had happened to them? The East End was the most dangerous part of London—

There weren't any daytime raids on the twenty-sixth, she told herself. But there weren't supposed to have been five fatalities at Padgett's either. If Mike was right and he *had* altered events by saving the soldier Hardy at Dunkirk, anything was possible. The space-time continuum was a chaotic system, in which even a minuscule action could have an enormous effect ...

But two additional fatalities – and civilians, at that – could scarcely have changed the course of the war, even in a chaotic system. Thirty thousand civilians had been killed in the Blitz and nine thousand in the V-1 and V-2 attacks, and fifty million people had died in the war.

And you know *he didn't lose the war*, Polly thought. *And historians have been travelling to the past for more than forty years. If they'd been capable of altering events, they'd have done it long before this.* Mr Dunworthy had been in the Blitz and the French Revolution and even the Black Death, and his historians had observed wars and coronations and coups all across history, and there was no record of any of them even causing a discrepancy, let alone changing the course of history.

Which meant that in spite of appearances, the five fatalities at Padgett's weren't a discrepancy either. Marjorie must have misunderstood what the nurses said. She'd admitted she'd only overheard part of their conversation. Perhaps the nurses had been talking about the victims from another incident. The air-raid warden had said Marylebone had been hit last night, too, and Wigmore Street. And Polly knew from experience that ambulances sometimes transported victims to hospital from more than one incident. And that people one thought had been killed sometimes turned up alive.

But if she told Mike about her having thought the theatre troupe was dead, he'd demand to know why she hadn't known St George's would be destroyed and conclude that was a discrepancy as well. Which meant she needed to keep him from finding out about the five casualties at Padgett's till she'd had a chance to determine if there actually were that many.

Thank goodness he wasn't here when Marjorie came, she thought. *You should be glad they're late.*

And thank goodness Miss Snelgrove had taken Marjorie back to hospital, though it meant Polly hadn't had a chance to ask her what exactly the nurse had said. Polly had offered to take Marjorie there herself so she could ask the hospital staff about the fatalities, but their floor supervisor Miss Snelgrove had insisted on going, 'so I can give those nurses a piece of my mind. What were they thinking? And what were *you* thinking?' she'd scolded Marjorie. 'Coming here when you should be in bed?'

'I'm sorry,' Marjorie had said contritely. 'When I heard

Padgett's had been hit, I'm afraid I panicked and jumped to conclusions.'

Like Mike did when he saw the mannequins in front of Padgett's, Polly thought. *Like I did when I found out Eileen's drop in Backbury didn't open. And like I'm doing now. There's a logical explanation for why Marjorie heard the nurses say there were five fatalities instead of three, and for why no one's come to get us. It doesn't necessarily mean Oxford's been destroyed. Research might have got the date the quarantine ended wrong and not arrived at the manor till after Eileen had left for London to find me. And the fact that Mike and Eileen aren't back yet doesn't necessarily mean something's happened to them.* They might simply have had to wait till Theodore's mother returned from her shift at the aeroplane factory. Or they might have decided to go on to Fleet Street to collect Mike's things.

They'll be here any moment, she told herself. *Stop fretting over things you can't do anything about, and do something useful.*

She wrote out a list of the times and locations of the upcoming week's raids for Mike and Merope – correction, *Eileen* – and then tried to think of other historians who might be here besides Gerald Phipps. Mike had said there was a historian here from some time in October to December eighteenth. What had happened during that period that a historian might have come to observe? Nearly all the war activity had been in Europe – Italy had invaded Greece, and the Royal Navy had bombed the Italian fleet. What had happened here?

Coventry. But it couldn't be that. It hadn't been hit till November fourteenth, and a historian wouldn't need an entire month to get there.

The war in the North Atlantic? Several important convoys had been sunk during that period, but being on a destroyer had to be a ten. And if Mr Dunworthy was cancelling assignments that were too dangerous …

But anywhere in the autumn of 1940 was dangerous, and he'd

obviously approved something. The intelligence war? No, that hadn't really geared up till later, with the Fortitude and V-1 and V-2 rocket disinformation campaigns. Ultra had begun earlier, but it was not only a ten, it *had* to be a divergence point. If the Germans had found out their Enigma codes had been cracked, it surely would have affected the outcome of the war.

Polly looked over at the lifts. The centre one was stopping on third. *They're here. Finally*, she thought, but it was only Miss Snelgrove, shaking her head over the negligence of Marjorie's nurses. 'Disgraceful! I shouldn't be surprised if she had a relapse with all her running about,' she fumed. 'What are you doing here, Miss Sebastian? Why aren't you on your lunch break?'

Because I don't want to miss Mike and Eileen like I missed Eileen when I went to Backbury, but she couldn't say that. 'I was waiting till you got back, in case we had a rush.'

'Well, take it now,' Miss Snelgrove said.

Polly nodded and, when Miss Snelgrove went into the stockroom to take off her coat and hat, told Doreen to send word to her *immediately* if anyone came in asking for her.

'Like the airman you met last night?'

Who? Polly thought, and then remembered that was the excuse she'd given Doreen for needing to know the names of airfields. 'Yes,' she said, 'or my cousin who's coming to London, or anyone.'

'I promise I'll send the lift boy to fetch you the *moment* anyone comes. Now, go.'

Polly went, running downstairs first to look up and down Oxford Street and see if Mike and Eileen were coming, and then going up to ask the shop assistants in the lunchroom about airfields. By the end of her break, she had half a dozen names which began with the correct letters and/or had two words in their names.

She ran back down to third. 'Did anyone ask for me?' she asked Doreen, even though they obviously hadn't come.

'Yes,' Doreen said, 'not five minutes after you left.'

4

'But— I told you to send word to me!'

'I couldn't. Miss Snelgrove was watching me the entire time.'

I knew I shouldn't have left, Polly thought. *This is exactly like Backbury.*

'You needn't worry, she hasn't gone,' Doreen said. 'I told her you were on lunch break, and she said she had other shopping to do and she'd—'

'She? Only one person? Not a man and a girl?'

'Only one, and definitely *not* a girl. Forty if she was a day, greying hair in a bun, rather scraggy-looking—'

Miss Laburnum. 'Did she say what she was shopping for?' Polly asked.

'Yes,' Doreen said. 'Beach sandals.'

Of course.

'I sent her up to Shoes. I told her it was likely too late in the season for us to carry them, but she was determined to go and see. I'll watch your counter if you want to go— Oh, here she is,' she said as the lift opened.

Miss Laburnum emerged, carrying an enormous carpetbag. 'I went to see Mrs Wyvern and obtained the coats,' she said, setting the carpetbag on Polly's counter, 'and I thought I'd bring them along.'

'Oh, you needn't have—'

'It was no bother. I spoke to Mrs Rickett and she said yes, your cousin could share your room. I also went to see Miss Harding about the room for your Dunkirk friend. Unfortunately, she'd already let it, to an elderly gentleman whose house in Chelsea was bombed. Dreadful thing. His wife and daughter were both killed.' She clucked sympathetically. 'But Mrs Leary has a room to let. A second-floor back. Ten shillings the week with board.'

'Is she in Box Lane as well?' Polly asked, wondering what excuse she could give after Miss Laburnum had gone to all this trouble if it was in a street on Mr Dunworthy's forbidden list.

'No, she's just round the corner. In Beresford Court.'

Thank goodness. Beresford Court wasn't on the list either.

'Number nine,' Miss Laburnum said. 'She promised me she won't let it to anyone else till your friend's seen it. It should do very nicely. Mrs Leary is an excellent cook,' she added with a sigh and opened the carpetbag.

Polly caught a glimpse of bright green inside. *Oh no*, she thought. It hadn't even occurred to her when she'd asked Miss Laburnum about the coats that she might—

'I hoped to get a wool overcoat for your gentleman friend,' Miss Laburnum said, pulling out a tan raincoat, 'but this mackintosh was all they had. There were scarcely any ladies' coats either. Mrs Wyvern says more and more people are making do with last year's coats, and I fear the situation will only grow worse. The government's talking of rationing clothing next.' She stopped at the expression on Polly's face. 'I know it's not very warm—'

'No, it's just what he needs. There's been so much rain this autumn,' Polly said, but her eyes were on the carpetbag. She braced herself as Miss Laburnum reached in again.

'That's why I got your cousin this,' she said, pulling out a bright green umbrella. 'It's a frightful colour, I know, and it doesn't match the black coat I obtained for her, but this was the only one without any broken spokes. And if it's too gaudy for your cousin, I thought we might be able to use it in *The Admirable Crichton*. The green would show up well on stage.'

Or in a crowd, Polly thought.

'It's lovely – I mean, I know my cousin won't think it too bright, and I'm certain she'll lend it to us for the play,' Polly said, chattering in her relief.

Miss Laburnum laid the umbrella on the counter and pulled the black coat out of the carpetbag, then a black felt hat. 'They hadn't any black gloves, so I brought along a pair of my own. Two of the fingers are mended, but there's still wear in them.' She handed them to Polly. 'Mrs Wyvern said to tell you that if any of Padgett's employees are in a similar situation to send them to her, and she'll see they get coats as well.' She snapped the bag neatly shut. 'Now, do you know if Townsend Brothers sells plimsolls, and if so, where I might find them?'

'Plimsolls?' Polly said.

'Yes, I thought they might work instead of beach sandals. The sailors on board ship might have been wearing them, you see, when it sank. I asked in your shoe department, but they hadn't any. Sir Godfrey simply doesn't *realise* how filthy the station floors are – discarded food wrappings and cigarette ends and who knows what else. Two nights ago, I saw a man' – she leaned across the counter to whisper – '*spitting*. I quite understand that Sir Godfrey has more pressing things on his mind, but—'

'We may have some in the games department,' Polly said, cutting her off in mid-flow. 'It's on fifth. And if we're out of plimsolls,' which Polly was almost certain they would be, with rubber needed for the war effort, 'you mustn't worry. We'll think of something else.'

'Of course you will.' Miss Laburnum patted her arm. 'You're such a clever girl.'

Polly escorted her over to the lift and helped her into it. 'Fifth,' she said to the lift boy, and to Miss Laburnum, 'Thank you ever so much. It was terribly kind of you to do all this for us.'

'Nonsense,' Miss Laburnum said briskly. 'In difficult times like these, we must do all we can to help each other. Will you be at rehearsal tonight?' she asked as the lift boy pulled the door across.

'Yes,' Polly said, 'as soon as I get my cousin settled in.'

If she and Mike are back by then, she added silently as she went back to her counter, but she felt certain now they would be.

You were worried over nothing, she thought, picking up the umbrella and looking ruefully at it. *And it will be the same thing with Mike and Eileen. Nothing's happened to them. There weren't any daytime raids today. Their train's been delayed, that's all, like yours was this morning, and when they get here, you'll tell Eileen the airfield names you've collected, and she'll say, 'That's the one,' and we'll ask Gerald where his drop is and go home, and Mike will go off to Pearl Harbor, Eileen will go off to VE Day, and you can write up your observations of 'Life in the Blitz' and go back to fending off the advances of a seventeen-year-old boy.*

And in the meantime, she'd best tidy up her counter so she wouldn't have to stay late tonight. She gathered up the umbrella, the mackintosh and Eileen's coat and put them in the stockroom and then put the stockings her last customer had been looking at back in their box. She turned to put the box on the shelf.

And heard the air-raid siren begin its unmistakable up-and-down warble.

'In all our long history we have never seen a greater day than this. Everyone, man or woman, has done their best.'

WINSTON CHURCHILL VE DAY, 1945

LONDON – 7 MAY 1945

'**D**ouglas, the door's closing!' Paige shouted at her from the platform.

'Hurry!' Reardon urged. 'The train will leave—'

'I *know*,' she said, attempting to squeeze past the two Home Guards who were still singing, 'It's a Long Way to Tipperary'. And forming a solid wall. She tried to go around them, but dozens of people were trying to board the carriage and pushing her back away from the door. She shoved her way back to it.

The door was sliding shut. If she didn't get off now, she'd lose them and never be able to find them again in these crowds of merrymakers. 'Please, this is my stop!' she said, squeezing her way between two very tipsy sailors to the door. There was scarcely enough room to slip through. She braced the door open with both elbows.

'Mind the gap, Douglas!' Paige shouted, and held out her hand.

She grabbed for it and half stepped, half jumped off the train, and before her feet even touched the platform, the train was moving, disappearing into the tunnel.

'Thank goodness!' Paige said. 'We were afraid we'd never see you again.'

You wouldn't have, she thought.

'This way!' Reardon called gaily and started along the platform towards the exit, but the platform was just as jammed as the train had been. It took them a quarter of an hour to get off it and through the tunnel to the escalators, where things were no better. People were blowing tin whistles, cheering, leaning over the top throwing confetti on them as they rode up, and somewhere someone was banging on a bass drum.

Reardon, five steps above her, leaned back down to shout, 'Before we get outside, we'd best settle on a meeting place. In case we get separated.'

'I thought we said Trafalgar Square,' Paige shouted.

'We did,' Reardon shouted, 'but *where* in Trafalgar Square?'

'The lions?' Paige suggested. 'What do you think, Douglas?'

That won't work, she thought. *There are four of them and they're right in the middle of the square, which will be jammed with thousands of people. Not only will we not be able to find the correct lion, but we won't be able to see anything from there if we do.*

They needed an elevated vantage point they could see the others from. 'The National Gallery steps!' she shouted up to them.

Reardon nodded. 'The National Gallery steps.'

'When?' Paige asked.

'Midnight,' Reardon said.

No, she thought, *if I decide I need to go tonight, I'll have to be there by midnight, and it will take me the better part of an hour to get there.* 'We can't meet at midnight!' she shouted, but her voice was drowned out by a schoolboy on the step above her blowing enthusiastically on a toy horn.

'The National Gallery steps at midnight,' Paige echoed, 'or we turn into pumpkins.'

'No, Paige!' she called. 'We need to meet before—'

But Reardon, thank goodness, was already saying, 'That won't work. The Underground only runs till half past eleven tonight, and the Major will have our heads if we don't make it back.'

Half past eleven. That meant she'd need to start for the drop even earlier.

'But we only just got here,' Paige said, 'and the war's over—'

'We haven't been demobbed yet,' Reardon said. 'Till we are—'

'I suppose you're right,' Paige agreed.

'Then we meet on the National Gallery steps at a quarter past eleven, agreed? Douglas?'

No, she thought. *I may need to be gone before that, and I don't want you waiting for me and ending up being late getting back.* She needed to tell them to go on without her if she wasn't there. 'No, wait!' she called, but Reardon was already to the top of the escalator and stepping off into an even larger crowd. She turned back to say, 'Follow me, girls,' and disappeared into the mêlée.

'Wait! Reardon! Paige!' Douglas called, pushing up the moving stairs to catch Paige, but the boy with the horn was blocking her way. By the time she reached the top of the escalator, Reardon was nowhere to be seen, and Paige was already nearly to the turnstiles. 'Paige!' she called again, and started after her.

Paige turned back.

'Wait for me!' Douglas called, and Paige nodded and made an effort to move to the side but was swept on through.

'Douglas!' Paige shouted and pointed to the stairs leading up to the street.

Douglas started that way, but by the time she reached Paige, she was halfway up the steps and clinging madly to the metal railing. 'Douglas, can you see Reardon anywhere?' she shouted down to her.

'No!' she called, bracing herself against the noisy, laughing crowd which was carrying them inexorably up the stairs to the street. 'Listen, if one of us isn't there on the steps when it's time to leave, the others shouldn't wait.'

'What did you say?' Paige shouted over the din, which was growing even louder. Just above them a man in a bowler shouted, 'Three cheers for Churchill!' and the crowd obligingly bellowed, 'Hip hip hurrah! Hip hip hurrah! Hip hip hurrah!'

'I said, don't wait for me!'

'I can't hear you!'

'Three cheers for Monty!' the man shouted. 'Hip hip—'

The cheering crowd pushed them up out of the stairway, rather like a cork from a bottle, and spewed them out onto the packed street – and into an even louder din. Horns were honking and bells were ringing. A conga line snaked past, chanting, 'Dunh duh dunh duh dunh UNH!'

She pushed up to Paige and grabbed her arm. 'I said, don't—'

'I can't hear a word you're saying, Doug—' Paige said, and stopped short. 'Oh my goodness!'

The crowd crashed into them, around them, past them, creating a sort of eddy, but Paige was oblivious. She was standing with her hands clasped to her chest and a look of awe. 'Oh, look: the lights!'

Electric lights shone from shops and the marquee of a cinema and the stained-glass windows of St Martin-in-the-Fields. The pedestal of Nelson's Monument was lit, and so were the lions and the fountain. 'Aren't they the most beautiful things you've ever seen?' Paige sighed.

They *were* beautiful, though not nearly as wonderful to her as they must be to the contemps, who'd lived through five years of the blackout. 'Yes,' she said, looking over at Trafalgar Square.

St Martin's pillars were draped in bunting, and on its porch stood a little girl waving a glittering white sparkler. Searchlights crisscrossed the sky, and a giant bonfire was burning on the far side of the square. Two months ago – two *weeks* ago – that fire would have meant fear and death and destruction to these same Londoners. But it no longer held any terror for them. They danced around it, and the sudden drone of a plane overhead brought cheers and hands raised in the V-for-victory sign.

'Isn't it wonderful?' Paige asked.

'Yes!' she said, shouting into Paige's ear. 'But listen, if I'm not on the steps at a quarter past eleven, don't wait for me.'

But Paige wasn't paying any attention. 'It's just like the song,' she said, transfixed, and began to sing, '"When the Lights Go On Again All Over the World ..."'

The people near them began to sing along with her, and then were drowned out by the man in the bowler, shouting, 'Three cheers for the RAF!' which was in turn drowned out by a brass band playing 'Rule, Britannia'.

The jolly mob was pushing her and Paige apart. 'Paige, wait!' she shouted, grabbing for her sleeve, but before she could catch hold, she was abruptly grabbed by a soldier who swung her into a dip, planted a wet kiss on her lips, swung her back to standing, and grabbed another girl.

The entire episode had taken less than a minute, but it had been long enough. Paige was nowhere to be seen. She attempted to find her, heading in the direction she'd last seen her going, and then gave up and struck out across the square towards the National Gallery. Trafalgar Square was, if possible, even more crowded than the tube station and the street had been. Huge numbers of people were sitting on the base of Nelson's Monument, astride the lions, on the sides of the fountain, on a jeep full of American sailors that was, impossibly, trying to drive through the centre of the square, horn honking continuously.

As she passed it, one of the sailors leaned down and grabbed her arm. 'Want a ride, gorgeous?' he asked, and hauled her up and into the jeep. He called to the driver in an exaggerated British accent, 'Buckingham Palace, my good man, and make it snappy! Does that please you, milady?'

'No,' she said, 'I need to get to the National Gallery.'

'To the National Gallery, Jeeves!' the sailor ordered, though the jeep clearly wasn't going anywhere. It was completely surrounded. She scrambled up onto its bonnet, to try to spot Paige. 'Hey, beautiful, where you goin'?' he said, grabbing at her legs as she stood up.

She swatted his hands away and looked back towards Charing Cross Station, but there was no sign of Paige or Reardon. She turned, holding on to the windscreen as the jeep began to crawl forward, to look towards the National Gallery steps.

'Get down, honey!' the sailor who was driving shouted up at her. 'I can't see where I'm going.'

The jeep crept a few feet and stopped again, and more people swarmed onto the bonnet. He leaned on the horn, and the crowd parted enough for the jeep to creep a few more feet.

Away from the National Gallery. She needed to get off. When the jeep stopped again, this time blocked by the conga line writhing past, she took the opportunity to slip off. She waded towards the National Gallery, scanning the steps for Paige or Reardon. A clock chimed, and she glanced back at St Martin-in-the-Fields. A quarter past ten. Already?

If she was going to go back tonight, she needed to be back at Charing Cross by eleven, or she'd never make it to the drop, and it could take longer than that just to reach the National Gallery steps. She needed to turn back now.

But she hated to leave without saying goodbye to Paige. She couldn't actually tell her goodbye, since her cover story was that she'd been called home because her mother had been taken ill. Technically, she wasn't supposed to leave without permission, but with the war over, she'd have been demobbed in the next few days anyway.

She'd intended to go back tonight because, with everyone from the post in London, it would be easier to slip away. But if she went tomorrow – even though it would be more difficult to effect her escape – it would give her a chance to see everyone one last time. And she didn't want Paige to wait for her, miss the last train, and get into trouble.

But surely Paige would realise she'd failed to show up because of the crowds and go on without her? Now that the war was over, it wasn't as if her absence would mean that she'd been blown up by a V-2. And even if she did stay, there was no guarantee she could find Paige in this madness. The National Gallery steps were jammed with people. She'd never be able to spot … no, there Paige was, leaning over the stone railing, anxiously peering out at the crowd.

She waved at Paige – a totally useless gesture amongst the hundreds of people waving Union Jacks – and elbowed her way determinedly towards the steps, veering left when she heard the 'dunh duh dunh' of the conga line off to the right.

The steps were packed. She pushed over to the farside, hoping it might be less crowded.

It was, marginally. She began to work her way up, stepping between and over people. 'Sorry … I beg your pardon … sorry.'

There was the sudden heart-stopping, high-pitched whine of a siren, and the entire square fell silent, listening, and then as they realised it was the all-clear – erupted into cheers.

Directly in front of her, a burly workman sat on a step, his head in his hands, sobbing as if his heart would break. 'Are you all right?' she asked anxiously, putting her hand on his shoulder,

He looked up, tears streaming down his ruddy face. 'Right as rain, dearie,' he said. 'It was the all-clear wot did it.' He stood up so she could pass, wiping at his cheeks. 'The most beautiful fing I ever 'eard in me 'ole life.'

He took her arm to help her up to the next step. ''ere you go, dearie. Let 'er through, blokes,' he called to the people above him.

'Thank you,' she said gratefully.

'Douglas!' Paige shouted from above, and she looked up to see her waving wildly. They worked their way towards each other. 'Where did you *go*?' Paige demanded. 'I turned round and you were gone! Have you seen Reardon?'

'No.'

'I thought perhaps I might spot her or some of the others from up here,' Paige said. 'But I haven't had any luck.'

She could see why as she looked out over the crowd. Ten thousand people were supposed to have gathered in Trafalgar Square on VE Day, but it looked like there were already that many here tonight, laughing and cheering and throwing their hats in the air. The conga line, now at the far corner, was weaving off towards the Portrait Gallery, to be replaced by a line of middle-aged women dancing an Irish jig.

She tried to take it all in, to memorise every detail of the amazing historical event she was witnessing: the young woman splashing in the fountain with three officers of the Royal Norfolk Regiment. The stout woman passing out poppies to two tough-looking soldiers, who each kissed her on the cheek. The bobby trying to drag a girl down off the Nelson Monument and the girl leaning down and blowing a party favour in his face. And the bobby laughing. They looked not so much like people who had won a war as people who had been let out of prison.

Which they had been.

'Look!' Paige cried, 'there's Reardon.'

'Where?'

'By the lion.'

'Which lion?'

'That lion.' Paige pointed. 'The one with part of his nose missing.'

There were dozens of people surrounding the lion and *on* the lion, perched on its reclining back, on its head, on its paws, one of which had been knocked off during the Blitz, and more trying to climb on. A sailor sat astride its back, putting his cap on the lion's head.

'Standing in front of it and off to the left,' Paige directed her. 'Can't you see her?'

'No.'

'By the lamppost.'

'The one with the boy shinning up it?'

'Yes. Now look to the left.'

She did, scanning the people standing there: a sailor waving his cap in the air, two elderly women in black coats with red-white-and-blue rosettes on their lapels, a blonde teenaged girl in a white dress, a pretty redhead in a green coat—

Good Lord, that looks just like Merope Ward, she thought. And that impossibly bright green coat was exactly the sort of outfit those idiot techs in Wardrobe would have told her was what the contemps wore to the VE Day celebrations.

And the young woman wasn't cheering or laughing. She was looking earnestly at the National Gallery steps, as if trying to memorise every detail. It was definitely Merope.

She raised her arm to wave at her.

'There won't be any next time if this war is lost.'

EDWARD R. MURROW 17 JUNE 1940

LONDON – 26 OCTOBER 1940

For a moment after the siren began its up-and-down warble, Polly simply stood there with the stockings box still in her hand, her heart pounding. Then Doreen said, 'Oh, no, not a raid! I thought for certain we'd get through today without one.'

We did, Polly thought. *There must be some mistake.*

'And just when we were finally getting some customers,' Doreen added disgustedly. She pointed at the opening lift.

Oh no, what a time for Mike and Eileen to finally arrive. Polly hurried over to intercept them, but it wasn't them after all. Two stylish young women stepped out of the lift. 'I'm afraid there's a raid on,' Miss Snelgrove said, coming over too, 'but we have a shelter that is very comfortable and specially fortified. Miss Sebastian will take you down to it.'

'This way,' Polly said, and led them through the door and down the stairs.

'Oh dear,' one of the young women said, 'and after what happened to Padgett's last night—'

'I know,' the other one replied. 'Did you hear? Five people were killed.'

Thank goodness *Mike and Eileen aren't here,* Polly thought. But they could easily have been on their way up when the siren sounded and would be down in the shelter when they got there, and there would be no way to avoid the subject. And no way to convince Mike this wasn't a discrepancy.

'Were the people who were killed in Padgett's shelter?' the first young woman was asking worriedly. She had to shout over the siren. Unlike at Padgett's, where the staircase had muffled the sirens' sound, the enclosed space here magnified it so that it was louder than it had been out on the floor.

'I've no idea,' the other shouted back. 'Nowhere's safe these days.' She launched into a story about a taxi that had been hit the day before.

They were nearly down to the basement. *Please don't let Mike and Eileen be there*, Polly thought, only half listening to the young women. *Please—*

'If I hadn't mistaken my parcel for hers,' the young woman went on, 'we'd both have been killed—'

The siren cut off. There was a moment of echoing silence, and then the all-clear sounded.

'False alarm,' the other young woman said brightly. They started back upstairs. 'They must have mistaken one of our boys for a German bomber,' which sounded likely. It wouldn't necessarily convince Mike. Polly hoped he and Eileen hadn't been within earshot of the siren.

But the fact that the woman knew about the five fatalities must mean it was in the papers, and if it was, it would be chalked on billboards and newsboys would be shouting it, and there'd be no way to keep it from him. And there was no way a shopgirl could ask a customer, 'How did you find out about the fatalities?'

Polly hoped the young women might bring it up again, but now they were solely focused on buying a pair of elbow-length gloves.

It took them nearly an hour to decide on a pair, and when they left, Mike and Eileen still weren't there. *Which is good*, Polly thought. *It means the chances that they didn't hear the siren are excellent*. But it was after two. Where *were* they?

Mike heard a newsboy shouting the headline Five Killed at Padgett's *and went to the morgue to see the bodies*, she thought worriedly, but when Mike and Eileen arrived half an hour later, they didn't say anything about fatalities or Padgett's. They *had* been delayed at Theodore's. 'Theodore didn't want me to go,' Eileen explained. 'He threw such a tantrum I had to promise to stay and read him a story.'

'And then on the way back we went to the travel shop Eileen had seen, to try to find a map,' Mike said, 'but it was hit last night.'

'The owner was there,' Eileen said, 'and he said there was another shop on Charing Cross Road, but—'

Miss Snelgrove was eyeing them disapprovingly from Doreen's counter. 'You can tell me when I get home,' Polly said. She gave them the coats, her latchkey and Mrs Leary's address. 'I may be late,' she added.

'Should we go to the tube station if the raid begins before you come home?' Eileen asked nervously.

'No. Mrs Rickett's is perfectly safe,' Polly whispered. 'Now go. I don't want to lose my job. It's the only one we've got.'

She watched them depart, hoping they'd be too busy settling in to their new accommodations to discuss Padgett's or daytime raids with anyone. She'd planned to go to the hospital tomorrow to try to find out if there really had been five fatalities, but if the deaths were in the newspapers, it couldn't wait. She'd have to go tonight, and poor Eileen would have to face her first supper at Mrs Rickett's alone.

But she might as well have gone straight home. She couldn't get in to see Marjorie or find out anything from the stern ward sister, and when she reached the boarding house, Eileen was sitting in the parlour with her bag, even though Polly could hear the others in the dining room. 'Why aren't you in there eating supper?' Polly asked.

'Mrs Rickett said I had to give her my ration book, and when

I told her about Padgett's, she said my board couldn't begin till I got a new one, and Mike wasn't here—'

'Where is he? At Mrs Leary's?'

'No. He arranged things with her and then went to check a travel shop in Regent Street and then to fetch his clothes from his rooms, but he said he'd be late and not to wait for him, to go ahead to Notting Hill Gate and meet him there. When do the raids begin tonight?' she asked nervously.

'Shh,' Polly whispered. 'We shouldn't be talking about this here. Come up to the room.'

'I can't. Mrs Rickett said I wasn't allowed to till I'd paid her.'

'*Paid* her? Didn't you tell her you were moving in with me?'

'Yes,' Eileen said, 'but she said not till I'd given her ten and six.'

'I'll speak to her,' Polly said grimly, picking up Eileen's bag. She took her up to the room, left her there, and went down to the kitchen to confront Mrs Rickett.

'When I moved in, you said I had to pay the full rate for a double,' Polly argued. 'It shouldn't be extra for—'

'There's plenty as wants the room if you don't,' Mrs Rickett said. 'I had three Army nurses here today looking for a room to let.'

And I suppose you plan to charge them three times the full rate for a double, Polly almost snapped, but she couldn't risk getting them evicted. Eileen would already have given Theodore's mother this address, and Mrs Rickett wasn't the type to tell a retrieval team where they'd gone if they did show up. Polly paid the additional ten and six and went back upstairs.

Miss Laburnum was just coming out of her room, carrying a bag full of shells and an empty glass bottle. 'For Ernest's message in a bottle,' she explained. 'Sir Godfrey said to get a whisky bottle, but with Mrs Brightford's little girls there, I thought perhaps orange squash would be more suitable—'

Polly cut her off. 'Would you tell Sir Godfrey I may not be at rehearsal tonight? I must help my cousin get settled in.'

'Oh yes, poor thing,' Miss Laburnum said. 'Did she know any of the five who were killed?'

Oh no, Miss Laburnum knew about the deaths too. Now she'd have to keep Mike and Eileen away from the troupe as well.

'Were they shop assistants?' Miss Laburnum asked.

'No,' Polly said, 'but the incident's left her badly shaken, so I'd rather you didn't say anything to her about it.'

'Oh no, of course not,' Miss Laburnum assured Polly. 'We wouldn't want to upset her.' Polly was certain she meant it, but she or someone else at the boarding house was bound to slip. She *had* to find a way to get in to see Marjorie tomorrow.

'It's dreadful,' Miss Laburnum was saying, 'so many killed, and who knows how it will all end?'

'Yes,' Polly said, and was grateful when the sirens went. 'I'd appreciate it if you told Sir Godfrey why I can't come.'

'Oh, but you *can't* be thinking of staying here with a raid on? Can she, Miss Hibbard?' she asked their fellow boarder as she came hurrying out of her room carrying a black umbrella and her knitting.

'Oh my, no,' Miss Hibbard said. 'It's far too dangerous. Mr Dorming, tell Miss Sebastian she and her cousin must come with us.'

And in a moment Eileen would open the door to see what was going on. 'We'll come to the shelter as soon as I've shown her where things are,' Polly promised, to get rid of them. She escorted them downstairs.

'Don't be late,' Miss Laburnum said at the door. 'Sir Godfrey said he wished to rehearse the scene between Crichton and Lady Mary.'

'I may not be able to rehearse with you, with my cousin—'

'You can bring her with you,' Miss Laburnum said.

Polly shook her head. 'She'll need rest and quiet.' *And to be kept away from people who know there were five people killed.* 'Tell Sir Godfrey I'll be there tomorrow night, I promise,' she said, and ran back upstairs.

She waited to make certain Mrs Rickett had gone with them and then ran back down to the kitchen. She put the kettle on, piled bread, margarine, cheese and cutlery on a tray, made tea, and brought it up to Eileen.

'Mrs Rickett said we weren't allowed to have food in the room,' Eileen said.

'Then she should have let you begin boarding immediately.' Polly set the tray on the bed. 'Though, actually, it was a blessing she didn't. This is much better than supper would have been.'

'But the siren,' Eileen said anxiously. 'Shouldn't we—'

'The raids won't start till 8:46.' Polly buttered a slice of bread and handed it to Eileen. 'And I told you, we're safe here. Mr Dunworthy himself approved this address.'

She poured Eileen a cup of tea. 'I found out some more names of airfields today,' she said and read them to her, but Eileen shook her head at each one.

'Could it have been Hendon?' Polly asked.

'No. I'm so sorry. I *know* I'd recognise it if I saw it. If only we had a map.'

'Did you get to the shop in Charing Cross Road?'

'Yes, but the owner demanded to know what we wanted with a map and asked us all sorts of questions. He even asked Mike what sort of accent it was he had. I thought he was going to have us arrested. Mike said he suspected us of being German spies.'

'He may have,' Polly said. 'I should have thought of that. There've been all sorts of posters up warning people to be on the lookout for anyone behaving suspiciously – snapping photographs of factories or asking questions about our defences – and trying to buy a map would obviously fall into that category.'

'But how are we to get hold of one, then?'

'I don't know. I'll check Townsend Brothers' book department to see if they have an atlas or something.'

'Would they have an ABC?' Eileen asked.

'Yes, I looked up the trains to Backbury in it,' Polly said, wondering why she hadn't thought of using a railway guide

– it listed the stations alphabetically, so they'd be able to find Gerald's airfield under D. Or T. Or P. 'Did you use an ABC when you brought the children to London?'

'No, they used an ABC in one of Agatha Christie's novels, to solve the mystery,' Eileen said. 'And we can use it to solve ours.'

If only it were that simple, Polly thought.

Eileen looked up at the ceiling. 'Is that sound bombers?'

'No, rain. But luckily,' Polly said lightly, 'we have an umbrella.'

She took the tea things downstairs, made a sandwich to take to Mike, then set off for Notting Hill Gate with Eileen. It was coming down hard – an icy downpour that made Polly glad Miss Laburnum had brought Eileen the coat and made her wish she'd brought a second umbrella. It was impossible to huddle under Eileen's and lead her along the wet, dark streets at the same time, and twice Polly stepped in an ankle-deep puddle.

'I hate it here,' Eileen said. 'I don't care if I *do* sound like Theodore. I want to go *home.*'

'Did you tell Theodore's mother your new address so your retrieval team can find you?'

'Yes, and her neighbour Mrs Owen. And on the train in from Stepney, I wrote to the vicar. I wanted to ask you about that. Do you think I must give Alf and Binnie my new address?'

'Are those the children you told me about? The haystack-fire starters?'

'Yes,' Eileen said, 'and if I tell them where I am, they're likely to take it as an invitation, and they're—'

'Dreadful,' Polly finished.

'Yes, and the only way the retrieval team would know where they are was if the vicar told them, and I've already told *him* where I am, so the retrieval team wouldn't need—'

'Then I don't see any reason you need to contact them,' Polly said, leading her down the steps into the tube station where their neighbours would be sheltering for the night. 'Where did

24

Mike say he'd meet us? At the foot of the escalator?'

'No, in the emergency staircase. There's one here just like the one in Oxford Circus.'

Good, Polly thought, following Eileen through the tunnel. *We'll be safe from the troupe there. And if Mike's been waiting in it, I needn't worry about his having overheard people discussing Padgett's.*

But Mike wasn't there. Eileen and Polly climbed up three flights and then down as many, calling his name, but there was no answer. 'Should we go to Oxford Circus?' Eileen asked. 'That's what he said to do if we got separated.'

'No, he'll be here soon.' Polly sat down on the steps.

'The raids weren't on Regent Street tonight, were they?' Eileen asked anxiously.

'No, over the City and—'

'The city?' Eileen said, looking nervously up at the ceiling. 'Which part of it?'

'Not the city of London. The City with a capital C. It's the part of London around St Paul's.' *And Fleet Street,* Polly added silently. 'It's nowhere near here, and the raids later on were over Whitechapel.'

'*Whitechapel?*'

'Yes – why? Mike wasn't going there, was he?'

'No. But that's where Alf and Binnie Hodbin live.'

Good Lord. Whitechapel was even worse than Stepney. It had been almost totally destroyed.

'Was it heavily bombed?' Eileen said anxiously. 'Oh dear, perhaps I shouldn't have torn up that letter after all.'

'What letter?'

'From the vicar, arranging to send Alf and Binnie to Canada. I was afraid they might end up on the *City of Benares*, so I didn't give it to Mrs Hodbin.'

Thank goodness Mike's late and wasn't here to hear that, Polly thought. She was going to have a difficult enough time persuading him that Padgett's five fatalities weren't a discrepancy, let alone having to convince him that Eileen hadn't saved the Hodbins' lives by withholding the letter.

There were lots of other ships to America they might have gone on. Or the Evacuation Committee might have decided to send them to Australia instead, or to Scotland. And even if they had been assigned to the *City of Benares*, they might not have gone. Their train might have been delayed, or – Eileen had said they were dreadful – they might have been thrown off the ship for painting blackout stripes on the deck chairs or setting them on fire.

But she doubted Mike would be convinced by her arguments, especially if he'd found out about Padgett's. He'd go into a tail-spin, certain he'd lost the war, and nothing short of telling him about VE Day would persuade him otherwise. But telling him meant their finding out about her deadline, and the rest of it. Which would give them even more to worry about. And now, with this discrepancy …

I must find out about those fatalities before he does, Polly thought. 'Don't bring up the subject of Alf and Binnie to Mike,' she said to Eileen. 'He needn't know about the letter. And there's no need to tell him you didn't write and tell them your address.'

'But perhaps I *should* write to them. To tell them Whitechapel's dangerous.'

I should imagine they already know that. 'I thought you didn't want them to know where you are.'

'But I'm the one responsible for them being there instead of in Canada. And Binnie's still not completely well from the measles. She nearly died, and—'

'You didn't tell me that,' Polly said.

'Yes, she had a horribly high fever, and I didn't know what to do. I gave her aspirin—'

And thank goodness Mike hadn't heard that either.

'If Alf and Binnie are in danger,' Eileen said, 'it's my fault. I—'

'Shh,' Polly said. 'Someone's coming.'

They listened. Far below them a door shut and footsteps began to ascend the iron steps.

'Eileen? Polly? Are you up there?'

'It's Mike,' Eileen said, and ran down to meet him. 'Where *were* you?'

'I went to the morgue,' Mike said.

Oh no, I'm too late, Polly thought. *He's already found out about the five fatalities.*

But when he came up the stairs, he said cheerfully, 'I found a bunch of airfield names, and I've got a job, so we don't have to live on just Polly's wages.'

'A job?' Eileen said. 'But if you're working, how will you be able to go and look for Gerald?'

'I've been hired as a stringer for the *Daily Express*, which means I go out and find news stories – including at airfields – and get paid by the story. I didn't have any luck finding a map, so I went to the *Express'* morgue to look through their back issues for mentions of airfields.'

The newspaper *morgue*, Polly thought, *not the actual morgue.*

'—and when I told them I was a reporter who'd been at Dunkirk, they hired me on the spot. Best of all, they gave me a press pass, which will give me access at the airfield. So now all we need is to figure out which one it is.' He pulled a list from his pocket. 'What about Digby? Or Dunkeswell?'

'No, it was two words, I think,' Eileen said.

'Great Dunmow?'

'No. I've been thinking. It might have begun with a B instead of a G.'

Which means she has no idea what letter it began with, Polly thought. 'Boxted,' she said.

'No,' Eileen said.

'B,' Mike murmured, going down the list. 'Bentley Priory?'

Eileen frowned. 'That sounds a bit like it, but—'

'Bury St Edmunds?'

'No, though that might ... oh, I don't know!' She threw her hands up in frustration. 'I'm sorry.'

'Don't worry, we'll find it,' Mike said, wadding up his list. 'There are lots more airfields.'

'Can you remember anything else Gerald said about where he was going?' Polly asked.

'No.' She frowned in concentration. 'He asked me how long I was going to be in Backbury, and I said till the beginning of May, and he said that was too bad, that if I'd been staying longer he'd have come up some weekend to "brighten my existence".'

'Did he say how?'

'How? You mean motor up or come by train?' Eileen asked. 'No, but he said, "Is backwater Backbury even *on* the railway?"'

'And the day I saw him,' Mike interjected, 'he said one of the things he had to do was check the railway schedule.'

'Good,' Polly said. 'That means the airfield's near a railway station. Mike, you said he went through to Oxford?'

'Yes, but that was just to set things up, not for his assignment. He could have been checking on a train to anywhere ...'

Polly shook her head. 'Wartime travel is too unreliable. Mr Dunworthy would have insisted he come through near where he needed to go. Troop trains cause all sorts of delays.'

'She's right,' Eileen said, 'some days the train to Backbury didn't come at all.'

'So we're looking for an airfield near Oxford,' Mike said.

'Or Backbury,' Polly said.

'Or Backbury. And near a railway station, and one that has two words in its name and begins with D, a P or a B. That narrows it down considerably. Now, if we can just find a map ...'

'We're working on that,' Polly said. 'And I'm working on writing down all the raids.' She gave them each a copy of the list for the next week.

'There are raids *every night* next week?' Eileen said.

28

'I'm afraid so. They let up a bit in November when the Luftwaffe begins bombing other cities, and later on when winter weather sets in.'

'Later on?' Eileen asked in dismay. 'How long did the Blitz *last*?'

'Till next May.'

'*May?* But the raids taper off, don't they?'

'I'm afraid not. The biggest raid of the entire Blitz was May tenth and eleventh.'

'That's when the worst raid was?' Mike asked. 'In mid-May?'

'Yes. Why?'

'Nothing. It doesn't matter. We'll be out of here long before that.' He smiled encouragingly at Eileen. 'All we have to do is figure out where Gerald is. Can you think of anything else he said that might give us a clue? Where were you when you had this conversation?'

'There were two – in the lab and then over at Oriel when I went there to get my driving authorisation. Oh, I remember something he said about that. It began to rain while he was telling me how important and dangerous his assignment was, and he looked up at the sky and held out his hand the way one does to see if it's really raining, and then pointed at my authorisation – you know, the printed form one has to fill up for driving lessons. You had one, Polly.'

'A printed red-and-blue form?'

'Yes, that's the one. He pointed at it and said, "You'd better put that away, or you'll never learn to drive. Or at any rate, where *I'm* going you wouldn't," and then he laughed as though he'd said something tremendously clever. He's always doing that – he fancies himself a comedian, though his jokes aren't funny in the least, and I didn't understand that one at all. Do you understand the joke?'

'No,' Polly said, and she couldn't think of anything the form would have to do with an airfield. 'Can you remember anything else he said?'

'Or anything at all about when you were talking to him,' Mike said. 'What else was going on?'

'Linna was on the phone with someone, but it didn't have anything to do with Gerald's assignment.'

'But it may trigger a memory of the name of the airfield. Try to remember every detail you can, no matter how irrelevant.'

'Like the dog's ball,' Eileen said eagerly.

'Gerald had a dog's ball?' Mike asked.

'*No*. There was a dog's ball in one of Agatha Christie's novels.'

Well, that's certainly irrelevant, Polly thought.

'In *Dumb Witness*,' Eileen said. 'At first it didn't seem to have anything at all to do with the murder, but then it turned out to be the key to the entire mystery.'

'Exactly,' Mike said. 'Write it all down, and see if it triggers something. And in the meantime, I want you to make the rounds of the department stores on Monday and fill out a job application at each one.'

'I can ask Miss Snelgrove if they need anyone at Townsend Brothers,' Polly said.

'This isn't about a job,' Mike said. 'It's so they'll have her name and address on file when the retrieval team comes looking for us.'

Which must mean the arguments I made to him this morning at Padgett's convinced him he didn't alter history after all, Polly thought. But after they'd curled up under their coats on the landing to sleep, he shook her awake and motioned her to tiptoe after him down past the sleeping Eileen.

'Did you find out anything more about Padgett's?' he whispered.

'No,' Polly lied. 'Did you?'

He shook his head.

Thank goodness, Polly thought. *When the all-clear goes, I'll take him straight to the drop. He can't talk to anyone there. He can sit there till I come back from the hospital. If I can get him out of here without Miss Laburnum latching onto us and blurting out something about how awful it is that there were five people kil—*

'You said there were three fatalities, right?' Mike asked.

'Yes, but the information in my implant could have been wrong. It—'

'And the supervisor – what was his name? Feathers?'

'Fetters.'

'Said everybody who worked at Padgett's had been accounted for.'

'Yes, but—'

'I've been thinking. What if it was our retrieval team?'

BETHNAL GREEN – JUNE 1944

Mary flung herself down in the gutter next to Talbot, half on top of her, listening to the sudden silence where the putt-putt of the engine had been.

'What in God's name are you doing, Kent?' Talbot said, trying to wriggle free from underneath her.

Mary pushed her back down into the gutter. 'Keep your head down!' They had twelve seconds before the V-1 exploded. Eleven … ten … nine … *Please, please, please let us be far enough away from it*, she prayed. Seven … six …

'Keep my—?' Talbot said, struggling against her. 'Have you gone mad?'

Mary pressed her down. 'Cover your eyes!' she ordered and squeezed her own shut against the blinding light that would come with the blast.

I should put my hands over my ears, she thought, but she needed them to hold down Talbot, who was, unbelievably, still attempting to get up. 'Stay down! It's a flying bomb!' Mary put her hand to the back of Talbot's head and forced it flat against the bottom of the gutter. Two … one … zero …

Her adrenalin-racing mind must have counted too quickly.

She waited, arms tight around Talbot, for the flash and deafening concussion ...

Talbot was struggling harder than ever. '*Flying* bomb?' she said, wrenching herself free and raising herself on her hands and elbows. '*What* flying bomb?'

'The one I heard. Don't—' Mary said, trying vainly to push her down again. 'It'll go off any second. It—'

There was a sputtering cough, and the putt-putting sound started up again. *But it can't have*, she thought bewilderedly. *V-1s don't start up again—*

'Is *that* what you heard?' Talbot asked. 'That's not a flying bomb, you ninny. It's a motorcycle.' And as she spoke, an American GI came around the corner on a decrepit-looking De Havilland, sped towards them and careened to a stop.

'What happened?' he asked, leaping off the motorcycle. 'Are you two all right?'

'No,' Talbot said disgustedly. She pulled herself to sitting and began brushing dirt off the front of her uniform.

'You're bleeding,' the GI said.

Mary looked at Talbot in horror. There was blood on her blouse, blood trickling down her mouth and her chin. 'Oh my God, Talbot!' she cried, and she and the GI began fumbling for a handkerchief.

'What are you talking about?' Talbot said. 'I'm not bleeding.'

'Your mouth,' the GI said, and Talbot felt it cautiously and then looked at her fingers.

'That's not blood,' she said, 'it's lipstick— Oh my God, my lipstick!' She began looking frantically around for it. 'I only just got it. It's Crimson Caress.' She started to stand up. 'Kent knocked it out of my hand when she— Oh! Ow!' She collapsed back onto the kerb.

'You *are* hurt!' the GI said, hurrying over.

'Oh, Talbot, I'm so sorry,' Mary said. 'I thought it was a V-1. The newspapers said they sounded like a motorcycle. Is it your knee?'

'Yes, but it's nothing,' Talbot said, putting her arm around the GI's neck. 'It twisted under me as I went down. It'll be fine in a moment— Ow! Ow! Ow!'

'You're not fine,' the GI said. He turned to Mary. 'I don't think she can walk. Or ride a motorcycle. Have you got a car?'

'No. We came up here from Dulwich by bus.'

'I'm all right,' Talbot said. 'Kent can give me a hand.'

But even supported by both of them, she couldn't put any weight at all on the knee. 'She's probably torn a ligament,' the GI said, easing her back down to sitting on the kerb. 'You're going to have to send for an ambulance.'

'That's ridiculous!' Talbot protested. '*We're* the ambulance crew!'

But he was already mounting his motorcycle to go and find a telephone. Mary gave him the exchange and number of the Bethnal Green post. 'No, not Bethnal Green,' Talbot protested. 'If the other units find out, we'll be laughingstocks. Tell him to ring Dulwich.'

She did, but when the ambulance arrived a few minutes later, it was from Brixton. 'Both of yours were out at incidents,' the driver said. 'Jerry's sending them over fast and furious today.'

Not over us, Mary thought ruefully.

Brixton's crew took the news that she had mistaken a motor-cycle for a V-1 in stride, but when she and Talbot got back to Dulwich, there was a good deal of merriment. 'The newspapers said they sound like a motorcycle,' Mary said defensively.

'Yes, well, the newspapers said they sound like a washing machine, too,' Maitland said. 'I suppose we'd best be careful when we do our laundry, girls.'

Parrish nodded. 'I don't want to run the risk of being flung down while hanging up my knickers.'

'It was a very *old* De Havilland,' Talbot said in Mary's defence, 'and it did sputter and then die, rather like a flying bomb.' But that only made it worse. The girls began calling her De Havilland and Triumph and any other motorcycle name that was handy, and whenever a door slammed or a pot boiled over, someone shouted, 'Oh no, it's a flying bomb!' and attempted to tackle her from behind.

The ribbing was all good-natured, and Talbot didn't seem to bear a grudge, even though she'd been taken off active duty and assigned secretarial tasks and had to hobble about on crutches. She seemed far more upset about her lost lipstick and having missed the dance than about her knee.

On their way home from an incident the next morning Mary and Fairchild went to see if they could find the lipstick, but either it had rolled into the storm drain or someone had seen it lying in the street and taken it. They *did* find Talbot's cap, which had been run over and was obviously beyond repair. And on the way home, they passed the railroad bridge Mary had gone to the dance to see – or rather, what was left of it. 'It was hit by one of the first flying bombs that came over,' Fairchild said casually.

And if you'd mentioned that sooner, Mary thought, *I'd have known my implant data was accurate, and I wouldn't have injured Talbot.*

To make amends, Mary offered Talbot her own lipstick, but Talbot said, 'No, that's too pink,' and set about concocting a substitute out of heated paraffin and merthiolate from the medical kit. The result proved too orange, and for the next few days the entire post was utterly absorbed – in between incidents, some of them grisly – in finding something which would reproduce Crimson Caress.

Currants were too dark, beet juice too purple, and there were no strawberries to be had anywhere. Mary, helping to carry the body of a dead woman with a broken-off banister driven through her chest, noticed that her blood was the exact shade they needed, then felt horrified and ashamed of herself and spent the rest of the incident worrying that one of the other FANYs might have noticed the colour too. It was almost a relief when they spent the journey home arguing over whose turn it was to have to wear the Yellow Peril.

If and when any of them got to go out again. With Talbot injured, they were shorthanded, and they'd already been pulling double shifts. And Hitler was sending more V-1s over every day. The newspapers reported that anti-aircraft guns had been placed in a line along the Dover coast and that the barrage balloons had been moved to the coast from London, but clearly neither of those defensive measures was working. 'What I want to know,' Camberley said, exasperated after their fourth incident in twenty-four hours, 'is, where are our boys?'

At least I know where the V-1s are, Mary thought.

The rockets were all coming over exactly when and where they were supposed to. The Guards Chapel was hit on June eighteenth, there was a near-miss of Buckingham Palace on the twentieth, and Fleet Street, the Aldwych Theatre, and Sloane Court were all hit on schedule. And since they had more than they could handle in their own district, they were no longer transporting any patients through Bomb Alley, so Mary was able to relax and concentrate on observing the FANYs and trying to live down her nickname.

The next week, Major Denewell came into the dispatch office, where Mary was manning the telephone, and asked, 'Where's Maitland?'

'Out on a run, ma'am. Burbage Road. V-1.'

The Major looked annoyed. 'What about Fairchild?'

'She's off-duty. She's gone with Reed to London.'

'How long have they been gone?'

'Over an hour.'

She looked even more annoyed. 'Then you'll have to do,' she said. 'We've had a telephone call from the RAF asking for a driver for one of their officers, and Talbot can't drive with her wrenched knee. You'll have to go in her place.' She handed Mary a folded slip of paper. 'Here's the officer's name, where you're to meet him, and your route.'

'Yes, ma'am,' she said. *And let's hope the airfield where I'm to pick him up isn't Biggin Hill or any of the other airfields in Bomb Alley*, she thought, unfolding it.

Oh good, it was Hendon. But there was no destination listed. 'Where am I to drive Flight Officer Lang to, ma'am?'

'He'll tell you that,' the Major said, obviously wishing Talbot was in a condition to do this. 'You're to drive him wherever he wishes to go and then wait for him and drive him back unless otherwise instructed. You're to be there by half past eleven.'

Which meant she needed to leave immediately. 'Take the Daimler,' the Major said. 'And you're to wear full-dress uniform.'

'Yes, ma'am.'

'And since you'll be in the vicinity, stop in Edgware and ask their supply officer if they have any stretchers they can spare.'

'Yes, ma'am,' she said, and went to change. And look at the map. Hendon was far enough northwest of London that it was completely out of rocket range, and only half a dozen had fallen between here and there this morning. The British Intelligence plan to convince the Germans to shorten the rockets' range must be working.

She looked at the route the Major had mapped out for her. Two of the six V-1s lay along it. She'd have to head west to Wandsworth instead and then north. It would take extra petrol, but she could say the road the Major had suggested had been blocked by a convoy or something.

She traced out the new route and set out for Hendon, hoping she'd arrive early enough to go on to Edgware and pick up the bandages first, but there was all sorts of military traffic. It was after twelve by the time she reached the airfield, and the officer was already waiting at the door, looking impatiently at his watch.

I hope he's not angry, she thought, but he grinned as she pulled up and bounded towards the ambulance. He was no older than she was and boyishly handsome, with dark hair and a crooked smile.

He opened the door and leaned in. 'Where have you been, you beautiful—?' He stopped in midsentence. 'Sorry, I thought you were someone I knew.'

'Apparently,' she said.

'Not that *you're* not beautiful. You are,' he said, flashing her the crooked smile. 'Rather devastatingly beautiful, as a matter of fact.'

She ignored that. 'I'm here from Ambulance Post #47 to pick up Flight Officer Lang,' she said.

'*I'm* Officer Lang.' He got into the front seat. 'Where's Lieutenant Talbot?'

'She's on sick leave, sir.'

'Sick leave? She wasn't hit by one of these blasted rocket bombs, was she?'

'No, sir.' *Only by a historian.* 'Not exactly.'

'Not *exactly*? What happened? She wasn't badly hurt?'

'No, only a wrenched knee. I knocked her down,' she confessed.

'Because you wanted to be the one to drive me?' he said. 'I'm flattered.'

'No, because I thought I heard a V-1. I pushed her down into the gutter, but it was only a motorcycle.'

'And so she's not able to drive, and they sent you as her replacement,' he said, grinning. 'It wasn't an accident you were sent, you know. It was Fate.'

I doubt that, she thought. *And why do I have a feeling you say the same thing to every FANY who drives you?* 'Where am I to take you, sir?'

'London. Whitehall.'

Which was better than somewhere in Bomb Alley, but not perfect. Once they got there, they'd be safe. No V-1s had fallen in Whitehall today, but more than a dozen had hit between Hendon and London.

'Whitehall. Yes, sir,' she said, and opened out the map to find the safest route.

'You won't need that,' he said, plucking it out of her hands and folding it up. 'I can show you the way.' There was nothing for her to do but start the engine. 'It's quickest to take the Great North Road. Follow this lane till the first turning, and then bear right.'

'Yes, sir,' she said, heading in the direction he indicated and trying to think of an excuse for getting the map back so she could see what towns lay along the Great North Road.

'Definitely Fate,' Flight Officer Lang was saying. 'It's clear we were destined to meet, Lieutenant – what's your name?'

'Kent, sir,' she said absently. She should have told him that the Major insisted her FANYs take the Edgware Road to London. That way they'd have been out of range nearly the entire way.

'*Lieutenant* Kent,' he said sternly. 'Lovers brought together by Fate do not call each other by their last names. Antony and Cleopatra, Tristan and Isolde, Romeo and Juliet. Stephen—' he pointed at himself, 'and—?'

'Mary, sir.'

'*Sir?*' His voice was filled with mock outrage. 'Did Juliet call Romeo sir? Did Guinevere call Lancelot sir? Well, actually, I suppose she may have done. He *was* a knight, after all, but I don't want you to do it. It makes me feel a hundred years old.'

A hundred and thirty-some old, actually, she thought.

'As your superior officer, I order you to call me Stephen, and I will call you Mary. Mary,' he said, looking over at her and then frowning puzzledly, 'have we met before?'

'No,' she said. 'Does this route take us through Edgware?'

'Edgware?' he said. 'No, that's the other direction. This road goes through Golders Green, and then we take the Great North Road south through Finchley.'

Oh no. There'd been a V-1 in East Finchley this afternoon, and two in Golders Green. 'Oh dear, I thought this went through Edgware,' she said, and didn't have to feign the distress in her voice. 'I was to pick up some stretchers for the Major at Edgware's ambulance post.' She slowed the car, looking for a place to pull off and turn around. 'We must go back.'

'You'll have to do it after we return, I'm afraid. I've a meeting at two, and I'll be cashiered if I'm not there on time. And we're late as it is. It's already half past twelve.'

The Golders Green V-1s had hit at 12:56 and 1:08. *And let's hope Flight Officer Lang isn't right about our meeting being Fate, and that fate is to be blown to bits by a V-1. I should have memorised the casualties from each rocket attack*, she thought, *so I'd know if an RAF flight officer and his driver were killed this afternoon.*

But there'd scarcely been room in her implant for all the rockets which had hit in the areas she was most likely to be in, so all she knew was that the 12:56 one had been on Queen's Road and the 1:08 one on a bridge somewhere outside the village. And they were heading straight towards both of them.

The net wouldn't have let her come through if her presence in the past would affect events, but that didn't mean she could blithely drive into the path of a V-1, certain that nothing would happen.

For one thing, *she* could be killed even if he wasn't. And for another, Flight Officer Lang had a constantly dangerous job. It might not make a difference to the course of history whether he was killed this afternoon or on a mission tomorrow.

But it made a great deal of difference to her, which was why she needed to get off this road. 'I promise you we'll go straight to Edgware after my meeting,' Lang was saying. 'And to make up for it I'll take you out for dinner and dancing. What do you say?'

I'd say that won't make up for my being dead, she thought.

There was a crossroads ahead. Good. She'd ask him again which way to turn, then pretend she'd misheard his instructions, turn right instead of left, and get them somehow onto a road which would lead them back out of range.

She waited till they were nearly to the crossroads and then said, 'Which road did you say I take?'

'We stay on this. In another mile it turns into Queen's Road.

Are you certain we haven't met before?'

'Yes,' she said, only half listening. She peered ahead, looking for another crossroads. She wouldn't ask this time, she'd simply turn off.

'You're certain you haven't driven me before?' he persisted. 'Last spring?'

Absolutely certain. She wished he'd stop talking so she could hear. She might be able to swerve – or stop – if she heard the V-1 soon enough, but the noise of a car engine sometimes masked the sound, and with him prattling on—

'Or last winter?'

'No, I've only been in Dulwich for six weeks,' she said, glancing at her watch. 12:53. She rolled down the window. She couldn't hear anything yet. And she didn't know where on Queen's Road the V-1 would—

'Stop!' he said ordered, 'there's a lorry ahead!'

There was – a US Army transport, apparently stopped. She nearly ran into the back of it, and as she did, she saw it was the last in a line of lorries loaded with what looked like crates of ammunition.

Oh no, she thought, and then realised the lorries were her salvation. 'It's a convoy,' she said, backing the Daimler up. 'We'll never get through.' She began turning it around, wishing the road wasn't so narrow.

'There's no need to turn round,' Stephen said, leaning out to look ahead. 'The front of the line's beginning to move.'

'You said you were late,' she said briskly, yanked on the wheel, completed the turn, and shot back the way they'd come.

'I'm not that late,' he said. 'And it would be a blessing if I missed the entire thing. It's one of those utterly pointless conferences on what should be done to stop these rocket attacks.' He had the map out and was poring over it. 'If we turn right at the next opportunity, it will take us—'

Straight back towards that V-1, she thought. 'I know a short-cut,' she said, and turned left instead and then left again.

'I'm not certain this is the road,' he said doubtfully, peering at the map.

'I've taken it before,' she lied. 'Why is it pointless?' she asked to prevent him from looking at the map. 'Your conference? Or can't you talk about it? Military secrets and all that?'

'It would be secret if there was anything to be done to stop them on this end which hasn't been done already – anti-aircraft defences, detection devices, barrage balloons, none of which has been at all effective, as you and your ambulance unit no doubt know.'

And none of which stopped the ones which are about to hit here, she thought, driving as fast as she dared to get them out of the danger zone. The lanes were narrow and rutted, and there was no room to turn. If they ran into a car going the other way …

Behind them, she heard a muffled explosion. The 12:56 V-1. She waited for the second one, which would mean it had hit the convoy, but it didn't come.

'As I was saying, none of our defences is at all effective,' Stephen said calmly. 'The only way to stop them is to prevent them from being launched in the first place.'

The lane was narrowing. She turned off it onto another which was just as narrow and even more rutted. She glanced at her watch. One o'clock.

She needed to get them out of the danger area before 1:08, when the second V-1 had hit the bridge. She drove faster, praying for a road to turn onto. They passed a field of barley and then an ammunition dump, from where the convoy had probably originated, another field, another, and then a small grove of trees. Beyond it lay a bridge.

Of course, Mary thought, and glanced at her watch again. 1:06.

*We are all going to have whistles as Mr Bendall thinks if we
are buried, it will be useful to our rescues. This I consider quite
useful and if buried shall whistle with all my might.*

VERE HODGSON'S DIARY 28 FEBRUARY 1944

LONDON – OCTOBER 1940

As soon as they reached the landing, Mike asked Polly, 'What
if the retrieval team was in Padgett's looking for Eileen, just
like we were?'

'But … they can't have been,' Polly stammered.

She'd thought he'd brought her down here to the landing to
ask her if she'd found out whether there'd been any fatalities. But
the idea that some of those fatalities might have been the retrieval
team had never occurred to her. The possibility so knocked her
back on her heels that for a moment it seemed entirely possible.
It would explain why there'd been five casualties – the three
there were supposed to be and the two-man retrieval team.

'Why couldn't they have been?' Mike pressed her. 'Who else
could they be? You heard Eileen's supervisor. Everyone who
worked there had been accounted for. And that would explain
why they haven't been found yet – because they don't know
there's anyone to look for.'

'But they knew Padgett's was going to be hit. They wouldn't
have gone—'

'We knew it was going to be hit, and *we* did. What if they saw

43

us go in and followed us? If they didn't realise we'd taken the elevator down, they might still have been looking for us when the HE hit.'

There was no reason why a retrieval team, like historians, couldn't be killed on assignment. And if that was what had happened, then Oxford hadn't been destroyed and Colin hadn't been killed. And Mike hadn't lost the war.

She wondered if that was why he was so determined that this was what had happened. Because, bad as it was, it was better than the alternative.

On the other hand, it could explain why their retrieval teams hadn't shown up, and why there were five fatalities.

You don't know for certain that there are, she reminded herself. *You need to find out*. And soon. Before Mike heard about the five. *I must go to the hospital tomorrow. And keep him away from Miss Laburnum and newspapers till then*. He'd said they needed to check her drop and see if it was working. If she could take him there as soon as they got out of here—

'As soon as the all-clear goes, I'm going back to Padgett's,' he said. 'I've got to tell them there may still be casualties in the wreckage. If it's the retrieval team, they won't be looking for them.'

'But you can't—'

'I won't tell them it's the retrieval team. I'll say I saw some people going in while I was waiting for Eileen. We can't just leave them there. They may still be alive.'

No, they aren't, Polly thought. *Whoever it is, they've already been pulled out of the wreckage dead*. But she couldn't say that.

'We have to help them,' Mike said.

'We can't—'

'Mike?' Eileen called from above them. 'Polly? Where are you?'

'Down here,' Mike shouted, and they heard her start down the clanking steps.

44

'Don't say anything to her about this till we know for certain,' Polly whispered to Mike. 'She's—'

'I know,' he whispered back. 'I won't.'

Eileen came down to where they were standing. 'You weren't leaving to go to the drop without me, were you?'

'Not a chance,' Mike said. 'We were just trying to figure out what other historians might be here besides Gerald Phipps.'

'Why did you come down *here* to do that?'

'We didn't want to disturb you,' Polly said.

Mike nodded. 'We couldn't sleep, and we thought we might as well make use of the time. Don't worry, we wouldn't go off and leave you.'

'I know you wouldn't,' Eileen said shamefacedly. 'I'm sorry. It's only that I can't bear the thought of being here all alone again.' She sat down on the step. 'So have you thought of anyone?'

And you'd better come up with something quickly, Polly said silently, *or she'll know we're lying.*

'Yeah,' Mike said, 'Jack Sorkin, but unfortunately, he's on the USS *Enterprise* in the South Pacific.'

'What about your roommate?' Eileen asked. 'Wasn't he doing World War II?'

'Yes, but that doesn't do us any good either. Charles is doing Singapore.'

Oh my God: Singapore! Polly thought. *And if his drop isn't working, like ours, he'll still be there when the Japanese arrive. He'll be captured and put in one of their prison camps.* She wondered if Mike realised that. She hoped not.

'Who else?' she asked to change the subject. 'Eileen, what about the other people in your year? Were any of them doing World War II?'

'I don't think so. Damaris Klein might ... no, I think she was doing the Napoleonic Wars. What about the historian who was doing the rocket attacks?' She turned to Polly. 'When did those begin, Polly?'

'June thirteenth of 1944,' Polly said, 'which is too late to be of any use. We need someone here *now*.'

'And we don't know who it was who did the V-1 attacks,' Mike said.

'But if we can't find anyone else—' Eileen said. 'Mike, are you certain they didn't say who it was?'

'They might have ...' he said, frowning as if trying to remember.

'Could it have been Saji Llewellyn?' Polly asked.

'No, she was observing Queen Beatrice's coronation. You know that, Polly,' Mike said. 'Do either of you know Denys Atherton?'

'I've seen him at lectures and things,' Eileen said, 'but I've never spoken to him. What's he doing?'

'I don't know,' Mike said, 'but it's something from March first to June fifth 1944, which is also too late to help us. What would he be observing then, Polly? The war in Italy?'

'No, he would have come through earlier for that. He's likelier to have been observing the build-up to the invasion, especially since his return date's one day before D-Day.'

'Which means he'll be here in England,' Mike said. 'Where? Portsmouth? Southampton?'

'Yes, or Plymouth or Winchester or Salisbury,' Polly said. 'The build-up was spread over the entire southwestern half of the country. Or he could be observing Fortitude, in which case he'd be in Kent. Or Scotland.'

'Fortitude?' Eileen said. 'What's that?'

'An intelligence operation to fool Hitler and the German High Command into believing the Allies were attacking somewhere other than Normandy. They built dummy Army installations and planted false news stories in the local papers and sent faked radio messages. Fortitude North was in Scotland. Its mission was to convince the Germans the invasion would be in Norway, and Fortitude South in southeast England's mission was to convince them it was coming at the Pas de Calais.'

'So Denys Atherton could be anywhere,' Mike said.

'And if he's working in Intelligence, he won't be using his own name,' Polly said.

'But I know what he looks like,' Eileen said. 'He's tall and has dark curly hair—'

'Christ,' Mike said, 'I hadn't even thought about names. That means Phipps could be here under some other name too. Eileen, did he say anything about whether he'd be using his own name or not?'

'No.'

Polly asked Mike, 'And you didn't see his name on the letters he was carrying?'

'No,' he said disgustedly.

'But you and Eileen both know what he looks like.'

'If I can only remember the name of his airfield,' Eileen said ruefully. 'I *know* I'd know it if I heard it.'

'It'll be in the railway guide,' Polly said. 'I'll see if Mrs Rickett has one in the morning, and if she doesn't, I know Townsend Brothers has one in the book department. I used it to look up the trains to Backbury. I'll buy it on Monday. And in the meantime, the best thing we can do is get some sleep. We'll all be able to think more clearly if we've had some rest.' *And I'll be able to think of a way to keep Mike from going to Padgett's in the morning*, she thought.

But how? Telling him that they couldn't help, that historians couldn't affect events, brought them back to Hardy. And telling him it had already happened and there were fatalities, and therefore there was no point in trying, not only sounded completely heartless, but was too much like their own situation. And hopefully Mr Dunworthy wasn't telling Colin the same thing at this very moment.

She would have to persuade Mike that she should be the one to go to Padgett's. 'Mr Fetters is less likely to recognise me than Eileen or you,' she could tell him, 'especially if I change my clothes and put my hair up. I can tell him I was waiting outside

47

for Eileen and saw people go in just as the store closed.'

But when she tried to persuade him, waking him up before the all-clear so the sleeping Eileen wouldn't hear, he insisted on going himself.

'But shouldn't I show you where the drop is first?' Polly asked. 'If it's working, you can go through and tell Oxford to send a team disguised as rescue workers.'

He shook his head. 'We'll go to Padgett's first and then the drop.'

'But what will we tell Eileen?'

He finally agreed to take Eileen back to Mrs Rickett's, tell her the two of them were going to the drop, and *then* go to Padgett's.

Which created a whole new problem. If they left now, they'd run straight into the troupe, and Miss Laburnum would almost certainly say something about the five fatalities.

'We need to wait here till everyone's gone so they don't see us leaving the emergency staircase,' she said. 'Once they realise it's not locked, all sorts of people will want to use it. And we should let Eileen sleep, poor thing. I doubt if she's had a good night's rest since she came to London.'

'All right,' he said, and agreed to let Eileen sleep another half an hour, during which Polly hoped he'd fall asleep and she could go and find out alone. But he didn't, and after they'd walked Eileen home and Polly had got her safely upstairs without seeing anyone, he insisted on going straight to Padgett's, even though it had begun to rain again. And there was nothing for it but to go with him and hope a rescue crew was digging, or Mike might insist on going down into the pit himself.

But they were there, at least a dozen men hard at work with picks and shovels, in spite of the rain, and the incident officer had just come on duty and didn't know if they'd recovered any victims or not. 'But they must think there are some of them under there,' he said when Mike told him he'd seen three people going in. 'Or they wouldn't be working like that.'

Which seemed to satisfy Mike, at least for the moment, and when Polly said they needed to go *now* or they'd run into people on their way to church – which was true, even though St George's was no longer there; the rector was conducting services at St Bidulphus' – Mike agreed to leave the dig and let her take him to the drop.

She felt guilty over it – it was raining harder than ever, and even with the mackintosh Miss Laburnum had got him, he'd freeze sitting on the cold steps. But she *had* to have time to find out the truth about the fatalities.

And Mike didn't seem dismayed by the rain. 'At least there won't be many contemps out in this,' he said, 'so there'll be less chance of the shimmer being seen.'

He was right about no one being out in the rain. The streets were deserted. Polly led Mike through the partially cleared rubble to the alley and over to the passage which led to the drop. The rain had washed away the chalked messages she'd scrawled on the walls and the barrels, but the ones on the door were still there, and she was glad to see that the overhang had largely protected the steps and the well.

'It seems fairly dry in here,' she said. But it was also untouched. The dust, leaves and spiderwebs were all still there.

'You put this "For a good time, ring Polly" here?' Mike asked, pointing at the door.

'Yes, and I put an arrow on that barrel,' she said, pointing, 'and Mrs Rickett's address and the name of Townsend Brothers on the back, though I imagine the rain's washed them away. I thought if the retrieval team came, it could help them find me.'

'It was a good idea,' he said. 'I had one like it when I was in the hospital.'

'You were going to put messages on your gun emplacement?'

'No, in the newspapers. We could put an ad in the classifieds.'

'An ad? What sort of ad? "Stranded travellers seek retrieval team to come and get them?"'

'Exactly. Only not in those words. They'll have to look like all the other classified ads, but be worded so someone from Oxford would recognise them as being from us and know what they mean.'

'"Wounds my heart with a monotonous languor",' Polly murmured.

'What?'

'That was the coded message they sent out over the BBC to the French Resistance the day before D-Day. It's from a Verlaine poem. It meant "Invasion imminent".'

'Exactly,' Mike said. 'Coded messages.'

'But that could be dangerous. If they decide we're German spies—'

'I'm not talking about "The dog barks at midnight" or "Wounds my heart with—"' whatever the hell you said. I'm talking about, "R.T. Meet me in Trafalgar Square noon Friday, M.D."'

Polly shook her head. 'Meetings in public places are nearly as suspect as "The dog barks at midnight".'

'All right, then, we'll make it "R.T. Can't wait to see you, darling. Meet me Trafalgar Square noon Friday. Love, Pollykins."'

'I suppose that might work,' Polly said thoughtfully. The classifieds were full of messages to and from lovers, and from people who'd gone to the country or been bombed out, notifying their friends and relations of their new addresses. 'But there are dozens of London newspapers. How will we know which one to put the message in?'

'We'll work that out later,' he said. 'In the meantime, we need to replace the messages you wrote here that have been washed off.'

'They'll only be washed off again.'

'Then we'll have to buy some paint.'

'And hope this rain stops,' Polly said, looking up at the rain dripping from the overhang. 'Do you want me to bring you an umbrella?'

'Not if it's that bright green one of Eileen's. It can be seen for miles. I'm trying *not* to be seen, remember?'

'Mine's black. I'll bring it,' she promised. 'And something to eat.'

And a Thermos of hot tea, she thought. *But not till I see Marjorie.*

Visiting hours weren't till ten, and – in spite of everything they'd already done this morning – it was still only half-past eight. But if she went back to Mrs Rickett's, Eileen might be awake and want to come with her. And perhaps this early the stern ward sister who'd refused to answer her questions wouldn't be on duty yet.

She wasn't. A very young nurse was. Good. 'Have you a patient named James Dunworthy here?' Polly asked her. 'I was told he was brought here the night before last. From Padgett's?'

The nurse checked the records. 'No, we've no one by that name.'

'Oh dear,' Polly said anxiously, calling on the acting techniques Sir Godfrey had taught her, 'my friend was certain he was brought here. She works at Padgett's with Mr Dunworthy, and she asked me to find out for her. She was a bit banged up and couldn't come herself. She's terribly worried about him. Mr Dunworthy would have been brought in early in the evening.'

'I wasn't on duty that night. Let me see what I can find out,' the nurse said, and went off. When she returned, she said, 'I spoke by telephone with the ambulance crew who handled the incident, and they only transported one' – a fractional hesitation – 'injured victim to hospital, and it was a woman.' And the pause meant the 'injury victim' had died on the way to hospital, just as Marjorie had said.

'But if he wasn't brought here, then that means—' Polly said, and clapped her hand to her mouth. 'Oh no, how dreadful.'

'You mustn't worry,' the nurse said sympathetically, and looked quickly round to make certain no one was in earshot. 'I asked the ambulance crew about fatalities, and they said both the others were women, too.'

Three fatalities, not five. 'Did they work at Padgett's?' Polly asked.

'No. They haven't been identified yet.'

So there was still a possibility that they might be the retrieval team. If it was Polly's or Eileen's team, they'd almost certainly have sent women to fit in at a department store, though they usually only sent two historians to retrieve. But what if they were Polly's *and* Eileen's teams?

At least it wasn't a discrepancy. 'Oh, my friend will be so relieved!' Polly said truthfully. 'There must have been some sort of mix-up.'

She thanked the nurse profusely and hurried out of the hospital and down the steps, where she nearly collided with a pair of young nurses in dark blue capes coming on duty. 'Last night I went to an RAF dance and met the most adorable lieutenant,' one of them was staying. 'He's a pilot. He's stationed at Boscombe Down. He said he'd come to see me on his next leave.'

Boscombe Down. Could that be the name of Gerald's airfield? It was two words, and it began with a B *and* a D. It had to be it.

She'd expected to need to spend the entire day tracking down the information about the casualties, but now that she'd solved both her problems, she could actually do what she'd told Eileen she intended to do and go and visit Marjorie. It would mean one less lie she could be caught out in.

But it wasn't ten yet, and at any rate she couldn't go in the front when she was supposed to be hurrying off to tell her friend from Padgett's that James Dunworthy was all right.

She knew which ward Marjorie was in from her earlier attempt to visit, so she wouldn't need to ask, but if the nurse saw her going up …

She found the emergency entrance and waited out of sight till an ambulance pulled in, bells clanging, and began to unload patients, and then walked purposefully past them and the attendants coming out to help.

From there, she darted up the first flight of stairs she saw to the fourth floor and into Marjorie's ward. And found she needn't have gone to all the trouble of inquiring after a fictitious patient to find out what she needed to know. She could have simply asked Marjorie.

'I was wrong about five people being killed. There were only three,' Marjorie said, sitting propped against her pillows, her arm in a sling. 'None of them worked at Padgett's. They've no idea who they were or what they were doing there. Like me. If I'd been killed, no one would have known what I was doing in Jermyn Street either.'

'What *were* you doing there?'

'I went to meet Tom,' she said, and at Polly's blank look, she added, 'the airman I told you about. He'd been after me to go away with him, and I wouldn't, but then when you were nearly killed at St George's, I thought, why not? I might be killed tomorrow. I've got to snatch at life while I can.'

Polly's heart began to pound. 'You changed your mind because of me?'

'Yes. When I saw you that morning, your skirt torn and your face all covered in plaster, it brought it home to me that you might have *died* – that *I* could die at any moment. And that working at Townsend's would have been all there was to my life. And I decided I wasn't going to die without ever doing anything, so the next time Tom came in – it was the Friday you went to see your mother – I told him I'd go away with him.'

And when she went to meet him, she'd been hit, buried, nearly killed. *And I did it,* Polly thought. *I'm the one who put her there.*

She'd been assuring Mike that he hadn't saved Hardy, that Hardy would have seen the boat even without Mike's pocket torch or been rescued by some other boat, but there was no other reason why Marjorie would have been in Jermyn Street that

Friday night. No other reason for her broken arm and cracked ribs, for her having spent all those hours in the rubble, for her nearly having been killed.

But that's impossible, Polly thought. *Historians can't alter events. The net won't let them.*

Unless Mike's right. And suddenly she thought of the UXB at St Paul's. What if it hadn't been an error in the historical record, that it had been removed on Saturday and not Sunday? What if the time difference was a discrepancy?

KENT – APRIL 1944

'**T**he *Queen*?' Ernest said. 'I can't visit the Queen. Cess and I have been up all night inflating tanks. I need to go to Croydon and deliver this week's newspaper articles and letters to the *Call*. I've already missed the *Sudbury Weekly Shopper's* deadline. I can't afford to miss another one.'

'Your royal sovereign,' Prism said, 'is far more important than – what is it you were writing up yesterday? A garden party?'

'Tea party. For the officers of the Twenty-first Airborne, newly arrived from Bradley Field. That's not the point. The point is that these stories must go in on schedule or the troop movements will have to be completely redone.'

'Prism will help you,' Moncrieff said. 'And at any rate, this will only take a couple of hours. We'll be back in plenty of time for you to deliver your stories.'

'That's what Cess said about the tanks last night.'

'Yes, but this is quite nearby. At Mofford House. It's only a few miles beyond Lymbridge.'

'Can't Chasuble go instead? Or Gwendolyn?'

'He's already there setting up. And Chasuble's over at Camp

Omaha, rigging up a chimney for the mess tent.'

'What does the mess tent need a chimney for? They're not cooking anything.'

'But they must *look* as if they are,' Prism said. 'And you must go. You're the one who's going to write this all up for the London papers.'

The London papers meant the story would get a good deal more notice than an article in the *Call*, particularly if there was an accompanying photograph, and it was a chance to meet Queen Elizabeth, which any Fortitude South agent – or any historian – would give his eyeteeth for. Plus, it looked as if he was going to go whether he wanted to or not. 'Do I need to bring my camera?' Ernest asked.

'No. The London papers will have their photographers there. All you need is your pyjamas,' Chasuble said, and Prism dumped them, his slippers and his robe into Ernest's arms. 'Now come along, we're late.'

'If it's not too much to ask,' Ernest said once they were in the staff car, with Moncrieff driving, 'w*hy* am I meeting the Queen in my pyjamas?'

'Because you've been wounded,' Moncrieff said. 'A broken foot would be appropriate, I think.' He looked back at Ernest in the back seat. 'We'll put you in a plaster and on crutches. Unless you'd rather have a broken neck.'

'Have you any idea what he's babbling on about?' Ernest leaned forward to ask Prism.

'We're attending the ribbon-cutting for a hospital,' Chasuble explained. 'They've turned Mofford House into a military hospital to deal with the soldiers who'll be coming back wounded from the invasion.'

'Which hasn't happened yet. So how can we be invasion casualties?'

'We're not. We were wounded at Tripoli. Or Monte Cassino, whichever you prefer.'

'But—'

'We're window dressing,' Prism said impatiently. 'The newspaper stories you'll write will say that the hospital has only a few patients at present, but that its capacity is six hundred, and that it's one of five new hospitals that will open in the area over the next four months.'

'Which plays nicely into the scenario that the invasion's scheduled for mid-July,' Ernest said. 'So the Queen will be seen visiting the wards?'

'Ward,' Prism said. 'We were only able to mock up one for the ribbon-cutting. The hospital in Dover couldn't spare the beds for more than that, and Lady Mofford wasn't keen on having her entire house turned into a hospital just for one afternoon's photographs.'

'Afternoon?' Ernest said. 'I thought you said this would only take a couple of hours.'

'It will. There'll be a speech welcoming the Queen, a visit to the ward, and then tea. The Queen's supposed to arrive at one.'

'One o'clock this afternoon?' Cess cried. 'That's *hours* from now. And Worthing and I haven't even had breakfast. Why did we need to leave now?'

'I told you,' Prism said imperturbably. 'The Queen will be there. One can't keep royalty waiting. And we need to help set up.'

'But I'm starving!' Cess said.

'And I must be in Croydon by four o'clock, or my articles won't make this week's edition.'

'Then they'll have to go in next week's.'

'That's what you said last week,' Ernest said. 'At this rate, they won't go in till *after* the invasion, and a bloody lot of good they'll do then.'

'Very well,' Prism said. 'When we get there I'll ring up Lady Bracknell and have Algernon take them to Bexhill for you.'

Which would completely defeat the purpose. 'They're not done yet,' he said. 'I'd intended to finish writing them up last night, and instead I ended up playing matador.'

'With a tank as his cape,' Cess said, and launched into an account of their adventures with the bull and his charging of the tank, which Prism and Moncrieff both found highly amusing.

'Today won't be nearly so dangerous,' Moncrieff said. 'And don't worry, we'll have you back to the castle in plenty of time.'

At which point, I will no doubt be sent to blow up more tanks.

'Speaking of dangers,' Prism said, 'you need to read this.' He handed a sheet of paper back to Ernest over the seat. 'It's a memo from Lady Bracknell.'

'Warning us,' Cess said, 'about' – he lowered his voice to a sinister whisper – 'spies in our midst.'

Ernest snatched the paper from Prism. 'Spies?'

'Yes,' Cess said. 'It says we're to look out for suspicious behaviour, particularly for people who seem unfamiliar with local customs. And we're not to discuss our mission with *anyone*, no matter how harmless and trustworthy they seem, because they might be German spies. That bull this morning, for instance.'

'It's not a joking matter,' Prism said. 'If there's a security breach, it could endanger the entire invasion.'

'I know,' Cess said. 'But whom exactly does Bracknell think we'd talk to? The only people we ever see are irate farmers, except for Ernest here—'

'And the only people I talk to are irate editors who want to know why my articles are always late,' Ernest said. He needed to get this conversation off the topic of spies. 'And I doubt very much that they'll believe I missed their deadline because I was having tea with the Queen. How are we supposed to address her, by the way? Your Majesty? Your Highness?'

'There! You see that?' Cess said, pointing an accusing finger at him. 'Unfamiliarity with local customs. Definitely suspicious behaviour. And he behaved *very* oddly around that bull. Are you a spy, Worthing?' he said, and when Ernest didn't answer, 'Well, *are* you?'

'We shall fight in the offices ... and in the hospitals ...'

WINSTON CHURCHILL, 1940

LONDON – 27 OCTOBER 1940

The moment Polly returned from seeing Marjorie, Eileen said, 'Mr Fetters rang up while you were gone. He said they'd found three bodies in Padgett's.' Which meant Polly hadn't had to go to the hospital after all.

She wished she hadn't. She'd gone there to prove the number of dead wasn't a discrepancy so that Mike could stop worrying that he'd altered events, only to find that she'd altered them.

Don't be ridiculous, she thought. *Historians can't do that.* And there were dozens of reasons why Mr Dunworthy could have got the time of the St Paul's UXB's removal wrong. The newspaper could have moved the time up to throw the Germans off. During the V-1 and V-2 attacks, they'd printed false accounts of where the rockets fell to trick the Germans into shortening their range. They might have done something like that with the UXB, to convince the Germans the bomb was easier to defuse than it had been. Or they could simply have got the time wrong, like the nurses at Padgett's.

You thought the number of fatalities was a discrepancy, she reassured herself, *and it turned out it wasn't. And look at your last assignment. For a few weeks there, you were convinced you'd altered events, but you hadn't. Everything worked out exactly the same as it would have if you hadn't been there.*

And this will, too. The doctors say Marjorie's going to make a full recovery, and it isn't as if she married her airman or got pregnant. In a few days she'll be out of hospital and back at Townsend Brothers, just as if nothing had happened. And all I have to do is make certain Mike doesn't find out what Marjorie said. And that Eileen kept the Hodbins from going on the City of Benares.

She wondered if she should caution Eileen again not to say anything about that, but she didn't want her inquiring why. And Eileen wasn't likely to bring up the subject of the Hodbins to Mike for fear that he'd make her write to them and tell them where she lived. At any rate, the only thing on Eileen's mind was what had happened at Padgett's.

'Mr Fetters says they were three charwomen,' Eileen said. 'They didn't work at Padgett's. They worked at Selfridge's. He said they must have been on their way to work when the raids began and took shelter in Padgett's basement.'

Which meant Mike could also stop worrying about the fatalities being the retrieval team, and so could she. *And now all I have to worry about is where the team is. And whether it will show up before my deadline. And about the possibility that Oxford's been destroyed.*

And about Eileen, who'd been badly shaken by the knowledge that, 'We could have been in that basement shelter, too.'

'No, we couldn't,' Polly had said firmly. 'Because I know when and where the raids are, remember?' *At any rate till January.*

'You're right.' Eileen looked reassured. 'It was a tremendous comfort yesterday going to Stepney, knowing there weren't going to be any sirens.'

Except the one that had sounded at Townsend Brothers. Had that been a discrepancy, too?

'Oh, and I wanted to ask you,' Eileen said, 'Mr Fetters said Padgett's is reopening "on a limited basis" next month, and asked me if I was interested in coming back to work there, and

I wondered what I should tell him. I mean, we mightn't be here by then—'

Or we might.

'I'll ask Mike,' Polly said. 'I'm going to check on him now and take him a blanket.'

'Can I come with you?'

'No, there are too many people about. I'll show you tonight where the drop is. Oh, I nearly forgot. I think I found the airfield Gerald's at. Was it Boscombe Down?'

'No,' Eileen said. She looked thoughtful. 'Though the B sounds right. I'm sorry ...'

'It's all right,' Polly said, fighting back disappointment. She'd been so certain that was it. 'I'll go and ask Mrs Rickett if she has an ABC. If she does, you can look through the names while I'm gone.'

Mrs Rickett didn't have one. Miss Laburnum was certain she had one 'somewhere' in her room before she said, 'Oh, that's right, I lent it to my niece when she was visiting from Cheshire.' And then insisted on showing Polly two coconuts she'd managed to scrounge up for the play and relating in detail the time she'd seen Sir Godfrey onstage when she was a girl. It was two o'clock before Polly was able to escape, by which time she was convinced that Mike would be dead from hypothermia.

He wasn't, and even though his teeth were chattering, he refused to leave the drop. 'There have been contemps in the area all day,' he told her. 'It'll have a much better chance of opening after the raids start tonight.'

'But it won't help to have you freeze to death,' she said and tried to persuade him to let her spell him long enough for him to go to Mrs Leary's and eat his supper, but he refused.

'The more coming and going there is, the greater the chance someone will see us,' he argued.

'Won't you at least let me bring you another blanket and something to eat?'

'No, I'll be fine. Where are the raids tonight?'

'The East End, the City and Islington.'

'Good. Then there won't be firemen or rescue workers around here to see the shimmer. Were you able to find out anything about the casualties at Padgett's?'

'Yes.' She told him about the three dead charwomen. 'So it wasn't the retrieval team. And there wasn't a discrepancy.'

'Good,' he said, sounding relieved. 'What about Phipps' whereabouts? Were you able to get hold of a railway guide?'

'Not yet, but I'll look at the one at Townsend Brothers to-morrow, and I should be able to find out some more airfields at Notting Hill Gate tonight,' she said, thinking of her troupe mates Lila and Viv. 'Is there anything else you want us to do?'

'Yes, buy some newspapers for us to use for our classifieds. And keep pumping Eileen about what else Gerald said. You haven't figured out what his joke about getting her driving authorisation meant, have you?'

'No. The only thing I've been able to think of is that RAF pilots carried their papers in a waterproof wallet in case they had to ditch in the Channel, but the wallet wasn't red, and I don't see what—'

'But at least that tells us we're on the right track with his being at an airfield,' he said. 'You'd better go. When are the sirens supposed to go tonight?'

'I don't know.' She explained about having left before Colin got the siren data to her. 'The raids begin at 7:50. Here, take my coat. I can borrow one for tonight,' she said, draping it over his knees. 'And if it begins to rain again, go home. Don't try to be a hero.'

'I won't,' he promised, and she hurried back to the boarding house, got Eileen, took her to Notting Hill Gate and sent her off to Holborn to see if the lending library had an ABC.

'If they don't,' she said, 'borrow some newspapers.' She told Eileen about Mike's idea of using the classifieds to tell the retrieval team where they were.

'*I* know where we can find examples of ads,' Eileen said eagerly. '*A Murder is Announced*.'

'What?' Polly said.

'It's a mystery novel. By Agatha Christie. It's full of classified ads— Oh no, that won't work,' she said glumly.

'Why not? The library at Holborn has several Agatha Christie novels, and if they don't have it there, I'm certain one of the bookshops in Charing Cross Road—'

'No, they won't. It wasn't written till after the war.' She cheered up. 'But I think there's one in *The Dawson Pedigree* that we could use.' She started towards the Central Line.

'Wait,' Polly said, 'you need to be back before half past ten. That's when the trains stop.'

'Yes, Fairy Godmother,' Eileen said. 'Any other instructions?'

'Yes. Keep a close watch on your belongings. There's a band of urchins at Holborn who pick people's pockets.'

'Of course. It's my fate to be surrounded by horrible children no matter where I go. But at least it's not the Hodbins,' she said, and went off to catch her train. Polly went out to the District Line platform where the troupe was rehearsing to talk to Lila and Viv.

They weren't there. 'They went to a dance,' Miss Laburnum reported.

'On a *Sunday* night?' the rector said, shocked.

'It's an American USO dance,' Miss Laburnum explained. 'I don't know *what* Sir Godfrey will say when he gets here. He *so* wanted to rehearse the shipwreck scene.'

What Sir Godfrey said, when he arrived a moment later, was, '"How all occasions do inform against me. False varlets! They have out-villained villainy!" Their foul perfidy leaves us no choice but to rehearse the rescue scene. We shall begin at the point at which the castaways have heard the ship's gun and have all rushed down to the beach.'

Polly and Sir Godfrey were the only ones in that scene, which meant she had no chance to look through Sir Godfrey's *Times* for airfields. And after rehearsal was over, when she asked Mrs Brightford if she knew the names of any, Sir Godfrey said dryly, 'Does this mean that you, too, will be abandoning us to "foot it featly here and there", Lady Mary?'

'No,' she said, hoping Holborn had had an ABC.

'It didn't,' Eileen reported on her return. 'And it only had two newspapers. The librarian said children keep taking them for the scrap paper drive. But she had *heaps* of Agatha Christies. Look,' she said excitedly, showing her '*Murder in the Calais Coach!*'

'It's the American edition of *Murder on the Orient Express.*'

'Is that the one you thought had a classified advert in it?'

'No, that's not by Agatha Christie, it's by Dorothy Sayers. At least I *think* that's what it was in. It might have been in *Murder Must Advertise* instead, and at any rate, the library didn't have either one. But' – she produced another paperback – 'it *did* have *The ABC Murders.*'

Which was not quite the same as an ABC. But, as Eileen said, it was full of place names which might help her remember. Eileen had also retrieved a wadded-up edition of the *Daily Mirror* from a dustbin.

She handed it to Polly, and Polly began looking through it for the names of airfields and any references to the afternoon raid. There was nothing about bombing – which was a relief – but nothing about a false alarm either, or an aeroplane crash.

There *was* a story about the Battle of Britain, which said the RAF's efforts had 'changed the course of the war', and which listed several airfields.

'Bicester?' Polly asked.

'No.'

'Broadwell?'

'No.'

It wasn't Greenham Common or Grove or Bickmarsh either. 'Have you had any luck remembering what else Gerald said?' Polly asked her.

'Nothing useful. I remember Linna was speaking on the phone to someone who was angry that the lab had changed the order of their French Revolution assignments.'

Let's hope they're not trapped there like we are here, Polly thought. *They might end up being guillotined.*

'I feel so stupid, not being able to remember,' Eileen said.

'You had no way of knowing it was important,' Polly re-assured her. 'We'll find the name of the airfield tomorrow when I buy the ABC.'

'Or your drop might have opened,' Eileen said, cheering up. 'And Mike will be waiting for us outside the station so we can all go through together.'

But when the all-clear went at five, he wasn't there, or at Mrs Rickett's. 'He probably went back to Mrs Leary's to sleep when the raids ended,' Polly said.

'Should we go to the drop to check?' Eileen asked.

'No, there are too many people about in the morning. And we need to get you a ration book before I go to work so you can start eating at Mrs Rickett's.'

But applying for a new ration book required an identity card, which had also been in Eileen's handbag, and since she'd been living in Stepney, she couldn't apply for a new one at the local council office. She had to go to the one nearest to where she'd been living.

'Which is where?' Polly asked the clerk at the Kensington council office.

'In Bethnal Green.'

'Bethnal *Green*?'

'Yes,' the clerk said, and told them the address.

'Are there raids in Bethnal Green today?' Eileen whispered as they left the counter.

'No,' Polly said.

'But you looked so—'

'I thought it might be where Gerald had said he was going. It begins with a B and has two words.'

'No, I'm almost certain the second word began with a P.'

Polly sent Eileen off and hurried to work and up to the book department, but the railway guide was no longer there. 'A man from the Ministry of War came in last week and took it,' Ethel said.

'*How all occasions do inform against us,*' Polly thought. 'Would you have a railway map, then?'

'No, he confiscated those as well. To keep them from falling into German hands. You know, in case of invasion. Though if they've got as far as Oxford Street, I shouldn't think they'd need maps, would you?'

'No,' Polly said, but that wasn't what worried her. What worried her was that the Ministry of War had come in *last week*. What did they know that had made them think invasion was coming now? Hitler had called off Operation Sealion at the end of September and postponed the invasion till spring.

What if he didn't? Polly thought. *What if this is a discrepancy?*

It could be a disastrous one. By spring he'd decided to abandon the invasion altogether so he could concentrate on attacking Russia. If he invaded now ...

'Are you all right?' Ethel asked her.

'Yes. If you haven't any railway maps, what about an ordinary map of England?' she asked.

'No, he took those as well. I take it someone in your family's a planespotter?'

'Yes,' Polly said, latching onto the explanation. 'My nephew. He's twelve.'

'My little brother spends all his time scanning the skies for Heinkels and Stukas.'

'So does my nephew,' Polly said and worked the conversation around to airfields. She got several more names from her, and another one on her lunch break, though none had two words of which the second began with a P.

But when she returned to her counter, there was good news.

66

Miss Snelgrove had told Doreen that Marjorie was being released from hospital and would be coming back to Townsend Brothers soon. Which meant this was just like her other assignment – it had *looked* like she'd altered events, but in the end things had worked out. She should have had more faith in time-travel theory and in the complexity of a chaotic system.

And she should have remembered her history lessons. The code for the D-Day invasion had been broken by the Nazis, which could have been catastrophic for the Allies – but when the wireless operator had shown Field Marshal von Rundstedt the message, he'd ignored it. 'I hardly think the Allies will announce the invasion over the wireless,' he'd said.

And there were hundreds of examples like that scattered throughout history. *'All's well that ends well,'* Polly thought, quoting Shakespeare and Sir Godfrey, and focused on quizzing Sarah Steinberg, whose brother was in the RAF, about airfields.

By the end of the day, she'd obtained a dozen names. She tried them out on Eileen when she came back from Bethnal Green, with no luck. Eileen hadn't been able to get an identity card either. 'The clerk in Bethnal Green told me I had to go to the National Registration office, but it isn't open on Monday.'

'It's probably just as well,' Polly said. 'Mrs Rickett serves trench pie on Monday night.'

'What's that?'

'No one knows. Mr Dorming's convinced she makes it out of rats.'

'It can't possibly be that bad,' Eileen said. 'And at any rate, I don't care. I can bear anything now that I've found you and Mike. I'd be willing to eat sawdust.'

'That would be Mrs Rickett's victory loaf, which we have on Thursdays,' Polly said. She tried to give Eileen some money for lunch, but she refused it.

'We'll need all our money for our train fare to the airfield,' she said, and went off to see if Selfridge's had an ABC.

It didn't. And neither did the *Daily Herald*'s office. When

Polly got off work, Eileen and Mike were both waiting for her outside the staff entrance, and they reported no luck in finding one.

And no luck with the drop. 'I stayed there till two,' Mike said, 'and nary a shimmer of a shimmer.'

He'd spent the rest of the afternoon at the *Herald*, going through July and August issues for airfield names. As soon as they got to Notting Hill Gate and the emergency staircase – which was colder than ever – he tried them on Eileen. 'Bedford?'

'No,' Eileen said, 'I'm convinced it was two words.'

'Beachy Head?'

'That sounds a bit like it ... no.'

'She thinks the second word begins with a P,' Polly said.

'He checked his list. 'Bentley Priory?'

Eileen frowned. 'No ... it wasn't Priory. It was Paddock or Place or ...' She frowned, attempting to remember.

He checked the list again. 'No Ps,' he said. 'How about Biggin Hill?'

Eileen hesitated. 'Perhaps ... I'm not certain ... I'm so sorry. I thought I'd know it when I heard it, but now I've heard so many ... I'm not certain ...'

'You're sure it's not Biggin Hill?' he asked. 'It would be a logical choice. It was in the thick of the Battle of Britain.'

'So was Beachy Head,' Polly said. 'And Bentley Priory. And that's the one that's nearest Oxford. Perhaps we should try that first.'

'But it's not just an airfield, it's the RAF command centre,' Mike said, 'which means security will be tighter. Biggin Hill's closest. I say we try that first and then the other two. Now, what about messages we can send? Did you tell Eileen my idea, Polly?'

'Yes,' she said, and to prevent Eileen from launching into an account of mystery novels that hadn't yet been written, she said, 'How's this for an ad? "Historian seeks situation involving travel. Available immediately"?'

'Great,' Mike said, scribbling it down. 'And we can do variations of your "meet me in Trafalgar Square" or Kensington Gardens or the British Museum.'

'There are lots of notices looking for soldiers who were at Dunkirk,' Eileen mused. 'What about "Anyone having information regarding the whereabouts of Michael Davies, last seen at Dunkirk, contact E. O'Reilly" and Mrs Rickett's address?'

Mike wrote their suggestions down. 'What about crosswords?' He pointed at the *Herald*'s puzzle. 'I could compose one with our names in the clues, like "This bird wants a cracker." Or "What an Italian tower might say if asked its name?"'

'Absolutely not,' Polly said.

'Because they're bad puns?'

'No, because a crossword nearly derailed D-Day.'

'How?'

'Two weeks before the invasion, five of the top-top-secret code words appeared in the *Daily Herald*'s crossword puzzle: "Overlord", "mulberry", "Utah", "Sword", and I forget the other one. The military was convinced the Germans had tumbled to the invasion and was ready to call the entire invasion off.'

'Had they?' Eileen asked. 'Tumbled to it?'

'No. The puzzle's author was a schoolmaster who'd been doing them for years. He told the military his students and dozens of other people composed the clues and that they'd have no way of knowing which puzzle they'd be in, and in the end they decided it was just a bizarre coincidence.'

'And was it?' Mike asked.

'No. Forty years later the *Herald* published a story about it, and a man who'd been one of the schoolmaster's students confessed he'd overheard two Army officers talking and had co-opted the words for clues with no idea what they meant.'

'But the puzzle incident wasn't till 1944,' Mike said. 'It isn't likely British Intelligence would be reading crossword puzzles now—'

'In which case the retrieval team won't be either. I think

they're much more likely to read personal advertisements. There are lots of "losts". Perhaps we could do something with that.'

'Like "Lost: historian. Reward for safe return"?'

'No,' Polly said, 'but we could say we'd lost something and give our name and address. Here's one. "Lost: pair of brown carpet slippers on Northern Line platform, Bank Station. If found—"'

'Oh,' Eileen said. They looked inquiringly at her. 'You told me to remember any detail, no matter how irrelevant, about my conversations with Gerald—'

'Does Gerald's airfield have the word "bank" in it?' Mike asked eagerly, grabbing for his list of names. 'Glaston Bank?'

'No, not that part. The bit about the slippers.'

They looked blankly at her.

'"Slippers" sounds like "slippage".'

'Slippage?'

'Yes. Linna was on the phone while I was talking to Gerald, and whoever she was talking to wanted to know how much slippage there was on someone's drop, and then when I went through to Backbury, Badri was talking to someone about an increase in slippage, and Linna asked me if the slippage the last time I went through had increased from the other times.'

'And had it?' Mike asked.

'No, and when I told her that, she said, "Good", and looked at Badri.'

'Who was she talking to, do you know?'

'No. I assume it was Mr Dunworthy. She called him sir.'

'And it was an increase?' Mike asked eagerly. 'Not a decrease? You're sure?'

'Yes. Why?'

Because then there wasn't too little slippage, Polly thought. *And it couldn't have let Mike – or me – go to a place where we could alter events.*

'They questioned Phipps on his slippage, too,' Mike said. 'Did they say anything to you about it when you came through, Polly?'

'They asked me to note how much there was and tell them when I reported in.'

'And how much was there?'

'Four and a half days. It was only supposed to be an hour or two. I assumed there was a divergence point that—'

'I don't think so,' Mike said excitedly. 'I think a bunch of drops were experiencing an increase in slippage, and it was enough to worry them. Which means it couldn't have been a few days' worth. It must have been weeks. Or months.'

'And that's why our retrieval teams aren't here?' Polly said. 'Because the slippage sent them to November or December instead?'

He nodded.

'So all we need to do is wait for them to come and fetch us?' Eileen said eagerly.

'No. It might be a while before they get here, and in case you haven't noticed, this is kind of a dangerous place. The sooner we can find a working drop and get out of here, the better.'

'But if there's slippage, then Gerald's drop won't open either, will it?' Polly asked.

'Even if it doesn't, he may know more about what the slippage problem is and how long we're looking at. That means finding him's still our first priority. And our second's to make sure the retrieval team can find us when they get here. Eileen, have you had a letter back from Lady Caroline?'

'No, not yet,' Eileen said, looking at Polly. She was obviously afraid he was going to ask her if she'd written to the Hodbins.

'What about you, Mike?' Polly asked hastily. 'Have you left a trail of bread crumbs for your team to follow?'

'Yes, I wrote to the hospital in Dover and Sister Carmody at Orpington, and I sent my address to the barmaid at the Crown and Anchor.'

'Barmaid?' Eileen said.

'Yes.' He told them about Daphne's coming to see him in hospital. 'She'll tell everybody in Saltram-on-Sea. I'll put this

"Meet me in Victoria Station" message in tomorrow's paper when I go down to the *Express* in the morning. I'm going to see if I can talk the paper into having me write a piece on "Our Biggin Hill Heroes". That'll help me get access, and I can earn some money while I'm at it. Maybe they'll even pay my way.'

'But aren't we *all* going?' Eileen asked.

'No, I'll be able to get there quicker and find out more in a shorter time if I'm on my own.'

'And I can't leave my job,' Polly said.

'I know,' Eileen said reluctantly, 'it's only … I think it's a bad idea for us to split up when it took us so long to find one another.'

'We're not splitting up,' Mike said, 'we're doing what Shackleton did.'

'Shackleton? Is he a historian?' Eileen asked.

'No, Ernest Shackleton, the Antarctic explorer. They were trapped in the ice, and he had to leave his crew behind to go and get help. If he didn't, none of them would get out. That's what I'm doing – going off to find help. If Gerald's at Biggin Hill, I'll ring you and have you come there.'

'You won't go through without us?'

'Of course not. I'll get you both out, I promise. In the meantime, Eileen, I want you get your name on file at the department stores, and Polly, keep trying to scout up an ABC.'

'I will,' she said.

She tried, with no luck at all. She also made a list of the next week's raids for Mike and Eileen to memorise, spent a fruitless evening in Victoria Station by the clock, waiting for the retrieval team and being accosted by soldiers, and then went to rehearsal in the hopes that Lila and Viv would be there. They were, but the troupe was rehearsing Act Two, which everyone was in, so she had no chance to ask them.

Mike returned from Biggin Hill Friday morning. 'No luck,' he told Polly leaning over her counter at Townsend Brothers. 'He's not at Biggin Hill. I got a look at every one of the ground crew *and* all the pilots. I don't suppose Eileen remembered the airfield name while I was gone?'

Polly shook her head.

'I was afraid of that. I brought a new list of names for her to look at. Is she at Mrs Rickett's?'

'No,' Polly said after a hasty look around to see if Miss Snelgrove was watching, 'she's still making the rounds of the department stores. She should be back soon. She said she was going to check in at lunch.'

'When's *your* lunch break?'

'Half-past twelve – yes, may I help you, sir?'

'May—? Oh yes,' he said, thankfully not looking over at Miss Snelgrove, who'd suddenly appeared. 'I'd like to see some stockings.'

'Yes, sir,' Polly said, bringing out a box and opening it. 'These are very nice, sir.'

He leaned forward to finger them. 'Do you have these in any other colours?' he asked, and then, under his breath, 'I'll meet you and Eileen at twelve-thirty at Lyons' Corner House.'

'Yes, sir. They also come in powder pink and ecru,' and, to give him an exit opportunity, 'I'm afraid we're out of ivory.'

'Oh, too bad. My girl had her heart set on ivory,' he said, and left, mouthing, 'Twelve-thirty' at her.

Eileen still wasn't back by then. Polly left a note for her and went to tell Mike, who'd got them a table in a secluded corner.

'I told her to meet us here,' she said, shrugging off her coat.

He handed her the menu. 'I'm afraid they're out of everything but fish-paste sandwiches.'

'Which is still better than anything at Mrs Rickett's,' Polly said. She handed him a sheet of paper.

'More airfield names?'

'No, next week's raids. The worst one's on the twelfth. Sloane Square Underground Station, seventy-nine casualties.'

'And no break in the nightly raids, I see,' he said, looking at the list.

'Not till next week. Then they shift to the industrial cities – Coventry and then Birmingham and Wolverhamp—'

'Coventry?'

'Yes. It was hit on the fourteenth. What's the matter?'

'I hadn't even thought of that,' he said excitedly. 'We've only been considering the historians who are here right now, not the ones who were here earlier.'

'Before 1940, you mean?'

'No, not earlier *now*,' he said, 'earlier in Oxford time. Historians who had World War II assignments last year. Or ten years ago. Like Ned Henry and Verity Kindle. Weren't they in Coventry the night it was bombed?'

'Yes, but that was two years ago— Oh,' she said, seeing what he was getting at. It didn't matter *when* historians had done it in their past. This was time travel. Here in 1940, they would do it two weeks from now.

'But there's no way we could get to Ned and Verity. We don't know where they were except that they were in the middle of Coventry, in the heart of the fire. And it's much too dangerous—'

'Not any more dangerous than Dunkirk,' Mike said. 'And we know one place they were – in the cathedral.'

'As it was burning down,' Polly said. 'You can't be thinking of trying to go there. The area around the cathedral was nearly a firestorm.'

'It might also be our fastest way out. We wouldn't necessarily have to find Ned and Verity. The drop was inside the cathedral, wasn't it? All we have to do is find *it*.'

'Mike, we can't go through their drop.'

'Why not? We *know* it was working.'

'But we can't use it because it was two years ago. We can't go through to a time we're already in. Their drop opens in Oxford two years ago, and two years ago—'

'*We* were all in Oxford,' he said. 'Sorry, I don't know what I was thinking. But we can send a message through them.'

'A message?'

'Yes. We find Verity and Ned before they go back and have them tell the lab where we are and that our drops won't open and to reset the drop so it opens in our time. There's no reason we can't do that, is there?'

'Yes, there is. Because we didn't.'

'You don't know that.'

'Yes, I do. If we'd found them and told them what had happened, Oxford would have known what was going to happen when it sent us through. *We'd* have known what was going to happen.'

He considered that. 'Maybe they couldn't tell us because it would create a paradox. If we knew we were going to be trapped, we wouldn't come, and we had to come because we *had* come.'

'But Mr *Dunworthy* wouldn't have let us come. You know how overprotective he is. He'd never have let you come knowing they couldn't get you out after you were injured.' *And he wouldn't have let me come knowing I had a deadline.*

But she couldn't say that. 'This is a man who was worried I might get my foot caught in a barrage-balloon rope,' she said instead. 'He'd never have let us get trapped in the Blitz. Or let you go to Coventry to get us out. The entire city burned. It would be suicide for you to go there. You're here to observe heroes, not die trying to be one.'

'Then we need to come up with somebody besides Ned and Verity. Who else was here? Didn't Dunworthy go to the Blitz at some point?'

'He went several times, but—'

'When?'

'I don't know. I know he observed the big raids on May tenth and eleventh, because he talked about watching the fire in the House of Commons, and that happened on the tenth.'

'And you said before that that was the worst raid of the Blitz?'

'Yes. Why?'

'Nothing. We need something sooner. When else was he here?'

'I don't know. I remember him telling a story about attempting to get to his drop, and the gates at Charing Cross Railway Station being shut and him not being able to get in.'

'But you don't know the date?'

'No.'

'But if he told you he was trying to get to his drop, that means it must have been somewhere near Charing Cross.'

'No, it doesn't. He might have been taking the train to his drop. He could have been going anywhere.'

'But it's a place to start, and we can't afford to leave any stone unturned. I want you to go and check it while I'm at Beachy Head. Unless one of these names I got at Biggin Hill turns out to be Phipps' airfield. Speaking of which, what's keeping Eileen?' he asked, glancing at his watch. 'I need to read them to her. I managed to wangle a ride to Beachy Head, and the guy's leaving at two, but I don't want to waste my time there if Gerald's at one of these other airfields.'

Eileen hurried in just as Mike was paying the bill, saying, 'Sorry, I was applying at Mary Marsh, and they kept me waiting.'

Mike read her the list. She shook her head decisively at each of the names.

'Okay, then, it's Beachy Head,' he said. He hurried off to catch his ride. 'I'll be back before the fourteenth.'

So you can go to Coventry, Polly thought.

She had to keep him from doing that, which meant she had to find Gerald's airfield. Over the next few days, she spent her lunch breaks going to Victoria and St Pancras Stations to copy down two-word names beginning with B and P from the departure boards and her evenings incurring Sir Godfrey's wrath by trying to get additional airfield names from Lila and Viv, but they were almost no help at all.

'We nearly always go to the dances at Hendon,' Lila said.

'There's one on Saturday,' Viv told her. 'You and your cousin could come with us.'

She nearly accepted. They could ask the airmen they danced with where else they'd been stationed. But she was afraid if they weren't there when Mike came back, he'd decide to go to Coventry, which would be not only dangerous but pointless.

Because if Mike had found Ned and Verity and given them the message, that would mean Mr Dunworthy had known for *years* that all this was going to happen and not only allowed it to but *arranged* it: arranged for Mike to go to Dunkirk, for Eileen to go to a manor where the evacuees had the measles, had manipulated and lied to all of them from the moment they entered Oxford.

It's impossible, she told herself.

But even as she thought it, she was remembering. *He made me bring extra money, he made me learn the raids through December. He insisted I work in a department store which was never hit during the entire Blitz.* And if they *had* managed to get a message through, then he'd have known they were pulled out in time and that they weren't in any actual danger.

But if Mr Dunworthy *had* lied, then why hadn't he sent Mike to Dunkirk in the first place instead of scheduling him to do Pearl Harbor and letting him get his L-and-A implant? And why had Linna and Badri been questioning everyone about increased slippage if they already knew about it?

Mike still wasn't back by the twelfth, and they'd had no word from him. It hadn't taken him this long when he went to Biggin Hill.

What if he went to Coventry without telling us? Polly thought. From behind the stocking counter, she looked over at the lifts, hoping one would open and Mike would emerge.

One of them finally did, but it wasn't Mike. It was Eileen. 'I came for two reasons,' she said. 'I'm determined to have the name of Gerald's airfield for Mike when he gets back from Beachy Head, so I came to tell you I'm going to go and scour the secondhand bookshops for an old ABC or a book about the RAF or *something* with airfield names, and I wanted to make certain there weren't any raids in Charing Cross Road today.'

'There aren't any daytime raids anywhere in London today,' Polly reassured her.

'Oh good. I'm sorry I'm such an infant about them—'

'It's not being an infant to be frightened of someone who's trying to kill you,' Polly said. 'You said you had two reasons for coming?'

'Yes. I wanted to tell you I found out why Lady Caroline didn't write. I got another letter from Mrs Bascombe. Lady Caroline's husband was killed.'

'Oh dear. Had you met him?'

'No, Lord Denewell worked in London at the War Office, and the house he was staying in was bombed—'

'Lord Denewell? You worked for Lady *Denewell*?'

'Yes, at Denewell Manor. Why? Is something wrong? Did you meet Lord Denewell?'

'No. Sorry. I saw Miss Snelgrove looking this way. Perhaps you'd better go—'

'I will. I only wanted to ask you if you thought it would be all right for me to send her a letter of condolence? I mean, with my being a servant and everything. I'm afraid she'll think I'm acting above my place, but—'

Polly cut her off. 'Miss Snelgrove's coming. We'll discuss it tonight. Go and look for your ABC.'

Eileen nodded. 'I won't come back till I have either a list of airfields or a map in hand.'

She started towards the lifts. 'Wait,' Polly said, running after her, 'if you have to ask for a map, tell them you want it for your nephew who's interested in planespotting. That way they won't be suspicious.'

'Planespotting … I never thought of that,' Eileen said. 'Polly, listen, I've just had an idea – uh-oh, Miss Snelgrove at eleven o'clock,' she whispered. 'I'll see you tonight,' and hurried off.

'Miss Sebastian,' Miss Snelgrove said.

'Yes, ma'am. I was only—'

'Miss Hayes will be returning to work today, and I'd like you to be here to assist her, so if you wouldn't mind waiting to take your lunch break till two—'

'I'm happy to,' Polly said and meant it. Marjorie was coming back to work. Polly'd been afraid she'd been too traumatised by her experience to stay in London, but she was coming back.

And when she arrived, she was nearly her old rosy-cheeked self. *I was right*, Polly thought. *I didn't alter the end result. Everything's worked out just as it would have if Marjorie'd never been injured.*

'I'll wrap your parcels for you till your arm's better,' she told Marjorie, 'though you can no doubt do better with one hand than I can with two. I never have got the hang of it, and now that the paper and string are rationed—'

But Marjorie was shaking her head. 'I'm not staying. I only came to tell everyone goodbye.'

'Goodbye?'

'Yes. I've handed in my notice.'

'But—'

'I— The nurses in hospital were so kind to me. I wouldn't have made it if it weren't for them, and it made me think about what *I* was doing to help win the war. I couldn't bear to see Hitler come marching down Oxford Street because I hadn't done all I could.' She took a deep breath. 'I've joined Queen Alexandra's Nursing Service. I'm going to be an Army nurse.'

> *'There are six evacuated children in our house. My wife and I hate them so much that we have decided to take away something for Christmas.'*

LETTER, 1940

LONDON – NOVEMBER 1940

I know exactly where I can get a map, Eileen thought, hurrying out of Townsend Brothers and up Oxford Street to the tube station to catch a train to Whitechapel. *Alf Hodbin has one. His planespotting map. Why didn't I think of it before?* She could get it from him and locate Gerald's airfield – she was positive she'd recognise the name when she saw it – and Polly and Mike would stop looking at her as though she were an imbecile for not remembering the name. And they could go to the airfield, find Gerald, and go home.

If Alf still has the map, she thought. *And if he'd give it to her.* He might well refuse, especially if he sensed how badly she needed it. Hopefully he and Binnie would still be in school and she could get it from their mother instead and not have to worry about Alf's refusing or about the children following her and finding out where she lived. Though it wouldn't matter – she wouldn't be here that much longer.

She looked at her watch. It was just one. She should be able to get to Whitechapel well before school let out. But Alf and Binnie had constantly played truant in Backbury, and Mrs Hodbin didn't seem the type who'd see to it they went to school. And if they were there ...

I'm going to have to bribe them, she decided. But with what?

I *know*, she thought, and took a train to the Tower of London, where she bought a book on beheadings at the first souvenir shop she could find and a film-star magazine for Binnie, then set out for Whitechapel.

Which proved nearly impossible to get to. The District Line was shut down.

Polly said there weren't any daytime raids today, Eileen thought nervously, going back upstairs to take a bus, but the damage turned out to have been from a raid the night before – damage which became apparent as she neared Whitechapel. There was a massive crater in the middle of Houndsditch, and a bit further on, the wreckage of a warehouse lying across the road.

Polly'd said the East End had been badly bombed, but Eileen hadn't expected it to be this bad. On every street some of the back-to-backs had collapsed inward in a heap of bricks and plaster; others had toppled sideways onto the next terraced house, and the next, and the next, like a line of falling dominoes.

Eileen was grateful there weren't any raids today. She didn't know how Polly and Mike stood them. 'You'll get used to them,' Polly'd said. 'A few more weeks, and you won't even hear them,' but it wasn't true. She still jumped every time she heard the crump of an HE and flinched at the *poom-poom-poom* of the anti-aircraft guns. Even the wail of the sirens sent her into a panic. If there *had* been raids in the East End today, she wasn't certain she could have summoned the courage to come, map or no map.

At Commercial Street, she was to change buses, but with every street barricaded, she decided it would be faster to walk the half-mile to Gargery Lane. It was already three o'clock. But even walking was difficult. Entire streets had been reduced to rubble, and the terraced rows which still stood had their sides smashed in or their fronts torn away, the furniture inside exposed to the street. In one, a kitchen table set for breakfast stood on a now-slanting floor, food still on the plates. In another, a staircase climbed up into empty space. And in between, everything was smashed flat, including the corrugated iron roof of an Anderson shelter exactly like the one she and Theodore had spent so many nights in.

In more than one place, rubble covered the street, too, and Eileen had to backtrack and go around, getting thoroughly lost in the process. She had to ask directions and then ask again – first of an elderly man pushing a pram full of household belongings and then from a middle-aged woman sitting on the kerb with her head in her hands. 'Gargery Lane? It's down that way,' the woman said, pointing towards a line of gutted buildings. 'If it's still there. They were hit hard last night.'

I should definitely have given Mrs Hodbin that letter, Eileen thought guiltily. Alf and Binnie would have been safer on the torpedoed *City of Benares* than in this dreadful place. She hurried past the blackened shell of a building. What if Gargery Lane was a burnt-out ruin or a heap of plaster and bricks? What if Alf and Binnie had been killed, and it was her fault?

But miraculously it was there, and fairly intact. The windows had been taped over and covered with bits of cardboard, but the row of houses still stood, and they were proudly flying Union Jacks. The one the Hodbins lived in had 'Weel Gett Our Own Bak, Adolff!' written across its brown front door in red paint – no doubt Alf's handiwork, since most of the words were mis-spelled. Its windows were boarded up, too, all except for one, which must have been just blown out. Shards of glass lay on the pavement in front of it.

The door stood ajar. *Good*, Eileen thought. She could hopefully avoid the alarming woman with the red hands this time. She stepped over the broken glass and squeezed into the tiny front vestibule past a bicycle, a stirrup pump and two buckets with ARP stencilled on them, one of which was full of soaking rags and the other full of potato peelings.

The door on her right shot open, and the woman with the red hands came charging out at her, brandishing a rag mop. 'Thought you could sneak past me, did you?' she shouted, raising the mop above her head with both hands like an axe. 'Not this time, you little bastard!'

Eileen shrank back against the wall, her hand up to ward off the mop. 'I'm Eileen O'Reilly. I was here before,' she said, and the woman lowered the mop and held it out in front of her like a bayonet. 'I'm looking for Mrs Hodbin.'

'You and the greengrocer and the off-licence,' the woman said scornfully. 'Owes me four weeks' rent, she does. And ten bob for the window in me parlour. As if 'itler wasn't breaking half the windows in England, that blooming Alf 'Odbin's got to smash the few we've got left. Threw a rock at it, 'e did, and when I get my 'ands on 'im and that sister of 'is—' She brandished the mop again.

It's like being back in Backbury, Eileen thought. She'd had conversations just like this one with irate farmers at least a dozen times. But at least Alf and Binnie were all right, and apparently undaunted by the Blitz.

'Them two'll end up 'anged, you see if they don't,' the woman said, 'just like Crippen and—'

'Mum!' a child's voice called from inside the flat.

'Shut it!' the woman shouted over her shoulder. 'If you find 'em,' she said to Eileen, 'you tell 'em to tell their mother either she pays me what she owes, or all three of 'em'll be out on the street—'

'Mum!' the child called again, shriller this time.

'I said *shut* it!' The woman stormed into the flat and slammed the door behind her. There was a smack and then a wail.

Eileen hesitated. It was clear Mrs Hodbin wasn't at home and there was no point in going up, but the thought of having to come all the way back here again made her determined to at least knock on the door. And she'd best do it before the woman reappeared with her mop.

She ran up the stairs to their flat and knocked on their door, but there was no response. 'Mrs Hodbin?' she called, and knocked again.

Silence. 'Mrs Hodbin, it's Miss O'Reilly. I brought Alf and Binnie home from Warwickshire.' She thought she heard a noise from inside. 'I'm sorry to bother you, but I need to speak with you about something.'

More muffled sounds, and then a 'Shh!' that sounded suspiciously like Binnie.

'Binnie? Are you in there?'

Silence.

'It's Eileen. Let me in.'

'Eileen? Wot's *she* doin' 'ere?' she heard Alf whisper, followed by an even fiercer, 'Shh!'

'Alf, Binnie, I know you're in there.' She took hold of the doorknob and rattled it. 'Open this door at once.'

More muffled voices, as if an argument was taking place, then a scraping sound, and a moment later the door opened a few inches and Binnie stuck her head out. 'Hullo, Eileen,' she said innocently. 'What're you doin' 'ere?'

She was wearing the same summer dress she'd worn on the train, with a holey cardigan over it, and the same bedraggled hair ribbon, the same falling-down socks. Her hair looked like it hadn't been combed in days, and Eileen felt a pang of sympathy for her.

She suppressed it. 'I need to speak—'

'You ain't 'ere to 'vacuate us again, are you?' Binnie asked suspiciously.

'No,' Eileen said. 'I need to speak with Alf.'

''E ain't 'ere,' Binnie said. ''e's in school.'

'I know he's here, Binnie—'

'Not Binnie. Dolores. Like Dolores del Rio. The film star,' she added unnecessarily.

'*Dolores*,' Eileen said through gritted teeth, 'I know Alf is in there. I just heard his voice.' She tried to peer past Binnie into the room, but all she could see was a line of not-very-clean-looking washing.

'No, 'e ain't. There ain't nobody 'ere but Mum and me. And Mum's asleep.' Her eyes narrowed. 'What d'you want with Alf anyways? 'e ain't in trouble, is 'e?'

Very probably, Eileen thought. 'No,' she said. 'Do you remember that map of the vicar's, the one Alf uses to do his plane-spotting?' She spoke loudly so Alf could hear her from inside the flat. She noticed Binnie didn't shush her on behalf of her sleeping mother.

'Alf never stole it,' Binnie said, instantly defensive, 'You give it to 'im.'

'I know,' Eileen said, 'I—'

'It's 'is planespottin' map,' Binnie said, and Eileen was surprised Alf didn't pop up to chime in in his own defence. Was he hiding? Or had he gone out of the window? She wouldn't put either past him.

''e *said* 'e didn't want it back.'

'Binnie – *Dolores* – I *know* the vicar gave the map to him. No one's accusing him of stealing it.'

'Then why're you taking it back?'

'I'm not – I only want to borrow it, so I can look at something.'

'At what?' Binnie asked suspiciously. 'You ain't a Nazi spy, are you?'

'*No!* I need to look for the town where a friend of mine lives. I've forgotten the name.'

'Then 'ow can you look for it?'

Eileen knew from experience that this sort of back-and-forth could go on all day. 'I'll give you this if you'll lend me the map,' she said, showing her the film-star magazine.

Binnie looked interested. 'Is Dolores del Rio in it?'

Eileen had no idea. 'Yes,' she lied, 'and lots of other good names – Barbara and Claudette and—'

'I dunno,' Binnie said doubtfully. 'Alf'd be awful mad if 'e found out. S'pose 'e needs to do some planespottin'?'

'If you'll let me in, I could look at it here,' Eileen said, but that had the opposite effect from what she'd expected.

'I dunno where it is. I'll wager Mum threw it out,' Binnie said, and tried to shut the door.

Eileen put her hand on it to stop her. 'Then wake your mother and tell her I'm here,' she said, 'and *I'll* ask her,' and was surprised to see Binnie look frightened.

'I got to go now.' Binnie glanced behind her and tried to pull the door to.

'No, wait!' Eileen said. 'Binnie, is anything wrong?'

'*No*. I got to go.'

'Wait, don't you want your film magazine?' Eileen asked, and the sound of an air-raid siren starting up suddenly filled the corridor. 'What—?' She looked up at the ceiling, frightened. Polly'd said there hadn't been any raids over the East End today. She'd said there hadn't been any daytime raids at all. And it was only half past three.

'Binnie! Where's the nearest shelter?' she cried, but Binnie had already drawn her head in and shut the door.

> *'You have always told me it was Ernest. I have introduced you to everyone as Ernest ... You are the most earnest-looking person I ever saw in my life. It is perfectly absurd your saying your name isn't Ernest.'*

THE IMPORTANCE OF BEING ERNEST, OSCAR WILDE

KENT – APRIL 1944

At Cess' question, Moncrieff slowed the car and Prism twisted around to look at them. 'Well, *are* you a spy?' Cess asked Ernest.

'Yes, Worthing,' Prism said, looking back at them from the front seat of the staff car, '*are* you a German spy?'

'If I were,' Ernest said lightly, 'I'd be working for our side, like all the other spies.'

'All the spies we've *caught*,' Moncrieff said, without taking his eyes from the road. 'Lady Bracknell evidently thinks there are some we haven't caught, hence the memorandum.'

'So Bracknell thinks one of *us* is a spy?' Cess asked.

'No, of course not,' Prism said, 'but it's a dangerous time. If the Germans were to find out that FUSAG's a hoax and we're invading at Normandy instead of Calais—'

'Shh.' Cess put his finger to his lips. 'For all we know, Moncrieff here is sending secret messages to the enemy. Or you are, Worthing. You're always typing up letters to the editor. How do we know some of them don't have secret codes in them?'

I have to get them off this subject, Ernest thought. 'I think the bull's your man. The image of Himmler. Is that Mofford House?'

'Where?' Cess said. 'I can't see anything.'

'There, beyond the trees,' Ernest said, pointing at nothing, and they spent the next quarter of an hour attempting to catch sight of it, after which Cess spotted a turret and then the gates.

'I say,' Cess said as they drove in through them, 'one can't have a hospital without nurses. Have we got some?'

'Yes,' Moncrieff said. 'Gwendolyn set it up.'

'Are they the same girls who helped us when we did the oil refinery opening?' Cess asked. 'The ones from ENSA?'

'No,' Chasuble said, 'these are the real thing. Gwendolyn borrowed them from the same hospital that lent us the beds.'

Ernest looked up alertly. 'The hospital in Dover?'

'Yes, and don't get any notions of flirting with them. There'll be all sorts of higher-ups and Special Means people here. I don't want any trouble.'

I don't either, Ernest thought, and the moment they pulled up, snatched up his nightclothes and the boxes of bandages and took off for the house.

It was obvious why they'd chosen Mofford House. It had a moat and a distinctive turreted tower that the Germans would recognise, even though his newspaper story would say only, 'One of England's stately homes, whose name cannot be disclosed for security reasons, has been converted to a hospital.'

He hobbled quickly across the drawbridge, hoping that since today this was supposed to be a hospital, he wouldn't run into a butler at the door who'd demand to know where he was going.

He didn't – only two soldiers attempting to wedge a hospital bed through the door. Beyond them he could see a hall and, off to the side, the room which was posing as the ward today. Inside it stood a cluster of older men in officers' uniforms and several white-clad nurses.

He squeezed past the wedged bed, keeping out of their sight, down a corridor and into the nearest unoccupied room, which turned out to be the dining room. He wedged chairs against both doors and, using the mirror above the sideboard, began winding bandages around his head.

He emerged ten minutes later in pyjamas, robe and slippers, his head and both hands swathed in bandages. 'Where have you been?' Prism asked. 'And what are you doing in that get-up? You look like an escapee from an Egyptian tomb.'

Ernest pulled him off to the side. 'You said they'd be taking photographs, and my picture was already in the newspapers from the opening of Camp Omaha. If the Germans see me in more than one photo, they'll spot a fraud.'

'You're right. Good show. Was Cess in the photo?'

'He wasn't there. He was off doing landing craft.'

'Good, then he can be the broken foot. Go and help bring in the wheelchairs.'

Ernest did, and then carried two oil paintings, three water-colours and an antique writing table upstairs for Lady Mofford, made up the hospital beds, bandaged several other 'patients', and helped lay out tea in the library.

The tea included sandwiches, and he ate two, hid four more for Cess inside the bandages on his hands, and went to find him. Cess said, 'You look like Boris Karloff in *The Mummy*. And don't try to convince me you did it to keep from being recognised in the photo. I know the real reason.'

'You do?' Ernest asked cautiously.

'Yes. You didn't want to be stuck in an itchy plaster cast all afternoon.'

'You're right. You can have my wheelchair and I'll do the crutches,' he offered, then regretted it. The crutches dug into his armpits, the afternoon turned beastly hot and he began to sweat under his bandages.

And the Queen was three-quarters of an hour late. 'She's royalty,' Moncrieff said when Ernest complained. 'She can keep us waiting, just not the other way round. Why don't you spend the time writing up those articles you said were due?'

'I can't.' He held up his bandaged hands.

'That's not *my* fault. You were the one who decided to come as the ghost of King Tut. I don't know why you felt it necessary to use so many bandages.'

Neither do I, he thought. Especially since it had turned out to be a false alarm. The hospital in Dover hadn't been able to spare any nurses. These were from Ramsgate.

He considered taking the facial bandages off, but just then the Queen – a stout, sweet-faced woman in pale blue – arrived along with half a dozen photographers from the London papers, and the affair commenced.

'You never did tell me how to address her,' Ernest whispered to Prism, who was in the bed next to him as she proceeded down the row.

'You don't say anything unless she asks you a direct question,' Prism whispered. 'And then it's "Your Majesty". Shh. Here she comes.'

He should have asked him if she knew this was a hoax or not. It was impossible to tell. She spoke to the 'patients' as if they actually had been injured in battle, asking them what unit they were with and where they were from. If she *did* know, she was doing an excellent job of acting. *We could use her in Special Means*, he thought.

The entire thing was over by half past two. The Queen declined to stay to tea and left at a quarter past, and the photographers took a few more pictures and departed. He could still make it to Croydon if they left now.

He put the case to Moncrieff. 'All right,' Moncrieff said. 'We'll leave as soon as we've loaded the beds back on the lorry.'

'And got me out of this plaster,' Cess said.

The former was no problem – they had the lorry loaded and off by three. But Cess' plaster cast was another matter. Both tin-snips and a hacksaw failed to work. A servant had to fetch a hammer and chisel.

'Can't we do this back at the post?' Ernest asked, but they couldn't get Cess through the door of the car with the cast on.

It was nearly seven before they got home. 'We'd better not have to blow up any more tanks tonight,' Cess said, limping inside.

They didn't, but Ernest had to write up the hospital event for the London papers and then phone it in, and it was past ten before he was able to start in on his own news articles. It was much too late for Croydon, but he'd made Moncrieff feel guilty enough about it on the way home that he'd promised to let him drive them over to Bexhill to meet the *Village Gazette*'s deadline, which meant he'd have an entire afternoon to do what he needed to do unobserved.

He rolled a new sheet of paper in the typewriter and typed the letter he'd thought up about the bull, and then an ad for a dentist in Hawkhurst. 'New patients welcome. Specialises in American dental techniques.'

Cess leaned in the door. 'Still at it?'

'Yes, and if you're here to ask me to go and blow up an aircraft carrier, the answer's no,' he said, continuing to type in the hope that Cess would take the hint and go away, but he didn't.

'I think I'm permanently crippled,' Cess said, coming in and perching on the desk. 'It was worth it, though, to get to meet the Queen. D'you know what she said to me? She thanked me for my bravery in battle. Wasn't that nice?'

'It would have been if you'd actually *been* in battle,' Ernest said, continuing to type.

'I was. When they were trying to get that plaster off my foot. And in that pasture with that bull last night. What did she say to you?'

'She asked me to elope. She said *The Mummy* was her favourite film and asked me to run off to Gretna Green with her.'

'All right, don't tell me,' Cess said. 'I'm off to bed.' He left and then leaned back in the door. 'I'll get it out of you eventually, you know.'

No, you won't, Ernest thought, though Cess wouldn't know what it meant if he did tell him, and she had probably told hundreds of soldiers the same thing. But it had cut a little too close to the bone.

He waited five minutes, typing up the fictitious wedding of Agnes Brown of Bexhill to Corporal William Stokowski of Topeka, Kansas, 'currently serving with the 29th Armored Division', while he waited to make sure Cess had really gone to bed. Then he took the manila envelope from the bottom drawer of the desk and rolled the story he'd been writing yesterday into the typewriter. But he didn't begin to type. Instead, he stared at the keys and thought about the Queen.

'Your King appreciates your sacrifice and your devotion to duty,' she'd said. 'He and I are grateful for the important work you are doing.'

'What of the future? ... Will the rocket-bomb come?
Will more destructive explosions come?'

WINSTON CHURCHILL 6 JULY 1944

GOLDERS GREEN – JUNE 1944

The bridge lay just ahead, and there were no turnoffs that Mary could see. *Out of the frying pan, into the fire*, she thought. The bridge was less than a hundred yards from the ammunition dump. If this was the bridge the V-1 had hit, they'd be blown to bits. She glanced at her watch. 1:07.

Beside her in the ambulance Stephen Lang was still talking about the ineffectiveness of their rocket defences. 'The only way to stop them is to prevent them from being launched at all. I say, slow down a bit. You'll get us both killed.'

Not if I can get us over this bridge before 1:08, she thought, stepping on the accelerator pedal. She shot over the bridge, bracing for the blast and trying to gauge how far away they had to be to not be hit by it.

'The meeting's not that important,' Stephen protested.

'I have orders to get you there on time,' she said, roaring down the lane.

And there was the road she'd taken to Hendon. *Thank God.* She turned south on it and, now that they were out of range, slowed down. 'You were saying the only way to stop the rockets is to prevent them from being launched?' she asked.

'Yes, which is why I should be flying a bomber in France instead of being stuck here – not that I'm complaining. After all, it affords me a chance to be with you again,' he said and smiled that heartbreakingly crooked smile. 'Where were you before?'

She looked at him, startled. 'Before?'

'Before Dulwich. I'm attempting to determine where it is we first met.'

'Oh. Oxford.'

'Oxford,' he said, and frowned as if he was truly trying to remember.

Oh no. She'd assumed he was only flirting. 'Haven't we met?' had been almost as common a pick-up line during the war as 'I'm shipping out tomorrow.' But there was a possibility she *had* met him. This was, after all, time travel. She might have known him on an upcoming assignment. And if she had, it could be a major problem, especially since she'd have been there under a different name. And if he'd seen her somewhere which didn't match the story she'd told the FANYs and the Major, and he told Talbot …

I need to get him off this topic before he remembers where he met me, she thought. 'What do you fly?' she asked. 'Hurricanes?'

'Spitfires,' he said, and for the rest of the way to London regaled her with tales of his flying exploits. But as they were coming into the city, he asked, 'Where were you before Oxford?'

'I was in training. Were you in the Battle of Britain?'

'Yes, till I was shot down. You weren't ever posted near Biggin Hill, were you?'

'No,' she said firmly. 'I'm quite sure we've never met. I'm certain I'd remember someone as cheeky as you.'

'You're quite right,' he said. 'And I could never have forgotten meeting someone as beautiful as you.' He stretched his arm across the back of the seat, shifted so he was facing her, and edged closer. 'Perhaps it's *déjà vu.*'

'Or perhaps you've flirted with so many girls you've got them mixed. That's what you get for having a girl in every port.'

'*Port?*' he said. 'I'm in the RAF, not the Navy.'

'A girl in every hangar, then. Tell me, does that "destined to be together forever" line of chat work on other girls?'

He grinned at her. 'As a matter of fact, it does.' Then he gave her a puzzled look. 'Why didn't it work on you?'

Because I'm a hundred years older than you, she thought. *You died before I was ever born*, and then regretted it. He was a pilot. He might very well die before the end of the war.

Or before they reached Whitehall. London had had eleven V-1 attacks between two and six. 'Where in Whitehall is your meeting?' she asked.

'The Ministry of Health,' he said wryly. 'In St Charles Street. Take Tottenham Court Road. It's quickest.'

And it had had a V-1 hit at 1:52. 'Turn left here,' he ordered, and as she turned right, 'No, left.'

'Sorry,' she said, continuing to drive away from Tottenham Court Road. 'It was Fate.'

'That's unkind,' he said. 'Isolde would never have said something like that to Tristan.'

'Sorry,' she said, turning down Charing Cross Road.

'Why is it you're completely immune to my charms?' he asked. 'Oh no, don't tell me you're *engaged*?'

She wished she could. It would be the simplest way to put a stop to his nonsense, but it might create complications if Talbot drove him again. She shook her head.

'Promised to someone?' he persisted. 'Betrothed at birth?'

'No,' she said, laughing, which was the worst possible thing to do. He wouldn't take her protests seriously now. But his determination and irrepressible spirits were utterly disarming. It was a good thing they'd arrived. 'Here we are,' she said and pulled up in front of the Ministry of Health.

'Bang on time,' he said, looking at his watch. 'You're wonderful, Isolde.' He got out of the Daimler and then leaned back in. 'I've no idea how long this will take, an hour, perhaps two, but as soon as it's done, I'll take you to tea, and then we'll go to the nearest church and post the banns.'

'I can't,' she said. 'Those stretchers, remember?'

'Stretchers be damned. This is destiny.' He gave her his crooked smile and loped off towards the building, and as he did, she had a sudden sense of *déjà vu* too, a feeling that she *had* met him before.

Which ruled out its having happened in the future. She couldn't remember something which hadn't happened yet. It had to have been here, on this assignment. Could they have met when she was on her way to Dulwich, in the railway station as she attempted to buy a ticket? Or in Portsmouth? No, she wouldn't have forgotten those rakish good looks or that crooked smile. And it wasn't so much that he seemed familiar as that he reminded her of someone.

Who? Someone in Oxford? Or on a previous assignment? She squinted, trying to remember, but she couldn't place him. Perhaps she'd only had the sensation of *déjà vu* because of Stephen's having suggested they'd met before.

She gave up, reached for the map and began plotting the coordinates of the V-1s which had fallen between two and five o'clock so she could plan a route back to Hendon which would avoid them. As soon as she'd finished, she mapped out a safe route back to Dulwich from Hendon. If Flight Officer Lang returned by four, and it didn't take too long to get the stretchers in Edgware, she should be able to return the way she'd come, except that she'd have to go around Maida Vale and then cut through Kilburn.

He wasn't back by four. Or half past. Or five. He'd clearly underestimated the time the meeting would take. She made a mental list of the V-1s that had fallen between five and six – no, best make it seven – and redid the route back to Hendon and then the one home, which was much longer and more complicated. She hoped she could follow it. If he wasn't here soon, she'd be driving home in the dark. And the blackout.

He finally emerged from Whitehall at a quarter past six, looking furious. 'Do you know what those fools said? "You in the RAF need to come up with more effective defensive tactics against the rocket bombs",' he fumed, getting in and slamming the door.

She started up the car and edged into traffic. 'Exactly what do they suggest?' he said angrily. 'It's not as though there's a pilot we can shoot, or a way to defuse the bomb en route. It's already triggered when it's launched.'

She nodded absently from time to time and concentrated on getting them out of London and onto the road to Hendon. At least he'd abandoned the 'Haven't I met you somewhere?' topic.

'And if we shoot them down,' he raved on, 'we can't control where they'll land and we may end up killing more people than would have been killed if we'd let them continue on to their target. But could I make them understand that? No.'

She drove through the evening with her foot down hard on the accelerator pedal, wanting to reach Edgware Road while she could still make out landmarks, as he ranted on about how the generals knew nothing about rockets or aeroplanes.

'They demanded to know why the RAF couldn't invent some method whereby the rockets would hit a woods or a meadow instead of a populated area,' he told her, incensed. 'But not a pasture, mind you. No, the explosion might disturb the cows!'

It was half past seven when they finally reached the turn-off to Hendon. By the time she dropped him off, went to Edgware, and talked the ambulance post out of the stretchers, it would be dark.

'And you can imagine what wonderful sorts of suggestions *they* came up with,' Stephen said. 'One of the generals suggested we use nets, and another – a hundred if he was a day; I shouldn't be surprised to find he'd led the Charge of the Light Brigade – asked why we couldn't toss a rope round the rocket's nose, like roping a mare, and lead it back to France. A brilliant suggestion. Why on earth didn't *I* think of that?

'Sorry,' he apologised. 'I didn't mean to inflict my raving on you, even though we are destined to spend the rest of our lives together. I don't suppose you gave any thought to where we should be married while I was in with that lot of fools, did you?'

'Yes,' she said. 'I decided we shouldn't, that wartime attachments are a bad idea. Particularly if you're going to be lassoing flying bombs.'

'Well, then, I'll simply have to think of something better. And in the meantime, I'll take you to tea and—' He seemed suddenly to take in their surroundings. 'We're not out of London already, are we? I intended to take you to dinner at the Savoy for being so patient. Where are we exactly?'

'Home.' She pulled up to the airfield gate.

'Wait,' he said as she brought the Daimler to a stop, 'you can't go yet.' He reached to take her hand.

She avoided taking it by reaching past him for the transport form at the same time. 'Have you a pen?' she asked innocently. 'Oh, never mind, I have one.'

He tried again. 'You can't go yet. We've only just met.'

'You forget, we met before,' she said, filling up the transport form. 'You really *do* need to keep your pick-up lines straight, Flight Officer Lang.'

'So I do,' he said ruefully. 'But just because I've failed in the romance department doesn't mean you should starve. You've already gone all day without food, thanks to me. Look, there's a nice little pub only a few miles from here.'

She shook her head. 'I must go to Edgware for those stretchers, remember?'

'I'll go with you. I'll help you load your stretchers, then we'll have dinner and work out where it was we met before.'

That was the last thing she needed. 'No, I must get back. My commanding officer's extremely strict.' She handed him the form to sign. 'Sorry,' she said and smiled at him. 'It's Fate.'

'All right. You win, Isolde.' He signed the form, climbed out of the Daimler, and then leaned back in. 'But keep in mind this is only round one. I have all sorts of techniques I haven't tried yet, which I promise you will *not* be able to resist – though I'm forced to admit you have better defences than any girl I've ever met. Perhaps we should use you to stop the V-1s. You could turn them away with a flick of your hand or a well-timed word—'

He stopped and looked blindly at her, as if he'd suddenly remembered something.

Please don't let it be where we met, she thought. 'I really must be going,' she said quickly.

'What?'

'The stretchers.'

'Oh. Right,' he said, coming back from wherever he'd been. 'Adieu, Isolde, but don't think you've seen the last of me. It's our destiny to meet again very soon. *Very* soon. It wouldn't surprise me if I needed a driver again tomorrow.'

'I'm on duty tomorrow, and you're lassoing V-1s, remember?'

'Quite right,' he said, and got that odd, looking-straight-through-her gaze again. She took the opportunity to say good-bye, pull the door shut and drive off quickly.

'One can't escape one's destiny by driving away from it!' he called after her. 'We were meant to be together, Isolde. It's Fate.'

I'll have to make certain I'm on duty or away from the post for the next few days, she thought, turning towards Edgware. *After which he'll forget all about attempting to remember where he met me and begin calling some other girl Isolde.*

She should have found a way to escape from him sooner. By the time she located Edgware's ambulance post and managed to talk them out of one lone stretcher, it was not only dark but past eight o'clock. She was in unfamiliar territory, her shuttered headlamps gave almost no light at all, and if she got lost and took the wrong road, she'd be blown up.

But she also couldn't creep along. Dulwich had had three V-1s tonight. They'd need every ambulance, and the route she'd mapped out was only good till twelve, and with the blackout, she'd have no way to look at the map. *I must be home by midnight*, she thought, leaning forward, both hands on the wheel, peering at the tiny area of road her headlamps illuminated. *Just like Cinderella.*

There wasn't enough light to see signposts by, even if there were any, which there weren't. *The threat of invasion's long since over*, she thought, annoyed. *There's no reason for them not to have put the signposts back up.*

But they hadn't, and as a result, she made two wrong turns and had to retrace her way for a tense few minutes, and it was half past twelve by the time she reached Dulwich.

The garage was empty. *They've already left for the V-1 that fell at 12:20. Good, that means I can have my tea before the next one.* But she'd no sooner pulled in than Fairchild and Maitland piled in beside her. 'V-1 in Herne Hill, De Havilland,' Fairchild said. 'Let's go.'

'They've had three in the last two hours,' Maitland said, 'and they can't handle it all.' And for the rest of the night, Mary clambered over ruins and bandaged wounds and loaded and unloaded stretchers.

It was eight in the morning before they came home. 'I heard you got stuck with my job, Triumph,' Talbot said when she went into the dispatch room. 'Which one was it? I hope not the Octopus.'

'The Octopus?'

'General Oswald. Eight hands, and cannot keep any of them to himself.' Talbot shuddered. 'And *very* quick, even though he's ancient and looks like a large toad.'

'No,' Mary said, laughing. 'Mine was young and very good-looking. His name was Lang. Flight Officer Lang.'

'Oh, Stephen,' Talbot nodded wisely. 'Did he convince you he'd met you somewhere before?'

'He attempted to.'

'He uses that line on every FANY who drives him,' Talbot said, which should have been a relief, but part of her had been secretly looking forward to the possibility of seeing him on her next assignment.

'I wouldn't set my cap for him,' Talbot was saying. 'He's *definitely* not interested in wartime attachments.'

'Good,' Mary said. 'I'm not either. If he rings up saying he needs a driver, would you—?'

'I'll see to it the Major sends Parrish.'

'*Thank* you. Talbot, I wanted to apologise again for knocking you down. I *am* sorry.'

'No harm done, Triumph,' Talbot said, and the next day she hobbled into the common room on her crutches and kissed her on the cheek.

'What was that for?' Mary asked.

'This,' Talbot said, waving a letter at her. 'It came in the post this morning. Listen, "Heard about your accident. Get better soon so we can go dancing. Signed, Sergeant Wally Wakowski",' she read. 'And in the parcel with it were two pairs of nylons! Your knocking me down was an absolute godsend, De Havilland! As soon as my knee's healed, I'll take one – no, two – of your shifts for you.'

But over the next week, the Germans increased the number of launchings till nearly two hundred and fifty V-1s were coming over every twenty-four hours, and everyone, including Talbot, went on double shifts. If Stephen had called and pretended he needed a driver, there wouldn't have been any drivers *or* vehicles to send. Mary and Fairchild drove the Rolls to three separate incidents, and the Major spent most of her time on the telephone attempting to talk HQ into an additional driver and/or ambulance.

But the next week, the number of V-1s arriving abruptly dropped. Polly wondered if the Germans had finally begun acting on the false information Intelligence had been feeding them and recalibrated their launchers to send the V-1s to pastures in

Kent. Or perhaps Stephen had thought of a way to shoot them down. Whichever it was, the ambulance unit was able to go back to regular shifts and going to dances.

Parrish, Maitland and Reed dragged Mary to one in Walworth. Since she now knew what a V-1 sounded like – she'd heard one on a run to St Francis' – and since there weren't any in a twenty-mile radius of Walworth on the day of the dance, she thought she could risk it.

She was wrong. She met an American GI with exactly the same, 'Haven't we met somewhere before?' line as Stephen Lang, none of Stephen's charm or wit and no dancing ability at all. She came home limping almost as badly as Talbot.

The GI rang her up every day for a week, and on Thursday, when she and Fairchild got back from their second incident of the day – one dead, five injured – Parrish met them as they came in from the garage with 'Kent, there's someone waiting to see you in the common room.'

'American?' she asked.

'I don't know. I'm only relaying a message from Maitland.'

'I do hope it's not that GI who couldn't dance.'

'Would you like me to come and rescue you?' Fairchild offered.

'Yes. Wait five minutes, and then come and tell me I'm needed at hospital.'

'I will. Here, give me your cap.'

She handed it to Fairchild, went down the corridor to the common room and opened the door. Maitland sat perched on the arm of the sofa, swinging her legs and smiling flirtatiously at a tall young man in an RAF uniform.

It wasn't the GI. It was Stephen Lang. 'Isolde,' he said, smiling crookedly at her. 'We meet yet again.'

'What are you doing here?' she asked. 'Do you need a driver?'

'No, I came to thank you.'

'Thank me?'

'Yes, on behalf of the British people. And to tell you I finally remembered.'

'Remembered?'

'Yes. I *told* you we'd met before. I finally remembered where.'

LONDON – NOVEMBER 1940

Eileen looked up wildly at the sound of the siren. It wound up to a full-throated wail, its rising and falling notes filling the corridor outside the Hodbins' flat. 'Binnie!' Eileen shouted through the door, 'where's the nearest shelter?'

She rattled the knob, but the door was locked. 'Binnie, you can't stay in there!' she called through it. 'We must get to a shelter!'

Silence except for the siren, which seemed to be right there in the building with her, it was so loud. 'Binnie! Mrs Hodbin!' She pounded on the door with both fists. The tube station they'd come from that day she first brought the children home was over a mile away. She'd never make it in time. It would have to be a surface shelter. 'Mrs Hodbin! Wake up! Where's the nearest shelter? Mrs Hod—!'

The door flew open and Binnie shot past her down the stairs, shouting, 'It's this way! Hurry!' Polly ran after her down the stairs and past the landlady's shut door, the siren ringing in her ears. She heard the outside door bang shut, but by the time she got outside, Binnie'd vanished. 'Binnie!' she called. 'Dolores!'

There was no sign of her, and no one else in sight to tell her where the nearest shelter was. She ran back inside and along the corridor, looking for steps that would lead down to a cellar, but she couldn't find any.

And these terraces collapse like matchsticks, she thought, panic washing over her. *I must get out of here.*

She ran outside and back along the street, searching for a shelter notice or an Anderson, but there were only smashed houses and head-high heaps of rubble. The planes would be here any moment. Eileen looked up at the sky, trying to spot the black dots of the approaching bombers, but she couldn't see or hear anything.

There was a thump, followed by the slither of falling dirt, and Alf leaped down from the rubble and landed at her feet. 'I thought I seen you,' he said. 'What're you doin' 'ere?'

She was actually glad to see him. 'Quick, Alf,' she said, grabbing his arm. 'Where's the nearest air raid shelter?'

'What for?'

'Didn't you hear the siren?'

'*Siren?*' he said. 'I don't 'ear no siren.'

'It stopped. Is there a surface shelter near here?'

'Are you *sure* you 'eard a siren?' he said. 'I been out 'ere ages, and I ain't 'eard nuffink, 'ave I?'

I take it back about being glad to see him, Eileen thought. 'Yes, I'm certain I heard it. I was in there,' she pointed back at their house, 'talking to Binnie—'

His eyes narrowed. 'What about?'

'It doesn't matter. Alf, we must get to a shelter now, before the raid—'

'You ain't here 'cause of Child Services, are you?'

Why on earth would she be here on behalf of Child Services? 'No. Alf—' She tugged on his arm.

'We don't need to go till the planes come,' he said maddeningly. ''sides, me and Binnie ain't afraid of a little raid. There was one last week wot blew up an 'undred houses. *Ka-boom!*'

He flung his arms up to show her. 'Bits of people all over. What did Binnie tell you?' he asked suspiciously.

We are going to be killed standing here, she thought desperately. 'Alf, we can discuss all this later.'

'Wait,' he said as if he'd suddenly had an idea, 'what did the siren sound like?'

'What do you mean, what did it sound like? An air-raid alert. Alf, we must—'

'Where was you when it went?'

'In the corridor outside your— Why?' she asked, suddenly suspicious.

'I'll wager you 'eard Mrs Bascombe.'

'Mrs Bascombe?' What would Mrs Bascombe be doing here in Whitechapel?

'Our parrot.'

A parrot.

'We taught 'er to do the alert and the all-clear,' Alf said proudly. 'And HEs. *Blooey! Ka-blam!*'

'You have a parrot that can imitate an *air-raid alert*?' Eileen said furiously, thinking, *Of course they do. This is the Hodbins.* Binnie had told it to do its siren imitation and then led her a merry chase down the stairs and hidden behind the building, where she no doubt still was, laughing her head off.

'Mrs Bascombe sounds just like 'em,' Alf was saying. ''specially the HEs. She scared old Mrs Rowe so bad she fell down the stairs. You thought it was a *real siren*,' he said, pointing at her and then doubling up with laughter. 'What a good joke! You shoulda seen your face. Wait'll I tell Binnie!' He started to run off, but Eileen hadn't spent nine months with them for nothing. She was *not* leaving without the map. She grabbed Alf's collar and held on in spite of his wriggling.

'Stop squirming and stand still,' she said. 'I want to talk to you. Do you still have the map the vicar gave you?'

'I dunno,' he said. 'Why?'

'I need to borrow it.'

'What for?' he said, his eyes narrowing again. 'You ain't one o' them fifth columnists, are you?'

'Of course not. I need it to look up something. If you'll lend it to me, I'll give you a book.'

Alf snorted. 'A *book*?'

'Yes,' she said, attempting to decide whether she dared let go of him long enough to take it out of her bag. 'About chopping people's heads off.'

He was immediately interested. 'Whose 'eads?'

'Anne Boleyn's. Sir Thomas More's. Lady Jane Grey's.' She took the book from her bag.

'Does it 'ave pictures?' he asked, and when she nodded, 'Can I see 'em?'

'Not till you bring me the map.'

He thought it over. 'No,' he said finally. 'What if a Messerschmitt comes over? 'ow'll I mark it if I ain't got—?'

'I only need it for a day or two. After they chopped their heads off, they put them up on spikes on London Bridge.'

His face lit up. 'Does it 'ave pictures of that?'

'Yes,' she lied.

'All right. Only you got to pay me. Five quid.'

'*Five quid?*' Eileen said. 'Do you know how much money that is? I have no intention—'

Alf shrugged. 'Suit yourself.'

Very well, Eileen thought. 'Where did you get that parrot, Alf?' she asked. 'You stole it, didn't you?'

'No!' he said, outraged, 'we *never*! We found it in the rubble. There's all *sorts* of fings in the rubble.'

'That's looting,' Eileen said, 'and looting's a crime.'

'It *ain't* looting!' he protested, his hands going defensively to his pockets. ''ow can it be looting if the people wot owned is all *dead*?'

Which was a good point, but Eileen needed that map, and they'd just taken ten years off her life with that parrot. 'It's still looting in the eyes of the law.'

'Mrs Bascombe would've *died* if we hadn't found her. We *rescued* 'er.'

'That may be, but I'm still going to have to call a constable and tell him you're keeping a stolen parrot in your rooms.'

He went white as a sheet. 'Wait. Don't!' he pleaded. 'You can borrow the map.'

'Thank you,' she began, and he wrenched suddenly free of her grasp, snatched the book out of her hands and went racing off across the rubble. 'Alf Hodbin, you come back here!' Eileen called after him, but he'd already disappeared.

And so had her chances of getting the map. She would have to admit defeat, go to Charing Cross Road, and hope she could find a map in a travel guide.

She began walking towards Mile End Road, hoping the journey back wouldn't be as—

'Eileen!' Alf called, running up to her, Binnie at his heels. 'You was s'posed to *wait*,' he said accusingly, and handed Eileen the map.

'You needn't bring it back,' Binnie said. 'You can keep it. He don't do planespotting no more. Now he collects shrapnel.'

'And UXBs,' Alf said.

Of course, Eileen thought.

'So you needn't come back,' Binnie finished.

Eileen needn't have worried about them following her back to Mrs Rickett's. On the contrary, they couldn't wait to be rid of her. Why – what were they up to now? Alf had turned pale when she'd mentioned calling a constable. Had he 'collected' a UXB and taken it home? But surely not even Mrs Hodbin would have let them bring—

''ad'nt you best be goin'?' Binnie said. 'It's gettin' late.'

She was right, and whatever mischief they were up to, it was no longer her responsibility. 'Yes,' Eileen said. 'Thank you for the map, Alf. Goodbye, Binnie.'

'Dolores.'

I'll almost miss you, Eileen thought. *Almost*.

'Goodbye, Dolores,' she said and pulled the film magazine from her bag and held it out to Binnie. 'Here.'

Binnie clutched it to her chest and ran off, as if she expected Eileen to change her mind and snatch it away from her.

Alf still stood there.

'It's all right,' Eileen said. 'I know you need your map for your planespotting. I'll bring it back to you.'

'You don't 'ave to if you don't want to. It's like Binnie said, I don't need it.'

They *definitely* did not want her coming around. 'I could send it back to you by post,' she suggested.

'That'd be heaps better,' he said, looking relieved, but he continued to stand there. 'You ain't goin' t' tell the constable, are you?'

'Not if you promise me you'll keep out of the rubble,' she said, with no hope of his actually obeying her. 'And that you won't collect any more UXBs.'

'I only collect *little* ones.'

'No bombs,' she said firmly.

'I can still collect shrapnel, can't I?'

'Yes,' she said, 'but no watching raids. I want you to promise me you and Binnie will go to a shelter as soon as the sirens go.'

Amazingly, he nodded. 'Do you want me to show you where to catch the bus?' he asked.

'No, that's all right. I know the way home.' *It's somewhere on this map*, and had to fight the impulse to open the map and look for the name of the airfield then and there, but it was growing late. It would have to wait till she got on the bus.

But the bus was filled to capacity, and ten minutes after Eileen got on, it drove over a piece of shrapnel which Alf *hadn't* collected and burst a tyre, and she had to walk several streets over to catch another one, which was even more crammed. She had to stand, hanging on to a strap, the entire way, and there were so many barricades and diversions that by the time the bus reached Bank Station, it was so late she was afraid if she went to Townsend Brothers she'd miss Polly.

Instead, she went to Mrs Rickett's and straight up to their room, sat down on the bed and opened out the map. It was badly worn, and ripped along the folds, and the panel where the index of place names should have been had been torn off. She'd have to locate the name on the map itself. Alf had marked Xs and dates all over the lower half of it, obscuring the names underneath. Luckily, they were in pencil and could be rubbed out; hopefully doing that wouldn't also rub out the names underneath. She hoped Alf hadn't spotted a Messerschmitt over the airfield where Gerald was, or that it wasn't on one of the torn folds.

Polly and Mike thought his airfield was near Oxford. She began searching the section between there and London, bending over the tiny print, looking for Bs. Boxbourne ... Bishop's Stortford ... Banbury.

There was a timid tap on the door. She opened it a crack, just like Binnie had, and poked her head out.

It was Miss Laburnum. 'We're just going down to dinner,' she said. 'Are you coming?'

'No, Polly's not here yet,' Eileen said. 'I'm waiting for her.'

'Wise decision,' Mr Dorming growled, passing in the corridor. 'It's boiled tripe tonight.'

Boiled tripe, Eileen thought, making a face as she shut the door. *I must find that name*. She bent over the map again. It wasn't anywhere on the railway line between Oxford and London, which must mean it was further east. Baldock ... Leighton Buzzard ... Buckingham ...

There it was. *I knew I'd recognise it if I saw it*, she thought. And she'd been right about it being two words. Now if Polly would only come. She went out into the corridor to look down the stairs. An appalling stench somewhere between rotting flesh and mildewed sponge-bag assailed her and she clapped her hand to her nose and mouth and retreated into the room. A moment later Polly came in the door, gasping, 'What *is* that wretched odour? Has Hitler begun using mustard gas?'

'It's boiled tripe,' Eileen said, 'but it's all right.'

'How can it possibly be all right?' Polly said, unbuttoning her coat. 'We have to *eat* that.'

'No, we don't,' Eileen said. 'We're going home. I know where Gerald is.'

Polly stopped in the act of taking off her coat. 'You found a map.'

'Yes. I got it from Alf Hodbin.'

'But I thought you said the Hodbins were horrid. They're not. They're wonderful. Oh, Alf, you darling boy!'

'I wouldn't go so far as that,' Eileen said. 'He and his sister have a parrot they've trained to imitate an air-raid siren. But it doesn't matter. I found the airfield.' She grabbed the map and shoved it under Polly's nose to show her. 'He's at Bletchley Park.'

KENT – APRIL 1944

'Worthing!' Cess shouted from the hallway, and Ernest could hear him opening doors. 'Ernest! Where are you?'

Ernest yanked the sheet of paper he was working on out of the typewriter, slid it under a stack of papers, and threaded a new one in. He called out, 'In here,' and began typing, 'On Tuesday, the Welcome Committee of Derringstone held a "Hands Across the Sea" concert. Mrs Jones-Pritchard—'

'There you are,' Cess said, carrying in some papers. 'I've been looking for you everywhere. Didn't you hear me?'

'No,' Ernest said, typing, '—sang "America the Beautiful"—'

'What does Mrs Jones-Pritchard have to do with the First United States Army Group?' Cess asked, coming round the desk to read it, as Ernest had been afraid he might.

'"—and Privates First Class Joe Makowski, Dan Goldstein and Wayne Turicelli",' Ernest recited, typing, 'of the Seventh Armored Division, gave a spirited rendition of "Yankee Doodle Dandy" on the spoons. A good time was had by all,' he typed with a flourish, pulled the sheet out of the typewriter, and handed it to Cess.

'Ingenious,' Cess said, reading it. 'The Seventh Armored

Division only moved to Derringstone last week, though. Would they have had time to practise?'

'All Americans are born knowing how to play "Yankee Doodle Dandy" on the spoons.'

'True,' Cess said, handing the sheet of paper back.

'Did you come to tell me something?' Ernest asked.

'Yes, we must go to London.'

'London?'

'Yes, and don't say you've got to stay here and finish your newspaper stories because you've been in here typing all day.'

'But I have to deliver them to Ashford and Croydon,' Ernest protested.

'Not a problem. Lady Bracknell said we can drop them off on the way.'

'Exactly where in London are we going?' Ernest asked, wondering if he was going to have to fake a sudden toothache.

'Bookshops. We're buying up travel guides to northern France and copies of Michelin Map 51. The Pas de Calais area.'

Bookshops should be safe enough. He just needed to be careful. And Cess said they were going as British Expeditionary Force officers, but after he handed in his articles to Mr Jeppers at the *Call* in Croydon, he put on a false moustache, just to be certain. He talked Cess into doing Oxford Street while he did the secondhand bookshops on Charing Cross Road, which meant he was able to make several calls, and the whole thing went off without a hitch, but he was still relieved when it was over – so much so that he didn't even complain when Lady Bracknell sent him to pick up a load of old sewer pipes for the dummy oil depot Shepperton Film Studios was building in Dover.

The assignment left him smelling so bad no one would come near him for two days, and he took advantage of the time to get caught up on his fake wedding announcements and roadway accident reports and irate letters to the editor, all referencing Americans and the fictional First United States Army Group. And to work on his own compositions. He also tried to wangle ways to deliver his work to the newspaper offices on his own, but without success, and on Saturday Cess informed him they had to go to London again.

'More travel guides?' he asked.

'No, rumour mill duty, and this time we get to be Yanks. Do you think you can manage an American accent?'

Absolutely, he thought. 'I believe so,' he said. 'I mean, you bet, kiddo.'

'Oh, good show,' Cess said, and Ernest went back to typing, 'Special Yank Movie Night at the Empire Theatre in Ashford on Saturday. American servicemen admitted half-price.''

Half an hour later, Cess reappeared with an American major's dress uniform. 'I thought you said we were on rumour mill duty,' Ernest said. 'Isn't that a bit dressy for a pub?'

'We're not going to a pub. We're going to London. To the Savoy, no less.'

'Is it the Queen again?'

'No. Someone *far* more important,' Cess said. He draped the uniform over the typewriter. 'Make certain you've a crease in your trousers and that your shoes are polished.'

'Lady Bracknell will have to find someone else. I haven't any shoes that could pass as a major's.'

'I'll find you a pair.' He came back in a few minutes with a pair of Lady Bracknell's.

'These are two sizes too small,' Ernest protested.

'Don't you know there's a war on?' Cess handed him a tin of shoe polish and a rag. 'They need to be shined to a high gloss. He's a stickler.'

'*Who* is?' Ernest asked, thinking, *It can't be the King. He's in Dover with Churchill touring the 'fleet'*. He'd just written up the press release. 'Is this reception for Eisenhower?'

'No,' Cess said. 'He's running the *real* invasion. We're in charge of the phony one, remember? And tonight's star attraction is in charge of us,' he said mysteriously.

Who did he mean? Special Means was in charge of them, but

they didn't frequent the Savoy, and neither did Intelligence's top brass. The whole idea was invisibility.

Prism came in, dressed as an American colonel. 'Did you hear we're going to dinner with Old Blood and Guts?'

'Who?'

'The Supreme Commander of the First United States Army Group.' He clicked his heels together and saluted. 'General George S. Patton.'

'*Patton?*'

'Yes, now do hurry along,' Cess said. 'We need to leave. The reception's at eight.'

'We're supposed to be Yanks,' Ernest said, trying on the shoes. 'It's not "Do hurry along". It's "Hurry up, chum, or you'll miss the bus". And "lieutenant's" pronounced "looten-ant", not "leftenant".'

'Not to worry,' Cess said and pulled a pack of Juicy Fruit chewing gum out of his jacket pocket. 'All I need to do is chew this and everyone will be convinced I'm a Yank.' He held out a stick to Ernest. 'Want some gum, chum?'

'No, I want a pair of shoes that fit.' But thanks to all the time spent in muddy fields and muddier estuaries, there wasn't another decent pair in the whole unit. He didn't change into Lady Bracknell's shoes till they got to London, but he could still scarcely walk by the time they entered the lobby of the Savoy. 'You'd best not limp like that in front of General Patton,' Moncrieff said. 'He'll likely slap you for being a weakling.'

But Patton wasn't there yet. A number of British officers and middle-aged civilians in evening dress stood in small clusters. 'Are they dummies as well?' Cess asked.

'I don't know,' Moncrieff said, 'but just in case they aren't, steer clear of them. I don't want any of you hanged for imper-sonating an officer. You've got two ideas to push tonight: one, the invasion can't possibly take place till the middle of July. And two, it will definitely be at Calais. But I don't want any of you talking outright about it. You're supposed to have been sworn to secrecy, and an obvious breach will look suspicious. I want subtle hints, and only if the subject comes up in the conversation. I don't want you introducing the topic yourself.'

'What about a careless lapse, the sort you'd make if you'd had a bit too much to drink?' Cess asked, eyeing the guests' cocktail glasses.

'Fine,' Moncrieff said. 'Chasuble, fetch them their drinks. Mingle – and remember, subtle.'

Cess nodded. 'This is just like a night at the Bull and Plough, only with superior food and liquor.'

'An American would say, "better chow and hooch",' Ernest corrected, but he soon found out that wasn't true. The 'cocktails' Chasuble handed them were weak tea.

'Sozzled lips sink ships,' he explained. 'Moncrieff doesn't want us spilling what we really know.'

'Are those dummy canapés, too?' Cess asked, watching the white-gloved servants circulating with small silver trays.

'No, but don't make pigs of yourselves. You're supposed to be officers.'

That turned out not to be a problem. The elegant-looking hors d'oeuvres on the silver trays turned out to be cubes of Spam and rolled-up pilchards on toothpicks.

'This damnable war,' said a red-faced man in the group Ernest had drifted over to, waving a toothpick. 'There hasn't been anything decent to eat in five years.' The conversation turned to the deprivations of rationing and the criminal shortage of sugar, fresh fruit, and 'a really nice brisket' – none of which would have afforded any opportunities for hints about the invasion, if they'd included him in the conversation, which they didn't. They hadn't even noticed him. He stared into the weak tea at the bottom of his cocktail glass and mentally composed a letter to the *East Anglia Weekly Advertiser*: 'Dear Editor, The present rationing situation is simply criminal, and it has been made much worse by the arrival of so many American and Canadian troops in our area ...'

'Oh, and that dreadful wheatmeal loaf,' one of the women was saying. 'What *do* they put in it? One's afraid to ask.'

Ernest let Chasuble give him another weak-tea cocktail and wandered over to where Cess was talking to an elderly gentleman. The gentleman appeared to be deaf – a good thing, since Cess seemed to have completely forgotten he was supposed to be using an American accent.

'So then the bloke says to me,' Cess said, '"I'll wager we won't invade till August."'

Ernest wandered back to within earshot of the first group. The woman was still talking. 'And jam's simply *disappeared* from the shops. Even Fortnum and Mason's haven't—' She stopped, staring at the door.

Everyone did, including the deaf gentleman and the white-gloved servants. 'Sorry I'm late,' General Patton boomed. He was standing in the doorway, flanked by aides and looking even more dramatic than Ernest had expected, in full brass-buttoned field uniform, from his star-studded helmet liner right down to his polished riding boots. There were spurs on his boots and more stars on his collar and his field jacket.

Cess had abandoned the deaf gentleman to come over for a closer look. 'He looks like the bleeding Milky Way!' he whispered to Ernest.

'Not bleeding. Goddamned Milky Way,' Ernest whispered back.

'And look at those guns!'

Ernest nodded, staring at the pair of ivory-handled revolvers on his hips. And at the white bull terrier standing, panting, at Patton's feet.

'Darforth!' Patton bellowed and strode into the ballroom and over to the host, followed by the bull terrier. And his aides. 'Sorry we didn't get here earlier.' He grabbed Lady Darforth's hand and began pumping it up and down. 'Came here straight from the field. Didn't have time to change. We were down in K—'

'Would you like me to take Willy outside for you, sir?' an aide cut in, stopping him in mid-word.

'No, no, he's all right,' Patton said impatiently. 'Willy loves parties, don't you, Willy?' He turned back to the host. 'As I was saying, I just got back from—' He glared at the disapproving-looking aide. '—from an undisclosed location, and didn't have time to change.'

'I quite understand,' Lady Darforth said. 'Allow me to introduce you to Lord and Lady Eskwith, who've been eager to meet you.' She led him over to the far side of the room.

'Thank God he isn't really in charge of the invasion,' Cess whispered. 'They'd never be able to keep it secret. He stands out – what's the American expression?'

'Like a sore thumb,' Ernest said. 'Which I'd imagine is why he was chosen for this assignment.'

'Mingle,' Moncrieff whispered, coming up behind them.

Ernest nodded and wandered over to the edge of another group who had watched Patton and then begun talking animatedly among themselves, but they were discussing food, too. 'Last night I dreamt of roast chicken,' a horsy-looking woman said.

'It's pudding I always dream of,' the woman next to her said. 'They say things will be better after the invasion.'

'Oh, I do hope it will come soon. All this waiting makes one so nervy,' the horsy-looking woman said, and Ernest moved closer.

'Of course it's coming soon,' the plump woman's husband said. 'The question is, *where* will it come?' He, and the rest of the group, turned to look pointedly at Ernest. 'Well, sir? You're undoubtedly in the know. Which is it to be, Normandy or the Pas de Calais?'

'I'm afraid I wouldn't be allowed to tell, sir,' Ernest said, 'even if I knew.'

'Oh bosh, of course you know. Wembley and I have a wager going,' he said, pointing with his glass to a moustached man. 'He says Normandy, and I say Calais.'

'You're both wrong,' a third, balding, man said, coming over. 'It's Norway.'

Which meant Fortitude North in Scotland was doing its job. 'Can't you at least give us a hint?' the horsy woman said. 'You can't know how difficult it is to make plans, not knowing what's going to happen.'

'Everyone knows it's Normandy,' Wembley said. 'In the first place, the Pas de Calais is where Hitler will be expecting it.'

'That's because it's the only logical point of attack,' the other man said, his face getting red. 'It's the shortest distance across the Channel and the shortest land route to the Ruhr is from there. It has the best ports—'

'Which is why we're going to invade at Normandy,' Wembley said loudly. 'Hitler will be concentrating his troops at Calais. He won't be expecting the attack to come at Normandy. And Normandy—'

Ernest had to stop this. It was all much too close to the truth. 'You both make interesting cases,' he said and turned to Mrs Wembley. 'Have you read Agatha Christie's latest mystery novel?'

'Hmmph,' Wembley said, drawing himself up.

Ernest ignored him. 'Have you?'

'Why, yes,' she said. 'Are you saying her book—?'

He leaned towards her confidentially. 'I can't say anything about the invasion – it's all top-secret, you know. But if *I* were in charge of it,' he lowered his voice, 'I'd take Agatha Christie's novels off the shelves till fall, or at any rate the American editions.'

'You would?' she said breathlessly.

'Or I'd have their titles painted over, like you English did with your train stations,' he whispered, emphasising the word 'train'.

'Now if you'll excuse me, ladies,' he said, bowed slightly, and limped back over to Cess and Chasuble, who were plotting how to get their hands on the real liquor.

'I don't see what detective novels have to do with the invasion,' he heard Wembley grumble as he walked away.

'It's a riddle, darling,' his wife said. 'The answer's in the American title of one of her books.'

'Oh, I do love puzzles,' the horsy woman said.

'He mentioned railway stations,' Mrs Wembley said musingly. 'Let's see, there's *The Mystery of the Blue Train*. And *The ABC Murders*. ABC. Could that be some sort of code, do you think?'

Cess looked over at the group. 'What did you say to them?' Chasuble asked curiously.

Ernest told them. 'I got the idea from those mysteries Gwendolyn's always reading. Moncrieff told us "subtle",' he said, picking up an impaled pilchard and eyeing it dubiously, 'but I think it may have been a bit too subtle.' He put the pilchard back on the tray and rejoined the group.

'It could be something with a place-name in it,' Mrs Wembley was saying. 'There's *Murder in Mesopotamia* ...'

'As much as the Allies cherish the value of a surprise,' the balding man said, 'I doubt very much they will invade by way of Baghdad.'

'Oh, of course,' she said, flustered, 'how silly of me. Oh, I can't think. What else did she write? There's *Murder at the Vicarage*, but that can't be it, and the one where *he* did it, and the one where the two of them—'

'I've got it,' the horsy woman said, looking triumphant. She turned to Ernest. 'Very clever, Major, particularly the clue about trains.'

'Well?' Wembley said impatiently to her, 'what is it?'

'We should have guessed it at once,' she said to Mrs Wembley. 'It's one of her best-planned-out books, and one the reader won't guess till the very last moment.' And when Mrs Wembley still looked blank, 'It's set on a train, dear.'

'Oh, of course,' Mrs Wembley said, 'the one where everyone did it.'

'Are you or are you not going to tell us what the title is?' Wembley said.

'I'm not certain we should,' Mrs Wembley said. 'As the Major said, it's top-secret.'

'But since all we're discussing is mystery novels,' the horsy woman said, 'you simply *must* read *Murder in the Ca—*'

'Anderson!' Patton's unmistakable voice bellowed, and everyone looked over at where he stood, riding crop raised, waving at a British officer on his way out. 'Goodbye! See you in Calais!'

LONDON – NOVEMBER 1940

*J*esus, Mike thought, *Bletchley Park. I should have gone to Coventry.* 'You're sure Gerald didn't say Boscombe Down or Broadwell?' he asked Eileen.

'No, it was definitely Bletchley Park,' Eileen said. 'Why? Isn't it an airfield?'

'No,' Polly said grimly.

'What is it then?'

'It's where they worked on Ultra,' Mike said. And at her blank look, he added, 'The top-secret facility where they decoded the messages of the German Enigma machine.'

'Oh, but then that's definitely where he is,' Eileen said eagerly. 'Decoding would be much more suited to him than the RAF, with his skill at maths and—'

'Blenheim has a park, too,' Mike interrupted. 'You're sure he didn't say Blenheim Park?'

'No,' Polly said. 'He's at Bletchley Park.'

He turned on her angrily. 'How do *you* know?'

'Because of the joke Gerald told Eileen about the rain getting her driving authorisation wet. Remember? And her not being able to drive?'

'What does that have to do with Bletchley Park?'

'The driving authorisation form is printed in red.'

'What?'

'The bigram codebooks the German Navy used on its U-boats were printed in a special red water-soluble ink, so if the submarine was sunk, the codes couldn't be captured.'

'And?'

'And those codebooks were what they used to break the Ultra naval code at Bletchley Park.'

'I can't believe this!' Mike said. 'The one person who can get us out of here, and he's in goddamned Bletchley Park.'

'I don't understand,' Eileen said, looking upset. 'Why don't you want him to be at Bletchley Park?'

'Because it's a *divergence point*,' Polly said.

'But Dunkirk was a divergence point,' Eileen said, bewildered, 'and Mike went there.'

'Bletchley Park isn't just a divergence point,' Polly explained. 'It's *the* divergence point. Ultra was the most critical secret of the war. It was essential to winning in the North Atlantic. And in North Africa. And Normandy. If the Germans had had so much as an *inkling* that we'd cracked their codes and had access to their top-secret communications, we'd have lost the advantage that won us the war. If we were to cause that to happen—'

'But how could we? Historians can't alter events,' Eileen said, 'can they?'

'No,' Mike said, 'she just means it'll be tough to get Phipps out with all the security they're bound to have.'

But as soon as he got Polly alone, he asked her, 'What's happened? Did you find a discrepancy while I was gone?'

'I don't know. Marjorie – the shopgirl I worked with at Townsend Brothers and who Eileen told she worked at Padgett's – is enlisting in the Royal Army Nursing Service.'

Which made no sense at all. He sat her down and made her explain it to him. When she finished, he said, 'But lots of women enlisted.'

'But she said she enlisted because of having been rescued

from the rubble, and she wouldn't have been *in* the rubble if it hadn't been for me.'

'You don't know that,' he said. 'She might have eloped even if nothing had happened to you.'

'But that's not all,' she said and told him about the UXB at St Paul's. 'Mr Dunworthy said it took three days to get it out, which means it should have been removed on Saturday, not Sunday.'

'No, it shouldn't,' he said, relieved that that was all. 'It's not a discrepancy.'

'You don't know that.'

'Yes, I do. While I was looking for you, I went to St Paul's. I figured any historian of Dunworthy's would have heard all about the cathedral from him and might show up there, and you did, just not on the same day as me. And anyway, this old guy who worked there—'

'Mr Humphreys?' Polly said.

'Yeah, Humphreys. He gave me a tour of the whole place – sandbags and all – and told me all about the UXB. And he said it hit the night of the twelfth, which would make it three days if they got it out Sunday afternoon. So there's no discrepancy there. And lots of women eloped with enlisted men during the war. And the increase in slippage would make it *harder* for us to alter events, not easier.'

'But if that isn't what's going on, and we *can* affect events—'

'Then Phipps has no business being at Bletchley Park, and the sooner we get him out of there, the better. If he's still there. If he went through just after his recon and prep, he might already have gone back.'

'I don't think so,' Polly said. 'His joke about the water-soluble ink makes me think he's probably there to observe the cracking of the naval Enigma code, and they didn't capture U-boat 110 and get the bigram books until May of 1941.'

Great, Mike thought. Phipps would have six months to louse up the war. If he hadn't already. Maybe *that* was why their drops wouldn't open. It wasn't something Mike had done – it was Phipps' fault.

Mike didn't say that. He just told them he intended to leave for Bletchley the next morning. 'Shouldn't we both go?' Eileen asked. 'I know what Gerald looks like. And with two of us, we'll be twice as likely to find him. We can split up—'

'No, I'm going alone.'

'If it's her being conspicuous you're worried about,' Polly said, 'there were more women than men working at Bletchley Park. They did all the transcribing of the intercepts and ran the computers, and some of them even worked on the decoding. So if you're worried about Eileen standing out—'

That's not *what I'm worried about,* Mike thought. 'Two people are more likely to attract attention than just one,' he said, 'especially if they're both snooping around and asking questions.'

'Mike's right,' Polly said. 'The people who worked there were under a good deal of surveillance.' Which wasn't exactly reassuring.

'If only one of us can go, it should be me,' Eileen said. 'Gerald knows me. He may spot me, even if I don't spot him.'

Which was true. 'He'll recognise me, too,' Mike said, though he wasn't at all sure he would. 'I need you and Polly here to meet the retrieval team if they answer our ads. And I'll have more freedom of movement than you would. A man can go into restaurants and pubs alone without attracting attention.'

'Not if you're an American,' Polly said. 'The Americans didn't come to the Park till February of '42. Do you think you could pass as an Englishman?'

'I *am* an Englishman. I had an American L-and-A, remember? But how am I supposed to pull off working there? It took clearance to get into Bletchley Park. I'd never be able to pass the background check.'

'Gerald did,' Eileen said.

'With carefully forged school records and letters of recommendation. That's probably what his recon trip was about, planting documents that could stand up to Bletchley Park's background check. My history wouldn't.'

'You needn't actually work there,' Polly said. 'And by the way, it's BP or the Park, not Bletchley Park. And not Bletchley – Bletchley's the town. Bletchley Park is the Victorian manor outside of town where the decoding was done. Only a few code-breakers lived on the estate. Everyone else was billeted in Bletchley or the surrounding villages.'

'Then why do I have to pretend at all? Why can't I go as a reporter and talk to them in the town, say I'm working on a story?'

'Because they've all been forbidden to talk to anyone. They've all signed the Official Secrets Act. They can get the death penalty if they talk. Besides, you'd be hauled in by the authorities *instantly* if they heard you were planning to write about Bletchley Park.'

'I could say I was doing a story on something else,' he said, but Polly was shaking her head.

'No, people will be much more likely to talk to you if they think you're one of them. If they ask what your job is, which they won't, you can say you work for the War Office. That was the official cover for intelligence work.'

'How can you be so sure they won't ask me what my job is?'

'No one was allowed to discuss what they were doing. People who worked in one hut didn't even know the names of the people in the other huts.'

Then how am I supposed to find out if Gerald's there? he wondered. 'What if Gerald's one of the people living on the estate?' he asked.

'He won't be. That was mostly the top code-breakers, like Dilly Knox and Alan Turing. Turing was Ultra's computer genius.' She was looking critically at him. 'You haven't any other clothes, have you?'

'No, these are the best I've got. Aren't they good enough?'

'They're too good. If you're going as a cryptanalyst – that's what they called the code-breakers – you'll have to look the part. Don't worry, we'll find you something.'

The 'something' turned out to be a secondhand tweed jacket with patches at the elbows, a scruffy-looking knitted waistcoat, and a tie with a large grease spot on it. 'Are you sure this is what they wore, Polly?' Mike asked doubtfully.

'Positive, although the jacket may be a bit too nice.'

'Too *nice*?'

'These are physicists and mathematicians we're dealing with. Can you play chess?'

'No. Why?'

'There weren't enough cryptanalysts in England at the beginning of the war, so they recruited anyone they thought might be good at decoding – mathematicians and Egyptologists and chess players. If you could play, it would make a good conversational opening.'

'I could teach you,' Eileen said.

'There isn't time,' he said. 'I want to leave tomorrow.'

'No, you need to wait till Sunday,' Polly said. 'It'll be less conspicuous. Lots of BPers will be coming back from the weekend then. And I need to fill you in.'

She did, telling him everything she knew about Bletchley Park and Ultra and the principal players in such detail that he wondered if she was still worried about his altering events, too, in spite of his reassurances. She even told him what the various code-breakers looked like.

So I can keep out of their way, he thought. Which wasn't a bad idea, just in case. He memorised the names she gave him: Menzies, Welchman, Angus Wilson, Alan Turing.

'Turing's blond, medium height, and stammers. Dilly Knox – he heads up the main team of cryptanalysts – is tall and thin and smokes a pipe. And he's absentminded. He's been known to fill his pipe with pieces of his sandwich. Oh, and he's usually surrounded by young women – Dilly's girls.'

'Dilly's girls?'

'Yes. They played a vital role in the decoding. They searched through millions of lines of code, looking for patterns and anomalies.'

'How do you know all this?' he asked. A horrible thought struck him. 'You didn't do an assignment at Bletchley Park, did you?' If she had, and she had a deadline—

'No,' she said, 'I considered it, but after I'd researched it, I decided the Blitz might be more exciting.'

Not if historians can alter the course of the war, he thought.

On Sunday Polly and Eileen went to the station to see him off and to give him last-minute instructions. 'The Park's in walking distance of the village,' Polly said, 'but I don't know in which direction, and asking might look suspicious.'

'I won't ask,' he assured her. 'I'll find a likely prospect and follow him when I get off the train.'

'And I'm not sure the project's called Ultra at this point. "Ultra" stood for ultra-top-secret, the most classified category of military secrets, and I think in 1940 the project may just have been called Enigma, and not—'

'It doesn't matter what it's called. I have no intention of mentioning either one. I intend to find Gerald and get out.'

'There's the boarding call,' Eileen said. 'Perhaps you'll be in the same compartment with someone who works there, and you can ask *them* if they know Gerald and how you can get in touch with him, and you won't need to go to Bletchley at all.'

Jesus, he hadn't thought about running into them on the train. 'What does Turing look like again?' he asked Polly.

'Blond hair. Stammer.'

'And Dilly Knox is tall and smokes a pipe.'

'And has a limp like yours. And Alan Ross has a long red beard, and when it's cold wears a blue snood over it.'

'Over his *beard*?' Mike said. 'And you're worried about *me* being conspicuous? They sound crazy.'

'Eccentric,' Polly corrected. 'Oh, and Ross has a little boy, and when he travelled, he doped him with laudanum—'

'Laudanum,' Eileen said wistfully, and when they looked at her, she added, 'Sorry, I was just thinking how useful laudanum would have been on that journey to London with the Hodbins.'

'Yes, well, I don't know if Ross' son was a terror or not,' Polly said, 'but he gave him laudanum and stowed him in the luggage rack, so if you see a little boy sleeping up in the luggage rack, you'll know that's the compartment Alan Ross is in.'

And I can make sure I keep out of it. 'Look, I'd better get out to the platform,' he said.

'Wait,' Eileen said, grabbing his sleeve. 'What happened?'

'What happened?' he repeated blankly.

'To Ross' son?' Polly asked.

'No, to Shackleton. When he left his crew on the island and went off to get help. Did he come back?'

'Yes, with a ship to take them all home. He didn't lose a single man.'

'Good,' she said, and smiled at him.

'Ring us as soon as you get there,' Polly said.

'I will,' he promised, thinking, *If I can get there.* Just because he'd gone to one divergence point didn't mean the continuum would let him near another, especially one where a single person could mess up everything. His train could be blown up *en route.* Or the train might just be too jammed, which looked like was going to be the case.

It was packed to the gills, but he managed to squeeze on, and on the train from Oxford, he was even able to find a seat – taking care to pick a compartment which didn't have any blond stammerers, tall pipe-smokers, or doped-up children in it. He picked one occupied by five soldiers and two elderly ladies. He slung his bag up onto the luggage rack – which held only brown-paper-wrapped parcels, no children – and sat down in the single empty seat.

He was almost instantly sorry. As soon as the train pulled out of the station, the soldiers left the compartment to go and have a smoke, and a bald, spectacled man dressed in tweeds, with a

129

knitted waistcoat even rattier and more full of holes than the one Eileen had found for him, came in and sat down between Mike and the door, stretching out his legs so it was impossible for Mike to get out of the compartment without asking him to move, and he didn't want to have any contact with him.

The man was too bald to be Turing and too short to be Knox, and he didn't have a red beard, but he definitely worked at the Park. The moment the train left the station, he pulled out a book titled *Principia Mathematica* and buried his nose in it, ignoring Mike and the two ladies, who were cheerfully discussing various physical ailments.

'The pain begins in my foot and works its way all up my spine,' the one in the brown hat said. 'Dr Granholme says it's sciatica.'

'I have a dull throbbing pain in my knees,' the other one, in a black hat with a bird on it, said. 'Dr Evers prescribed a course of nutrient baths, but it didn't do a bit of good.'

'You should go to Dr Sheppard in Leighton Buzzard. My friend Olive Bates says he's wonderful with knees. I didn't tell you, her son was called up last week. Poor Olive, she's frightfully worried he'll be sent somewhere dangerous.'

Like Bletchley Park, Mike thought, pretending to look out the window. It was an exponentially more dangerous divergence point than Dunkirk because it involved a secret, and secrets were the most fragile and easily altered divergence points in the continuum. Because even though it took the combined efforts of many people to *keep* a secret, a single person, a single careless remark, could reveal it, like a delayed-action bomb which the slightest touch could set off.

All he had to do was ask the wrong question. Or too many questions. Or blow his cover. That meant he'd have to watch every word. His American L-and-A still hadn't worn off, so he'd have to remember to keep his vowels clipped and to use the English terms for things. No 'flashlights' or 'elevators', though he doubted Bletchley was a big enough town to have elevators – correction, lifts – and it—

The train jerked to a stop. Black Hat with Bird looked nervously out of the window. 'Oh dear, I do hope it's not an air raid. I'd hoped to arrive in Bletchley before dark.'

And I'd hoped to arrive in Bletchley, period, Mike thought, hoping a passing troop train had delayed them, but they weren't on a siding, and after a minute the guard came through apologising for the delay and asking them to pull down the blackout blinds.

'Is it a raid?' Brown Hat asked.

'Yes, madam' the conductor said, 'but I'm certain there's no danger.'

Except from me, Mike thought, listening for approaching planes, but nothing happened. They didn't start up again either, and as they sat there, everything Polly'd told him about how she'd influenced the shopgirl Marjorie came back to him, and he found himself thinking about Dunkirk and all the other things he'd done besides unfouling that propellor, from tossing those diesel cans overboard to hauling that dog up over the side. He'd lost his life-jacket in the water. Had it floated off somewhere to entangle itself in some other propellor? And what about the body? And now here he was going to a place where a single mistake, a single word could—

The train jerked sharply and started moving again, and the ladies went back to discussing their ailments. 'All autumn I've had a dreadful pain in my heel,' Brown Hat said. 'A friend of mine told me about Dr Pritchard's manipulation treatments, so I'm going to his clinic in Newport Pagnell.'

'Newport Pagnell?' Black Hat with Bird cried. 'Why, that's quite near Bletchley. You must come for tea one day. Are you getting off there, too?'

'Yes. Dr Pritchard's sending a car.'

Good, that meant he wouldn't have to ask the spectacled man which station was Bletchley.

'If Dr Pritchard's treatment isn't satisfactory,' Black Hat with Bird went on, 'you must go to Dr Childers in St John's Wood.'

St John's Wood. The lab had had a permanent drop there in the early days of time travel, before they'd figured out how to set up remotes. He wondered if Polly or Eileen knew where it was. When their drops malfunctioned, the lab might have re-opened it to use as an alternative. He would have to tell Eileen and Polly that when he called them – correction, rang them up – to tell them he'd arrived safely.

If they ever got there. He had to sit through a seemingly end-less discussion of bunions, rheumatism, lumbago and palpita-tions before Black Hat with Bird said, 'Oh, good, we're coming into Bletchley,' and both ladies began collecting their things. The man continued reading, even when they pulled in to the station, and Mike wondered if he'd been wrong about him being one of Bletchley Park's cryptanalysts. But the second the train stopped, he clapped his book shut and, without so much as a glance at any of them, was out of the door and walking rapidly along the platform towards the station. Mike stood up, intend-ing to follow him, but the ladies asked him to help them take their packages down from the overhead rack, and by the time Mike did, the man had vanished.

But there were plenty of people still in the station and outside – cycling and walking away from the station – who he could follow. As soon as he found a phone. He'd promised Polly he'd call to tell her he'd got there okay. He only hoped it didn't take forever to put the call through.

The phone booth – correction, telephone *box* – wasn't occu-pied, and the operator put the call through fairly quickly, but Mrs Rickett answered, and when he asked for Polly, said sourly, 'I don't know if she's here,' and when he asked her to go and check, heaved a put-upon sigh and went off for so long he had to put more coins in.

When Polly finally answered, he said, 'I've got to make this quick.' The stuff about St John's Wood could wait till next time. 'I got here all right.'

'Have you found a room? Or Gerald?'

'Not yet for either one. I just got off the train. I'll call you as soon as I know where I'm staying,' he said, hung up and hurried out into the station, but it had already emptied out, and when he went outside into the gathering dusk, there was no one in sight.

I should've watched to see which way they were all going and then called, he thought, kicking himself. Well, it was too late now. It was already getting dark. He'd have to wait till tomorrow morning to find out where Bletchley Park was. Right now he needed to find the centre of town and a room. But there wasn't a taxi in sight either, and no sign saying 'To Town Centre'.

He set off along the likeliest-looking street, but its brick buildings quickly gave way to warehouses, and when he reached the corner, he couldn't see anything promising in either direction. *This is ridiculous,* he thought. *How big can Bletchley be?* If he kept walking, he'd eventually have to come to *something,* even if it was only the edge of town, but it would be completely dark in a few more minutes, and his bad foot was beginning to ache. He looked up the side street again, trying to decide which way to go.

And glimpsed two people in the dusk. They were a block and a half away – too far ahead for him to catch up to them with his limp – but he hobbled after them anyway.

The pair reached the corner and stopped, as if waiting to cross, even though there weren't any cars that he could see. Mike laboured to catch up to them. It was two young women, he saw as he got closer, obviously two of the hundreds Polly had said worked at the Park. Good. After he'd asked them for directions, he could say, 'You wouldn't happen to know a Gerald Phipps, would you?' and since Phipps was such a stick, they'd make a face and say, 'Why, yes, unfortunately we do,' and he could be on the train back to London to pick up Eileen and Polly by tomorrow.

Only half a block to go. The young women were still standing there talking, totally caught up in what they were saying and oblivious to his approach. And no wonder they'd been known as 'girls' – they didn't look more than sixteen. They were talking animatedly and giggling, and it was clear as he got closer to them that they weren't waiting to cross. They'd simply stopped to talk.

Keep talking till I catch up, he willed them, but when he was still half a block away, they crossed the street, walked to the second building and started up the steps to the door.

Oh no, they were going in. He hobbled quickly to the corner. 'Hey!' he called, and both girls turned at the door and looked back at him. 'Wait!' He stepped out into the street. 'Can you tell me the way to—?'

He didn't even see the bicycle. His first thought as his bag flew out of his hand and both palms and his knee hit the pavement was that a bomb must have exploded and the blast had knocked him down, and he looked towards the girls, afraid they'd been hit, too. But they were running down the steps and over to him, exclaiming, 'Are you all right? Did he injure you?'

'He?' he said blankly.

'When he ran his bicycle into you,' the first one said, and it was only then that he realised he'd been knocked down by a bicyclist. He looked on down the street to see the bicycle wobble and swerve and then crash into the kerb, spilling its rider onto the pavement and clattering onto its side.

The girls saw the bike crash too, but they paid no attention, even though it looked like the rider had taken a much worse fall than Mike had. They were busy picking Mike up. 'Are you injured?' the first girl asked again, putting her hand under his arm to help him up.

'I think he only clipped me,' Mike said.

The other was standing with her hands on her hips, staring at the rider, who was getting slowly to his feet. 'He shouldn't be allowed on the streets,' she said, annoyed.

'Do give us a hand, Mavis,' the first one said to her, and Mavis came over to take Mike's other arm. Mike stood up, more or less. 'Are you certain you're not hurt?' she asked.

'I don't think I am,' he said, taking stock. His knee was beginning to throb, but he was able to put weight on it, so it wasn't broken or sprained, and it and his hands had struck the pavement first. He flexed his fingers. 'I think I'm fine. Anyway, nothing's broken. I should have been looking where I was going.'

'*You* should have?' Mavis exploded. '*He* should have. It's the third time he's knocked someone down this week, isn't it, Elspeth?'

Elspeth nodded. 'He nearly killed poor Jane on her way to the Park last week.' She glared at the rider, who was righting his bicycle.

He got on and rode off down the street, apparently unharmed.

'Watch where you're going!' she shouted after him, to no effect. He didn't even look back.

'You're certain you're all right?' Mavis was asking. 'Oh, you're limping.'

'No, that isn't from—'

'I *knew* he'd end up injuring someone,' Mavis said angrily. 'He never watches where he's going.'

'My foot's not hurt,' Mike said, but neither girl was listening.

'He's an absolute *menace*,' Mavis said angrily. 'He should be forbidden from riding a bicycle.'

Elspeth shook her head. 'He'd only begin driving his car again, and that would be even worse,' she said and turned to explain to Mike. 'Turing's a wretched driver.'

'In wartime the truth is so important it must be accompanied by a bodyguard of lies.'

WINSTON CHURCHILL, IN A SPEECH TO BLETCHLEY PARK

LONDON – NOVEMBER 1940

Polly and Eileen waited to make sure Mike's train actually left for Bletchley Park, and then Eileen went to Whitechapel to return Alf Hodbin's map. 'I told them I'd post it to them, but I promised Theodore Willett I'd go and see him, so I may as well run it by. And I want to talk to Alf. I got the feeling last time that he and Binnie are up to something.'

'Like what?' Polly asked.

'I'm not certain, but knowing the Hodbins, it's something illegal. There weren't any Nazi child spies, were there?'

Polly saw her onto her tube and then went to the British Museum – 'Darling, so sorry. If you can forgive me, meet me by the Rosetta stone Sunday at two' – to wait for the retrieval team. And fret.

In spite of Mike's reassurances that they hadn't affected events, she was still worried. Her actions hadn't affected only Marjorie. They'd also affected the warden who'd found her and the rescue squad and ambulance driver, her nurses and doctors, the airman she hadn't met, who'd gone off on his mission thinking she'd changed her mind, even Sarah Steinberg, who'd been given Marjorie's job, and the shopgirl Townsend Brothers had hired to replace Sarah. The ripples spread out and out. And now Marjorie was going to be a nurse. She was going to be saving soldiers' lives.

Like Mike had saved Hardy's. And unlike Hardy, there was nothing else which could have caused what had happened. Marjorie had said quite plainly that she'd decided to run off with her airman because of having seen Polly standing there looking so upset the morning after St George's was hit. That had led directly to her having been in Jermyn Street when it was hit, and to her deciding to become a nurse and thus altering who knew what other events. Polly saw now why Mike had been so worried that morning outside Padgett's when he thought he'd saved Hardy.

And now Mike was on his way to Bletchley Park, where he could do far more damage to the war than a hospital nurse could. If Gerald Phipps hadn't beaten him to it.

But if he had, there should be more discrepancies than just a siren going off when it shouldn't have. And Mike was right, there were all sorts of instances in history when an action which should have had a major effect had been counteracted by something else, like the Verlaine-poem invasion signal. Or the appearance of 'Omaha' and 'Overlord' in the *Herald*'s crossword puzzle, which hadn't affected the invasion after all.

But that was also an example of how a single small action could have tremendous consequences. A few words in a cross-word puzzle had nearly derailed an invasion involving years of careful planning and two million men. If D-Day had had to be delayed, the invasion's target would almost certainly have leaked out, and Rommel's tanks would have been waiting for the invasion troops at Normandy. And all because of a bit of carelessness and a teenage boy. 'For want of a nail ...'

So what sort of impact could the combined actions of Marjorie and Hardy and Gerald and now Mike wandering around the place where the most important secret of the war was being kept have? If Mike got there. Just because he'd gone to Dunkirk didn't mean he'd be allowed to reach Bletchley Park.

She gave the retrieval team another half an hour to show and then went back to Mrs Rickett's to see if Mike had phoned. He hadn't, and by the time Eileen returned, there'd still been no word from him. 'Did you find out what the Hodbins were up to?' Polly asked her.

'No, no one was there,' Eileen said, frowning. 'I had to slide the map under the door. Did Mike ring up?'

'No, not yet. His train was probably delayed by a troop train or something.'

But she must not have succeeded in hiding her anxiety, because Eileen asked, 'No trains were bombed today, were they?'

'No.' *Not in London.*

'Was Bletchley?'

'I don't know, but there were never any casualties at Bletchley Park. Come along, it's time for supper. One of Mrs Rickett's Sunday-night "cold collations".'

Tonight it consisted of sliced tongue and nettle salad.

'I'm sorry I ever got my ration card,' Eileen said when she saw it. 'I can't wait till Mike finds Gerald and we can go home. Perhaps that's why he hasn't rung us, because someone on the train knew where Gerald was, and he's gone off to find him.'

But when Mike finally rang up, moments before Polly had to leave for Notting Hill Gate for rehearsal, it was only to say he'd arrived. He hadn't even left the station yet. And he was in a hurry. He told them he'd phone them again when he knew where he was staying and rang off before Polly could warn him to be careful.

But if the problem's an increase in the slippage, then it would have prevented him from going to Bletchley Park if he could affect events. There's nothing to worry about, she told herself, and forced herself to concentrate on the problems of the admirable Crichton and Lady Mary.

The troupe was in their final week of rehearsals, and Sir Godfrey was in a foul mood. 'No, no, no!' he shouted at Viv. 'You say, "Here comes Ernest" *before* Ernest makes his entrance! Again. From "Father, we thought we should never see you again."'

They started through the scene again.

'No, no, no!' Sir Godfrey thundered at Mr Dorming, 'why can't you remember? This is a comedy, not a tragedy. At the end of Act Three you are *rescued* from this island.'

'By a prince?' Trot asked.

'No, by a ship. Or, considering the rate at which this production is progressing, by the end of the war.'

'*I* think it should be by a prince,' Trot said.

'Take it up with the author,' Sir Godfrey growled. 'Try it again. From "Here comes Er—'

'Sir Godfrey,' Lila interrupted, 'you keep saying it's a comedy, but how *can* it be when Lady Mary and Crichton are separated at the end?'

'Yes,' Viv said, 'and why *can't* they be together?'

'Because *he* is a butler and *she* is a lady. You and Mary,' he said, glaring at Polly as though this were her fault, 'are far too young to ever have loved someone whom, for reasons of social class or age or circumstance, you could not be with, but I assure you lovers *do* sometimes face insurmountable obstacles.'

'But if they didn't have to part,' Viv said, 'it would make the ending so much more romantic.'

'As I told Trot,' Sir Godfrey said dryly, 'take it up with the author. Again. From the beginning. We are going to get this right if it kills me. Which it may very well do. Unless the Luftwaffe gets me first,' he added, looking up at the ceiling. 'The raids seem rather excessive tonight.'

They did, but they began and ended when they were supposed to and hit the correct targets, and there was nothing in Sir Godfrey's *Times* the next night about security breaches or captured spies, though Mike hadn't phoned again.

Tuesday there was a letter for Eileen. 'Is it from Mike?' Polly asked. Perhaps he had decided to write instead of phoning.

'No, it's from the vicar, Mr Goode,' Eileen said, and smiled. She opened it and began to read. 'Oh no, he says he's writing with bad news ... But that can't be right—'

'What can't?'

'He says Lady Caroline's son's been killed, but it was Lord Denewell—'

'Read the letter,' Polly ordered.

"Dear Miss O'Reilly, I am writing with sad news. Lady Caroline's son was killed on the thirteenth of November.'

So it couldn't have been an error in the death notice the vicar had read. Lord Denewell had been killed on the second.

'His plane was shot down over Berlin,' Eileen went on, 'during a bombing run.'

It's a discrepancy, Polly thought, a chill going through her. *The son was killed instead of the father.*

'This is such sad news,' Eileen read on, 'coming as it does so soon after Lord Denewell's death.'

So it wasn't a discrepancy, after all, only a horrible coincidence of the war, and she should have felt reassured, but that night after rehearsal, as she and Eileen composed more messages for the retrieval team, she found herself looking through the newspapers for possible discrepancies, and the next morning she told Eileen she had to be at work early to tidy the workroom and went to Westminster Abbey to see if it had been hit.

It had, and the damage to Henry VII's chapel and the Tudor windows and the Little Cloisters matched that which she'd read of during her prep.

You didn't alter events, she told herself. *The drops won't open because there's been an increase in slippage. That's why your retrieval team's not here. Unless Mike was right, and they're in the wreckage of Padgett's.*

Just because the three fatalities had turned out to be charwomen didn't mean there couldn't be other bodies buried in that pit. Or in the wreckage opposite her drop. The retrieval team could have come looking for her that night when she was trapped in Holborn. They could have been leaving her drop to look for her just as the parachute-mine exploded. No one would have had any idea they were there. Like Marjorie. If the warden hadn't heard her, no one would have ever thought to look for her in the rubble in Jermyn Street.

Or the retrieval team could have been killed on their way to her drop, in that burnt-out bus she'd seen on her way to Townsend Brothers. Or on the way to Backbury or Orpington. Or what if Colin had come after her when he found out about the increased slippage? He'd promised to come and rescue her. What if he'd followed her to Padgett's? Or been killed in a raid on his way to Oxford Street?

Don't be ridiculous, she thought. *He'd know better than to get himself killed. Besides, if he came here, he couldn't catch up in age.*

But she immediately began thinking she saw him – on the escalators at Oxford Circus after work, in a knot of soldiers, stepping off a train onto the District Line platform at Notting Hill Gate.

It wasn't him. The soldier she saw was speaking fluent French. The man on the escalator had Colin's sandy hair and grey eyes, but when he saw Polly looking at him, his answering smile was nothing at all like Colin's crooked grin, and he was far too old. He was at least thirty, and Polly knew instantly that he wasn't Colin, but in that first moment, her heart jerked painfully.

When the seventeen-year-old who looked like him stepped off the train, she was in the middle of the rescue scene with Crichton, and she stopped in mid-line and stared after him till Sir Godfrey said, 'We are doing *The Admirable Crichton*, Lady Mary, not *Romeo and Juliet*.'

'What? I— Sorry, I thought I saw someone I knew.'

'And I thought this misbegotten play was opening two nights from now,' Sir Godfrey grumbled and kept them rehearsing till the all-clear went.

On the way home Eileen asked, 'Did you think you saw Mike?'

'Yes,' Polly lied.

'I'm certain he'll ring us soon. Perhaps he hasn't found a room yet. Or perhaps he's having difficulty finding a place to phone from where he won't be overheard.'

Or his asking about Gerald has attracted attention, and he's been taken in for questioning, Polly thought, but she had no time to worry over it. Christmas shoppers were already beginning to come in. On Tuesday, Polly had asked Miss Snelgrove if Townsend Brothers planned to hire extra help for the holidays, and when she said yes, Polly told her about Eileen having lost her job at Padgett's.

Miss Snelgrove had hired her on the spot to help on third, and then had to move her up the next day to the book department when Ethel, who'd discussed ABCs and planespotters with Polly, was killed by shrapnel. But even though they weren't working on the same floor, Eileen was grateful to be working in a department store which hadn't been bombed, delighted at being surrounded by so many Agatha Christie novels, and certain there was an innocent explanation for why Mike hadn't phoned yet.

Eileen was the only one who was cheerful. The troupe was nervy about the play, and everyone was jumpy and ill-tempered from lack of sleep, even though the raids only happened intermittently now. Or perhaps *because* they did. In those first weeks, the raids had become background noise which it was possible to ignore, but now that they didn't occur every night, there was constant discussion of whether and when 'they' would come and in what nasty new forms – like delayed-action bombs wired to go off as they were being defused and magnetic mines which exploded when a wristwatch came near them – and discussion of the damage they could do.

By now everyone had a horror story. The rector's sister had found a blown-off arm in her rose garden, a man Lila had gone dancing with had been blinded by flying glass, and everyone knew someone who'd been killed. It was no wonder everyone's nerves were frayed.

The weather didn't help – it had rained steadily since the day Mike had left – and neither did the shorter days. 'It's as if the darkness were closing in all round us,' Miss Laburnum said, shivering, on their way to Notting Hill Gate on Thursday night.

It is, Polly thought, and was glad to enter the brightly lit tube station, in spite of its crowdedness and the overpowering smell of wet wool.

Friday and Saturday night they performed *The Admirable Crichton* in the lower-level hall of Notting Hill Gate. Opening night went perfectly except for the moment at the end of Act Two when the rescue ship arrived. Mr Simms was supposed to cock his head and ask uncertainly, 'Was that a gun I heard?'

Unfortunately, he had to shout the line over a deafening anti-aircraft barrage.

The audience roared, and an elderly man shouted out, 'What are ya, lad, deaf?'

Mr Simms was mortified.

'Nonsense!' Sir Godfrey, clad in rolled-up trousers and the plimsolls Miss Laburnum had actually managed to track down, told him during the interval. 'It was marvellous. You must see if you can work it into the show again tomorrow.'

The rest of the show came off without incident. 'You and Sir Godfrey were simply wonderful together,' Miss Laburnum enthused to Polly.

'This has been wonderful for morale,' Mrs Wyvern said. 'It's a pity we can't do more than two performances. Perhaps we could arrange to do it in other stations.'

Sir Godfrey looked appalled.

'We can't,' Polly said quickly. 'We're only allowed to do two performances without paying royalties,' she lied.

'Oh, what a pity,' Mrs Wyvern said, and Sir Godfrey whispered, 'Again do I owe my life to you, fair maid.'

Saturday night went even better. After the curtain, which consisted of Trot holding a placard reading 'Curtain', rang down and the cast had taken their bows to a necessarily standing ovation, Mrs Wyvern gathered everyone on the platform to present Sir Godfrey with a copy of J.M. Barrie's *Complete Plays*.

'"Thus were the Trojans murderously undone, by treacherous gifts as these",' Sir Godfrey murmured to Polly.

She was afraid he was right.

'I have wonderful news!' Mrs Wyvern said. 'Today I met with the head of London Transport, and he has agreed to allow us to perform in the other Underground stations during Christmas week.'

'But the royalties—' Polly began.

'Not *The Admirable Crichton*,' Mrs Wyvern said, 'a Christmas play.'

'*Peter Pan!*' Miss Laburnum enthused. 'How wonderful! I love the scene where Wendy asks, "Boy, why are you crying?" and Peter Pan says—'

'No, not *Peter Pan*,' Mrs Wyvern said. 'Charles Dickens' *A Christmas Carol*!'

'The very thing,' the rector pronounced. 'It has a message of hope and charity which is badly needed in these dark times.'

'And Sir Godfrey will make a wonderful Scrooge!' Miss Laburnum cried. And they were off and running.

'But at least it's not Barrie,' Sir Godfrey whispered, and on the way home after the all-clear, Eileen said, 'It's good that all the female roles are small. When Mike finds Gerald, they'll be able to easily replace you.'

If *Mike finds Gerald*, Polly thought. *If he's not in the Tower, awaiting trial as a German spy*, and instead of going to the London Zoo to meet the retrieval team, as per the advertisement they'd put in the papers, sent Eileen instead so she wouldn't miss his call.

Eileen didn't mind. 'I'll take Theodore,' she said. 'He's been wanting to go. The zoo wasn't hit, was it?'

'Yes.' Fourteen HEs. 'But not today.'

'Oh good. If Mike's found Gerald and wants us to come to Bletchley, we'll be in the elephant house. I won't be home to supper, thank heavens. I'll eat at Theodore's.'

Mike didn't phone, and Eileen was back by three. 'What happened?' Polly asked. 'How was the zoo?'

'Dreadful. The retrieval team wasn't there, and neither were the animals. Nearly all of them have been moved to the country for safekeeping, including the elephants, which Theodore particularly wanted to see, and ten minutes after we got there he decided he wanted to go home. And when I got him home, his mother was just going out, so I wasn't even asked to stay to supper,' she said and looked as if she was about to burst into tears. 'And now I'll have to eat one of Mrs Rickett's horrid cold collations.'

'No, you won't,' Polly said. 'I can't face it either. The play's over, so there's no rehearsal tonight. As soon as Mike phones, we'll go to Holborn's canteen and have sandwiches.'

'What if he doesn't phone?'

'We'll wait till seven – he'll expect us to have left for Notting Hill Gate by then – and then go. And while you're waiting, you can think about whether you'll order a cheese sandwich or fish paste.'

'Both,' Eileen said happily and went off to sit on the stairs with Agatha Christie's *Murder in the Calais Coach* so she could hear the phone. Polly ironed her blouse and skirt for work and worried over Mike's failure to call. And about the retrieval team and Colin and her deadline and discrepancies.

It can't be all of them, she told herself sternly. *They're mutually exclusive. If it's increased slippage that's keeping your drops from opening, then you can't have altered events and the retrieval teams can't come through, so they can't be buried in the rubble at Padgett's or your drop. And if they are, then the drops must be working again, so you didn't lose the war, and you needn't worry about your deadline. You can worry about one or the other, but not all of them at once.*

Unless they were connected. Unless the slippage had increased *because* they'd altered events, and the net was ensuring that other historians didn't make the discrepancies worse.

No, that wouldn't work. The increase had happened *before* Mike rescued Hardy, and before she'd come through to the Blitz. And before Gerald had gone to Bletchley Park. And it couldn't have been anything she did before because she'd been able to go back through after VE Day. And Eileen had—

'It's seven,' Eileen said, coming back upstairs.

Polly insisted they wait another half an hour, and then they went off to Holborn, after first extracting a promise from Miss Laburnum to take down any messages for them and promising in turn to try to find a suitable candle for the Ghost of Christmas Past's crown.

'And a green fur-lined cloak for the Ghost of Christmas Present,' Miss Laburnum said.

'If I had a green fur-lined cloak, I'd wear it myself,' Eileen said as they walked over to Notting Hill Gate. 'My coat isn't anywhere near warm enough for this horrid weather. And black is so grim.'

'Everyone's wearing black,' Polly snapped. 'There's a war on. And no one has a new coat. Everyone's making do.'

'I didn't …' Eileen said, turning puzzled eyes on her. 'I was joking.'

'I know, I'm sorry,' Polly said. 'It's only—'

'You're worried about Mike,' she said. 'I know. He knew you were busy with the play. He probably didn't want to distract you by phoning.'

Distract me? Polly thought bitterly.

'I'm sure he'll ring us tomorrow.'

Eileen linked her arm through Polly's and chattered the rest of the way to Holborn about how wonderful the play had been and how hungry she was and about Agatha Christie.

'Wouldn't it be wonderful if I actually saw her? She lived in London during the war. She worked as a dispenser in the hospitals. Unfortunately, she didn't use the tube shelters. She had an irrational fear of being buried alive.'

Not all that irrational, Polly thought, remembering Marble Arch. And Marjorie.

But it was a pity they had no chance of encountering her. They could have used her help, though Polly doubted whether even Agatha Christie could solve *The Mystery of the Drops Which Wouldn't Open.*

'I wonder if she took the tube to work,' Eileen said. 'If she … here's our stop … if she did, we might see her on her way home.'

They got off the train.

'I do hope the queue for the canteen isn't very long,' Eileen said, starting through the clot of passengers getting off and on and down the platform past a band of urchins up to no good towards a group of young women in FANY uniforms.

Polly stopped. 'Come along, I'm starving,' Eileen said, beckoning to her.

A sailor passed, going the other way.

Polly turned and walked swiftly after him along the platform to the archway as the train pulled out and then, as she reached the safety of the archway, looked back. Eileen was coming after her, pushing through the FANYs, calling 'Polly!'

She hurried through the arch and along the tunnel to the hall and onto the escalator.

'Where are you *going*?' Eileen asked breathlessly, catching up to her halfway up.

'I thought I saw someone,' Polly said.

'Who? Agatha Christie?'

'No, a historian. Jack Sorkin.'

'I thought he was in the South Pacific.'

'I know, but I could have sworn—' Polly said. They reached the top of the escalator. Polly looked around at the crowd, frowning.

'Oh, it isn't him, after all,' she said, pointing at a sailor on the far side of the hall. 'Too bad.'

'It's all right,' Eileen said. 'We can still go to the canteen.' She started over to the escalator to go back down.

'Wait, I've just had a brilliant idea,' Polly said. 'Let's go to Lyons' Corner House instead.'

'Lyons'?' Eileen repeated doubtfully. 'Why?'

'There aren't any raids tonight. They're bombing Bristol. We can have a proper meal, and you can tell me all about *Murder on the Whatever It Is*.'

'The Calais Coach,' Eileen said. 'Or Orient Express. Do you think they may have bacon? Or eggs?'

They had both, and tea that didn't taste like dishwater. And pudding that didn't taste like wallpaper paste.

'That was the most wonderful meal I've ever had,' Eileen said blissfully on the train home. 'I'm glad you thought you saw Jack.'

'You were going to tell me about *Murder on the Calais Coach*,' Polly said.

'Oh yes. It's wonderful. Everyone has a motive for the crime, and you think, "It can't be all of them. It's got to be one or the other," but then it turns out ... but I don't want to spoil it for you. Would you care to borrow it? I'm sure the librarian at Holborn wouldn't mind if I kept it a bit longer.'

Polly wasn't listening. She was thinking about the slippage and their altering events. 'Eileen,' she asked, 'did Linna or Badri say anything about what was *causing* the increase in slippage?'

'No, not that I remember,' Eileen said, and when they got back to their room, she handed Polly a sheet of paper. 'Here, I wrote down everything I could remember, the way you and Mike told me to.'

On the sheet was scrawled, 'G had umbrella, ddn't offer it – Badri wking console – Linna on phne – mad abt. Bastille – L sd she kn R of T first.'

'What's R of T?'

'The Reign of Terror. Linna was talking to this person on the telephone about the lab changing whoever it was' drop to the Storming of the Bastille, and the person on the other end was obviously angry, and she said, "I *know* you were scheduled to do the Reign of Terror first." But she didn't say anything about slippage to them.'

Whoever it was had been scheduled to the Reign of Terror, and they'd changed it so he or she went to the Storming of the Bastille. Which had happened before the Reign of Terror.

'Where was Mike going before his assignment got changed to Dunkirk?' she asked Eileen. 'Was it Pearl Harbor?'

'I don't know. I think so. They'd changed his entire schedule.'

'Where else was he supposed to go?'

'I don't remember. Salisbury, I think, and the World Trade Center. I wasn't—'

Really listening, Polly thought, wanting to shake her. *Of course not. Just like you weren't listening to Gerald Phipps.*

'You can ask Mike when he rings us,' Eileen was saying. 'Why do you need to know?'

Because Pearl Harbor happened on December seventh, 1941. And the Storming of the Bastille was before the Reign of Terror.

Mike had said Mr Dunworthy had been shuffling and cancelling dozens of drops. What if he'd been doing it because the slippage increase wasn't a matter of months but of years? What if Mr Dunworthy had been putting all the drops in chronological order and cancelling ones where there was already a deadline because he had been afraid their drops wouldn't open in time? What if the increase had been four years? Or the length of the war, and that was why she'd seen Eileen at VE Day? Because they hadn't got out. But if that was it, then why hadn't he cancelled her drop?

Perhaps the increase isn't that large, she thought. Pearl Harbor was only a year and a half after Dunkirk. She didn't know how far apart the two events in the French Revolution were. The Storming of the Bastille was July fourteenth, 1789, but she didn't know when the Reign of Terror had begun. If it was less than three years—

Or that might not be the reason they'd changed the schedules at all. It might be something else altogether. *When Mike phones, I need to ask him the original order of his assignments and what it was changed to,* she thought. *If he phones. And in the meantime, it's pointless to worry.*

Which was impossible. She spent her lunch break going to Selfridge's and Bourne and Hollingsworth's to look at women's coats – which were luckily all far too expensive for Eileen to afford, even at Bourne and Hollingsworth's 'Bomb Damage' sale. And when clothing rationing went into effect, it would be impossible to save up enough points to buy one. But it still made Polly feel better to see that the only colours available were black, brown and navy blue.

Mike phoned Monday night, and it was exactly as Eileen had predicted. He'd had difficulty finding a phone where he could speak without being overheard. 'Either I'm going to have to find a telephone box that's closer,' he said, 'or we'll have to conduct our conversations in code.'

'You're surrounded by England's greatest cryptanalysts,' Polly said. 'I wouldn't recommend that.'

'You're right. It'll have to be letters. Does Mrs Rickett steam open your mail?'

'I wouldn't put it past her.'

'Well, don't worry. I'll think of something. I don't suppose the retrieval team's answered one of our ads yet?'

'No. You were supposed to do your Pearl Harbor assignment first, is that right?'

'Yes, and then the World Trade Center and the Battle of the Bulge, so I could use one L-and-A implant for all three.'

'And what did they change it to? Were Dunkirk and Pearl Harbor the only two they switched?'

'No, they switched them all around. After Pearl Harbor they wanted me to do El Alamein and then the Battle of the Bulge—'

I was right. They put them in chronological order, Polly thought and felt the familiar flutter of panic. *But El Alamein's only nine months after Pearl Harbor, and the Battle of the Bulge is only two years after that. It's still not as great a length of time between as mine.*

'—followed by the second World Trade Center attack—'

Which had been nearly sixty years after the Battle of the Bulge.

'—and the beginning of the Pandemic in Salisbury,' Mike said. Twenty years later. But that didn't prove anything. The lab might have put his assignments in chronological order because of Pearl Harbor, not the others.

I need to find out when the Reign of Terror began, she thought, and tried to think who would know. Not Eileen. Polly didn't want her to begin asking questions. And because Eileen was working in the book department, she couldn't look it up in a book on the French Revolution.

Sir Godfrey would no doubt know – he'd almost certainly played Sydney Carton on the stage. But he'd ask questions as well, and he saw far too much as it was. *The librarian at Holborn,* she thought.

When they got to Notting Hill Gate, she told Eileen she'd forgotten to give Doreen a message and had to go to Piccadilly Circus to tell her, and took the train to Holborn.

'The Reign of Terror?' the ginger-haired librarian said promptly. 'It began in September of 1793.' Four years and two months after the Storming of the Bastille.

OXFORD – APRIL 2060

M r Dunworthy went over Dr Ishiwaka's calculations again and then called, 'Eddritch, come into my office, please.' When his secretary appeared in the doorway, he said, 'I need you to ring up the lab and see why they haven't sent over that slippage analysis yet.'

'They did send it, sir,' Eddritch said, and just stood there.

I should never have let Finch become a historian, Dunworthy thought, lamenting the loss of his previous secretary. 'Well, then, where is it?'

'On my desk, sir.'

'Bring it to me,' Dunworthy said. When Eddritch came back with the file, he asked, 'Has Research telephoned?'

'Yes, sir.'

'What did they say?'

'They said they had the information you requested and that you were to ring them back,' Eddritch said. 'Would you like me to ring them for you?'

No, because you would very likely fail to inform me you'd put the call through, Dunworthy thought. 'I'll do it myself,' he said and rang them up.

'There were two hundred fatalities that night,' the tech who answered the telephone said. 'Twenty-one in the area you asked about. But that figure doesn't include those who might have been injured on that date and later died of their wounds.'

Or anyone who was killed days – or weeks – later as a consequence of what they did, Dunworthy thought.

'Do you want us to attempt to find out about those who suffered eventually fatal injuries?' the tech asked.

'We'll see. Give me what you've found thus far. You said twenty-one that night?'

'Yes, sir,' she said. 'Six firemen, an ARP warden, a Wren, an officer in the Lancaster Rifles, a WAAC, a seventeen-year-old boy and two charwomen.'

'No naval officers?'

'No, sir. But as I said, this is only the people who died that night.'

'Have you the exact locations where they were killed?'

'For some of them. The officer and two of the firemen were killed in Upper Grosvenor Street, and the others fighting a fire in the Minories. The ARP warden was killed in Cheapside. The post was hit.'

'What about the Wren?'

'She was killed in Ave Maria Lane.'

Only a few streets away from St Paul's. 'Is there a photo of her?'

'No, not with the death notice. Do you want me to try to find one?'

'Yes. And I need the names of the fatalities and, if possible, photographs. As soon as you can. When you have it, phone me directly.' He gave her the number, rang off, and started through the slippage analysis, afraid that it held more bad news. But although there was a slight increase in the average amount of slippage per drop, it wasn't as large as Ishiwaka had predicted, and several of the drops were in areas where their opening was highly likely to be observed, which could account for the increase. And there was nothing to indicate a spike.

But the analysis didn't include this week's drops. He told Eddritch to ring him at the lab if Research phoned, and went out of the gate and over to the Broad.

As Dunworthy turned up Catte Street, Colin Templer caught up with him. 'I'm glad I found you,' he said breathlessly. 'That idiot secretary of yours wouldn't tell me where you were.'

He should reprove Colin for calling Eddritch an idiot, but there was a certain amount of truth to his assessment. 'Why aren't you in school?' he demanded instead.

'We had a holiday,' Colin said, and at his look, added, 'No, truly. You can ring up the school and ask them. So I came up to see you. I've an idea for an assignment,' he said, walking beside Dunworthy. 'Do you know the land girls?'

'The *land* girls?'

'Yes. In World War II. They were these women who—'

'I am familiar with the land girls. You're proposing to pose as a female and enlist in the Women's Land Army?'

'No, but the *reason* they had to have land girls was because the farm labourers had all gone off to the war, and the farmers hired boys as well, so I thought I could say I was fifteen – that way I'd be too young to be called up – and I could observe wartime farm life. You know, food shortages and all that.'

'And what's to stop you from enlisting the moment you get there? Or haring off to London to see Polly Churchill?'

'That's the *last* thing I'd do,' Colin said fervently, and Dunworthy wondered what *that* was all about. Had she laughed at him and hurt his feelings? 'And I promise I won't enlist. I'll swear to it if you like, or sign an oath in blood or something.'

'No.'

'But I've found a farm in Hampshire where there wasn't a single bomb or V-1 for the entire war. And I've researched milking cows and gathering eggs—'

They'd reached the lab. Dunworthy stopped outside the door. 'I am not sending you anywhere until you have passed your examinations, been admitted to Oxford, and completed your undergraduate degree – none of which look likely at this point.'

'That's unfair. I rewrote my essay on Dr Ishiwaka and got a 98 on it, even though I still think his theory's rubbish.'

And let's hope you're right, Dunworthy thought. 'Run along,' he said. 'I have business to conduct.'

'I don't mind waiting.'

'There's no point. I do not intend to change my mind. And in case you were hoping to sneak into the drop with me the way you did when I went after Kivrin Engle, I am not here to use the net. I am here to talk to Badri.'

'Then there's no need to bar me from the lab, is there?' Colin said, sidling in before Dunworthy could shut the door. 'I'll wait till you're done and then tell you my *other* idea. You won't even know I'm here.'

'See that I don't,' Dunworthy said, and started over to Badri, who was at the console.

'If you're here about your drop to St Paul's,' Badri said, 'we just finished calculating the coordinates, so you can go at any time.'

'Good,' Dunworthy said. 'I want to see the slippage for this week's drops. Is the amount still increasing?'

'Yes.' Badri called it up on the screen. 'But the rate of increase is less than last week.'

Good, Dunworthy thought. Perhaps it was only a temporary anomaly.

'I've been looking at the individual drops,' Badri said. 'The elevated slippage seems to be confined to drops back to World War II, so the increase could be due to the greater incidence of divergence points wars produce. Or to wartime conditions – civilian observers, ARP patrols – that sort of thing.'

But scores of historians had gone to World War II over the years, and there'd been no increase in the average slippage. 'Have all the historians I spoke to you about been cancelled or rescheduled?'

'Yes, sir,' Badri said, and Linna handed him a list.

'What about Michael Davies?' Dunworthy asked, looking at it.

'We rescheduled him to do his Dunkirk evacuation observation first. He left' – he consulted the console screen – 'four days ago. He'll be back six to ten days from now.'

'And the Pearl Harbor drop's scheduled for when?'

'The end of May.'

Good, Dunworthy thought. *I'll have six weeks before I need to make a decision.* 'Why the uncertainty in when he'll return? Was the projected slippage high?'

'No, sir, but his drop's outside Dover, so it may take him a day or two to make it back there after the end of the evacuation.'

'We had a dreadful time finding him a drop site,' Linna volunteered. 'The only one we could find was five miles from Dover.'

Dunworthy frowned. Difficulty in finding drop sites was one of the signs Dr Ishiwaka had predicted. 'An abnormal amount of difficulty?'

'Yes,' Linna said.

'No,' Badri said, 'not considering the large number of people in the area. And the high level of secrecy surrounding the operation.'

'Any other instances of difficulty finding a drop site?' Dunworthy asked.

'We had some minor difficulty finding Charles Bowden one in Singapore, but we were finally able to send him through on the British colony's polo grounds. And we had a good deal of difficulty with Polly Churchill's, but that was because of your location requirements and the blackout.'

'Send her to see me as soon as she returns from the Blitz. When is that?'

'She should be reporting in tomorrow or the day after with the address of the boarding house where she'll be staying.'

'What? Do you mean to tell me she hasn't reported in *yet*?'

'No, sir, but there's nothing to worry about,' Badri said. 'She may have had difficulty finding a room to let, or she may have decided to wait till she had a job as well. That way she could tell us the name of the department store—'

'She's been there a *month*,' Dunworthy said. 'It can't possibly have taken her that long to find a job. Why wasn't I told she hadn't reported in?' He turned accusingly to Colin. 'Did *you* know about this?'

'I don't even know what you're talking about,' Colin said. 'She hasn't been there a month. Has she, Badri?'

'No. She's only been there two days.'

'What? Eddritch told me a month ago that she'd left on assignment.'

'She did, sir, but not for the Blitz,' Linna said. 'We were having difficulty finding a drop site for her, so she suggested we send her to one of the other parts of her project first.'

'And you did? You sent her to the Zeppelin attacks on London without obtaining my approval first?'

'You'd already approved the project, so we thought … but we couldn't send her to the Zeppelins. She hadn't done her World War I prep yet. We sent her to the third part.'

'The *third* part?' Dunworthy thundered. 'And then you sent her to the *Blitz*?'

'Yes sir, we—'

'In spite of the fact that I'd told you to cancel all out-of-order drops?'

'Out-of-order?' Badri said. 'I … you didn't say that was what you were doing. You only gave us a list—'

'Of drops which were to be rescheduled so they'd be chronological. Or cancelled if that wasn't possible.'

'You didn't say anything about chronology,' Linna said defensively.

'I … I'd no idea,' Badri stammered. 'If we'd known—'

'Is something wrong?' Colin asked, coming over. 'Has something happened to Polly?'

Dunworthy ignored him. 'What do you mean you had no idea?' he said to Badri. 'Why else did you think I was re-scheduling them? And if Polly Churchill was on assignment, why wasn't she on the list you gave me?'

'You asked for a list of every historian in the past,' Linna said, 'and she'd already returned.'

Dunworthy wheeled on Colin. 'You knew she'd gone, didn't you? Why didn't you *tell* me?'

'I thought you knew,' Colin said. 'What's *wrong*? Why wasn't she supposed to go to the Blitz?'

Dunworthy turned back to Badri. 'Badri, how long will it take to set up the coordinates on Polly's drop?'

'Has something happened to Polly?' Colin persisted.

'No, because I'm pulling her out of there.'

'You're sending a *retrieval team* after her, sir?' Badri said.

'No. That will take too long. I'll go myself. How long?'

'But you don't know where she is,' Badri argued.

'She'll be checking in in another day or two. Wouldn't it be easier to wait till—?'

'I know she's looking for a job on Oxford Street. How long?'

'I'd have to change her drop to send mode,' Badri said. 'It's set up for a return drop at the moment. A day or two.'

'Too long,' Dunworthy said. 'I want her out of there now. And I don't want anything to interfere if she tries to check in. How long to set up a new drop nearby?'

'A *new* drop?' Badri said. 'I've no idea. It took us weeks to find Polly's. The blackout—'

'What about the St Paul's drop?' Dunworthy asked Badri. 'How long to set new temporal coordinates?'

'An hour perhaps, but you can't go through to St Paul's. John Bartholomew was there in—'

'Not in early September. He didn't go through till the twentieth.'

'But you can't go through in early September. It's too dangerous.'

'St Paul's wasn't bombed till October,' Mr Dunworthy said.

'I'm not talking about St Paul's. I'm talking about your—'

'What day did Polly go through?' Dunworthy interrupted.

'September tenth.'

'Has something *happened* to her?' Colin said. 'Is she in some sort of trouble?'

'What time was her drop set for?' Dunworthy asked Badri.

'Five a.m. The raids on the night of the ninth were over at half past four, and the all-clear didn't go till 6:22.'

'Set mine for four a.m. That way the fire watch will still be up on the roofs and I'll have the entire day to find her.'

'You're pulling her out the same day she went *through*?' Colin asked.

Badri said, 'Sir, you can't go through with a raid in progress. And the tenth is too close to—'

'I'll only be there the few hours it takes to find her, and there's a tube stop just down from the cathedral. I can go straight to Oxford Street from there. And the raids that night were over the East End, not the City.'

'*Tell* me why you need to pull her out,' Colin said, his voice rising. 'What's *happened*?'

'Nothing's happened,' Dunworthy said. 'I'm merely pulling her out as a precaution.'

'What do you mean, a precaution? Against what?'

I knew I shouldn't have let Colin into the lab, Dunworthy thought. 'There's been a slight increase in the amount of slippage,' he said. 'And until we know what's causing it, I'm not sending historians on multi-part drops, that's all. I was unaware that Polly had left on hers or I would have stopped her from going. Since she's already there, I'm bringing her back.'

'I'm going with you.'

'Don't be ridiculous.'

'No, I must,' Colin said earnestly. 'I promised her I'd come and rescue her if she was in trouble.'

'She is *not* in trouble—'

159

'Then why are you pulling her out? And what do you mean, a slight increase? How much?'

'Only a few days.'

'Oh,' Colin said, and Dunworthy could see the relief in his face.

But he was a bright lad; he'd make the connection. Dunworthy needed to get him out of here. 'Colin, I need you to go to Props and tell them I need a 1940 identity card,' he said, afraid Colin would balk at leaving, but he was eager to help.

'What name do you want on the card?' he asked.

'There's no time to make up a special one. Have them give you whatever they have on hand.'

Colin nodded. 'You'll need a ration book, as well, and a shelter assignment card and—'

'No, I'm only going through for a few hours,' he said. 'Just long enough to locate Polly and bring her back.'

'But you'll need money for the tube and things. And what about clothes? Should I go to Wardrobe and—?'

I can just imagine what Wardrobe would come up with, Dunworthy thought. 'No, I'll wear what I have on,' he said. A tweed jacket and wool trousers had, thankfully, been wardrobe staples for well over a century.

'But you'll need a gas mask. And a steel helmet,' Colin said. 'It's the Blitz—'

'I am fully aware of the Blitz's dangers,' Dunworthy said. 'I have been there several times.'

'Sir?' Badri interrupted. 'I think you should send a retrieval team instead of going yourself. It would only take a short time to set one up and a day or two to prep them—'

'There is no need for a retrieval team.'

'Then at least someone who hasn't been to 1940—'

'You could send me,' Colin said eagerly. 'I know all about the Blitz. I helped Polly with her prep—'

'*You* are not going anywhere,' Dunworthy said, 'except to Props to fetch me an identity card.'

'But I know when and where all the raids were, and—'

'Go,' Dunworthy said. 'Now.'

'But— Yes, sir,' Colin said reluctantly, and ran out.

'How long before Linna will have those coordinates set up?' Dunworthy asked Badri.

'A few minutes. But I really think you should send someone who hasn't been to 1940 before. You're clearly worried about the increase in slippage making it impossible to pull people out by their deadlines, which means you shouldn't—'

'The increase in slippage at this point is only two days, which would put me through on the twelfth at the latest, and I will be there less than a day. I'll be in no danger. Linna, do you have those coordinates?' he called over to her.

'Nearly,' she called back, and Dunworthy took off his watch and began emptying his pockets.

The door to the lab banged open, and Colin came skidding in, waving a handful of papers. 'You're Edward Price,' he said. 'You live at 11 Jubilee Place, Chelsea. I brought you two five-pound notes.'

'And I see you've changed out of your school blazer into something Wardrobe fondly imagines young boys were wearing during the Blitz,' Dunworthy said.

Colin flushed. 'I think I should go with you. With two people looking, we can find Polly twice as fast, and I know where every single bomb fell on the tenth.'

'As do I. Give me my money and identity card.'

'And here's your ration book,' Colin said, handing them to him. 'You might get hungry. I brought you a pocket torch. To help you see where you're going.'

Dunworthy handed it back. 'All that will do is get me arrested by the local ARP warden. Pocket torches weren't allowed in the blackout.'

'But that's all the more reason for me to go with you. I can see really well in the dark—'

'You are not going, Colin.'

'But what if you're hit by a bus? That happened a lot in the blackout. Or get into some other sort of trouble?'

'I will *not* get into trouble.'

'You did last time,' Colin said, 'and I had to rescue you, remember? What if that happens again?'

'It won't.'

'Mr Dunworthy?' Linna said from the console. 'I have the coordinates if you're ready.'

'Yes,' he said and saw Colin dart a calculating glance at the draped folds of the net and the distance between it and where they were standing. 'Thank you, Linna, but I need a few more minutes. Colin, on second thought, I believe you're right about the torch. If I'm to get Polly out quickly, I can't afford to sprain an ankle falling off a kerb.'

'Good,' Colin said, holding the torch out to him.

'No, this one won't work,' he said. 'It's too modern. And it needs to be fitted with a special blackout hood to eliminate the beam's being seen from above. Go and ask Props if they have one with a hood, and if they haven't, then paste strips of black paper over the glass. Hurry.'

'Yes, sir,' Colin said, and dashed out.

'You have the coordinates ready?' Dunworthy asked Linna as soon as Colin was gone.

'Yes, sir,' she said. 'We can do it as soon as Colin—'

He went over to the door and locked it. 'Send me through.'

'But I thought—'

'The last thing I need is a seventeen-year-old tagging along while I'm trying to find a missing historian,' he said, walking over to the net and ducking under its already descending folds. 'A seventeen-year-old who, as Badri can attest, has a history of stowing away on journeys to the past.' He centred himself on the grid. 'Ready,' he said to her.

'I think you should at least wait until we've set up the return drop,' Badri said. 'If there's increased slippage, and you go through later than—'

162

'You can set it up after you send me through. Now, Linna.'

'Yes, sir,' she said. She began typing, and he saw the beginnings of the shimmer.

'Don't send anyone else through on assignment till I return. And if Polly comes back to check in, keep her here.'

'Yes, sir.'

'And Colin's not to be allowed anywhere near the net while I'm gone.'

The shimmer was beginning to grow and flare, obscuring Linna's features. 'He's not to come through after me – or Polly – under any circumstances,' he said, but it was too late. The net was already opening.

'Very well met, and well come!'

WILLIAM SHAKESPEARE, *MEASURE FOR MEASURE*

BLETCHLEY – NOVEMBER 1940

Turing. Oh God. He'd collided with Alan Turing and nearly got him killed. 'That was Turing?' Mike asked and grabbed for the wall, his legs suddenly unsteady.

'Oh, you *are* hurt!' Elspeth said. 'Here, come inside and sit down. And you're limping!'

'No, that's not—' he began, but the girls were already helping him up the steps and inside.

'People like that should be forbidden from riding bicycles,' Mavis said indignantly. 'Let me see your foot.'

'Did you say Turing?' Mike said. 'Alan Turing?'

'Yes,' Elspeth said. 'Do you know him?'

'No, I knew a guy named Turing in college. A math—'

'That's him. They say he's a genius at maths.'

'Well, I don't care if he's a genius or not,' Mavis said. 'I intend to give him a piece of my mind!'

'No! Don't say anything to him. I'm all right.'

'But he may have broken your foot—'

'No, he didn't. It was shot off.'

Their eyes widened and Elspeth, obviously impressed, said, 'Were you at *Dunkirk*?'

'Yes – the point is, he didn't hurt me. I was just shaken up for a minute. There's no need to say anything to Mr Turing. I was the one who wasn't watching where I was going.'

'*You* were the one?' Mavis said indignantly. 'Turing never pays the slightest attention to where he's going. He simply ploughs through pedestrians.'

Elspeth nodded. 'Someone needs to tell him he must be more careful! He could have injured you!'

And I could have injured him, Mike thought. *Or killed him.* If Turing had lost control of his bicycle and crashed into a lamppost instead of the kerb, or into a brick wall—

Mavis said, 'I've a good mind to tell Cap—'

'No. There's no need to tell anybody. I'm fine. No harm done. Thank you for picking me up and dusting me off.' He picked up his bag, which Mavis had carried in.

'Oh, don't go,' Elspeth said. 'We want to hear about Dunkirk.' She perched on the arm of the couch. 'Was it exciting? It must have been dangerous.'

'Not half as dangerous as this place,' he said.

Elspeth laughed, but not Mavis. She was looking curiously at him. 'Why were you at Dunkirk? Aren't you an American?'

Oh Jesus, worse and worse. He hadn't even been thinking what he was saying, he'd been so upset about nearly killing Turing, and now he'd just blown his cover. 'Yes,' he admitted.

'I *knew* it,' Mavis said smugly, and Elspeth added, 'Oh good, we *adore* Americans. But what were you doing at Dunkirk?'

You can't say you're a reporter. 'A friend of mine had a boat. We thought we'd go over and see if we could lend a hand.'

'Oh, how thrilling!' Elspeth said. 'You've no idea how exciting it is to meet someone who's actually doing something *important* in the war.'

'You must stay to tea and tell us all about it,' Mavis said. 'I'll go and put the kettle on.'

'No, don't.' He stood up. 'I'm sure you're busy, and I'm interrupting—'

'No, you're not,' Elspeth said. 'We're off duty tonight.'

'But it's getting late, and I have to find a place to stay. I don't suppose you know of any rooms that are available?'

'In *Bletchley*?' Elspeth said, as if he'd asked for an apartment on the Moon.

'I'm afraid everything's filled up for miles around,' Mavis said. 'We're three to a room here.'

'Did I hear someone say we're getting a new roommate?' a female voice called down from upstairs. 'Tell her there's no room.' She came running down the stairs. She was very buxom and very blonde. 'We're crammed in like pilchards as it is – oh, hullo,' she said, coming over to meet Mike. 'Are you going to be billeted here? How lovely!'

'He's *not* billeted here, Joan,' Mavis said. 'Even if we weren't full up, Mrs Braithewaite only lets to girls,' she explained to Mike. 'She says it saves complications.'

I can imagine, Mike thought, looking at Joan.

'Have you been to the billeting office yet?' Elspeth asked.

Billeting office? 'No,' he said. 'I just arrived.'

'Well, when you go,' Elspeth said, 'tell them it's essential you live close in, or they'll put you up in Glasgow.'

'And you must insist on seeing your billet first,' Mavis added. 'Some of them are dreadful. *Bedbugs*!'

He was still thinking about what they'd said about a billeting office. He should have thought of that. Of course the administration at Bletchley Park would be in charge of assigning lodgings. He'd been thinking he could rent a room and hint to his landlady that he worked out at the Park, but if everyone who worked there got lodgings through the billeting office—

'He might try the Empire Hotel,' Joan said to Mavis.

'It's full up,' Mavis said, and to Mike, '*Everything's* full up. Even cupboards. Our friend Wendy's sleeping in the pantry at her billet, in among the bottled peaches.'

'The billeting office isn't open on a Sunday,' Joan said. 'We could sneak him upstairs for tonight.'

'*No*,' the other two said in unison.

'What about the Bell?' Elspeth asked.

Mavis shook her head.

'Well, maybe they'll let me sleep in the lobby,' Mike said, and went to the door.

'You're certain you can't stay a bit longer?' Joan asked.

'Afraid not. Thanks for all your help. Do any of you happen to know—?' but before he could ask whether they knew a Gerald Phipps, they began giving him directions to the Bell. 'And if it hasn't any rooms, the Milton's two streets down—'

'Watch out for Turing on your way there,' Joan cut in.

'And for Dilly,' Elspeth said. 'He's even worse about not watching where he's going, and he has a car! Whenever he comes to a crossing, he speeds *up*.'

'Dilly?' Mike said hoarsely.

'Captain Knox,' Mavis said. 'We work for him. He has some sort of mathematical theory that by going faster he'll hit fewer people, because of being on the crossing a shorter time.'

My God. First Alan Turing and now Dilly's girls. He was smack in the middle of Ultra, and he'd only been in Bletchley half an hour. 'I refuse to accept lifts from him anymore,' Elspeth was saying. 'He forgets he's driving and takes both hands off the— Are you all right? You're pale as a ghost.'

'Turing *did* injure you,' Mavis said. 'Come and sit down while we phone for the doctor. Elspeth, go and put the kettle—'

'No!' he said. 'No. I'm fine. Really,' and left before they could protest. Or Dilly Knox showed up.

'But we don't even know your name!' Mavis called after him.

Thank God for that at least, he thought, pretending he hadn't heard her. And thank God he hadn't asked about Phipps. He hurried off towards the Bell. What next? Would there be an Enigma machine in his room?

If you can find a room, he thought. But surely they'd have saved a hotel room or two for people passing through, billeting or no billeting.

Wrong. The desk clerk hooted when he asked.

'You don't know of anywhere—?' Mike said.

'In *Bletchley*?' the clerk said and turned to the young man who'd just come up to the counter. 'Yes, Mr Welchman?'

Gordon Welchman? Who'd headed up the team which had broken the German Army and Air Force Enigma codes? Christ, he thought, retreating hastily, at this rate he'd have met all the key players by morning. He headed for the Milton, wondering if he should go back to the station right now and catch the first train going anywhere.

No, with his luck, Alan Ross would be on it with Menzies sound asleep in the luggage rack. But it didn't look as if he could stay here either. Neither the Milton nor the Empire had a room, and going back to the Bell was out of the question. 'You might try one of the boarding houses on Albion Street,' the clerk at the Empire said, 'but I doubt you'll find anything.'

He was right. Every house had a 'No Rooms Available' or 'No Vacancy' placard in its front window. *Maybe the reason the Germans never found out about Ultra was because their spies couldn't find anywhere to stay*, Mike thought, crossing the street – after first looking carefully in all directions – and starting down the other side, peering through the dark at the signs: 'No Rooms', 'Full Up', 'Room to Let—'

'Room to Let.' It took a moment for that to sink in, and then he was up the steps and pounding on the door. A plump, rosy-cheeked old lady opened the door, smiling. 'Yes?'

'I saw that you have a room. Is it still available?'

She stopped smiling and folded her arms belligerently across her stomach. 'Did the billeting office send you?'

If he said yes, he might have to produce some sort of official form, and if he said no, she was likely to tell him all her rooms had already been co-opted. 'I saw your notice,' he said, pointing at it. The smile came back, and she motioned him to come in.

'I'm Mrs Jolsom,' she said. 'I didn't think you looked like one of them.'

Polly and Eileen won't be happy about that, after all their efforts, he thought, wondering what was wrong with his appearance.

'I don't let rooms to that lot at the Park. Unreliable. Coming and going at all hours, scattering papers everywhere, and when you try to tidy up after them, shouting at you not to touch anything, like it was something valuable instead of a lot of papers covered with numbers. Ten and four.'

For a moment he thought she was talking about the numbers on the papers, and then realised she meant the price of the room. 'Paid by the week. In advance,' she said, leading him upstairs. 'Room only, no board – the rationing, you know. I ask two weeks' notice if you're leaving,' she said, leading him up a second flight, 'so the room won't stand empty.'

She apparently hasn't heard about Wendy having to sleep in the pantry, Mike thought, following her down a hall. The room was the size of a closet, but it was a room, and it was in Bletchley. 'I'll take it,' he said.

'I've had them go off without a word,' she said indignantly, 'or not come when they said they would – and after I'd saved the room for them. "There must have been a miscommunication," the billeting officer said. "Miscommunication!" I said, "what about this letter? And what about my four weeks' rent?"'

Mike finally stopped her by handing her the week's rent and asking if she had a telephone. 'No, but there's one at the pub two streets over,' she said. 'Claimed he hadn't sent the letter, he did. "Well, then, that's the last one you billet here," I told him. "What about your patriotic duty?" says he. "What about *their* patriotic duty?" I says. "Lazing about here messing with multiplication tables like a lot of schoolboys when they ought to be in the Army?" She looked at Mike suspiciously. 'Why aren't *you* in the Army?'

He wasn't about to blow it now, when this was the only room for miles, *and* in the one house where he wouldn't have to worry about running into a famous cryptanalyst on the way to the bathroom. 'I was injured at Dunkirk.' He pointed at his foot. 'Dive bomber.'

'Oh my,' Mrs Jolsom said, pressing a hand to her bosom, 'only just think, a hero here under my own roof,' and bustled off to make him tea and a soft-boiled egg. He'd have felt ashamed of himself for passing himself off as a war hero if he hadn't still been spooked by his encounters with Turing, Dilly's girls and Welchman.

You didn't do any damage, he told himself. Turing wasn't hurt, and all he'd done to Dilly's girls was talk to them. *And blow your cover*, he thought. But they hadn't thought there was anything odd about an American being in Bletchley. And if Dilly's girls and Turing were this easy to find, then Gerald Phipps should be a snap. And *you have a room and, since Mrs Jolsom's making you supper, you don't have to go out so you can't get in any more trouble tonight*. But he'd have to go out tomorrow to look for Phipps, which meant being in places he was likely to run into BPers.

Or maybe not. Instead, he could pretend to be looking for a room to rent. Nobody could be suspicious of that, given the housing situation, and after they'd turned him down, he could say casually, 'Oh, by the way, you don't have a boarder named Gerald Phipps, do you? Sandy-haired guy with spectacles?' And he wouldn't have to go anywhere near Bletchley Park.

His plan worked like a charm – except that he didn't find Phipps. And if he'd really been looking for a room, he wouldn't have found that either. He'd apparently got the last one in Bletchley. After four days of knocking on doors and asking at every hotel and inn, he was certain Phipps wasn't living anywhere in the town.

Which meant he was billeted in one of the surrounding villages, but according to Dilly's girls, BPers were scattered all over the area. It would take him forever to find Phipps that way. Looking at Bletchley Park would be much more efficient.

If he could find it. He doubted if Mrs Jolsom would tell him, given her enmity against it, and he didn't dare ask a passerby. With his luck it would turn out to be Angus Wilson. Or Winston Churchill.

But the Park turned out not to be that hard to find. All he had to do was follow the stream of naval officers and professors and pretty girls out of town along a paved road clogged with bicycles ridden by people who didn't pay any more attention to where they were going than Turing.

Polly'd been right. He didn't need to get into Bletchley Park to see who worked there. He could watch them all from the cinder-covered driveway that led up to the guarded gate. Beyond it lay long grey-green buildings and a gabled red-brick Victorian mansion. He limped a few feet up the drive and then stopped and knelt, pretending to tie his shoe, though nobody was taking any notice of him. The pretty girls were chattering to each other, and the professors were in another world. The guard paid no attention either. He checked off names on a roster and glanced cursorily at the identity cards people held out to him. Mike had the feeling he could hold out his press pass and get in.

He finished tying his shoe and stood up. Several men were standing around smoking and apparently waiting for someone. *I need to buy some cigarettes*, he thought. No, a pipe. He could spend a long time filling it, trying to light it, patting his pockets for matches. For now, he glanced impatiently at his watch and scanned the people coming out. He didn't see Phipps, though there were several sandy-haired, bespectacled, tweed-clad men, and he caught a glimpse of two more inside the grounds.

Let's hope I don't have to sneak inside to find him, Mike thought, though if he did, at least it wouldn't be hard. There was a fence, but no barbed wire, and the gate's bar wasn't even lowered. It didn't look at all like a military installation, let alone the site of the most closely guarded secret of the war. It looked like Balliol in mid-term. The young women walking between the buildings, file folders clasped to their breasts, could be students; the men playing a game on the lawn could be the cricket team.

He could imagine what the regimented, spit-and-polish Germans would make of this place and its inhabitants. Maybe that was why they'd never figured out that the British had cracked the Enigma code. It wouldn't have occurred to them that these giggling young women and dishevelled daydreamers could be a threat. The Nazis would have had nothing but contempt for Dilly's girls and the stammering Turing.

Which was why they'd been defeated. They shouldn't have underestimated them. And he'd better not underestimate them either. For all he knew, the scruffy professor smoking over by the gate or the blonde dabbing powder on her nose worked for British Intelligence and would shortly knock on his landlady's door to 'ask him a few questions'. In which case he'd better get out of here before he attracted their attention.

He waited till a staff car pulled up to the gate and the guard leaned in the window to talk to the driver and then casually joined the stream of people walking back to town. Once there, he bought a pipe, tobacco and a newspaper, went to the lobby of the Milton, looked around to make sure Wilson or Menzies weren't there, and sat down in a chair by the window to wait for the four o'clock shift change and look for Gerald.

When he didn't see him, he followed two men who looked like cryptanalysts to a pub, ordered a pint of beer, and spent the evening nursing it and observing everyone who came in.

He did the same thing at a different pub the next night, and the next. The first night he pretended to be reading a newspaper, but it was awkward seeing over it, so the next night he folded it open to the crossword and pretended to be working on it, like he had in the hospital sunroom at Orpington. That way he could stare thoughtfully into space as if trying to think of an answer while scanning the room, though he wasn't sure it was necessary. No one paid any attention to him. The men either talked in heads-bent-together groups, scribbled busily, or sat with their heads in a book – Haas' *Atomic Theory*, De Broglie's

Matter and Light, and in one instance, an Agatha Christie. He'd have to tell Eileen.

He didn't run into Turing again – literally or figuratively. Or Welchman. He did see Dilly Knox at the wheel of a car, and the girls hadn't exaggerated about his bad driving. The two naval officers ahead of him had to leap for the kerb. He glimpsed the girls twice, but managed to escape both times without their seeing him.

His only problem (aside from not having found Phipps) was staying in contact with Eileen and Polly. On Wednesday night he'd realised he hadn't told them his address yet and had spent the next few days trying to find a phone where he could talk and not be overheard. He finally went back to the railway station – after first watching Dilly's girls leave for their shift so he wouldn't run into them – and called from there, but no one answered, and the station was full of people all through the weekend.

He wasn't able to get hold of Polly till Monday. He told her where he was living and asked her if the retrieval team had responded to any of their ads. 'No,' Polly said and asked him what the original order of his drops had been.

He told her. 'Why?' he asked curiously.

'I was just trying to remember other historians who might be here,' she said, 'or might be Historian X, and I wanted to make certain they weren't you.'

'Speaking of that, I had another idea.' He told her about possibly using St John's Wood or one of the other older drops. He didn't tell her about Dilly's girls or Welchman or about colliding with Turing that first night. There hadn't been any repercussions from that. The accident hadn't even made Turing mend his ways. On Saturday night he'd overheard an officer complaining loudly about his having nearly run her down the night before.

Nobody seemed to worry about being overheard, and, listening to them and watching their casual comings and goings, he wondered how the government had ever managed to keep

Ultra's secret from getting out. New people arrived every day, jamming the already overcrowded town.

And the station. He gave up on the idea of calling Polly and Eileen again and sent them a note hidden in the squares of a torn-out newspaper crossword puzzle, telling them to check the old remote drop in St John's Wood and hoping Polly would realise it was a code, and then went back to trying to find Gerald.

He made the rounds of the Park gates, the boarding houses, the hotels, and then went back to sitting in the pubs, though they were so crowded he couldn't find an empty table. On Sunday night Mike had to squeeze to the counter to order his pint and then lean against the bar for over an hour, waiting for one where he could sit, pretend to work his crossword, eaves-drop, and watch for Phipps.

A small knot of men stood in the far corner, talking and laughing, but they were too tall to be Phipps. At the table next to them sat a bald man, doing calculations on the back of an envelope, and next to him, his back to Mike, was a sandy-haired guy. He was talking to a pretty brunette, and from the annoyed look on her face, he might very well be telling her an unfunny joke.

Mike moved his chair, trying to see his face. No luck. He looked down at his crossword for a moment, then up again, tapping his pencil against his nose, waiting for the guy to turn around.

The men in the corner were leaving, stopping as they went out to talk to the girls at the table between Mike and the sandy-haired guy.

Get out of the way, he thought, leaning so he could see past them.

'Good Lord,' a man's voice behind him said, 'you're the *last* person I expected to see here.'

Mike looked up, startled. He'd completely forgotten about the possibility that Phipps might recognise him. But it wasn't Phipps standing over the table. It was Tensing, the officer he'd conspired with in the sunroom of the hospital.

DULWICH – JULY 1944

'What do you mean, you've remembered where we met, Officer Lang?' Mary said, trying not to look as cornered as she felt, seeing him standing there in the common room of the ambulance post. 'I thought we agreed that line of chat didn't work.'

'It's not a line, Isolde,' he said, and smiled his crooked smile. 'I *have* remembered where we met.'

Oh no. Then she *had* met him – or rather, *would* meet him – on her next assignment. And now she'd have to pretend she remembered him, too, without knowing how well she'd known him or under what circumstances. And she'd have to hope he hadn't remembered what her name had been – correction, *would* be.

Where's Fairchild? she thought, looking towards the door. *She promised she'd come and rescue me.*

'You said you have good news to tell me as well?' she said, stalling.

'I have indeed.' He bowed formally. 'I'm here to deliver my thanks and the thanks of a grateful nation.'

'The thanks—? For what?'

'For giving me a smashing idea, which I shall tell you all about when I take you to that dinner I owe you, and don't say you can't because I've already found out from your fellow FANY here that you're off-duty tonight. And if it's flying bombs you're worried about, I can assure you there won't be any more tonight.'

'But—' she said, glancing hopefully back at the door. *Where was Fairchild?*

'No buts, Isolde. It's destiny. We're fated to be together through all time. I told you, I've remembered where we met, and I also know *why* you don't remember that meeting.'

You do? Could she somehow have betrayed her identity? Did he know she was a historian?

I should have told Fairchild to come in immediately instead of waiting five minutes. 'I only just remembered, I forgot to log in,' she said, starting towards the door. 'I'll be back straightaway,' but he grabbed her hand.

'Wait. You can't go till I've told you about the flying bombs. I've found a way to stop them. Remember how I told you the generals were after me to invent a way to shoot them down before they reached their target?'

'And you thought of one?'

'I told you, shooting them down doesn't work because the bomb still goes off.'

'So you've found a way to keep the bomb from going off?' she said, thinking, *He can't have. The RAF was never able to devise a way to disable the V-1s' bombs in flight.*

'No. I found a way to turn them round and send them back across the Channel. Or at any rate away from the target.'

'This isn't the lassoing it with a rope plan, is it?'

'No.' He laughed. 'This doesn't require a rope *or* cannons. All that's needed is a Spitfire and some expert flying. That's the beauty of it. All I do is catch up to the V-1 till the Spitfire's just below it—'

And edge your wing under the V-1's fin, she thought, *and then angle your plane slightly so the fin tips up and disrupts the airflow and sends the rocket careening off-course.*

She had read about the practice of V-1 tipping when she was prepping for this assignment. But it was an incredibly danger-ous thing to attempt. The contact could send the Spitfire into a disastrous tailspin. Or, if the Spitfire came up on the V-1 too fast, they could both explode.

The sickening thought flickered through her mind that this was the reason the net hadn't prevented her from driving him out of the way of those V-1s. It hadn't mattered that she'd saved his life because he was going to be killed tipping them.

'And then we come up under the wing,' he was saying. He demonstrated, bringing one of his hands up under the other, 'and tilt it ever so slightly.' He nudged the hand on top, 'so that it tips—'

The hand on top angled up and then veered off. 'The rocket's got a delicate gyroscopic mechanism. Most of the time we needn't even touch it.'

He demonstrated it again, this time without his hands touch-ing, and as she watched him, boyishly intent on explaining how it worked to her, she had the same feeling she'd had in Whitehall that afternoon, that there *was* something familiar about him.

'The slipstream does the work for us,' he said, 'and the V-1 goes spiralling down into the Channel, or, if we're *truly* lucky, back to France and the launcher it came from, without us so much as laying a finger on it. We've downed thirty already this week.'

And that's why the number of rockets has been down the past two weeks, she thought. *Not because of Intelligence's misinformation campaign, but because Stephen and his fellow pilots have been playing, 'Tag, you're it' with the rockets.*

'—and not a single casualty on the ground,' he was say-ing happily, 'but that's not the best of it. What I came to tell you—'

'Triumph!' someone called from the corridor.

Finally, she thought. 'In here!' she called back.

'Triumph?' Stephen said. 'I thought your last name was Kent.'

'They've been calling me that since the motorcycle incident,' she explained, wondering why Fairchild hadn't appeared. 'That, and De Havilland and Douglas and Norton,' she said. 'The name of every motorcycle they can think of. Oh, and Lawrence of Arabia, because that's how he died, in a motorcycle crash.'

'I quite understand,' he said, grinning. 'My nickname at school was Spots. And the name Triumph suits you. Which reminds me, I was going to tell you where we met.'

Where was Fairchild? 'I really must go and log in. The Major—' she began, and the door opened.

But it was only Parrish. 'Oh, sorry,' she said when she saw Stephen, 'didn't mean to interrupt. You haven't got the keys to Bela, have you, De Havilland?'

'No,' she said. 'I'll come and help you look for them—'

'No, I wouldn't dream of dragging you away from such a handsome young man,' Parrish said, smiling flirtatiously at Stephen. 'You wouldn't happen to have a twin, would you? One who's fond of jitterbugging?'

'Sorry,' he said, grinning.

'Truly. I can help you look—' Mary began.

'Don't bother. They're probably in the dispatch room,' Parrish said. 'Ta,' and left, closing the door behind her.

'Lieutenant Parrish is a very good dancer,' Mary said. 'And she's very much in favour of wartime attachments. You should ask her to go—'

'It won't work, you know,' he said. 'You can't get rid of me. It's our destiny to be together. I told you we'd met before, and we have, even though you don't remember it. And the reason you don't is because it was in another lifetime.'

'Another ... lifetime?' she stammered.

'Yes,' he said, and smiled that devastatingly crooked smile.

178

'Far in the distant past. I was a king in Babylon, and you were a Christian slave.'

And that was a poem by William Ernest Henley. *He's quoting poetry, not talking about time travel*, she thought. *Thank goodness*. And was so relieved she laughed.

'I'm deathly serious,' he said. 'Our souls have been destined to be together throughout history. You may not remember our meetings, but I do. I told you, we were Tristan and Isolde.' He moved in closer. 'We were Pelleas and Melisande, Heloise and Abelard.' He leaned towards her. 'Catherine and Heathcliff—'

'Catherine and Heathcliff are *not* historical figures, and there weren't any Christian slaves in Babylon,' she said, slipping neatly away from him. 'It was BC, not AD.'

'There, you see,' he said, pointing delightedly at her. 'What you did just then, that's exactly it! That's what—'

'Norton!' a voice called from the corridor. 'Kent!'

And there's Fairchild, she thought wryly, *when I no longer need to be rescued*.

She hadn't met him on an upcoming assignment, or on any assignment. He was only flirting – and he was so good at it she was almost sorry she'd asked Fairchild to come and drag her away. Though it was probably just as well. Stephen was entirely too charming, and it was entirely too easy to forget that she was a hundred years too old for him, that they were even more star-crossed than the lovers he'd named. If he'd been from 2060 instead of 1944—

'Kent!' Fairchild called again. 'Mary!'

'I'd best go and see what's wanted,' she said and started for the door, but Fairchild had already flung it open. 'Oh good, there you are. You're wanted on the telephone. It's the hospital. You can take it in the— Oh my goodness!' she shouted and, astonishingly, shot past her and launched herself at Stephen. 'Stephen!' she cried, flinging her arms about his neck. 'What are you *doing* here?'

'Bits and Pieces! Good God!' he said, hugging her and then

holding her at arm's length to look at her. 'What am *I* doing here? What are *you* doing here?'

'This is my FANY unit,' Fairchild said. 'And I'm not Bits and Pieces. I'm Lieutenant Fairchild.' She saluted smartly. 'I drive an ambulance.'

'An ambulance?' he said. 'You can't possibly. You're not old enough.'

'I'm nineteen.'

'Don't be ridiculous.'

'I *am*. My birthday was last week, wasn't it, Kent?' she said, looking over at Mary. 'Kent, this is Stephen Lang, the pilot I told you about.'

The person Fairchild had been in love with since she was six, the one she'd said was in love with her as well, only he didn't know it yet. *Oh God.*

'Our families live next to each other in Surrey,' Fairchild said happily. 'We've known each other since we were infants.'

'Since *you* were an infant,' Stephen said, smiling fondly at her. 'The last time I saw you, you were in pigtails.'

'You still haven't told me what you're doing here,' Fairchild was saying. 'I thought you were stationed at Tangmere. Mother said—'

'I was, and then at Hendon,' he said, looking at Mary. 'But I've just been transferred to Biggin Hill.'

'Biggin *Hill*? What good news! That means you'll be only a few miles away.'

And squarely in the heart of Bomb Alley. It was already the most-hit airfield, and when Intelligence's misinformation made the rockets begin to fall short, it would be even more dangerous. As if tipping V-1s wasn't dangerous enough.

'How lovely!' Fairchild was saying. 'How did you find out I was here? Did Mother write to you?'

'No,' he said. 'As a matter of fact, I had no idea you were here. I came to see Lieutenant Kent.'

'Lieutenant Kent? I didn't know you two knew each other.'

'I drove him to a meeting in London last month after Talbot wrenched her knee. The Major asked me to substitute. But I had no idea you knew him,' Mary said, thinking, *Please believe me.*

'And I had no idea you knew my little sister,' he said.

'I'm not your sister,' Fairchild said, 'and I'm not an infant. I told you, I'm nineteen. I'm all grown up.'

'You'll *always* be sweet little Bits and Pieces to me.' He tousled her hair. He smiled at Mary. 'I hope you girls are taking good care of this youngster.'

Oh, worse and worse. 'She doesn't need taking care of,' Mary said. 'She's the best driver in our unit.'

'Oh no, she's not. *You* are,' he said. 'That's one of the things I came to tell you. Do you remember when I told you to turn down Tottenham Court Road on our way to Whitehall, and you turned the wrong way? Well, it was fortunate you did. A V-1 smashed down in the middle of it not five minutes later.'

He turned to Fairchild. 'She saved my life.' He smiled at Mary. 'I told you our meeting was destiny.'

'Destiny?' Fairchild said, looking stricken.

'Abso—'

'Absolutely not,' Mary cut in before he could ruin things even more completely, 'and I fail to see how making a wrong turn constitutes expert driving. And the reason we met was because I couldn't tell a flying bomb from a motorcycle.'

She turned to Fairchild. 'Did you say there was a trunk call for me? I'd best go and take it.' She started for the door. 'It was nice seeing you again, Flight Officer Lang.'

'Wait, you can't go yet,' Stephen said. 'You still haven't said you'll go out to dinner with me. Bits, convince her I'm not a bounder.'

You are *a bounder,* Mary thought. *You're also an utter fool. Can't you see the poor child's in love with you?*

'Tell her what a nice chap I am,' he said to Fairchild. 'That I'm entirely trustworthy and upstanding.'

181

'He is,' Fairchild said, looking as though she'd been cut to the heart. 'Any girl would be lucky to get him.'

'There, you see? You have my little sister's endorsement.'

'Oh, but the two of you must have tons of catching up to do,' Mary said desperately. 'Childhood memories and all that. I'd only be in the way. You two go.'

'I can't,' Fairchild said, managing somehow to keep her voice natural. 'I must go and collect a shipment of medical supplies for the Major,' and Stephen at least had the decency to say, 'Can't you get one of the other girls to go in your place?'

'No – we'll do it next time you come round. You go, Kent.'

And if I do, Mary thought, watching her make her escape, *she'll never forgive me.* She might not forgive her anyway, but Mary had no intention of making it worse than it already was. 'I really must go and take that call from HQ,' she said, 'and if it's about what I think it is, I won't be able to go to dinner either.'

'Then tomorrow.'

'I'm on duty, and I told you, I don't believe in wartime attachments. There must be scores of other girls dying to go out with you.'

'None I knew in a previous life. The day after tomorrow?'

'I can't. I really *must* take that call.' She started for the door.

'No, wait,' he said and grabbed her hands. 'I haven't thanked you yet.'

'I told you, I didn't save your life. Tottenham Court Road is a very long road, and—'

'No, not for that. This is about the V-1s.'

'The V-1s?'

'Yes. Do you remember how you managed to slip out of my grasp just as I was about to kiss you before Bits and Pieces came in?'

'About to kiss—?'

'Yes, of course. That was the entire point of all that Babylon rot, don't you know,' he said, and grinned. 'And just as I thought it was working, you eluded my grasp, more's the pity.'

'I thought you were going to tell me about the V-1s.'

'I was. I am. You did the same thing that day you drove me. Twice. My line of attack was working splendidly, and then suddenly I found myself totally thrown off-course, even though I'd never got near enough to lay a hand on you.'

'I still don't know what this has to do with—'

'Don't you see?' he said, squeezing her hands. 'That was where I got the notion of throwing the V-1s off-course. You're the one who gave me the idea. If it hadn't been for you, I'd have been blown up by now, trying to shoot them down.'

BLETCHLEY – NOVEMBER 1940

Mike stared at Tensing, stunned.

'This is the chap I was telling you about, Ferguson,' Tensing said. 'The one who served as lookout for me when I was in hospital.'

'The American?' his companion said.

Christ, if he'd gone ahead with his plan to pose as an Englishman ...

'Yes,' Tensing said. 'I'd still be lying in that wretched hospital bed in Orpington if it weren't for his unique talent for deception.'

'It's a distinct pleasure to meet you, Mr Davis,' Ferguson said, shaking Mike's hand and then turning back to Tensing. 'I do hate to hurry you, but we really should be going.'

Thank God he can't stay and ask me what I'm doing here, Mike thought, *because he's obviously connected to Bletchley Park.* Mike suddenly remembered Tensing saying he worked at the War Office. He should have realised he was in Intelligence.

'No, we've enough time,' Tensing said. 'You go and settle the bill while I catch up with Davis. This *is* lucky, running into you! I'm just on my way to London. I can't believe you're here in Bletchley, of all places. When did you get out of hospital?'

'September. Let me get you a chair,' Mike said to stall.

'That's all right, I'll get it,' Tensing said, waving him back down and looking around for a vacant chair. 'Hang on.'

Hang is exactly what I'll do if I don't come up with a plausible reason for being here, Mike thought. 'I'm here on special assignment' was out of the question. *Should he say he was visiting a friend?*

Tensing was back with a chair. 'Mavis told me there was an American here,' he said, sitting down, 'but I never imagined it was you. I understand you had an unfortunate encounter with a bicycle. I must warn you, this place has some shockingly bad drivers. But you still haven't told me what brings you here. It's not an assignment for your newspaper, I hope. Bletchley's deadly dull, I'm afraid.'

'I'm finding that out. No, actually, I'm here about my foot. I came here to see Dr Pritchard,' he said, calling up the name of the doctor the old ladies on the train had said had a clinic in Newport Pagnell. 'He has a clinic in Leighton Buzzard. He's supposed to be an expert at reattaching tendons. I'm hoping he can fix me up enough to get back in the war.'

'A sentiment with which I can completely sympathise,' Tensing said. 'I thought I'd go mad in hospital, listening to the bad news on the wireless day after day and not being able to do a damned thing about it.' He looked down at Mike's newspaper. 'Still interested in crosswords, I see.'

Mike shrugged. 'It passes the time. As you say, Bletchley isn't particularly exciting.'

Tensing nodded. 'It's a good deal like the sunroom. All that's wanted is a potted palm and Colonel Waring, rattling his *Telegraph* and harrumphing.' He tapped the crossword. 'You were quite good at these, I recall.'

'As *I* recall, I had help.'

'Still, though, most Americans find our crosswords completely unintelligible.' His tone had changed.

Did I say something to give myself away? Mike wondered. What?

He'd purposely said Dr Pritchard was at Leighton Buzzard instead of Newport Pagnell to make it harder for Tensing to track the doctor down if he checked up on Mike's story. Had Tensing by some horrible coincidence gone to see Dr Pritchard, too?

No, Tensing had hurt his back, not his foot. But something had made him suspicious. Could it be the crossword puzzle? he wondered, remembering the story Polly'd told him about D-Day and the suspicious clues. Could Tensing suspect him of sending messages to the Germans?

But he was solving a crossword, not constructing one. And Tensing had seen him doing the same thing countless times in the hospital.

Ferguson was working his way back towards them between the tables. Good, this conversation couldn't end too soon.

'All set,' Ferguson said.

'In a moment,' Tensing said over his shoulder, and then to Mike. 'Were you serious? About wanting to get into the war?'

I'm already in it, Mike thought, *and can't get out.* 'Yes.'

'How long will you be here seeing this doctor – what was his name?'

'Pritchard,' Mike said. 'I'm not certain. It all depends. He thinks I may have to have surgery.'

'But you'll be here for a week at the least?'

So you can check and see whether I've been to see Dr Pritchard or see if the Omaha Observer *exists?* 'Yes, I have another full month of treatments.'

'Good. I must go down to London for three or four days, but when I get back, there's something I want to have a chat with you about. Where are you staying?'

'I haven't found a room yet. Every place I've tried so far is full.'

'So you're at the Bell?' Tensing said, and thankfully didn't wait for an answer. 'Is this pub where you take your meals?'

Not after tonight. 'Usually, unless the doctor's treatments go too long.'

'Good. I'll see you when I return.' Tensing stood up. 'It's odd your happening to turn up here. Almost as if it was meant.' He turned to Ferguson. 'Come on, let's catch that train,' he said, and they went out.

And what the hell had just happened? Was Tensing suspicious, or did he just want to reminisce about their time together in the hospital? And if he *was* suspicious, what had given Mike away? *The crossword puzzle,* he thought. But why? He'd seen other BPers working them.

I need to talk to Polly, he thought, but the only secure phone was at the station, and Tensing and Ferguson were on their way there. If they missed their train, he'd run smack into them. Besides, Polly and Eileen wouldn't be home. They'd be at the shelter.

He waited till the pub closed, then walked over to the station and called, hoping the all-clear might have gone early, but it apparently hadn't. They weren't there.

They weren't there the next morning either. Were there raids in London this week? He should have asked Polly before he left. If there were, it could take all week to get them.

He went over to the Bell and, after making sure Welchman wasn't in the lobby, bought a paper, tore out the crossword, wrote a message saying, 'URGENT WILL CALL TUES NITE,' in it, mailed it, and then walked out to the Park. He didn't find Gerald, but on the way back he overheard a conversation between two Wrens. 'Do you know anything about the new man in Hut 8?' one asked.

'Yes,' the other Wren said disgustedly. 'His name's Phillips, he's billeted in Stoke Hammond, and you can have him. He's a dreadful stick.'

The 'dreadful stick' part definitely sounded like Phipps, and Phillips would be a natural cover name for him. Mike took the bus to Stoke Hammond and spent the rest of the day and half of Wednesday pretending to look for a room there and asking, 'You don't happen to have a lodger named Phillips, do you?'

On the tenth try Tuesday, the landlady said, 'No, a young man by that name came looking for a room, Monday it was, I sent him to Mursley.'

Mursley was six miles further on. By the time Mike had caught the bus there, tried half a dozen places without success before he found a woman who said she remembered someone named Phillips and that she'd sent him over to Little Howard, and Mike had come back to Bletchley, it was nearly seven. He took off immediately for the railway station to call Polly.

And ran straight into Dilly's girls. 'Hullo!' Elspeth said happily. 'We'd been wondering what happened to you!'

'We've looked for you every day at the Park,' Joan said.

'This is the American we were telling you about, Wendy,' Mavis said to the fourth girl. 'The one Turing nearly killed.'

'The handsome one,' Wendy – who looked none the worse for sleeping in the larder – said and batted her eyes at him. 'I've been dying to meet you!'

'I saw him first,' Joan said.

'*I* picked him up after Turing ran him down,' Elspeth said, linking her arm possessively in his.

'Girls, girls, this is no time to be greedy,' Mavis said, taking his other arm. 'In wartime we must share and share alike.' And how the hell was he going to get away from them? He couldn't even get a word in edgewise. 'Did the billeting officer find you a place to stay?' Mavis asked him.

'Of course he hasn't,' Wendy said bitterly. 'I've been after him for weeks. There hasn't been a vacancy anywhere for *months*.'

'We've been out looking for a room for Wendy,' Elspeth explained.

'Not only does she have to sleep among the bottled peaches,' Mavis added, 'but now the billeting officer's assigned her two roommates.'

'We heard a rumour there was a vacancy on Albion Street,' Wendy said, 'but when we got there it was already taken.' She sighed. 'I should have known it was too good to be true.'

'And now you've got to come and buy all of us a drink to cheer us up,' Joan said.

'I'd love to, but I can't. I'm meeting someone—'

'I *knew* it,' Elspeth said morosely.

'Is she pretty?' Joan asked.

'Not a girl, an old friend,' Mike said.

'Well, then, Friday,' Mavis said.

'Friday,' he said, 'and I promise I'll let you know if I hear of any vacant rooms,' and was finally able to escape, but it was nearly eight. *Please, please, let Polly still be there*, he thought, hobbling to the station.

Eileen answered. 'Have you found Gerald?' she asked eagerly, and there was a terrific crashing sound.

'What was that?' Mike asked.

'An HE. We're in the middle of a raid.'

Of course. Jesus, could their luck get any worse?

'Did you?' Eileen persisted. 'Find Gerald?'

'Not yet. Is Polly there? Put her on.'

There was a loud whistle and another crash, and Polly came on the line. 'What's happened?' she said.

'I ran into this guy I was in hospital with. Tensing, his name is.'

'And he knows you're an American, not an Englishman. Did he blow your cover?'

'No. I mean, I'd decided not to tell people I was an Englishman, after all, which was a good thing. Anyway, I'm pretty sure he works at Bletchley Park. I told him I was here to see a doctor about my foot, and he bought that. Anyway,' he said, shouting over the racket on Polly's end – the anti-aircraft guns must have started up, 'he saw me in a pub, and we talked for a few minutes, and then he asked me if I was still interested in doing crossword puzzles.'

'In what? I can't hear you. It's rather noisy here.'

'*Crossword puzzles*,' he shouted. 'I'd done them in the hospital, and I was pretending to work on one while I sat there looking for Phipps. He asked me if I was still interested in doing them, and when I said yes, he asked me how long I'd be in Bletchley, that he had to go to London for a few days but that he wanted to talk to me when he got back.'

'Did he say anything else? About the crossword puzzles?'

'Yeah, he said he remembered I was good at them and that most Americans weren't able to solve English crosswords. Do you think they could already be looking for spy messages in crossword puzzles, like the D-Day thing you told me about?'

'No. He's going to offer you a job at Bletchley Park. Remember how I told you Bletchley Park recruited anyone they thought might be good at decoding – mathematicians and Egyptologists and chess players? Well, they recruited people who were good at solving crosswords, too. They even had the *Daily Herald* sponsor a crossword contest, and then offered jobs at the Park to all the winners. But they were still short of decoders, and they were always looking for potential prospects. When did you say he was coming back from London?'

'I'm not sure. Tomorrow or the next day.'

'You need to get out of there.'

'Hang on. Maybe I should take the job. If Gerald's staying at Bletchley Park—'

'No, that's a dreadful idea. You'd never get out. They couldn't afford to let their people leave because of the secrets they knew, so the people who worked at BP were there for the duration. You need to get out of there tonight.'

'But I just got a lead on Phipps—'

'Eileen will have to follow it up for you. Is there a train out tonight? You probably won't be able to get to London – the raids are too bad – but you can at least get out of Bletchley.'

'But I don't see what all the hurry is. Why can't I just turn the job down, now that I know what he's going to ask? I already told him I was having treatments on my foot. I could tell him I have to have surgery—'

'That won't be enough of an excuse. It's a desk job, and remember, Dilly Knox has a limp.'

'Well, then, I just tell him I'm not interested.'

'An American reporter who smuggled his way aboard a boat so he could get to Dunkirk isn't interested in being involved in the most exciting espionage work of the war? He won't buy it.'

She was right. Someone like Tensing, who'd been so determined to get back in action that he'd defied his doctor's orders, would never understand why Mike was turning down a chance to 'get back in the war' – especially since he'd told him that was why he was seeing Dr Pritchard. He'd begin to wonder what was behind the refusal and start snooping around. And find out he'd lied about Dr Pritchard.

'You need to get—' A deafening whistle drowned out the end of Polly's sentence. Another bomb, he thought, and then realised it was a train.

He glanced at his watch. 8:33. The train from Oxford. 'Sorry, I didn't hear what you said. A train's coming in.'

'I said, get out of there now,' Polly said urgently. 'If Tensing's thinking of offering you a job, he may already be doing a background check and have realised you're not who you say you are. You can't take the risk of running into him and—' There was a screech, and the line went dead.

'Polly?' he said. 'Polly?'

'I'm sorry, sir,' the operator said. 'There's a disruption on the line. I can attempt to reconnect you, if you like—'

But if the disruption was a bomb, the lines might not be repaired for days, and Mike was just as glad. If he talked to Polly again, she'd just insist he get out, and she was right, he had to, but there was no need to do it tonight. Tensing wouldn't be back till tomorrow at the earliest, and he didn't know where Mike was living. And since Mike hadn't got his room through the billeting office, it would take Tensing awhile to find him, and by the time he'd tried the pub and then the hotels, Mike would have found out whether Phipps was in Little Howard. 'Thanks, I'll try later,' he told the operator, hung up, and stepped out of the telephone box.

The train had apparently arrived. Passengers were coming along the platform. An elderly army officer, two Wrens, a—

Jesus, it was Ferguson, and just stepping down from the train after him was Tensing. They hadn't looked this way yet. Mike ducked instinctively back into the telephone box, but he was still afraid he might be recognised. There wasn't enough time for him to hobble across the station and out of the door before they saw him so he lurched through the other door to the deserted eastbound platform and all the way down to the end of it, listening for pursuing footsteps and trying to think what to do.

Polly was right – he needed to get out right now – but not on this train. With his luck, Tensing would have left his hat on it or something and come back to catch him in the act of leaving. He'd have to take the next one. It wasn't till 11:10, but he'd still better stay here. If he tried to go back to Mrs Jolsom's for his bag, he was liable to run straight into Tensing. Or Dilly's girls. He needed to sit right here, out of sight.

But if he didn't go and collect his bag and Tensing *did* manage to find out where he'd been staying, his suddenly disappearing and leaving his luggage behind would look wildly suspicious, and Mrs Jolsom was bound to tell him. And if Tensing concluded he was a spy, that would do as much damage as his being caught by Tensing and offered a job. And even if Tensing was suspicious of him and that was why he'd come back early, he wouldn't go to Mrs Jolsom's. He'd try the pub first, and the hotels, and by the time he got around to knocking on boarding house doors, Mike would be long gone.

He waited another fifteen minutes on the platform to give Tensing and Ferguson time to get well away from the station, and then hurried back to Mrs Jolsom's, taking a roundabout route so he didn't have to pass Dilly's girls' house or the Bell, and looking carefully in all directions before he crossed each street.

It was after ten by the time he got to Mrs Jolsom's. *Maybe she'll have already gone to bed, and I can leave her a note*, he thought hopefully, but she opened the front door before he could put his latchkey in the lock. She was wearing an apron and drying her hands on a tea towel. 'Oh, it's you, Mr Davis,' she said. 'I was doing the washing up and heard someone at the door. How are you this evening?'

'Not very well, I'm afraid,' he said, following her into the kitchen. 'I don't know if I told you, but I came here for medical treatment. For my foot. I've been seeing Dr Granholme in Leighton Buzzard, and I was sure he could help me, but he said he couldn't, and sent me to Dr Evers in Newport Pagnell, and *he* says I'll have to have surgery, so he's sending me to Dr Pritchard in Banbury,' he said, giving the wrong villages for all three doctors in the hope that when Tensing couldn't find him, he'd conclude Mrs Jolsom had got the names and places mixed up. 'The problem is, he wants to do the surgery right away, so I can't give you the two weeks' notice, you—'

'Oh, you mustn't worry yourself over that,' Mrs Jolsom said, drying a cup and saucer and putting them away in the cupboard. 'I only asked for that because of the boarders from the Park going off without bothering to notify me.' She folded the tea towel and hung it over the edge of the counter. 'Or not coming at all, and me left holding the room for weeks. And do you know what the billeting officer said when I told him? He said he didn't know anything about it. He even denied sending the letter!'

The letter. That day in the lab, when Phipps had returned from his drop, he'd said he'd sent the letter. Could it have been the letter reserving a place to stay? But he was supposed to have come through in the summer, not the fall.

You don't know that, Mike thought. July was when the recon and prep was, not necessarily the assignment. Maybe that was why the first drop had been necessary – because of the lodging

193

shortage and the necessity of making arrangements months in advance. And if there'd been increased slippage on his drop, Mrs Jolsom would have been left holding the room. Which was why she had the only vacancy in Bletchley.

I should have made that connection, Mike thought.

'Do you leave in the morning, Mr Davis?' Mrs Jolsom was asking.

No, tonight, he started to say and then remembered there wasn't a train to Banbury till morning. 'Yes, but I need to go and see Dr Pritchard first, so I'll probably be leaving before you're up. Your boarder who didn't show up, what was his—?'

The doorbell rang. *Jesus*, Mike thought, *it's Tensing. I shouldn't have underestimated him.*

Mrs Jolsom took off her apron and went to answer it. Mike tiptoed to the kitchen door and opened it a crack. A man's voice, and Mrs Jolsom answering him, but he couldn't make out what they were saying.

Mike heard the door shut and moved away from the door. Mrs Jolsom came in. 'It was a young man looking for a room.'

And what if it was Phipps? 'Did he leave?' Mike asked and ran to the door, opened it, and looked out, but he couldn't see anyone on the blacked-out street. 'What did he look like?' he asked Mrs Jolsom, who'd followed him to the door.

'He was an older gentleman,' Mrs Jolsom said, clearly taken aback. 'Why—?'

'I thought it might be a patient I met yesterday at Dr Pritchard's,' Mike said, cursing himself. Talk about behaving suspiciously. 'I was going to tell him I could get out tonight so he could move in. I can go to a hotel.'

'I wouldn't think of doing that to you, Mr Davis,' she said, 'and certainly not for someone who would come looking for a room this time of night. You stay as long as you like.' She started for the stairs. 'Good night.'

Mike reached across and put his hand on the railing to stop

her. 'I just didn't want to leave you stuck with a vacant room like that boarder of yours who didn't show up—'

'Oh, you mustn't worry about that, Mr Davis.' She patted his hand. 'I quite understand your needing to leave. Is it quite a serious surgery?'

If he said yes, she'd ask a bunch of worried questions, but if it wasn't serious, then why was it so urgent? And neither answer would get them back to the subject of the border who hadn't showed up, and he had to know his name. Before the 11:10 train.

'I should imagine I'll come through all right,' he said. 'It's funny the billeting officer making a mistake like that. They're usually extremely efficient. You said the officer said there'd been a miscommunication. Couldn't you have got the dates wrong or—?'

'I most certainly did not,' she said, bristling. '*Miscommunication*? The billeting officer wouldn't even admit he'd sent me the letter, when his signature was right there on it.' She marched into the parlour and came back with a letter. 'There's his name, plain as day, Captain A.R. Edwards.'

She thrust the letter in Mike's face. It read, 'Billeting order for Professor Gerald Phipps, arriving 3 October 1940.'

'We are hanging on by our eyelids.'

GENERAL ALAN BROOKE, CHIEF OF CHURCHILL'S GENERAL STAFF

LONDON – NOVEMBER 1940

After Polly found out that the Reign of Terror had been more than four years after the Storming of the Bastille, she attempted to convince herself that there couldn't possibly be that much slippage. The most on record for a non-divergence point had been three months and eight days. Someone had had six months' slippage, and Mr Dunworthy had overreacted and cancelled everyone's drops, that was all. And the fact that he hadn't cancelled hers proved it.

But the fear still nagged at her, so much so that she redoubled her efforts to find a way out. She put a new batch of ads in the papers and went to Charing Cross to see if there was any spot in the sprawling station where Mr Dunworthy could have come through on his earlier drops.

There wasn't. Even the emergency staircase was filled with amorous couples. His drop had to have been somewhere else.

There was no sign of a younger Mr Dunworthy either, though she wasn't certain she'd recognise him if she saw him. The first few times he'd gone to the past, he'd been scarcely older than Colin. She tried to imagine him Colin's age – lanky, eager, taking the escalator steps two at a time – but she couldn't manage it, anymore than she could imagine Mr Dunworthy sending them knowingly into danger. Or not coming to get them if he could.

She wondered suddenly if it was not just an increase in slippage that was keeping him from pulling them out, but the fact that he was already here on a previous assignment and couldn't come through till after his younger self had returned to Oxford. Which would be when?

Mike didn't phone on Tuesday or Wednesday, or write, which Eileen was convinced was a good sign. 'It means he's found Gerald, and they're on their way to check his drop,' she said. 'You mustn't worry so. Just when things are in a complete mess, and you can't see how they can possibly work out, that's when help arrives.'

Not always, Polly thought, remembering the thousands of soldiers who hadn't made it off Dunkirk's beaches, or the victims who'd died in the rubble before the rescue teams reached them.

'When I took Theodore to the station on the train,' Eileen was saying, 'he grabbed hold of my neck and wouldn't let go, and the train was leaving. And just as I was about to despair, who should show up in the very nick of time but Mr Goode, the vicar, to rescue me.' She smiled at the memory. 'And we'll be rescued, too. You'll see. I'm certain we'll hear from Mike tomorrow. Or from the retrieval team.'

They did, a scrawled note saying, 'Arrived safely and am in comfortable lodgings. More later, Mike.' There was also a newspaper clipping in the envelope, of a sale on men's suits at Townsend Brothers.

'Why did he write that? We already know it. And why did he put the clipping in?' Eileen asked. 'Is he saying the jacket and waistcoat we sent him in were the wrong sort of clothes?'

'I don't know,' Polly said, turning the clipping over, but the only thing on the back was a filled-in crossword puzzle. When he'd phoned, he'd said he was doing crosswords as cover while he looked for Gerald in pubs. Could he have accidentally stuck it in the envelope along with the note?

'Oh, Miss O'Reilly,' Miss Laburnum said, coming in from the parlour, 'you had another letter in the afternoon post.' She handed it to her.

'Perhaps it explains this one,' Polly said, but it was from the vicar.

Eileen went up to their room to read it. Polly stayed in the vestibule, looking at the clipping. Mike had talked about sending a message in code, and she'd told him about the D-Day code words appearing in the *Daily Herald* puzzle. Could he have hidden some message in the crossword answers? She grabbed a pencil, went up to the bathroom, locked the door, and sat down on the edge of the bath to decipher it. *I hope the code's not too complicated*, she thought.

It wasn't – it wasn't even a code. He'd simply printed his message in the puzzle's squares, beginning with 14 Across: NO LUCK YET CHECKING BILLETS DO U NO SITE OLD REMOTE DROP ST JOHNS WOOD OR DROPS HISTS USED B4 CLD B HOLDING OPEN EMERG XIT.

The lab had had a remote drop in St John's Wood which they'd used for a number of years. Apparently Mike thought they might have opened it and other drops historians had previously used so they could employ them as emergency exits, though why those drops would open if what was preventing their drops from opening was an increase in slippage, Polly didn't know.

But she wasn't in a position to leave any stone unturned, so instead of going to meet the retrieval team at Trafalgar Square on Thursday after work, she took the tube to St John's Wood. She didn't know where the old remote drop was, but she hoped it might have been in some immediately obvious spot.

It wasn't, and she didn't know of any other London drops earlier historians had used, except for hers, on Hampstead Heath, which she'd last used just before midnight on the eve of VE Day. At this point, it didn't exist yet, but the lab might have reset its coordinates for 1940, so the next morning she put an ad in the *Times*, telling 'R.T.' to meet her at St Paul's on Sunday.

Eileen was unexpectedly argumentative about it. 'But we already placed one meeting the retrieval team at the National Gallery concert,' she said.

'You can do that one, and I'll do St Paul's,' Polly said.

'But I've always wanted to see St Paul's,' Eileen persisted. 'Mr Dunworthy was always talking about it. Why don't I do it, and you do the concert?'

Because it's more difficult faking having been to a concert, Polly thought. *And besides, I'm not certain how long this will take.*

'No,' she said, 'I know one of the vergers at St Paul's – Mr Humphreys – and he'll know if any strangers have been in.'

'I could go with you. The concert isn't till one.'

I should have said I was going to Westminster Abbey or something, Polly thought. 'But I don't know when the retrieval team will be there. I forgot to give a time,' she said. 'I'll meet you after the concert and we'll go to Lyons' Corner House for tea, and then I'll take you on a guided tour of St Paul's,' and made certain she was gone before Eileen was up the next morning.

She took the tube to Hampstead Heath and climbed the hill. It was raining, a fine mist, which was good – there wouldn't be that many people about – but she wished she'd brought her umbrella. She hadn't been able to find it in the dark this morning, and she'd been afraid to switch on the light for fear of waking Eileen and having her insist on coming with her.

She hurried across the heath and into the trees, hoping she'd recognise the spot. The last time she'd been here, it had been May. Now the trees were russet and brown and heavy with rain.

No, there was the weeping beech, its golden-leaved branches sweeping the ground. The rain was coming down harder. *Good*, she thought, pushing the curtain of leaves aside. *If anyone catches me, I can say I was taking shelter from it.*

She stepped quickly under it, let the concealing leaves fall together behind her, and looked around at the dim tent-like space. The ground was covered with curling yellow leaves and twigs. A lemonade bottle and a torn paper ice lolly wrapping lay half-buried in the leaves, but both were weather-faded.

The retrieval team hasn't been here, Polly thought, looking at the undisturbed leaves.

But the drop might only have been set up for them to return through. She sat down against the beech's mottled white trunk, checked her watch, and settled in to see if the drop would open.

It was cold. She pulled her knees up under the coat of her skirt and hugged her arms to her chest. The rain wasn't coming through the leaves, but the leaf and bark-covered ground was icily damp, its wetness soaking through her coat and skirt.

And as she sat there, all the things she was worried about began to soak through her, too – her deadline, and Mike and whether the incident which had destroyed St George's and the shops hiding her drop was a discrepancy. She'd assumed the church hadn't been on Mr Dunworthy's forbidden list because she'd intended to stay in the tube shelters, but it hadn't been in the implant Colin had made for her either.

Which meant he *could* have been near her drop when the parachute-mine exploded.

No, he couldn't, she thought, fighting down sudden nausea. *He didn't put it in the implant because he thought I'd be safely in a tube shelter when it went off. Which I was.*

And Colin had talked to her about parachute-mines. He'd lectured *her* on the dangers of shrapnel and the blackout, and he was endlessly resourceful. And she knew from experience he wouldn't take no for an answer. If anyone could find a way to get them out of here, he could.

Unless Oxford's been destroyed, and he's dead, she thought. *Or there was an increase in locational slippage as well, and the net sent him through to Bletchley Park. Or Singapore.*

She sat there as long as she could stand it, and then wrote her name and Mrs Rickett's address and phone number on the lolly wrapping, took an Underground ticket stamped Notting Hill Gate out of her pocket, wrote 'Polly Churchill' on it, stuck it under the lemonade bottle, and went to St Paul's, even though the retrieval team wouldn't be there either.

The trip back into London took forever. There were three separate delays due to air raids, and she was glad she'd refused to trade with Eileen and go to the concert. She didn't reach St Paul's Station till after noon, and it was pouring outside. By the time she made it to the cathedral, she was drenched.

On the porch lay an order of worship someone had dropped. She picked it up. She could show it to Eileen as proof she'd spent the entire morning here. The sermon this morning had apparently been on the subject 'Seek and Ye Shall Find'.

If only that were true.

She shook out her wet, clinging skirts, and went into the cathedral. The partition in front of the Geometric Staircase was still up. The fire watch must have decided preserving the stairway was more important than providing access to the west end.

She walked out into the nave. It was dim and gloomy today, grey instead of golden and so dark she couldn't even see the far end of it. And *cold*. The elderly volunteer selling guidebooks at the desk had her coat on.

A guidebook was a good idea. She could pretend to be reading it while she looked for the retrieval team. She went over to the desk.

The volunteer was helping a middle-aged woman choose a postcard like the ones Mr Humphreys had shown her. 'This one of the Wellington Memorial is very nice,' she said. 'It shows Truth Plucking Out the Tongue of Falsehood.'

'You haven't any of the High Altar?' the woman asked.

'I'm afraid not. They went very quickly.'

'Of course,' the woman said, shaking her head, 'such a shame,' and began browsing through the rack of postcards again. 'Have you any of the Tijou Gates?'

They've been removed for safekeeping, Polly thought, blowing on her numb hands and wishing the woman would make up her mind. It was even colder in here than it had been on Hampstead Heath, and there was an icy draught from somewhere.

She looked up. Two of the gallery's stained-glass windows had been blown out, and fairly recently. No attempt had been made to cover them, and jagged edges of red and blue and gold still lined the frames. A bomb must have exploded near the cathedral and the blast had broken them.

'What about *The Light of the World*?' the woman was asking. 'Have you any postcards of it?'

'No, but we've a lovely colour print,' the volunteer said, indicating it on its stand. 'It's sixpence.'

Polly looked at the print. Its colour was slightly bluer than the painting, and Christ looked as chilled as she was, his face pinched with cold.

It's too bad that lantern he's holding isn't real, she thought, gazing at its warm glow. Mr Humphreys was right about seeing something new each time one looked at it. She hadn't noticed before that the door Christ was about to knock on was mediaeval. Neither it nor the lantern he was carrying could possibly have existed in AD33.

He must be a time-traveller like us, Polly thought, *and now he's trying to get back home, and his drop won't open either.*

The woman had finally made up her mind and paid. Polly stepped up to buy her guidebook. 'Thruppence,' the volunteer said, and Polly reached in her purse for the coins, but her hands were so stiff with cold, she dropped them. They made an unholy, echoing clatter on the marble floor.

Well, thought Polly, *if the retrieval team* is *here, this is one way to get their attention,* but no one turned around.

'Sorry,' she said, gathering up the tuppenny piece and the penny and paying for the guidebook.

The volunteer handed it to her. 'I'm afraid the Crypt and the choir are closed today.'

The choir? Polly thought, wondering why, but asking would mean continuing to stand there in the draught from the windows. She thanked the volunteer and walked up the nave. No one approached her, and she didn't see anyone who looked like they were there to meet someone. Several people knelt, praying in the middle of the nave. Two Wrens stood in front of the bricked-up Wellington Memorial, looking puzzledly up at it, and a pair of soldiers stood a few feet away, looking at the Wrens.

Just past the next pillar, a young woman stood, wearing a pair of open-toed shoes that looked like one of Wardrobe's bright ideas for an icy 1940 November and gazing around as though searching for someone. But before Polly could make her way around the chairs and across the nave to her, a member of the fire watch came up to the woman, and it was obvious from his smile, and hers, that they knew each other.

So clearly not the retrieval team, Polly thought. She turned to go and see if anyone was in the transept, and nearly collided with a beaming Mr Humphreys.

'I thought you'd come when you heard about our incident,' he said. 'We've had any number of people come to see the damage.'

'Yes. It's dreadful about the windows,' Polly said.

'It is,' he agreed, looking back at them. 'They should have been taken to Wales for safekeeping along with the other treasures. Still, it may turn out to have been a blessing in disguise. Sir Christopher Wren designed St Paul's to have clear panes of glass in the windows, and now there's a good chance he will see his dream realised.'

He would. At the end of the Blitz, there'd be only one intact window left in the entire cathedral, and that would be broken in 1944 by a V-1 which had exploded nearby, and all the replacement windows would be of clear glass.

'In the case of the altar, however,' Mr Humphreys went on, 'I'm afraid it's another matter.'

The altar?

'Luckily, the bomb damage was confined to it and the choir.'

The choir. That's why the volunteer at the desk had said the choir was closed today.

Mr Humphreys walked across the space under the dome and over to the entrance and to the choir. It was blocked off with a sawhorse.

He moved it aside and led Polly through. 'And the bomb went through to the Crypt, unfortunately just at the spot where our fire watch sleeps,' he said, but she wasn't listening. She was staring at the choir, and the destruction beyond.

Where the altar had been was a tumbled heap of timbers and shattered stone. Polly looked up. There was a gigantic jagged hole in the ceiling. A grey tarpaulin half-covered it, water dripping from its edges onto a rickety-looking scaffold beneath. *But St Paul's wasn't hit,* she thought, staring unseeing at the gaping hole, at the rubble. *It survived the war.*

'When did this happen?' she demanded.

'The morning of October tenth, just as we were making one last round of the roofs. I was—' he said and must have seen her face. 'Oh, I *am* sorry. I thought from what you said that you knew. I should have prepared you. It gives one a shock, I know, seeing it for the first time.'

Mr Dunworthy hadn't said a word about a bomb hitting the altar. He'd spoken of the UXB and of the incendiaries on the twenty-ninth, but nothing about an HE on the tenth.

'The altar was entirely destroyed and these two windows were broken,' Mr Humphreys explained.

'And the windows in the nave,' Polly said. It hadn't been blast from a bomb the next street over which had broken them. It had been this bomb. Which Mr Dunworthy had never mentioned.

'Yes. The bomb brought down more of the lower courses there,' Mr Humphreys said, pointing up at the edges of the hole, 'which hit the reredos. You can see where it's chipped, and where St Michael's nose was broken off.'

He went on, pointing out the damage, but she could scarcely

hear him over the thudding of her heart. What if the reason Mr Dunworthy hadn't told her about it was because it hadn't happened? Till now. She'd persuaded herself there weren't any discrepancies, that the problem was increased slippage, which was frightening enough. But this was even worse.

This is the proof we've altered events, she thought.

'How bad is the damage to the structure?' she asked, afraid of the answer.

'Dean Matthews is hopeful the underlying supports weren't cracked,' Mr Humphreys said worriedly, 'but we won't know till the engineers have completed their examination. The explosion lifted the roof off from end to end, and when it came down it may have damaged the supporting pillars.'

In which case the blast from the bombs falling all around the cathedral on the twenty-ninth might bring the weakened pillars down, and St Paul's with it. And what would that do to civilian morale? St Paul's had been the heart of London. The photo of her dome standing firm above the fire and smoke had lifted the contemps' spirits and hardened their resolve for the remaining long, dark months of the Blitz. What would its destruction do to them? And to the outcome of the war?

'We were actually very lucky. It could have been far worse. The bomb struck the crown of the transverse arch and detonated in the space between the roofs. If it had hit further down the apse or in the choir, or if it had fallen on through the roof before it exploded, the damage would have been far greater.'

But this much damage might well be enough to alter the course of the war.

I must write to Mike, she thought. *He's got to get out of Bletchley Park.*

'The organ case was badly damaged,' Mr Humphreys was saying. 'Luckily, the pipes had been taken down to the Crypt for safekeeping—'

'I must go,' Polly said. 'Thank you for showing me the—'

'Oh, but I haven't shown you what the bomb did to the choir. Luckily, these pillars protected the stalls from—'

'Mr Humphreys!' someone called. It was the firewatcher who'd been talking to the young woman with the open-toed shoes. He pushed past the barricade and came up to them. 'Sorry to interrupt,' he said, nodding to Polly, 'but we need the duty roster, and Mr Allen said you had it.'

'You're busy,' Polly said, taking advantage of the interruption. 'I mustn't keep you. Goodbye,' and walked quickly away from them.

'I gave it to Mr Langby,' she heard Mr Humphreys say as she squeezed past the barricade.

Polly hurried down the nave and out of the cathedral. It had stopped raining, but she scarcely noticed, she was so intent on getting home and writing to Mike.

I hope Eileen's not there, she thought, and only then remembered she'd promised to meet her.

She glanced at her watch to see if she had time to go home, write the letter and come back, but it was after two. The concert would be nearly over. *And if you're not there, she'll know something's wrong.*

And she might know if it's truly a discrepancy or not, Polly thought. *She said Mr Dunworthy spoke to her about St Paul's. He may have told her about the altar's being hit. If it was hit. It could easily have been hit without my knowing about it*, Polly tried to persuade herself. The tenth of October would have been when she was preoccupied with Marjorie, not with reading newspapers, and before she'd gone to the morgue to look for her own death notice.

Or the bombing might not have been in the papers, given St Paul's vital importance to the war, she thought, heading for Charing Cross. *They wouldn't have wanted the Germans to know about it.*

She reached Trafalgar Square just as the concert was letting out. Concertgoers were streaming out of the doors and onto the porch where she'd seen Paige standing on VE Day Eve, buttoning coats and pulling on gloves, holding their hands out to see if it was raining, opening umbrellas.

Polly looked for Eileen. She was standing off to one side. Her face looked drawn and pinched with cold, and she'd pulled her black coat tightly about her. The National Gallery must have been as frigid as St Paul's.

'Eileen!' Polly called and hurried across the wet square, the pigeons scattering before her, flying up to perch on the lions and the base of the Monument.

Eileen saw her and raised her hand in recognition, but she didn't wave. Or smile.

Polly glanced at her watch. It wasn't that late, and the concert had obviously just let out. And Eileen was always so cheerful and optimistic. Some of Polly's anxiety these last few weeks must have infected her.

Perhaps I shouldn't say anything about St Paul's, she thought. *It will only make things worse.*

But Polly had to know. And there was no one else to ask. She ran up the steps and over to her.

'Eileen, I need to ask you something,' she said urgently. 'Was St Paul's—?' but Eileen cut her off.

'The retrieval team didn't come to the concert,' she said. 'Did *you* find them?'

'No, there was no one at St Paul's.'

'No one?' Eileen said, and there was an edge to her voice. Was she angry at her for insisting she go to the concert? If she was, it couldn't be helped. There were more important matters at stake. 'No historians at all?' Eileen persisted.

'No, and I was there from nine o'clock on. Eileen, do you know if St Paul's was hit by any HEs during the Blitz?'

She looked surprised. 'Hit by HEs?'

'Yes. Not incendiaries, high-explosive bombs. Did Mr Dunworthy say anything about its being hit?'

'Yes,' Eileen said, 'but you—'

'Did he say when and which part of the cathedral?'

'I don't know all the dates. A UXB landed under the—'

'I know about the UXB. And the twenty-ninth.'

'And the altar was hit on October tenth.'

Thank God, Polly thought, reaching out to the stone railing in her relief. It was supposed to have been hit.

Eileen was frowning. 'If you were at St Paul's this morning, then you saw the damage, didn't you?'

Oh no, in her anxiety about the bombing, she'd totally forgotten Eileen knew nothing about her and Mike's fears that they'd altered events. 'Yes, I mean, I did see it,' she stammered, 'but I didn't know ... Mr Dunworthy'd told me all about the UXB and the incendiaries, but not about the altar, and when I saw it, I—'

'—thought it might have happened this morning?'

This *morning*? What did that mean? But at least Eileen hadn't guessed the real reason she'd asked all these questions. 'No, last night,' Polly said. 'And there was so much damage, it looked like the entire thing could collapse any minute, and even though I knew St Paul's had survived, I thought ... I mean, I wasn't thinking. It was such a shock, seeing it. I hadn't realised St Paul's had ever been hit by an HE.'

'Two,' Eileen said.

Two? Mr Humphreys had said one—

'The other one was in the transept,' Eileen said. 'I don't know when.'

'The north transept?' Polly asked, thinking irrelevantly of the memorial to Captain Faulknor. Mr Humphreys would be so upset if that was destroyed.

'I don't know which transept. Mr Bartholomew didn't say.'

'Mr Bartholomew?' Who was Mr Bartholomew? Had someone here at the concert told her about the bombing of the altar? If so, then it could still be a discrepancy. 'Mr Bartholomew?' Polly asked.

'Yes, John Bartholomew. He gave a lecture about it when I was a first-year.'

Oh thank goodness, it was someone from Oxford. 'He's a professor at Balliol?'

'No, a historian. He gave a lecture about his experiences on the St Paul's fire watch during the Blitz.'

'He's *here*?' Polly grabbed Eileen's arms. 'Why didn't you say something?'

'No, he's not here *now*. He was here years ago.'

'In the Blitz. In 1940,' Polly said, and when Eileen nodded, 'It doesn't matter when he was here *Oxford* time. This is time travel. If he was here in 1940, he's still here now.'

'Oh!' Eileen clapped her hand to her mouth. 'I didn't even think of that. Is that why you—?'

'How could you not *think* of it?' Polly burst out. 'Mike asked us to try to think of any past historians who might be here,' she said, but even as she said it, she thought, *That was that day he came to Townsend Brothers before he left for Beachy Head. Eileen wasn't there.* And immediately after that, all their attention had turned to Bletchley Park.

'Mike never said a *word* to me about past historians,' Eileen said defensively. 'How—?'

'It doesn't matter. Now that we know he's here—'

'But he's *not*. He was injured when the bomb fell and went back to Oxford.'

'How long after the bombing?'

'The next day.'

Which meant he'd been gone back two weeks before Mike had found her and the two of them had found Eileen.

'Oh, if I'd only *realised*,' Eileen lamented, her voice filled with anguish.

'It wouldn't have made any difference,' Polly said, sorry she'd upset her. 'By the time we found each other and realised there was something wrong with our drops, it was already too late. He was already gone. You're certain he went back on the eleventh?'

'Yes. I don't remember very much about the lecture because

it was in 1940, and the only part of World War II I wanted to go to at that point was VE Day—'

So you didn't pay attention, just as you didn't pay attention to Gerald, Polly thought bitterly. But that was unfair. Eileen could scarcely be expected to know that three years later the details of a first-year lecture would prove to be vitally important.

'—but I do remember Mr Bartholomew talking about going back the morning after St Paul's was attacked,' Eileen went on, 'because I assumed it was because he was injured and needed medical attention.'

Like Mike had, Polly thought. Only no one had come to pull him out. 'I don't suppose he said where his drop was, did he?'

'No. But if he's gone back, his drop wouldn't be working now, would it?'

It might, Polly thought, but she couldn't tell Eileen that, or she might begin questioning Polly about her earlier assignments. Might it have been in St Paul's?

No, not with people there all day and the fire watch there at night. She wondered suddenly if John Bartholomew had been in the cathedral that first day she'd gone there. He might very well have been that firewatcher she'd seen coming on duty as she left. Or one of the men out by the UXB.

If I'd known he was there, I could have gone back to St Paul's and told him I was in trouble as soon as I found out my drop was open, she thought, *and he could have got word to Mr Dunworthy—*

'Would it?' Eileen was asking. 'Still be working? Mr Bartholomew's drop? I thought drops shut down when the historian returned and the assignment was over.'

'They do,' Polly said. Standing here was only going to get her in trouble. 'It's beginning to rain again,' she said. 'We don't want to get drenched.'

But Eileen made no move to leave the shelter of the porch. 'You still haven't told me about St Paul's. Nobody came in all morning who might have been the retrieval team?'

'No, there was scarcely anyone there at all, not even for the morning service.'

'The morning service?'

Polly nodded, glad she'd picked up that order of worship. 'The place was almost completely deserted. Let's go before it gets any worse.'

Eileen still didn't budge. 'You needn't protect me, you know. I know this is my first assignment, but that's no reason for you and Mike to treat me like a child. I know how much trouble we're in—'

No, you don't, Polly thought, *you have no idea.*

'—and I know how dangerous it is here. You needn't keep things from me.'

'No one's keeping anything from you,' Polly said. 'If this is about our not telling you about the historians who were here before, I intended to, but then you remembered Gerald was at Bletchley Park, and I didn't think we'd need to find anyone else—'

'Then why have we been putting all those personal ads in the paper?' Eileen said belligerently. 'Why did you send me to the concert today and go to St Paul's?'

'As back-up. In case Mike can't find Gerald. Come along—'

Eileen shrugged off her hand. 'Has something happened to Mike?'

'To Mike?'

'Yes. We haven't heard from him in days.'

'No, nothing's happened to Mike. He very likely doesn't want to communicate any more than necessary so as not to arouse suspicions.'

'And you haven't been in touch with him? You didn't go and meet him today?'

'Meet him?' Polly said, surprised. Was that why Eileen had been so upset since she got here? Because she thought Mike had returned and the two of them were meeting secretly?

'Yes, meeting him. Was that clipping Mike sent a signal the two of you'd arranged for you to go and meet him?'

'No, of course not,' Polly said, and Eileen must have heard the bewilderment in her voice because she looked relieved. 'Is that why you think I went to St Paul's, to meet Mike? I didn't. I haven't seen Mike since he said goodbye at the station weeks ago. I went to St Paul's to see if the retrieval team showed up in answer to our ad, that's all. And I nearly froze to death. I had to sit through an absolutely interminable sermon on the subject of "Seek and Ye Shall Find".'

Eileen stiffened. '"Seek and Ye Shall Find?"'

'Yes. It wasn't nearly as good as the one your vicar gave that day I went to Backbury. And it was twice as long. You should be glad you didn't come with me. Now come along. You'll be soaked. We'll go to St Paul's another day, when it's warmer. Now come along. You'll get soaked.' She took Eileen's arm and propelled her across the wet square. 'We'll have a nice tea, and *no* cottage pie. Do you know, I think Mrs Rickett makes hers from actual cottages.'

Eileen didn't even crack a smile. 'I don't want tea,' she said, hugging her arms to herself against the cold. 'I want to go home.'

DULWICH – SUMMER 1944

Flight Officer Stephen Lang telephoned Mary nineteen times
over the next two weeks. She instructed the other girls to
tell him she was out on a run or fetching supplies. 'Or tell him
I was hit by a V-1,' she said to Talbot in exasperation when he
rang up for the sixteenth time. 'Tell him I'm dead.'

'I doubt that would stop him,' Talbot said. 'You *do* realise
you're only making things worse, don't you? There's nothing a
man finds so attractive as a woman who plays hard to get.'

'So you think I should go *out* with him? Fairchild's my *part-
ner*, and Stephen's her true love. She's been mad about him
since she was six!'

'I'm only saying that the more you run, the more he'll pursue
you.'

'So what do you think I should do?'

'I've no idea.'

Mary had no idea either. She obviously couldn't go out
with him – just the fact that he wanted her to was killing poor
Fairchild – and she didn't dare talk to him on the telephone. But
he refused to take no for an answer.

'*I* think you should go out with him, Triumph,' Parrish said, 'and use the occasion to convince him Fairchild's the one he should be going out with.'

Which had been a dreadful idea ever since the days of the American Pilgrims, when John Alden had attempted to persuade Priscilla Mullins to go out with Miles Standish, and Priscilla had said, 'Speak for yourself, John.' The last thing she needed was for Stephen to say, 'Speak for yourself, Isolde.'

She wondered if John Alden had been a time traveller, who'd then had no idea how to get out of the muck-up he was in. And it was a muck-up. Everyone at the post got involved, and Reed and Grenville were both furious with Mary. 'I think it's positively beastly to steal another girl's man,' Grenville said, and when Mary attempted to explain, she added, 'Well, you must have done *something*.'

'Look at her,' Reed whispered, glancing over at Fairchild. 'She's absolutely heartbroken.'

She was, though she hadn't said a word of reproach to Mary. She hadn't said *anything* to her. She was silent on their runs, except for saying, 'I need a stretcher over here!' and 'This one's got internal injuries,' and at the post she kept carefully out of hearing of the telephone, but she was obviously suffering. And Mary was clearly responsible for that suffering, which either meant her being here had altered events, which was impossible – historians couldn't do that – or that her coming between Fairchild and Stephen didn't matter, which meant they wouldn't have got together even if Mary hadn't been here. Because Stephen had been killed.

Of course he'd been killed. He was not only tipping V-1s but living in the middle of Bomb Alley. And hundreds of thousands of charming young men just like him had been killed at Dunkirk and El Alamein and Normandy.

But it will kill Fairchild, she thought, and was afraid it might have done exactly that. She wouldn't have been the first person in World War II to have lost someone and volunteered for dangerous duty. And Mary couldn't help feeling that if Fairchild did that, it would have been her fault, that both their deaths would be on her head. If she hadn't been here and knocked Talbot in the gutter, Talbot wouldn't have wrenched her knee. She wouldn't have had to substitute for her, and Stephen would never have come to the post.

Or perhaps he would have. Perhaps he'd have asked Talbot out to dinner, and exactly the same thing would have happened, with Talbot the villain. Or perhaps Talbot would have gone to that dance they never got to and met a GI who promised her nylons, and he'd made a date with Talbot for that day, and she'd asked Fairchild to drive to Hendon in her place. And she and Stephen had fallen in love on the way to London, and they'd had a wartime wedding and lived happily ever after.

Fairchild could just as easily have driven him through Golders Green or down Tottenham Court Road and they'd both have been killed, Mary told herself. *And either way, you can't change the outcome. If you could have, the net wouldn't have let you come through.*

But just because historians couldn't affect events, it didn't mean they should intentionally create problems, so she made certain she was unavailable when Stephen rang up, spent her off-duty time away from the post, and volunteered to go after the supplies the Major was constantly wangling out of other posts, hoping Stephen would get bored and turn his attentions to Fairchild, where they belonged.

But he continued to ring her up, Fairchild looked more and more wan, and nothing, not even the arrival of a new ambulance – which the Major had managed against all odds to get from HQ – stopped the FANYs from discussing 'poor Fairchild'.

And on the first of September, the Major made it worse by issuing a new duty roster on which she and Fairchild were no longer partnered, leading to endless speculation over whether she or Fairchild had asked for the change.

Mary was almost grateful when the V-2 attacks began. It gave them all something else to think about, and it gave Stephen's squadron a new challenge. His calls became less frequent and then ceased as the RAF wrestled with the problem of how to stop these new, much more deadly attacks.

Even Spitfires had no chance of catching up to the V-2s – they flew at nearly four thousand miles an hour, which was faster than the speed of sound, and took only four seconds to reach their target. As a result, there was no siren or warning rattle. The only sound they made was a sonic boom, and if one heard that, they'd already survived the explosion.

The rockets struck out of nowhere, and it was amazing just how terrifying that was. Even the unflappable FANYs began staying indoors and stealing surreptitious glances at the sky when they were on a run. Sutcliffe-Hythe moved all her belongings down to the cellar, and Parrish told a GI who wanted to take her to a jitterbugging contest that she had to stay in and wash her hair.

On the way home from a run one morning, they saw a group of children with suitcases, with cardboard tags around their necks, being loaded onto buses. 'What's happening?' Mary asked.

'They're being evacuated to the north,' Camberley explained, 'out of range.'

Reed said wistfully, 'I wish I could go with them.'

The damage from the V-2s was terrifying, too. Instead of smashed houses, there were entire flattened areas, so obliterated it was impossible to tell what had been there. The number of victims taken away from incidents in mortuary vans went up sharply, and so did the number who died en route to hospital. Some casualties simply vanished, vaporised by two thousand pounds of explosives. And the things the FANYs saw at the sites became markedly more grisly and unspeakable.

But within the month they'd adjusted to the V-2s and invented a new – and totally spurious – mythology regarding them. 'They never land where any other rocket's hit,' Maitland pronounced, 'because of the magnetism. So we're perfectly safe while we're at the incident. The trick is in getting there.'

But they had that covered as well. 'They never come till an hour after the first V-1 volley of the day,' Sutcliffe-Hythe said, and Talbot reported that one of her beaus at the motor pool had told her the V-2 motor wouldn't work when it got cold, so the number would be less as winter approached – neither of which was true. But it made it possible for the FANYs to face sleeping and working and driving to incidents every day, knowing they might be blown to bits at any moment.

And before another fortnight had passed, they were back to discussing clothes – Mary's blue organdy had got a tear in the skirt, and there was a debate over whether to mend the sheer cloth or take out an entire width – and men. Sutcliffe-Hythe had met an American sailor from Brooklyn named Jerry Wojeiuk, and Parrish had broken it off with Dickie.

Unfortunately, they also went back to discussing 'poor Fairchild'. 'Perhaps you could get engaged to someone else,' Reed suggested to Mary when Stephen began telephoning again.

'Or married,' Maitland put in – suggestions that were so ridiculous that it was a relief when Talbot came in and said the Major wanted her to drive to Streatham to pick up bandages.

'I suppose I've got to drive Bela Lugosi,' Mary said.

'No, it's in the shop. And Reed's not back yet. She had to drive the Octopus to Tangmere. Your luck is in. You get to drive the new ambulance. Camberley's going with you. I'll tell her to meet you in the garage.'

But when the passenger door opened, it was Fairchild who got in. 'Camberley's feeling under the weather. She asked me to fill in for her,' she told Mary, and sat silently as Mary pulled out of the garage and set off for Streatham. She wondered if she should try one more time to explain about Stephen, but she was afraid she'd only make things worse.

Streatham couldn't give them any lint or bandages. 'We're nearly out ourselves. Those horrid V-2s,' the FANY at the post told them. 'I'm going to have to send you to Croydon for them.'

'Croydon?' Croydon had been hit by more rockets than any other borough, and it was outside the area Mary'd memorised. 'Couldn't we get them from Norbury?' she asked. 'It would be a good deal closer.'

The officer shook her head. 'They're worse off than we are. I've telephoned, and Croydon said they'd have them ready for you so you won't need to wait.'

Well, that was something, and no ambulance post had been hit in 1944. Which didn't help as far as the way there and back were concerned. *I'll just have to drive very fast and hope the Germans aren't paying attention to British Intelligence tonight.*

At least she didn't have to worry about Fairchild's talking distracting her – she sat stonily silent. And Mary had no attention to spare for conversation. She had all she could do to find the post in the blanketing darkness. The FANYs would have a dreadful time dealing with their incidents tonight. There was no moon at all, and a heavy October mist seemed to swallow up the headlamps. She couldn't see a thing.

It took her over an hour to find the post in Croydon, and then the FANY on duty couldn't find the supplies. 'I know they were set aside,' she said vaguely and looked all over while the sirens went three separate times. She finally had to box up more lint and bandages and make Mary fill up a different requisition form.

By the time she'd finished, Fairchild was in the ambulance in the driver's seat. Mary considered telling her she should drive because she knew the way, but the set look on Fairchild's face made her decide not to. They'd only waste more time in arguing, and she wanted to get out of here before the sirens went again.

She climbed in the passenger side, and Fairchild drove along Croydon's blacked-out high street and turned onto the road to Dulwich. *Good*, Mary thought, *in another ten minutes we'll be safely back inside the area I've memorised.*

Fairchild pulled the ambulance over to the side of the road and stopped. 'What are you doing?' Mary asked.

Fairchild switched off the ignition and pulled on the hand brake. 'I lied about Camberley,' she said. 'I was the one who asked to change shifts so I could come with you. I needed to talk to you, Mary.'

Mary. Not Triumph or De Havilland or even Kent.

'That is, if you're still speaking to me.' Fairchild's voice faltered. 'After the beastly way I've behaved to you. Are you?'

It was too dark to see her face, but Mary could hear the anxiety in her voice. 'Of course I am,' she said. 'You haven't been beastly, and I wouldn't blame you if you had been. But can't we discuss this when we get home?' Or at least inside the area where she'd memorised the rockets.

'No,' Fairchild said. 'This can't wait. Yesterday Maitland and I pulled a thirteen-year-old boy out of the wreckage of his house in Ulverscroft Road. It was a V-2. His mother was killed. Direct hit, nothing left of her at all. The boy kept sobbing that he'd been angry with her for making him sleep in the Anderson, and he had to tell her he was sorry he'd called her an old cow. It was dreadful watching him, and I began thinking about how either of us might be killed at any moment, too, and how important it is to mend things before it's too late.'

'There's nothing to mend,' Mary said. 'Let's at least go somewhere warmer to talk. There's a Lyons' in Norbury. We'll have a cup of tea—'

'Not till I've told you how sorry I am for the way I've been acting. It's not your fault that Stephen fell in love with you and not me—'

'He's not in love with me. He's only interested because I represent a challenge by refusing to go out with him.'

'But that's what I wanted to tell you. You *should* go out with him. I'd much rather he was in love with you than Talbot, or someone else who might hurt him.'

'He's *not* in love with me,' Mary insisted, 'and I'm not in love with *him*.'

'You needn't try to spare my feelings. I've seen the way you look at him.'

'No one's in love with anyone, and I have no desire to go out with him. He's your—'

'No, he'll never think of me as anything but his little sister. I thought when he saw me in uniform, he'd realise I'd grown up, but he'll always see me as little Bits and Pieces, six years old and in pigtails. Which isn't your fault, Mary, and I don't want this to ruin our friendship. It's dreadfully important to me, and I couldn't bear it if—'

'Shh,' Mary said, putting her hand up to stop her, even though Fairchild couldn't see it in the dark.

'No, I need to say this—'

'*Shh*,' Mary ordered. 'Listen. I thought I heard a V-1.'

'Hie you, make haste, for it grows very late.'

WILLIAM SHAKESPEARE, *ROMEO AND JULIET*

LONDON – DECEMBER 1940

Mike had phoned from Bletchley on the Monday after Polly'd gone to Hampstead Heath to say he'd run into Tensing, and Polly had told him to leave Bletchley immediately, which meant he should have been back by Friday morning at the latest, but he wasn't. He didn't come on Friday afternoon either, or telephone, or write, and Polly was nearly frantic. Where *was* he?

Tensing found him before he could get out of Bletchley, she thought, *and talked him into working for him. He'll never survive the background check.*

'You didn't tell Mike about the troupe deciding to do *A Christmas Carol*, did you?' Eileen asked. 'Perhaps he's been ringing up while we were at rehearsal. I'll stay home tonight in case he telephones again.'

But he didn't phone Friday night either, or over the weekend, and Polly could tell Eileen was just as worried as she was. She'd been irritable and jumpy, and she didn't offer any optimistic theories or say anything about being rescued just when she thought all was lost.

She scarcely said anything, and she was getting no sleep at all. Because of the rehearsals for *A Christmas Carol* they'd abandoned the emergency staircase for the District Line platform, and whenever Mr Dorming's snoring woke Polly, she found Eileen sitting against the platform wall, arms huddled around her knees, staring bleakly into space.

Polly did her share of that too over the next few nights, and spent hours trying to think of a plausible reason Mike hadn't phoned or sent a message. *He found Gerald*, she thought. *He said he had a lead.* What if Mike had run into him as he left Bletchley, and they'd gone back to Oxford?

They couldn't have. If they had, the retrieval team would be here already. Unless there was slippage. *Or it was Tensing Mike ran into, not Gerald, and Mike's under arrest.*

He knew how much danger he was in, she told herself. *He wouldn't have been stupid enough to stay. He's simply having difficulty getting back to London. He'll be here tomorrow morning.*

But he wasn't. *If he hasn't contacted us by Monday, we'll have to go to Bletchley and find out what happened to him*, Polly thought.

But what if he was fine and by going, by inquiring after him, they jeopardised his safety, or the safety of Ultra's secret? Or what if Mike had already jeopardised it? Polly hadn't found any large discrepancies – Southampton and Birmingham and the air raid shelter at Hammersmith had all been bombed on schedule – but the raids on Tuesday had begun ten minutes earlier than they were supposed to, and on Friday Townsend Brothers was evacuated for two hours because of a UXB on Audley Street which wasn't in her implant.

Because it didn't go off, she told herself, and while they were waiting in the shelter for the bomb to be removed, forced herself to concentrate on composing messages for the retrieval team: 'Lost, near Notting Hill Gate Station, cocker spaniel, answers to Polly. Contact O. Riley, 14 Cardle Street' and 'Dearest T., Sorry couldn't come to Oxford as planned. Meet me Peter Pan Statue 10 a.m. Sunday'.

'But if Mike comes on Sunday,' Eileen protested, 'how will he find us if we're in Kensington Gardens?'

'Not *we*, I. I'm supposed to be meeting my dearest Terence or Tom or Theodore. This is supposed to be a romantic tryst. If Mike arrives, the two of you can come and fetch me.'

Eileen looked as if she was going to argue, then turned away and began reading her Agatha Christie again, and when Sunday came made no attempt to go with Polly.

Kensington Gardens didn't look much like a place for a romantic rendezvous. Two anti-aircraft guns stood on either side of the Round Pond, rows of half-tracks filled the lawns, and the Victorian railings edging the bounds of the park had been taken down, presumably for the scrap-metal drive.

So many slit trenches had been dug in the area near the Peter Pan statue that Polly began to worry it might have been re-moved for safekeeping, but the bronze statue was still there in a little wooded glade, its base crawling with fairies and woodland creatures. If Sir Godfrey were here, he'd no doubt have some pithy comment to make about J.M. Barrie.

But he wasn't here, and neither was the retrieval team. Polly glanced at her watch. It wasn't ten yet. She sat down on a bench across from the statue from which she could see anyone ap-proaching and prepared to wait.

Ten came and went, but no one appeared, not even any children or nannies with prams – and by a quarter past she was sorry she hadn't let Eileen come with her. Sitting here gave her time to think. What if Mike never came back? What if their drops never opened and—?

She caught a sudden flash of movement beyond the bushes off to the left. A bird? Or someone standing there watching her? It couldn't be the retrieval team; they'd have revealed themselves as soon as they recognised her. A purse snatcher? Or worse?

She was suddenly aware of just how isolated the spot was.

But it was mid-morning, and there were soldiers within screaming distance.

But what if British Intelligence had thought there was something suspicious about the advertisement? What if they were watching to see whom she met? Had there been something suspicious in the ad? She didn't think so.

She needed to act the way she would if her young man was late. She glanced at her watch, frowned, stood up and walked along the path a short way as if looking for someone, trying to look hopeful and bit annoyed, and then strolled back to the statue.

There was definitely someone there in the bushes. 'Hullo?' Polly called. 'Who's there?'

A hushed silence, as if someone was holding his breath. 'I know you're in there,' Polly said, and Eileen emerged from the bushes. '*Eileen*? What on earth are you doing here? Has Mike come back?'

'No. I decided to come along and see if anyone had answered your ad. I told Mrs Rickett where we'd be, and I left a note for Mike with Mrs Leary.'

Which didn't explain what she had been doing lurking in the bushes, and Eileen seemed to realise that because she added, 'But then I couldn't find the statue, and I ended up in among the trees,' which was clearly untrue. The signposts pointing the way to the Peter Pan statue were the only ones in England that hadn't been taken down, and at any rate Eileen was looking guilty of something, though Polly had no idea what.

'What's going on?' she asked. 'Why did you really come?'

'Eileen!' Mike called, 'Polly!'

He was limping up the path towards them, waving.

Mike. Oh thank God. He wasn't dead.

'Mike!' Eileen cried and ran to meet him. 'You're back! Thank heavens – we've been so worried!'

'Tensing didn't find you, did he?' Polly asked anxiously.

'No.'

'Then where were you?'

'In Oxford.'

'*Oxford?*' Eileen gasped. 'Oh God, you've found Gerald! Thank heavens.'

'No, no, Oxford right now. In 1940. I'm sorry,' he said, looking in dismay at her disappointed face. 'I didn't mean to get your hopes up like that. I didn't find Gerald. I—'

Polly cut him off. 'We want to hear all about your journey,' she said loudly, and then in a whisper, 'but not here. Somewhere where we can't be overheard. Come along. I know just the place.'

She tucked her arm in Mike's and led him down the path, chattering brightly. 'We thought you'd never come, didn't we, Eileen?'

'Yes – if you'd told us which train you'd be on,' Eileen said, playing along, 'we'd have come to meet it.'

'I didn't know myself,' Mike said. He dropped his voice to a whisper. 'What's going on? Was someone spying on us back there?'

Only Eileen, Polly thought. 'I don't think so,' she said, 'but loose lips sink ships. Come along.'

She led them past the trenches to an open lawn with a large monument in its centre. From here, they'd be able to see anyone coming from any direction. 'All right,' she said, sitting down on the monument steps. 'Now we can talk.'

'What did you mean, "loose lips sink—?"' Mike stopped, staring at the statuary around the monument. 'Jesus, what *is* this thing?'

'The Albert Memorial. Possibly the ugliest monument in all of England.' Polly smiled happily at the elephant, the water buffalo, the semi-naked young women clustered round them, at Prince Albert sitting on top reading a book. She felt giddy in her relief that Mike wasn't in the Tower. Or dead.

'It's hideous. It wasn't destroyed in the Blitz, was it?' he asked hopefully.

'No, only minor damage, I'm afraid, though supposedly at

one point someone put up a large arrow to guide the Luftwaffe to it.'

'It's too bad it didn't work,' Mike said, still staring, appalled. 'Christ, is that a *buffalo*?'

'Who *cares* what it is?' Eileen said impatiently. 'Tell us what happened and why you went to Oxford.'

'Okay. After I called you about Tensing, I went back to Mrs Jolsom's to pack my stuff, and she told me the room I'd rented was supposed to have been Phipps'.'

'It was *Gerald's* room?' Polly said.

'Yes. He was supposed to have come two months ago, but he never arrived, so I went to Oxford to see if I could find out whether something had happened to him on the way.'

'And?'

'He never came through. He'd made a reservation at the Mitre in Oxford for the night he arrived, but he never showed up there either.'

'The increased slippage could have sent him through late,' Eileen said, 'and he decided to go straight to Bletchley instead of stopping in Oxford.'

Mike shook his head. 'He'd mailed a package addressed to himself to the Mitre. He never picked it up.'

'Do you know what was in it?' Polly asked.

'Yeah, that's why I was gone so long. It took me forever to steal it.' He pulled a sheaf of papers from his pocket and laid them out on the steps of the monument. 'It's all the papers documenting he was who he said he was – letters of recommendation, school records, security clearances, everything he'd need to pass a background check. Plus train tickets and money. And a letter from his sister in Northumbria informing him his mother was ill. Addressed to Mrs Jolsom's address.' He looked up at them. 'He obviously never came through.'

The net wouldn't let him, Polly thought, *which means its safeguards are still functioning*.

Only it didn't necessarily mean that at all. It might just

as easily mean that there was no Oxford from which to send him.

She glanced anxiously at Eileen to see how she was taking the news, but she didn't look upset. *Because she doesn't believe it*, Polly thought. *In a moment she'll say Mr Dunworthy must have rescheduled Gerald's assignment and Mike shouldn't have taken the parcel because Gerald will need it.*

Mike said it instead. 'I intended to put the package back, but when I saw what was in it, I thought I'd better not leave it there for some curious hotel clerk to open.'

'Will the Mitre notice it's missing?'

'No. I wrapped my waistcoat up in the brown paper – and had a hell of a time doing it, I might add. I couldn't get the string tied around it for the life of me – and sneaked it back on the shelf, and I stuck a Notting Hill Gate ticket stub in the pocket, so if Phipps *does* come through, he'll know where to look for us.'

'If he can get to London,' Polly said, looking at the money on the steps.

'I stuck enough money for the train fare to London in the pocket, too,' Mike said. 'I was going to leave all of it, but I decided we might need it to tide us over till we find some other way out. I assume our retrieval teams still haven't shown up?'

'No,' Eileen said. 'Have you heard from Daphne?'

'I don't know. I haven't been to Mrs Leary's yet. I came straight to Mrs Rickett's to find the two of you. I'll check when we go back. But if Phipps' drop didn't open, then our retrieval teams' drops probably can't either, which explains why they're not here. But if that's what happened, then Oxford knows something's wrong, and they'll start working on figuring out a way to get us out of here. We'll be home in no time. We just need to make sure they can find us when they get here, so we need to—'

'*Will* we be home in no time?' Eileen asked challengingly. 'Or will we still be here when the war ends, Polly?'

'When the *war* ends?' Mike said. 'What are you talking about? None of us know how long we'll—'

'*She* does,' Eileen said. 'She was already here.' She turned to Polly. 'That's why the night you found me in Padgett's you asked me if the manor in Backbury was my first assignment. Because you were afraid I had a deadline like you.'

'A deadline?' Mike said. 'You were here before, Polly?'

'Yes,' Eileen said, looking steadily at Polly. 'That's why she asked me whether you were supposed to go to Pearl Harbor first. She was afraid that you had one, too. And that the increased slippage means we won't get out before her deadline.'

I should never have underestimated her and her mystery novels, Polly thought.

All those weeks Polly'd been trying to protect her from the truth, Eileen had been patiently collecting clues and piecing them together. *But she can't know when—*

'I don't understand,' Mike said. 'When I asked you if you'd been to Bletchley Park, you said no.'

'Not Bletchley Park,' Eileen said. 'VE Day.'

'*VE Day?*'

'Yes,' Eileen said, her face stony. She turned to confront Polly. 'That's why when I saw you in Oxford, you asked me if that was where I was coming back from. And why, when we asked you who'd gone to VE Day, you changed the subject. You saw me there, didn't you?'

As long as VE Day was all Eileen knew about, it would be all right. She could tell them.

'Is what she's saying true?' Mike asked. 'Were you at VE Day, Polly?'

'Yes.'

'Jesus.'

'And you saw me there,' Eileen said.

Polly hesitated so it would sound like she was reluctantly admitting to it. 'Yes.'

'Why didn't you tell us?' Mike asked.

'I— At first, in Oxford, I didn't want Eileen to be angry with me. I hadn't known Mr Dunworthy wasn't going to let her go to VE Day. I didn't want her to think I'd stolen the assignment from her. And then when we found out the drops weren't working, we were already in so much trouble, and you were both so upset, I didn't want to add to your worries.'

'But if we'd known—' Mike began.

'If you'd known, what? There wasn't anything either of you could do about it,' Polly said angrily, hoping the anger would stop them from asking any more questions. 'And you already had more than enough to deal with.'

'You say you saw Eileen,' Mike said. 'Are you certain it was her? Did you talk to her?'

'No. I saw her from a distance. In the crowd in Trafalgar Square the night before VE Day. She was standing next to one of the lions. The one whose nose had been knocked off in the Blitz.'

'You were in Trafalgar Square on VE Day,' Mike said. 'When did you come through?'

Polly thought rapidly. They'd never believe she'd only been there for the two days of the victory celebration. 'April eighth,' she said. 'I was there to observe the winding-down of the war during its last few weeks. I posed as a Wren working as a typist in the War Office.'

'A typist,' Eileen said.

'Yes.'

'April eighth,' Mike said. 'That gives us four years—'

'Four years and five months,' Eileen said.

'Right,' Mike said, 'nearly four and a half years. And when I was talking about increased slippage, I meant a few months, not years. We'll be out of here long before your deadline, Polly.'

'Which is what?' Eileen asked.

Mike looked at Eileen in surprise. 'You heard her. She said she came through on April eighth—'

'She's lying. That isn't her deadline.'

There was a silence, and then Mike said, 'Is she right, Polly? Are you lying?'

'Yes,' Eileen answered for her. 'When I told her about one of the historian's drops to the Reign of Terror and the storming of the Bastille being switched, she went absolutely white, and they were only four years and two months apart.'

And I'm obviously not as good an actress as Sir Godfrey's always telling me I am, Polly thought, cursing herself for not having said she'd gone through earlier than April. 'It was Pearl Harbor I was worried about, not—'

'Wait. Stop,' Mike said. 'Pearl Harbor? The storming of the Bastille? I have no idea what either of you is talking about. Explain.'

Polly said, 'After you and I talked about an increase in slippage possibly being the problem, it occurred to me that Mr Dunworthy might have been putting all the assignments in chronological order.'

'Chronological—? You're right. He *did* put all mine in chronological order. That's why you asked me about the order of my drops when you called.'

'Yes.' Polly explained about Eileen's notes, and concluding that the increase might be much longer than a couple of months. 'And I was frightened. A lot of the worst raids of the Blitz will be after the first of the year, and we don't even know when and where they are. And I'm not even certain our boarding houses are safe from January on.'

Which had the advantage of being true. *And let's hope it convinces them*, Polly thought.

'That isn't the only reason,' Eileen said grimly. 'Ask her why, if she was a typist in the War Office, she knows all about driving an ambulance. When I told her I had to learn to drive that day we talked to you in Oxford, Mike, she offered to teach me. On a Daimler, because that was what all the ambulances were.'

'I'd learned that from my prep for the Blitz,' Polly said. 'I studied the Civil Defence—'

'And ask her why she turned and ran from a group of FANYs we saw on the platform in Holborn. She knew them from her assignment, that's why. She never tried to avoid walking past Wrens.'

And all the time I was worried she was fretting over Mike, she was actually playing detective, like a character in one of her Agatha Christies, Polly thought. *I underestimated her. But she can't have figured it all out.*

'And ask her where she went when she said she was going to St Paul's to meet the retrieval team.' She turned on Polly. 'When I got to the National Gallery it was pouring rain and the concert wasn't till one, so I thought I'd come to St Paul's and meet you. But you weren't there.'

'Yes, I was. We must just have missed each other. St Paul's is huge, and there are so many chapels and bays—'

'I saw you come in. I saw you buy that guidebook and spill pennies all over the floor. She was drenched,' Eileen said to Mike, 'like she'd been out in the rain all morning. And don't bother pretending you were up in the Whispering Gallery, Polly. It's closed. And the sermon wasn't "Seek and You Shall Find". It was "The Lost Sheep". You must have picked up an order of service for the early mass by mistake. Where were you?'

At least this was a question she could answer. 'I was at Hampstead Heath. That was where my drop for VE Day was.' She looked at Mike. 'When you sent that message from Bletchley about older drops, I went to see if they might have opened mine to use for an emergency exit. And I couldn't tell you, Eileen, because I didn't want you to find out I'd been here before.'

'Is that the truth?' Eileen said.

'Yes.' *And please, please, let that be all you know.*

'You swear?' Eileen said.

'Yes.'

'Then why didn't you know about the bomb at St Paul's, but you knew all about V-1s and V-2s?' She turned back to Mike. 'She knew the exact date the V-1 attacks began. Don't you see, *she* was the historian who did the rocket assignment. She drove an ambulance in Bethnal Green. Didn't you, Polly? That's why you were so upset when I told you that was where we had to go to get me a new identity card. Because you were afraid someone in Bethnal Green would recognise you. You were attached to the ambulance unit there, weren't you?'

'No,' Polly said, 'to the ambulance unit in Dulwich.'

> *'Wars are not won by evacuations.'*

WINSTON CHURCHILL, SPEAKING OF DUNKIRK

OXFORD – APRIL 2060

The shimmer flared. 'Colin's not to come through after me,' Dunworthy said again, though the shimmer was too bright. Badri would never be able to hear him, but he tried nonetheless. 'No matter what excuse he gives you.'

It was too late. He was already through. And definitely in St Paul's, though he couldn't see a thing. His words echoed and then died away into the hush of a high, open, vaulted space. He'd have recognised it anywhere, just as he'd have recognised the distinctive chill. It always felt like the dead of winter in St Paul's. He peered into the solid darkness, waiting for his eyes to adjust. It clearly wasn't four a.m. Or if it was, there'd been locational slippage, and he'd come through in the Crypt instead of the north transept.

No, this couldn't be the Crypt. The fire watch had their headquarters down there, and there'd be lights. But he might be inside one of the staircases. No, the sound wasn't that of an enclosed space. He wasn't willing to take chances, though. He'd come through on a flight of stairs one time early in his career and nearly pitched off it and killed himself. He slid one foot forward and then the other, feeling for an edge.

He was on a flat surface. A stone floor, so this had to be on the main floor of the cathedral, which meant it was far earlier than four a.m. But even if it were midnight, there should be *some* light. The raids in the early morning hours of the tenth had been less than half a mile from here, and some of the docks had still been burning from the first two nights' raids. And there should be searchlights.

And noise. But he couldn't hear anything – no clatter of incendiaries, the bane of St Paul's. No muffled thud of bombs. No droning of planes overhead. No sound at all, except the distinctive hush. What if Linna had got the coordinates wrong in her haste, and this wasn't 1940? Or what if Dr Ishiwaka had been right?

But when Dunworthy put his hand out, it connected with canvas and a yielding weight which could only be a sandbag. He patted around it. More sandbags, and when he felt his way around them to the wall and along it, he came to a carved wooden doorway. The north doors. Which meant he was exactly where he was supposed to be, and the sandbags meant he was in the general vicinity of when.

There should be two steps leading down to the doors. He felt his way carefully down and tried to open them. They were locked. Locked? John Bartholomew had said they kept the cathedral unlocked. But he wasn't here yet. He wouldn't arrive till the twentieth, and perhaps St Paul's hadn't unlocked the doors till later, after the necessity of getting fire hoses in quickly became apparent.

It should have been apparent from the beginning, Dunworthy thought irritably, groping his way back up the steps. Now he'd have to go all the way down the nave to the west doors. Which would take him an hour at this rate.

Perhaps he should sit down and wait for it to grow light enough to see, but it was too cold. His teeth were already chattering. And the longer he waited, the more likely he was to run into the fire watch and have to explain what he was doing here.

He could always tell them he'd come in looking for shelter

when the sirens went and had fallen asleep, but if he and Polly were seen when he brought her back here, there could be complications. Worse, they might decide they needed to make a sweep of the cathedral every night. Or lock the west doors.

He needed to get out now, before anyone saw him. And if he was lucky, and it was as early as the darkness and the lack of raids suggested, the trains would still be running, and he could make it to Notting Hill Gate before they stopped. He could spend the night searching that station, search High Street Kensington and the others on the list as soon as the trains began again in the morning and find Polly before nightfall and have her back in Oxford before breakfast. And he could stop worrying over what might happen to her if Dr Ishiwaka was right.

He patted his way cautiously back along the wall, around the sandbags. Wall, more sandbags, pillar—

His foot hit something metal, and it fell over with a terrific, echoing clatter. He dived to silence whatever it was, and his hand came down in a bucket of freezing water and nearly knocked it over. He felt frantically for the thing he'd banged into.

A stirrup pump. He could tell by the metal handle, the rubber hose. He straightened, clutching the pump in both hands and peering anxiously into the blackness, listening for running footsteps or a shouted 'What was that?'

Neither came, which meant the entire fire watch was still up on the roofs, thank heavens, and if he could just reach the nave with its high windows, there should be a bit more light and he'd be able to see where he was going.

There wasn't any more light. The wall he'd been patting his way along ended and the quality of the hush changed, so that he could tell he was in a wider, higher space, but it was still pitch-black. Bartholomew had said they'd kept a small light burning on the altar at night for the fire watch to orient itself by, but when he looked towards where the choir and the altar should be, there was nothing but a black blankness.

And I will have a few things to say to Mr Bartholomew on

the accuracy of his historical reporting when I return to Oxford, he thought, feeling for the angled and fluted pillars that formed the corner of the wall. He didn't dare go out into the middle of the nave. It was full of wooden folding chairs to crash into. He'd better keep to the north aisle.

He felt along the aisle's wall, one hand on the cold stone and the other hand in front of him, attempting to remember what lay along it. Lord Leighton's statue, he thought, and promptly stumbled over it, the sandbags breaking his fall.

I'm too old for this, he thought, getting to his feet again and working his way past it, past an alcove, a rectangular pillar, another alcove, and another bucket, this one full of sand – which he nearly broke his toe against but thankfully, did not knock over.

Colin was right, I should have brought a torch, he thought, feeling his way around another pillar and up against what was unmistakably a brick wall.

There aren't any brick walls in St Paul's. Could I be somewhere else altogether? Then he realised what it was: the Wellington Monument, which they'd bricked up because it was too large to move. He worked his way quickly along its face to the next pillar. After this there should be only the All Souls' Chapel and then St Dunstan's Chapel before he reached—

A door slammed somewhere behind him, and footsteps hurried down the nave towards him. Dunworthy ducked behind the pillar, hoping he was out of sight. 'I'm certain I heard something,' a man's voice said.

'An incendiary?' a second voice asked.

No, you heard me crashing about, Dunworthy thought. They were obviously members of the fire watch.

A pocket torch flashed briefly. Dunworthy shrank further behind the pillar. 'I don't know,' the first man said. 'It might have been a DA.'

A delayed-action bomb, Dunworthy thought.

'Bloody hell, that's all we need,' the second one said. And bloody hell was right. They'd search the entire cathedral.

'It sounded like it was in the nave,' the first one said, and Dunworthy braced himself, wondering what sort of tale he could concoct to explain his presence. But when the torch flashed again, it was over towards the south aisle, and their footsteps grew softer as they moved away from him.

Dunworthy stayed where he was, trying to hear what they were saying, but he only caught snatches. '... have been on the south chancel roof? ... likely put it out ...'

They must have decided it was an incendiary after all. They were all the way to the west end of the nave. He caught, '... over for tonight ...' and something that sounded like 'Coventry', though that was unlikely. He didn't think Coventry had been bombed before the fourteenth of November.

'... north aisle ... ?' one of them said, and Dunworthy looked back towards the transept, wondering if he should retreat there.

'No ... check the gallery first.' There was a brief flash of light, and Dunworthy heard a clank of metal and then footsteps ascending.

They're going up Wren's Geometric Staircase, he thought, and took advantage of the covering sound of their footsteps to walk quickly along the aisle, his hand on the wall for guidance. Pillar, pillar, iron grille. That was St Dunstan's Chapel. The vestibule and the door should be just beyond.

'... find anything ... ?' he heard from somewhere above him. He ducked for cover moments before the pocket torch's light flared down.

'Here it is!' one of them shouted; it must have been the first one because he said triumphantly, 'I told you I heard something. It's an incendiary. Get a stirrup pump.'

Dunworthy heard the second one racket along the gallery overhead. He felt his way quickly to the door, opened it, and slipped out to the porch and the steps.

And into pouring rain. *Which explains why it's so dark*, he thought, ducking back under the porch's roof. It was nearly as dark out here as inside. If he hadn't known there was a pillared porch and then steps, he couldn't have found his way down to the courtyard.

He squinted across it. He could only just make out the dark outlines of the buildings opposite. The rain also explained the absence of searchlights and of bombers droning overhead – the Luftwaffe would have had to call off the raids when this started. And it explained there not being any fires. The rain would have put all of them out – except for the incendiary that had come through the gallery's roof.

Dunworthy glanced up at the bell tower to see if the fire watchers were up there and then splashed down the steps. To reach the tube station, he needed to find Paternoster Row and then Newgate. And watch where he was going, though that was almost impossible to do in this rain. It beat against him icily, more like sleet than rain. He hunched forward, ducking his head against its onslaught.

At any rate, no one else will be mad enough to be out in this, he thought, pulling the collar of his tweed jacket up tightly round his neck, but he was wrong. There were two figures walking straight towards him. Members of the fire watch? Or civilians on the way home from the tube station? Or an ARP warden who would demand to know what he was doing out on the streets and hustle him off to a surface shelter?

He splashed quickly across the road and down the narrow lane to his left. It was scarcely six feet across, and what little light he'd had to see by was utterly shut out by the buildings on either side. It was as dark as it had been inside the cathedral. He had to return to feeling his way, and it took him forever to reach Paternoster Row.

If it was Paternoster Row. It didn't look like it. It was no wider than the lane and was lined with ramshackle houses instead of publishers and book warehouses. It also seemed to have a deeper descent than it should, though that might be a trick of the darkness.

Its abrupt end in a courtyard wasn't. He must have missed Paternoster Row in the dark. He retraced his way back to the lane and up the way he'd come.

But it wasn't the same lane. This one ended in a wooden stable. *You're lost,* he thought furiously. *You should have known better than to wander about in the dark in the City.* There was no worse place in London – or history – to be lost. The area surrounding St Paul's had been a rabbit warren of confusing lanes and mazelike passages, most of them leading nowhere. He could wander in here forever and never find his way out. And the rain was coming down harder than ever.

'I am *too old* for this,' he muttered, craning his neck to catch a glimpse of St Paul's, but the buildings were too tall, and there was nothing to orient himself by. He no longer even knew which direction the cathedral lay in.

Yes, you do, he thought. *You know exactly where it is. On top of Ludgate Hill. All you need to do is climb up the hill.* But that was easier said than done. There were no streets going up. They all led inexorably downhill, away from St Paul's and from the tube station. But if he continued downhill, he'd eventually come to Blackfriars, or, if he was too far east, Cannon Street. Either tube station would have trains which could take him to the station where Polly was. He turned down a lane and then another.

After two more turns and another cul-de-sac he came to a broader street. Old Bailey? If so, Blackfriars lay at the foot of it. It was finally growing light, at least enough to see that the street was lined with shops, and the shops had awnings. He splashed across the street, eager to get even partially out of the rain.

Nearly all the shop windows were boarded up. Only the second from the corner still had glass in it, and as he drew nearer, he saw it was boarded up as well. What he'd thought was glass was actually a reflection from a garland of silver-paper letters nailed to the wood. They spelled out 'Happy Christmas'.

It can't be Christmas, he thought. If it was, there'd have been a Christmas tree in the nave and another outside in the porch. John Bartholomew had talked about its having been repeatedly knocked over by blast.

But the trees could very well have been there. He wouldn't have seen them in the darkness. *But if it's Christmas*, he thought, *that means there's been nearly four months' slippage, and that's impossible. The increase was only two days.* But he knew it was true. That was why it was so cold. And so dark. The net *had* sent him through at four a.m., but in December four a.m. would be pitch-black.

'Ascertain your temporal location immediately upon arrival.' Wasn't that what he was always enjoining his students to do? He should have realised it couldn't be September tenth when there weren't any fires. They hadn't got the ones on the docks out for nearly a week.

But he'd ignored the clues, and now he'd have to climb all the way back up that hill in the rain. Because Polly wasn't here. Her assignment had ended on the twenty-second of October. She'd been safely back in Oxford for at least a month and a half, and this had been an exercise in futility.

Except that now he had the proof he'd been looking for that the slippage was beginning to spike. He had to return to St Paul's immediately, go back to Oxford, and tell Badri to pull all the historians out. He started back up the hill, looking for a taxi, but the streets were completely deserted.

No, wait, there was one, in the darkness at the end of a side lane. He stepped into the lane and hailed it.

It had seen him. It pulled out and began to move towards him, and thank God Colin had insisted on his bringing money. Dunworthy pulled out his papers and shuffled through them, looking for the five-pound notes, and then looked up again.

The taxi was moving away. It hadn't seen him after all. 'Hullo!' Dunworthy shouted, his voice echoing in the narrow street, and rushed towards it, waving.

There, it had seen him now. The taxi began to move towards

him again. It must be further away than he'd thought because he couldn't hear the engine at all. He hurried towards it, but before he'd gone half the distance, he saw it wasn't a taxi. What he'd thought was the vehicle's bonnet was the rounded edge of a huge black metal canister, swinging gently back and forth from a lamppost. A dark shroud was draped over the lamppost. A parachute.

It's a parachute-mine, he thought, watching as the canister swung gently back and forth, missing the lamppost by inches. And if the wind shifted slightly, or the parachute ripped …

He took two stumbling steps backwards, and then turned and ran for the mouth of the lane, listening for the tearing of parachute silk, for the scrape of the mine against the lamppost, for the deafening boom of the explosion.

It didn't come. There was a faint sigh, and he was suddenly on the ground, his hands out in front of him on the pavement. He thought at first he must have tripped and fallen, but when he got to his feet, he was covered with dust and glass. *It must have broken the stationer's window*, he thought, and then confusedly, *the mine must have gone off.*

He brushed the glass and dirt off his trousers, his coat. And he must have cut himself in the process because the palms of his hands were scraped and bloody, and blood was trickling down behind his ear. He could hear ambulance bells.

I can't let them find me here, he thought. *I must get back to Oxford. I must pull everyone out.* He started down the lane, wishing there was a wall to lean against for support, but all the buildings seemed to have fallen down except the one at the very end. He walked towards it as quickly as he could. The bells were growing louder. The ambulance would be here any second, and so would an incident officer. He needed to be out of the lane, across the road, around the corner—

He made it just past the corner before he collapsed, falling to his knees.

Colin was right. He said I'd get into trouble, he thought. *I should have let him come with me.* And he must have been un-conscious for a few minutes, because when he opened his eyes, it was nearly light and the rain had stopped. He got heavily to his feet and then stood there a moment, looking confused. What had he—?

Oxford, he thought. *I must get back to Oxford.* And he started down the hill to Blackfriars to take the tube to Paddington Station to catch the train.

'For the rain it raineth every day.'

WILLIAM SHAKESPEARE, *TWELFTH NIGHT*

LONDON – DECEMBER 1940

Mike stared at Polly, stunned, as she sat there on the steps of the Albert Memorial. '*You* were the historian we were talking about that day in Oxford?' he said angrily. 'The one we couldn't believe Mr Dunworthy would let do something so dangerous?'

Polly nodded.

'Which means your deadline's *not* April second, 1945. It's what? When did the V-1 attacks start?'

'A week after D-Day.'

'A week – in 1944?'

'Yes. June thirteenth.'

'Jesus.' VE Day had been bad enough, but D-Day was only three and a half years away, and if the slippage had increased enough for Dunworthy to be cancelling drops right and left ... 'Why didn't Dunworthy cancel your assignment if you had a deadline?' he asked.

'I don't know,' Polly said.

'But if he didn't, then perhaps he was changing the order for some other reason,' Eileen suggested. 'Because he was putting the less dangerous ones first or something. The Reign of Terror was more dangerous than the storming of the Bastille, wasn't it? And Pearl Harbor was more dangerous than—'

She stopped, flustered, and looked down at Mike's foot.

'It would have been more dangerous,' Mike said, 'if I'd gone to Dover like I was supposed to. Eileen's right, Polly. The assignments could have been switched for lots of reasons. And the fact that they didn't cancel yours is a good sign Oxford doesn't think you're in danger.'

'And her seeing me at VE Day might be a good sign, too. I could have gone there after we got back to Oxford. Because Mr Dunworthy felt badly about our having been trapped. He knows I've always wanted to go to VE Day.'

You may get your wish, Mike thought grimly.

He looked at Polly, who hadn't said anything. Her expression was guarded, wary, as if there was still something she hadn't told them, and he thought about her saying, 'You asked me if I'd been to Bletchley Park.' Could she still be lying to them and carefully answering exactly what they asked and nothing else?

'Is the V-1 assignment your only one to World War II?' he asked, and Eileen looked, horrified, at him and then Polly.

'Is it?' he pressed her. 'Or did *you* go to Pearl Harbor? Or the end of the Blitz?' he asked, remembering she'd known all about those attacks, too.

'No,' she said, and looked like she was telling the truth. But then he'd thought she was telling the truth before.

'You weren't here in World War II on any other assignment besides this one and the V-1s and V-2s?'

'No.'

Thank God, he thought, but the V-1s assignment was bad enough. Denys Atherton wouldn't be here till March of 1944, which was cutting it awfully close.

If he'd come through. And to get to him, they had to survive the next three years and the rest of the Blitz, and in another few weeks they wouldn't know when or where the bombs were going to be. And if the increase in slippage was bad enough for Dunworthy to have switched drops that were years apart, there might not be anything they could do till well after Polly …

But they didn't *know* the increase was that big. And even if it was, the increase might only be on a few drops. And there might be some other reason Phipps hadn't come. Bletchley Park was still a divergence point, and, for all they knew, so were these months of the Blitz. And the soldiers at Dunkirk had thought they were licked, and look how that had turned out.

'Don't worry, Polly,' he said, 'we'll get you out of here. We've got three years to figure out something. And there's still Denys Atherton.'

'And Historian X,' Eileen said. 'The historian who's here till the eighteenth.'

He'd hoped they'd forgotten about that. 'Afraid not,' he said.

'Why not?' Eileen said.

'Because Historian X was Gerald,' Polly said, 'wasn't it, Mike?'

'Yes.' He told them about the date on the letter. 'And there was a train ticket to Oxford for December eighteenth, and his departure letter was postmarked the sixteenth.'

'Oh dear,' Eileen said.

'But we still have the drop in St John's Wood,' Mike said. 'And on my way here, I saw hoardings have gone up on the site in front of your drop, Polly.'

'So if the drop wouldn't open because people could see into it,' Eileen said eagerly, 'it may begin working again.'

'Exactly,' Mike said. He stood up. 'What say we get out of here and give the Luftwaffe a clear shot at this atrocity?' he suggested, looking around at the Albert Memorial statuary. 'I'll take you two to lunch and we'll plan our strategy for finding X and for finding the St John's Wood drop. Eileen, did you hear from Lady Caroline?'

'Yes, but not from the officer at the manor.'

'Write to them again, and write to your vicar and see what you can find out about the training school. Maybe they've moved it. And I'll write to my barmaid and see if they've taken the beach defences down. You said the invasion had been called off, didn't you, Polly?'

'Yes, but that doesn't mean they'll take the defences down.'

'You don't know that,' Eileen said. 'Or maybe Mike's barmaid's written to say the retrieval team's been there, and all our problems will be solved.'

'Eileen's right. We'll stop by Mrs Leary's on our way to lunch and pick up my mail. Come on,' he said, pulling Polly and then Eileen to their feet and walking them back to Mrs Leary's.When they arrived, Eileen said, 'While you're collecting your post, I'll go and see if we've had any.'

'It's Sunday,' Polly said. 'There's no post on Sunday.'

'But the retrieval team may have rung up,' she said, and hurried off towards Mrs Rickett's.

Mike watched her till she rounded the corner and then turned to Polly. 'You said you saw Eileen on VE Day. Was she the only person you saw?'

'What do you mean? There were thousands of people in Trafalgar Square that night—'

'Was I one of them?' If she had seen him, it *would* be proof they hadn't got out, that they'd still been there when Polly's deadline passed.

'No,' Polly said. 'I didn't see you.'

'Did you see something else, something that made you think she was there because we didn't get out?'

'No, nothing except that our drops won't open and Mr Dunworthy was worried about a slippage increase and was changing assignments to chronological—'

'But he didn't change yours. And the fact that you didn't see me there with Eileen means she's right. She was there on a later assignment. Otherwise, I'd have been there with her. How did she look? Excited? Sad?'

'Not sad,' Polly said, frowning as if trying to remember. 'Optimistic,' she said finally.

He looked hard at her, trying to decide if she was still keeping something from him. 'You're sure it was Eileen? That it wasn't just somebody who looked like her?'

'No, I'm certain it was her.'

'Then why, when I left for Bletchley Park, were you so worried about Marjorie?'

'Because I *did* change what happened. And a nurse is in a position to save who knows how many lives—'

'But whatever she does, we know it can't lose the war. You may have gone to VE Day before all this other stuff happened, but Eileen didn't. She hasn't gone yet. She went *after* I saved Hardy and after Marjorie was dug out of the rubble.'

'I hadn't thought of that,' Polly said.

'Well, it's true. Either we didn't alter events, or there was no lasting harm done,' Mike said. 'I wish you'd told me all this before I left for Bletchley Park. I got worried after that encounter with Turing.'

'Turing? Alan Turing?' Polly cried. 'What encounter?'

'He nearly ran me down with his bicycle,' Mike said. 'He swerved at the last minute and crashed into a lamppost. He wasn't hurt and neither was his bike, but when I found out it was him, it scared me to death. But thank God it didn't do any damage. I'll be right back.'

He ran inside to ask Mrs Leary if he'd received anything while he was gone and then came back out. 'No letter and no messages,' he said. 'Where's Eileen? Isn't she back?'

'No, she must have got caught by Miss Laburnum. She's doing the costumes for the play. We'd best go rescue her.'

But as they came round the corner they saw Eileen running towards them, waving a letter.

'I thought you said there wasn't any mail delivery on Sunday,' Mike said to Polly.

'You've had a letter from Daphne,' Eileen called excitedly, running up. 'It came yesterday, but since it was addressed to you, Mrs Rickett thought it had been sent to the wrong address and she was planning to send it back. Thank goodness I saw it before she did.'

She handed it to Mike. He opened the letter and then frowned. 'What's wrong?' she asked.

'The letter's dated a week ago. She must have forgotten to mail it.' He began reading the letter. 'She also misplaced the other address I gave her. That's why she sent it to Mrs Rickett's. And—'

He stopped short, reading silently, then said, 'Oh my God!'

'What?' Eileen and Polly said in unison.

'I don't believe this. Listen to this,' he said excitedly, '"You said to tell you if anyone came round asking after you. Two men came in to the Crown and Anchor last night, asking all sorts of questions. They said they were friends of yours and that they needed to get in touch with you and did I know where you were."' He looked up at Eileen. 'Christ, you were right. The retrieval team's here. They've been here for over a week.'

'I told you they'd find us,' Eileen said smugly. 'Did she tell them where you were?'

Obviously not, or they'd have been here by now.

'No,' he said, 'I should leave tonight for Dover.'

'I think we should go with you,' Eileen said, 'or at least Polly should. She's the one it's the most urgent to get out.'

He shook his head. 'I'm going to have to get the information out of Daphne, and she wouldn't appreciate my showing up with another woman.'

'She wouldn't need to go with you to the pub,' Eileen argued. 'She could stay at the inn or—'

'The inn and the pub are one and the same,' he said, 'and even if they weren't, Saltram-on-Sea's a tiny village. Daphne'd know about Polly within five minutes of her arrival. Besides, I have no idea how I'm going to get there.'

He explained about the bus service having been discontinued and the petrol rationing making it hard to get hold of a car. 'I'll probably have to hitchhike, and it could take two or three days.

Plus, it's a restricted area. I've got a press pass, but neither of you do.'

Polly agreed. 'The trains will be jammed with Christmas travellers and soldiers home on leave. Perhaps instead of going there, you should write to Daphne. It might be quicker.'

'Unless the retrieval team's there in Saltram-on-Sea. Or unless she doesn't know where they are. I may have to track them down after I've talked to her. I'll phone you as soon as I've found them.'

'But if they're in Saltram-on-Sea, how will we get there?' Eileen asked worriedly. 'You said it was a restricted area.'

'We'll cross that bridge when we come to it,' Mike said.

Eileen was still looking anxious.

'Don't worry. If the retrieval team's here, they can go back through to Oxford and get you all the passes and papers you need. Or they may decide it's easier to set up another drop closer to London. Look, I'll call you as soon as I know what the plan is.'

'How much money do you think you'll need?' Polly asked, digging in her shoulder bag. 'Never mind. Take this.' She handed him some money.

'What about you two?' he asked.

'I've kept back enough for our tube fares, and we'll get paid the day after tomorrow.'

She handed him a handwritten list. 'Here are the raids on London and the southeast for the next week. The Luftwaffe was concentrating mostly on the Midlands and the ports in mid-December, so it's not a very long list and I'm sorry I don't know more about the raids on southeastern England. I didn't have those implanted. Oh, and when you get to Dover, you need to be especially careful. It was under bombardment for nearly the entire war. The list I made for you only goes to the twentieth. If you think you'll be gone longer than—'

He shook his head, folded up the paper, and put it in his pocket. 'We'll be back in Oxford long before that.'

'Oh! Wouldn't it be heaven if we were home by Christmas?'
Eileen said rapturously.

'It would,' Mike said, 'but first I've got to get to Saltram-on-
Sea, which means I've got to get to Victoria Station before the
Underground shuts down. Are there any raids tonight, Polly?'

'Yes,' she said, 'but not till 10:45.'

'Then if I want to be out of London before they start, I'd
better get going.'

'Do you want us to go with you to Victoria?' Polly asked.

'No, you need to be here where the retrieval team can find
you, in case they gave up on me. Is your play group still putting
on *The Admirable Crichton*?'

'No, now we're in rehearsals for *A Christmas Carol*.'

'You'd better tell them you can't do it,' he said.

He gave both of them a peck on the cheek, said, 'I'll call as
soon as I know anything,' and took off. If he could get an express
to Dover, he could be there by midnight and on the main road to
Saltram-on-Sea by dawn and maybe be able to hitch a ride with
a farmer heading up the coast early.

But Polly had been right. The trains were jammed, and as the
agent informed him when he bought his ticket, military personnel were being given first priority.

'I'm willing to stand in the corridor,' Mike said.

'First priority *is* standing in the corridor,' the ticket agent
said. 'I can get you out on the 2:14 Tuesday.'

'*Tuesday?*'

'Sorry, sir. It's the best I can do. The holidays, you know.
And the war, of course.'

Of course. 'You don't have anything sooner than Tuesday?'

'No, sir. I can get you on the 6:05 to Canterbury tomorrow.
You might be able to get a train to Dover from there.' And after
Mike had attempted unsuccessfully to buy a ticket off several
people in the queue for the 9:38 to Dover, that was what he
opted for, a move he regretted almost immediately.

Since the train went before the tube began running in the

morning, he couldn't go back to Notting Hill Gate to spend the night, and there wasn't anywhere in Victoria to sleep. He had to sit up all night on an unbelievably uncomfortable wooden bench.

And once he got on the train, he was even sorrier. Not only did it turn out to be a local, and even more packed than the *Lady Jane* had been on the way back from Dunkirk, but less than five miles out of London it was shunted onto a siding while three troop trains and a freight train loaded with military equipment passed.

After nearly an hour and a half, the train started up again, went half a mile and stopped again, this time for no reason at all. 'Air raid,' a soldier close to the window said, looking out. 'I hope the jerries aren't out hunting trains today. We're sitting ducks, aren't we?' after which everyone spent the next few minutes looking up at the ceiling and listening for the deadly hum of approaching He111s.

'I'd rather be back on the front line than here,' another soldier said after a few minutes. 'Waiting about for the blow to fall, and not a bloody thing you can do about it.'

Like Polly, Mike thought. It must have been hell for her when she realised her drop wouldn't open, and worse keeping it to herself these last weeks while he and Eileen talked about options she knew wouldn't work. But the worst must have been not being able to *do* anything about it. Lying there in the hospital worrying about what had happened to the retrieval team and whether he'd messed things up by saving Hardy had been bad enough. He couldn't imagine what it would have been like if he'd already been to Pearl Harbor, even if it was a year from now, or, like the day the V-1s started, three and a half years off. It didn't matter *when* it was. It was still heading straight at you. Like the German Army getting closer and closer to Dunkirk, and you sitting there helplessly on the beach, listening to the guns in the distance, and hoping to God a ship would show up and take you off before the Germans got there, and nothing for you to do in the meantime but wait.

Which is what all three of them would have been doing right now if he hadn't got Daphne's letter. Thank God it had come when it did. He couldn't have stood just sitting there cooling his heels. It was a hell of a lot easier to fire a machine gun at the Zeroes or hand up ammunition than to just sit there and be shot at, a hell of a lot easier to take a leaky launch over to Dunkirk than to sit on a beach waiting for the Germans to come.

Or the Japanese. He'd assumed, when he found out Gerald hadn't come through, that his roommate Charles hadn't either, but what if he had? What if he was in Singapore, and *his* drop wouldn't open, and the Japanese would be there any minute, and he didn't dare leave Singapore for fear he'd miss the retrieval team?

Charles won't be in Singapore, Mike told himself, *because as soon as I find them, I'll tell them they've got to pull him out. I'll go with them to get him if I have to.*

But that wouldn't take anywhere near as much courage as Charles having to sit there at the country club in his dinner clothes and listen to radio bulletins describing the Japanese Army's approach.

When he'd read that book Mrs Ives had given him in the hospital, he'd thought Shackleton was the hero, taking off in a tiny boat and braving Antarctic seas to bring help, but now he wondered if it hadn't taken more courage to stay on that barren island and watch the boat disappear, and then wait as weeks and months went by, with no guarantee that anybody was ever coming, while their feet froze and the food ran out and the weather got worse and worse.

Back when he'd been scanning the newspapers, looking for the names of airfields, there'd been a story about an old woman being dug out of the wreckage of what had been her house and the rescue crew asking her if her husband was under there with her. 'No, the bloody coward's at the front!' she'd said indignantly.

He'd laughed when he read it, but now he wasn't so sure it had been a joke. Maybe England *was* the front, and the real heroes were the Londoners sitting in those tube stations night after night, waiting to be blown to smithereens. And Fordham, lying there in the hospital in traction. And everyone on this train, waiting patiently for it to begin moving again, not giving way to panic or the impulse to call Hitler and surrender just to get it over with. He was going to have to rethink the whole concept of heroism when he got back to Oxford.

If he got back to Oxford. At this rate, he wasn't sure he'd even make it to Canterbury, let alone Saltram-on-Sea.

He did, but it took him two more days of delayed departures, waits on sidings and fruitless trips to garages. He ended up hitching rides in a half-track, a sidecar and a lorry full of turnips.

The lorry was driven by a pretty land girl who'd grown up in Chelsea and was now slopping hogs and milking cows on a farm a few miles west of Saltram-on-Sea.

'The work ruins your hands,' she said when he asked her how she liked it, 'and I despise getting up before dawn and smelling of manure, but if I didn't have something to do, I'd go mad with worry. My husband's serving in the North Atlantic, escorting convoys, and sometimes I don't hear from him for weeks at a time. And I feel as though I'm contributing something.'

She smiled at him. 'There are four of us girls, and we all get along famously, so that helps, and Mr Powney's not nearly so gruff as some of the other farmers round here.'

'Wait, you work for Mr Powney?'

'Yes. Why?'

'I can't believe it,' he said, laughing. 'Does he have a bull?'

'Yes, why? Have you heard of it? It hasn't killed anyone, has it?'

'Not that I know of.'

'Well, I wouldn't be surprised if it had. It's the worst, most ill-tempered bull in England. How do you know of it?'

He explained about having waited around for Mr Powney to

253

come back from buying it so he could get a ride. 'And I finally have.'

'Well, I wouldn't be too glad about that just yet, if I were you,' she said. 'This lorry has the worst tyres in England.'

She wasn't exaggerating. They had two flats between Dover and Folkestone, and there was no spare. They had to take the tyre off both times and patch it, the second time in driving sleet, and then reinflate it with a bicycle pump.

It was half past three and beginning to grow dark before they came within sight of Saltram-on-Sea. He could see the gun emplacement, flanked now by row after bristling row of concrete tank traps and sharpened stakes.

There was barbed wire all along the top of the cliff, and signs warning, *Danger – This Area Mined*. He wondered what the retrieval team had thought when they'd seen all that.

'Do you mind if I drop you at the crossroads?' the land girl, whose name was Nora, asked him. 'I want to get home before dark.'

'No, that's fine,' he told her, but was sorry from the moment she let him out. The wind coming off the Channel was bitter and the sleet was turning to snow.

Damn it, the retrieval team had better be here after all this, he thought, limping down into the village, his head bent against the wind, his coat collar pulled up around his neck. And the drop they'd come through had better be here, too.

At least Daphne will be, he thought, going into the inn, but she wasn't behind the bar. Her father was.

'I'm looking for Daphne,' Mike said.

'You're that American reporter, aren't you?' her father said. 'The one who went to Dunkirk with the Commander?' and when Mike nodded, 'Sorry, lad. You're too late.'

'Too late?'

'Aye, lad,' he said. 'She's already married.'

'I pray you tell me, hath anybody enquir'd for me here today?'

WILLIAM SHAKESPEARE *MEASURE FOR MEASURE*

SALTRAM-ON-SEA – 18 DECEMBER 1940

'**D**aphne's *married*?' Mike said, clutching the edge of the pub's counter.

'Aye,' her father said, placidly towelling a glass dry. 'To one of the lads what was putting in the beach defences.'

I obviously didn't need to worry about accidentally breaking her heart and keeping her from marrying anybody else, Mike thought.

'Beach defences,' the pipe-smoking fisherman he'd talked to on the quay snorted. 'Didn't know much about defences, if you ask me. Couldn't defend himself against your Daphne, could he now?' He nudged Mike. 'Looks like you couldn't either, eh, lad?'

There was general laughter, under cover of which Mike asked, 'Can't you tell me where I can find her?'

Daphne's father frowned. 'I don't know as that's a good idea, lad. She's Mrs Rob Butcher, and there's nowt you can do about it.'

'I don't want to,' Mike said.

Her father scowled.

'I mean, I don't want to make trouble. I just need to talk to her about something. She wrote me a letter – about some men who were asking for me – and I need to ask her if she knows where I can get in touch with them. Or maybe you can help me. Daphne said they came in last month—'

Her father shook his head. 'I know nowt about any men, and as for Daphne, she's in Manchester. Her husband was sent there, and she went with him.'

Manchester? That was more than two hundred miles from Saltram-on-Sea. It would take him at least two days to get there by train. If he could even get on one. They'd be jammed with soldiers going home on leave for Christmas.

'I don't suppose you have a phone number where she can be reached?' Mike asked. 'Or an address?'

'You're not thinkin' of goin' there to make mischief, are you?'

'No, I just want to write to her,' Mike lied, hoping the address wouldn't be a post office box.

It wasn't. It was an address on King Street. 'Though I had a letter from her yesterday saying their lodgings were very unsatisfactory,' Daphne's father told him, 'and they were hopin' to find somethin' better.'

Let's hope they didn't, Mike thought, writing the address down.

'If anyone comes in asking for me, tell them I can be reached here,' he said, giving him Mrs Rickett's address and telephone number. He congratulated him on his daughter's marriage, then set out for Manchester.

It didn't take two days. It took nearly four of fully-booked trains, delayed departures, missed connections, and compartments crammed full not only of soldiers but of civilians with parcels, plum puddings and, on one leg of the journey, an enormous unplucked Christmas goose. Apparently no one in England was obeying the government order posted in every station to 'avoid unnecessary travel'.

He didn't reach Manchester till late afternoon on December twenty-second – by which time Daphne and her new husband had found 'something better'. He limped all the way to King Street, only to be sent back across town to Whitworth Street. And then the landlady, who looked exactly like Mrs Rickett, wasn't sure Daphne was in. 'I'll go and see,' she said, and left him standing at the door.

Please let her be in, he thought, leaning against the doorjamb to take the weight off his aching foot.

She was. She came halfway down the stairs and stopped, just like she had that first day in Saltram-on-Sea. 'Why, Mike,' she said, her eyes widening, 'I never expected to see you in Manchester. Whatever are you doing here?'

'I came to find you, to ask you—'

'But didn't Dad *tell* you? Oh dear, this is dreadful! I didn't mean for you to find out like this! You're a lovely boy, and now you've come all this way. But the thing is, I was married last week.'

'I know. Your father told me,' he said, trying to get the right mixture of heartbreak and resignation into his voice. 'I really came about your letter.'

'My letter?' she said, bewildered. 'But I didn't ... I thought about writing and telling you about Rob, but I didn't know where you were or what you were doing, and I thought if you were off covering the war, it would be unkind ...'

'No, the letter you wrote me about the men who came in asking about me,' he said, pulling it out of his coat. 'There was a mix-up with the mail, and I just got it this week.'

'Oh,' she said, sounding vaguely disappointed.

'I went to Saltram-on-Sea to talk to you about it, and your father told me you'd gone to Manchester and that you'd got married. Congratulations to both of you. Your husband's a very lucky man.'

'Oh, but I'm the lucky one,' she said, blushing. 'Rob's wonderful, so kind and brave. He's working on repairing the docks just now, but he's put in for combat duty. He's determined to do his bit for England. I said, "You *are* doing your bit. You're seeing to it England doesn't starve, aren't you? It may not *look* as grandly heroic as shooting Germans or sinking U-boats, but—"'

And if he didn't cut her off, he'd be here all night. 'If I could just ask you a couple of questions?'

'Oh, of course. Where are my manners, keeping you standing in the door like that? Come through to the parlour. Would you like some tea?'

He'd love some tea – he hadn't had anything to eat since breakfast – and he'd love to take the weight off his foot, but he didn't want to do anything to encourage her to talk longer than she already was. 'No, thanks, I have a train to catch. You said these two men came into the pub asking for me.'

Daphne nodded. 'Twice. The first time they asked everyone in the pub if they knew a war correspondent named Mike Davis, and Mr Tompkins said *I* did, and they asked me if I knew how they could get in touch with you.'

'And did you tell them?'

'No. I remembered what you said about letting you know straightaway if anyone came round asking for you. That's why I wrote to you instead of giving them your address.'

Mike groaned inwardly. 'Did they say why they were trying to get in touch with me?'

'No, they said it was something to do with the war, and that it was very important that they contact you, but they didn't say what it was.'

'Did they tell you their names?'

'Yes. Mr Watson and Mr …' She frowned and bit her lip. '… I can't remember, it began with an H, like Hawes or …'

'Mr Holmes?'

'Yes, that was it. Mr Watson and Mr Holmes.'

That cinched it. It was the retrieval team.

'They knew all about you having been at Dunkirk and in hospital,' Daphne said. 'They said one of the nurses told them you might have gone to Saltram-on-Sea.'

Which meant they'd traced him as far as Orpington, but they

obviously hadn't talked to Sister Carmody or she'd have told them he was in London. 'What did they look like?' he asked. 'Were they in uniform?'

'No. Civilian clothes. Very posh, and very posh accents, and they were both *terribly* handsome' – she cocked her head flirtatiously – 'though not so handsome as you, speaking quite impartially. I'm a married woman, you know.'

Yes, I know. 'You said they came in twice,' he said, trying to get her back to the subject at hand. 'The same day?'

'No, they came in on, let me see, when was it? The first Saturday in December, I think.'

When he was in Oxford, trying to find out whether Gerald Phipps had been there.

'And then they came in again the next night and that was when Rob got jealous and told me to stop flirting with them, and I said, "I wasn't flirting, and even if I was, you've got no call to tell me not to, Rob Butcher. I'm not your wife," and he said, "I wish you were," and the next thing you know he's been to Dover and got a special licence so the vicar could marry us straightaway. Dad wanted us to wait, but Rob said no, who knew what might happen tomorrow or how much time we might have together, and then he found out he was being sent here, and—'

'When the men came the second time,' Mike finally managed to get in, 'what did they say?'

'They said if I *did* hear from you, to contact them immediately, and they wrote down their address for me. I meant to send it on to you, but then in all the excitement of the wedding and all, I forgot. Oh, it was a lovely wedding. Rob looked terribly handsome in his uniform, and the church was all decorated with holly and—'

'Do you remember the address?'

'No—'

Of course not.

'—but I've got it. I put it' she frowned in consternation – 'now, where *did* I put it?'

Please don't say you stuck it behind the bar, and now I'll have to trudge all the way back across the country to Saltram-on-Sea for it, Mike thought.

'I put it ... oh, I know,' she said. 'I put it in my vanity case so I wouldn't go off without it. It's upstairs. Hang on.' She started up and then turned to look at him over the railing. 'You're not in any trouble, are you?'

Not any more, he thought.

'I mean, the authorities aren't after you or anything?' he asked, concerned.

'No. I think I know who the men were. They're a couple of guys who were on the boat with me coming back from Dunkirk. Reporters.'

'Oh, I wish I'd known they'd been at Dunkirk. I could have asked them about the Commander and Jonathan. They might know what happened to them.'

'I'll ask them when I see them,' Mike lied. 'You were going to go and get the address?'

'Oh yes,' she said, and pattered up the stairs, turning as she ran to give Mike one of those over-the-shoulder smiles that had no doubt snared her new husband. 'I'll only be a moment.'

She was as good as her word, reappearing almost immediately with a sheet of lined paper torn from a notebook like the one he himself carried. 'Here it is,' she said, handing it to him.

He looked down at the address. It was in Edgebourne, Kent. That must be where their drop was.

'It's near Hawkhurst,' Daphne said.

Hawkhurst. Well, he wouldn't have to go all the way back to Saltram-on-Sea, but almost. He'd have to make that whole long, uncomfortable trip back in a packed train.

At least it wasn't on the coast, so he wouldn't have to deal with guards and checkpoints. But he was afraid it wasn't big enough to have a railroad station. But it didn't matter. Nothing mattered. He felt all the near-panic of the last six months melt away. The retrieval team was here, and they were going home.

'Thank you,' he said, and kissed Daphne impulsively on the cheek. 'You're wonderful.'

'Now, then,' she said, blushing, 'you mustn't do that sort of thing, you know. I'm a married woman. Rob—'

'Is a very lucky guy.' *And so am I. You have just saved my life. All our lives.* 'Listen,' he said. 'Be careful. When the sirens go, don't be a hero. Get yourself to the shelter. I don't want anything to happen to you.'

'Oh dear, I *did* break your heart, didn't I?' She smiled sympathetically at him. 'You mustn't worry. You'll meet someone, and you'll be just as happy as Rob and I are. You'll see; it will all work out for the best. Rob says—'

The sirens went, and Mike used them as an excuse to leave. 'Remember what I said,' he told her, 'You get to that shelter.' And he limped off before she could tell him what Rob had said and what her wedding dress had looked like and how he'd find a nice girl.

I already have a nice girl, he thought. *Two of them.*

Who he needed to call and tell the good news to as soon as he got to the station. He hadn't wanted to call them before for fear he wouldn't be able to find Daphne or for fear she wouldn't have the retrieval team's address, but now they needed to quit their jobs and get ready to go. And he needed to ask Polly if Manchester had been bombed on the twentieth and how badly.

In spite of the sirens having gone nearly fifteen minutes before, he still didn't hear any planes. Manchester must have a longer warning period than London, since they were further north and west. He didn't hear any guns either, and the only searchlights were out towards the docks. But they gave off enough light to see his way by.

He hobbled on towards the railway station, cursing his limp. *Which I won't have in a few more days,* he thought. *I'll have a brand-new foot, and Polly won't have to worry about still being here on her deadline, and Eileen won't ever have to suffer through another raid.*

A man hurried past him, carrying a spray of holly.

We'll be home for Christmas, Mike thought. He pushed through the station door and headed for the line of red telephone boxes along the far wall to call Polly and Eileen. Would it be better for him to go back to London and get them, and the three of them go to Edgebourne together, or should he have them meet him there? That would be faster, and it would mean Eileen and Polly were safely out of London sooner. But if something went wrong and they got separated—

Maybe he'd better go and get them. That way they'd all be together and—

What am I talking about? he thought. *All I have to do is get to Edgebourne and tell them where Polly and Eileen are, and they can have another team go and get them. Tonight if they want. Or the night I left for Saltram-on-Sea.* This was time travel. Eileen and Polly were probably already in Oxford. In which case all he needed to do was get back to Kent and tell the retrieval team where they were the day he'd left.

He looked up at the departures board. There was an express leaving for Reading in six minutes. He limped over to the ticket counter. 'One way to Reading on the 6:05,' he said.

The ticket agent shook his head.

'Or on the next train east I can get a space on.'

'No departures during a raid,' the agent said, and pointed up at the high ceiling, where a sudden buzz of planes was becoming a dull roar. 'You're not going anywhere tonight, mate. I'd find a shelter if I were you.'

'Happy Blitzmas!'

CHRISTMAS CARD 1940

LONDON – DECEMBER 1940

Three nights after Mike left for Saltram-on-Sea, Eileen asked anxiously, 'Shouldn't we have heard from him by now?'

Yes, Polly thought. They were at Mrs Rickett's. The sirens hadn't gone and the rehearsal for *A Christmas Carol* didn't begin till eight, so Eileen had insisted on their waiting till the last moment to leave for Notting Hill Gate, hoping Mike would phone, but he hadn't.

'I doubt if he'll phone before next week,' Polly said reassuringly.

'Next *week*?'

'Yes – he may not even be there yet, given all the wartime travel delays and no bus service from Dover. And the retrieval team may not be in Saltram-on-Sea. They may be in Folkestone or Ramsgate, or they may have gone off looking for Mike after they spoke to Daphne—'

'In which case it might take Mike *days* to locate them,' Eileen said, sounding relieved.

'Exactly,' Polly said, not mentioning that it didn't matter how long it took Mike to contact the team because this was time travel. If he did find them, all he needed to do was tell them where she and Eileen were and a second team could have

263

been at Mrs Rickett's immediately after Mike left for Victoria Station. Which meant either he hadn't found them, or something had happened to him, and she had no intention of telling Eileen that. It would only frighten her, and Polly was already frightened enough for both of them – correction, for all three of them.

The letter from Daphne combined with Eileen having told him she'd witnessed the end of the war seemed to have convinced him they hadn't altered the future. He'd even brushed off his collision with Alan Turing.

But he didn't know about Eileen's withholding the *City of Benares* letter from Alf and Binnie Hodbin's mother, or about Eileen's having given Binnie aspirin when she had the measles.

Mike had said Turing hadn't been injured by the collision, but he wouldn't have had to be. This was Alan Turing, the man who was behind Bletchley Park's success, and he still hadn't cracked the naval Enigma code. What if Mike's colliding with him had interrupted his train of thought at a critical moment, and he didn't crack the code? Or what if Mike had done something else while he was in Bletchley that – combined with Hardy's rescue and what she and Eileen had done – would tip the balance of the war later on? Or what if he'd done something now in Saltram-on-Sea?

I should have warned him, she thought. *I should have told him about the* City of Benares *and about the possible discrepancies.* But she wasn't certain they *were* discrepancies. And he'd been so distraught when she told him about her deadline, and then, after he'd got the letter from Daphne, so certain the retrieval team had come.

And if they have, then there's no reason to worry him with any of this. 'Sufficient unto the day is the evil thereof.'

But what if they haven't?

'You *are* worried, aren't you?' Eileen asked anxiously. 'About Mike's not phoning.'

'No,' Polly said firmly. 'Remember, he said the phone at the

Crown and Anchor wasn't at all private. He may have to wait till he arrives back in Dover to find one that is. Or the telephone lines may be out.'

From the shelling Dover is taking every night, Polly thought, wishing Mike would find a way to phone so she could tell him about the shelling and the upcoming raids. He'd be all right for the next few days – the raids would all be in the Midlands or the west: Liverpool on the twentieth, Plymouth on the twenty-first, and Manchester the night after that. But on the twenty-fourth Dover would undergo a major shelling, and two trains in Kent would be machine-gunned from the air.

They waited another quarter of an hour, hoping he'd phone. 'It's twenty to,' Polly said finally. 'We really must leave, or I'll be late for rehearsal.'

'All right,' Eileen said reluctantly. 'Wait, was that the phone? It's Mike. I *knew* it!' She pelted down the stairs to answer it.

It was Mrs Rickett's sister, and it was clear they intended to talk for some time. 'She's phoned twice in the past three days. Mike's very probably phoned already and couldn't get through,' Eileen said as they walked over to Notting Hill Gate. She paused. 'You knew Lady Caroline, didn't you? When you were in Dulwich.' And when Polly looked at her in surprise, 'The day I got the letter from the vicar about Lord Denewell, you said, "Lady Caroline is Lady *Denewell*?"'

And what else has she worked out? Polly wondered.

'Yes,' she said, 'she was my commanding officer.'

Eileen nodded as if she already knew that. 'And she made you do all the work.'

'No. She was a wonderful commanding officer, hardworking, always thinking of her girls, determined to get us the supplies we needed. That's why I was so surprised. from what you'd told me about her—'

'I think it must have been because of losing her husband *and* her son. War changes people,' Eileen said thoughtfully. 'In Mrs Bascombe's last letter, she said Una's become quite a good driver in the ATF. You don't suppose the war will improve Alf and Binnie Hodbin, do you?'

'I very much doubt it.'

'So do I,' Eileen said as they turned onto Kensington Church Street. 'Have you told the troupe that you may not be here for the performance of *A Christmas Carol*, and that they need to arrange for an understudy?'

'Not yet,' Polly said, wishing she could believe Mike had simply been delayed and that the retrieval team would be waiting for them when they arrived at the tube station, or that when Mrs Rickett came, she'd tell them Mike had phoned after she'd rung off.

She didn't, and there was no one at the tube station or at Townsend Brothers the next morning. 'He'll phone today, I know it,' Eileen said confidently, going up to the book department. 'I'll see you at lunch.'

But there was no time for lunch. There were Christmas decorations to put up – evergreen and cellophane garlands and paper bells (the aluminium foil ones had gone to Lord Beaverbrook's Spitfire drive) and banners reading, 'There'll Always Be A Christmas' – and there was a horde of customers to contend with.

'The only good thing,' Polly told Eileen when they met after work,' is that we've sold so many gifts we've run completely out of brown paper.'

But when she arrived at Townsend Brothers the next day there was a large stack of Christmas paper on her counter. 'Miss Snelgrove found it in the storeroom,' Doreen said. 'From Christmas two years ago. Wasn't that lucky?'

Polly stared hopelessly at the holly-sprigged sheets. 'Haven't we a duty to turn it in to the War Ministry for the war effort, to make stuffing for gun casings or something?' she asked.

Miss Snelgrove glared at her. 'We have a duty to our customers to make this difficult Christmas as happy as possible.'

What about my *Christmas?* Polly thought.

She attempted to convince her customers it was their patriotic duty to take their purchases home unwrapped, but to no avail. It was the only wrapping paper they were likely to get their hands on for the duration, and they didn't intend to pass up the chance. Some of them even bought things just to obtain the paper, as witness all the bilious lavender-pink stockings she sold over the next few days. She spent nearly all her time struggling with knots and corners and the rest of it struggling to learn her lines for *A Christmas Carol*.

She had been wrong about the play. The female roles *were* small, but there were a great many of them, and Polly found herself playing not only Scrooge's lost love, Belle, but also the eldest Cratchit daughter, one of the businessmen soliciting a charitable donation from Scrooge (in a false moustache and sideburns), the boy sent to buy the turkey (in a cap and knee pants) and the Ghost of Christmas Yet to Come.

How appropriate, she thought. She hadn't realised till now that the play was about time travel, and that Scrooge was a sort of historian, journeying to the past and then back to the future.

And he had altered events. He'd given Bob Cratchit a rise, he'd improved the lot of the poor, he'd saved Tiny Tim's life. But in *A Christmas Carol*, there wasn't the possibility that what he'd done would have a bad effect. In Dickens good intentions always resulted in good outcomes. And none of his characters had deadlines.

They can occupy the same time twice, Polly thought enviously, watching the rector playing the young Scrooge and Sir Godfrey playing the elder in the same scene.

When Sir Godfrey wasn't onstage, he was berating Miss Laburnum for her failure to secure a turkey for the Christmas-morning scene.

'There are simply none to be had, Sir Godfrey,' she said, 'the war you know.'

Or he was shouting at Viv (Scrooge's nephew's wife) and Mr

Simms (the ghost of Marley) for their inability to learn their lines.

'I suppose you don't know your lines for the tombstone scene either, Viola,' he growled at Polly when she missed a cue.

'I haven't any lines,' Polly reminded him. 'All I do is point at Scrooge's grave.'

'Bah, humbug!' he said, bellowed at Tiny Tim (Trot) to get her cane out of the way, and started them through the Scrooge-confronts-his-own-death scene. 'Before I draw nearer to that stone to which you point,' he said, quailing from the cardboard tombstone, 'answer me one question. Are these the shadows of the things that will be, or are they shadows of things that may be only?'

I don't know, Polly thought.

The war still seemed to be on track. Liverpool, Plymouth and Manchester had been bombed, Victoria Station had been hit, and the British had counterattacked the Italian forces in North Africa, all on schedule.

But would things stay that way? Or would Marjorie – who'd sent Polly a card from Norwich, where she was doing her training, saying, 'Wishing you anything but a Jerry Christmas!' save the life of someone who would make a decisive error at El Alamein or on HMS *Dorsetshire?*

'Spirit!' Sir Godfrey shouted. 'Lady Mary! Viola! Kindly remember this is a holiday play, and you are the Ghost of Christmas Yet to Come, not Dark Unyielding Doom. I realise the thought of performing in Piccadilly Circus is grim, but if you look like that during the performance, you'll terrify the children. This is a *comedy*, not a tragedy.'

I haven't seen any proof of that, Polly thought. But she attempted – both onstage and off – to put on a face more in keeping with the season. Like everyone else was doing, in spite of their facing a future that was just as uncertain as hers and civilian casualties that were mounting daily. The contemps entered wholeheartedly into the Christmas spirit, pinning decorations to their blackout curtains and greeting one other gaily with 'Happy Christmas!'

And preparing presents to give each other. 'I went in to Miss Laburnum's room just now to borrow her iron,' Eileen reported, 'and caught her trying to cover up something on her writing table. I think she's making us Christmas gifts.'

'Or she's a German spy,' Polly said, 'and you caught her writing messages in code.'

Eileen ignored that. 'What if we're still here on Christmas, and she gives us a gift and we haven't one for her? We must get something for her and for Miss Hibbard and Mr Dorming ... oh dear, do you think Mrs Rickett will expect a gift?'

'She won't be here. I heard her tell Miss Hibbard she's going to her sister's in Surrey for the holidays.' Polly started to say she doubted any of them would expect gifts in light of all the government admonitions to have a 'frugal Christmas' to assist the war effort, and then thought better of it. Planning gifts might keep Eileen from fretting about Mike. 'What about Theodore?' she said instead.

'Oh yes, I must definitely get Theodore and his mother something,' Eileen said, making a list. 'I know we can't spend much money because we've got to save for our train fares to the drop, but I *should* send a gift to Alf and Binnie as well. Speaking of which, do you think you could steal some Christmas paper at work to wrap them in?'

'Gladly, if it will make us run through our supply sooner,' Polly said. 'You'd best do your shopping soon, or the shops will be sold out.'

Which was true. Townsend Brothers' shelves were becoming barer and barer, and Polly spent half her time bringing out ancient, dusty stock from the storeroom to sell in place of the stockings and gloves she was out of – old-fashioned garters and bedjackets and Victorian nightgowns. Customers snapped them up.

Both Townsend Brothers and Oxford Street were jammed with

shoppers, parents bringing children to see Father Christmas, and elderly women soliciting donations for the Air-Raid Distress Fund, the Minesweepers Fund, and the Evacuated Children's Fund. In front of bombed-out John Lewis', Victory bonds were being sold from the back of a lorry. Banners went up on government buildings proclaiming 'Not a Merry Xmas but a Happy Xmas – Devoted to the Service of Our Country', and Christmas trees went up in the shelters. Mistletoe hung from the tunnel arches, the canteen was swathed in fir branches, and WVS volunteers handed out sweets and toys and tickets to pantomimes.

One of them gave two tickets for *Rapunzel* to a mortally offended Sir Godfrey, 'because you like plays and things'. He promptly gave them to Polly. She gave them to Eileen to pass along to Theodore and his mother.

'But they're for Sunday the twenty-ninth, and she has to work that day,' Eileen said. 'And I can't take Theodore because we won't be here. What do you think I should do? Give them to someone else?'

No, Polly thought, *because if Mike's still not here by the twenty-ninth, you'll definitely need something to keep your mind off things.*

'Hang on to them for now,' she told Eileen. 'Mike may have difficulty travelling this near the holidays. The trains and buses are jammed with soldiers coming home on leave. Did you get a gift for Miss Hibbard?'

'Yes. Did you manage to pinch the wrapping paper?'

'I did. Not that it helped the situation. We appear to have an endless supply. And Miss Snelgrove told us we're to use less string. Have you ever tried to tie a knot with an inch of string?'

'Give me the paper,' Eileen ordered. She vanished into the bathroom for several minutes, and came back with a neatly wrapped parcel. 'I'm giving you your Christmas present early,' she said, handing it to Polly.

'But I haven't anything for—'

Eileen waved her objection away. 'You need it now, and if Mike comes back tonight, you won't have any use for it. Open it.'

She did. It was two rolls of cellophane tape.

'It was all I could find,' Eileen said. 'I do hope it's enough to get you through Christmas.' She looked anxiously at Polly, who was still staring down at the tape. 'You like it, don't you?'

'It's the nicest Christmas present anyone's ever given me,' Polly said, and, to her horror, she burst into tears.

'Except for getting to go home, and we'll get that soon. Don't *cry*. You're making the paper wet, and I need to use it again for Theodore's gift.'

'We'll wrap it this minute,' Polly said, and waited impatiently as Eileen ironed the paper out and fetched the toy Spitfire from the bureau drawer. The tape was wonderful. It held the ends of the paper beautifully.

And now what was she going to get Eileen? And when? Christmas was nearly here, Townsend Brothers was a zoo, and she'd promised Miss Laburnum, who was nearly hysterical about the prospect of their performing in other stations – 'Leicester Square is in the *heart* of the West End, and who *knows* who might be in the audience?' – to help her with costumes and props. And she still hadn't learned Belle's lines. And tomorrow night Dover would be shelled, and Mike still hadn't phoned. Or written. Or sent another crossword puzzle. *Because he's dead,* she thought.

You don't know that, she told herself. *You thought something had happened to him when you didn't hear from him when he was in Bletchley, and he was perfectly all right. And there could be all sorts of reasons why you haven't heard from him. The retrieval team's drop site is in Northumberland or Yorkshire, and Mike's having trouble getting there. Or Daphne's gone off to visit relatives for the holidays, and Mike has to wait for her to come back. Or the shelling on the coast has taken out the* telephone lines, and it takes longer for a letter to be delivered because of the Christmas rush.

We'll hear from him tomorrow, she thought. But they didn't.

'Do a good turn for Christmas.'

MAGAZINE ADVICE, DECEMBER 1940

LONDON – DECEMBER 1940

Mike still wasn't back by Christmas Eve.

'Do you think he'll come tonight?' Eileen asked Polly as they rode down the escalator to Piccadilly Circus Station to perform *A Christmas Carol*.

The man behind them said, laughing, 'Ain't you a bit old to believe in Father Christmas, dearie?'

'You fool, she wasn't talking about Father Christmas,' his companion said. 'She was talking about 'itler.' He nodded at Eileen. 'I'll give you six to one odds 'e'll come tonight. It'd be just like 'im to try to ruin our Christmas, the little bastard.'

They had obviously both had more than a little Christmas cheer.

'That's no way to talk in the presence of ladies, you bleedin' sod,' the first man said belligerently, and Polly hoped they wouldn't come to blows there on the escalator.

But the other man tipped his cap and said, 'Beggin' your pardon, misses. I shouldn't 'ave called 'itler a little bastard. 'e's the biggest bastard wot ever lived. And I'll wager five bob 'e's up ter somefink. A nasty Christmas surprise, you mark my words. Them sirens'll go orf any minute now.'

They wouldn't, but it was obvious he wasn't the only one

273

who thought that. There were more people in the station than there had been in the last two weeks, all with their bedrolls and picnic baskets. The woman just below them on the escalator was carrying a Harrods carrier bag full of Christmas presents, and two toddlers had each brought a long brown stocking with them.

The two men weren't the only ones who'd been drinking. There were periodic outbursts of too-loud laughter and unsteady choruses of 'God Rest Ye Merry, Gentlemen' on the platforms. And during their performance, when Sir Godfrey as Scrooge launched into his 'Bah, humbug!' speech, someone shouted from the audience, 'What you need is a spot of rum, you auld sod!'

The troupe gave two performances, the first in the main hall and the second on a stage built out over the tracks on the westbound Piccadilly Line platform after the trains had stopped. Even with the stage, the platform was still too small to accommodate the crowd. 'Do you see that crutch by the fireplace, tenderly preserved?' Sir Godfrey muttered to Polly. 'That's Tiny Tim's. He was pushed onto the track by his adoring public and run over by a train.'

'But at least he wasn't doing panto when he died,' Polly whispered back.

'Or, God forbid, *Peter Pan*,' Sir Godfrey said, and made his entrance.

Scrooge bahhed, humbugged, saw the ghost of Marley (Mr Simms), travelled to the past and back to the future, learned the error of his ways, made amends and prevented Tiny Tim from dying, in front of a large and enthusiastic crowd which Polly and Eileen both scanned for Mike.

But he didn't come. He wasn't waiting for them outside Notting Hill Gate or at Mrs Leary's either. And all that was waiting for them at their boarding house was the news that Mrs Rickett had taken the Christmas goose and plum pudding, purchased with her boarders' ration points, with her when she went to her sister's and left them turnip soup for their Christmas dinner.

'No matter,' Miss Laburnum said. 'My nephew in Canada sent me a Christmas box, and the convoy got safely through.' She brought down a tin of biscuits, a packet of tea and a bag of walnuts. Eileen and Polly chipped in their emergency stash of tinned beef, marmalade and chocolate, and Mr Dorming produced a tin of condensed milk and one of peaches.

'In *syrup*,' Miss Laburnum said, as if it were ambrosia, and insisted on serving it separately in Mrs Rickett's best sherry glasses.

They put everything else in the centre of the table. 'Just like a picnic,' as Miss Hibbard said.

'This is a far better dinner than we would have had had Mrs Rickett been here,' Miss Laburnum said, 'goose or no goose.'

'There is no need to call Mrs Rickett names,' Mr Dorming said, and they all collapsed in giggles.

After dinner, they listened to the King's speech on the wireless. 'This time we are all in the front line and the danger together,' he said in his stammering voice. 'The future will be hard, but our feet are planted on the path of victory.'

I fervently hope so, Polly thought.

After the speech, they drank the King's health – in tea, the peach syrup having all been consumed – and then they exchanged gifts. Miss Laburnum presented Polly and Eileen each with a homemade lavender sachet, and Miss Hibbard gave them knitted scarves.

'I made them for the soldiers, but after I'd finished them, I was afraid they were perhaps too bright and might endanger them.' They might indeed. They were a bright pumpkin orange, which would stand out like a target to the enemy.

Polly gave Eileen tattered secondhand paperbacks of *Murder at the Vicarage*, *Three Act Tragedy* and *The Murder of Roger Ackroyd*, which Eileen clutched rapturously to her breast. Eileen and Polly gave Mr Dorming a packet of tobacco, Miss Hibbard a box of soaps with a picture of the King and Queen on it, and Miss Laburnum a secondhand copy of *The Tempest*, all wrapped in smuggled-out Townsend Brothers Christmas paper. 'Look at the frontispiece of your book,' Polly told Miss Laburnum. 'Sir Godfrey signed it to you.'

'"To my fellow player and costumer extraordinaire,"' Miss Laburnum read aloud, '"the best of Christmases, from your fellow thespian, Sir Godfrey Kingsman,"' and burst into tears. 'It *is* the best of Christmases,' she said. 'I don't know how I should get through this war without all of you.'

And I don't know how we'd have got through today – and these months – without you, Polly thought, grateful that Townsend Brothers would be open on Boxing Day.

But even post-Christmas exchanges and taking down decorations and preparing for the New Year's sales weren't enough to take Polly's mind off Mike, and she and Eileen raced home after work to see if he'd phoned.

He hadn't, and he didn't come on the twenty-seventh, or the twenty-eighth. What if he's dead? Polly thought, taking down paper bells. *What if he was killed when they shelled Dover last night? Or on the day he left for Saltram-on-Sea, and he's been dead all this time? Like Mr Dunworthy and Colin.* Or what if the retrieval team was in Liverpool or Plymouth, both of which had been bombed, and he'd gone there to find them?

There was a photo of Manchester's ruined railway station in the *Daily Mirror. I should have told him about Manchester before he left*, she thought. *I should have told him about the raids tonight. And about the ones on Sunday.*

On Sunday morning Eileen said, 'I'm to take Theodore to the pantomime this afternoon, but perhaps I'd better not. If Mike comes—'

'I'll tell him where you are,' Polly said, thinking, *If you're at the pantomime, you won't be here watching the clock and making me nervy.*

She was already nervy enough for both of them. Tonight

was the attack on the City and St Paul's. The Germans had dropped eleven thousand incendiaries and damaged half the railway lines into town. If Mike attempted to come to London tonight ...

'What time is the pantomime over?' she asked Eileen.

'I've no idea. It begins at half past two, so I should think four. Or half past.'

'And then you must take Theodore back to Stepney?'

Eileen nodded.

'If the trains are running late and you're still in Stepney when the sirens go, stay there. The raids will be bad tonight.'

'But I thought the East End was the hardest-hit—'

'Not tonight. Tonight the City will be the target, and several of the tube stations. You're safer in Stepney.'

'I hate to leave you.'

'I'll be quite all right. I need to wash out some things.' *And be here to warn Mike about tonight if he telephones.*

'If I get bored,' Polly said, 'I'll read one of the Agatha Christies I gave you and see if I can guess the murderer.'

'You can't,' Eileen said, 'she's far too clever. I always think I know who did the murder, but it always turns out to be someone I've never even *thought* of, though the clues were right there in front of me. You realise your theory of the crime was all wrong, that something else entirely was going on.'

The frizzy-haired librarian at Holborn had said almost the same thing, that the ending made her realise she'd been looking at things the wrong way round.

Eileen put on her coat. 'The theatre's the Forrest on Shaftesbury Avenue,' she said, and went off to Stepney to fetch Theodore. Polly washed out her blouse and stockings, hung them up to dry, fended off an invitation from Miss Laburnum to go to a prayer service at Westminster Abbey, 'for our dear boys in uniform', and ironed her skirt, keeping one ear cocked the entire time for the telephone.

It finally rang at half past eleven.

It was Mike. 'Mike! Oh thank goodness!' she said. 'Where *are* you?'

'In Rochester. I've only got a couple of minutes to talk. The train's about to leave. I just wanted to tell you I'm okay, and I'll be there in a couple of hours.'

'Did you find—?' She stopped and looked into the kitchen and then the parlour. She couldn't see anyone, but she lowered her voice anyway. 'Did you find what you were looking for?'

'No,' he said, 'it turned out to be a guy I knew in the hospital. In the bed next to me. Guy named Fordham. He'd finally got out and thought he'd look me up.'

She had known for days it wasn't the retrieval team, but she still felt a lurch of panic at his words. They were nearly out of options, and in two more days they wouldn't know where or when the raids were, and what then?

Mike was saying, 'I'm sorry I didn't call before, but it took me forever to track Daphne down. She'd got married and moved to Manchester.'

'Manchester? Oh God, you weren't there during the bombing, were you?'

'As a matter of fact, I was, and then couldn't get out because the railway station had been hit. I couldn't call you either. The lines were down. I had to hitch a ride to Stoke-on-Trent and take the train from there.'

'Oh, it's my fault!' Polly cried, 'I should have warned you. But I didn't think you'd have any reason to be in the Midlands. I'm so sorry. Listen, I have to tell you' – she lowered her voice again and cupped her hand over her mouth and the receiver – 'tonight's a horrible raid, one of the worst of the war. A huge part of the City burned and St Paul's was nearly destroyed, and several of the railway lines and stations were hit – Waterloo and—'

'What did you say?' Mike asked.

'I said, Waterloo Station and—'

'No, about St Paul's. You said it was nearly destroyed?'

'Yes,' she whispered. 'It was hit by twenty-eight incendiaries, and everything else around it burned, Paternoster Row and—'

'I thought the incendiaries at St Paul's were on May tenth.'

'No, you're thinking of the House of Commons. It—'

'But you said May tenth was the worst raid of the Blitz.'

'It was,' Polly said, wondering what this had to do with anything. 'It had the most casualties, and it caused the most damage, but the worst fire was on the twenty-ninth.'

'So the twenty-ninth is the night the fire watch is famous for? The night they saved St Paul's?'

'Yes.'

'Was St Paul's hit on May tenth?'

'No. What's this all—?'

'Listen,' Mike said urgently. 'I know where – damn it, my train's pulling out. I've got to run for it. But I need you to—'

'Do you want me to meet you somewhere?'

'No, you and Eileen both stay right where you are. And be ready to go when I get there. I know how we can get out. Bye.'

'Eileen's not here,' she said, but he'd already rung off.

Polly replaced the receiver.

At least I warned him about tonight, she thought, though she wasn't at all certain he'd been listening. But if he was in Rochester and there weren't any delays, he'd be here well before the raids began. Or if his train was delayed, he'd ring up again in a few minutes, and she could warn him.

She stood there, looking down at the telephone, trying to decide whether she should go and fetch Eileen. He'd said to be here and be ready to go when he arrived. But Eileen wouldn't be at the theatre yet – it was scarcely noon – and if Polly set out for Stepney, they'd be certain to miss each other.

She rang the Forrest, but no one answered then. Or at half past. Or one, and Mike didn't phone again, which meant he was on his way.

He'd obviously thought of a historian who was here now, and it had something to do with St Paul's. She doubted if another historian would have been assigned to observe the fire watch besides Mr Bartholomew, so he – or she – must be observing something else in that area: the Guildhall fire or one of the eight Wren churches which had burned. But why wouldn't Mike have thought of him or her before now? And how could he know for certain where this historian would be?

Polly tried the theatre again at half past one, but there was still no answer. She'd have to go to there after Eileen herself, but she was afraid of missing Mike, and there was no one home to leave a message with. Miss Hibbard was visiting her aunt, Mr Dorming was at a football match in Luton, and Miss Laburnum wasn't back from Westminster Abbey yet. And a note left for Mike could easily go unnoticed or astray.

She decided to keep ringing the theatre and to wait another quarter of an hour and hope Miss Laburnum came home.

She did.

Polly didn't give her a chance to tell her about the service. She said, 'Will you be in this afternoon?' and, when Miss Laburnum said yes, ran upstairs to fetch her coat and hat.

She pulled her coat on, snatched up her hat and bag from the bureau, and turned to see Mike burst, panting, through the door. 'Oh thank goodness,' she said. 'I didn't think you'd be here so soon.'

'Where's Eileen?' he demanded.

'She took Theodore Willett to a pantomime.'

'I *told* you two to stay put.'

'She'd already gone when you phoned. I was just going to fetch her.'

'Which theatre is she at? Can we call her and tell her to meet us?'

'I've tried. There's no answer.'

'Then we'll have to go and get her. Come on.'

'What's this all about, Mike? Did you think of someone who's here?'

'Yes. I'll tell you on the way. Which theatre is it?'

'The Forrest, but I don't know if they'll let us in after the play's begun.'

'Which is when?'

'Half-past two.'

'Then we have to get there before that. Come on.' He hustled her down the stairs.

Miss Laburnum was standing at the foot of them. 'What was it you wished me to do, Miss Sebastian?' she asked.

'Nothing, never mind, goodbye,' Polly said, hurrying outside after Mike, who, in spite of his limp, was already several doors down.

'What's the fastest way to the Forrest?' he asked when she caught up to him.

'A taxi, if we can find one,' she said. 'Otherwise, the Underground.'

'Where's the best place to find a taxi?'

'Bayswater Road. Now, tell me where we're going after we fetch Eileen.'

'To St Paul's,' he said without breaking stride, 'to find John Bartholomew.'

'John Bartholomew!' Polly said, halting. 'But he's already gone back, in October.'

He stopped and faced her. 'Who told you that?'

'Eileen. She said he went back immediately after he was injured in the bombing on October tenth.'

'Eileen *knew* about Bartholomew?' he said, grabbing Polly by the arms. 'Why the hell didn't she say something?'

'She wasn't there when you and I discussed past historians who'd been here, and I didn't find out about him till after you'd left for Bletchley Park. And since he was already gone—'

Mike shook his head. 'He's not gone. She got her dates wrong. And he wasn't injured – another member of the fire watch was, and Bartholomew saved his life. And it didn't happen in October, it was tonight.' They'd reached the Bayswater Road. 'Damn it,' he said, looking up and down the empty street, 'what the hell's happened to all the taxis?'

'It'll have to be the tube,' Polly said.

They hurried into Notting Hill Gate and down to the Central Line. A train was just pulling in, and the carriage they got on was, thankfully, empty so they could talk. 'You're certain Bartholomew was here on the twenty-ninth?' she asked.

'Yeah, I heard him give a lecture on it. He told us all about the incendiaries and the tide being out so they didn't have any water to fight the fires and the Wren churches burning and the fire watch saving St Paul's. He was up there on the roofs with them. Damn it! He's been here this whole time! If I'd only known—' He broke off. 'Well, it can't be helped now. I just hope we can get to him in time—'

'In time? But if you know he's at St Paul's—'

'He's there tonight, but that's all. Eileen was right about that part of it. He went back to Oxford immediately after the raid – which means he leaves tomorrow morning. We've only got a few hours. What time do the raids start tonight?'

'Six-seventeen, though that doesn't mean the attack on St Paul's began then. It might have been later.'

'When did the sirens go?'

'I don't know, but all the ones this month have gone at least twenty minutes before the planes arrived.'

'So we've got till at least a quarter to six.' He looked at his watch. 'It's a quarter to two now. That gives us four hours, which should be more than enough to find him.'

'But I don't understand. If you knew he was here—'

'I *didn't* know. He said the night St Paul's nearly burned down was the worst night of the Blitz, and *you* said that was May tenth, and since he'd said in his lecture that his assignment had lasted three months, I didn't think he'd be here till February.'

And if I'd told him about Bartholomew when he came home, we could have contacted him weeks ago, Polly thought guiltily. *'How all occasions do inform against us.'*

'Don't worry. We've still got plenty of time,' Mike said. The train pulled into Leicester Square. 'What time is it?' he asked as they got off.

'Five to two,' Polly said. 'We'll never make it.'

'Yes, we will,' Mike said. 'This is our lucky day.' And surprisingly, when they reached the Forrest, there were still children and parents in the lobby and a queue in front of the box office. Polly sprinted up the stairs to the usher, followed by a limping Mike.

'Tickets, please,' the usher said.

'We're not here to see the performance,' Mike said. 'We just need to talk to somebody in the audience.'

'I'm sorry, sir. You'll have to wait till the interval to speak to them.'

'We *can't* wait.'

'It's terribly important we speak to her,' Polly pleaded. 'It's an emergency.'

'I could have someone take her a message,' the usher said, relenting. 'Where is she sitting?'

'I don't know,' Polly said. 'Her name's Eileen O'Reilly. She has red hair. She has a little boy with her—'

'Look,' Mike said, 'we're not trying to sneak into your lousy pantomime.'

The usher stiffened.

'All we want—'

'Are there still tickets available for this performance?' Polly cut in before Mike could do any more damage.

'I believe so,' the usher said coldly.

'Thank you,' Polly said. 'Come on,' she said to Mike, and ran back down the steps to the box office.

'We don't have time for this,' Mike said.

'If we get thrown out of here, we won't be able to speak to Eileen till the play's over.' She leaned towards the ticket seller's cage. 'Have you any tickets left for this performance?'

'I'm afraid all I have is two seats in the orchestra at eight and six. Row F, seats nineteen and—'

'We'll take them,' Mike said, slapped down two half crowns, and grabbed the tickets.

They hurried back up the stairs, handed the tickets to the still-vexed-looking usher, and let him lead them to their row. He pointed at their seats, which were in the middle of the row, handed them back their stubs, and left. The man in the aisle seat stood up so they could go by him.

'We need to find somebody first,' Mike said. 'Can you see them, Polly? What colour hat was she wearing?'

'Black,' Polly said, scanning the audience, but every adult in the place was wearing a black hat, too, and the theatre was a sea of children, bouncing up and down in the seats, chattering, laughing, wriggling, standing on the plush seats to talk to someone behind them. And all the mothers and nannies and governesses had their heads turned, attempting to make them sit down. 'We'll never find her in this mob.'

'I know. Wait, there she is,' Mike said, pointing up at the balcony. 'There, in the first row. Eileen!' He waved to her, but Eileen was speaking to Theodore, who was the only child sitting still in the entire theatre, his feet stuck straight out in front of him, his hands sedately on the arms of his seat. 'Eileen!'

'She can't hear us,' Polly said.

She crossed over to the side aisle, as if headed for the ladies' lounge, and then sprinted up the steps, flashed her ticket and programme at the usher standing at the head of the staircase, and sped up and into the balcony, Mike keeping pace with her somehow in spite of his limp.

Eileen was four seats from the end of the row, past a governess and three little girls, two of whom were hanging over the edge of the balcony tearing their programmes to bits and dropping them on the heads of the people below while the governess remonstrated uselessly with them. 'Girls, don't! You'll fall! You're both being *very* naughty.'

Eileen still didn't see Polly and Mike. 'Eileen!' Polly called to her across the girls and the governess who was blocking her view.

'Pauline! No, you mustn't stand on the seat! You'll tear the cloth. *Violet!*' the governess cried as one of the paper droppers threatened to topple over the edge.

Eileen made a grab for Violet's dress and hauled her back to safety.

'Oh thank you,' the governess said.

'You're wel—' Eileen said, and finally saw them standing there. 'Mike! Polly! What are you doing here? Thank heavens you're all right, Mike. We've been so worried! Did you—?' She went suddenly pale. 'You've found the retrieval team,' she breathed.

'No,' Mike said, 'but we've found a way out.'

Polly looked nervously at the governess, wondering what she was making of this, but she was still attempting to persuade the little girls to sit down. 'Oh Henrietta, *do* be a good girl,' she said helplessly.

'We've got to hurry,' Mike was saying.

'But—' Eileen said, 'I promised Theodore—'

'It can't be helped. We've only got a few hours.'

Eileen stood up, pulled her coat on, and reached for Theodore's coat. 'I'm afraid we can't stay for the pantomime, Theodore,' she said, holding his coat out to him. 'We must go home now.' She put his arm in his sleeve.

'*No!*' Theodore cried in a piercing, siren-like wail that was audible all over the theatre. 'I don't *want* to go home!'

LONDON – 29 DECEMBER 1940

'**I** don't *want* to go home!' Theodore shrieked. 'I want to see the *pantomime!*'

'We can't,' Eileen said, trying to put his wildly flailing arms into the sleeves of his coat. 'We must go.'

'*Why?*' Theodore wailed.

'Here, let me take him,' Mike said, edging past the nanny and the three little girls to pick him up.

'Oh, don't—' Eileen said, but Theodore had already kicked him.

Mike let go of him with a grunt.

'Sorry. I should have warned you.' She turned sternly to Theodore. 'No kicking. Now put your coat on, there's a good boy—'

'*No!* I don't *want* to go!' he shrieked, and every child and adult in the audience turned to look disapprovingly at him.

'Here, what's all this then?' the balcony usher said, coming up followed by – oh no – the one who'd refused to allow them in without tickets. 'We can't have this sort of disruption. The performance is about to begin.'

'Are these two bothering you, miss?' the usher who'd refused to let them in asked Eileen.

'No. Hush, Theodore,' Eileen said, 'they—'

'They attempted before to enter the theatre without paying,' the usher who'd refused to let them in told the balcony usher.

'The hell we did,' Mike said.

'We have tickets,' Polly said quickly, handing the usher hers. 'Show him your ticket, Mike. We only wanted to speak with our friend for a moment. Something's happened at home—'

'I don't *want* to go home!' Theodore wailed and burst into noisy tears.

The governess tugged on Polly's sleeve. 'You said something had happened at home? Has there been a raid? Has someone in his family been—'

'No,' Polly said, and was instantly sorry. It would have been the perfect excuse for getting him out of there.

But their usher had already pounced. 'Then it's scarcely an emergency,' he said, snatching the tickets from the balcony usher. He looked at them. 'These tickets are for row eight in the orchestra. You don't even belong in this section.'

'I *know*,' Mike said angrily. 'We were only trying to speak to this young lady—'

The lights blinked off and then on again.

'The curtain's about to rise,' the balcony usher said. 'I'm afraid I must ask you to return to your seats. You can speak to your friend during the interval.'

'But—'

'I want to see the *pantomime*!' Theodore wailed.

'And so you shall, young man,' the usher said, glaring at Mike and Polly. 'Sir, madam, either take your seats or I'll be forced to escort you from the theatre.'

'Go and sit down,' Eileen said, leaning across the little girls to put her hand on Mike's. 'It'll be all right.'

'But we don't have time—'

'I know. It'll be all right. I promise.'

How? Polly wondered as they were led ignominiously back down to their seats.

'What does she mean, it'll be all right?' Mike asked her.

'I don't know. Perhaps she can persuade Theodore to leave—'

'*Persuade* him? Fat chance.' He rubbed his leg where Theodore had kicked him. 'And what if she can't?'

'Then I'm afraid we must wait for the interval,' Polly said, looking back up the centre aisle where their usher stood guard, his arms militantly folded. 'Perhaps you'd better go on to St Paul's, and I'll bring Eileen when I can.'

He shook his head. 'We're all going together or we're not going at all.' They sat down. 'How many acts till the interval?'

Polly opened her programme to see. The pantomime, which was titled, *Rapunzel: A Wartime Christmas Pantomime*, consisted of only two acts, but under Act I were listed at least a dozen songs, as well as dance numbers, magic acts, juggling acts and performing dogs.

Oh no, we'll be here forever, she thought. And no wonder Sir Godfrey hated pantomime so. It looked more like a vaudeville show than a play.

'I want it to *begin*,' the little boy next to Polly said.

'So do I,' she told him.

The asbestos fire safety curtain went up, revealing red velvet curtains, and the audience applauded wildly. *Good,* she thought, but nothing else happened.

'Maybe Theodore'll have to go to the bathroom,' Mike said, looking up at the balcony where Eileen was talking earnestly to him, 'and we can throw a coat over him or something.'

'*Shh,*' the little boy leaned across Polly to say sternly. 'It's beginning.'

At last, Polly thought.

The orchestra played a fanfare, and a pretty girl in tights and doublet came out onstage with a large white card and said, 'In case of an air raid, this notice will be displayed.' She flipped the card over to reveal, 'Air Raid in Progress,' then flipped it back to its blank side and set it on an easel at the side of the stage. 'Thank you.'

More raucous applause, and the curtains parted to reveal a forest of cardboard trees and a tall cardboard tower. Near the top was a small window with a blonde sitting in it, combing her long hair. 'Oh, woe is me,' she said, 'here I sit, trapped in this tower! Who will come and rescue me?' She leaned out of the window. 'Oh no! Here comes my cruel jailer, the wicked witch!'

There was ominous music from the orchestra pit, and a Nazi officer goose-stepped onstage and stopped under her tower. 'Sieg heil, Rapunzel, let down your hair!' he barked in a German accent. 'Zhat's an order!'

Rapunzel dumped a huge mass of yellow yarn hair on him, knocking him flat, and then brushed her hands together briskly. The audience erupted in cheers and laughter, and above the deafening roar floated Theodore's clear, piercing voice. 'I don't *like* the pantomime. I want to go *home*!'

'That's our cue,' Polly whispered, and she grabbed Mike's hand and hustled him up the aisle, and down the stairs to the lobby.

Eileen was already there, an impatient Theodore tugging on her hand. 'I told you it would be all right,' she said.

'I want to go *home*!' Theodore declared.

'So do we,' Polly said, grabbing his other hand, and they hurried out of the theatre, the glaring usher holding the door open for them.

'What's happened?' Eileen asked as soon as they were outside. 'You said you didn't find the retrieval team. Did you find some other historian?'

'Yes,' Mike said. 'John Bartholomew.'

'Mr Bartholomew?' Eileen said, looking from him to Polly. 'But didn't you tell Mike he's already gone back?'

'He hasn't,' Mike said, 'you heard wrong. He was here for the attack on St Paul's, which is tonight.'

Theodore was listening avidly to them.

'Shouldn't we discuss this after we see Theodore home?' Polly said.

'Yes, we need a taxi,' Mike said, looking down the street for one. 'You know his address, don't you, Eileen? We can pay the driver up front and tell him to—'

'We can't send him home *alone*,' Eileen said. 'His mother's not there. She's at work. That's why I had to bring him to the pantomime.'

'Well, there must be a relative or a neighbour—'

'There's Mrs Owens, but she may not be home either, and I can't send him off not knowing whether there'll be anyone at the other end,' Eileen said. 'He's six years old.'

'You don't understand,' Mike said, 'we've only got today to find Bartholomew. He leaves tomorrow.'

'But we're not going with him, are we?' Eileen said. 'We're only sending a message telling Oxford where we are. So couldn't you two go and I'll take Theodore home and you tell the retrieval team to come and get me at Mrs Rickett's tomorrow? Like Shackleton. And that way you'll be certain to get Polly back since she's the one with the deadline.'

'Polly doesn't know what Bartholomew looks like, and you do,' Mike said. 'And tonight's' – he glanced at Theodore and lowered his voice – 'one of the worst raids of the war, and Bartholomew's going to be right in the middle of it. Which means we need to be out of here before it starts. We need to find him, get him to take us to his drop, and go through with a message telling them to pick us up this afternoon.'

'I know,' Eileen said, 'but Theodore's my responsibility. I can't leave him.'

'Perhaps we could find someone to take him,' Polly suggested. 'Didn't you say you sent him home from Backbury in the care of a soldier?'

'Yes, but I knew his mother would be waiting for him at the station. And I can't turn him over to a perfect *stranger*.'

'Not a stranger,' Polly said. 'We could go back to Mrs Rickett's and see if Miss Laburnum—'

'Are you sure she'll be there?' Mike asked.

'No.'

He frowned a moment, thinking, and then said, 'It looks like it'll be faster to take him ourselves. Do you think you'll be able to find someone in the neighbourhood to leave him with if we do?'

'Yes, I'm certain we can.'

'Then let's go. Where's the best place to find a taxi?'

'The tube will be faster,' Eileen said. 'There are so many diversions between here and Stepney.'

And now let's hope the trains to Stepney are running, Polly thought, *and that Theodore doesn't suddenly announce that he doesn't want to go on the train.* But he boarded the carriage eagerly, peeled a corner of the blackout paper back from the window, pressed his nose against the glass, and gazed happily out, even though they'd still be underground for several more stops and there was nothing to see.

The three of them moved over to the opposite seats so they could talk. 'What if we don't reach him before the raids begin?' Eileen asked.

'Then we get him to tell us where his drop is,' Mike said, 'and we go there and wait for him to come when the raid's over. I figure his drop's got to be outside London to have been able to open the morning after the twenty-ninth.'

'And you're certain it will open?' Eileen asked.

'It already *did* open,' Mike said. 'Six years ago.'

'Oh, that's right, I'm sorry. And I'm sorry I thought he went back in October. I should have listened more closely to his lecture.'

'And I should've told you both about Bartholomew when I thought of him,' Mike said.

And I should have told Eileen what Mike said about trying to think of historians who'd been here earlier, Polly thought, *but I didn't want her to ask me about my last drop or my last assignment. So here we all are, making a last-minute dash to find a historian who was here six years ago.*

And if we succeed, Mr Bartholomew will take a message through to Mr Dunworthy, and he will wait six years and then send us through, he will lie to us for six years and then send us through to Dunkirk and an epidemic and the Blitz, knowing full well Mike will lose half his foot, knowing full well how terrified Eileen will be.

She refused to believe it, in spite of the extra money he'd made her bring, the limitations he'd placed on where she could live. He wouldn't lie to them like that.

How do you know he wouldn't? she thought. *You've been lying to Eileen and Mike for weeks.*

What if, like her, Mr Dunworthy had had a good reason for lying? What if he was trying to protect them, too? What if lying to them was the only way to save them?

Save us from what? she thought. And even if he was convinced lying was the only way, there'd have been no way he could have kept it from Colin, and Colin would never have gone along with it. He'd have warned her.

Perhaps he had. *He'd said, 'If you get in trouble, I'll come and rescue you,'* she thought, but he'd seemed boyishly earnest when he'd said it, not worried she might be in actual danger. *If he thought you were, he'd have stopped you. Or moved heaven and earth to come and fetch you. And he wouldn't let a little thing like an increase in slippage stop him.*

Which means we didn't find Mr Bartholomew, we didn't get a message through. We didn't get there in time. Mike's wrong, and Mr Bartholomew went home in October or won't be here till May. Or we won't be able to find anyone to leave Theodore with, or the train back to St Paul's will be delayed. It will jerk to a stop, and we'll sit in a tunnel for hours and won't be able to get to St Paul's.

Or perhaps the delay's already happened, she thought, remembering the fatal minutes they'd spent arguing with the usher, that they'd spent arguing over how to get Theodore home. *We're already too late.*

But they had to find Mr Bartholomew. It was the only chance they had of getting out before her deadline.

And not just *her* chance, but theirs. Mike and Eileen would never be able to find Denys Atherton among the hundreds of thousands of soldiers preparing for D-Day. They hadn't even been able to find her at Townsend Brothers.

Eileen had been at VE Day because they hadn't been able to get out. They'd still been here when Polly's deadline arrived. And Mike ...

We've got to find him, she thought, trying to think what they should do if there was no one to leave Theodore with.

But Mrs Owens was there. 'I was afraid he might not last through the whole pantomime,' she said, greeting them at the door. 'I'm glad 'e didn't. I've 'ad a feeling all day there was going to be a raid tonight.'

'Well, if there is,' Eileen said, 'take Theodore to the shelter. That cupboard under the stairs isn't safe.'

'I will,' she promised, 'and you three should be 'eading for 'ome.'

'We are,' Eileen said.

'Theodore, tell Eileen goodbye, and thank her for taking you.'

'I don't *want* to,' Theodore said, and launched himself at Eileen. 'I don't want you to go!'

This is the delay, Polly thought. *We're going to spend the next two hours attempting to pry Theodore loose from Eileen's legs.*

But Eileen was ready for him. 'I must go,' she said, 'but I brought you a Christmas present.' She pulled a box wrapped in Townsend Brothers' Christmas paper out of her bag and handed it to him.

As Theodore sat down to open it, they made a hasty exit and were back on the train in a thankfully empty carriage by half-past four. 'We should have plenty of time to get to St Paul's before the raids start,' Mike said.

'But in case we don't,' Polly said, 'and in case we get separated, you need to tell me what Mr Bartholomew looks like.'

'He's tall,' Eileen said, 'dark hair, early thirties – no, wait, I keep forgetting he was here six years ago. He'd be in his late twenties.'

'The fire watch's headquarters are in the Crypt,' Polly said, 'and the stairs to it are—'

'I know,' Mike said, 'I've been to St Paul's.'

'To look for Mr Bartholomew?' Polly asked.

'No. I told you, I thought he came in the spring. I was looking for you. It was when I was trying to find you, before I found you and Eileen at Padgett's. I thought you might have gone to St Paul's, since Dunworthy was always talking about it, and this old guy—'

'Mr Humphreys,' Polly guessed.

'Yeah. He grabbed me and gave me a whole tour of the place. He told me all about this Captain Faulknor guy who saved the day by tying two ships together and showed me all the staircases and—'

'But he didn't show Eileen,' Polly said. 'Or did he, that day you came looking for me, Eileen?'

'Yes, but I had other things on my mind. Where did you say the steps down to the Crypt are?'

'Here,' Polly said, drawing a map of St Paul's with her finger on the leather back of the seat and pointing to where the stairway down to the Crypt was.

'Where are the stairs to the roof?' Eileen asked.

'I don't know, and it's not roof, it's *roofs*. There are layers and layers of levels and roofs. That's what made putting out the incendiaries so difficult. But there'll be someone in the Crypt who can take a message up to Mr Bartholomew,' she said and filled Eileen in on the raid. 'St Paul's didn't burn—'

'—because of the fire watch,' Mike said.

'Yes, but the entire area around it did. And Fleet Street and the Guildhall and the Central Telephone Exchange – all the operators had to be evacuated – and at least one of the surface shelters. I don't know which one.'

'Then we need to stay out of all of them,' Mike said. 'You said some of the tube stations were hit? Which ones?'

'Waterloo, I think,' she said, trying to remember. 'And Cannon Street, and Charing Cross Railway Station had to be evacuated because of a land mine.'

'St Paul's Station wasn't hit?'

'I don't know.'

'Did they drop lots of high explosive bombs?' Eileen asked nervously.

'No,' Mike said. 'It was nearly all incendiaries, but the tide was out, and the primary water main got hit. And it was really windy.'

'The fires nearly became a firestorm like Dresden,' said Polly.

'Which means it will be a great time to have already gone home,' Mike said. 'How many more stops do we have till we get to St Paul's?'

'One more till Monument, where we change to Bank for the Central Line, and then one to St Paul's,' Polly said.

But when they got to the Central Line platform, there was a sandwich board in the entranceway: 'No service on Central Line until further notice. All travellers are advised to take alternate routes.'

'What other line is St Paul's on?' Mike asked, starting over to the tube map.

'None. We'll have to use another station,' Polly said, thinking rapidly. Cannon Street was the nearest, but it had been hit, and she didn't know at what time. 'We need to go to Blackfriars,' she said. 'This way.'

She led them out to the platform.

'Blackfriars isn't one of the stations that burned, is it?' Eileen asked.

'No,' Polly said, though she didn't know. But it was only a bit past five. It wouldn't be on fire now.

'How far is Blackfriars from St Paul's?' Mike asked.

'A ten-minute walk.'

'And from here back to Blackfriars, what? Ten minutes?'

Polly nodded.

'Good, we've still got plenty of time,' he said and headed for the platform.

But they had just missed the train and had to wait a quarter of an hour for the next one, and when they got off at Blackfriars, they had to work their way through scores of shelterers putting down their blankets and unpacking picnic hampers.

Oh no, the sirens must already have gone, Polly thought, looking at the crowd, *and the guard won't let us leave*.

A band of ragged children ran past them and Polly grabbed the last one and asked him, 'Have the sirens gone?'

'Not yet,' he said, wriggling free of her, and tore off after the other boys.

'Hurry,' Polly said, pushing her way through the mob pouring in. Mrs Owens must not have been the only one who'd 'had a feeling' about there being a raid tonight.

Polly led Mike and Eileen quickly towards the entrance, fearful that at any moment the siren would sound and that, even if they did make it out, it would be too dark to see anything. The tangle of narrow dead-end lanes around St Paul's was bad enough in daylight, let alone after dark and in the blackout.

But when they came up the stairs and emerged onto the street, St Paul's dome was clearly outlined against the searchlit sky. They started up the hill towards it.

We're actually going to make it, Polly thought. Which meant it was true. Mr Dunworthy and Mr Bartholomew – and Colin – had kept what had happened secret all these years, had been willing to sacrifice them to keep the secret.

Like Ultra, she thought. That secret had been kept by hundreds and hundreds of people for years and years – because it was absolutely essential to winning the war. What if their getting trapped, their coming back had had to be kept secret for some reason equally vital to time travel? Or to history? And that was why they couldn't be told, why they'd had to be sacrificed …

'What time is it?' Mike asked.

Polly squinted at her watch. 'Six.'

'Good, we've still got plenty of time—' Mike said, and a siren cut sharply across his words.

I knew it, Polly thought, and took off at a trot, Mike and Eileen following.

'It's only the siren,' Mike said, panting. 'That still gives us twenty minutes till the planes, doesn't it?'

I don't know, Polly thought, sprinting up the hill. *Please let there be twenty minutes. That's all we need.*

And it looked like they'd be granted their wish. They were nearly at the top of Ludgate Hill before the searchlights switched on, and the anti-aircraft guns still hadn't started firing by the time they came to the iron fence surrounding the cathedral. And why couldn't it, of all the fences in London, have been taken down and donated to the scrap metal drive so they could go in the north transept door? They'd have to go around to the west front.

She started along the fence.

'Damn it,' Mike said behind her.

'What is it?' she asked, and heard what he had, the drone of a plane. 'There's still time. Come along,' and rounded the corner to the west front and started up the broad steps to where a Christmas tree stood in front of the Great West Doors.

'You there!' a man's voice called from behind them. 'Where do you think you're going?' A shuttered pocket torch fixed its narrow beam on Polly and then on Mike and Eileen. A man in an ARP helmet emerged from the darkness at the foot of the steps. 'What are you lot doing outside? You should be in a shelter. Didn't you hear the sirens?'

'Yes,' Mike said. 'We were—'

'I'll take you to the shelter.' He started up the steps towards Polly. 'Come along.'

Not again, Polly thought, *not when we're so near.* She glanced up the steps, wondering if she could make it the rest of the way up to the porch and over to the door before he caught her. She didn't think so. 'We weren't looking for a shelter, sir,' she said. 'We're looking for a friend of ours. He's on the St Paul's fire watch.'

'We *have* to talk to him,' Mike said. 'It's urgent.'

'So's that,' the warden said, jamming a thumb skyward. 'Hear those planes?'

It was impossible not to. They were nearly overhead, and the fire watch would already be heading up to the roofs, preparing for them.

'In a minute those planes'll be here,' the warden said, 'and the watch'll have more than they can deal with. They won't have time for any conversations.' He extended his hand towards Polly. 'Now, come on, you three. There's a shelter near here. I'll take you there.'

'You don't understand,' Eileen said, 'all we need to do is to get a message to him.'

'It'll only take a minute,' Mike added, backing down the steps and to the side so the warden had to turn to face him.

He's doing that to distract him, Polly thought, and took a silent backwards step up the broad stone stairs, and then another, grateful for the growing roar of the planes which hid the sound of her footsteps. 'I know right where to find him!' Mike shouted over the noise. 'I can be in and out in no time.'

Polly took another step backwards up the stairs.

An anti-aircraft gun behind her started up, and the warden turned at the sound and saw her. 'You there, where do you think you're going?' He scrambled up the steps towards her. 'What are the three of you up to?'

There was a strange, swooping swish above them. Polly looked up and had time to think, *If that's a bomb, I shouldn't have done that.* Then there was a clatter, like an entire kitchenful of pots and pans falling on the floor.

Something landed on the stair between her and the warden and burst into a furious, fizzing fountain of sparks. Polly backed away from it, putting up her hand to shield her eyes from the blinding blue-white light. The warden had jumped away from it too as it sputtered and spun, throwing off molten stars.

It'll catch the Christmas tree on fire, Polly thought, and had turned to run into the cathedral for a stirrup pump when she realised this was her chance. She darted up the stairs and across the porch to the door. She grabbed the handle.

'Hey, you there!' the warden shouted. 'Come back here!'

Polly yanked on the heavy door. It didn't budge. She yanked again, and this time it opened a narrow crack.

She glanced back down at Mike and Eileen, but the incendiary was jerking and spitting too violently and erratically for them to risk running past it, and the warden was already nearly upon her.

'Go!' Mike shouted, waving her on. 'We'll catch up with you!'

Polly turned and fled into the blackness of the cathedral.

ST PAUL'S CATHEDRAL – 29 DECEMBER 1940

The door clanged shut behind Polly. It was pitch-black inside
the cathedral. There was supposed to be a light under the
dome for the fire watch to orient themselves by, but she couldn't
see it – she couldn't see anything. She couldn't hear anything
either, except the still-reverberating echo of the door shutting
behind her. Not planes, not the sputtering incendiary, nothing,
not even the sirens.

But the warden had been just below her on the steps. He
would come through that door any moment. She had to hide.

She paused a second, willing her eyes to adjust, trying
to remember what lay on this side of the cathedral. Not the
Wren staircase – it was blocked off – and the copy of *The Light
of the World* was too small to hide behind. She should have
paid more attention when Mr Humphreys was showing her
around.

She still couldn't see *anything*, not even outlines. She groped
for the wall, arms outstretched in front of her like a child playing blind man's buff. Stone and then open space and narrow
iron bars. The chapel's grille. She ran her hand hurriedly along

the bars, anxious to get past the chapel, and felt the gate open under her touch.

She was through it instantly and into the chapel, feeling her way. The chapel had had an altar with a tall carved reredos behind it. She could hide behind that.

She crashed into something wooden, banging her knee. *The prayer stalls*, she thought, reaching down to feel their waist-high fronts. They had lined either side of the chapel, which meant the altar was—

A door opened somewhere. Polly dived down behind the prayer stall and crouched there, holding her breath, listening.

A voice, too soft and too distorted to make out, and then a second, answering, and then footsteps. The warden? Or a member of the fire watch making the rounds?

It must be the fire watch. She heard more footsteps, quicker this time and walking away, and then a door – too quiet to be the heavy door she'd come in through – shutting.

She waited a bit longer, hoping Mike or Eileen – or both of them – would have got away from the warden and come back. They both knew what John Bartholomew looked like, and Mike could pretend to be a volunteer on the fire watch. There hadn't been any women, and it was unlikely they'd let one up on the roofs to look for someone, even if she knew how to get there.

But she *did* know how to get to the Crypt. She could ask the officer in charge to take a message to Mr Bartholomew.

She crept cautiously out from behind the prayer stall, checked to make certain there was no sweep of a torch in the aisle or in the nave beyond, and felt her way towards the gate.

Light flashed suddenly in her face, blinding her. Polly dived for the haven of the stall, cracking her knee again, and then realised what she'd seen: a flare. A rattling clatter overhead like someone tossing a handful of pebbles made her look up. Incendiaries on the roofs. And then voices from the direction of the dome and more banging of doors and footsteps running up stairs.

Still blinded, Polly felt for the gate and opened it, trying not to make any noise. She went out into the nave, and stood for a minute, waiting for her eyes to recover. When they did, she could just discern the shadowy outlines of the arches, the bricked-up Wellington Memorial across the nave, and the choir, and she thought her eyes must finally have adjusted to the darkness. But when she glanced up behind her, she saw the windows were lit with yellow.

Fire, she thought, guiltily grateful for the light. There was just enough for her to find her way and not to crash into the tin baths full of water sitting at the base of the massive pillars, or into the stirrup pumps propped against them.

They'll need all of those tonight, she thought, hurrying along the south aisle, past *The Light of the World,* although nothing of the painting but the lantern was visible in the near-darkness. It glowed dimly golden, though the light from the windows seemed to be growing steadily brighter and redder and to be coming from the north transept as well.

Out here in the aisle she could hear the drone of the planes, punctuated by the thud of the anti-aircraft guns. Another batch of incendiaries clattered onto the roofs as she passed the ranked rows of wooden chairs, so loud she looked up, expecting them to clatter onto the marble floor in front of her, but there were no more running footsteps. The fire watch must all be up on the roofs already.

A door banged heavily at the end of the cathedral she'd just come from, and this time it was definitely an outside door. Polly looked wildly about for a place to hide, then ducked behind the nearest pillar and flattened herself against it, listening. Whoever it was was running this way, straight down the middle of the nave, his footsteps ringing on the marble floor.

Polly inched her way around the pillar to get a look at him. If it was a member of the fire watch, she could ask him to take her to Mr Bartholomew. There wasn't enough light to see him clearly, but she could see that he was wearing an overcoat. It flapped about his legs as he ran. *It's Mike*, she thought.

No, it wasn't him. He wasn't limping. Someone looking for shelter? People had taken shelter in the Crypt, hadn't they? But whoever this was knew exactly where he was going. He ran between the rows of wooden folding chairs set up for evensong and towards the dome.

He had to be one of the fire watch. She ran out from behind the pillar, but he was already across the wide floor under the dome. 'Wait!' Polly called. 'Sir!' She ran after him, but he'd already vanished into the shadows.

A door slammed. Where? Had he gone into the south choir aisle or into the transept? She darted down the near side of the transept and then around to the other side, looking for a door. The stairs up to the Whispering Gallery were along here somewhere, but she didn't know if they led on up to the roofs. Here were the stairs leading down to the Crypt, but they were barred by a gate, not a door, and what she'd heard was definitely a door. It must be somewhere in the choir. She started into it.

And ran into a young man in a black robe. She jumped a foot, and so did he, but he recovered immediately.

'Were you looking for the shelter, miss? It's this way.' He took her arm and led her back to the Crypt stairs.

'No, I'm looking for someone,' she said. 'A member of the fire watch.'

'They're all on duty just now,' he replied, as if she'd asked for an appointment. 'If you'll come back tomorrow—'

She shook her head. 'I must speak to him now. His name is John Bartholomew—'

'I'm afraid I don't know most of the watch by name.' He unlatched the gate. 'I'm only filling in tonight, you see.'

'Is Mr Humphreys here?'

'I don't know if he's on duty. As I said, I'm only—'

'Then is there someone in charge I could speak to?'

'No, I'm afraid Dean Matthews and Mr Allen are both up on

the roofs. The raids are very bad tonight. The shelter's down these stairs,' he said, motioning for her to precede him.

'I don't …' she began, and thought better of it. She didn't want him taking her out through the nave and delivering her into the hands of the air raid warden.

They started down the stone steps. 'Mind your step,' he said. 'I'm afraid these stairs are rather badly lit. The blackout, you know.'

Badly lit was an understatement. Below the first landing there was no light at all, and Polly had to put her hand on the cold stone wall and feel her way.

'I'm only a chorister, you see. One of the volunteers fell ill, and Dean Matthews asked me to help out. Nearly there,' he said helpfully, and pulled aside a black curtain for Polly.

She slipped through it into the Crypt.In spite of the vaulted ceiling and the tombs in the floor, it didn't look like a Crypt. It looked like an ARP post. A paraffin lamp sat on a wooden table next to a gas ring with a kettle on it, and beyond the table was a row of made-up cots, with overalls and helmets hanging on hooks behind them. But no members of the fire watch.

'Will they come back down during the night to rest and have a cup of tea?' Polly asked.

'It's not likely they will tonight,' he said, looking up at the low ceiling, through which the droning planes could be heard faintly. 'The shelter's along here.'

He led her past what had to be Wellington's tomb – an enormous black and gold sarcophagus – towards the west end. 'I expect they'll be up on the roofs all night, with all these bombs.'

'Then could you go up and tell John Bartholomew that I *must* speak with him?'

'Go up? Onto the roofs, you mean?' He shook his head. 'I wouldn't know the first thing about how to get up there. That's why Dean Matthews put me in charge down here. Our shelter's just over here,' he added and led her into a sandbagged arch at the end of the church where half a dozen women and a young boy huddled against one wall on folding chairs.

'Here's another for your little band,' the chorister said to them. He explained to Polly, 'These ladies were evacuated from a shelter in Watling Street.'

'It was on fire,' the boy explained, sounding disappointed that they'd been forced to leave.

'You'll be safe here,' the chorister said to all of them, and walked rapidly back to the watch's headquarters. But not back upstairs, and it didn't look like he was going to go upstairs. He was messing about with the kettle.

Polly looked about for a stairway at the end of the Crypt, but she couldn't see one. What now? Should she wait here on the off chance one of the fire watch would come down here and try to persuade him to take a message to John Bartholomew?

From the sound of things, that wasn't likely to happen. More and more incendiaries were spattering overhead, and the roar of the planes was growing louder even down here. 'Will St Paul's burn down?' the boy asked his mother.

'It can't,' the woman said. 'It's built of stone.'

But that wasn't true. The cathedral had wooden inner roofs, wooden supports, wooden beams, wooden choir stalls, wooden screens, wooden chairs. And hard-to-reach spaces between the roofs that seemed to have been designed just for incendiaries to melt through and lodge in. Which was what the fire watch were working frantically to keep from happening. And would be working frantically on all night. The chorister was right. They wouldn't be down before morning.

She couldn't wait that long. But to get to the roofs, she'd have to get past the chorister. And away from the shelterers, which would be difficult. When the boy wandered a short way down the Crypt, the women made him come and sit down, saying, 'The gentleman in charge told us to keep to this end.'

'I only wanted to look at the tombs,' the boy said, which gave Polly an idea.

'Isn't the artist who painted *The Light of the World* buried down here?' she asked no one in particular, and walked over to read the memorial tablets on the north wall, working her way slowly along them and waiting for her chance.

The chorister looked at his watch, took the kettle off the gas ring and disappeared into one of the bays. Polly waited for the next batch of incendiaries and, when the shelterers automatically looked up at the ceiling, darted into the next bay and down the Crypt, keeping next to the wall and looking for another way up to the main floor. Or to the upper levels.

Two of the bays had mounds of sandbags covering something – the organ pipes? John Donne in his shroud? – and the next had a grille across it with a padlocked and locked gate, but in the one after that there were several shovels and coils of rope and a large tub of water. And a stairway.

It was the twin of the one she'd come down, which meant it would only go up to the main floor, but it would get her up out of the Crypt and away from the chorister. She ran quickly up the not-nearly-as-dark steps and out into the north transept.

And into the arms of the chorister. 'Not that way, miss,' he said, catching her with both hands. 'Down this way.'

He took her back down the steps.

'I was only—'

'Quickly,' he said, and he didn't seem angry, only in a great hurry.

He hustled her at top speed through the Crypt to where the shelterers were sitting. 'Attention, everyone,' he said, 'please collect your things. We need to evacuate the building.'

The women began gathering up their belongings. 'This is the second time I've had to move tonight,' one of them said disgustedly.

'Is St Paul's on fire?' the boy asked.

The chorister didn't answer. 'This way,' he said, and led the way to a narrow door in the northwest corner. 'I'll see you all get to another shelter.'

'But you don't understand,' Polly said. 'I must speak to Mr Bartholomew.'

'You can speak to him outside,' he said, herding them through the door. 'The fire watch is being evacuated as well.'

The fire watch? Why were they being evacuated? They were supposed to be putting out incendiaries. *It doesn't matter*, she thought. *It means you can tell Mr Bartholomew.*

'Will they come out this way?' she asked.

'No, they'll have gone out through the nave. It's quicker,' he said, pushing Polly through the doorway, up the short flight of steps to the surface and through the outer door. They emerged into the churchyard and a cacophony of sound – droning bombers, clanging fire bells, the deafening thud of anti-aircraft guns, the wind. It was blowing hard, fanning the flames of a Victorian house on fire just beyond the churchyard.

The flames lit the churchyard with an eerie reddish light. The shelterers stood in a huddle among the tombstones, waiting for the chorister to take them to the shelter.

Polly darted past them and around to the west front of the church. The fire watch was already there, standing in the courtyard. But there were far too many of them – an entire crowd – and they weren't the watch, they were civilians. And beyond them, firemen were playing water on several buildings on fire in Paternoster Row. The people in the courtyard must have fled those buildings and come here for shelter.

But they were making no attempt to go inside St Paul's. They were all standing well back from the steps, in the centre of the courtyard, and they seemed oblivious to the fires behind them and to the deafening drone of planes overhead. They were looking, transfixed, up at the dome.

Polly followed their gaze. Halfway up the dome was a small gout of blue-white flame. 'An incendiary!' a man behind her shouted at her over the roar of the planes. 'It's too far up for the fire watch to reach.'

'Once the dome catches,' the woman on her other side said, 'the whole building will go up like a torch.'

No, it won't, Polly thought. *St Paul's didn't burn down. The fire watch put out twenty-eight incendiaries and saved it.*

The fire watch. She looked over at the porch, but no one was on it or on the steps or coming out either of the side doors. The chorister had said coming out through the nave was quicker. That meant the fire watch was already out here, somewhere in this crowd. Polly started through it, looking for men in overalls and helmets.

'Mr Bartholomew!' she called, pushing between people, hoping someone would turn his head. 'John Bartholomew!' but there was too much noise from the guns and the planes and the fire engines' bells. She couldn't make herself heard. And she couldn't see any helmets.

'Oh, look!' the woman she was shoving past said. 'She's going!' and Polly, shocked, turned and looked up. Where the small flame had been, large yellow flames were spurting, whipped by the wind. Even as she watched, the fire seemed to grow larger and brighter.

'She's done for,' someone said.

'Can't they *do* something?' a woman asked plaintively.

A man's voice in the middle of the crowd said with authority, 'I think a prayer would be in order,' and the crowd went silent. 'Let us pray.'

That had to be Dean Matthews. The chorister had said he was up on the roofs. He and the fire watch would be standing together.

Polly headed for his voice, but the crowd, spellbound by the drama on the dome, refused to let her through. Polly pushed out of the crowd and ran towards the cathedral and up the steps to see where Dean Matthews and the fire watch were standing. If she could spot Mr Bartholomew from Eileen's description and wave to him …

She clambered up next to the lamppost at the end of the stairs and scanned the crowd, looking for a clerical collar. She still couldn't see Dean Matthews or the fire watch. She moved a bit to the right, attempting to get a better angle to see their up-turned faces, lit by the orange light from the fires in Paternoster Row. She noted and discarded the ones who couldn't be on the fire watch – woman, woman, too young, too old—

Oh God. She grabbed for the lamppost, suddenly weak in the knees.

It was Mr Dunworthy.

'How all occasions do inform against me.'

WILLIAM SHAKESPEARE *HAMLET*

ST PAUL'S CATHEDRAL – 29 DECEMBER 1940

Eileen watched the warden start around the incendiary and up the steps after Polly. 'You there! Stop!' he called after her, but Polly was already inside and the door had closed behind her.

For a split second, Eileen was afraid he was going to go in after her, but the incendiary suddenly began gyrating and throwing off violent sparks and blobs of molten magnesium and the warden stopped where he was, brushing wildly at his coat and arms. Mike leaped to his aid, slapping at the sparks.

The incendiary's spinning was bringing it closer to the men and to the edge of the step.

'Look out!' Eileen shouted. It rolled over the edge, still spinning, and down two steps, sending off a shower of stinging sparks. Eileen instinctively backed away from it and fell off *her* step, stumbling and flailing her arms to keep her balance.

There was another, higher-pitched swish. 'Jesus!' Mike shouted, running towards her. 'Here come some more. We've got to get out of here!' He grabbed her hand. They skirted the incendiary and ran up the steps, but too late. Another incendiary rattled down onto the porch, directly between them and the door, fizzing. They backed away from it.

And straight into the arms of the warden. 'This way!' the warden shouted. 'Quick!'

He grabbed their arms and herded them back down the stairs and around the side of the cathedral. More incendiaries fell, glittering among the trees and shrubs in the churchyard and along the lane as he propelled them down the hill.

'Where are we going?' Mike shouted.

'Shelter!' the warden yelled back over the roar of the planes. 'Keep near the buildings!'

There was another clatter, several streets away, and a heavier thump. *That's an HE,* Eileen thought. *But Polly said it was all incendiaries.*

They rounded a corner. A woman and two children were huddling in a doorway. 'Come along,' the warden said, letting go of Mike's arm to take charge of them, too. 'We must get out of this.'

He was right. Fires were springing up all around them, turning the garish white light of the incendiaries to orange. The group went faster, heads down, hugging the line of wooden warehouses, and two elderly men fell in behind them.

Mike leaned close to Eileen as they ran. 'If we get separated,' he said, 'go to Blackfriars with him and wait for me there.'

'Why? What are you going to do?'

'I've got to get into St Paul's.'

'But—' Eileen said, looking fearfully back up the hill. Fires were burning all along its crest.

'We've only got tonight to find Bartholomew,' Mike said, 'and Polly doesn't even know what he looks like.'

'But I thought you said we needed to keep together.'

'We do. But if we should happen to get separated, we can't afford to waste time running around looking for one another. We may only have a couple of hours' leeway to get to the drop—'

He broke off as the warden turned his head to say, 'We're nearly there.' The warden pointed down a side street. 'There's a surface shelter just round the corner from here.'

A surface shelter. Polly had said one of them had been hit. 'I thought you were taking us to Blackfriars,' Eileen shouted over the anti-aircraft guns.

'This is nearer,' the warden shouted.

They rounded the corner and stopped. The building at the end of the block was on fire, flames and smoke boiling from its upper story. In front of it, filling the narrow street, was a fire engine. Firemen swarmed around it, uncoiling the hose, spraying a stream of water on the blaze. Eileen stepped back involuntarily and bumped into another fireman. 'This lane's out of bounds,' he shouted at her, and then at the warden, 'What are these people doing here?'

'I was taking them to the shelter in Pilgrim Street,' the warden said defensively.

'This whole area's restricted,' the fireman said. 'You'll have to take them down to Blackfriars.'

'Wait,' another fireman said, coming over from the engine. He was carrying an infant.

He thrust it into Eileen's arms. 'Here. Take this with you,' he said, as if it were a parcel.

The baby immediately began to scream. 'But I can't—' Eileen protested, and turned to look at Mike for support.

He was nowhere to be seen. He must have taken advantage of the confusion to go and attempt to assist Polly. And left her here. With an infant.

The fireman was already walking away. 'Wait, where's its mother?' she shouted over the baby's ear-splitting screams. 'How will she know where to find it?'

He looked at her and then back at the burning building and shook his head grimly.

'Come along,' the warden said, and led Eileen and the others back to the corner and down the hill, stepping over the tangle of fire hoses which seemed to be everywhere.

The infant was screaming so loudly that Eileen couldn't even hear the guns. 'Shh, it's all right,' she whispered to it. 'We're going to the shelter.'

It redoubled its screams.

I know just how you feel, Eileen thought.

The couple and the teenaged girl had all hurried ahead, and the warden called back impatiently to Eileen, 'Can't you keep that child quiet?' as if she were violating some rule of the blackout.

At least they were going to Blackfriars. And between the fires and the searchlights, she could see the street ahead and the tube station below them. 'Shh, we're here, sweetheart. We're at the shelter,' she told the baby, hurrying to the entrance, down the stairs, and inside.

The baby abruptly stopped crying and looked around at the busy station, rubbing its eyes. It was perhaps a year old, and covered with soot. *Perhaps it got burned and that's why it's screaming*, Eileen thought, and examined its chubby arms and legs.

She couldn't see any injuries. Its cheeks were very red, but that was probably from crying, which it looked like it was winding up to do again. 'What's your name, sweetheart?' she asked to distract it. 'Hmm? What's your name? And what am I going to do with you?'

She needed to find someone in a position of authority to give the infant to. She went over to the ticket office. 'Can you—?' she said, and the baby began to scream again. 'This child's got separated from its mother,' she shouted over its shrieks, 'and the fireman asked me to take her to the authorities.'

'Authorities?' the ticket seller shouted back blankly.

A bad sign. 'Have you an infirmary here?'

'There's a first-aid station,' he said doubtfully.

'Where?'

'On the eastbound platform.'

But it wasn't there, though she walked the full length of the platform, the baby squalling the entire time. 'I don't recall ever seeing one,' a shelterer said when she asked him. 'Is there a first-aid station here, Maude?' he asked his wife, who was putting her hair up in pincurls.

'No,' Maude said, opening a hairgrip with her teeth. 'There's a canteen in the District Line hall.'

'Thank you,' Eileen said and started along the tunnel. Surprisingly, it was deserted.

Or perhaps not so surprisingly, she thought, walking through a puddle and then another. Water was dripping from the ceiling, and there was a distinctly unwaterlike odour. She walked rapidly towards the stairs at the end.

Halfway there, she was suddenly surrounded by a gaggle of children. They ranged in age from about six to twelve or so, and were incredibly grubby. *Fagin's band of pickpockets*, she thought, and tightened her grip on her handbag and the baby.

'Give us tuppence?' one of them asked, holding out his hand.

'Sorry,' she said.

'Why's your baby cryin'?' the eldest one asked challengingly.

'Is it sick?'

'Wot's its name? 'as it got the colic?' the others chimed in, dancing around her.

'It's crying because you're frightening it,' she said. 'So run along.'

'I 'eard 'er tell the ticket seller it weren't 'er baby,' the girl said. '*I* think that's why it's crying.'

'I bet she *pinched* it,' the eldest boy said.

The girl circled around behind her.

'*That's* why she won't tell us its name,' the smallest one said, pointedly not looking at the girl, who was edging closer to Eileen's handbag. 'Because she don't know it. If it *is* your baby, wot's its name?'

'Michael,' Eileen said, and walked rapidly away.

They ran to catch up with her. 'What's *your* name?'

'Eileen,' she said without breaking stride and rounded the corner to a stairway crowded with people.

The sitting and reclining bodies made it nearly impossible to get up the stairs, but it didn't matter. The children had melted away so quickly she thought there must be a guard at the head of the stairs and scanned the crowd eagerly for him, but there was no one who looked official, only people in coats and night-clothes: shelterers and evacuees. Eileen shifted the baby to a more comfortable position and picked her way up the stairs and out into the District Line hall.

Where there was no canteen, and no first-aid station. 'Oh dear,' she said, and was immediately sorry. The baby, whose crying had subsided slightly during the interesting encounter with the urchins, went off again.

'Shh,' she said, walking over to two women standing in an alcove, talking. 'I'm supposed to deliver this baby to the au-thorities,' she said without preamble. 'It lost its mother in a fire. But I can't find—'

'You need to take her to the WVS post,' one of the women said promptly. 'They're in charge of incident victims.'

'Where's that?' Eileen asked, looking round at the hall.

'Embankment.'

'Embankment? Oh but—'

'The westbound platform,' the woman said, and the two of them walked quickly away.

Before I could fob the baby off on them, Eileen thought. What now? She couldn't take it to Embankment. Mike had told her to wait for him here. If he found John Bartholomew ...

But she couldn't go with him with this infant on her hands. And Embankment was only two stops away.

But Polly'd said some of the lines had been hit. What if she couldn't get back? She couldn't risk it. She'd have to find some-one here to take the baby. She surveyed the platform, looking for a motherly type.

There was one, bathing a baby in a dishpan. 'Shh, sweetheart, don't cry,' Eileen said, stepping carefully between people's shoes and their stretched-out stockinged feet to get to her.

'I was wondering if you could help me,' she said to the woman, who was wringing out a washcloth. 'I'm trying to find this baby's mother.'

'I'm not it,' the woman said, and began washing her baby's face.

It didn't like it. It began to cry, and so did Eileen's.

'I know,' Eileen shouted over the din. 'I was wondering if you could watch the baby since you have one of your own.'

'I've *six* of my own,' the woman said, grabbing a bar of soap and rubbing it vigorously over her baby's hair. It screamed even louder. 'I can't take on another. You'll have to find someone else.'

But everyone Eileen asked refused to help. *Maybe I should just wait till no one's looking*, she thought, *and set the baby down in the middle of them and walk off. They won't even notice it's not one of theirs.* And even if they did, they'd surely take care of it when they realised it didn't belong to anyone.

And if they didn't, and the baby toddled out to the edge of the platform and fell onto the tracks?

I'm going to have to take it to Embankment after all, Eileen thought, and went out to the westbound platform.

It was even more jammed than the others. She stepped gingerly around picnic hampers and over a game of Parchesi. 'You! Watch where you're going!' someone called, but they weren't speaking to her. They were shouting at two of the urchins who'd accosted her before.

They dashed up to her, just missing the Parchesi game. Eileen instinctively tightened her grip on her handbag. 'You said you was named Eileen,' the boy said. 'Eileen wot?'

'Why?' Eileen said eagerly. 'Is someone looking for me? A tall man with a limp?'

The boy shook his head.

'Is it the baby's mother?' she asked, though it couldn't be. The fireman had indicated that she was dead.

'I *told* you she pinched it,' the girl said to the boy.

'Eileen wot?' he repeated doggedly.

'O'Reilly,' she said. '*Who* asked what my name was?' but they were already tearing back down the platform at breakneck speed, vaulting over shelterers and darting between passengers who were getting off the train that had just pulled in.

'Mind the gap,' the guard called, standing inside the door of the train.

The train guard. She wouldn't have to take the baby to Embankment after all. She could give it to the guard, and he could take it to the WVS post. If she could get to him.

But the platform was jammed, and the doors were already closing. 'Wait!' she cried, but it was too late. *I'll have to wait for the next one*, she thought, working her way out to the edge so she could hand the infant to the guard as soon as the doors opened.

It had been snuffling, but as soon as Eileen stood still, it set up a howl again. 'Shh,' Eileen said. 'You're going to take a nice train ride. Would you like that?'

The baby howled louder.

'You're going to go on a nice train, and then have some nice milk and biscuits.'

'If the train comes,' the old man next to her said. 'They're saying there's been a disruption in service.'

'A disruption?' Eileen peered down the track into the tunnel, looking for an engine light in the blackness. Nothing.

This is the story of my life, she thought, *standing on platforms waiting for trains which never come with children who don't want to go on them.*

'That infant should be in bed,' the old man said disapprovingly.

'You're quite right.' She looked at him consideringly, but he looked frail. And ill-tempered. 'I'll speak to Hitler about it,' she said and noticed that people waiting had perked up and were looking down the track. She still couldn't see a light, but there was a faint rumble, and a gust of air caught the skirt of her coat and blew it against her.

'Can you see it?' she turned to ask the old man. The baby gave a sudden ear-splitting shriek and launched herself out of Eileen's arms.

'Don't—' Eileen gasped, lunging for it.

'Maaah!' the baby shrieked, its little arms outstretched, and Eileen looked up the platform.

A woman was running towards them, her arms outstretched, too, stumbling over the shelterers sitting against the wall. Her face and arms were smeared with soot, and there was a nasty-looking gash on her cheek, but her face was alight with joy.

'Oh, my darling!' she sobbed, pushing past the old man, nearly knocking him down.

She snatched the baby out of Eileen's arms and hugged it to her. 'I thought I'd never see you again, and here you are! Are you all right?' she said, holding the baby out to look at it. 'You're not hurt, are you?'

'It's fine,' Eileen said. 'Only a bit frightened.'

'The bomb knocked you out of my arms, and I couldn't find you and the fire ... I thought ...'

'I need to get to the train,' the old man said, and Eileen was surprised to see that the train had pulled in. He pushed past her to the opening doors.

'Mind the gap,' the guard to whom Eileen had intended to give the baby said, and passengers began to get off, buffeting mother and baby, but neither of them noticed.

The baby gurgled happily and the mother cooed, 'Mummy's been looking for you everywhere.'

One of the passengers crashed into Eileen, hurrying to get past. 'Sorry,' he muttered, and darted past her, so quickly he was halfway to the end of the platform before she realised who it was. John Bartholomew.

He wasn't wearing the fire-watch uniform – he had on an overcoat and a dangling woollen scarf – but it was him. Eileen was certain of it, in spite of his looking younger, in spite of the fact that he was supposed to be at St Paul's, not here at Blackfriars. He must have been somewhere else and had returned as soon as the raid began. That was why he was pushing his way desperately through the crowd, to get to St Paul's.

'Mr Bartholomew!' Eileen shouted and ran after him down the platform.

He didn't turn his head, he just kept plunging through the crowd, over to the exit and into the tunnel.

Oh no, he's here under another name, Eileen thought. And what were the fire watch called? 'Officer!' she shouted as she ran along the tunnel to the stairs. 'Firewatcher! Wait!'

He was halfway up the stairs. 'Officer Bartholomew!' she shouted, and stepped squarely into the Parchesi game. The board flipped up, and dice and wooden pieces flew everywhere. 'What the—?' the boys who'd been playing the game cried.

'Sorry!' she called without stopping, and ran on up the stairs, sidestepping teapots and shoes.

'Watch where you're going!' someone shouted as she raced along the tunnel and over to the escalators. 'This isn't a race-course, you know.'

John Bartholomew was already at the top of the nearly empty escalator and stepping off. 'Mr Bartholomew!' she shouted desperately, vaulting up the moving escalator two steps at a time.

At the top, the station was full of people swarming in carrying children and bedrolls and, improbably, a tall stack of books. For a moment she couldn't see him, and then she spotted his dark head. He was going towards the turnstiles.

She started after him, swimming upstream through the crowd, calling, 'Mr Bartholomew! Wait!' But there was no way he could hear her in this din.

She pushed past a cluster of women, all in robes and night-gowns, and ran towards him. 'Mr Barthol—' she shouted, and two urchins jumped out in front of her.

'I told you it was 'er,' Binnie said.

'Alf, Binnie!' Eileen said, looking desperately past them at John Bartholomew, who was through the turnstile and heading towards the exit. 'I haven't time—' She tried to elbow past.

But they planted themselves firmly in front of her, blocking her way, and Binnie grabbed her arm. 'We been lookin' for you *everywhere*,' she said.

'Yeah.' Alf folded his arms belligerently. 'Where's my map?'

LUDGATE HILL – 29 DECEMBER 1940

Mike rounded the corner and flattened himself into the first doorway he came to and waited, hoping the ARP warden wasn't right on his heels. When the fireman had begun shouting at the warden, Mike had started backing away from the group, keeping close to the buildings, and as soon as he was even with the corner, had darted up the lane they'd just come down and into the next side street. It was narrow and pitch-black after the light of the fires, which was why he'd ducked into the doorway – so his eyes could adjust and he could see if he was being followed.

He wasn't. There was no one in the street or at the end of it, though he'd half hoped Eileen would manage to get away from the warden, too. He'd hated abandoning her, but he'd been afraid he might not have another chance. Once inside the shelter, they'd have had a hell of a time getting out. And he had to get to St Paul's. Polly didn't know what John Bartholomew looked like, and besides, there was no way they'd let a woman up on the roofs, which was where Bartholomew was bound to be. Another wave of incendiary-bearing planes was already coming this way, the rumbling drone growing louder by the second.

The fastest way back to St Paul's was the way they'd come

with the warden, but he didn't dare risk it. That warden had been doggedly determined. When he discovered Mike was missing, he was liable to come after him. *I'd better take the next street over*, Mike thought. He emerged from the doorway, looked quickly in both directions and took off running, thinking, *At least I don't have to worry about being heard.* The roar of the planes drowned out everything else.

Before he'd gone a hundred yards, he regretted his decision to come this way. The street curved sharply, and the lane branching off it was *not* the next street over. It was no wider than an alley, with several other darker alleys opening off it. Mike picked the one that looked like it led out of the maze, hampered by the fact that he couldn't *see* anything.

The alley didn't lead anywhere. It ended in a brick wall. Mike retraced his steps, cursing. Why couldn't they have figured out John Bartholomew was at St Paul's two weeks ago, two *months* ago, so all they'd have had to do was walk into the cathedral and ask for him? He'd known where he was. He should have asked Polly when St Paul's had nearly burned down, instead of assuming it had been in May, and he should have asked Eileen what John Bartholomew's assignment was. But they'd all been so focused on airfields and then Bletchley Park. And now, instead of walking into St Paul's and politely asking Polly's Mr Humphreys for Bartholomew, he had to fight his way through a raid at the last minute *in the dark.*

He realised he must have missed a turning. The street he found himself on led back downhill, and when he turned and went in the opposite direction, twisted back on itself and ran downhill, too. The drone grew louder, so loud he could barely hear the clatter of incendiaries falling on all sides. They were several streets over, but they lit the whole area in a garish, white light.

Good, Mike thought. *At least I'll be able to see where I am.* But nothing looked familiar at all. He glanced up, searching for the dome of St Paul's to orient himself by, but the buildings on either side of the narrow street were too tall. He ran down to the corner, but he couldn't see it from there either. The only thing visible was thick, roiling smoke, reflecting the light from the fires in a pinkish orange, and above it thick clouds. And flames. There were fires everywhere. The lack of water to fight them with was supposed to have been the problem, but no amount of water could have made a dent in this many fires.

Another batch of incendiaries rattled down, making him dive into a doorway for cover. 'Heddson and Poldrey, Booksellers, has moved to 22 Paternoster Row,' a notice posted on the door said, and there was an arrow pointing up to the next street. Paternoster Row ran right alongside the cathedral.

But the entrance to it was blocked by a blaze which filled the whole street. He backtracked and went up the next lane over, but it didn't go through. He tried the next.

And there was the blaze which had blocked his way to what had to be Paternoster Row. He had to be really close to St Paul's, though he still couldn't see it. The dome was supposed to have floated like a beacon above the smoke and flames that night, so where the hell was it? All he could see was smoke. And more flames. The entire far side of the street was on fire, red flames leaping from the windows of the warehouses and book depositories that lined it, but he couldn't afford to backtrack again. He had to get to St Paul's.

He ducked his head against the intense heat and started along the street.

A man with an axe grabbed him by the sleeve. 'Where do you think you're going?' he shouted over the roar of the fire.

'St Paul's!'

'You can't get through that way,' the man shouted. 'Help me break this door down!'

Mike shook his head. 'I'm not a fireman!' he shouted back.

'Neither am I!' the man bellowed, hacking at the door. 'I'm a reporter. I'm supposed to be covering this fire, not fighting it, but there's no one else here!'

I don't have time *for this*, Mike thought.

'I'll go and get the fire brigade!' he shouted to get away from the man.

'No use! That's the fire station,' the man shouted, pointing with the axe at a flaming building down the street and chopping ineffectually at the door again. 'I just saw an incendiary land on the roof!'

And if it burned through to the floor below, the building and this whole end of the street would go up and he'd never get through. Mike grabbed the axe from the reporter and began hacking at the door, splintering the heavy wood while the reporter ran to get one of the sandbags piled up against the corner lamppost.

'Why in God's name they've locked every one of these buildings when they know there were bound to be raids, I don't know,' the reporter said, coming back with the sandbag. 'And what good did they think putting a bucket of water and a stirrup pump *outside* the door would do?'

Mike had the door open. The reporter dumped the sandbag across his arms, grabbed the stirrup pump and bucket and raced up a rickety staircase. Mike ran up after him, but by the time he got there with the sandbag, the reporter already had the incendiary out.

Mike smothered it with sand, just in case, and the reporter said, 'That's one less fire I'll have to cover tonight,' but by the time they got downstairs again, flames from the warehouse next door were licking at the side of the building, and yet another wave of planes was buzzing overhead.

'Do you hear that?' the reporter said unnecessarily, and then Mike realised he was talking about a jangle of bells. The fire brigade.

A fire engine pulled into the street, and men swarmed off it and began hooking up a hose to the hydrant. Water belched from the hose and then slowed to a trickle. 'There's no water in the main!' one of the firemen shouted.

'We'll have to hook them up to the pumps!' the one in charge said, and the men hooked the hoses up to portable pumps and began playing water on the flames.

Good, Mike thought, *the professionals can take over.* The reporter seemed to be thinking the same thing. He picked up his camera from where he'd left it on the doorstep and began snapping pictures of the firemen training a hose on the fire station.

Mike edged away from him, gauging whether he could get down Paternoster Row to the cathedral or was going to have to go around. The flames didn't seem to be any bigger, but the wind was starting to pick up, fanning the flames.

'Here,' a fireman said, shoving a hose into Mike's hands, 'take this branch pipe down to Officers Hunter and Dix.'

'I'm not one of your firemen,' Mike said, determined not to get caught again. He thrust the hose back at him and said what he should have said to the reporter. 'I have to get to the cathedral. I'm a member of the St Paul's fire watch.'

The fireman slapped the heavy nozzle and hose back into Mike's hands. 'Then this is where you belong.'

'But—'

'If we don't stop it here, nothing you can do at the cathedral will save her. Run it along there, where Hunter and Dix are,' he ordered, pointing at two firemen, barely visible through the smoke, playing water on a warehouse fifty yards or so up the street.

And fifty yards closer to St Paul's, Mike thought.

'Praise the Lord and pass the ammunition,' he muttered, and slung the hose over his shoulder and limped off with it down the wet street, stepping over two other hoses and going around a pile of burning debris. He'd hand the branch pipe to Hunter and Dix and take off, and hopefully the smoke would keep the first fireman from seeing what he'd done. Or at least give him a head start.

If he could get past the fire they were trying to put out. It was a bookshop – he could see the wrought-iron signboard above the door: T.R. Hubbard, Fine Books – and the inside of the store was an inferno, flames leaping from every single window all the way up to the roof and lunging out into the middle of the narrow street.

Hunter and Dix, playing a pathetic stream of water – which turned instantly to steam – on it, were backed almost up against the warehouse across the street, even though it was on fire, too – as if they were afraid the flames in front of them would make a sudden lunge for them – and their helmeted heads were ducked against the blaze.

And the heat. The air was hideously hot and full of burning cinders. One landed on Mike's ear, sizzling, and he swiped wildly at it as if it was a wasp.

The hose snagged on something, jerking him back so hard he nearly stumbled. He hobbled back to see what it had caught on. A piece of stone coping. It must have fallen from the top of one of the buildings. He kicked it aside and began hauling the hose again towards Hunter and Dix, who had backed up even further against the warehouse behind them so that it seemed to loom over them.

It *was* looming over them. 'That wall's going!' Mike shouted, but even he couldn't hear his voice over the roar of the flames and the wind. 'Get out of there!'

He dropped the hose and waved his arms wildly, but they didn't see him either. Their heads were down, and the top of the wall arched out above them like a breaking wave.

'Look out!' he shouted, and dived forward, half tackling, half shoving them into the middle of the street and out of the way.

The wall crashed down, spraying bricks and sparks. Hunter and Dix scrambled to their feet, slapping at their uniforms. The hose they'd been holding flailed and writhed like a huge snake, spraying icy water all over the three of them.

Mike made a dive for it, but it was too strong for one person to hold. 'You have to help me!' he shouted to Hunter and Dix, but they were just standing there next to the heap of bricks that had been the warehouse wall.

They shouted something at him. It sounded like 'You saved our lives.'

Oh no, Mike thought, wrestling with the writhing hose. *Just like Hardy.*

But it doesn't matter, he told himself. *We won the war. Polly was there.*

But that wasn't what they were shouting after all – it was something about the bookshop.

'What?' he said and turned around to see it, signboard and all, come crashing down on him.

BLACKFRIARS TUBE STATION – 29 DECEMBER 1940

Eileen tried to push past Alf and Binnie, but they'd planted themselves immovably between her and the turnstile, and John Bartholomew was already going through it.

'We been lookin' all over the station for you,' Binnie said.

They were both filthy, and Binnie was wearing the same too-small dress she'd worn the day Eileen went to borrow the map. 'Ain't you glad to see us?'

No, Eileen thought, looking desperately over to where John Bartholomew was elbowing his way towards the exit.

'What're you doin' 'ere?' Binnie asked.

''ow come you never sent my map back like you said?' Alf said.

I haven't got time for this, Eileen thought frantically. Bartholomew was nearly at the exit. 'I can't talk to you now,' she said, shoving the children aside and running after him.

An arm shot out to bar her way. 'Where do you think you're going, miss?' the station guard demanded.

'The man who just left – I must catch him.'

'Sorry, no one allowed out till the all-clear.'

'But you let *him* out,' she said, straining against his arm.

'He's one of St Paul's fire watch.'

'I know. I *must* catch him,' Eileen said, and made a dive to get past him.

The guard grabbed her around the waist. 'No, you don't, miss,' he said, and then more kindly, 'It's too dangerous out there.'

'Dangerous?' she said, nearly crying with rage, '*dangerous?* You don't understand. If I don't get a message through to—'

'The fire watch is too busy for messages just now. So you be a good girl and go back down below where it's safe. Whatever you need to tell him can wait till morning.' He turned her around and gave her a push back towards the turnstiles. And Alf and Binnie.

'We thought you'd be glad to see us,' Binnie said reproach-fully. 'Tom told us 'e seen a lady named Eileen, and I says, "Eileen what?" and Tom says 'e don't know, and I says, "Well, go and ask 'er then—"'

Eileen grabbed Binnie by the shoulders. 'Listen, I must get past the guard. Can you help me?'

''course,' Alf said scornfully.

'Wait 'ere,' Binnie ordered her, and the two of them shot over to where the guard was standing.

Eileen couldn't see what they were doing, but moments later the guard shouted, 'Hey, you two! Come back here!' and took off after them.

Eileen didn't wait to see where they went. She shot through the gate and up the steps.

And into a nightmare. There was smoke everywhere, and just up the hill a building spurted red-orange flames from its roof. Half a dozen firemen had their hoses trained on it, and more moved purposefully around the fire pumper and the ambulance standing in the middle of the street, hooking up hydrants, load-ing a stretcher into the back of the ambulance.

But there was no sign of Mr Bartholomew. Those few minutes

she'd been delayed had given him too much of a head start. At least she knew where he was going. But there was no sign of the cathedral either, only smoke and more smoke, great billowing grey and pink and rose-coloured clouds of it.

You don't need to see it, she thought. *It's at the top of the hill. She* started up it, past the pumper, trying to hurry, but speed was impossible. The pavement was a snakepit of hoses and water and mud. She squelched through it past the fire, past the ambulance, where they were loading in a second stretcher.

'This one's bad,' one of the firemen loading it shouted to no one in particular. 'He's lost a good deal of blood.'

A hand grabbed Eileen's arm.

Oh no, it's the station guard, she thought, but it was the ARP warden who'd forced her to come to Blackfriars.

'Can you drive?' he asked.

'Drive?' she repeated blankly. 'What—?'

'I need someone to drive that ambulance to hospital. The driver's unconscious. Hit on the head. And I've got an Army officer who's bleeding bad. Do you know how to drive?'

'Yeah,' Binnie said, appearing out of nowhere with Alf.

'The vicar taught her,' Alf put in.

''e taught me, too,' Binnie said. '*I'll* drive the ambulance.'

'You will not,' Eileen said, and to the warden, 'These children have no business—'

'Do you know first-aid?' the warden asked Binnie.

''course.'

She scrambled into the back of the ambulance. 'Show her what to do,' the warden shouted to the stretcher-bearers. He turned back to Eileen. 'I've no one else to send.'

'You don't understand,' she said. 'I must get to St Paul's. It's a matter of life and death.'

'So's this. I've got a driver!' he called to the men, opened the ambulance door and pushed Eileen in. 'It's already running. Take them to Bart's. It's nearest.'

'I don't know the way.'

'I do,' Alf said, getting in. 'I know this 'ole side o' London. Even if you *didn't* bring my map back.'

'You better 'urry,' Binnie said from the back. ''E's really bleedin'.'

And Binnie no more knew first-aid than the man in the moon. Eileen scrambled over the seat into the back where Binnie squatted between two stretchers, holding a folded gauze pad on the lieutenant's blood-soaked leg. 'Press down as hard as you can. *Push,*' Eileen said, thinking, *Thank goodness Lady Caroline insisted I attend those first-aid lectures.*

'How bad is it?' the officer, a lieutenant, asked weakly.

Eileen hadn't realised he was conscious. 'Not bad,' she said.

'Not *bad?*' Binnie exclaimed. 'Look at all that blood.'

'You mustn't worry,' Eileen said, glaring at Binnie. 'We're taking you to hospital.'

She took a quick look around the back for bandages or plasters, to fix the pad more tightly to the wound, but there was no sign of a first-aid kit, and the driver on the other stretcher was in no shape to tell her what had happened to it. She was unconscious, her face grey even in the orange light from the fire.

They both needed to get to hospital immediately – if Eileen could find it. And if she could get out of here. Another fire pumper had arrived, bells clanging, and it blocked her way. She had to back and turn the ambulance – which was at least three times the size of the Austin – twice to get it past it. 'Which way?' she asked Alf.

'That way.' He pointed, and they took off through the burning streets.

It seemed as if every road had at least one fire, and in the few that didn't, incendiaries glittered and spat white sparks. 'Take the next turning,' Alf said.

'Which direction?'

'Right,' he said. 'No, left.'

'Are you certain you know the way to Bart's?'

'Course. We was there when—' He stopped short.

'When what?' Eileen said, glancing over at him.

He didn't answer her. 'If I 'ad my map, I'd know the way for sure,' he grumbled. ''ow come you never sent it?'

'I brought it back, but you weren't home, so I put it under your door.'

'Oh,' he said. 'That's why. After—'

'You never said what you was doin' in Blackfriars,' Binnie interrupted from the back.

'I was trying to get to St Paul's. What were you two doing there?' Eileen asked, though she had a good idea.

'We was goin' to a shelter durin' the raids like you told us to,' Binnie said virtuously.

Alf nodded. 'Bank Station's the best, but sometimes we go to Liverpool Street. Or Blackfriars, like tonight. It's got a canteen.'

'Can't you drive *faster*?' Binnie called from the back.

No, Eileen thought, gripping the wheel. There was too much smoke, and too many obstacles. Half the streets Alf told her to take were filled with fire equipment.

Or with flames. Glowing embers clattered onto the bonnet of the ambulance, and halfway along Old Bailey, the darkened buildings on either side suddenly flared into burning torches, and Eileen had to back up and take a lane so narrow she wasn't certain the ambulance could get through. And if the tall wooden buildings crowding in on either side caught fire the way the others had, there'd be no way out.

'This is fun, ain't it?' Alf said. 'Are we gonna be *killed*?'

'No,' Eileen said grimly. *You were born to be hanged.*

'Now where?' she asked.

'That way.' He pointed off to the east.

'I thought the hospital was north.'

'It *is*, but we can't go that way. There's fires.'

'Binnie!' Eileen called back into the back seat. 'Is the driver coming round yet?'

'No,' Binnie said, 'and the lieutenant's asleep.'

Oh no.

'Is he still breathing?' she asked.

'Yeah,' Binnie said, but uncertainly. ''ow long do I got to push on this bandage?'

'Till we get there,' Eileen said. 'You can't let up for even a moment, Binnie.'

'I *know*.'

'Go down there,' Alf directed, pointing along a street that led downhill towards the river.

'You're certain this is the shortest way, Alf?' Eileen asked, veering around an incendiary in the middle of the street.

'Yeah. We got to go *round* the fires.'

Which was easier said than done. New waves of planes flew overhead every few minutes, followed by scattered spurts of white and then yellow flame at a dozen places among the roofs. *We'll have to drive to Dover to get around all these fires*, Eileen thought.

'Now down there,' Alf said.

'The bandage is bleedin' through,' Binnie said.

'Keep pressing. Don't let up.'

'The blood's comin' through to my hands. It's all over 'em,' Binnie said.

'Can I see?' Alf said eagerly.

'No,' Eileen said, dragging him back down into the front seat with one hand. 'I need you to navigate. Binnie, press *hard*!'

'I *am*.'

'Good girl. We'll be there in a bit,' she said, even though she didn't believe it, even though it seemed she would spend the rest of eternity turning down street after street at Alf's direction while all around them London burned to the ground.

'There's blood all *over*,' Binnie said, and there was a tone of desperation in her voice that was totally unlike her.

Eileen pulled the car over to the kerb, stopped it and climbed over the seat to look.

Binnie was right. There was blood everywhere. Binnie was

pushing down manfully, but she wasn't strong enough to stanch the bleeding. 'Here, let me,' Eileen said, and Binnie immediately let go and scooted aside. Blood spurted.

'Wow!' Alf exclaimed. 'Look at that!'

Eileen pressed down on the towel as hard as she could. The bleeding slowed, but didn't stop. She got on her knees, bent forward so her full weight was over him, and pushed down.

'It's stoppin',' Binnie said.

But how did that help? The moment she let up on the towel, the wound would begin spurting again, and they couldn't stay here indefinitely. The lieutenant's only hope lay in their getting him to hospital, and soon. 'Binnie? Do you think you could drive?' Eileen asked.

''course,' Binnie said, and scrambled over the seats and into the driver's seat.

'Do you remember where first gear is?'

In answer, Binnie stepped on the clutch, put the car in gear, and shot down the street at breakneck speed.

She's going to get us all killed, Eileen thought, but she didn't tell her to slow down. Speed was their only hope, both for the officer and the driver, who looked as though she was already dead. Even bending over her, Eileen couldn't hear her breathing.

'Go right,' Alf said. 'Now down there. Now bear left,' and Binnie was apparently going the way he told her because he didn't call her a noddlehead.

She hoped to goodness he knew where he was going and wasn't only making it up as he went along. But he only hesitated once, to say, 'It's the next one, I think, or the one after. No, go back, it was the first one.' Binnie threw the car into reverse, backed up, and turned into the street he'd indicated.

Eileen didn't have time to ask if they were getting close. She had her hands full with the lieutenant, who was coming back to consciousness and attempting to pull away from her, and it was all she could do to keep the pad in place.

'Now bear right down that lane,' Alf said, 'all the way to the end.'

There was a brief silence, and then Binnie said accusingly, 'You told me wrong. There ain't no way out, just buildings.'

'I know,' Alf said. 'We're 'ere.'

Eileen bent forward to look out of the front window. They were. The stone buildings of Bart's towered beautifully ahead of them.

'Which door do we go in?' Binnie asked Alf.

'I dunno,' Alf said. 'Eileen, where do we go?'

'Binnie, come back here and take over,' Eileen said. Binnie scrambled over the seat and took Eileen's place, and Eileen squeezed past her into the driver's seat, but in the darkness she couldn't tell which door she should pull the ambulance up to either. There were a dozen doors, none of them marked and none of them lit.

'I'll go and see,' Alf said and was out of the ambulance and out of sight before she could stop him.

Hurry, Eileen thought, her hands gripping on the steering wheel, ready to move the car the instant he returned.

'Why don't 'e come?' Binnie asked, sounding panicked. 'The blood's comin' through again.'

There was no sign of Alf. Eileen honked the horn, but no one came.

'I think the driver lady's stopped breathin',' Binnie said.

They're both going to die right here outside Bart's, Eileen thought desperately.

She said, 'I'm going to go and find help,' and flung herself out of the ambulance and across the drive to the nearest door.

It was locked. She banged on it for what seemed like an eternity and then ran to the next one, and the next. The last one opened onto a narrow, dimly lit corridor, and at one side a counter and sign: Dispensary. Eileen ran up to the counter, praying there was someone behind it.

There was – a plump, sweet-faced woman in a grey dress with

white cuffs and collar and a cameo at her throat. She looked out of place, as if she should be presiding over a tea party.

She won't be of any help at all, Eileen thought, but there was no one else.

'I have two patients outside, and I can't find where to go, the doors are all locked, and the ambulance driver's unconscious and the other one's bleeding badly,' she said, thinking, *I'm babbling, she'll never be able to understand,* but amazingly, the woman did.

'Where's the ambulance?' she said, snatching up a telephone. 'Outside this door?'

'Yes, I mean, no. It's— I kept trying doors and they were all locked. I—'

'Bring the ambulance round to this door,' the woman ordered, and said into the telephone, 'I have an emergency here in the dispensary. I need a stretcher crew immediately, and tell them we'll need a transfusion.'

'Thank you,' Eileen breathed, and ran back out to the ambulance, scrambled in, said to Binnie, 'I've found help,' and started the ambulance. By the time she'd backed it up to the dispensary door, a group of attendants were already there, opening the back doors, loading the driver and the officer efficiently onto wheeled carts and draping them with white sheets.

'He's bleedin',' Binnie said, scrambling out of the ambulance after them. 'You got to apply direct pressure.'

The attendant nodded. 'Go with her and make your report,' he said to Eileen, pointing to the nurse standing next to the stretchers.

'I'm not—' Eileen began.

The nurse herded her and Binnie through the door. 'Where are you injured?' she asked as soon as they were inside.

'She *ain't*,' Binnie said. 'It's them wot's 'urt.' She pointed at the stretchers they were bringing in.

'Come with me,' the nurse said and led them down the

corridor after the carts, which the attendants were pushing at breakneck speed.

The nurse was walking almost as quickly. 'I'm not the ambulance driver,' Eileen said, trying to keep up with her. 'The injured woman is. They recruited me because I could drive—'

The nurse wasn't listening. She'd raised her head and was listening to a drone of planes which was growing louder and louder.

Oh no, Eileen thought, *was Bart's hit on the twenty-ninth?*

They turned down another corridor, and then another, at the end of which the carts disappeared through a pair of double doors. 'Wait here,' the nurse said, and went through them, too.

'You ain't gonna have to file a report, are you?' Binnie asked.

'A report?'

'Yeah, about us takin' the ambulance. We won't 'ave to tell 'em our names, will we?'

'Where'd you two *go*?' Alf asked, appearing out of nowhere.

'Where'd *we* go?' Binnie said indignantly. 'You were the one wot disappeared.'

'I never. I went to find where to go, like you *told* me—'

'Shh,' Eileen said. 'This is a hospital.'

Alf looked around. 'What are you standin' 'ere for? I thought you said you 'ad to go to St Paul's.'

'I do, but the nurse—'

'Then we better go before she comes back. The ambulance is this way,' Alf said.

'We can't drive the ambulance to St Paul's,' Eileen said. 'The hospital needs it.'

'But if they ain't got nobody to drive it, it ain't no good to 'em. We might as well take it,' Alf said practically.

'And if we don't, 'ow'll you get there?' Binnie asked. 'It's *miles*, and the trains've stopped running.'

'They have? What time is it?' Eileen said, glancing at her watch.

It was nearly eleven. Mike would have long since have come back to Blackfriars looking for her. He'd have no idea where she'd gone. She had to get back there.

But how? The planes were growing steadily louder, and fires were already blocking nearly every street that led back to Black-friars. And they'd have spread during the time they'd been here. Soon no one would be able to get anywhere near it, or St Paul's. The entire City would be ablaze, and there'd be no way to get to Mike or Polly. Or to Mr Bartholomew, whom they'd surely found by now. They'd each promised they wouldn't go without the others, but what if the drop was only open for a short time? What if they hadn't any choice but to go without her?

'Where did you say the ambulance was?' she asked.

'This way.' Alf plunged along a corridor.

'Wait,' Eileen said. 'How do you know it's still there? Someone else might have taken it out.'

Alf reached in his pocket and held the key up. 'I took it out when I was lookin' for you. So nobody could pinch it.'

'Alf!'

'There's lots of thieves about during raids,' he said inno-cently.

'We better go before that nurse comes back and asks us our names,' Binnie said.

'This way,' Alf said, 'quick,' and led them back through a maze of corridors to the one that led to the dispensary.

Binnie balked. 'I don't think we should go this way. What if that lady's there?'

'What if she is?' Alf said. 'We ain't *doin'* nuffink, only walkin' past. This way's the nearest.'

'All right,' Binnie agreed reluctantly, dropping her voice to a whisper, 'but tiptoe.'

'Tiptoeing will look suspicious,' Eileen whispered back. 'Just walk past normally. She won't even notice us.'

Binnie didn't look convinced. 'She looked like the sort wot don't miss a trick.'

Alf nodded. 'Like the ticket guard at Bank Station.'

'That's your guilty conscience speaking,' Eileen said. 'She was no such thing.' She started confidently down the corridor.

The door to the dispensary stood half open. Inside, the woman who'd helped her was counting out white tablets with a metal stick, her head bent over the tray. *Don't look up*, Eileen willed her as they passed.

She didn't. Eileen opened the door, and they scooted through it. She'd counted on the darkness hiding them once they were outside, but the drive was nearly as bright as the corridor had been. The cloudy sky above them was orange-pink, and the hospital buildings cast odd, wrong-angled, blood-red shadows across the ambulance parked there.

Eileen made Alf and Binnie get in back. 'Get down so they can't see you till we're away from the hospital,' she said, putting the key in the ignition and hoping she could start it. It had been running when the rescue worker had handed it over to her.

She pulled on the choke and let the clutch out, praying for the engine to catch.

It did and then promptly died. 'Come *on*,' Alf said from the back seat. ''*urry*.'

Eileen tried again, pulling the choke out slowly and easing up steadily on the clutch as the vicar had taught her. This time it didn't quite die, and she glanced in the rear-view mirror and began to back away from the door.

A fist pounded on the passenger-side window.

Eileen nearly jumped out of her skin and killed the engine. A man in a white coat was standing there knocking. 'We're for it now,' Alf said.

'Step on it!' Binnie ordered, leaning over the seat. 'Go!'

'I can't!' Eileen said, trying desperately to start the engine.

It wouldn't catch. The man, in his sixties, opened the door and leaned in. 'Are you the young woman who brought in the ambulance driver?'

She nodded.

'Good,' he said, getting in. He was carrying a black leather bag. 'Mrs Mallowan told me you were out here. Thank goodness you hadn't left. I'm Dr Cross. I need you to take me to Moorgate.'

Both children had ducked down out of sight. 'Moorgate?' Eileen said.

He nodded. 'There's a young woman at the tube station there. She's too badly injured to be moved.' He shut the ambulance door. 'We'll have to treat her at the scene.'

'But I can't— I'm not a real ambulance driver—'

'Mrs Mallowan told me you'd been recruited to bring the injured driver and the lieutenant in.'

'She can't take you,' Alf said, popping up from the back.

'Good Lord, a stowaway,' Dr Cross said, and as Binnie appeared beside him, 'Two stowaways.'

'We're 'er assistants,' Binnie said. 'She can't take you to Moorgate. She's got to go to St Paul's.'

'To pick up a patient?'

'Yeah,' Alf said.

'One of the fire watch was injured,' Eileen lied.

'They'll have to send another ambulance.'

He reached across and honked the horn. An attendant appeared in the doorway. 'As soon as Dawkins gets back,' the doctor called to him, 'send her to St Paul's.'

He turned to Eileen. 'All right, let's go.'

'We ain't sure it'll start,' Alf said.

'It wouldn't before,' Binnie added.

And if I can't start it, Dr Cross will have to find some other transport, Eileen thought and yanked roughly on the choke the way she had on her first driving lesson.

The ambulance started up immediately. She put it in gear and let out the clutch with a motor-killing jerk that didn't do anything either. The motor was practically purring.

'Turn left onto the street,' the doctor directed, 'and then left on Smithfield.'

Eileen began to back out of the courtyard. An ambulance was pulling in. Why couldn't it have been here five minutes sooner?

She slowed, trying to think of something she could say to persuade him to take the other ambulance.

Two men in helmets and overalls were clambering out of the back. They pulled out a man on a stretcher. Attendants converged on them.

'Hurry,' the doctor said to Eileen, 'we haven't much time.'

'Paradoxically one might say that the most important incident of that night was one that failed to happen.'

W.R. MATTHEWS, DEAN OF ST PAUL'S, WRITING
ABOUT THE NIGHT OF 29 DECEMBER 1940

ST PAUL'S CATHEDRAL – 29 DECEMBER 1940

'**M**r Dunworthy,' Polly breathed. She grabbed for the lamppost at the end of the steps of St Paul's, legs suddenly wobbly. Eileen had said he would come, and he had. And this was why she hadn't been able to get a message to John Bartholomew, because she didn't need to. Mr Dunworthy had found them before they found him. It was only a spike in slippage, after all, and not some horrible catastrophe that had killed everyone in Oxford, not their having changed the outcome of the war.

And not Mr Dunworthy – and Colin – having lied to them. Colin. *If Mr Dunworthy's here, Colin may be, too*, she thought, her heart soaring, and glanced at the people on either side of Mr Dunworthy, but she couldn't see him. Mr Dunworthy was flanked by two elderly women who were staring raptly up at the dome.

'Mr Dunworthy!' Polly called to him, shouting over the roar of the planes and anti-aircraft guns.

He turned, looking vaguely about to see where the voice was coming from.

'Over here, Mr Dunworthy!' she shouted, and he looked directly at her.

It wasn't him after all, even though the man looked exactly like him – his spectacles, his greying hair, his worried expression. But the face he turned to her showed no recognition, no relief at finding her. He looked stunned and then horrified, and she turned and glanced automatically behind her to see if the fire in Paternoster Row had reached St Paul's.

It hadn't, though half the Row's buildings were now ablaze. She looked back at the man, but he'd already turned and was working his way to the rear of the crowd, away from her, away from St Paul's.

'Mr Dunworthy!' she called, not quite able to believe it wasn't him, and ran across the forecourt after him. 'Mr Dunworthy!'

But as she followed him, she became even more convinced it wasn't him. He'd never had that defeated stoop to his shoulders, that old man's walk. The likeness of his features must have been a trick of the red, flickering light. And of her wishful thinking, like the times she'd thought she'd seen Colin.

But she had to be absolutely certain. 'Mr Dunworthy!' she called again, ploughing through the crowd.

'Look!' a man shouted, and several hands shot up, pointing at the dome. 'It's falling!'

Polly glanced up. The fiery yellow star that was the incendiary wavered and began to slide down the dome and then tumbled off and disappeared into the maze of roofs below. The crowd erupted in cheers.

She turned back to Mr Dunworthy, but in the moment it had taken her to glance at the incendiary, he'd vanished. She pushed her way through to the back of the crowd, which was already beginning to disperse, the people hurrying away from the cathedral as if they'd suddenly realised how close the fires were and how much danger they were in.

'Mr Dunworthy! Stop! It's me, Polly Sebastian!' she shouted. The guns and planes and even the wind had stopped for the moment, and her voice rang out clearly in the silence, but no one turned, no one slowed.

It wasn't him, she thought, *and I've been wasting valuable minutes I should have spent looking for John Bartholomew. He'll be going back into the cathedral any moment.*

She turned to look at St Paul's, but no one was going up the steps yet, and a knot of people were still gazing up at the dome.

'Have they put it out?' a boy shouted, and Polly looked up to see the silhouettes of two helmeted men at the dome's base, bending over the incendiary, shovelling sand on it. More men were hurrying towards them with shovels and blankets.

The fire watch hadn't been evacuated. Of course they hadn't. They had to be there to put out the incendiary when it fell off. John Bartholomew had been up there on the roofs the entire time.

She had to get up there, too. She looked around to see where the chorister was. He stood at the foot of the steps – the women and the boy gathered around him as he gave directions to the shelter, blocking the way into the nave.

Polly kept the dispersing crowd between her and the chorister and crossed the courtyard, then walked quickly over to the churchyard and in through the door to the Crypt. She hurried down the steps, through the gate, and down the length of the Crypt, running at full tilt past the sandbags and Wellington's tomb and the fire watch's cots, her footsteps echoing hollowly on the stone floor.

At the foot of the stairway she paused, panting, to risk a look back, but there was no sign of the chorister. She ran up the steps he'd brought her down and out onto the cathedral floor.

The nave was as bright as day, the gold of the dome and the arches shining richly in the orange light from the windows, the transepts and the pillars and the chairs in the centre of the nave lit more brightly than they were in the daytime.

Good. It will make the door to the roofs easier to find, she thought.

She heard someone running up the north aisle. *The chorister,* she thought, ducking into the south aisle and behind a pillar. He'd seen her come in and intended to intercept her before she could get to the roofs. He'd head straight for the door that led up to them, and all she had to do was see where he went.

And keep from being caught, which would be difficult with so much light in here. She waited, pressed against the pillar, listening intently. His footsteps echoed, paused, echoed again. Oh no, he was checking in every bay and behind each pillar. She couldn't stay here. There was nowhere to hide. She leaned against the pillar, took off her shoes, stuck them in her coat pockets and waited for the pause that meant he was checking in one of the bays.

When it came, she ran silently down the south aisle to the chapel where she'd hidden before. She lifted the latch up slowly, trying not to make any noise, opened the gate and slipped silently through. She debated leaving the gate open, decided that would be a dead giveaway, and pulled it shut. It clanked, but not loudly, and the chorister's footsteps didn't slow at the sound.

He was at the far end of the nave. *Go to the door,* she willed him, but he was crossing the nave to this side and coming quickly this way, pausing, coming again.

Polly retreated further into the chapel, looking for a hiding place. Not the prayer stalls – there was too much light to hide in their shadow.

Under the altar cloth? she thought, and ran stocking-footed up the aisle to the back row of stalls, and into the narrow, shadowed space between them and the wall behind them.

She crouched down out of sight, thinking, *This is ridiculous. I've been here over two hours, and I'm no nearer the roofs than I was when I started.* And this was a dreadful hiding place. She couldn't hear his footsteps from here. All she could hear was the planes, which were coming over again.

She was about to abandon her hiding place when she heard the chorister at the gate. He rattled the latch, satisfied himself it was fastened, and went on.

He's going into the vestibule, she thought, *and then he'll go and check the door,* but instead she heard the rattle of another gate, and then a clank, and footsteps ascending a staircase. The Wren Geometrical Staircase.

But it's boarded up, she thought, and then remembered Mr Humphreys saying they were debating whether to open it again, in spite of its fragility. Because the staircase led to the roofs.

I must have gone straight past it in the darkness when I ran into the church, she thought, cursing herself. If she'd remembered it, she could already have found John Bartholomew by now.

The chorister climbed up a few more steps and then walked back down. She heard him latch the gate and head back down the aisle towards the dome.

It took every ounce of self-control she had not to plunge out of the chapel and over to the staircase. She waited till the chorister's footsteps had died away, counted to ten, squeezed out of her hiding place and tiptoed over to the gate. The south aisle and the nave beyond were full of smoke which stung her eyes and made her want to cough. She forced the cough back, holding her breath, and looked up the nave towards the dome – and saw flames.

Oh God, the roofs caught fire after all, she thought, and then saw that the flames were from scraps of burning paper and pieces of wood swirling in the air below the dome.

They must be blowing in through the shattered stained-glass windows from the fires in Paternoster Row. The air was full of them. A burning order of worship danced down the nave and sank to the stone floor, still alight and dangerously close to the Christmas tree that stood next to the desk where she'd bought her guidebook. And even here, in the south aisle, the air was full of ash and glowing sparks. One landed on Polly's coat, and she batted at it as she ran towards the spiral staircase. She opened the gate and started up the curving steps.

And heard flames crackling. *The tree,* she thought, and darted back down the steps and out into the nave, but it wasn't the

Christmas tree. It was the visitors' desk. Flame and smoke curled up from the counter.

Perhaps it's only the guidebooks, she thought. But as she watched, the wooden rack caught fire, the postcards Mr Humphreys had shown her of the Wellington Memorial and the Whispering Gallery going up like struck matches.

Where's the fire watch? she thought. *This is their job. I have to find John Bartholomew.*

But by the time they found it, the fire might have spread. Scraps from the burning postcards were floating, still aflame, up the nave towards the wooden chairs, the wooden pulpit.

And what if this was a discrepancy, the result of Mike's having saved Hardy or of her having decided Marjorie to go and meet her airman? *What if, thanks to us, St Paul's* did *burn down?* she thought.

The sixpenny print of *The Light of the World* caught fire, the edges curling up, the shut door in the picture burning away to black, to ash. Polly darted down the aisle to the nearest pillar, snatched up one of the pails of water, heaved the contents over the desk and the burning print, and then ran back to fill it again from the tin tub.

But the first pailful had put the fire out. She poured the second pail over the counter and the card rack anyway, then pulled the postcards out of the rack and threw them and *The Light of the World* onto the floor several feet from the desk, in case the fire wasn't completely out.

She set the bucket down and ran back to the staircase and up the twisting steps, round and round, to the gallery.

It was even more full of smoke and ash and cinders. *And it will get worse as you go up,* Polly thought, ducking her head to protect it from the embers as she ran along the gallery, trying doors, searching for a stairway that would take her further up. A library. A closet, filled with choir robes.

The stairway must be in the transept, she thought, and hurried towards the dome.

It *was* in the transept, just past the corner of the gallery. It led up to a dark and stiflingly hot corridor roofed with low wooden beams that she had to duck under and huge bumps in the floor she had to edge around or crawl over. The tops of the arches' vaults?

But she must be going the right way, because coils of hose and tubs of sand and water stood every few yards against the walls and, in one case, in the middle of the corridor. She splashed into it as she tried to step over a hump, and it was only then that she realised she was still in her stockinged feet and her shoes were still in her pockets. She sat down next to the tub, put her shoes on and went on, looking for a stairway leading further up.

She finally found one. It led up to a maze of even lower-roofed, narrower and smokier passages that had to be just beneath the roofs. She could hear planes and anti-aircraft guns through the ceiling.

And voices, coming from further along the passage and above her. 'Easy, easy,' she heard one voice say, and then a second voice from a bit below the first, saying, 'Watch the turning.'

They're coming down a flight of stairs, Polly thought. And they were no more than a few feet away, which meant this passage had to connect to the stairs. She scuttled along the passage, trying not to crack her head against ceiling beams she could only half see in the dimness, straining to spot the doorway to the stairs.

'No, no, you'll—' the first voice said. 'Come back this way.'

And the other said, 'Wait, I haven't got a good grip.'

They must be carrying something between them. They were nearly even with her. She needed to hurry or she'd miss them. She rushed towards their voices.

And straight into a wall. The stairway lay on the other side of it – she could hear the two men only inches from her – but there was no door, no connecting link. The passage she was in was a dead end. And in the meantime, the men had already passed below her with their burden, their voices still repeating, 'Easy,'

348

and 'Careful,' as they got further away.And now she had the entire maze to crawl back along, hoping she could remember the way she'd come and find a way out.

She was so focused on retracing her steps that she nearly missed the door. It stood behind an angled beam and was so narrow that she had to squeeze through it and up the shallow stone steps, not certain she wouldn't get stuck as she did. The stairs ended in a trapdoor, which she had to push up mightily on with both hands to budge. It fell back, opening on the suddenly deafening roar of planes and a rush of heat and wind which blew her hat off. She grabbed for it, but her hat was already gone, caught in an updraft.

But it didn't matter. She was through it and finally, *finally*, out on the roof. *On one of the roofs*, she amended, pushing her blowing hair out of her eyes and looking at the long, flat roof and the stone wall and steep slant above her.

In spite of the distance she'd climbed, this was only one of the lower aisle roofs which ran the length of the nave. The pitched central roof and the dome were still a full story above her, and she had no way to get to them.

I'll need to go all the way back down and find another way up, she thought despairingly.

But if an incendiary fell down here, they had to have a way to get to it quickly. There must be something here to make that possible – ropes or a ladder or something.

A ladder. It stood against the wall, hidden by the shadows of the transept roofs above it. She began to climb it. Blustery as it had been on the aisle roof, the surrounding walls had protected her from the brunt of the wind. And from the cold. As she climbed higher, freezing gusts whipped around her, flapping the tail of her coat and blowing her hair across her face. She leaned forward to grab at the leaded gutter and then the parapet. Her foot accidentally kicked the side of the ladder as she pulled herself over the edge, and it fell away and down with a muffled clang.

Polly clutched at the parapet with both hands, squinting against the driving wind, and pulled herself up over it and onto the roof. The wind was even icier up here, though it shouldn't have been. It was filled with darting sparks and flecks of fire and ash. She slitted her eyes against them and pulled herself to standing, holding on to a stone projection, and looked out over the edge of the roof.

And gasped. There were flames below her as far as she could see, building after building, roof after roof on fire.

Oh God, Mike and Eileen are down there somewhere in that, she thought.

Off to the right, a church spire was blazing like a torch. One of the Wren churches? Beyond it a scattering of just-fallen incendiaries sparkled like stars. It had no business being beautiful, but it was, the white searchlights piercing the billows of crimson and orange and gold smoke, the shining pink curve of the Thames, the burning windows glowing like row after row of Chinese lanterns. And nearer in, a solid ring of fire, closing inexorably on St Paul's.

'It can't possibly survive,' Polly murmured, looking down at the flames. *Pails of water and sandbags and stirrup pumps and a score of firewatchers can't stop that.*

'Where is it?' a man shouted behind her, and she whirled around.

One of the firewatchers was standing there. It was too dark to make out his features. 'Where'd the incendiary fall?' he shouted at her over the wind. 'Down there?' He peered over the edge at the roof she'd just climbed up from.

'Are you John Bartholomew?' she shouted at him.

'What?' He straightened and looked at her, astonished. 'You're a girl. What the bloody hell are you doing up here?'

'I'm looking for—'

'How did you get up here? Civilians aren't allowed on the roofs!'

'Peters!' he shouted, grabbed her arm, and pushed her ahead

of him, the two of them half walking, half crawling over the steep roof to the base of the dome, where half a dozen men were flailing at the roof with wet burlap bags. Sparks sizzled as the sopping bags smothered them. The firewatcher pushed her towards the nearest man. 'Peters! Look what I found over on the pocket roof.'

'How'd you get up here?' Peters demanded, looking around for someone to blame. 'Who the bloody hell let her up here?'

'No one,' Polly said. 'Is any of you John Bartholomew?' she called over to the other men, but the wind carried her words away, and a new batch of planes was approaching, droning off to the east.

The men all looked up alertly. 'You can't stay up here!' Peters bellowed at her. 'You're in danger.'

'I'm not leaving till I speak with John Bartholomew!'

He ignored her. 'Nickleby, take her down and see that she stays there.'

Nickleby pulled on her arm.

She wrenched away from him. 'Please,' she said to Peters, 'it's an emergency.'

'Emergency,' he said, looking out at the burning City, the encroaching fires. 'Bartholomew's not here. He's gone.'

'Gone?' she echoed. 'He can't have gone yet. He— When did he leave?'

'A quarter of an hour ago. He took one of the watch who was injured to hospital.'

And I heard him carrying the man down, Polly thought sickly. *He was just on the other side of the wall.*

'Then let me speak to Mr Humphreys,' she said.

She could at least give him a message to give John Bartholomew when he returned. If he returned. Eileen had said he'd left immediately after he'd been injured. She'd had it wrong – he wasn't the one injured – but she might have got the part about his leaving then right. He might have gone to hospital and then not been able to get back to St Paul's because of the fires.

'Humphreys went with them.'

'To which hospital?'

'I don't know.'

'Bart's,' Nickleby said.

'Where is that?' Polly asked.

'Over there,' the first firewatcher said, and pointed over the northern edge of the roof at a sea of smoke and flame. 'But you've no business going out there. You need to be in a shelter.'

An anti-aircraft battery just below them started up. 'Nickleby, take her down to the Crypt,' he shouted over it, 'and then get back up here.' He looked up at the smoky sky, listening to the planes, now nearly overhead. 'We're due for another round.'

Polly let Nickleby lead her over to a doorway at the base of the dome, then wrenched free of him and ran down the spiralling stone steps to the Whispering Gallery – Oh God, those stairs did go all the way up! If she'd only come that way! – and the telephone post of the watch just below it.

She shot past the startled fire-watch volunteer on the phone and on down the steps and out into the nave. And down it, through the whirlwind of burning cinders and orders of worship, past the visitors' desk, past the charred print of *The Light of the World*, and fled out of the door and down the steps into the fire.

THE CITY – 29 DECEMBER 1940

Eileen and the children made five runs to and from Bart's with Dr Cross over the next few hours. There was no opportunity to get away from him. When they returned to Bart's, he never even got out of the ambulance. Instead, he had Eileen back up to the entrance, where attendants unloaded the patients while he gave instructions to the house officer through the window and was told their next assignment.

'St Giles, Cripplegate,' he'd say to Alf. 'Do you know where that is?' and they were off again.

On the third run, Eileen had said, 'We're nearly out of petrol,' hoping she'd be sent to fill the tank when they arrived back at Bart's and they could escape, but Dr Cross had simply asked the incident officer for a can, which he'd poured into the tank as flames licked less than five feet away.

We'll have to make a run for it when we arrive back at Bart's this time, Eileen thought.

But they didn't go back. At the last moment the incident officer leaned in to say, 'Injured ARP warden in Wood Street. Bart's wants to know if you can pick him up on the way back.'

'Tell them yes,' Dr Cross said.

'But what about the patient in the back?'

'He's stable for the moment,' the doctor said, and they took off for Wood Street through streets filled with reddened smoke and lined with orange flames, manoeuvring around spills of bricks and sparkling, sputtering incendiaries.

'HE,' Dr Cross said as Eileen edged past a huge crater.

Alf nodded. 'Five-hundred-pounder.'

I thought Polly said they didn't drop any HEs, Eileen thought. *And she said the raids were over by midnight.*

But even though the all-clear had gone while they were on the way back from Moorgate, she could still hear the low growl of the planes, and so could Binnie. ''ow come they done the all-clear when them bombers is still comin'?' Binnie asked.

'It ain't bombers makin' that sound, you noddlehead,' Alf said. 'It's the fires. Ain't it?' he asked Dr Cross.

'Yes,' Dr Cross said absently, wiping the windscreen with his hand to clear it, but it wasn't the windscreen. It was the smoke, which seemed to be growing thicker by the moment as the number of fires increased.

When it began to rain a few minutes later, Eileen thought, *Good, that should help put out the fires,* but all it did was send up smothering clouds of steam that came down over the streets like a blackout curtain.

Even Alf couldn't find his way in it. He got them lost twice, and even when he was able to tell which way to go, more often than not the route was blocked with debris or with fire pumpers and miles of snaking hose.

They detoured around fallen masonry and a broken gas main shooting a jet of flame across the road. It was impossible to avoid all the broken glass – it was everywhere, testament to the HEs Polly had said the Luftwaffe hadn't dropped.

Eileen drove cautiously over it, praying she wouldn't get a puncture and strand them in the midst of the flames. She backed, turned, bore left in response to Alf's directions and then right, trying to get to the incident and the injured warden and then trying to find a way back to Bart's in an endless nightmarish round of darkness and flame and smoke.

Occasionally, a gust of wind would blow the smoke aside, and she'd catch a glimpse of St Paul's dome, floating above the smoke. It was never any closer, always just out of reach. Even if she could somehow have got free of Dr Cross and the patients in the back, she couldn't have got to it. When they tried to go to Creed Lane, a soot-blackened warden had stopped them and said, 'You can't get through this way. You'll have to go round by Bishopsgate to Clerkenwell.'

'*Bishopsgate?*' Alf said. 'That's *miles*. Can't we take Newgate?'

The warden shook his head. 'The whole of Ludgate Hill's on fire.'

'Even St Paul's?' Dr Cross asked anxiously.

'Not yet, but it won't be long now, I'm afraid.'

'What about the fire brigades? Can't they do anything?'

He shook his head. 'Can't get to her, and even if they could, there's no water. She hasn't a chance.' And he gave them directions to make their way back to Bishopsgate.

'There's got to be some way to go to Creed Lane without goin' all that way,' Alf said after the warden walked away. 'Try Gresham. Second left.'

But Gresham Street was a solid wall of flame, and so was the Barbican. They ended up having to go all the way to Bishopsgate after all, and by the time they reached Creed Lane, the burn victim had died.

'Young woman in her twenties,' the incident officer said, shaking his head. 'Flames jumped the lane.'

He indicated the body that lay in the street, covered with a grey blanket. 'That could've been you if I wasn't navigatin',' Alf said to Eileen.

'She should've been in a shelter,' the incident officer said. 'She'd no business being out in this.'

'Can Alf and me go and look at the body?' Binnie asked.

'No,' Eileen said. They had no business being out on the streets in this either. 'Is there a shelter near here?' she asked the officer. 'These children—'

'You can't *leave* us 'ere,' Alf said. 'We're your *assistants*.'

'But your mother will be worried about you—'

Alf said, 'We ain't—'

Binnie cut him off. 'Mum ain't 'ome. She's at work.'

'And if you make us go to a shelter, who'll tell you 'ow to get back to Bart's?' Alf asked.

He was right. She wouldn't have a prayer of getting the ambulance back to the hospital without him. She was completely disoriented in the smoky fog, and Dr Cross was even worse. 'No sense of direction, even in the daytime, I'm afraid,' he'd said on the first trip. 'That's why I never learned to drive.'

'You can leave us behind in some shelter,' Binnie said, 'but you can't make us stay there.'

She was right, and God knew what the two of them would do or where they'd go if they weren't with her. 'Get in the ambulance,' Eileen said, and went over to Dr Cross and the incident officer.

The doctor was speaking on a field-telephone. As she came up, the incident officer said, 'Are you injured, miss?'

'Doctor,' he said, turning to Dr Cross, 'this young lady is—'

'I'm not injured. I'm Dr Cross' driver.'

Dr Cross took the receiver from his mouth and said, 'I've just been in contact with Wood Street Fire Station. They've a fireman in Alwell Lane with burns and a broken leg. Guy's was supposed to send an ambulance, but they can't. The hospital's on fire, and they're busy evacuating their own patients.' He handed the telephone back to him and turned to Eileen. 'We need to go and pick up the fireman.'

He started for the ambulance.

'Wait,' Eileen said. If she could phone the fire watch and get a message to John Bartholomew, she could tell him they were trying to get to him and to wait till they arrived.

'Can you get through to St Paul's on that telephone?' she asked the incident officer. 'My husband's a member of the fire watch. I was on my way there to take him his supper when I was recruited into driving. He'll be frantic with worry over where I— where the children and I are. If I could only telephone him to let him know I'm all right—'

The incident officer looked doubtful. 'These phones are supposed to be for official business only.'

'This is official business,' Dr Cross said. 'We don't want any of those lads worrying. We want their full attention on saving that cathedral.'

The incident officer nodded, cranked up the telephone, then put it to his ear and said, 'Put me through to the fire watch at St Paul's,' and handed it to her. 'It'll take some time to patch it through.'

Eileen nodded, listening to a series of hums and trying to think what to say. She couldn't mention their drops or time travel with the incident officer listening. And Mr Bartholomew hadn't met her yet. Who should she say was calling?

Mrs Dunworthy, she thought, *and I'll tell him I'm trying to get to St Paul's so we can go home together, and to—*

There was a sharp crackle, and a man's voice said, 'St Paul's Fire Watch here.'

'Yes, hello, I'm trying to reach—'

There was a volley of static, and then silence.

'Hello? Hello?'

The incident officer took the telephone from her. 'Hullo?' He flicked the switching mechanism back and forth. 'Are you there? Hullo?'

He listened for a moment. Eileen could hear a woman's voice on the line.

'They just lost the telephone exchange at Guildhall,' the incident officer said. 'They're trying to get it back.'

But they won't, Eileen thought. *The Guildhall's on fire. They're evacuating the telephone operators.*

'I'll see if I can patch you through,' he said.

But that didn't work either. 'The operator says lines are down all over the city. If I do get through, what should I tell him?'

She thought quickly. 'Tell him Eileen said that we can't get through, but the three of us are coming to him as soon as we can, and to stay at St Paul's till we arrive. Tell him on no account is he to leave for Mr Dunworthy's in Oxford without us,' Eileen instructed, and at his curious look, she added, 'We were to have gone to our friends in Oxford for the New Year.'

He nodded, then ran up to the ambulance as she was pulling away. 'You didn't tell me your husband's name.'

'*Husband?*' Alf said incredulously. 'She ain't—'

'Bartholomew, John Bartholomew,' she said quickly, and drove off before Alf could do any more damage.

'Bartholomew,' Dr Cross said musingly. 'How fitting that you and your children, the angels who've come to St Bartholomew's aid, should be named Bartholomew.'

Binnie began, 'We ain't—'

'Angels,' Eileen finished neatly.

'Oh, but you are,' Dr Cross said. 'I don't know what we should have done without you. Half of our drivers were caught on the other side of the fire and couldn't make it in. If it hadn't been for you and your children—'

'We *ain't*—'

'Which way do I turn up here?' Eileen cut in to ask

'Left,' Alf said, 'but—'

'It was extraordinarily good luck that Mrs Mallowan told me she'd seen you leaving,' Dr Cross said, and Eileen realised she'd heard him say that name before, when they were leaving Bart's on that first run. But it had to be some other Mrs Mallowan.

'Mrs Mallowan?' she asked to be certain.

He nodded. 'Our dispenser, though actually she's not ours. Our regular dispenser couldn't make it in, and Mrs Mallowan kindly offered to—'

'Her given name isn't Agatha, is it?'

'Yes, I believe so.'

'Agatha *Christie* Mallowan?'

'I believe so. She lives in Holland Park.'

Binnie had said, 'The dispenser looks like she don't miss a trick,' and she was certainly right about that.

I finally get to meet Agatha Christie, Eileen thought ruefully, *and when I do, she stops me from making my getaway and going to St Paul's.*

'Are you acquainted with Mrs Mallowan?' Dr Cross was asking.

'Yes— No, I've heard of her.'

'Oh yes, I believe she writes some sort of novels. Are they good?'

'People will still be reading them a hundred years from now,' Eileen said, and turned into Alwell Lane.

And into a scene of chaos. Nearly every building on both sides of the narrow street was on fire, bright yellow flames shooting from the windows and boiling up violently from the roofs and over the narrow street, threatening to engulf it at any moment. Three firemen had their hoses aimed at the burning buildings, even though there was no way they could save any of it. The stream from their hoses was only a thin trickle.

But they kept on spraying the buildings, oblivious to the flames arching dangerously over their heads. And to Dr Cross. He had to shout at them twice before they told him where to find the injured fireman, and there turned out to be three other casualties as well – two firemen unconscious from smoke inhalation and a young boy with badly burned hands. They had to cram the four of them into the rear of the ambulance, and Binnie had to sit on the doctor's lap on the way back to Bart's.

The journey back took even longer than the others had. Every road they turned up was blocked with fallen masonry or roaring flames, or both. They could no longer catch even glimpses of St Paul's. It had been swallowed up in a boiling mass of smoke that filled the entire sky. When they pulled in to Bart's, the smoke stood like a great red wall stretching from horizon to horizon.

There was no one at the entrance to take the patients inside. Binnie had fallen asleep on Dr Cross' lap. Eileen had to shake her gently awake to get her off him so he could go in to get help.

'I'm *awake*,' Binnie murmured crankily and curled up again next to the drowsing Alf.

'Shove *off*!' he said, then sat up, rubbed his eyes sleepily. ''e's gone. Why ain't you takin' off for St Paul's?'

'Because we have four patients in the back.' And Dr Cross was coming out of the door with a trolley.

'I couldn't find anyone,' he said. 'We'll have to take them in ourselves.'

Somehow they managed – with Alf and Binnie helping – to get all four patients onto trolleys, into the hospital and through an endless maze of corridors to a place where they could be turned over to the staff.

And it was no wonder there hadn't been anyone at the entrance. Every ward, every examining room, was filled with patients, scurrying nurses, soot-covered rescue workers, doctors shouting orders, harried-looking attendants – one of whom detached himself at Dr Cross' order from the ARP warden he was bandaging to come and take Eileen's end of the trolley from her. 'What are you doing?' he asked. 'You're injured. Sit down. I'll fetch a doctor.'

Why did everyone keep saying that? 'I'm Dr Cross' driver.'

'What are *you* doing?' Dr Cross said impatiently to the attendant. 'Grab hold of the trolley.' To Eileen he said, 'Wait here.'

Eileen nodded, and he and the attendant disappeared with the trolley through a pair of double doors. And she was suddenly free to leave and go to St Paul's, as long as she wasn't waylaid by some other doctor on the way out.

And if I can get to the cathedral, she thought, remembering that wall of red and what the warden had said about all of

Ludgate Hill being on fire. She looked at Alf and Binnie, drooping beside her. *I can't take them back into the middle of those fires*, she thought, though she wasn't at all certain she could find her way to St Paul's without them.

I must. I've already exposed them to too much danger tonight as it is. Which meant she had to get away from them, a feat that she knew from experience was nearly impossible. Perhaps if she persuaded them to sit down, they'd fall asleep again.

But when she suggested it, Binnie said, 'Sit *down*? He'll likely be back any minute.'

'Come along,' Alf said, grabbing her hand.

'In a moment,' she said. 'I need to tell Matron we've gone out to the waiting room so the doctor won't know where we've gone,' which was duplicitous enough for them to fall in eagerly with the scheme. 'Stay there,' she ordered, and walked quickly down the corridor.

She wasn't certain she could find her way back to the ambulance, let alone to St Paul's. She hadn't paid any attention to which way they'd come when they brought the trolley in. And she had to be quick, or Alf and Binnie would tumble to what she was doing, and she'd find them waiting for her outside.

She looked in vain for someone to ask. There – walking away down that side corridor, was someone, not a nurse. She was hatless and wearing a navy-blue coat. *An ARP warden*, Eileen thought. She'd very likely just brought a patient in.

'Miss,' Eileen called, 'can you tell me where the emergency ward is?' and the young woman turned.

She looked dishevelled, her fair hair badly windblown, and smears of soot on her cheeks and forehead. *Not an ARP warden*, Eileen thought, *a patient*.

'Eileen! Oh thank God!' the young woman cried, and began to run towards her.

'*Polly?*'

Polly flung her arms around her. 'I was so afraid I'd be too late. It took me *hours* to get here,' she said, nearly sobbing.

'There were fires everywhere, and I couldn't get through ... and I thought I'd never find the hospital ... but here you are, thank God!'

They were both talking at once. 'How did you find me?' Eileen asked. 'I thought you were at St Paul's. I was just leaving to look for you. Where's Mike?'

Polly pulled back from her. 'Isn't he here with you?'

'No, I— We got separated. I thought he went to St Paul's. He's not with you?'

'No. Where did you see him last?' She stopped, staring at Eileen in horror. 'What's happened? Are you hurt?'

'*No*. You mean because I'm here at Bart's? I was dragooned into driving an ambulance and—'

'But you're bleeding.'

'No, I'm not,' Eileen said, and looked down at herself. The entire front of her coat was covered in dried blood. Her hands were bloody, too. A crooked line of blood had trickled down the back of her hand and wrist and into her sleeve. No wonder people kept asking her if she was injured.

'It's not mine,' she said. 'There was an Army officer who was bleeding. I had to apply direct pressure.'

'And *I* 'ad to drive,' Binnie said, popping up beside her.

'*I* told you where to go, you puddinghead,' Alf said. 'You'd 'ave ended up bein' burnt to ashes if I 'adn't.'

'I would *not*,' Binnie said.

'You would *so*.' Alf turned to tug at Eileen's bloody sleeve. 'What're you doin' 'ere? The ambulance is that way.' He pointed back down the corridor. 'And who's she?'

'My friend Polly. Are you certain Mike didn't come to St Paul's?' Eileen asked Polly. 'That's where he said he was going.'

'Who's Mike?' Binnie asked.

'Hush,' Eileen said. 'Might you have missed each other some-how?'

'Yes ... I don't know. He might have come while I was on the roofs—'

'Or he might have gone back to Blackfriars tube station to find me,' Eileen said. 'He told me to wait there for him. Come along, we've got transport. We'll go to St Paul's first. Mike may have told Mr Bartholomew where—'

'Who's Mr Bartholomew?' Alf asked.

'*Shh,*' Eileen said. 'Mike may have told him where he was going, and if he didn't, we'll tell Mr Bartholomew to search between St Paul's and Pilgrim Street – that's where we got separated – and we'll go to Blackfriars and look—'

'*No,*' Polly said. 'Mr Bartholomew's *here*!'

'Here?'

'Yes, in the hospital.'

'Oh, well, then, that makes it simple. He can go back to St Paul's and look for Mike there, and we can go to Black—'

'You don't understand,' Polly said, 'I came here to *find* John Bartholomew, but I don't know where he is. I've been asking the staff, but no one will tell me anything. I know he's somewhere here in the hospital—'

Eileen stared blankly at her. 'You haven't found him yet?'

'No, I only just missed him. The fire watch said he'd left for hospital – he brought the man who was injured here – and I came to find him, but it's taken me *hours*, and—'

'He brought him *here*? When?'

'I'm not certain,' Polly said. 'A bit before eleven.'

John Bartholomew had been here at Bart's the entire time she was transporting patients. If she'd only known! 'What's the name of the firewatcher who was injured?' Eileen asked.

Polly looked stricken. 'I don't know. I should have asked, but I thought I might still be able to catch them—'

'It's all right. I know what Mr Bartholomew looks like and what he had on. I saw him earlier tonight. He was wearing street clothes and an overcoat and scarf. We'll go through the wards—'

'You *saw* him?' Polly said. 'Where?'

'At Blackfriars. He—'

'Why didn't you say so before?' Polly said eagerly. 'If you told him about us— Did he tell you where the drop was?'

'Drop?' Binnie said alertly.

Alf cut in, 'You mean like when they 'ang somebody?'

'I didn't have a chance to tell him anything,' Eileen said. 'I was on the train platform when he ran past, and I tried to go after him to catch him, but—'

'Alf got in the way,' Binnie said.

'I did *not*,' Alf responded indignantly. 'It was that guard wot stopped 'er.'

'Shh, both of you,' Eileen said. 'I tried to go after him, but I was shanghaied into driving two bombing victims—'

'We been rescuin' people all night,' Alf said.

'Except for this one what died,' Binnie put in. 'We got there too late.'

'Too late,' Polly murmured.

'You mustn't worry,' Eileen told her. 'We'll find him. What sort of injury did the firewatcher he brought in have? Burns? Broken bones? Internal injuries?'

If it was internal injuries, he'd be in surgery, but Polly didn't know. 'All I know is they had to carry him down from the roofs on a stretcher.'

'They? There was more than one firewatcher with him?'

'Yes. The other one was Mr Humphreys. Elderly, balding.'

'Good,' Eileen said. 'You know what *he* looks like, and I know what Mr Bartholomew looks like.'

'I'll find 'em,' Alf said, and started to dash off. Eileen grabbed him by the scruff of the neck and Binnie by her sash.

'Wot're you doin' that for?' Alf demanded indignantly. 'I'll wager I can find 'em sooner'n you. I'm good at spottin'.'

'I know you are,' Eileen said, 'but neither of you is going anywhere till we've worked out a plan. Mr Bartholomew is tall and has dark hair. How tall is Mr Humphreys, Polly?'

'Shorter than me,' she said. 'They should both be wearing

blue overalls and tin helmets, unless Mr Bartholomew didn't have time to change, in which case—'

'He'll be wearing street clothes and an overcoat,' Eileen said. 'You and Binnie check the waiting rooms, and I'll go and ask Dr Cross—'

'Wot if 'e makes you drive 'im someplace again?' Binnie asked.

She was right. 'I'll ask the Matron, then, and Polly, you go and describe the patient to the admitting nurse. We'll all meet back here. Alf, Binnie, if you find Mr Humphreys, ask him where Mr Bartholomew is, and tell him—'

'You're lookin' for 'im,' Alf finished for her.

Polly gave Eileen a rapid look.

'No,' Eileen said, 'he won't know who we are. Tell him someone from Oxford needs to speak to him.'

'*You* ain't from Oxford,' Alf said. 'You're from Backbury.'

''ow come 'e won't know who you are?' Binnie asked.

'I'll explain later. If he won't come with you, tell him to stay where he is, and then come and fetch us.'

'What if we get thrown out?' Alf asked.

Always a possibility where the Hodbins were concerned. 'Go round to the door of the ambulance entrance and wait for us there,' Eileen said.

'What if 'e's unconscious so we can't tell 'im?' Alf asked.

'We ain't lookin' for the one wot's hurt, you dunderhead,' Binnie said. 'We're lookin' for the ones wot're *with* 'im. Ain't we, Eileen?'

'Yes,' she said, and Alf nodded and took off like a shot down the deserted corridor.

Binnie started after him and then stopped. 'You sure you ain't tryin' to ditch us like you done when you said you was goin' to tell Matron we was in the waitin' room, are you?'

She should have known better than to think she could fool them. 'I'm sure.'

'You swear?'

'I swear,' Eileen said.

Binnie pelted down the corridor. 'I take it those are the fabled Hodbins,' Polly said, looking after them.

'Yes, and if anyone can find Mr Bartholomew, they can.' She led Polly back to the spot where Dr Cross had told her to wait, said, 'Someone inside will be able to tell you where the admitting desk is, Polly. And the ambulance room entrance,' and hurried upstairs.

She'd hoped the busyness and disorganisation would enable her to sneak unnoticed into the wards, but the ward sister stopped her. 'No one's allowed up here— You're injured. Orderly!' she called. She took Eileen's arm and attempted to steer her to a chair. 'Where are you bleeding?'

'It's not my blood,' Eileen said, cursing herself for not taking off her coat. 'I'm Dr Cross' driver. He sent me to ask about a patient who was admitted here tonight, a member of the St Paul's fire watch.'

'The men's wards are on the second and third floors.'

'Thank you,' Eileen said, and ran upstairs, pausing on the landing to shed her coat, drape it over the railing, and use her handkerchief and spit to rub the worst of the caked blood off her wrists and hands before going on up.

There was no ward sister on second, but an SEN came out of the first ward as she was going in. She went through her story again. 'What's the patient's injury?'

'Dr Cross didn't tell me,' Eileen said. 'Two other firewatchers brought him in, Mr Bartholomew and Mr Humphreys.' She described them.

The nurse shook her head. 'They wouldn't be on the ward. Only patients are allowed on this floor.' But Eileen went through the litany with nurses outside each of the wards, hoping one of them might know where Mr Bartholomew was, and then went up to third. It took forever, and she felt as if she was still in the ambulance, dealing with endless detours and blocked-off passages.

There was no sign of Mr Bartholomew or Mr Humphreys. Or of Alf and Binnie. *They've probably already managed to get themselves thrown out*, she thought, but as she ran down to Admitting, she thought she glimpsed them darting around a corner.

Polly hadn't had any luck either. 'The nurse on Admissions went to ask if anyone in the emergency ward knows anything,' she said, 'but she's been gone forever. I'm afraid she may have been waylaid to help out with patients.'

The way I was with the ambulance, Eileen thought. 'The firewatcher wasn't in the patient roster?'

'No.'

'Are you certain he was brought here?'

'Yes,' Polly said, then looked uncertain. 'That is, the firewatcher I talked to said he thought they'd come here, but if the roads were blocked, they might have taken him to Guy's.'

'No, it caught fire. They had to evacuate.'

'Where were they taking the patients?'

'I don't know,' Eileen said. And if they set off to some other hospital, they might miss him, the way she and Polly had missed each other when she'd gone to Townsend Brothers.

'They might not even be here yet,' she said. 'You may have been able to come here faster on foot, there are so many roads blocked. I'll go and check the ambulance entrance.'

If I can find it, she added silently, and set off to look for it, but before she was halfway down the corridor Polly called her back.

The nurse had returned. 'I found the patient you were looking for,' she said. 'Mr Langby.'

'Where is he?' Polly asked.

'He's just been taken upstairs from surgery.'

Eileen and Polly started towards the stairs, and the nurse moved swiftly to block their way. 'I'm afraid no one's allowed in the recovery room. If you'd like, you can wait in the waiting room.'

'Two men brought him in,' Polly said. 'Members of the fire watch. Can you tell us where they are?'

And when the nurse seemed to hesitate, Eileen put in, 'Dr Cross sent me to find out. I'm his driver.'

'Oh,' the nurse said, 'of course. I'll go and see.'

'One's elderly and the other's tall with dark hair,' Eileen called after the nurse, and described what she thought they were wearing.

'And let's hope she doesn't run into Dr Cross while she's finding out,' she said to Polly.

Binnie came tearing up. 'I been to all the wards, and 'e ain't there. You want me to go and look someplace else?'

'No, stay here till the nurse comes back,' Eileen said. If the nurse didn't bring any information, they could send her to surgery. 'Where's Alf?'

'I dunno,' Binnie said. 'Me and 'im split up. Should I go and look for 'im?'

'No.' Eileen grabbed her to ensure she didn't.

The nurse returned. 'I spoke with the ambulance driver who brought Mr Langby in. She said only one member of the fire watch came with Mr Langby – a Mr Bartholomew – and he left as soon as Mr Langby was safely inside the hospital.'

'Left?' Polly said, looking as though she'd been kicked in the stomach.

'Left to go where?' Binnie asked, and the nurse seemed to suddenly become aware of her presence.

'Children aren't allowed in—' she began.

'Left to go where?' Eileen cut in. 'It's *essential* Dr Cross speak with him immediately. When did he leave?'

'Over an hour ago,' the nurse said. 'You'll have to take that child to the waiting room.'

'She's Dr Cross' niece,' Eileen said. 'I'll go and tell him.'

She let go of Binnie's arm, grabbed Polly's and propelled her down the corridor. 'Don't worry. We can still catch him.

We'll drive to St Paul's,' she said. 'Binnie—' But Binnie had disappeared.

An orderly was coming towards them, looking angry – no doubt the reason Binnie'd vanished, and she'd reappear as soon as he passed – but she didn't.

Good, Eileen thought, steering Polly through the maze of corridors, looking for something familiar to show her they were headed in the right direction. They obviously couldn't take Alf and Binnie with them, and this way they wouldn't have to waste time arguing with them over their staying here.

But Alf popped up moments later and said, 'If you're lookin' for the ambulance, you're goin' the wrong way.'

'Where's your sister?' Eileen asked.

He shrugged. 'I dunno. We split up. Where's your coat?'

'I took it off. Show us the way.'

'Come along,' he said, and led her and Polly quickly and expertly to the dispensary.

Agatha Christie wasn't there, which Eileen supposed was good, considering what had happened last time, but she'd have liked to have seen her again now that she knew who she was. *And what? Tell her how much you love her novels?*

London's burning to the ground, and you've got to get to St Paul's. She pushed out through the emergency doors.

The ambulance wasn't there.

Of course not. There were hundreds of casualties, and Guy's ambulances couldn't get through. *I should have taken the keys*, she thought, feeling sick, staring at the empty spot where the ambulance had been.

Polly was staring at the sky. The wall of smoke was still there, but the red had faded to a pinkish charcoal grey, and above the pall the overcast sky was beginning to show a hint of paler grey. 'It's nearly morning,' she said. 'We'll never make it in time.'

'No, it isn't,' Eileen said staunchly. 'That's the light from the fires reflecting off the cloud cover.'

Polly shook her head. '"It is the lark."'

'It isn't. It's only—' Eileen held her watch up, trying to see the time, but it was too dark to make out see the hands. 'There's still time to get there before he leaves,' she said, though she didn't see how. The Underground wouldn't start running till half past six, and even if they could get to Blackfriars, they'd have to climb Ludgate Hill.

Polly was still staring blindly at the sky. 'We won't be able to find him,' she murmured as if to herself. 'We'll be too late.'

'Alf,' Eileen said, 'do you think you could find us a taxi?'

'A *taxi*?' Alf said. 'Wot d'you want a taxi for?'

Wretched child. 'We must get to St Paul's immediately. It's an emergency.'

'Why don't you take the ambulance?' he said, and Binnie came driving around the corner of the hospital.

She leaned out of the window. 'I thought I better 'ide it so nobody else took it.'

Alf opened the passenger door, scrambled in and rolled down his window. 'Well?' he said. 'Are we goin' or what?'

BARTHOLOMEW'S HOSPITAL – 30 DECEMBER 1940

Mike woke up with a splitting headache, and when he tried to put his hand to his forehead, a searing pain shot along his arm.

He opened his eyes. His arm was swathed in gauze, and he was lying in a white-painted iron bed in a dimly-lit ward. He turned his head to look at the sleeping patient in the bed next to him. It was Fordham, with his arm still in traction. 'Oh God,' he murmured, trying to sit up. 'How did I get here?'

'Shh,' a pretty, wimpled nurse – not Sister Carmody – said, pushing him back down and pulling the blankets up over him. 'Lie still. You've been injured. You're in hospital. Try to rest.'

'How did I get to Orpington?' he asked.

'Orpington?' she said. 'You *did* get a knock on the head. You're in St Bartholomew's – Bart's.'

Bart's. Good. He was still in London. he must have ... but then what was Fordham doing here? He looked over at him, and it wasn't Fordham after all. It was a young boy.

'What time is it?' Mike asked, looking over at the windows, but they were completely covered by sandbags piled against them.

'Never you mind about that. Would you like some breakfast?'

Breakfast? Oh Christ, he'd been out cold the whole night.

'You must try to rest,' the nurse was saying. 'You've a concussion.'

'A concussion?' He felt his head. There was a painful bump on the left side.

'Yes, a burning wall fell on you,' she said, pulling out a thermometer. 'You were extremely lucky. You've a burn on your arm, but it could have been far worse.'

How? he thought. *I was supposed to be finding John Bartholomew, and I've been out of commission all night.*

'Eight other firemen were killed in Fleet Street when a wall collapsed,' she said.

Mike tried to sit up. 'I've got to go—'

She pushed him back down. 'You're not going anywhere,' she said, sounding exactly like Sister Carmody.

A horrible thought struck him. What if he'd been here for weeks, like in Orpington? 'What day is it?'

'What day?' she said, looking worried. 'I'll fetch the doctor.' She stuck the thermometer in her pocket and hurried off.

Oh God, it *had* been weeks. He'd missed the drop.

No, Eileen and Polly wouldn't have gone without you, he told himself. *They'd have made John Bartholomew wait.* Or sent a retrieval team back for him.

But they wouldn't have had any idea where he was. Even if they'd thought to search the hospitals, the nurse obviously thought he was a fireman ...

'I heard you ask what day it was,' the boy in the next bed said. 'It's Monday.'

'No, the *date*,' Mike asked.

The kid gave him the same look the nurse had given him. 'December the thirtieth.'

Relief washed over Mike. 'What time is it?'

'I don't know,' the boy said, 'but it's early. They haven't brought breakfast round yet.'

If Bart's was like Orpington, they brought everybody's breakfast at the crack of dawn, which meant there was still time. But not much. The nurse would be back with the doctor any minute.

Mike sat up carefully, testing for dizziness. His head was splitting, but not so badly that he couldn't stand up, and he didn't have time to wait till the pain lessened. He swung his legs over the side of the bed.

'What are you doing?' the boy asked, alarmed. 'Where are you going?'

'St Paul's.'

'St *Paul's*?' the boy said. 'You'll never get anywhere near it. Our fire brigade tried. We couldn't get any nearer than Creed Lane.'

'You're a *fireman*?' Mike asked. The kid couldn't be fifteen.

'Yes. Redcross Street Fire Brigade,' he said proudly. 'You won't be able to get through. They had to take me all the way round to Bishopsgate when they brought me here.'

'I *have* to get through.' Mike stood up, his head swimming. 'Did you see what the nurse did with my clothes?'

'But you can't just get dressed and walk out of here,' the boy protested. 'You haven't been discharged.'

'I'm discharging myself,' Mike said, yanking open the drawers of the nightstand.

His clothes weren't there. 'I said, did you see what the nurse did with my *clothes*?'

The kid shook his head. 'You were already here when I was brought in,' he said, 'and you heard what the nurse said. You've a concussion. Why don't you wait for her to come back and—?'

And have her what? Tell him not to worry? Promise to ask Matron and then disappear for hours? It could be *days* before they'd let him out of here.

'Or at least wait till the doctor's had a chance to examine

you,' the boy said, his eyes straying towards the bell on the nightstand between their beds.

Mike snatched the bell up and jammed it under his own pillow. 'Did you see what the nurse did with *your* clothes?'

'In the cupboard there,' the kid said, pointing at a white metal cabinet. 'But I don't think you should—'

'I'm fine,' Mike said, limping over to the cupboard. His own clothes were on the top shelf, neatly folded on top of his shoes. He began pulling on his trousers, keeping one eye on the ward doors. The nurse would be back with the doctor any second. He tried not to wince as he eased his shirtsleeve over his bandaged arm. 'Where's the nearest tube stop?'

'Cannon Street,' the boy said, 'but I doubt the trains are running. Waterloo and London Bridge were both hit last night.'

'What about Blackfriars?' Mike asked, buttoning his shirt and jamming the tail into his trousers. 'Was it hit?'

'I don't know. That whole part of the City was pretty much destroyed.'

Destroyed. Mike shoved his bare feet into his shoes and jammed his socks and his tie into his trouser pockets. 'Did you see what they did with my raincoat?'

'No. Look, you're not thinking clearly ...'

There was no time to look for the coat. The nurse had already been gone longer than he'd had any right to expect. Mike pulled his jacket on, grunting with the pain, limped quickly to the doors, and opened one a crack. There were two nurses at the far end of the hallway, talking, but no one at the ward sister's desk. A third of the way down the hall, another hallway branched off it.

And I don't look like a patient, he thought, glancing at his sleeve to make sure the bandage wasn't showing and then smoothing down his hair.

Don't limp, he told himself, and pushed the left-hand door open.

The nurses glanced up briefly and went back to talking. He

walked quickly – but not too quickly – down the hallway, trying not to wince as he forced the weight onto his bad foot.

'Absolutely swamped all last night,' he could hear one of the nurses saying, 'what with the patients from Guy's Hospital and the firemen and all. And then, just as we'd got everyone settled, two horrid children came running through the wards ...'

He reached the side hallway and turned down it, praying it was empty and that it led out of the hospital. It did, but it was raining outside – a drizzle so icy he debated going back inside to find his raincoat, especially since this seemed to be some sort of courtyard at the rear of the hospital. He wasn't even sure he could get to the street from here.

'No, doctor,' he heard someone say behind him, and he hobbled across the yard and through some bushes to the front of the hospital. He'd hoped he might be able to see St Paul's from here so he'd know which way to go, but a low pall of smoke and pinkish-grey clouds hung over the buildings in every direction, hiding every possible landmark, including the Thames, and the fires were no help. Every way he looked there were flames.

And not a single pedestrian to ask directions of. The only person in sight was the red-coated attendant standing at the door of the hospital, his white-gloved hands clasped behind him. Mike supposed that was a good thing – at least there wasn't a huddle of doctors and nurses around him, asking if he'd seen an escaped patient. But he would come to that conclusion on his own if Mike asked, 'Which direction is St Paul's?' and there wasn't time to wander around till he saw it on his own—

'Need a ride, guv'nor?' a voice called from behind him, and to his amazement, a taxi pulled up to the kerb, and a cabbie stuck his head out of the window. 'Where to, guv?'

Mike hesitated, debating whether to have the cabbie take him to Blackfriars first to pick up Eileen. If she was still there. He'd told her to wait there for him, but if the all-clear had sounded, she might have tried to get to St Paul's on her own. 'Has the all-clear gone?' he asked.

'Hours ago,' the cabbie said. 'And a good thing. If the jerries had kept it up all night, I doubt this hospital'd still be standing. Now then, where to?'

St Paul's, he decided. If Eileen wasn't there, he'd go and get her in Blackfriars after he'd found out from Bartholomew where the drop was.

But he'd better not tell the cabbie where he wanted to go till he was inside the taxi. He didn't want him saying, 'Sorry, guv'nor, I'm not driving into that muddle,' and driving off. And he'd better not phrase it as a question.

Mike scrambled into the back, shut the door, and waited till the cabbie'd pulled away from the kerb before leaning forward and saying, 'I need to get to St Paul's.'

'You're an American,' the cabbie said.

'Yes.'

Now he was going to ask if the United States was coming into the war or not, and Mike was too tired to think what the correct answer for December of 1940 was, but instead the cabbie said, 'In that case, guv, I'll take you wherever you want to go.'

If only you could, Mike thought.

'St Paul's, you say? That may take a bit of doing. Most of the streets are blocked off this morning, but I've got me own ways. I'll see you get there right 'n' tight. Take you right to her front door, I will.'

'Thank you,' Mike said. He took a deep breath. *It's only half past six at the latest,* he thought. *The fire watch doesn't come off duty till seven, and Polly's had all night to find Bartholomew, even if she doesn't know what he looks like. And all she had to do was tell him, and he'd wait for Eileen and me.*

He leaned back, cradling his arm, which was throbbing badly. So was his head. *It doesn't matter. They can fix them both in Oxford.*

'Want to see the old girl for yourself, eh, guv'nor?' the cabbie called back to him. 'Make certain she's still there? I don't blame you. I thought she was a goner myself last night. It looked like London was a goner, too.'

He turned down a succession of smoky streets. 'I was taking a passenger to Guy's Hospital – a doctor, it was, trying to get there to take care of casualties. And when we got to Embankment, it looked like the sky itself was on fire, so bright you could read a newspaper by it, and this queer red colour it was.

'"Guy's won't be there," I told him, and blow me if the hospital wasn't on fire when we got there. I had to take him back across London Bridge to Bart's, and a good thing I got him there. I've never seen so many casualties.'

He stopped at a crossing to look down a street. 'Newgate's blocked off, but there's a chance Aldersgate's open.'

It wasn't. A wooden barricade stood across it.

'What about Cheapside?' the cabbie asked the officer standing next to it.

'No, this sector's blocked off all the way to the Tower. Where were you trying to go?'

The cabbie didn't answer him. 'What about Farringdon?'

The officer shook his head. 'They still haven't got the fires out. The whole City's impassable.'

The cabbie nodded and backed around. 'Don't worry,' he said to Mike. 'Just because one way don't work don't mean another won't, does it? I'll get you there.'

Mike hoped he was right. Every street they tried was either roped off or blocked by fallen masonry. A huge crater had been blown out of the middle of one lane, and in the next one over, two portable fire pumps and an ambulance had been abandoned. He was obviously going to have to walk, which meant he'd better put his socks on. He pulled them out of his pockets, took off his shoes, and began putting them on.

'You wanted a look at her,' the cabbie called back to him. 'Well, there she is.'

Mike looked up, and there was St Paul's, the dome framed by

the opening of the lane they were passing, and the ball and gold cross standing out clearly against the dark grey sky.

'Not a scratch on her,' the cabbie said admiringly. 'Not that Hitler didn't try his best. Beautiful, ain't she, sir?'

Beautiful, yes, but at least two miles away. They'd been closer at Bart's. *I need to get out of this cab before we get any further away*, Mike thought, but the cathedral had disappeared as the cabbie dived back into the maze of twisting streets, turning and backing and retracing so much Mike had no idea which direction it lay in.

And neither does he, Mike thought, tying his shoes and buttoning his jacket. *He's just driving. And meanwhile I'm running out of time.*

'Stop,' he said aloud, reaching for the door handle. 'I'll walk from here.'

The cabbie shook his head. 'It's rainin', guv, and you with no coat. No, I said I'd take you straight to St Paul's front door, and so I will.'

'No, really, I—'

But the cabbie had already turned down a narrow alley. He nodded at the blackened buildings on either side. 'Getting near it now, we are.'

Near to where the fires had been, anyway. Whole streets were gutted, with patches still burning in spite of the rain. It looked like vids Mike had seen of London after the pinpoint. Through the charred timbers, he could see the wreckage the next street over, and the next, but no sign of St Paul's.

We must be in the Barbican, he thought, *or Cheapside*—

'And here we are,' the cabbie said, pulling over to the kerb alongside a still-smouldering warehouse.

There, just past it, was St Paul's courtyard, and beyond, the pillared west front of the cathedral. Mike fumbled in his jacket for his wallet.

'Told you I'd get you here,' the cabbie crowed.

The nurse must have taken his wallet. He fumbled in his

trouser pockets and brought up a shilling and a threepenny piece. Oh no, not after he'd made it to within a few hundred yards.

'I must have lost my wallet last night, in the raid,' he stammered, searching through his pockets again. His papers weren't there either. Or his ration book. The nurses must have locked them up for safekeeping. 'I only have—'

'You don't owe me nothin', guv'nor,' the cabbie said, waving the coins away, 'not after what your lot's done.'

'My lot—?'

'You Yanks.' He held up the newspaper. The banner headline read, *Roosevelt Pledges Support to Britain.*

'Nothing can stop us winning the war now,' the cabbie said.

Thank you, President Roosevelt, Mike thought. *You came through in the nick of time.*

'And any rate, it was worth the fare just to see for myself she's still all in one piece. A sight for sore eyes, ain't she, guv?' He pointed towards the cathedral. 'Looks like we're not the only ones wanted to take a look at the old girl.'

He was pointing at knots of people standing in the courtyard, looking up at St Paul's. Mike was too far away to see if Bartholomew and Polly were among them.

He got out of the taxi. 'Thanks – for everything.'

'The same to you, mate,' the cabbie said and drove off.

Mike limped up the street towards St Paul's, looking for Polly and John Bartholomew, but he didn't see them among the people in the courtyard. He hoped they hadn't gone off looking for him.

No, they wouldn't have any idea where to look, he thought. *And they know I'd try to come here. This is where they'd wait.* He looked over at the porch and the broad steps where more people stood and sat. *Unless Polly and Bartholomew have gone to Blackfriars to find Eileen.*

No, Polly didn't know he'd told Eileen to wait there …

A hand grabbed his sleeve. Mike turned, expecting it to be Polly, but it was a thin, dazed-looking man. 'This is where I work,' the man said urgently, pointing at the still-standing door in the wreckage behind Mike. It hung in its frame, held up by two blackened supports. The rest of the warehouse was completely gutted. 'What do I do now?'

'I don't know. Sorry,' Mike said, trying to pull away.

'It's past time for them to open.' The man held up his wrist-watch for Mike to look at. It read nine o'clock.

Nine o'clock. It had taken him three hours to get out of the hospital and over here. The fire watch would have gone off duty long since and gone back down to the Crypt.

That's where Polly and Bartholomew will be, he thought, breaking away from the man's grasp and starting across the courtyard, picking his way over fire hoses and around ash-edged puddles.

The man trailed after him, murmuring, 'It's gone. What do I do now?'

Mike reached the foot of the steps. A score of people sat slumped against the steps, like the soldiers on the *Lady Jane* at Dunkirk, sooty, worn out, unseeing. And he'd been right – Polly was here waiting for him, sitting halfway up the steps next to two ragged children. And so was Eileen. Beside her on the step was a charred mark like a deformed star. The incendiary.

Eileen caught sight of him. She stood up and started down the steps to tell him what had happened, why John Bartholomew wasn't there, but he already knew. One look at Polly's face had told him everything.

'I didn't make it in time,' he said.

Eileen shook her head. 'The dean said he left an hour ago. He—'

'The door's locked,' the man said, clutching at Mike's sleeve. 'What do I do now?'

'I don't know,' Mike said, and sat down on the wet steps next to the girls. 'I don't know.'

ST PAUL'S CATHEDRAL – 30 DECEMBER 1940

Polly sat there on the broad steps of St Paul's, looking at Mike, standing below her, and Eileen. He looked as exhausted as she felt. He was in his shirtsleeves, and there was a bandage on his arm. She wondered what had happened to his coat.

'Bartholomew's gone?' he repeated blankly, looking from her to Eileen. 'Maybe we can still catch him. He can't have got far in this mess. If we can find out which way he went—'

Polly shook her head. 'He took the tube.'

'From Blackfriars? Maybe he's not to the station yet. If we hurry—'

'From St Paul's.'

'St Paul's? You mean the drop's here at the cathedral?'

'No, he left from St Paul's Station.'

'But last night it wasn't—'

'It's up and running this morning,' Eileen said.

'I bet *we* could catch 'im,' Alf said, and Binnie nodded. 'We're *quick*.' They stood up as if ready to dart off after him.

She looked over at them and then back at Polly. 'Do you think—?'

381

Polly shook her head. 'He'd been gone nearly an hour when we got here.'

'Did you ask the fire watch if Bartholomew said where he was going?' Mike asked. 'I mean, not where he was really going. But he might have told them where his—'

'Yes,' she said, cutting him off before he could say 'his drop' and looking pointedly over at Alf and Binnie, who were all ears. 'He told them his uncle in Wales had sent for him.'

'Did you ask them what else he said? He might have dropped some hint about where he was really going—'

Where he was going was Oxford. 'Mike—'

'Did you ask them which train he was taking? That'll at least tell us which direction he was heading.'

No, it wouldn't. St Paul's was only two stops away from access to every other line on the Underground. 'Mike, it's no use. He's gone,' Polly said, but he was already striding up the steps and into St Paul's.

Polly scrambled to her feet and went inside after him. He was already halfway to the transept, his footsteps echoing in the deserted nave. She called, 'Half the fire watch has already gone home, and the other half's gone to bed. Mike!' She ran after him.

It was last night all over again – her running endlessly after a man she couldn't catch, and she was suddenly too weary to try. She stopped and walked back down the dank, smoky nave through the charred scraps of paper that lay everywhere, the flaming orders of worship that had danced through the air last night. Now they littered the floor like black leaves.

There was still a puddle of water from where she had doused the burning postcards, and next to it lay the half-burnt print of *The Light of the World*. Polly bent to pick it up. The left-hand side of the picture where the door was supposed to be was blackened and curled, and when Polly touched it, that half crumbled into flakes and fell away, so that Christ's hand was raised to knock on nothingness.

Polly looked at the print a long moment, then laid it gently on the desk and went outside and sat down on the broad step next to Eileen and the children, and in a moment Mike came back outside and sat down between them. 'Bartholomew didn't say anything to anybody,' he said. 'He just left. I am so sorry, Polly.'

'It's not your fault,' she said. 'You tried your—'

'I beg your pardon,' said the man whom she'd seen speaking to Mike before as he got out of the taxi. He was standing at the foot of the steps, looking beseechingly up at Mike. 'Should I go home, do you think? Or should I wait here?'

'The place he worked was destroyed last night,' Mike explained to them.

'What do I do now?' the man said.

I have no idea, Polly thought.

'Stay here,' Mike said decisively. 'The owners of the business are bound to show up sooner or later.'

But what if they don't come till it's too late? Polly thought.

'Thank you,' the man said. 'You've been very helpful.'

They watched him go back down the steps and across the puddle-filled courtyard.

'Helpful,' Mike said bitterly. 'It's my fault we didn't find Bartholomew, you know. If I'd asked you about him and about St Paul's nearly burning down instead of *assuming* he'd been here at the end of the Blitz. Or seen that damned wall coming down—'

'What wall?' Eileen asked.

He told them how he'd been knocked unconscious and woken up in Bart's.

'You were there?' Eileen said incredulously. 'At *Bart's*?'

We were all at Bart's last night, Polly thought.

The injured firewatcher might have been in the bed next to the unconscious Mike. Mike might have been only inches away from Mr Bartholomew, as she had been up in the rafters of St Paul's, separated from him by only a wall. They had been so close.

But everything had conspired against them, from Theodore's refusal to leave the pantomime to the blocked streets that had kept them from getting here before he left this morning. It was as if the entire space-time continuum had been engaged in an elaborate plot to keep them from reaching John Bartholomew. Just as it had kept her and Eileen from finding each other last autumn. *How all occasions do inform against us,* she thought.

'It isn't your fault, it's mine,' Eileen was saying. 'If I'd listened properly to Mr Bartholomew's lecture, I'd have known he was still here, and we could have found him weeks ago. And now it's too late—'

''ow come you can't go to Wales an' get 'im?' Alf asked.

''cause they don't know *where* 'e is in Wales,' Binnie said. 'And you 'eard 'im.' She pointed at Mike. ''e ain't really goin' there. 'e only said 'e was,' and Polly was glad she'd stopped Mike from saying any more than he already had. They'd obviously been listening to every word the three of them had said. And she was almost certain they were the two delinquents she'd seen stealing the picnic basket that night in Holborn, though she hadn't said anything to Eileen.

'Well, if 'e ain't in Wales, then where's 'e gone?' Alf was asking Eileen.

'We don't know,' Polly said. 'He didn't tell us.'

'I bet *I* could find 'im.'

'How?' Binnie said. 'You don't even know what 'e looks like, you dunderpate.'

'I *ain't* a dunderpate. Take it back,' Alf said and dived at Binnie. She darted away down the steps and across the forecourt, Alf in hot pursuit.

Eileen was still blaming herself. 'I should simply have told the incident officer I couldn't take the ambulance to St Paul's.'

And I shouldn't have rushed off to Bart's without finding out the injured firewatcher's name and who'd gone with him to hospital, Polly thought. If she hadn't, she'd have found out what Mr Humphreys had told her a few minutes ago, that he'd helped Bartholomew put the injured man in the ambulance and then gone back up to the roofs. She could've told Mr Humphreys to tell Mr Bartholomew not to leave till they got there.

'It's no one's fault,' she said.

They couldn't have found him, no matter what they did, because it had all happened already, and when he got back to Oxford, he hadn't been bearing a message from them. It had been a hopeless enterprise from the beginning. It had all – the attempts to contact Mike's retrieval team and the search for Gerald – been hopeless.

The door behind them opened, and Mr Humphreys came out bearing a tray with a teapot and cups on it. 'Your friend Mr Davis said you were still out here,' he said to Polly, handing her and the others cups and saucers. 'And I thought you might like some tea. It's such a cold morning.'

He poured out their tea, then went down the steps and over to the man who'd asked Mike what he should do and then over to Alf and Binnie, who were playing in the still-smouldering wreckage.

He gave them biscuits and then came back. 'I'm so sorry you missed your friend, Miss Sebastian,' he said. 'I'll ask Dean Matthews if he had an address where Mr Bartholomew might be reached. Do you need assistance in getting home?'

Yes, she thought, *but you can't help us.* She shook her head.

'If you need bus fare or—'

'No,' Polly said. 'We have transport.'

'Good. Drink your tea,' he ordered. 'It will make you feel better.'

Nothing will make me feel better, she thought, but she drank it down. It was hot and sweet. Mr Humphreys must have put his entire month's sugar ration into it. She drained the cup, feeling suddenly ashamed of herself. She wasn't the only one who'd had a bad night. She wasn't the only one facing a frightening future. And the outlook wasn't totally bleak. The fact that they hadn't found Mr Bartholomew meant that Mr Dunworthy hadn't betrayed them, that Colin hadn't lied to her.

And her actions, and Mike's and Eileen's, didn't seem to have affected events. Last night had gone just as it was supposed to. St Paul's was still standing, and the rest of the City wasn't. History was still on track.

For the past two months Polly'd been terrified of finding proof Mike had altered the course of the war, but now she almost wished historians *were* able to alter events, to alter *this* – the Guildhall and the Chapter House and all those beautiful Christopher Wren churches destroyed. And all the horrors that were still to come – Dresden and Auschwitz and Hiroshima. And Jerusalem and the Pandemic and the pinpoint bomb which would obliterate St Paul's. To repair the whole bloody mess.

But what could do that? The three of them had attempted all last night to find a single man and deliver a single message, to no avail. What made her think they could repair history, even if they knew how to go about it? And there was no way to know. The continuum was far too complex, too chaotic to ensure that an attempt to avert a disaster wouldn't lead to a worse one. And, as horrific as World War II had been, at least the Allies had won. They'd stopped Hitler, which had been an unarguably good thing.

But at such a terrible, terrible price – millions dead, cities in ruins, lives destroyed. *Including mine,* she thought. *And Eileen's and Mike's.*

She glanced over at them, sitting hunched on the steps, Eileen looking half-frozen and about to cry, Mike with his arm bandaged and his foot half shot off. They looked all in, and Polly felt a wave of love for both of them. They had done all this, quite literally risked life and limb, for her, because of her deadline. And they would both have sacrificed their lives if it had meant getting her safely home. Which meant the least she could do was to pull herself together.

Mr Humphreys had managed to, and so had London. The

day after they'd watched half their city burn down around their ears, Londoners hadn't sat around feeling sorry for themselves. Instead, they'd set about putting out the fires that were still burning and digging people out of the rubble. They'd repaired water mains and railway tracks and telephone lines, shown up at their jobs even if where they worked was no longer there, swept up glass. Gone on.

If they could do it, she could, too. '*Once more into the breach,*' she thought and stood up and brushed the soot off her coat.

'We should be going,' she said. She gathered up their cups and saucers, took them inside, set them on the desk next to the half-burned print of *The Light of the World*, and started out, then went back to look at it again – at the lantern raised to light the nothingness which lay before it, the darkness on all sides, at Christ's robe, smeared with soot from the charred, flaking edge.

She'd expected his face to look as done in, as defeated as Eileen's and Mike's, but it didn't. It was filled with kindness and concern, like Mr Humphreys'.

She fished a sixpence out of her bag, laid it on the desk, folded the picture into quarters, put it in her pocket and went outside.

'We need to go,' she said to Mike and Eileen. 'We'll be late for work. And we must take the ambulance back to Bart's.'

'And get my coat,' Mike said. 'And Eileen's.'

'I need to take the children home first,' Eileen said. 'Alf! Binnie!' she called to them.

They were still messing about in the ruins, poking at a smouldering timber with sticks and then jumping back as it crumbled into glowing embers.

'Come along. I'll take you home.'

''ome?' Binnie said. The children looked at each other and then up at her.

'We don't need nobody to take us,' Alf said. 'We can get there on our own.'

'No, the trains to Whitechapel may not be running, and your

mother will be worried to death,' Eileen said. 'I want to tell her where you've been all night and how much help you were.' She started down the steps towards them.

Alf and Binnie exchanged glances again, and then dropped their sticks and tore off down the street, running as fast as they could.

'Alf! Binnie! Wait!' Eileen called, and took off after them, Polly and Mike in pursuit, but they'd already vanished into the tangle of smoking ruins beyond Paternoster Row.

'We'll never catch them in that maze,' Mike said, and Eileen nodded reluctantly.

'Will they be all right, do you think?' Polly asked.

'Yes, they're expert at taking care of themselves,' Eileen said, looking after them and frowning. 'But I wonder why—'

'They were probably afraid if you took them home they'd have to go to school,' Mike said, and when they reached the ambulance, he peered at the petrol gauge and said, 'We couldn't have taken them home anyway. We don't have enough gas to get to Whitechapel and back. We'll be lucky if we've got enough to get us to Bart's.'

'If we can *find* Bart's,' Eileen said. She started the car. 'Alf was my navigator, remember?'

Polly nodded, thinking of all the blocked streets and barricades.

'I think I can get us there,' Mike said.

And he did.

Eileen's coat was still hanging over the railing where she'd left it, but Mike's was nowhere to be found, and he refused to ask the staff. 'I left without being discharged,' he told them, 'and they're liable to try to put me back in the hospital.'

'I thought you said you'd scarcely burned your arm at all,' Polly said.

'I did – it's nothing. But that doesn't mean they'll let me out, and I can't afford to be stuck in here doing nothing like I was all those weeks in Orpington. I don't need a coat.'

'But it's winter,' Eileen said. 'You'll catch your death—'

'I'll go and find it,' Polly said, taking charge. 'Eileen, go and turn the ambulance in. Mike, wait for us out the front.' He nodded and limped off towards the door.

'You don't suppose they'll arrest me for stealing the ambulance, do you?' Eileen asked.

'Considering the blood-covered state of your coat, no. But if they do, I'll help you escape,' Polly said, and went up to the ward to ask about Mike's coat.

The nurse thought it likely they'd had to cut it off him when he was brought in. 'You might check in A&E.'

It wasn't there either, or with the Matron. Polly went out front to tell Mike. He and Eileen were both there. 'You weren't arrested?' Polly asked Eileen.

'No, they were extremely nice about it. You didn't find Mike's coat?'

'No, sorry. I'll have to ask Mrs Wyvern to get you another. Here.' Polly took off the pumpkin-coloured scarf Miss Hibbard had given her. 'Take this till we get you a coat.' She wrapped it around his neck, and they set out for the tube station.

It was open, but nothing much was working.

'This means there may still be a chance of catching Bartholomew,' Mike said. 'If the train he needed to take was destroyed or wasn't running, he may not have gone back yet. He may still be here in London.'

'Mike,' Polly protested, 'he left two hours—'

'You two go on to work. If I catch him, I'll come and get you at Townsend Brothers,' Mike said and took off before they could stop him.

'Do you think there's a chance—?' Eileen asked Polly.

'No,' Polly said, though it took them an hour and a half just to reach Townsend Brothers.

'Thank goodness you're here,' Miss Snelgrove said. 'Neither Doreen nor Sarah can make it in, and the New Year's sales begin day after tomorrow – good heavens, you're hurt!' she said to Eileen, and ordered Polly to telephone an ambulance.

'It's not my blood,' Eileen said, looking down at her coat. 'I don't suppose you know of anything that will take out bloodstains?'

'Benzene,' Miss Snelgrove said promptly, 'though it looks as if it's soaked through.'

She sent Eileen up to Housewares for a bottle of the cleaning fluid and set Polly to lettering placards for the New Year's sales while she went to fill in for Sarah.

Polly spent the rest of the day printing 'Special New Year's Markdown' and worrying about why Mike didn't come and about his burned arm and what they were going to do after tomorrow.

As of January first, they wouldn't know where and when any of the raids were or what was safe, except for Townsend Brothers and Notting Hill Gate. She assumed Mrs Rickett's and Mike's boarding house were, too, though Badri hadn't said whether the list of allowed addresses was safe for the duration of the Blitz or only till the end of her assignment. But Mr Dunworthy had been so insistent that she stay in a tube station which hadn't been hit at all that he was unlikely to have let her stay in a boarding house that had been.

But unlikely wasn't certain, which meant they'd best spend their nights in Notting Hill Gate – and hope they got there before the raids began.

Which was impossible with the short winter days. The sirens routinely went before five. And Mike's job took him all over London. And there were daytime raids to worry about. And UXBs and dangling parachute-mines. And the fact that by closing time Mike still hadn't shown up.

Where was he? And what if he got blood poisoning in his burned arm? Or caught pneumonia? Though that at least she could do something about, and after work she and Eileen went straight to Notting Hill Gate to speak to Mrs Wyvern.

She wasn't there. 'She and the rector are helping with a fund-raiser for families who've been bombed out,' Miss Hibbard told her.

'Do you know where?' Polly asked. There weren't any raids tonight, so she could go and find her, but they hadn't told Miss Hibbard the location of the fund-raiser.

I'll have to ask Miss Laburnum, Polly thought. 'Did she say when she was coming over?'

'She has a bad cold,' Miss Hibbard said. 'I told her she should stay at home. The station's so drafty and cold.'

It was, and the emergency staircase was even icier. When Mike finally arrived, Polly and Eileen took off their coats and the three of them huddled together under them as Mike told them where he'd been, which had apparently been in every tube station in London, with no luck. 'I should have gone to St Paul's Station as soon as I got to the cathedral,' he said. 'If I had—'

'You still couldn't have caught him,' Polly said.

'I'll figure out a way to get you out of here before your deadline, Polly,' he said fiercely.

'What about the retrieval team?' Eileen asked. 'You still might be able to find them,' and Polly realised that in all the excitement the night before, they hadn't told her what had happened.

'I *did* find them,' Mike said, 'but it wasn't the retrieval team. It was a guy I knew in hospital.'

Eileen's face fell. 'But they still might come. I could write to Mr Goode again. And the manor. And we could check Polly's drop again. It might be working by now.'

'You're right,' he said. 'We'll do all those things. And I'll figure out a way to get you both out of here. But right now we need to concentrate on staying alive till I do. Where are tomorrow's raids?'

'There aren't any tomorrow either,' she said, 'but I'm afraid I have more bad news.' She told them about not knowing about the raids after the first of the year.

'But Notting Hill Gate's safe, right?' Mike said. 'And Townsend Brothers, so you two are safe during the day.'

'No,' Eileen said. 'My supervisor told me today they plan to let all the Christmas help go as soon as the New Year's sales are over.'

'And we have another problem,' Polly said. 'Sometime – I don't know when – Eileen and I are going to be conscripted.'

'*Conscripted?*' Mike said. 'Into the Army?'

'Not necessarily, but into some sort of national service. The ATS or the land girls or working in a war-industry factory. It's the National Service Act. All British civilians between the ages of twenty and thirty must sign up.'

'Can't you get a deferment from Townsend Brothers or something?' Mike asked.

'No,' Polly said, 'and if we don't volunteer before it goes into effect, we run the risk of being assigned somewhere outside of London.'

'Which means we'd better find a way out of here fast,' Mike said, frowning.

'Don't you know when *any* of the raids are, Polly?' Eileen asked nervously.

'Some of them,' Polly said. 'And some nights they attacked other cities.'

'And they can't attack when the weather's bad,' Mike said, 'which should help for the next couple of months. And the Blitz ends in May, right?'

'Yes, May eleventh,' Polly said. *But between now and then nearly twenty thousand civilians will be killed.*

'So all we have to do is get through the next four and a half months,' Mike said, 'and then we're safe till Denys Atherton gets here.'

Safe, Polly thought.

'And that's a worst-case scenario. We're bound to figure out a way to get home before—' He stopped. 'What is it, Polly? Why are you looking like that?'

'Nothing. What *is* that dreadful odour?'

'My coat,' Eileen confessed. 'I'm afraid I used a bit too much benzene on it to get the blood out.'

'A *bit*?' Mike said, laughing, but the fumes grew so overpowering they had to abandon the staircase and go and sleep in the station, which was no warmer.

'We *must* get Mike a coat,' Eileen said on the way to work the next morning. 'Perhaps there'll be one marked down that we can buy.'

But they had no time to look amid the preparations for the New Year's sales and then the sales themselves, which people flocked to in spite of the wretched weather. The next few days there was bone-chilling fog and almost constant sleet.

'But that's good, isn't it?' Eileen asked as they hurried to Oxford Circus after work. 'It means there won't be any raids.'

It also meant that getting Mike a coat was more urgent than ever – and that the benzene was increasingly overpowering as Eileen's coat dried out. 'Miss Snelgrove said the odour would fade,' Eileen said, 'but it doesn't seem to be, does it?'

'No,' Polly said. It was a good thing there was a ban on smoking in the shelters. A stray flicked match and they'd both go up in flames.

'I've been thinking about what you said about our having to volunteer,' Eileen said as they got on the train. 'Perhaps I could volunteer to be an ambulance driver at Bart's. When I took the ambulance back, Dr Cross said if I hadn't got those passengers to hospital when I did, they'd have died.'

'What passengers?'

Eileen told her about the unconscious ambulance driver and the Army lieutenant. *Thank goodness Mike isn't here to hear this*, Polly thought. The last thing he needed was to begin worrying all over again about the possibility of their having altered the course of the war.

It couldn't have, she told herself. *We won the war. And the twenty-ninth went just like it was supposed to*, but after Mike and Eileen were asleep, she stole away to look at a discarded newspaper and make certain.

The Guildhall had burned just as it had in the historical records, and so had St Bride's and St Mary-le-Bow. But All Hallows by the Tower had burned, too. She'd thought it had been only partially destroyed, and the *Evening Standard* said the Germans had dropped fifteen thousand incendiaries instead of eleven thousand.

But those could easily be errors in reporting, she thought, crawling back under Eileen's reeking coat. *We won the war. Eileen and I were both there on VE Day.*

But the discrepancies haunted her all the next day, and on her lunch break she bought the *Herald* and the *Daily Mail* to check and then went up to the book department to tell Eileen not to say anything to Mike about her possibly driving an ambulance for Bart's. 'Or what Dr Cross said. He'd think driving an ambulance was too dangerous.'

'That's true,' Eileen said absently, much more concerned with getting Mike a coat.

'It's supposed to snow tonight,' she said, and an hour later she came down to report that she'd persuaded her supervisor to let her leave an hour early to go to the Assistance Board. She asked what size coat Mike wore and said, 'I'll try to get you a hat as well, Polly. Tell Mrs Rickett I won't be in to supper. And you needn't wait for me. I'll meet you at Notting Hill Gate. Have you a rehearsal tonight?'

'I'm not certain,' Polly said. 'The troupe's still arguing over what play to do next.'

And when she arrived, she found them discussing whether to do another play at all, given the fact that the intermittency of the raids and the winter weather were causing people to stay at home instead of using the shelter.

Including some of the troupe. Miss Laburnum was still recovering from her cold, and neither Sir Godfrey nor Mr Simms were there. 'We can't put on a play without a cast,' Mr Dorming grumbled. 'Or an audience.'

'But if we did, that would encourage people to come to Notting Hill Gate,' the rector said. 'We'd be doing our bit to help keep the populace safe.'

'Perhaps instead of a play, we could give a series of dramatic readings,' Miss Hibbard suggested. 'That way we wouldn't need everyone to be here.' While they discussed possible ones to do, Polly was able to sneak away to the emergency staircase to see if Eileen was there yet.

Halfway there she ran into Mike, who'd apparently just arrived. His hair and the pumpkin-orange scarf were wet, and he looked half-frozen. Polly was glad Eileen had gone to get him a coat.

She told him where Eileen had gone. 'She said she'd meet us here, but I don't know if she's arrived yet. I was just going to check the staircase.'

'I'll do that,' he said. 'You check the canteen, and I'll meet you back at the escalator.'

Eileen wasn't in the queue for the canteen. Polly went back down to the District Line to wait, standing in the southbound archway so she could spot Eileen and Mike but still duck back into the tunnel if any of the troupe descended the escalator. She didn't want to get dragged off to the platform to discuss the merits of reading scenes from *The Little Minister* versus *The Importance of Being Earnest*. But Mr Simms was the only one she saw come down. He was carrying his dog Nelson, who was afraid of the slatted escalator treads, in his arms.

There weren't nearly as many people in the station as usual, and most of those who were there were carrying umbrellas, not bedrolls and picnic baskets. The rest of the shelterers must have decided, as Mr Dorming had said, to take their chances that with the inclement weather there wouldn't be a raid. She hoped they were right.

And that Eileen would be here soon. *I hate not knowing when and where the bombs are going to fall,* she thought.

Mike came back. 'Eileen's still not here?'

'No. Did you hear planes on your way to the station?'

'No.' He looked up the escalator. 'Where did she say she was going for the—? Here she is.'

He pointed up at the top of the escalator and two men who'd just stepped on, and behind them, only her red hair visible, Eileen. Mike waved at her. 'It looks like she was successful.'

Polly caught a glimpse of a grey tweed overcoat over Eileen's arm and a woman's dark blue hat in her hand. Mike waved again.

Eileen saw them. She waved back with the blue hat.

Polly put her hand to her mouth.

'Looks like she was able to get a new coat too,' Mike said.

Yes, Polly thought sickly, watching Eileen push past the two men and hurry down the moving steps towards them. She was wearing a bright green coat, and there was no mistaking it.

It was the coat she had been wearing in Trafalgar Square on VE Day.

'Time present and time past
Are both perhaps present in time future,
And time future contained in time past.'

FOUR QUARTETS, T.S. ELIOT

CROYDON – OCTOBER 1944

Mary rolled down the window of the ambulance and leaned out, straining to hear. She was certain she'd heard the rattling putt-putt of a V-1.

'A flying bomb?' Fairchild said. 'I don't hear anything.'

'*Shh,*' Mary ordered, but she couldn't hear anything either. Could it have been another motorcycle or—?

An enormous boom shook the parked ambulance.

'Oh my God,' Fairchild said, 'that was nearly on top of us.' She leaned forward to turn the ignition and start the ambulance's bells. 'You don't think it hit the ambulance post, do you?'

'No, it was nearer than that.'

It was. The rocket had fallen just off the High Street they'd driven through only minutes before, smashing shops and stores. At the near end, an estate agent's was still recognisable, and at the other the marquee of a cinema stood at an awkward angle. Fires burned here and there among the wreckage.

Good, Mary thought, *at least we'll have light to see by.* She wished she'd worn her overalls and boots instead of her skirted uniform, since it looked like they were the first ones here and were going to have to clamber over the wreckage looking for victims.

Fairchild drove the ambulance as close to the wreckage as she could and parked, and they scrambled out. 'At least we've plenty of bandages,' she said. 'I'll go and find a telephone and ring the post.'

'Good, though I should imagine the post heard the explosion.' Mary put on her helmet and fastened the strap. 'I'll go and see if there are casualties in the cinema.'

'It doesn't show films on Wednesday,' Fairchild said. 'I know because Reed and I came down to see *Random Harvest* Wednesday last, and it was shut. And none of these shops would have been open at this time of night, so perhaps there won't have been any casualties.' She ran off to find a telephone box, and Mary pulled on her gumboots and started through the wreckage, hoping Fairchild was right.

Halfway down the street she thought she heard a voice. She stopped, listening, but she couldn't hear anything for Fairchild's hurrying back towards her, dislodging bricks and chunks of mortar as she came. 'I notified Croydon,' she reported. 'Have you found any—?'

'Shh. I thought I heard something.'

They listened. 'Jeppers!' Mary heard a man's voice call from somewhere at the other end of the destroyed area, and a word she couldn't make out.

'It came from over there,' Fairchild said, pointing, and began picking her way through the rubble.

Mary followed, stopping every few feet to look about her.

She'd been wrong about the fires. They gave off only enough light to manoeuvre by, not enough to see the hazards in her way or to make out more than silhouettes, and the flickering flames made her think she saw movement where there wasn't any.

Midway across, Mary thought she heard the man again. She stopped, listening, and then called, 'Where are you?'

'Over here.' It was so faint she could scarcely hear it.

'Where? Keep talking.'

'Over ...' He went off into a spasm of coughing.

Which she *could* hear. 'Fairchild, he's this way!' she called, and set off towards the sound, picking her way over the tangle of bricks and broken wood.

The coughing stopped. 'Where are you?' she called again.

'Here he is!' Fairchild called from several yards off, and then, as Mary clambered over to her, 'I found him.'

She was bending over a dark form, but she straightened as Mary reached her. 'He's dead.'

'Are you certain?' Mary said. It was so dark, Fairchild might have made a mistake. She squatted down next to the body.

Not body: half a body. The man had been sliced in two. Which meant he couldn't have been the one coughing. 'There's another one here somewhere,' she told Fairchild. 'You take that area over there and I'll look over here.' She walked back the way she'd come, calling, 'Where are you? If you can hear us, make a sound,' and then waiting, listening for the slightest sound before moving on again.

She stepped carefully over a broken window. A large black object lay on its side next to it. *What is that?* Mary wondered. *A piano?* No, it was far too large, and there was paper tangled in it and lying in drifts all round it. *It's a printing press*, she thought. *This must have been a newspaper office*, and saw an arm.

Let's hope it isn't only an arm, she thought, scrambling over to it. *Or that the rest of him isn't under that printing press.*

It wasn't. The man lay next to it, and the reason she hadn't been able to see him was that he was covered in newspapers, and his face was so white and so spattered with blood – which looked black in the orange light from the fires – that it was barely recognisable as a face.

He's dead as well, she thought, squatting down next to him, but his chest was rising and falling. And as she bent closer, she saw that the white was from plaster dust, which he was caked with. 'Are you all right?' she asked, but he didn't respond. 'Don't worry. We'll get you out of here straightaway. Fairchild!' she called into the darkness. 'Over here!'

She tried to see what the blood was from, wishing she had her pocket torch. She could scarcely see him in the reddish firelight. But she could see the blood. It was all over his coat and the newspapers covering him. 'Bring a torch!' she shouted, and began brushing the newspapers aside, looking for the wound that had to be there. She opened his coat. There was no blood on his shirt.

It's someone else's blood, she thought, and then remembered the printing press. She touched the black on his coat and then brought her fingers up to her nose. Ink. It must have splattered on him when the V-1 hit.

But even if it wasn't blood, he was clearly injured. *Perhaps the blast only knocked him unconscious*, she thought hopefully, but when she moved the remaining newspapers off, he was buried from his waist down in bricks and chunks of plaster. She dug through them with both hands. His left leg was covered in blood, and this time it wasn't printer's ink. All the blood and the darkness made it difficult to see just how bad the injury was, but the lower half of the leg looked as if it was badly mangled, and his foot had been severed.

Mary fumbled in her pocket for a handkerchief and tied it round his leg just below his knee. She broke off a short length of wood, tied it into the knot, and twisted the tourniquet till it was tight.

'Is he alive?' Fairchild asked, appearing out of the darkness to kneel down next to him and peer into his face.

'Yes,' Mary said, trying to see if the bleeding from his leg had stopped. 'Did you bring the torch?'

'No, I'll go and fetch one. How bad is he?'

'He's unconscious and his leg's crushed. His foot's been cut off,' she said, and the man murmured something.

'What is it?' Mary asked, bending over him, putting her ear close to his lips.

'Wasn't … ' he said, and his voice was hoarse and rasping.

From the plaster dust, she thought.

'… done …' His eyes closed again.

Done for. 'You're going to be all right,' she said, patting his chest. 'I'll get you out of here, I promise. I've tied a tourniquet,' she told Fairchild. 'Is Croydon here yet?'

'No,' Fairchild said, looking off towards where their ambulance was parked. 'I thought I heard a motor a moment ago, but I must have been mistaken.'

'We'll have to get him to the ambulance ourselves then,' Mary said. 'Go and fetch the stretcher.'

Fairchild nodded and ran off. 'Don't forget the torch,' Mary called after her, and went back to uncovering his other leg, shifting bricks and a metal case of type which was impossibly heavy. 'You mustn't worry. We'll have you out of here in no time.'

He seemed to flinch at the sound of her voice. 'No,' he murmured. 'Oh no … no …'

'You mustn't be frightened. You're going to be all right.'

'No.' He shook his head feebly. 'I'm *so* sorry.'

'It's all right.' *Poor man.* 'It's not your fault. You've been injured by a flying bomb,' but her words had no effect on him.

'Still been here …' he said, his hoarse voice anguished, '… dead …'

'Shh. Don't try to talk.'

'I thought I could … not supposed to be here …'

'Just lie still. I need to look at your leg.'

She went back to uncovering his other leg and his foot, which, thank God, wasn't cut off, but it was bleeding badly, and she didn't have another handkerchief for a tourniquet. She pressed on it with both hands. 'Fairchild!' she called. 'Paige! I need the medical kit.'

'Dulwich …' the man murmured. He must be asking where they were going to take him.

'We'll take you to Norbury,' she said. 'It's quicker. You mustn't worry about that. It's our job.'

'I can't get the stretcher out,' Fairchild called from the ambulance. 'It's stuck.'

'Leave it! Just bring the medical kit.'

'What?' Fairchild called back. 'I can't hear you, Mary!'

The man made a sound, part moan, part gasp. 'Mary?' he murmured.

'Yes,' she said, 'I'm here.' She pressed down as hard as she could.

This wasn't working. Blood was still oozing through her hands. It would have to be a tourniquet. 'Paige!' she called. 'Bring the kit! Hurry.'

'Mary,' the man said urgently, 'you mustn't go.'

'I'm not leaving. I'm right here,' she reassured him.

He'd been wearing a tie. If she could get it off, she could use that for a tourniquet. She opened his coat and began to untie the knot.

'Something wrong ...' he said, and the rest of his words were lost in a spasm of coughing.

The knot wouldn't come undone. She dug at the silk with her fingernails, trying to loosen it.

'Don't,' he said, distressed.

'I need to untie your tie so I can use it for a bandage. I'm going to tie a tourniquet to stop your leg from bleeding.' *Where is Fairchild? And Croydon's ambulance?*

The knot finally came loose. Mary untied it quickly. 'I'll get you out of here,' the man murmured, repeating what she'd said. 'I promise.'

She pulled the tie from his collar and began to crawl back down to his foot.

He grabbed hold of her wrist. 'Mary,' he said urgently, choked, and began to cough again. 'Don't go ...'

'I'm not going anywhere. I'm only going to bind your foot up. I won't leave you. I promise.'

'No,' he said, and caught hold of her wrist. 'You can't go!'

'I won't,' she said. 'I promise.'

'No,' he said furiously. 'Don't go. It won't ...' And the world went white and then black, splattering them with printer's ink, with blood, and she bent over him to tackle him, to push him into the gutter, but it was too late. It had already gone off.

'Once more unto the breach, dear friends.'

WILLIAM SHAKESPEARE *HENRY V*

LONDON – WINTER 1941

Eileen hurried down the escalator steps towards them in her new green coat, calling, 'Mike, I got you a coat!' She waved the dark blue hat. 'Polly, look, a hat!'

She reached the bottom. 'And it matches your coat—' She stopped short. 'What's wrong?' She looked anxiously at Polly and then at Mike. 'Has something happened?'

Yes, Polly thought, feeling sick.

'What's wrong?' Eileen said.

I've got to keep this from them, Polly thought. *Just now, it will kill them if they find out. I've got to look as though nothing's happened.* But it was impossible, like trying to stand up after being kicked in the stomach. She couldn't even think what excuse ...

'Are you ill?' Eileen was saying, alarmed. 'You're white as a sheet.' Mike turned to look questioningly at her.

'No, I'm fine,' Polly managed to say. 'I was afraid something had happened to you. You're so *late*. Where have you been?'

'The Assistance Board hadn't any coats at all,' Eileen said. 'The woman in charge there said they've had an absolute *run* on them since these last attacks and with the cold weather and everything, so I had to go to the one near St Pancras, and then I had difficulty getting a bus back. I'm sorry I worried you.'

Mike was still looking suspiciously at Polly.

'It's this not knowing when the raids are,' Polly said. 'It's got me a bit nervy, that's all. When the sirens went, and you still weren't here ...'

'I *am* sorry, but I did get you a hat.' Eileen handed it to Polly. 'And most importantly, I got you a coat, Mike. I'm afraid it's a bit too large,' she said, helping him try it on, 'but I thought it would prove easier to take in a large one than to let out one which was too small. Mine's not really warm enough for winter, but it was such a bright, hopeful colour that I couldn't resist. I was so sick of black and brown. This cheered me just to look at it. Doesn't it make you think of spring, Polly?'

No.

'Yes, it's very pretty,' she said.

Mike was still watching her.

'And what a lovely hat!' Polly said. She tried it on and made Eileen hold up her compact so she could see how it looked in the tiny mirror, and when she saw her own image, she was relieved to see that some of the colour had come back into her cheeks. 'Thank you so much. You're a miracle-worker, Eileen. Mike, hold out your arm.' She turned his cuff inside out to look at the lining. 'This should be easy to turn up. Now, take it off and let me see the seams.'

'We can do that later,' he said. 'The three of us need to talk.'

Oh no, Polly thought, *he's guessed.*

But when they got to the emergency staircase, he only wanted to know if she'd made a list of the raids she could remember. 'Yes,' she said, relieved to change the subject. 'I'm afraid it's rather spotty. The only two I know of in January are the ones on the nights of the eleventh and the twenty-ninth.'

Mike wrote the dates down. 'Do you know which parts of London were hit?'

'The East End was hit on January twenty-ninth, and central

London on Saturday the eleventh. Liverpool Street and Bank Underground Stations were both hit—'

'Bank?' Eileen interrupted.

'Yes, and several hospitals – I don't know which ones.'

'And you don't know about any other January raids?'

'No. I do know the weather was bad enough during January and February to keep the Luftwaffe grounded part of the time,' she said, 'and some nights they were bombing outside London – Portsmouth and Manchester and Bristol.'

'Were people killed at Bank Station?' Eileen asked.

'Yes, and at Liverpool Street,' Polly said. 'I'm not sure exactly how many. More than a hundred. But the raids weren't over this part of London, and this station was never hit.'

She told them the February and March raids she remembered. Buckingham Palace had been bombed again, and the shelter at London Bridge Station and the popular nightclub, the Café de Paris, had been hit. She was starting on April when Eileen said, 'Before we do any more, can we go to the canteen? I'm starving. What with getting the coats and all, I hadn't any supper.'

'I'll go with you,' Polly said, and got to her feet, but Mike said, 'We'll catch up with you. I want to ask Polly about something first.'

Eileen nodded and clattered down the steps. The door clanged shut, and Polly braced herself.

'What happened back there at the escalator?' Mike asked.

'Nothing,' Polly said. 'I told you, I was worried because she was so late. Not knowing when the raids are has—'

'It was the coat, wasn't it?' Mike said. 'Is that what she was wearing on VE Day?'

'No. I told you—'

He grabbed her by the arms and shook her. 'Don't lie to me – it's too important. That green coat was the one she was wearing on VE Day.' He shook her again. 'Wasn't it?'

It was no use. He knew.

'Tell me,' he said, tightening his grip. 'It's important. Is that what she was wearing?'

'Yes,' she said, and his grip slackened, as if all the strength had gone out of his arms.

'I kept hoping the fact that she didn't own a coat like that meant she was there on a different assignment,' Polly said, 'that we'd got out after all, and she'd talked Mr Dunworthy into letting her go to VE Day later.'

'It could still mean that,' Mike said. 'The coat's obviously the correct period. Wardrobe could have had one just like it. They could have *that* coat for that matter. Or it could have been someone else you saw. You said yourself you were too far away to be sure it was Eileen. She could have left it behind when we went back through, and it ended up at the Assistance Board again, and they gave it to someone else.'

Or it might have found its way to an applecart upset, Polly thought, wishing she could believe that was what had happened.

'And if she was there at VE Day because we didn't get out,' Mike said, 'I'd have been there, too.'

Unless you'd been killed, Polly thought.

'If something had happened to us, she'd hardly have been there celebrating.'

'That's not true. Everyone there that night knew someone who'd died in the war. And you and I could both have been killed a long time before—'

'Or we could all have been pulled out, and she was back to do the assignment she'd always wanted to do. Or maybe she decided not to go back after our drops opened. You know how she's always wanted to see VE Day—'

'So she stayed on through four more years of air raids and National Service and rationing to see *one* day of people waving flags and singing, "Rule, Britannia"?' Polly asked incredulously. 'She *hates* it here. And she's terrified of the bombs. Do you honestly believe she'd be willing to go through an entire year of V-1s and V-2s for *any* reason?'

'Okay, okay, I agree that's not very likely. I'm just saying there are all kinds of explanations for why she – or her coat – was there besides our not getting out. We missed contacting Bartholomew, but it's not like we're out of options. There's still the St John's Wood drop, and Dunworthy will be here in May, right? And there are bound to have been historians who were here in 1942 and 1943. And if we can't find them, we've still got Denys Atherton.'

Denys Atherton.

'You're right,' she said. 'I'm sorry. The shock of seeing the coat just unnerved me for a moment.' She started quickly down the steps. 'Eileen will wonder what's become of us, and I'm starving, too. Mrs Rickett outdid herself tonight. She made a sort of dishwater soup—'

He grabbed her arms and pulled her around to face him. 'No. You're not going anywhere till you've told me the truth. It isn't just the coat. It's something else. What?'

'Nothing,' she said, flailing about for some excuse. 'It's only that I'm worried that Denys' drop might not open. Gerald's didn't, and the build-up to D-Day may be a divergence point. It was terribly important that Hitler not find out when and where they were invading, and—'

'You're lying,' he said. 'When did you come through?'

'When did I … ? The fourteenth of September. I was supposed to come through on the tenth, but there was slippage, and I ended up coming through—'

'Not to the Blitz. To your V-1 assignment.'

You can still do this, Polly thought. *You can still pull it out.* 'I told you, the V-1s began on June thirteenth.'

'That isn't what I asked you.'

'I didn't make it to Dulwich till after the first rockets hit. I'd intended to be there on the eleventh, and I'd started for Dulwich from Oxford on the eighth of June, two days after D-Day,' she chattered, 'but it took me forever to get there. The invasion made travel simply imposs—'

'That isn't what I asked you either. I asked you what day you came through the net. And don't tell me June eighth.' He looked at her, waiting, and it was no use. He'd worked it out on his own.

She took a deep breath. 'December twenty-ninth, 1943.'

Mike closed his eyes and his hands tightened on her arms, gripping them so hard he hurt her.

'I couldn't just show up at Dulwich,' she said, trying to make him understand. 'I had to arrange to be transferred there, and that meant spending time in a unit in Oxford first. Major Denewell knew virtually everyone in the FANY. I'd never have got away with lying about my experience.'

'Like you've got away with lying to me all these weeks?' he said angrily. 'You've known all along that Denys Atherton came through after your deadline. That even if we found him, it wouldn't be in time to do any good.'

'I know, I'm sorry. I wanted—'

'Wanted to what?' He shook her. 'To *spare* me?'

Yes. I didn't want to put you through what I've been going through since the night we found each other and I realised your drops wouldn't open either. I didn't want you to look the way you're looking now, the way I felt when I found out, like someone who's just heard a death sentence pronounced.

'I'm sorry,' she repeated helplessly.

'What else are you sparing me from?' he said furiously. 'How many other assignments were you here on that you haven't told me about? Were you here in 1942, too? Or the summer of '41? Or *next week*, maybe?' He gripped her arms so hard she cried out with the pain. 'Was I there in Trafalgar Square with Eileen?'

'No.' Why was he asking that? 'Why—?'

'Was I? Missing an arm or a leg, and you decided you wanted to spare me that, too?'

'No,' Polly said tearfully, 'I only saw Eileen.'

'You swear?'

'I swear.'

'Hullo!' Eileen called up from below. 'Mike? Polly?'

Polly clutched at Mike's arm. 'Don't tell her,' she whispered. '*Please*. She'll … please don't tell her.'

'What happened to you two?' Eileen said, running up the stairs to them. She was carrying a sandwich and a bottle of orange squash. 'I thought you said you were coming.'

Mike looked at Polly, then said, 'We were talking.'

'About the raids,' Polly said quickly. 'We're trying to fill in the gaps in the list we made. You said Trafalgar Square was hit sometime during the winter. Do you know which month?'

'No,' Eileen said, sitting down on the steps and unwrapping her sandwich. 'Do either of you want a bite?'

Mike didn't answer, but Eileen didn't seem to notice anything was wrong. She was preoccupied with the subject of Alf and Binnie. 'I do hope they got home all right the other day.'

'I thought you said they could take care of themselves,' Polly said, trying to make her tone light.

'They can. But I couldn't shake them all night, and then, when I said I was going to take them home, they vanished. And I've been wondering why.'

'Because they were afraid you'd discover the thermometers and stethoscopes they'd stolen from Bart's,' Mike suggested.

Eileen didn't even hear him. 'They were both so grubby,' she said thoughtfully.

Polly wondered what that had to do with Alf and Binnie's running wild in Blackfriars, but whatever the connection was, she was grateful Eileen's mind was on that and not on them, or she'd have surely noticed how pale Mike looked.

I shouldn't have told him, she thought, even if he had already guessed the truth. *I should have lied and said I went through in May, or April.*

He looked so desperate, so *driven*. And on their way home after the all-clear, he pulled Polly aside to say, 'I'll think of some way to get you out of here before your deadline. Both of you. I promise.'

The next night he met her outside Townsend Brothers after work. 'Tell me about the build-up to D-Day,' he said.

'The build-up? But—?'

'We don't know for sure that Denys Atherton came through in March. Mr Dunworthy may have rescheduled his drop.'

Or cancelled it, she thought. *Or his drop wouldn't open, like Gerald Phipps', and he wasn't able to come through.*

'Or Atherton may have had to come through early like you did,' Mike said, 'so he could be in place when the invasion build-up started.'

She shook her head. 'That wouldn't have been necessary. There were hundreds of thousands of soldiers pouring into the camps. He wouldn't have been noticed at all.'

'Pouring in where?' he persisted. 'Where was the build-up?'

'Portsmouth, Plymouth, Southampton. But it covered the entire southwestern half of England,' she said, and then was sorry. She shouldn't have made finding him sound so difficult. She didn't want Mike to decide it was hopeless and do something rash like go to Eileen's drop, training school or no training school. Or to Saltram-on-Sea to blow up the gun emplacement on his drop.

But he didn't speak of doing either. And the next night when he told them he'd thought of a plan, it involved nothing more than taking turns checking Polly's drop and composing additional classified ads to be put in the newspapers.

'But we already did that,' Eileen said, 'and no one answered.'

'These aren't messages to the retrieval team,' Mike said. 'They're messages to Oxford.'

'But how can we send messages to the future unless we find another historian?' Eileen asked. 'We don't know where Mr Bartholomew's drop is.'

'We send them the same way we sent the messages to the retrieval team. Remember those messages you told us about,

411

Polly, that British Intelligence put in the newspapers to fool Hitler into thinking the invasion was coming at Calais instead of Normandy?'

'The wedding announcements, and letters to the editor?'

'Yes. And the night before Pearl Harbor, the Navy intercepted a coded telephone message to Japan telling how many aircraft carriers and battleships would be in harbour at the time of the attack.'

'But those messages weren't to the future,' Polly said.

'No, but they *made* it to the future. After World War II, historians went through all the newspapers of the time and all the radio recordings and telegrams of the time, looking for clues to what had happened, and they found the Fortitude South and BBC messages.'

'But they were looking through the 1944 newspapers,' Polly said. 'Why would they look for messages in 1941 newspapers?'

'Because we're in 1941. They'll be trying to find out where we are,' he said, 'and we're going to tell them.'

It won't work, Polly thought. If they were looking for messages, they'd already have found the ones the three of us sent to the retrieval team, and they'd have been in Trafalgar Square or at the Peter Pan statue.

And if they weren't looking, if Mike was counting on some random historian stumbling across their messages, that historian wouldn't understand it. Unless it read, 'Mr Dunworthy: Trapped in 1941. Need transport home. Polly, Mike, and Eileen,' there was no guarantee the historian would even recognise it as a message.

And that was if the message managed to survive till 2060. Fleet Street would be bombed several times before the end of the war, and countless more records had been destroyed by the pinpoint bomb which had taken down St Paul's and during the Pandemic. A message in the classified advertisements of the *Evening Express* had as much chance of reaching Mr Dunworthy as a message in a bottle, and Mike surely knew that.

Polly wondered if he was simply having them do this to keep her and Eileen from realising there was nothing they *could* do.

But no matter what the reason, he no longer had the driven, desperate look he'd had when Polly'd told him. And if Mike was waiting in St Paul's – 'Meet me in the south aisle by *The Light of the World*' – or at Hyde Park Corner, he wasn't off in Backbury or Saltram-on-Sea getting shot. So Polly diligently wrote, 'R.T. Sorry I couldn't come last Saturday. Leave cancelled. Meet me in Paddington Station, Track 6, at two. M.D.' and 'Gold ring, lost in Oxford Street, inscribed "Time knoweth no bounds". Reward. Contact M. Davies, 9 Beresford Court, Kensington.'

On Friday Mike asked her again whether she was positive he hadn't been in Trafalgar Square with Eileen. 'Did you look at the people standing around her?'

'Yes,' she said. 'There was a teenaged girl in a white dress, and a sailor ...' She frowned, trying to remember. 'And two elderly ladies. Why?'

'Because even if you and I had both been killed, she still wouldn't have been there alone. She'd have been there with the shopgirls from Townsend Brothers or something, and the fact that she wasn't proves she was there on another assignment.'

No, it didn't, but if he believed that, he was less likely to do something rash.

'The elderly ladies weren't Miss Laburnum and Miss Hibbard, were they?' he asked. 'Or Miss Snelgrove?'

'No,' Polly said, and didn't mention that she had scarcely glanced at them, or that at that point she hadn't met them yet.

On Saturday the eleventh, Townsend Brothers had to be evacuated again due to a gas leak in Duke Street, and Mr Witherill sent half the staff – including Polly – home. Eileen wasn't there, and before she could go and see if Mike was at Mrs Leary's, Miss Laburnum waylaid her to look through plays for dramatic readings the troupe could do.

'Scenes with only a few parts,' she instructed Polly, 'so it won't matter if not all the troupe is there.'

'I'm sorry I've been gone the last few nights,' Polly said. 'I promise I'll come this evening.'

'Oh, I wasn't referring to you,' Miss Laburnum said. 'I meant Mr Simms. He's volunteered to be a firespotter, and Lila and Viv scarcely ever come. They're always off to service club dances.'

'They're not going to one tonight, are they?' Polly asked anxiously. The big raids which had hit Bank and Liverpool Street stations were tonight.

'I do hope not,' Miss Laburnum said. 'We're reading a scene from *A Midsummer Night's Dream*, and we'll need them for Mustardseed and Peaseblossom.'

Neither Mike nor Eileen were back when the sirens went, or at Notting Hill Gate when Polly got there. Before they'd left last night, she'd reminded them to take shelter the moment they heard the sirens and not to board any train that would go through Bank or Liverpool Street Station, which meant they might be some time getting here.

She left a note for them on the staircase and went out to the platform. Lila and Viv, thankfully, were there, and so was everyone else except Mr Simms, who was on duty, and Mrs Rickett, who Mr Dorming reported was convinced the weather was too bad for raids. 'She may be right,' he said. 'It looks as though it might snow.'

That won't stop the Luftwaffe tonight, Polly thought. The troupe did Titania and Bottom's scene from *A Midsummer Night's Dream*, the rector recited the Lord Admiral's song from *HMS Pinafore*, and Polly and Sir Godfrey did a scene from *The Importance of Being Earnest*, raising their voices over the screech and thud of what sounded like hundreds of bombs.

Polly kept expecting Eileen and Mike to come at any moment, but they didn't. Mrs Rickett did, looking annoyed at having been wrong about the raids. 'Did Miss O'Reilly come home after I left for here?' Polly asked her.

'No, she hasn't been there since this afternoon.'

'This afternoon?'

She nodded. 'She told me she wouldn't be in to dinner and to give you this.'

She handed Polly an envelope. Inside was a scrawled note from Eileen: 'Dear Polly, Worried about Alf and Binnie. They said Bank was one of the stations they're often in. Have gone to make certain they're not there. Eileen.'

Gone to make certain they're not there? Polly thought, horrified. On the night Bank Station was bombed?

She grabbed up her coat and began putting it on. 'Where are you going?' Sir Godfrey asked.

'To find Miss O'Reilly.'

'But it's nearly eleven,' Miss Laburnum said. 'The trains will have already stopped for the night.'

'She'll surely have gone to a shelter when the raids began,' the rector said.

That's just the problem, Polly thought. *She's gone to a shelter which is going to be bombed.*

But Eileen *knew* it was going to be bombed. She'd find Alf and Binnie and get them out of there immediately. If they didn't refuse to go. They'd delayed her on the twenty-ninth. What if they delayed her tonight and kept her from leaving the station?

'I'm certain nothing will happen to your friend,' the rector said reassuringly.

He's right, Polly thought. *You're forgetting about VE Day. You saw her there in her green coat, which means she can't have been killed at Bank Station.*

But Mike hadn't been there on VE Day. What if he'd gone with her? 'Did Mr Davis come to the boarding house this afternoon?' she asked Mrs Rickett. 'Did you show him this note?'

Mrs Rickett drew herself up angrily. 'I most certainly did not. I haven't even *seen* your Mr Davis today. I am *not* in the habit of handing over my boarders' post to their gentleman friends.'

'No, of course not,' Polly said hastily. 'It's only that I'm so worried. They should both have been here hours ago, and the raids are so bad tonight.'

'There's nothing you can do till morning,' Mr Dorming said.

Nothing except worry, Polly thought, listening to the *crumping* of the bombs and wishing she knew when Bank Station had been hit and what else had been bombed. And where Mike was. What if he'd spotted Eileen as she was leaving Mrs Rickett's and followed her? And then lost her in the crowd at Bank and didn't realise she'd taken Alf and Binnie to another station? What if he was still at Bank looking for her?

You don't know that he followed her, she thought. *He could very well have gone to check your drop. Or to Fleet Street to deliver an ad and couldn't get back.* He'd been late last night because he'd been working on a story. *He's very likely in the cellar of the* Herald *and Eileen's at a tube shelter which wasn't hit, trying to prevent Alf and Binnie from picking other shelter-ers' pockets, and the best thing you can do is get some sleep.*

But the bombs kept waking her, and she crept off twice to see if either of them had come back to the emergency staircase.

The all-clear went at half past five. 'But they'll have to wait till the trains start,' the rector said.

'I know,' Polly said, and gave them half an hour extra, in case the first trains were too crowded to squeeze onto, but they still didn't come.

'They may have gone home and assumed they'd meet you there, Miss Sebastian,' Miss Laburnum said, folding up her blanket.

'I thought of that, but I'm afraid if I leave—'

'You'll miss them,' Miss Laburnum said. 'I quite understand. You stay here, and if Miss O'Reilly's at home, I'll tell her where you are. And I'll stop at Mrs Leary's on the way and tell her to tell Mr Davis.'

'I'll be here for at least another hour,' Mrs Brightford said, pointing at her still-sleeping girls, 'so if you want to go and look for her, I can have her wait here till you return.'

'*Thank* you!' Polly said gratefully, and ran out to each of the platforms to see which lines weren't running, and then stationed herself at the foot of the District and Circle level escalator so she'd be able to spot Eileen and Mike no matter which way they came in from, searching the crowd anxiously for an orange scarf or a green coat.

There was Eileen, emerging from the northbound tunnel. 'Eileen!' Polly called, and ran over to her. 'Thank goodness!' She looked past her into the tunnel. 'Is Mike with you?'

'Mike? No, he told me yesterday morning he had to work last night. Isn't he here?'

'No, but the Central Line's down. Damage on the line. He probably couldn't get back. I was afraid he might have gone to Liverpool Street or Bank looking for you.'

'Alf and Binnie weren't *in* Bank. They were at Embankment, but the only way I could be sure of keeping them there was to stay with them. I couldn't very well tell them' – she lowered her voice – 'that Bank and Liverpool Street were going to be hit, and you know Alf and Binnie, if I'd forbidden them to go there *without* giving them a reason, they'd have gone there immediately to see why. And besides, I needed to find out something.'

Exactly how many crimes they've committed? Polly thought, looking up at the people coming down the escalator. Miss Laburnum should have got to Mrs Leary's by now and told Mike, if he was there.

'I've been thinking about how Alf and Binnie ran away the other morning when I said I'd take them home,' Eileen said. 'And the day I borrowed the map from them, they wouldn't let me in.'

More and more people were coming down the escalators, shelterers with their bedrolls under their arms, making the trek back to the East End, and factory workers on the early shift, but there was still no sign of Mike.

'And Alf and Binnie are so dirty and ragged. I mean, I know their mother doesn't take proper care of them, but Binnie's wearing the same dress she had at the manor, and it was too short for her even then. And—'

Miss Laburnum was coming down the escalator towards them. 'It's all right,' Polly called up to her. 'I found her. You were right. She spent the night—'

And saw the ARP warden on the step above her. And the look on Miss Laburnum's face. 'What is it?' she asked. 'What's happened?' But she already knew.

No, she thought. *No.*

'Are you Miss Sebastian?' the ARP warden said, and she must have nodded because the warden said, 'I'm sorry to be the bearer of bad news, but I'm afraid your friend Mr Davis was killed last night.'

LONDON – WINTER 1941

Mike wasn't the only one who had been killed in the raid. Mr Simms had, too. He'd been filling in for a warden who had the flu when the ARP post was hit. Nelson had been with him, and the dog's whimpering had led the rescue crew to his master, but it was too late. Mr Simms had already bled to death.

Nelson was unhurt, except for a lacerated paw, but Mr Simms had no family, and there was concern among the troupe over what would become of him. But the next night Mr Dorming brought Nelson to Notting Hill Gate and announced that he had paid a guinea for him.

'Mr Dorming doesn't even *like* dogs,' Polly said when Miss Laburnum told her. 'And I thought Mrs Rickett didn't allow her boarders to keep pets.'

'I told you, my dear. Mr Dorming's moved out. He's taken Mr Simms' old rooms.'

Polly didn't remember Miss Laburnum having told her that. She didn't even remember having been told that Mr Simms had been killed, though she must have been because she recalled wondering if he had been in Houndsditch, too. She remembered scarcely anything of those first few days. It was all she could manage to absorb the fact that Mike was dead and to do all the things which had to be done.

She had always wondered how the contemps had found the courage to go on after their husbands, mothers, children, friends had been pulled lifeless from the rubble. But it wasn't courage. It was that there were so many things which had to be taken care of that by the time one had done all of them, it was too late to give way.

She had to go with the warden to the ARP post to identify Mike's effects and sign for them, had to talk to the incident officer, had to telephone Townsend Brothers to tell them she and Eileen wouldn't be in to work, and to remove Mike's belongings from his room so new tenants could move in. 'I do hate to worry you so soon,' Mrs Leary said, 'but it's a couple who were bombed out last night and have nowhere to go.'

'It's quite all right,' Polly said. And because she didn't want Mrs Leary going through his things and finding a list of upcoming raids and thinking he had been a spy, she went straight over.

But there was nothing incriminating in his room, only his clothes and his suitcase, his towel and shaving things, and a paperback biography of Shackleton.

She packed them up, took them back to Mrs Rickett's, and went to the *Daily Express* to tell his news editor, all the while protected by a barrier of numbness through which the pain would presently begin to work its way.

But there was no time to worry about that. She had to respond to Mike's news editor's questions and to the condolences of the troupe and Sir Godfrey's anxious concern, had to put the flowers Doreen had brought 'from everyone on Third' in water. And, worst of all, had to deal with Eileen, who refused to believe Mike was dead.

'It's all a mistake. It was someone else,' she insisted, even though the warden had shown them Mike's identity card and ration book and the reporter's notebook he'd carried. And the pumpkin-coloured scarf Miss Hibbard had knitted and Polly had lent him at Bart's the morning after they'd tried to find John Bartholomew.

The edges of his papers were charred, and all of the things were sodden. 'The fire hoses,' the warden explained apologetically.

'Those could have been stolen from him,' Eileen said. 'Alf and Binnie stole that sort of thing from people all the time. I won't believe it till I've seen the body.'

But there wasn't a body, as the warden gingerly explained. 'It was a thousand-pounder, and then incendiaries, you see.'

Polly saw. There would only have been fragments too small for the rescue squad to have collected. She thought of Paige Fairchild telling her at one of her first V-1 incidents, 'Don't bother with anything smaller than a hand.'

'It can't have been Mike,' Eileen insisted. 'What would he have been doing out in the middle of a raid? We all promised we'd go to a shelter the moment the sirens went.'

'Perhaps it was too far away and he hadn't enough time—'

'No,' Eileen said. 'I asked the warden. She said Houndsditch wasn't hit till eleven. And what would he have been doing in Houndsditch? He never mentioned it to you, did he?'

'No. But remember Marjorie? She didn't tell anyone she was going to meet an airman either. There was no reason anyone knew of for her to have been in Jermyn Street.'

'And Marjorie wasn't dead. Mike isn't either.'

'Eileen—'

'He might have been injured and wandered away, or got hit on the head and can't remember who he is,' Eileen argued and insisted on checking the hospitals – even though the authorities had already done that – and waiting at the foot of the escalator in Oxford Circus Station where they'd agreed to meet if something went wrong.

'You can't go on doing this,' Polly said after the third night. 'You must get some sleep.'

Eileen shook her head. 'I might miss him,' she said, and when he still hadn't come by the fifth night,' she said. 'Perhaps he found the retrieval team, and they pulled him out. And he wanted to come and fetch and us, but there wasn't time—'

Polly shook her head, remembering how adamant he'd been about them splitting up when he realised Mr Bartholomew was at St Paul's. 'He'd never have gone through without us.'

'Perhaps he hadn't any choice. Like Shackleton. He had to leave us behind to go and fetch help. Perhaps the drop was in Houndsditch, and if they didn't go through immediately, it would have been destroyed, so he went and now he's working with Badri and Linna to find another drop site for us.

'And don't say, "This is time travel" like that,' she said, even though Polly hadn't said anything. 'There are scores of reasons why they might not have been able to come through yet. Slippage and divergence points and ...'

But the most likely is that that isn't what happened at all, Polly thought. *Mike didn't go through, and there was no drop in Houndsditch.* Only an HE, followed by incendiaries.

'He *can't* be dead,' Eileen said. 'He promised he'd get us out.'

Yes, and Colin promised he'd come and rescue me if I got into trouble, Polly thought. *Sometimes promises can't be kept.*

'Perhaps he got a new lead on the retrieval team and went off to find them,' Eileen said. 'He went to Manchester without telling us.'

Which didn't account for his half-burnt papers being in Houndsditch, or his things being at Mrs Leary's. If he had gone off, he would have taken his razor and shaving soap with him.

Polly had hoped there would be some clue among his belongings as to what he had been doing in Houndsditch, though she was almost afraid to find out. What if he'd caught sight of Eileen going to find Alf and Binnie and followed her? Houndsditch wasn't that far from Bank Station. Or what if he'd been on some dangerous mission to get the three of them out? He'd looked so desperate and distracted after she told him about Eileen's coat. What if, in his desperation, he'd seen someone he thought might be the retrieval team and followed them to Houndsditch? To his death.

I shouldn't have told him, she thought. *I should have lied about the coat.* If he had died attempting to save them, to get her out before her deadline, she didn't think she could bear it.

But if they knew what he'd been doing in Houndsditch, Eileen might come to her senses, so the next night Polly stayed behind at Mrs Rickett's and dried out Mike's still-wet notebook in the oven and then went carefully through its crinkled leaves. The ink on some of the pages had run or washed away. *Like the code in the bigram books,* she thought, peering at the blurred words, attempting to decipher them.

There were notes for a newspaper story on an all-female AA-gun battery, the list of names she'd given him before he went to Bletchley Park – 'Alan Turing, Gordon Welchman, Dilly Knox' – and what looked like a list for possible newspaper stories: 'Wartime Weddings', 'Is Your Journey *Really* Necessary?', 'Winter and War: Ten Survival Strategies'.

Survival strategies, Polly thought, and felt the pain begin to seep through, like blood through a shirt.

Several pages had been torn out of the notebook. *The list of upcoming raids,* Polly thought.

The remaining pages were notes for an article called 'Doing Our Bit: Heroes on the Home Front', and a list of names, addresses and times. 'Canteen worker, Mrs Edna Bell, 6 Cuttlebone Street, Southwark, Jan. 10, 10 p.m.', and below that, 'Firespotter', and a name which might have been 'Mr Woodruff' or 'Mr Walton' and 'Jan. 11, 11 p.m., 9 Houndsditch, corner of H and Stoney Lane'.

He hadn't been following Eileen or looking for the retrieval team. He had gone to Houndsditch to interview a firespotter for a story he was writing on home-front heroes for the *Daily Express*. It wasn't her fault. He hadn't been killed attempting to save them.

She had thought that knowledge would be a comfort, but it wasn't, and she realised that she had been hoping as much as Eileen that there was some mistake, some other explanation. That he wasn't truly dead. But he was.

And if he was dead, then no one was coming to rescue them. She might have been able to convince herself that Mr Dunworthy would have allowed Mike to be left here with an injured foot and her here with a deadline, but there was no way he would have allowed one of them to be killed, not if he could help it.

Which meant he couldn't help it. He couldn't get them out. And it scarcely mattered if the reason was slippage or their having altered events or some catastrophe in Oxford. Mike was dead. 'Mike Davis, 26, died suddenly. Of enemy action.'

She took Mike's things back to Mrs Rickett's, and put them in a drawer of the bureau, then took out the half-charred print of *The Light of the World* she had retrieved from the floor of St Paul's and sat there on the bed, looking at it, at Christ's hand, still raised to knock on the door though the door had burned away to nothing, and at His face. It held no expression at all.

'Would you care for me to make arrangements for a memorial service for your friend, Miss Sebastian?' the rector asked her on Friday. 'I should be glad to officiate. I've arranged with the rector of St Bidulphus' to have Mr Simms' funeral there, and I could speak to him about a service for Mr Davis.'

But Eileen wouldn't hear of it. 'He *isn't* dead,' she insisted, and when Polly showed her the entry in his notebook, she said, 'That doesn't say the eleventh. It says the seventeenth. Or the seventh. Look how the water's blurred the numbers. And even if it does say the eleventh, it doesn't mean he kept the appointment.'

On Tuesday, Polly went to Mr Simms' funeral. She had attempted to persuade Eileen to go, too, but she'd refused to leave her post at the foot of the escalator. 'I might miss Mike,' she'd said, looking hopefully up at the people descending.

The entire troupe was at St Bidulphus', including Nelson.

Miss Laburnum and Miss Hibbard both wore black-veiled hats and carried black-edged handkerchiefs.

Sir Godfrey recited the St Crispin's Day speech: 'They shall not speak of this, from this day to the ending of the world, but we in it shall be remembered – we few, we happy few, we band of brothers. For he today that sheds his blood with me shall be my brother.'

And the rector, giving the eulogy, said, 'Mr Simms was no less a soldier than the men in Henry V's army, and no less a hero.'

So was Mike, Polly thought, and it didn't matter what he had been doing when he died any more than it mattered whether the RAF pilot was killed in a dogfight or while he was on leave. Mike had still died trying to get them out. He had devoted every moment since he'd found them to doing that. And it didn't matter that he'd failed either. History was full of failed attempts – Thermopylae, Scott's trek back from the South Pole, the siege of Khartoum. He was still a hero.

After the funeral, the rector asked Polly again about scheduling a service. 'I could speak to the Reverend Mr Unwin now, or perhaps you'd like to have it in some other church ...'

Yes, Polly thought, *St Paul's. It's where all the heroes are: Wellington and Lord Nelson and Captain Faulknor. Mike should be there as well*, though she knew they'd never allow it.

But she asked Mr Humphreys anyway, and to her surprise, he said that they could hold a small private service in the Chapel of St Michael and St George. 'I am so sorry about Mr Davis,' Mr Humphreys said. 'It's difficult sometimes to see God's plan in all this violence and death, but with His help, it will all come right in the end.'

He asked Polly what day she'd like to have the service, and she told him about Eileen. 'People often find death difficult to accept,' he said, shaking his head, 'particularly when it is sudden. Is there someone she's close to who could help her through this? Her mother or father, perhaps, or a friend from school?'

None of them have been born yet, Polly thought, going to Oxford Circus to attempt to persuade Eileen to return to Mrs Rickett's and get some sleep. Things couldn't go on this way. Eileen was eating almost nothing and sleeping scarcely at all. There were dark hollows under her eyes and a driven, distracted look about her.

Like Mike had, Polly thought. She must get through to her somehow.

But Eileen wouldn't listen to her. *And there's no one else here she's close to,* Polly thought, and then realised that wasn't true. She wrote to the vicar in Backbury, and when she didn't hear back from him after several days, she went in search of Alf and Binnie Hodbin.

They were hardly ideal comforters, but Eileen cared about them – she'd been talking about them just before they found out about Mike. And the important thing now was to jar Eileen back to reality, something Alf and Binnie were experts at.

Polly didn't know where they lived except that it was in Whitechapel, and according to Eileen, no one was ever at home. Which left the tube stations.

She started with Embankment, where Eileen had last seen them, and then searched Blackfriars and Holborn. When she still couldn't find them, she began collaring urchins and questioning them as to the Hodbins' whereabouts, which didn't work either. The children clearly thought she was a Child Services officer or a schoolmistress and weren't about to tell her anything, so she switched tactics, giving them tuppence to deliver a message to Alf and Binnie and promising another tuppence on delivery.

They were waiting outside Townsend Brothers when she left work the next day. So was the urchin she'd promised the tuppence to. She paid him, and he darted off.

As soon as he'd gone, Binnie said, 'Did somefink 'appen to Eileen?'

'Was she killed?' Alf demanded.

'No, nothing's happened to Eileen.'

'Then why ain't she 'ere?' Binnie asked.

'Does she need us to go with her in the ambulance again and tell her which way to go?' Alf asked.

'No,' Polly said, frustrated. Eileen was liable to come out through the staff door at any moment. Polly needed to tell them about Mike before she got here. 'It's about her friend, Mr Davis. You met him that morning at St Paul's.'

'The bloke wot didn't 'ave no coat?'

'Yes,' Polly said, remembering with a sharp pang him sitting there defeatedly in his shirtsleeves on St Paul's steps, remembered wrapping the pumpkin-coloured scarf round his neck. 'He was killed last week, and—'

'Eileen won't 'ave t'go to an orphanage, will she?' Alf asked.

'No, you noddlehead,' Binnie said, 'only *children* get sent to orphanages.'

'Eileen's been feeling very sad since Mr Davis was killed,' Polly said, 'and I was hoping you two might cheer—'

'Was it a bomb wot killed 'im?' Binnie cut in.

'Yes, and Eileen—'

'What sort've a bomb?' Alf demanded. 'A thousand-pounder or a parachute-mine?' Before Polly could answer, he added, 'Parachute-mines is the worst. They blow you up! *Ka-blooie!*' He flung his arms out. 'And bits of you go *everywhere*!'

What was I thinking? Polly asked herself. *These two have no business going anywhere near Eileen.*

But now how would she get rid of them? Especially when Binnie was saying, 'So we should cheer Eileen up?'

'Yes, but Eileen's too sad to see anyone yet. I thought perhaps you could send her a condolence card.'

'We ain't got no money,' Alf said.

'We could come to the funeral,' Binnie said. 'When is it?'

'We don't know yet,' Polly said, fumbling in her bag for money. She had to get rid of them before Eileen came out.

''ow can we send 'er a card?' Binnie said. 'We don't know where she lives.'

And I have no intention of telling you, Polly thought. 'You can send it to Townsend Brothers.'

'And we ain't got money for a stamp,' Alf said.

'Yes, you do,' Polly said, coming up with a shilling. 'Here.'

Alf snatched it, and the two of them darted off immediately, thank goodness.

But she was back to square one, and Eileen was more determined than ever that Mike was alive. 'People don't just *disappear.*'

Yes, they do, Polly thought.

'Perhaps Mike went to Bletchley Park again, to see if Gerald came through after he'd left, and he can't tell us because of Ultra's being so secret and everything. So he had to make it *look* like he was dead.' Which made no sense. 'He didn't want to, but it's the only way he could get you out before your deadline.'

And that's what this is about, Polly thought. *If she admits Mike's dead, that they weren't able to pull him out before he was killed, then it's also admitting they won't be able to pull me out either.*

But this couldn't go on. Eileen would have a breakdown. Polly wondered if she should write to the vicar again, but she didn't have to. He walked up to her counter, wearing his clerical collar, just before closing. 'Miss Sebastian?' he said. 'I'm Mr Goode. I believe we met briefly in Backbury last autumn. I'm sorry I wasn't able to come sooner. Your letter didn't reach me until two days ago, and I had difficulty making arrangements—'

'Thank you *so* much for coming,' Polly said, smiling at him. 'I can't tell you how much this will mean to Eileen.'

'Were Miss O'Reilly and Mr Davis … ?' He hesitated.

'Romantically attached? No. He was like a brother to us, and Eileen's taking his death very hard.' Polly glanced at her watch. It was nearly closing time, and she didn't want Eileen to see the vicar till she'd had a chance to explain the situation to him. 'If you'll give me a moment, I'll ask my supervisor if I can leave early,' she said, and hurried off to speak to Miss Snelgrove, who was nowhere to be found.

'She went up to sixth,' Sarah said, and the closing bell rang.

Polly hurried back, but she was too late. Eileen was already there. 'I was so sorry to hear of your loss, Miss O'Reilly,' Mr Goode was saying.

Eileen stiffened.

Oh no, Polly thought, *she's not going to listen to him more than she has to anyone else.*

'I'm sorry I didn't come sooner,' he said.

Eileen was glaring at her.

She knows exactly why I sent for him, Polly thought.

'Miss Sebastian's letter had to be forwarded on to me,' the vicar said. 'And then it took several days to arrange for leave.'

'Leave?' Eileen said.

'Yes. I haven't told you, I've enlisted as a chaplain in His Majesty's Army.'

The colour drained from Eileen's face.

Oh no, Polly thought, *I've only made things worse.*

'I couldn't stay in Backbury,' he said, 'preaching sermons and heading up committee meetings when so many others were making sacrifices – like you, facing danger every day here in London. I felt I had to do my bit, as it were.'

'But you can't,' Eileen said, and burst into tears. 'You'll be *killed*. Just like Mike was.'

CROYDON – OCTOBER 1944

Mary was lying flat on her back.

I must have slipped on something and fallen when I came through, she thought. *The shimmer must have blinded me.* She remembered the light had been much too bright and then …

There was a sudden deafening *cr–rack* and, immediately after it, a second one. *That was the double-boom of a V-2*, she thought, suddenly panicked, *I've come through too late*, and then remembered where she was. She and Fairchild had heard the V-2 – no, that was wrong – it had been a V-1, and they'd come back to Croydon to see if there were casualties, and Fairchild had—

Fairchild! She tried to sit up, but she couldn't. There was something on top of her, crushing her so she couldn't get any breath in her lungs, couldn't—

Oh God, don't let it be the printing press, she thought, gasping for breath, and then, *I'm buried in the rubble.*

She tried to feel what was pressing down on her, but there was nothing on her chest, no fallen beams or bricks on her throat, so why … ?

Somewhere far off, she heard an ambulance's bells. *Croydon*, she thought, straining to hear better, and in the attempt she stopped gasping for breath. And as soon as she did, she found herself able to breathe again, able to raise her head.

She had had the breath knocked out of her, that was all, and she wasn't buried, she was lying atop the rubble. The explosion must have knocked her flat. She drew a long, ragged breath, then stumbled to her feet, wishing there was something to lean on, but she couldn't see the printing press, couldn't see anything at all. The explosion must have blown out the fires. 'Fairchild!' she called. 'Fairchild! Where are you?'

She didn't answer.

Because she's dead, Mary thought.

'Fairchild!' she cried frantically. 'Answer me!'

No answer. No sound at all, not even the ambulance's bells. *The V-2 must have punctured my eardrums,* she thought detachedly, and then, *Oh God, I won't be able to hear Fairchild calling.*

And remembered that Paige was dead.

She heard ambulance bells again, but from the wrong direction, from behind her, and when she turned, she saw that she had been wrong. Not all of the fires had been blown out. One was still burning, more brightly than ever. She could see their ambulance silhouetted against it.

It was moving slowly past the fire. She stared at it stupidly for a long minute, unable to make sense of what she was seeing. If it was moving, then Fairchild must not be dead, she must be driving it, but she wouldn't leave without her, she wouldn't …

'Fairchild, don't leave!' she cried, and staggered forward.

'No,' a scarcely audible voice said, just off to her left.

Fairchild. Mary groped for her in the darkness, but it wasn't her, it was the man with the severed foot. How could she have forgotten him? She had been tending him when—

'Where—?' the man asked, and his voice was hollow, as if he was speaking from the bottom of a well.

'I'm here. It was a V-2,' Mary said, and her voice sounded just as echoingly hollow.

The man's foot had been severed. She needed to tie a tourniquet on his leg, and she'd taken off his tie to use as one.

No, I already tied it, she thought, but when she bent over him, trying to see if the tourniquet was holding, it wasn't a tie, it was a handkerchief.

But I remember untying the tie, she thought, confused. His other leg must have been bleeding as well. And it was, but she couldn't find the tie. She must have dropped it when the V-2 hit.

She got to her knees, pulled off her jacket and tried to tear it. The rough cloth wouldn't tear, but when she tried again, the lining ripped and she was able to yank a strip free, able to tie it around his thigh. But he'd already lost a good deal of blood. She had to get him to hospital. She bent over him. 'I need to go and fetch the ambulance,' she said.

'Go,' he murmured. 'Have to ...' and then, very clearly, 'leave.'

'I'll be back straightaway,' she said, and stumbled off across the dark wreckage, over bricks and roof slates she couldn't see, looking for the ambulance.

'Mary,' a muffled voice said at her feet. 'Here.'

'Fairchild!' She'd forgotten about Fairchild. Mary groped for her in the darkness and found her hand. 'Are you all right?'

'I can't ... breathe ...' Fairchild gasped, clutching her hand, '... can't catch ...'

'You've only had the breath knocked out of you,' Mary said. 'Breathe out.' She pursed her lips and exhaled, showing her how to do it. Which was ridiculous. Fairchild couldn't see her. 'Exhale. Blow out.'

'Can't,' Fairchild said, 'there's something on me.'

'It only feels that way,' Mary reassured her, but when she patted around her, feeling to see if Fairchild was intact, she encountered splintered wood. She tried to lift it, but Fairchild cried out.

Mary stopped. 'Where are you hurt?'

'What happened?' Fairchild asked. 'Did a gas main blow up?'

'No, it was a V-2,' she said, and tried to move the piece of wood to the side.

Fairchild cried out again.

She didn't dare try to do anything when she couldn't see. She might make things worse. She'd have to wait for the ambulance.

But the ambulance was already here. She'd seen it pulling up. She turned to look over at it, silhouetted against the fire, and could see the driver's door opening and someone in a helmet getting out. 'Injury over here!' she shouted, and the driver started towards them and then, inexplicably, moved away across the rubble.

'No, over here!'

'I don't think the ambulance is here yet,' Fairchild said. 'Listen.'

Mary listened. She could hear ambulance bells in the distance. Another unit, from Woodside or Norbury, must be coming. 'Croydon's already here,' she told Fairchild, 'but they can't hear us. We need to signal them. Is there a torch in the ambulance?'

'There's one in the medical kit.'

'Where's the kit? In the ambulance?'

'No, you sent me to fetch the kit. I was bringing it to you when ...'

Mary had no memory of sending her to fetch anything. She must still be a bit dazed from the blast. 'Where is it?'

'I think it must have been knocked out of my hand,' Fairchild said.

And I'll never find it in the darkness, Mary thought, but she put her hand on it, and on the torch, almost immediately. And, amazingly, it wasn't broken. When she pushed the switch, it lit up. She held it up and waved it back and forth so the ambulance driver would see it.

'You're not supposed to do that,' Fairchild said, 'the blackout – the jerries'll—'

Will what? Hit us with a V-2? She stripped off the tape shielding the lens.

'It's a good thing we had our ... talk when we did, isn't it?' Fairchild said.

Oh God.

'Shh. You mustn't talk like that.' Mary shone the torch on her, afraid of what she'd see, but there didn't seem to be any blood except for a cut on Fairchild's arm where a broken-off slat was jabbing it. It and several planks lay crisscrossed over her chest and stomach, but there was no blood on them and nothing lying on her legs or feet.

I need to fetch the ambulance, she thought, *and—*

'I told you things could happen just like that, with no warning,' Fairchild said. 'If anything happens to me—'

'Shh, Paige, you'll be fine.' Mary attempted to move the pieces of wood, but they were too entangled. She needed both hands. She propped the torch against a heap of bricks so that it shone on Fairchild and set to work.

'If anything happens,' Fairchild repeated, 'I want you to – oh! You're hurt! You're bleeding!'

'It's printer's ink,' Mary said, trying to extract her from the planks of wood.

It was like a child's game. She had to carefully pull one piece out at a time, all the while not disturbing the slat stabbing into Fairchild's arm.

There was a sudden *whoosh* and boom, and orange flames boiled up behind the silhouetted ambulance. 'Was that another V-2?' Fairchild asked.

'No, I think *that* was the gas main,' Mary said, looking over at the flames. She saw two ambulances and a fire engine pull up. 'The rescue squad's here. Over here!' and heard the slamming of several doors and voices. 'Casualty here!'

She stood up and waved the torch, sweeping it back and forth like a searchlight, and then knelt back down next to Fairchild. 'They'll be here in a moment.'

Fairchild nodded. 'If anything happens to me—'

'Nothing's—' she began, and thought with horror, *It wasn't Stephen who was killed. It was* Fairchild – *that's why I was allowed to come through the net, to come between them, because nothing I did made any difference. Because Fairchild was killed by a V-2.*

But she wouldn't have been here in the rubble if I hadn't come between them. She wouldn't have switched with Camberley, she wouldn't have stopped the car to talk to me.

And if she hadn't stopped the car, they wouldn't have heard the V-1—

'No, listen, Mary,' Fairchild said. 'If anything happens to me, I want you to take care of Stephen. He—'

There was the sound of running feet, and a girl in a St John's Ambulance overall ran up and knelt over her.

'Not me,' Mary said, 'she's the one who's hurt. Her arm—'

'I'll need a stretcher!' the girl shouted, and someone else raced up to them.

'Oh heavens, is that Fairchild?' the new arrival said, and Mary saw that it was Camberley. 'It's Fairchild and Douglas! Get over here quickly!' and instantly Reed was there with the first-aid kit, and Parrish and the stretcher were right behind her.

'What are you *doing* here, De Havilland?' Reed asked, bending down beside Mary. 'I thought you'd gone to Streatham.'

She was right, they were supposed to have gone to Streatham. Why hadn't they? She couldn't remember.

'You're supposed to go to the incident *after* the flying bomb hits, Douglas, not before,' Camberley said cheerfully, squatting down next to Mary.

'We did,' she said. 'There was a V-1, and then—'

'I was joking, dear,' Camberley said. 'Here, let me a have a look at your temple.'

'Don't bother about me. It's Paige's arm,' she said, trying to see past her to where Parrish and the St John's girl were working on Fairchild, lifting the wood off her, lifting her onto the stretcher, covering her with a blanket.

'Is she all right?' Mary asked. 'Her arm—'

'You let us worry about her,' Camberley said, holding Mary's chin and turning her head to the side. 'I need iodine,' she said to Reed, 'and bandages.'

'They're in the ambulance,' Mary said, and Camberley and Reed exchanged glances.

'What is it?' Mary asked. 'What's wrong?'

'Nothing. Let me see that head.'

Parrish and the St John's girl lifted Fairchild's stretcher and started across the rubble with it.

Mary attempted to go with her, but Reed wouldn't let her. 'You're bleeding.'

'It's not blood,' she said, but Reed ignored her and began to bandage her head.

'It's not blood,' she repeated, 'it's printer's ink.' And remembered the man whose leg she'd tied the tourniquet on. 'You need to go and fetch him,' she said.

'Hold still,' Reed ordered.

'He's bleeding,' Mary said, attempting to get to her feet.

'Where do you think you're going?' Camberley said, pushing her back down to sitting. 'We need a stretcher over here!' she called.

'No, he's over there,' Mary said, pointing across the dark rubble.

'We'll see to him,' Camberley said. 'Where the bloody hell is that stretcher?'

'Can you walk, do you think, Douglas?' Reed asked.

'Of course I can walk,' Mary said. 'He was bleeding badly. I tied a tourniquet on one leg, but—'

'Put your arm round my neck,' Reed said, 'there's a good girl. Here we go,' and began to walk her slowly across the rubble, and it was a good thing she was holding on to her. The ground was very rough. It was difficult to keep one's balance.

'He was over by the fire,' Mary said, but the fire was in the wrong place. It was near the ambulances, in the road.

That's not the right fire, she thought, stopping to look about at the rubble, trying to see where he was, but Camberley wouldn't let her, she kept urging her along. 'His foot had been severed,' Mary said. 'You need—'

'Stop worrying about everyone else and concentrate on this last bit. You can do it. Only a bit further.'

'He was over there,' Mary said, pointing, and saw two FANYs carrying a laden stretcher from that direction.

Oh good, they got him out, she thought, and let Camberley walk her the rest of the way to the ambulance. Two ambulances were already driving away. One of them was from Brixton. She could read its lettering in the firelight. And here was Bela Lugosi. But where was their ambulance? 'Did you take Fairchild to hospital in the new—?'

'Here we are then,' Camberley said, opening up the back of Bela Lugosi. Mary sat down on the edge, suddenly very tired.

'I need some help over here,' Camberley called.

Two FANYs Mary didn't know came over, helped her into the ambulance and onto a cot, covered her with a blanket, and hooked up a plasma bag.

'It's not blood,' she told them. 'Was he all right?' But they were already shutting the doors, the ambulance was already moving, and then they were at the hospital and she was being unloaded, carried in, deposited in a bed.

'Concussion, shock, bleeding,' Camberley told the nurse.

'It's printer's ink,' Mary said, but when she held out her hands to show them, they were covered in red, not black. Fairchild's arm must have bled more than she thought.

'Has Lieutenant Fairchild been brought in yet?' she asked the nurse. 'Lieutenant Paige Fairchild?'

'I'll ask,' she said, and went across the ward to another nurse.

'Internal bleeding,' she heard the other nurse whisper and saw her shake her head.

She's dead, Mary thought. *And it's my fault. If I hadn't tackled Talbot, I'd never have met Stephen, he'd never have come to the post.*

But that couldn't be right. Historians couldn't alter events. *But I must have*, she thought, unable to work it out because her head hurt too badly. *Because Fairchild is dead.*

But just after dawn Fairchild was brought in and put in the bed next to her, pale and unconscious, and in the morning Camberley, covered in dirt and brick dust, sneaked in to see how Mary was doing and to tell her Fairchild had been in surgery most of the night for a ruptured spleen, but that the doctors had assured her she'd recover completely.

'Thank goodness,' Mary said, looking over at Fairchild, who lay with her eyes closed and her hands folded across her breast, like Sleeping Beauty. She had a bandage on her arm.

'I feel so guilty,' Camberley said, 'knowing I should be the one who was in that ambulance instead of Fairchild. It's my fault—'

No, it isn't, Mary thought, *it's mine.*

'It was so lucky you were on the far side of the incident when the V-2 hit,' she said.

I was tying off the man's leg, she thought.

'Did he make it?' she asked, and when Camberley looked blankly at her, she said, 'The man we were working on. With the severed foot.'

'I don't know,' she said. 'We didn't bring him in. I'll ask the nurse.'

But the nurse said the only other patients who'd been admitted the night before were a woman and her two little boys.

'He may have been taken to some other hospital,' Camberley said, and promised to ring up Croydon and ask.

But she didn't return, and when Talbot came during visiting hours with flowers and grapes, she said, 'Camberley said to tell you the man you asked about wasn't taken to St Francis', and that Croydon said the only person they transported was

Fairchild. But Camberley said he must be somewhere because she checked with the mortuary van, which *was* there, and the only person they'd transported had died instantly.'

The man we found who'd been cut in half, Mary thought. 'Tell her to ring up Brixton and ask them if they transported him,' she said. 'They had an ambulance there.'

Talbot looked over at Fairchild. She still hadn't come out of the ether, though now she looked like she was only sleeping, and her colour was better. She looked even younger and more childlike than usual.

'What about Flight Officer Lang?' Talbot asked. 'Shall I ring him up and tell him what happened?'

'Not till after I've been discharged,' Mary said.

Talbot nodded approvingly. 'When will they let you go home, do you think?'

'This afternoon, I should imagine.'

And then I'll go and look for the missing man myself, Mary thought. But the doctor refused to let her go due to her possibly having a concussion, and when she attempted to explain about the man to her nurse, the nurse told her to 'try to rest'.

Which was impossible when there was a chance that no one had transported him, that they'd missed him in the darkness and he was still lying there in the rubble.

She wished she'd asked Talbot to bring her her bag. If she had some money she could ring up Brixton herself. If the nurses would let her anywhere near a telephone. Thus far they wouldn't even let her out of bed. They'd even reprimanded her for walking the two feet over to Fairchild's bed when she woke and called for her.

'I'm so glad you're all right,' she'd said groggily, clutching Mary's hand. 'I was so afraid—'

'So was I,' Mary had said, 'but the doctors say we're both going to be perfectly fine, though a bit banged up.'

And it's a good thing I'm going to be here through VE Day, she thought. *If I went back to Oxford looking like this, Mr*

Dunworthy would never let me go to the Blitz.

Camberley came late that afternoon as Mary was about to be taken up for X-rays, on her way home from a run. 'Did you ring up Brixton?' Mary asked.

'Yes,' Camberley said, 'but they said they weren't at the incident. Might the ambulance have been from Bromley?'

'I suppose so.' She could have misread the name in the flickering firelight.

'Or might he have been examined and discharged?' Camberley asked, but the hospital wouldn't even discharge her, and she only had a few cuts and bruises.

'No,' she said, 'he was much too badly injured. Did you check the morgue here and at St Francis'? He might have died on the way to hospital, and that's why they don't show him as being admitted.'

'I'll check,' Camberley said, and hesitated. 'Are you certain you saw him *last* night? You were rather badly concussed. You might have been muddled—'

'I wasn't muddled. He—'

'You were muddled about Brixton's being there. You might have got someone you administered first-aid to at some other incident confused with—'

'No, I saw him, too,' Fairchild said from the other bed, and Mary could have kissed her. 'That's who I was fetching the medical kit for.'

The orderly arrived with a wheelchair to take Mary to X-ray. 'When you come again, bring my bag,' she told Camberley. 'It's in the ambulance.' On the way to the X-ray, she looked for a telephone box.

There was one just outside the ward. *Good*. And luckily, their beds were just inside the ward's doors. As soon as she got her bag, she'd sneak out and ring up Croydon and ask them to go and check the incident again.

But when she got back, Fairchild was crying.

Dread gripped her. 'Did they find him?' Mary asked.

Fairchild shook her head, unable to speak for the tears spilling down her cheeks.

'What is it?' Mary asked. *Oh God, it's Stephen.* 'What happened?'

'Camberley ...' she said, and broke down.

'What about Camberley? Has something happened to her?'

'*No,*' she sobbed, 'to the ambulance.'

'What ambulance? The one from Brixton?' Oh God, they'd been transporting the man to hospital, and there'd been another rocket—

'No, *our* ambulance. Camberley said the V-2 hit it.'

Mary's first thought was, *My bag was in it. Now how will I get the coins to phone Croydon?*

And then, *That was the second explosion I heard, the fire I saw.* It hadn't been a gas main, after all. It had been the ambulance's petrol tank blowing up.

And then, *If I hadn't called Fairchild to leave the stretcher and bring the first-aid kit, she'd have still been in the ambulance when it hit.*

But if that were the case—

'We'd only just got it,' Fairchild said, sobbing, 'and we'll never be able to get another one.'

'Nonsense,' Mary said. 'This is the Major we're talking about. If anyone can talk HQ out of another ambulance, she can. I don't suppose you've any money with you, have you?'

'Yes,' Fairchild said, wiping at her eyes, 'at least, I do if my shoes made it with me to hospital. Mummy insists I always carry a shilling in my shoe. She says I might get in a sticky situation and need to telephone.'

'And she was right,' Mary said, hoping the shoes were in the nightstand between their beds.

They were, and so was the shilling. Mary hid it under her pillow and got back into bed, and the next time the nurse left the ward, she tiptoed out to the telephone box. She rang up Brixton.

'We weren't in Croydon last night,' they told her.

'But I saw—'

'It must have been Bethnal Green's ambulance you saw.'

No, it wasn't, Polly thought, but she rang them up. They hadn't been at the incident either.

She rang up Croydon, and they promised to go and recheck the area where the newspaper office had been, 'though the rescue crew went over every inch of it,' the FANY said.

Mary asked them what other ambulances had been at the incident, and she said, 'Norbury', but Norbury hadn't transported anyone of that description either, or seen an ambulance from any other post.

'Except yours,' the Woodside FANY said. 'It was difficult to miss. Could this man you're looking for have been military? If he was, he might have been taken to Orpington.'

He'd been wearing civilian clothes, but she rang Orpington and then the morgue there and the one at St Mark's to make certain he hadn't died on the way to hospital.

He hadn't, which meant he had to have been taken to some other hospital. Unless he was still lying in the wrecked newspaper office.

She rang up Croydon again. 'We looked where you told us to,' the FANY who answered assured her, 'but there was no one there. He must have been taken to Bart's or Guy's Hospital for some reason.'

And those were trunk calls, so she'd have to wait and ring them from the post. At any rate, she needed to get back before the nurse came looking for her. She stood up and opened the door of the telephone box.

Stephen was at the far end of the corridor in front of the Matron's desk, shouting at the Matron, who was attempting to block his way. 'You're not allowed on the floor, sir!' she said. 'Visiting hours are over.'

'I don't bloody *care* when visiting hours are. I intend to see Lieutenant Fairchild.'

442

Mary ducked quickly back into the telephone box and pulled the door shut behind her. She sat down, put the receiver to her ear and turned away so that Stephen wouldn't see her as he charged past with the nurse in pursuit.

'This is most irregular,' she heard the nurse say, and then the double doors of the ward banged open and shut again. Mary waited for the sound of Stephen being ejected or of the nurse going angrily for help, but she couldn't hear anything.

She ventured a cautious look out, then crept out and over to the doors to the ward and peeked through the small glass pane. Fairchild was sitting up in bed, looking very young and absolutely radiant. Stephen was sitting on the side of the bed.

Mary glanced back down the corridor and then pushed half the door open a crack so she could hear.

'I only just heard you were here,' Stephen was saying. 'A chap I know who's seeing a FANY in Croydon, Whitt's his name, told me, and I came as soon as I could. Are you certain you're all right, Paige?'

'Yes,' she said. 'Did they tell you Mary was hurt, too? She has a concussion.'

Oh, don't mention me, Mary thought, but he said, 'Whitt told me. He said it was a miracle you weren't killed when the V-2 hit.'

'Mary saved my life,' Fairchild said loyally. 'If she hadn't called to me to bring the medical kit, I'd still have been in the ambulance when it hit.'

'Remind me to thank her,' he said, gripping Paige's hands. 'When I think ... I might have *lost* you—'

Mary eased the door silently shut and then stood there, staring wonderingly at it. She'd been so afraid that the reason the net had let her come through and inadvertently muck up their romance was that it had already been star-crossed. That Stephen, or Paige, or both of them, had been killed. It had never occurred to her that it might have been because they had got together in spite of what she'd done.

She should have known she couldn't have affected events, even if it seemed for a time that was what she was doing. She should have known it would all come right in the end.

'And he simply *barged* in,' a woman's voice said behind her – a nurse, coming round the corner of the corridor. And if they saw her they'd take her back into bed, to Fairchild and Stephen.

She dived for the telephone box, reaching to pull its door shut, but she needn't have bothered. The nurse, flanked by the Matron and the orderly, marched past her without noticing her and pushed open the ward's double doors.

'You mustn't worry, darling,' she heard Stephen say. 'I'll see to it no other rocket ever gets near you if I have to shoot every last one of them down myself.'

'Flying Officer Lang,' Matron said sternly, 'I'm afraid I'm going to have to ask you to leave.'

'In a minute,' he said. 'Fairchild, when I heard what had happened, all I could think of was what an idiot I'd been for not realising how much you mean to me. You know that bit in the Bible about the scales falling from one's eyes? Well, that was *exactly* it.'

The doors swung shut, cutting off the rest of what he was saying. Mary pulled the door of the telephone box shut and sat down to wait for Stephen to be escorted out so she could go back to the ward and her bed. Even if historians couldn't affect events, she wasn't going to run the risk of coming between them again and somehow mucking things up. Not when things had worked out so well for everyone.

The FANYs would all be delighted, and the Major would change the schedule back to the way it had been. Reed and Grenville would stop being angry with her, the discussion would go back to who had to wear the Yellow Peril and how to get Donald to propose to Maitland, and she could go back to doing what she'd come here to do: observe an ambulance post during the V-1 and V-2 attacks.

And there was no reason at all for her to feel so ... *bereft*. It was ridiculous; she should be overjoyed. It must be some sort of delayed reaction to shock, like Fairchild's being so upset over the ambulance. There was certainly no reason to *cry*. He was a lovely boy, and that crooked smile of his was admittedly devastating, but it could never have worked out. He had died before she was born.

'But not in the war,' she murmured, and then, thinking of the nine months and the thousands of V-1s and V-2s still to come, 'I hope.'

'Whatever happens at Dunkirk, we shall fight on.'

WINSTON CHURCHILL 26 MAY 1940

LONDON – WINTER 1941

M r Goode only had a forty-eight-hour leave, so they held
Mike's memorial service the next afternoon. The troupe
attended, and Mrs Willett. She didn't bring Theodore, who had
a cold. He was staying with her neighbour.

Mrs Leary came, and Mike's editor and Miss Snelgrove and
two men, awkward and stiff in black suits, who for one heart-
jarring moment Polly thought might, against all odds, be the
retrieval team, but who turned out to be two firemen whom
Mike had rescued on the night of the twenty-ninth. They told
Polly and Eileen that Mike had warned them when a wall was
about to fall on them and saved their lives, and they were sorry
they hadn't been there to save his in return.

Alf and Binnie came, too, bearing a bouquet of browning lilies
Polly was convinced they'd stolen off someone's grave. 'We
saw when it was. In the papers,' Binnie said, looking around St
Paul's in awe.

'Coo, this church ain't 'alf fancy!' Alf said. 'There's lots of
nice things in 'ere—'

'Yes, and anyone who tries to pinch one of them goes straight
to the bad place,' Eileen said, sounding almost like her old self
for the first time since Mike had died.

446

With the vicar's arrival, she had abandoned her vigil at the foot of the escalator and had agreed to a memorial service. And when Miss Laburnum told her she simply *couldn't* wear her green coat to it, she'd let Miss Laburnum lend her a much-too-large black coat.

Too willingly, Polly'd thought. Eileen was still quiet and withdrawn, and Polly feared she'd gone from denial to despair, though it was difficult not to, with Mike and Mr Simms dead, and the gentle vicar going off to war. Eileen was right. He was almost certain to be killed.

Polly had wanted her to face reality, but now she was afraid that that reality might crush her, and she was glad to see some of her spirit return as she took charge of the Hodbins. 'You must sit still and be absolutely quiet,' Eileen told them.

'We *know*,' Alf said, offended, 'when— Ow!' he wailed, and his voice echoed through the vast spaces of the cathedral.

Mr Humphreys came scurrying down the south aisle towards them.

'Binnie *kicked* me!'

'Kicking's not allowed in church,' Mr Goode said calmly.

'And neither is hitting each other with floral offerings,' Eileen said, extracting the lilies from them and handing them to the vicar.

She steered Alf and Binnie through the gate and into the chapel, told them to sit down and stay put, and then took Polly by the arm and led her out into the south aisle. 'Alf and Binnie said you found them and told them about Mike.'

'Yes,' Polly said, afraid Eileen would consider that somehow a betrayal. 'I thought they might be a comfort—'

'Where did you find them? In Whitechapel?'

'No, I didn't know where they lived, so I looked in the tube stations.'

Eileen nodded as though that had confirmed something.

'We're about to begin the service,' the vicar said, coming out.

'Yes, of course,' Eileen said.

They went back in, and Eileen sat down between Alf and Binnie, telling them they had to be quiet, and showing them the correct place in the prayer book, and Polly felt reassured all over again.

But after the service began, sitting there looking like a child in her too-large coat, Eileen got that odd, withdrawn look again, as if she was somewhere else altogether.

But we're not, Polly thought, listening to the litany. *We're here in 1941 and Mike is dead.* It seemed impossible that they were at his funeral – and it *was* his funeral, whether there was a body or not. No wonder Eileen had refused to believe it. It couldn't possibly be true.

And not only had he died here, far from home, but he wasn't even being laid to rest under his own name. It was Mike Davis, an American war correspondent from Omaha, Nebraska, who'd died, not the historian Michael Davies, who had come to the past to study heroism and died there, abandoned, shipwrecked, trying to rescue his companions.

Polly had asked Mr Goode to do the eulogy, remembering his sermon that day in Backbury. He spoke of Mike and his bravery at Dunkirk and then said, 'We live in hope that the good we do here on earth will be rewarded in heaven. We also hope to win the war. We hope that right and goodness will triumph, and that when the war is won, we shall have a better world. And we work towards that end. We buy war bonds and put out incendiaries and knit stockings—'

And pumpkin-coloured scarves, Polly thought.

'—and volunteer to take in evacuated children and work in hospitals and drive ambulances—'

Here Alf grinned and nudged Eileen sharply in the ribs.

'—and man anti-aircraft guns. We join the Home Guard and the ATS and the Civil Defence, and we cannot know whether the scrap metal we collect, the letter we write to a soldier, the vegetables we grow, will turn out in the end to have helped win the war or not. We act in faith.

'But the vital thing is that we act. We do not rely on hope alone, though hope is our bulwark, our light through dark days and darker nights. We also work, and fight, and endure, and it does not matter whether the part we play is large or small. The reason that God marks the fall of the sparrow is that he knows that it is as important to the world as the bulldog or the wolf. We all, all must do "our bit", for it is through our deeds that the war will be won, through our kindness and devotion and courage that we make that better world for which we long.

'So it is with heaven,' the vicar was saying. 'By our deeds here on earth, in this world so far from the one we long for, we make heaven possible. We not only live in the hope of heaven, but, by each doing our bit, we bring it to pass.'

Mike did his bit, Polly thought. *He did everything he could do to save us. Like Mr Dunworthy. Like Colin.*

Because sitting there watching the vicar, she was absolutely convinced that Colin had searched desperately for her, had turned Oxford and the lab upside down, trying to find out what had gone wrong, trying to come up with a plan to get them out.

She could see him demanding action, trying drop site after drop site for one which would open, scouring historical records and newspapers and books on time travel, searching for clues to what had happened, refusing to give up. And if he had failed, if he had died before he was able to get them out, it wasn't his fault any more than it was Mike's. They had tried. They had done their bit.

As soon as the service was over, Mr Humphreys dragged the vicar off to look at Captain Faulknor's memorial, and Eileen hustled Alf and Binnie out of the chapel, leaving Polly to thank everyone for coming and listen to their condolences.

'We must trust in God's goodness,' Miss Hibbard said, patting her hand.

Mrs Wyvern patted it, too. 'God never sends us more than we can bear.'

'Everything which happens is part of God's plan,' the rector intoned.

Sir Godfrey came up to her, his hat in his hand.

If he has some appropriately cheerful Shakespeare quote, like 'There's a divinity that shapes our ends' or 'All will yet be well' I'll never forgive him, Polly thought.

'Viola,' he said, and shook his head resignedly. '"The rain it raineth every day."'

I love you, she thought, tears stinging her eyes.

Miss Laburnum came up. 'We must have faith at trying times like these,' she said and turned to Sir Godfrey. 'I have been thinking, we should do a dramatic reading from *Mary Rose*. There's a heartbreaking scene where her son comes looking for his dead mother ...'

She dragged him off, and Polly went to look for Eileen. She couldn't see her or the Hodbins anywhere, and she didn't want her to have to listen to the rector's or Mrs Wyvern's platitudes. She went out into the nave and towards the dome.

Eileen was looking at *The Light of the World* with Alf and Binnie. Or rather, Alf and Binnie were looking at it, and Eileen was staring at Alf and Binnie with the same blind, withdrawn look. Polly'd hoped the vicar's words would aid Eileen in coming to terms with Mike's death, but they didn't seem to have.

And the Hodbins were certainly of no help. 'Why's 'e wearin' a dress?' Alf asked, pointing at the painting. 'And wot's 'e standin' there for?'

''e's knockin' up the people wot live there, you dunderpate,' Binnie said.

'*You're* the dunderpate,' Alf said. 'Nobody lives there. Look at that door. It ain't been opened in years. I'll wager the people wot lived there went off and didn't tell 'im. Or else they're *dead*. 'e can go on knockin' forever, and nobody'll come.'

That is the last thing Eileen needs to hear, Polly thought, and

450

said, 'We should be going. We don't want to be caught out when the sirens go.' But Eileen gave no indication that she heard her. She continued to stare blindly at Alf and Binnie.

Polly tried again. 'Eileen, we need to go and rescue the vicar. Mr Humphreys took him to look at Faulknor's memorial and—'

'Alf, Binnie, come with me,' Eileen said abruptly, and herded them back to the now-deserted chapel. She opened the gate.

'Why're we goin' back in 'ere?' Binnie asked as Eileen motioned them inside.

'We didn't nick nuffink,' Alf said.

Oh no, Polly thought, *what did they steal now?*

'We wasn't even *in* 'ere,' Alf said, 'we was lookin' at that picture the whole time.'

Eileen shut and latched the gate and then turned to face them. 'We didn't steal nuffink,' Binnie said. 'Honest.'

Eileen didn't even seem to have heard that. 'How long has your mother been dead?' she asked.

Dead?

'You're daft,' Alf said. 'Our mum ain't dead.'

'She's down at Piccadilly Circus right this minute,' Binnie said, sidling towards the gate. 'We'll go and fetch 'er.'

Eileen stepped firmly between them and the gate. 'You're not going anywhere.' She looked across at Polly. 'Their mother was killed in a raid last autumn, and they've been covering it up ever since. They've been living on their own in the shelters.

'Haven't you?' Eileen demanded, looking steadily at the children. 'How long has she been dead?'

'We told you,' Alf said, 'she ain't—'

'She died at Bart's, didn't she?' Eileen said. 'That's why you knew where the hospital was, and why you wanted to leave, because you were afraid a nurse would recognise you and tell me what happened.'

'No,' Alf said, 'you said you needed to get to St Paul's. That's why we was—'

'How long has she been dead, Binnie?'

'We *told* you—' Alf began

'Since September,' Binnie said.

Alf turned on her furiously. 'What'd you go and tell 'er that for? Now she'll turn us in.'

Binnie ignored him. 'We didn't find out till October, though,' she said. 'Sometimes Mum din't come home for two or three days, so we din't think nuffink of it, but after a bit we got worried and went lookin' for her, and one of Mum's friends said she was in a pub what got 'it by a thousand-pounder.'

And there wasn't a body left to identify, Polly thought. *Like Mike*. And the 'friend' was either a fellow prostitute or one of Mrs Hodbin's clients, neither of whom would have wanted to have anything to do with the police, so her death hadn't been reported to the authorities.

'She'd already been killed when I came to borrow the map, hadn't she?' Eileen asked. 'That was why you wouldn't let me in and told me she was sleeping.'

Binnie nodded. 'That's wot we told the landlady, too. Mum always slept a lot when she was 'ome, and we 'ad the ration books, so it was all right. Till we run out of money and couldn't pay the rent.'

'And the landlady found out about Mrs Bascombe,' Alf said.

'Their parrot,' Eileen explained to Polly.

'So we told 'er we was all goin' to live with Mum's sister in the country.'

'And you went to live in the shelters,' Eileen said.

'But what did you live on if you hadn't any money?' Polly asked, and then thought, *Picking pockets and stealing picnic baskets.*

Mr Humphreys and the vicar were coming back, Mr Humphreys still talking of Captain Faulknor.

Binnie looked stricken. 'You ain't gonna tell the vicar, are you?'

'Promise you won't tell nobody,' Alf said, 'or we'll 'ave to go to an orphanage.'

'Ah, here you are,' Mr Humphreys said.

The vicar looked at them, taking in the latched gate, Eileen's sentry-like stance, the children's expressions. 'What's going on here, Miss O'Reilly?' he asked.

'*Please*,' Binnie mouthed.

Eileen turned, unlatched the gate and let them into the chapel. 'Alf and Binnie were just telling me about their mother,' she said. 'She was killed last autumn. They've been living on their own in the shelters.'

Binnie looked utterly betrayed.

'What'd you do that for?' Alf wailed. 'Now they'll send us away, and you're the only one wot's nice to us.'

'We don't need no one to take care of us,' Binnie said belligerently. 'Me 'n' Alf can take care of ourselves.'

'I'll take them in,' Eileen said.

'*What?*' Polly said. 'You can't—'

'Someone must. They obviously can't go on living in the tube stations,' Eileen said. 'Mr Goode, can you arrange for me to be named their guardian?'

'Yes, of course, but—' He turned to Mr Humphreys. 'Would you mind terribly showing the children round the cathedral for a bit? We need to discuss—'

'Of course,' Mr Humphreys said. 'Poor things. Come along with me, children.'

'It'll be all right,' Eileen said to Binnie.

'You swear?'

'I swear. Go on, go with Mr Humphreys.'

They'll bolt, just as they did the morning after the twenty-ninth, Polly thought, but they went docilely off with the verger.

'Come, I'll show you *The Light of the World*,' Polly heard him say as they went up the aisle.

'We already seen it,' Alf said.

'Oh, but you'll find that you see something different in it each time,' Mr Humphreys replied.

I can imagine, Polly thought.

Their footsteps died away. 'Are you quite certain you want to do this, Miss O'Reilly?' the vicar asked. 'After all, the Hodbins are—'

'I know,' Eileen said.

'Mrs Rickett will never allow it,' Polly said. 'You know her rules.'

'And it would be better if they were safely out of London,' the vicar said. 'The Evacuation Committee—'

'No,' Eileen said, 'if they're evacuated, they'll run away, and they won't survive on their own. Alf plays with UXBs, and Binnie's a young girl. She can't just run wild in the shelters or …'

She'll end up like her mother, Polly thought.

'They haven't anyone else,' Eileen said to Polly. 'If we don't rescue them—'

'But what about Mrs Rickett?' Polly said. 'You know her rules – no cooking in the room, no pets, no children. And Mr Goode's leave is up today—'

'I'll see if I can get additional time, since this is a matter involving my parishioners,' he said. 'And perhaps I can persuade Mrs Rickett to relax her rules, given the circumstances.'

I highly doubt that, Polly thought, and just as she expected, Mrs Rickett was not impressed by either the vicar's clerical collar or his arguments.

'You know the rules,' she said, her arms folded militantly across her chest. 'No children.'

'But their mother was killed in a raid,' the vicar said, 'and they've nowhere else to go. The Church will provide cots and bedding for them.'

'And we'll see that they don't cause you any bother,' Eileen added.

That's not the way to Mrs Rickett's heart, Polly thought.

'We'll pay extra for their board,' she said, 'and children are allowed an extra milk ration.'

'How large a ration?' Mrs Rickett demanded, her eyes glittering at the thought of the milk puddings and cream soups she could cook up into inedible messes.

'Half a pint a day,' the vicar said.

'Very well,' Mrs Rickett said, nearly snatching the children's ration books out of Eileen's hands, 'but their board won't begin till the day after tomorrow.'

Of course not, Polly thought.

'And if there's any playing on the stairs, or any noise—'

'There won't be,' Eileen said earnestly. 'They're very nicely behaved children.'

'You should join the troupe,' Polly said after Mrs Rickett had gone. 'You're a far better actress than I am.'

Eileen ignored her. 'Thank you so much, Mr Goode,' she said. 'We couldn't have managed it without you. You've been wonderful.'

He had. In the two extra days' leave he'd managed to wangle, he'd not only obtained new ration books and new clothes for Alf and Binnie but had had Eileen named their temporary guardian and had arranged for a school.

'*School?*' Alf and Binnie said, as if he'd suggested burning them at the stake.

'Yes,' the vicar said sternly, 'and if you don't go every day and do everything Miss O'Reilly tells you, she'll write to me, and I'll have you sent straight to the orphanage.'

Polly doubted the Hodbins were any more capable of being intimidated than Mrs Rickett, but then again, she'd expected them to bolt when Mr Humphreys took them off to *The Light of the World* and again when she and Eileen had told them to wait for them at Notting Hill Gate while they spoke to Mrs Rickett, and they hadn't. In fact, when they took the vicar to the station to see him off, Alf asked him, 'Is Eileen going to be our mum now?'

Polly didn't hear what the vicar said, but she saw how cheerful Eileen was and couldn't be sorry they'd decided to take in the Hodbins. Especially since the vicar had told Eileen he was being assigned to active duty.

Chaplains hadn't been armed – even though they were often in the thick of battle – and the vicar, with his slight frame and mild manner, was scarcely the soldier sort. And how many earnest young men, eager like him to help the war effort, had died in the sands of North Africa and on the beaches of Normandy? Polly wasn't certain Eileen could bear another loss.

They all went to see him off at Victoria Station. 'We got to,' Alf said, ''cause he seen us off that day we come to London. Remember, Vicar? How you come to tell us goodbye that day?'

'I do,' the vicar said, looking at Eileen.

'And now we're tellin' you goodbye. It's funny, ain't it, Eileen?'

'Yes,' she said, blinking back tears, 'thank you so much for everything, Mr Goode.'

'It was a pleasure,' he said solemnly. He picked up his duffel bag. 'I'd best board. You have my address for now, and I'll let you know where I'm going as soon as I'm able. Promise me you'll write to me if you need any further assistance with Alf and Binnie, and I'll see to it.'

If you can, Polly thought. *If you're not killed.*

They said goodbye, and the vicar boarded the train, the romance of it somewhat spoiled by Alf and Binnie shouting after him, 'Shoot heaps of Germans!' and 'Kill that ol' 'itler!'

Eileen watched the train out of sight.

'Whatcha waitin' for?' Binnie asked curiously.

'Nothing,' Eileen said. 'Come along, we're going home.'

'We can't,' Alf said, 'we got to go to Blackfriars to get our things.'

'*What* things?'

'You know,' Binnie said innocently, 'our clothes and things.'

'And that book wot you gave me about the Tower of London,'

Alf said, heading for the entrance to the Underground. 'The best part was when they cut off Mary Queen of Scots' head.'

And after they'd boarded the train to Blackfriars, he regaled them with the details. 'The executioner chopped it off, whack, like that.' He demonstrated for the benefit of the other passengers in the car. 'And then he picked it up by the 'air. That's what they done back then. They picked up the 'ead, all gory and dripping blood, and said, "This is what 'appens to queens wot commits treason."'

'And then they stuck it up on London Bridge,' Binnie finished.

'Not 'er they didn't,' Alf said. 'She was wearin' a wig, and when they picked up 'er 'ead, it fell on the floor and rolled under the bed, and 'er *dog* ran after it and—'

'This is Blackfriars,' Eileen said, standing up and pushing them both off the train ahead of her.

'Stop pushin'—' Binnie said.

'Don't you want to know wot Mary Queen of Scots' dog done?'

'No,' Polly said.

'You said you needed to get your things,' Eileen said. 'Where are they? On the platform?'

'Are you a noddlehead?' Binnie said, leading the way. 'People'd pinch 'em.'

'They're in the tunnel,' Alf said as they reached the platform. 'Wait 'ere.' And before Eileen could stop them, both children had darted to the end of the platform and disappeared into the blackness of the tunnel.

'They'll be killed,' Eileen said.

'No such luck,' Polly said, and in a moment they each reappeared with an armful of belongings – a cap, a ragged-looking cardigan, a pair of Wellingtons, a stack of film magazines.

Alf dumped his in Eileen's arms. 'I got to get Mrs Bascombe,' he said, and darted back towards the tunnel.

'Mrs Bascombe?' Polly asked. 'Who's Mrs Bascombe?'

'Their parrot,' Eileen said despairingly. 'I assumed it had been left behind when the children moved into the shelters.' She turned to Binnie. 'I thought animals weren't allowed in shelters.'

'They ain't,' Binnie said. 'That's why we 'ad to keep 'er 'idden in the tunnel.'

'This isn't the parrot who can imitate an air-raid alert, is it?' Polly asked, afraid she already knew the answer.

'And the all-clear,' Alf said, appearing with a large, rusty cage in which sat a grey-and-red parrot. 'But we've taught 'er lots of things since then.'

LONDON – 7 MAY 1945

That is *Merope*, Mary thought, leaning out over the National Gallery's stone railing to get a better look at the young woman in the green coat, standing there in Trafalgar Square. *Oh good. She wanted to do VE Day.*

She raised her arm to wave and shout to her, and then decided against it. She didn't know what name she was here under. Probably not Merope. That name hadn't become popular till the twenties. And she didn't know what her cover was, or if she was here with one of the contemps. A middle-aged man in an RAF uniform stood next to her on her left.

She lowered her arm, but Paige had already seen her begin to wave. 'Do you see Reardon *now*?' Paige asked her.

'No, I thought I saw someone I knew.'

'You very probably did. I think everyone in England is here tonight.'

Past and *present*, she thought.

'Reardon!' Paige shouted, waving wildly. She glanced over to where Paige was looking and then back to where Merope had been standing, but she was no longer there. She searched through the crowd for her – by the lamppost, by the lion, over by the Monument, but there was no sign of the green coat, which she should be able to spot, it was so bright. Or of her red hair.

'Oh no, I've lost sight of her,' Paige said, scanning the sea of people. 'Which way did Reardon go? I can't see her anywhere. She – there she is! And there's Talbot.' She began waving wildly. 'Talbot! Reardon!'

'I don't imagine they can hear you,' she said, but amazingly, they were ploughing determinedly through the crowd and up the steps towards them.

'Fairchild, Douglas, thank goodness,' Reardon said when she reached them. 'I thought I'd never see you again!'

Talbot nodded. 'It's bedlam out there,' she said cheerfully. 'Have any of you seen Parrish and Maitland? I got separated from them. They were over by the bonfire.' They all obediently looked in that direction, although there was no hope of recognising anyone with the fire behind them like that.

'I don't see them anywhere,' Talbot said. 'Wait— Fairchild, isn't that your true love?'

'It can't be,' Paige said, looking where Talbot was pointing. 'He's in France. He … oh, Douglas, look!' Paige grabbed her arm. 'It's Stephen! Stephen! I was afraid he wouldn't get here in time, and he'd miss all this. Oh Mary, I'm so glad he's here!'

So am I, she thought. It was wonderful seeing him without the fear and strain that had been in his face when Paige was in hospital, without the fatigue and concentration he'd had when he'd been tipping V-1s every day. He looked years younger than the last time she'd seen him.

But he's still too old for me, she thought regretfully. Though it wouldn't matter if she were a FANY and not a historian. She still couldn't have him. He hadn't found Paige in the crowd yet, but he was clearly looking for her, and when he did, he'd only have eyes for her.

I'm still glad I get to see him one last time, she thought, watching him work his way cheerfully through the jostling crowd, looking for Paige, his dark hair …

'He doesn't see us!' Paige wailed. 'Wave, Mary!'

She waved along with the others, and shouted, and Parrish emitted an ear-splitting whistle which would have made her titled parents shudder, but which did the trick. He looked up, saw Paige, grinned that devastatingly crooked smile of his, and started straight for them.

'Oh good,' Talbot said. 'He's seen— Good God! Is that the Major?'

Talbot pointed three-quarters of the way across the square, beyond the bonfire, but they all spotted her instantly. And worse, she'd spotted them. 'This is all your fault, Fairchild,' Talbot said. 'If we hadn't been waving at Stephen, she'd never have seen us.'

'What do you think she's doing here?' Reardon asked apprehensively.

'If I know her,' Parrish said, 'she's probably come to tell us we're all on report.'

'Or to send us to Edgware for sticking plaster,' Paige said.

'Should we start a pool on it?' Reardon asked.

Talbot laughed. 'Oh I'm going to *miss* all of you.'

'We'll see each other again,' Paige said confidently. 'You're all invited to my wedding. Douglas is going to be my maid of honour, aren't you, Mary?'

I can't, she thought.

'Only if you promise not to make me wear the Yellow Peril,' she said lightly.

'I knew I was glad the war was over,' Parrish said. 'It means I'll never have to wear the Yellow Peril again.'

'Or drive the Octopus,' Talbot said.

Or be afraid you're going to be killed any moment. Or dig body parts and dead children out of the rubble again, Mary said silently and thought of the man in the wrecked newspaper office in Croydon. After she'd got out of hospital, she'd telephoned Bart's, and Guy's Hospital, and then every ambulance unit within forty miles, but she hadn't found any trace of him. He must not have been as badly injured as she'd thought, though that seemed impossible.

I hope he made it, she thought. *I hope he's here tonight to see this.*

'Oh no,' Talbot said. 'The Major's coming this way!'

'Do you think she'll make us go home?' Reardon said.

No, just me, Mary thought. With the Major here, it was a perfect time to go back to the post, leave her note saying, 'My mother's very ill. Must go', and then head for the drop.

She was sorry she hadn't got to see Maitland or Sutcliffe-Hythe or Reed one last time – she had grown amazingly attached to all the FANYs over the last year. But she was only experiencing what every person here in Trafalgar Square would be in the next few days and weeks. This wasn't only an end to the war. It would be the end to who knew how many friendships, romances and careers. All sorts of partings, all sorts of goodbyes.

And if she was going, she needed to do it now, before the trains stopped for the night – and before the Major and Stephen got here. Stephen had nearly reached the foot of the steps. She gave him one last regretful glance and then looked at the other girls. Their eyes were still on the Major, on whose head an air-raid warden had just plunked a Nelson-like tricorn hat.

'Do you think we'd best flee while we can?' Parrish asked.

'No, it will only make it worse when she *does* catch us,' Talbot said.

'Perhaps she's come to celebrate with us,' Reardon said.

'Does she *look* like she's celebrating?' Talbot asked.

She didn't, despite the festive tricorn. *I'll miss you, too, Major*, Mary thought, and leaned towards Paige, who was still calling and waving to Stephen, and kissed her on the cheek. Paige didn't even notice.

Mary edged slowly away from her and then turned, squeezed quickly along the porch to the steps, and down the same way she'd come up, taking her cap off and keeping her head down in case Paige realised she was gone and began looking for her.

If she did, Paige would hopefully assume she'd tried to get down to Stephen and been carried away by the crowd. *Which could be true*, she thought, reaching the front of the steps.

She set out at an angle across the square towards Charing Cross. Halfway across, she caught a current which swept her in the direction she wanted to go and let it carry her. It looked like it might even deliver her neatly at the entrance to the station.

With time to spare, she thought, stopping at the edge of the square to look at her watch.

The little man in the bowler was still in exactly the same place. 'Three cheers for Patton!' he shouted, but the 'Hip, hip, hurrahs' were drowned out by the approaching beats of the conga line. She pushed through the crowd towards the Underground station. Hopefully, it would be less jammed than when they'd come. Certainly none of these people showed any sign of going home any time soon, and once the train got past Holborn, it should be—

'Come on, ducks!' a burly merchant marine shouted in her ear. He grabbed her around the waist, thrust her into the conga line ahead of him and forced her hands onto the waist of the soldier in front of her.

'No! I haven't time for this!' she cried, but it was no use. The marine had an iron grip on her waist, and when she tried to plant her feet firmly on the ground and refuse to go, he simply picked her up and held her out before him.

She was carried remorselessly back into Trafalgar Square and across it by the snaking *dunh duh dunh duh UNH'ing* dancers. They were heading straight back to the National Gallery. 'You don't understand,' she shouted, 'I've got to get to the Underground station! I must—'

'Here then, let her go, that's a good chap,' a man's voice said, and she felt herself grabbed by the waist and plucked neatly out of the conga line. The marine and the rest of the line danced past her and away.

'*Thank* you,' she said, turning to look at her rescuer, but before she got a good look at his face – she scarcely had time to register the fact that he was a soldier and that he was wearing a clerical collar – there was a loud explosion over by the fountain.

'Sorry, I believe I know who did that,' he said, and strode off through the crowd, presumably to rescue someone else.

'Thank you again, whoever you are,' Mary said, and set off for the tube station again, this time keeping to the very edge of the Square and the street.

The little man in the bowler was still standing outside leading cheers. 'Three cheers for Dowding!' he shouted.

He's going to run out of heroes to cheer, she thought, squeezing past him to the entrance, but she was wrong. As she ran down the stairs, she heard him shout, 'Three cheers for the firespotters! Three cheers for the ARP! Three cheers for all of us! Hip hip hurrah!'

'Father, we thought we should never see you again.'

SIR J.M. BARRIE *THE ADMIRABLE CRICHTON*

LONDON – WINTER 1941

They lasted less than a fortnight at Mrs Rickett's, even though Alf and Binnie proved quite adept at keeping their parrot out of sight – and earshot – of the landlady. Mrs Bascombe was a quick study, and it only took Alf a day to teach her not to do her air-raid imitations except when the actual sirens were going, and not to screech, ''itler's a bloody bastard!' at anyone who came near her cage.

But she was, unfortunately, also quick to pick up whatever she happened to overhear and to repeat it in a dead-on imitation of their voices – which explained how Alf and Binnie had been able to keep the masquerade of their mother's still being alive going for so long.

But that skill also led to Mrs Rickett's hearing what she thought was Binnie saying, 'What is this swill? It tastes bloody awful,' and using her key to get in, expecting to find, as she told Eileen, cooking going on in the room – and finding herself instead face-to-face with the beady-eyed Mrs Bascombe.

'Not to worry,' the parrot had said in a spot-on imitation of Alf's voice. 'We'll 'ide 'er. The old witch'll never find out,' and all five of them had found themselves out of a place to live and forced to take up residence in Notting Hill Gate Station for the next two nights.

Polly told the station guard that Mrs Bascombe was a prop in the troupe's new play, and Sir Godfrey, coming in behind them, exclaimed, 'Good God! Don't tell me they've decided to do *Treasure Island*!'

And when Miss Laburnum saw it, she said, 'Oh, it would be perfect for *Peter Pan*!'

'It's not staying,' Polly said, and asked if anyone knew of a vacant flat. No one did, and Polly wasn't able to find anything in the 'To Let' ads in the *Times* Sir Godfrey lent her.

'There's 'eaps of 'ouses nobody lives in 'cause the people wot lived in 'em are dead,' Binnie suggested.

'We know how to get into 'em,' Alf said.

'We are *not* breaking into dead people's houses.'

'Not all of 'em are dead,' Binnie protested, 'some of 'em are just empty.'

'We are not breaking into *any* houses.'

'Wait, that gives me an idea,' Eileen said. 'I remember one of Lady Caroline's friends telling her they were having difficulty finding someone to stay in their London house and look after it, and the situation's probably worse now, with the bombing.'

She turned to the *Situations Vacant* column. 'Listen to this. "Wanted, live-in caretaker". The address is in Bloomsbury.'

Eileen went to see the estate agent listed in the advertisement the next day and came back to Townsend Brothers jubilant. 'When I told him we had two children and a parrot—'

'You *told* him?' Polly said.

'Yes, and he said, "I've had four of the houses in my charge blitzed in the past month. Two children and their pet can scarcely do more damage than that."'

I wouldn't say that, Polly thought, *these* are *the Hodbins.*

'The house is in Millwright Lane,' Eileen said. 'Is that a safe address?'

Polly didn't know. Her list of addresses had only been good through to the end of December, but at least it wasn't near the British Museum or in Bedford Square. And she thought most of the attacks in Bloomsbury had been in the autumn. But it was still London.

'I think we should take Alf and Binnie to the country,' she told Eileen. 'You researched the statistics on children who stayed in London. You know they'd be much safer in the country.'

'But that means you'd have to leave Townsend Brothers. How would the retrieval team ever find us?'

The retrieval team's not coming, Polly thought.

'We could put messages in the newspapers, like the ones we put in before,' she said, 'telling them where we'd gone.'

'No, the best lead they have is Oxford Street.'

'We could go to Backbury, then. Or I could stay here and you go – I'm the one with the deadline. And then if the retrieval team comes, I can tell them where you are.'

'No, there's twice the chance of finding us with two of us. We're *not* splitting up. We're staying *here*,' she said, and the next day she told Polly she'd spoken to the estate agent and taken the position.

'But what about your National Service?' Polly objected.

'When I tell them about my caretaking job and about the Hodbins, they'll *have* to give me something here.'

Polly hoped she was wrong, that they'd assign her to something safely out of London, but they didn't. They gave her a job with the ATS, driving military officers.

Which is safer than working on an anti-aircraft gun crew, Polly thought. Or in a munitions factory. Factories were frequently targeted by the Luftwaffe.

And the house they moved into was near Russell Square, which was safe. But the house next door had been reduced to rubble and the one across from it had had its roof smashed in. 'That means ours won't be hit,' Alf said.

Binnie nodded wisely. 'Bombs never 'it the same spot twice.'

Polly knew from experience that that wasn't true, but she didn't contradict them. Nowhere in London was safe, but at least this wasn't the East End, which continued to be hammered;

the house had a sturdy-looking cellar; and even Eileen's and her own cooking was better than Mrs Rickett's, 'though I'm beginning to sympathise with her,' Eileen said after a week. 'How exactly does one produce meals for a family of four with one pound of meat and eight eggs a week?'

'We can get you some birds to cook,' Binnie said. 'There's lots of pigeons here.'

'And squirrels,' Alf said, brandishing his slingshot.

It really is too bad we can't smuggle them into Nazi Germany to drive Hitler to distraction instead of us, Polly thought, though on the whole things were going better than she'd expected. The children were going to school, the deserted houses meant there were scarcely any neighbours for Alf and Binnie to annoy, and Eileen seemed much more cheerful.

'I've been thinking about Dunkirk,' she said. 'Mike said the soldiers sitting waiting on the beaches thought no one was coming for them, and they'd be captured by the Germans. But they didn't know about the launches and rowboats and ferries that were being rounded up to come and fetch them. And the soldiers wading ashore on D-Day didn't know about all the things going on behind the scenes, like the deception campaign – what did you call it?'

'Fortitude.'

'Fortitude,' Eileen said, 'or about all the things the French Resistance was doing, or Ultra. And it may be the same with us. There may be all sorts of things going on we don't know about. Mr Dunworthy may be working on a plan to get us out this very minute. Or he may already be on his way here.'

But this is time travel, Polly thought, despairing of ever making her understand. *If they were coming, they'd already be here.*

'We mustn't give up hope,' Eileen said. 'Dunkirk worked out all right in the end.'

'Never give up,' Alf said behind them, and they both jumped.

Oh no, Polly thought, *how much did he hear?*

But when she turned around, it was only the parrot. 'I'm sorry,' Eileen said. 'I told Alf and Binnie to teach her something patriotic to say instead of "Hitler's a bloody bastard."'

'Loose lips sink ships,' Mrs Bascombe squawked.

'Well, she's certainly right about that,' Polly said. 'We need to watch what we say with the children here.'

'Donate your scrap metal,' the parrot croaked. 'Dig for victory. Do your bit.'

Eileen was certainly doing her bit by taking in Alf and Binnie. She deserved some sort of medal. But everyone they knew was doing theirs, too – the vicar and Mr Dorming, who'd taken on Mr Simms' job as a firespotter, and Doreen, who'd given her notice at Townsend Brothers and signed up for the ATA.

'I'm going to be an Atta Girl and fly a Tiger Moth,' she said proudly.

Her departure, and Sarah Steinberg's – she was going to do her National Service as an RAF plotter – left the third floor terribly shorthanded, and Miss Snelgrove told Polly that Townsend Brothers was applying for an Employer Hardship Exemption for her so she could remain in her job.

Eileen was overjoyed. 'I've been ever so worried about how the retrieval team would find you after you left to do your National Service.'

'I told Miss Snelgrove no,' Polly said. 'I'm going to try to get assigned to a rescue squad.'

'A rescue squad?' Eileen said. 'But why?'

Because I have a deadline, and if I simply sit here waiting for it, I'll go mad. And I keep thinking of Marjorie, lying there in that rubble with no one coming to dig her out. I know exactly how that feels. I can't bear to think of anyone else going through that. And if Colin was here – if he was the one who was trapped – that's what he would do.

She didn't say any of that to Eileen. She said, 'If they don't get the waiver, I'll almost certainly be assigned to somewhere outside of London. I need to sign up now.'

'But a rescue squad,' Eileen said, 'it's so dangerous. Couldn't you drive an ambulance instead? That's what you did before, isn't it?'

'Yes, but I can't risk it. I might be assigned to a unit with one of the FANYs I knew and create a paradox. And rescue work's not that dangerous. We don't go to the incident till after the bomb falls. And you heard Binnie. Bombs never fall in the same place twice.'

'But what about the retrieval team? How will they find us?'

'I'll tell Miss Snelgrove which unit I've been assigned to,' Polly said.

The next morning Polly gave her notice at work and went to the Works Board. She filled up a registration form and eventually had her name called by a stern woman with a pince-nez.

'I'm Mrs Sentry. Please be seated,' the woman said without looking up from the form. 'I see your last employment was as a shop assistant with a department store. I assume you can do sums. Can you type?'

If she said yes, she would end up in Whitehall, typing requisition forms for the War Office. 'No, ma'am,' she said. 'I was hoping to be assigned to a rescue squad.'

Mrs Sentry shook her head. 'You're far too slight to do the lifting involved.'

'Well, then, some sort of Civil Defence work.'

Mrs Sentry looked at her over her pince-nez. '*My* job is to match you with the job for which you're best suited. Are you married?'

'No, ma'am.'

Mrs Sentry wrote 'single' on the form below 'good at sums'. 'Are you good at puzzles?' she asked. 'Acrostics, crosswords, that sort of thing?'

Oh God, Polly thought, *she's planning to send me to Bletchley Park. That's why she asked me if I was married. I can't go to Bletchley Park. It's the last place I should be.*

'I'm not good at puzzles at all,' she said, 'or sums, really. My supervisor at Townsend Brothers was always having to correct my sales slips. And I'm not married, but I do have obligations. My cousin and I have two war orphans living with us.'

'How old are the children?'

How old do they have to be to keep me from going to Bletchley Park? Polly thought, wondering if she dared lie about their ages, but Mrs Sentry looked the type who'd check. 'Alf's seven and Binnie's twelve,' she said. 'Their mother was killed in a raid.'

And it was a good thing she'd told the truth because Mrs Sentry was looking suspiciously at her. 'What did you say your name was?'

Oh no, she knows Alf and Binnie. They've tried to steal her handbag in the tube station.

'Polly Sebastian,' she said.

'Sebastian,' Mrs Sentry said thoughtfully. 'You look extremely familiar. Have we met before?'

It was Stephen Lang all over again. *What if she knew me as a FANY?* Polly thought. She didn't look familiar, but ...

But this wasn't 1944. *Even if I did meet her then, it hasn't happened yet.*

'I'm almost certain we've met before,' Mrs Sentry was saying, 'but I can't think where ... It was at Christmas ...'

I hope she wasn't at the pantomime, Polly thought, recalling that episode with Theodore.

'Could it have been when you were at Townsend Brothers Christmas shopping?' she asked to throw her off the scent.

'No, I shop at Harrods. It was something to do with a theatre ...' She frowned, trying to remember.

Polly had to get her to assign her to a job before she did. If she remembered Theodore's screaming, 'I don't *want* to go home!' she was likely to decide Polly was an unfit mother and ship her off to Bletchley Park after all. 'If I could be assigned to an ARP post or—'

'*I* know where I saw you. In a play in the tube station at Piccadilly Circus. *A Christmas Carol.* When you said "anti-aircraft gun" I remembered you having to shout over them. You played the girl Scrooge was in love with, didn't you?'

'Yes,' Polly said, relieved that at least it hadn't been the pantomime.

'You were simply wonderful,' Mrs Sentry said, beaming at Polly through her pince-nez, no longer stern. 'I can't tell you how much the play meant to me. I'd been feeling rather glum about the war and everything, but seeing it brought back the Christmases of my girlhood – the family all together, reading Dickens round the fire. It gave me hope that we'll see Christmases like that again when this war is over. And it made me determined to do my bit to see that we do. Why didn't you say on your application that you were an actress?'

'I'm not,' Polly said. 'That was only an amateur troupe. We put on plays in the shelters, but they weren't—'

But Mrs Sentry wasn't listening. 'I have just the job for you. Wait here.' She stood up, hurried over to a file cabinet, extracted a sheet of paper and hurried back. 'It's perfect. *And* you'll be able to stay here in London with your family. Let me just write down the address for you,' she said, and printed 'ENSA' on a card.

ENSA, the Entertainments National Service Association, put on shows and musical revues for the soldiers. Mrs Sentry handed the address to her. 'You're to go to the Alhambra and report to Mr Tabbitt. It's just off Shaftesbury Avenue, near the Forrest.'

Which was the theatre where the pantomime had been.

'I'm so glad I remembered where I'd seen you,' Mrs Sentry said. 'If you hadn't given that performance in Piccadilly—'

I'd have the address of an ARP post to report to instead of a theatre, Polly thought disgustedly.

But there was no point in trying to talk Mrs Sentry out of this. She was looking far too pleased with herself. She'd have to come back and speak to someone else and, in the meantime, hope Mr Tabbitt wouldn't want her.

Which I doubt he will, she thought. *ENSA does musical revues, not plays, and I can't sing or dance.*

But when she told that to Mr Tabbitt, who turned out to be a large, beefy man who looked like *he* belonged on a rescue squad, he said, 'Neither can anyone else in this cast.'

She'd interrupted a rehearsal, and the chorus girls standing hands on hips on the stage above them hooted derisively when Mr Tabbitt said that, and one of them – with a mop of black curls – retorted, 'We're only trying to live up to our name, ducks. ENSA: Every Night Something Awful.'

Mr Tabbitt ignored her. 'What professional stage experience have you had?' he asked Polly.

'None. I told you, there's been an error. I was supposed to be assigned to an ARP post.'

'This is *far* more dangerous than the ARP,' the curly-haired chorus girl said. 'The audience were throwing turnips at the Amazing Antioch the other night.'

'Turnips?' one of the other girls said.

'No one's willing to waste a tomato, you see,' the first chorus girl explained, and one of the other girls said, 'I keep hoping they'll throw something good, like oranges.'

'Or ration stamps,' a redhead put in.

'Five-minute break,' Mr Tabbitt snapped, and the girls sauntered off the stage.

'Sorry,' he said, turning back to Polly. 'You were saying something about a mistake?'

'Yes. I was supposed to be assigned to the ARP. If you ring up the Bureau and tell Mrs Sentry that you don't want me, I'm certain she'll send over—'

'Who says I don't want you?' he said. 'I assume you can memorise lines. Lift your skirt.'

'What?'

'Lift your skirt. I want to see your legs.'

'But—'

'And don't go all maiden aunt on me. This isn't the Windmill.

I'm not asking you to take off your clothes. Come on then.' He motioned her to raise her skirt. 'Let's see them.'

She lifted her skirt to her knees and then her hips. He nodded briefly and then bellowed, 'Hattie!' and the curly-haired chorus girl came back onstage, eating a sandwich. 'Take her backstage and see if she'll fit into the ARP warden costume. If she does, bring her back, and we'll run through the skit.'

Hattie nodded.

'Go along now,' he said to Polly. 'You said you were supposed to be assigned to the ARP, and now you are.'

He turned back to Hattie and snatched the sandwich out of her hand. 'And have her try on your costumes as well, since *you* won't be able to fit into them if you keep eating like that.'

'Oh, that's such a clever line. You should put it in the show,' Hattie said, and led Polly backstage.

'And tell her the rules!' Mr Tabbitt shouted after them.

'No smoking backstage – fire regulations,' Hattie said, leading Polly through an obstacle course of ropes and flats. 'No drinking. No pets.'

This is just like Mrs Rickett's, Polly thought, following her down a rickety-looking iron spiral staircase.

'No male admirers allowed in your dressing room, if you *had* a dressing room of your own, which you won't. You'll be in here with Lizzie, Cora and me.'

She opened a door on a tiny, untidy room with a single make-up mirror and then shut it again and led Polly down the corridor to an even tinier room crammed with costumes.

Hattie rummaged through them and came up with a tin helmet, an ARP armband and a dark blue sequined bathing suit. 'Here, try this on.'

'*This* is the ARP warden's costume?' Polly said.

'Yes, and be careful getting into it. I sewed on all those sequins myself. You don't happen to know how to sew, do you?'

'No. I can't act either. As I told Mr Tabbitt, there's been a mistake. I was supposed to be assigned to—'

'The ARP, I know.' Hattie thrust the bathing suit at her. 'Go on, try it on.'

Polly stepped out of her skirt and wriggled into the bathing suit.

'A perfect fit,' Hattie pronounced. 'And you needn't worry about people throwing turnips at you with those legs. Tabbitt will definitely keep you.'

Polly's dismay must have shown in her face because Hattie said, 'If you truly want to be a real air-raid warden instead of a stage one, though personally I can't imagine why anyone would, you'd best go back to the Works Board before Tabbitt sees you in that costume. Once he does, he'll have your name put on the bill, and once that's printed, you'll never get away, not with the paper shortage. You'll be stuck at ENSA for the duration.'

Just like Bletchley Park, Polly thought. 'I'll tell him I sent you home to let out the seams and learn your lines,' Hattie said, handing her a script, 'and that you'll be at rehearsal at three tomorrow.'

'*Thank* you,' Polly said, stepping out of the costume and scrambling into her own clothes. 'You don't know what this means to me.' She hurried out of the stage door and back to the Board, hoping Mrs Sentry had gone off duty, but she was still there. She'd have to come back early the next morning.

'Well?' Eileen asked when she arrived home. 'Were you assigned to a rescue squad?'

'No. To ENSA, putting on shows for the troops.'

'Singin' and dancin', you mean?' Alf asked.

'Yes.'

'Do you even know how?' Binnie asked.

'No, but that doesn't appear to be an impediment.'

'You won't have to go to Egypt to entertain the troops, will you?' Eileen asked worriedly.

'No, I'll be performing at the Alhambra here in London.'

'Oh good,' Eileen said, looking relieved, and as soon as she and Polly were alone, she said, 'The Alhambra wasn't hit, was it?'

'No,' Polly said, though she didn't know that for certain. She knew that no theatre had been bombed during a performance, but that still left before and after performances and during rehearsals, and the *Alhambra* looked like an absolute firetrap.

But she wasn't about to tell Eileen that. 'The job's not definite yet,' she said. 'I may be assigned to an ARP post instead.'

She went to the National Service Bureau early the next morning to see to it that she was. Mrs Sentry, thankfully, wasn't there. She picked out the most sympathetic person she could find and laid out her case, but all she got was a not-at-all-sympathetic lecture on the importance of every service job – 'Each task, no matter how humble or seemingly insignificant, is vital to the war effort' – and the impossibility of being reassigned to an ARP post 'unless you have authorisation from the commander of the unit. You haven't, have you?'

Not yet, Polly thought, and went to every ARP post in Bloomsbury and Oxford Street and Kensington.

All of them were 'fully staffed at the moment'. 'Perhaps in six months,' the warden at the Notting Hill post told her.

The Blitz will only last four, she thought, frustrated, and asked to speak to the post commander.

'She won't be in till three o'clock,' the warden told her.

But by three she needed to be at rehearsal, and it was already after one. She had two hours to find a post that would take her. She couldn't keep going from post to post. She needed to talk to someone who'd know which posts were shorthanded, someone who—

Mr Humphreys at St Paul's, she thought. He'd know all the Civil Defence personnel in the area. He might even be able to talk one of them into taking her on.

She hurried to the tube station, caught the train to St Paul's and raced up the stairs and out of the station towards the cathedral.

And was appalled all over again. She hadn't been here since Mike's memorial service, and in the meantime, work crews had cleared away the charred hulks of the buildings on Paternoster Row and Newgate and Carter Lane, leaving St Paul's standing all alone in a flat grey wasteland.

'It looks like a pinpoint bomb went off here,' Polly murmured as she hurried up the street, and thought suddenly of Oxford. Was this what it looked like?

'Watch where you're going,' a female voice said, and she came out of her reverie just in time to avoid colliding with a woman in a WAAF uniform.

'Sorry,' Polly said, hurrying around her and up the hill. She ran across the forecourt, up the steps and into the cathedral.

There was no one at the desk or in the south aisle. *What if Mr Humphreys isn't here today?* she thought, starting up the nave, but he was in the north transept, standing with a trio of sailors in front of the piled sandbags which covered Captain Faulknor's memorial.

'Being in His Majesty's Navy, you'll be interested in this,' Mr Humphreys said, though the sailors showed no sign of it. They looked bored and fidgety. 'Captain Faulknor was one of our greatest naval heroes, though he's not so well known as Sir Francis Drake or Lord Nelson. He—'

'Mr Humphreys,' Polly said, hurrying over, 'I'm sorry to interrupt, but I—'

'Miss Sebastian,' he said, turning in mid-gesture. 'I've been hoping you'd come in! How fortuitous that you're here today.'

He turned back to the sailors. 'Gentlemen, if you'll excuse me for a moment, I need to speak with Miss Sebastian. I'll be back directly.' He dragged Polly off towards the choir.

'There's someone I want you to meet,' he said, leading her into the choir. 'He's a great admirer of *The Light of the World,* just as you are. He spends hours and hours looking at it.'

'I'm afraid I'm in rather a hurry today—' she began, but Mr Humphreys wasn't listening.

'I saw him come this way when we were in the nave.' He led her into the apse. The altar was still blocked off for repairs.

'Oh dear,' he said, looking around at the ladders and scaffolding. 'He's not here. I'm certain I saw him—'

'Mr Humphreys, I have a favour to ask,' Polly cut in. 'I was hoping you could help me get taken on as an ARP warden.'

'A warden? That's no job for a young lady,' he said, still looking vaguely around. 'It's dirty, dangerous work, what with the raids and all. And out in the winter cold all night. You'd catch your death.'

I'm going to catch my death no matter what I do, she thought.

'Being a warden's no more dangerous than being on the fire watch,' she said, but Mr Humphreys was still looking for this person he wanted her to meet.

'I do hope he hasn't left,' he fretted, starting back along the choir aisle. 'I did so want you to meet him. I've told him all about you. Such a nice gentleman. Do you know what he said the first time he saw *The Light of the World*? He said, "He looks as though he could forgive anything." So interesting, isn't it, what people see? Each time one looks at it, one sees something diff—'

'If not an air raid warden, then some other Civil Defence job—'

'Mr Hobbe – that's the gentleman I want you to meet – has only just got out of hospital.' He peered into the dim recesses of the south transept. 'He's had rather a hard time of it, I'm afraid. He was wounded in a bomb blast, a head wound, and he's still not entirely recovered. Let me just check the north transept,' he said, though Mr Hobbe obviously wasn't there – they'd just come from there.

The sailors weren't there either. They must have seen their chance and fled. 'Mr Hobbe is almost as fond of Captain Faulknor's memorial as he is of *The Light of the World*,' Mr Humphreys said, which Polly doubted. She wondered if he'd fled, too.

'Last week I found him here after the sirens had gone,' Mr

Humphreys went on obliviously, 'sitting against one of the pillars, looking at Captain Faulknor's statue.'

Which is impossible, Polly thought. *It's covered in sandbags.*

'And when I began to tell him about Captain Faulknor's tying the two ships together, he knew all about it. "It bound them into one," he said—'

'I think Mr Hobbe must have gone home,' Polly said, 'and I must go, too. If you could just tell me the name of someone I could speak to about getting hired on by Civil Defence, I—'

'But he can't have gone home. I don't believe he has one. I think it may have been destroyed in the same bomb blast. I've found him here at night several times since then.'

'At night?'

'Yes, and that first night, when I said I'd have one of the watch accompany him home – he's not well, and I hated to think of him out in the blackout – I asked him where he lived, and he said, "It doesn't exist."'

'It doesn't—?'

'Yes, dreadful, isn't it, to think of him bombed out in this weather, with only a shelter to—'

'You said he's been coming in every day,' Polly said. 'For how long?'

'Several weeks,' he said, walking back out to the dome. 'He began coming in shortly before the New Year. I'm afraid you've just missed him. What a pity. I did so want you two—'

'What does he look like?'

'Look like? He's my age, or perhaps a bit older. Tall, thin, spectacles. I think he may have been a schoolmaster. He knows all about the history of St Paul's. He's clearly troubled about something. I fear his family may have been killed in the bombing, he looks so sad. That's partly why I wanted you to meet him. I thought your being interested in *The Light of the World*, too, might cheer—'

He stopped in mid-word. '*I* know where he'll be,' he said. 'He never leaves without taking a last look at it.' He started across the nave, but Polly had already passed him, running towards the south aisle, praying he was still there.

He was. He stood in front of the painting, his hat in his hands, his shoulders slumped tiredly, looking up at Christ's face under its crown of thorns.

'One sees something different each time one looks at it,' Mr Humphreys had said, and it was true. This time Christ looked not bored, not frightened, but infinitely sorry for both of them.

Polly stepped forward and put her hand on Mr Dunworthy's sleeve. 'It's all right,' she said, and began to cry.

LONDON – WINTER 1941

Polly looked at Mr Dunworthy standing there in front of *The Light of the World,* and for a moment she thought she must have been wrong, as she had been wrong that night outside St Paul's, and it wasn't him after all, but only someone who resembled him.

He seemed far older than the Mr Dunworthy she knew, and his shabby coat, his worn hat, had an authenticity Wardrobe could never have managed. And he looked so weary. Mr Humphreys had said he was 'troubled' and 'not well', but it was far worse than that. He looked exhausted, broken. Defeated. Mr Dunworthy had never been defeated by anything in his life.

But Polly had known even before she saw him that it was him – and worse, that the man she'd seen looking up at the dome of St Paul's that night had been him, too. And the reason he looked so defeated, so … beaten, was that he was as trapped and helpless as she and Eileen were. He wasn't here as a rescuer. He was a fellow castaway.

But the mere fact that he was here at least meant that Oxford still existed. They hadn't altered history and lost the war. And Oxford hadn't been destroyed in some catastrophe. Everyone there wasn't dead. And even if Mr Dunworthy was shipwrecked, too, he was *here*, and she was overjoyed to see him.

'I'm so glad—' she began, and he turned and looked at her, but there was no surprise, no joy in his face, and as she stepped towards him, he backed away from her till he came up hard against *The Light of the World*.

Oh God, Mr Humphreys had said he'd been injured by a bomb blast, that he'd been in hospital. Could he have suffered brain damage? Could that be why he'd stared at her without recognition that night, and why he looked so afraid now? Because he didn't know her? 'Mr Dunworthy?' she said softly because Mr Humphreys would be here any moment. 'It's me …'

'Polly,' he murmured. 'It's really you, isn't it? It isn't a dream? There were times in hospital when I thought that all of it – Oxford and time travel and you – was only a dream.'

'It wasn't,' Polly said, 'and I'm really here. Eileen – Merope – she's here as well. She'll be so glad to see you! This is wonderful!' She moved to embrace him.

'No,' he said and put up his hands to ward her off. 'Not wonderful. Not when you …'

'It's all right. We already know about the drops not working. Michael—' She stopped herself in time. She would have to tell him about Michael's death, but not yet. He didn't look strong enough to bear it.

'We know we're stranded here,' she said instead, but he was shaking his head.

'You *don't* know,' he said fiercely. 'Polly,' he began, and then stopped, as if he couldn't bear to tell her. And what could be worse than knowing they couldn't get out? What could make him look so … *Oh God,* she thought, *it's Colin. He came through with Mr Dunworthy.*

Colin had talked him into letting him come along. Or tricked him and ducked under the net at the last moment, as he had when he was twelve. Whichever, they had both been here, they'd both been hit by the bomb blast. And the fact that he was here alone, that he'd been at St Paul's alone on the twenty-ninth, could only mean one thing.

'Did Colin—?'

'Oh, my goodness!' Mr Humphreys said, bustling up. 'Do you two *know* each other? But what a happy coincidence! I knew I was right in thinking you should meet.' He beamed at both of them. 'But I had no idea you were acquainted. How do you know Miss Sebastian, Mr Hobbe?'

'He taught me at school,' Polly said so Mr Dunworthy wouldn't have to answer.

'I *told* Miss Sebastian I thought you were a schoolmaster,' Mr Humphreys said happily. 'You knew so much about St Pau—'

'And you were right, Mr Humphreys,' she said. 'Thank you so much for bringing us together and giving us this chance to talk,' she added, hoping he'd take the hint, but he took no notice.

'What was your subject, Mr Hobbe?' he asked.

'History,' Polly said.

'I *knew* it! I told you he knew all about history, didn't I, Miss Sebastian?'

Mr Dunworthy winced.

'And I was right, you *are* a historian.'

She had to stop this, had to get Mr Dunworthy away somehow. 'Mr Humphreys, I'm afraid we're tiring Mr Hobbe.'

She took Mr Dunworthy's arm. 'You've only just got out of hospital. Perhaps—' She had intended to say, 'I should take him home,' but Mr Humphreys was too quick for her.

'Oh, of course, how thoughtless of me. Let me fetch you a chair.' He bustled off towards the nave.

The instant he was out of earshot, Polly said, 'Mr Dunworthy, it's Colin, isn't it? He came through with you, didn't he?'

'Colin? No, I wouldn't let him come.'

Polly's knees nearly buckled from the force of the relief she felt, and she had to put a hand out to the pillar to steady herself.

'I wanted to get you out as quickly as possible,' Mr Dunworthy said. 'I was afraid the slippage might spike, and you'd be trapped here past your deadline.'

'But then why didn't you come in September?'

'I did, but the slippage sent me through in December.'

Four months' slippage. That meant the reason their drops hadn't opened could have been because of slippage after all, and the entire first few months of the Blitz had been a divergence point. And now that the twenty-ninth was over—

But if it was merely slippage, Mr Dunworthy wouldn't look so utterly devoid of hope. Unless the bomb blast had destroyed his drop.

'Where's your drop?' she asked, and then remembered what Mr Humphreys had said about him frequenting the north transept. 'It's here, isn't it? In St Paul's? Is that why you've been coming here every day? You've been waiting for it to open?'

He shook his head. 'It isn't going to open.'

'What do you mean?'

A horrible thought struck her. He'd been to the Blitz before. What if it had been in February? 'Mr Dunworthy,' she said urgently, 'when were you here before?'

'*Here* we are,' Mr Humphreys said, arriving with a wooden folding chair. He opened it out with a snap and set it in front of the painting. 'Come, sit down.' He took Mr Dunworthy's arm.

Mr Dunworthy sank down heavily onto the chair, and Polly saw with dread how painfully he moved, how frail he was. She'd assumed she'd be killed just before her deadline by a bomb or shrapnel, but there were other ways of eliminating someone who might create a paradox – complications following an injury, or pneumonia.

'I should have thought of this before,' Mr Humphreys was saying. 'There should always be chairs in this bay, so that visitors can sit and contemplate *The Light of the World*.' He smiled happily up at it. 'It's a painting which cannot be understood in a few moments of looking. It requires time.'

'Time,' Mr Dunworthy said bitterly.

Oh God, Polly thought, *he does have a deadline.*

'Did you tell Mr Hobbe you were a fellow admirer of *The Light of the World*, Miss Sebastian?' Mr Humphreys asked brightly. 'That was why I wished the two of you to meet, Mr Hobbe. I knew I was right to insist on its being here in St Paul's, even though only as a copy. "It belongs here," I told Dean Matthews. "Who knows what good may come from some visitor seeing it?" And now look, it's brought the two of you together. God truly does work in mysterious—'

Mr Humphreys stopped at a sound of voices and looked out across the nave. The three sailors who'd been in the north transept were looking at the bricked-up Wellington Monument.

'Oh good, they didn't leave after all,' Mr Humphreys said. 'If I may take leave of you for a moment, I need to speak with them. I did not finish telling them the story of Captain Faulknor.'

He hurried off. Polly knelt in front of Mr Dunworthy. 'When were you here in the Blitz before?'

'When I was seventeen,' he said. 'And again when I was—'

'No, no, the dates – what dates were you here doing observations?'

'In May and in October and November.'

'And that's all?'

'No,' he said, and she could tell from his face that this was it, the bad news.

Oh God, she thought.

'September the seventeenth.'

But both that and his assignments to October and November were safely past. Might he have come through early for the May raids to set things up as she'd done for Dulwich? 'When did you come through for the big raids?'

'May first.'

'And those were the only times? You weren't here in February or March or April?'

He shook his head.

Thank goodness. She'd been terrified he'd say he'd been here

485

tomorrow – or tonight. May was dreadful enough, but it was three months off, and if the problem was just slippage …

'You mustn't worry,' she said. 'One of our drops is bound to open by then, Eileen's or mine or the one in Hampstead Heath. And if you know what's causing the problem … You do, don't you?'

'Yes,' he said dully. 'I know what's causing the problem. I kept hoping it meant something else. When I found out I'd come through in December, I thought perhaps it was all right and you'd completed your assignment and were safely back in Oxford, but when I saw you at St Paul's—'

'I saw you, too,' Polly said, but he went on as if she hadn't spoken.

'—and when I saw the three of you the next morning, sitting on the steps, I was afraid he was right.'

'You saw Merope and Michael and me?' Polly said, bewildered. Why hadn't he come over and told them he was there? And who was he afraid was right? Right about what?

There was clearly a good deal here she didn't understand, but this was no time to ask questions. Mr Dunworthy looked exhausted and ill. His face was pinched with cold, and he'd begun to shiver. And Mr Humphreys had said he'd been here all afternoon. He'd had no business spending the day in such a chill, drafty place when he was only just out of hospital. He'd had one relapse already. And *The Light of the World*'s lantern, for all its golden orange glow, didn't give off any warmth. She needed to get him home to a real fire.

'Mr Dunworthy,' she said. 'I think we should go—'

'And then, when I heard about Michael, when I learned he'd been killed, I was certain. Polly, I am so sorry.'

'There's nothing to be sorry for. It wasn't your fault,' she said briskly. 'We mustn't stay here in this cold.'

She took both his hands in hers. They were like ice. 'Let me take you home, and—'

He cut her off with a bitter laugh. 'Home.'

'I meant home here. In Bloomsbury, mine and Merope's,' she said, wondering how on earth she was going to get him there. A taxi would be best, but she hadn't enough for the fare. She supposed she could leave Mr Dunworthy in the taxi when they got there and run inside to fetch the fare, but it was a good deal of money. Till she was actually taken on as an air-raid warden, they shouldn't be spending …

She thought suddenly of her promise to Hattie to be at the Alhambra for rehearsal by three. Even though everything was changed now that Mr Dunworthy was here, she still owed it to Hattie to let her know she wouldn't be there, especially after Hattie had covered for her, and it would be well after five before they arrived home. She'd have to try to get him to the tube station and ring from there.

'Come along,' she said. 'Merope and I will make you some nice hot tea and some supper.'

He shook his head. 'There's something I must tell you.'

'You can tell me at home.' She buttoned up his coat as if he was a child and helped him to his feet. 'We need to go. The sirens will be going soon, and we mustn't be caught out in the raids.'

He shook his head. 'The raids won't start till midnight to-night. Over Wapping.'

He knew when the raids were, and where. Thank God. She needn't worry about their house or Alf and Binnie's school being blown up anymore. Or about having changed the future beyond all recognition. Or losing the war. *The only thing I have to worry about is getting him home*, she thought.

'We still need to go. We don't want to be out in the blackout,' she said, taking his arm, but he was looking at the painting. 'Mr Dunworthy—'

'It will never open,' he said, sinking back down on the chair.

If only Mr Humphreys was here to help her, but there was no sign of him. 'I'll be back straightaway,' she told Mr Dunworthy and hurried across to the north transept, but the verger wasn't there, or in the nave. He must have taken the sailors up to the Whispering Gallery. She hurried back.

Mr Dunworthy was gone.

She ran down the south aisle.

He was nearly to the door. 'Where are you going?' she asked, but it was obvious. He'd intended to steal away while she was gone.

He's much more ill than I realised, she thought. *Perhaps I should take him to hospital.*

But he would never agree to that. He was already opening the heavy door, going out onto the porch. It was raining. He couldn't be out in this, even for the short walk to the tube station. It would have to be a taxi.

'Stay here,' Polly ordered, 'and I'll go and hail a taxicab,' but he was already starting down the steps. 'It's raining,' she said, grabbing his arm to stop him. 'Go back up on the porch.'

'No,' he said, shivering. 'There are things you don't know.'

'You can tell me at home.'

'No. After I've told you, you won't want—'

'Of course we'd want you,' she said, truly alarmed now. 'You're talking nonsense. You can tell me on the way.'

'No. Now.' He began to cough.

'All right,' she said hastily, 'but we can't do it standing out here in this freezing rain. We need to find somewhere warm. The place you've been staying, is it near here?'

He didn't answer.

He doesn't want me to know where he lives, she thought. *He doesn't want me to be able to find him.* Which meant at the first opportunity he intended to attempt to get away from her again. She had to get him somewhere warm before he had the chance.

But everything along Paternoster Row had burnt down on the night of the twenty-ninth. She'd seen a pub off Newgate on her way home from St Paul's that first Sunday. She'd have to hope it was still there.

It was, and thank goodness the fires, the blackout and the

weather had almost completely destroyed business. The place was all but empty. Polly sat Mr Dunworthy, who was now shivering uncontrollably, down on the wooden settle in front of the fire, put her own coat around his shoulders and went to the counter.

'My friend has had a bad shock,' she told the middle-aged, ginger-haired barmaid. 'I daren't leave him alone. Could you bring us a pot of tea?'

''course, dearie,' the barmaid said. 'Bombed out, was 'e?'

'Yes,' Polly said, and hurried over to the fire. Mr Dunworthy had stood up, folded her coat over the back of the settle, and was going towards the door.

She headed him off, said, 'Our tea's coming,' steered him back to the settle and draped her coat over his knees. 'It'll be here in a moment.'

The barmaid came out of the kitchen bearing a teapot, tea-spoons, a pair of saucers, two chipped teacups dangling from her crooked fingers and a glass full of a brown liquid. 'I was bombed out meself in November,' she said to Mr Dunworthy. 'Dreadful. Fair knocks the stuffin' out of you, don't it? This will do you up right.'

She set the glass in front of Mr Dunworthy. 'A spot of brandy,' she explained to Polly. 'Nothin' like it to bring the fight back into you.'

'Thank you,' Polly said. She poured Mr Dunworthy out half a cup of tea, filled it the rest of the way with brandy, and handed it to him. 'There. Have some tea and then you can tell me what-ever it is. Drink it down,' she ordered.

He did, and she poured him a second, but he didn't drink it, in spite of her urging. He sat staring blindly at the fire, his hands wrapped around the teacup, not as if he was warming them on it but as if he was clinging to the cup for dear life.

I need to get him home and into bed, Polly thought. *And telephone the doctor.*

'Mr Dunworthy,' she said, 'whatever it is you have to tell me, it can wait. Merope will have made supper, and you'll feel better after you've had a hot meal.'

No response.

'You can stay with us tonight, and then tomorrow we can go and collect your things, and then when you're feeling better, we can decide which drop—'

'The drops won't open.'

'But if the problem's the slippage—'

'The slippage was an indicator.'

'We're trapped here for good, is that what you're afraid to tell me?' she said.

'Yes.'

'What about Michael's roommate, Charles? Did he go to Singapore, or did you realise we couldn't get out before—?'

'No.'

No. Which meant Charles would still be there when the Japanese invaded. He would be rounded up with the rest of the British colonials and herded off to a jungle prison camp to die of malaria or malnutrition. Or worse.

'What about the other historians with deadlines?' she asked.

'You're the only one. I'd pulled out all the others. I didn't realise you'd done the 1944 segment of your assignment first. That's why you weren't pulled out when the others were.'

'And there's no way we'll get out before our deadlines?'

'No,' he said. But there was no relief in his voice at having told her. Which meant there was worse to come. And if it wasn't Colin, there was only one thing it could be.

'The reason we're trapped,' she said, 'it's because we altered events, isn't it?'

He nodded.

So Mike had been right.

'How did you find out?' Mr Dunworthy asked.

'Mike – Michael – saved a soldier's life at Dunkirk, and the soldier went back across and brought home more than five hundred others, and Michael couldn't see how that couldn't have caused changes, so we began looking for discrepancies.'

'And did you find them?' he asked.

'None that I could determine for certain were discrepancies,' Polly said, 'but Michael wasn't the only one who'd done something. Eileen – Merope – stopped two of her evacuees from sailing on the *City of Benares*, and I was responsible for a shopgirl being injured and nearly killed. But we didn't know it was possible to alter the course of events. We thought the slippage kept historians from—'

Mr Dunworthy shook his head. 'We were wrong about the slippage's function. It wasn't a line of defence guarding against damage we might do to the continuum. It was a rearguard action against an attack that had already happened – an attempt to hold a castle whose walls had already been breached.'

'By time travel,' Polly said.

'By time travel. And in most cases over the years, the defences were sufficient to hold the castle. But not all. It couldn't hold it against multiple simultaneous attacks or in instances where the breach was at a particularly vital spot—'

Like Dunkirk, Polly thought. *Or the autumn of 1944, when the lightest touch of a Spitfire's wing on a V-1's fin could change who lived and who died.*

'Or in instances where the initial breach was too great,' Mr Dunworthy was saying. 'In those cases, no amount of slippage would have been sufficient to prevent the enemy from breaking through, so the only thing the continuum could do was to attempt to isolate the infected area—'

Like Eileen's quarantine.

'—and attempt to repair the damage.'

'To shut down access to the past,' Polly said, 'which is what you think the continuum did.'

He nodded. 'Trapping you here.'

And you. 'I'm so sorry, Mr Dunworthy.'

He shook his head. 'You are not to blame.'

'But if I'd told you I'd done the rocket attacks first ...' she said. 'I knew you were cancelling drops and changing schedules, even if I didn't know the reason. I was afraid you'd cancel mine, so I didn't report in, and I made Colin promise he wouldn't tell you.'

He nodded as if he wasn't surprised. 'Colin would do anything for you,' he said.

'Oh, this is all my fault! If I hadn't made him promise, if I'd reported in, you wouldn't have let me come. You wouldn't have had to come after me—'

'No, you don't know the whole story,' he said, putting up his hand to stop her. 'There was an increase in slippage even before you went to 1944, but it wasn't large, and I didn't think it was serious. The amount of slippage had often been greater than the circumstances seemed to merit, at other times far less, and I thought there was a simpler explanation than the one Ishiwaka had arrived at, even after he showed me his equations. I certainly didn't see any need to pull out my historians and shut down all time travel. I thought cancelling the drops of historians with deadlines and putting the others in chronological order was sufficient till I had more data, but Dr Ishiwaka was right. I should have pulled you all out.'

'But you couldn't have known what the increase meant—'

'Dr Ishiwaka had told me exactly what it meant, but I refused to believe him. We'd been travelling to the past for forty years without incident. I found it impossible to believe that we were a danger to the course of history. I should have listened to him. If I'd pulled you out, Michael Davies would still be alive, and you and Merope—'

'Merope?' she said, alarmed, 'she doesn't have a deadline. This was her first assignment. *Wasn't* it?'

'Yes,' he said, and she knew there was still more.

'The shutdown might not be a result of the continuum's attempt to correct itself,' he went on. 'It might be some sort of reflexive response to the damage, like shock in a trauma patient. And even if it is an attempt at self-correction, there's no guarantee it will be successful. The damage may be too great or too widespread to be repairable.'

'But it's not,' Polly said. 'We didn't lose the war. I was at VE Day—'

'That was before Michael saved the soldier, and you and Merope—'

'I know, but Merope was there too. I saw her. And she hasn't gone yet. She went there – will go there – after Mike saved Hardy and we did all the other things, so they can't have affected the outcome of the war.'

But Mr Dunworthy was shaking his head. 'At the point when you saw her, there would still have been a VE Day to which she could go. The course of history – past and present – would have remained as it had always been until the alterations reached a tipping point. That is why we are able to be here, even though we're part of that unaltered future. And why Eileen could have gone to VE Day. It would have remained unaltered until the moment the final alteration occurred and the continuum could not correct for it—'

'And then everything would change.'

'Yes.'

'But you said …' She frowned, trying to grasp it. 'I don't understand. Hadn't that tipping point already happened? The drops had stopped working.'

'Not entirely. Mine was still working in mid-December.'

'So the tipping point happened between our finding Merope and mid-December?'

'No, it may have been after that. I don't know when exactly. I wasn't able to get to my drop till the night after I saw you all on the steps of St Paul's.'

It was something one of us did the night of the twenty-ninth, Polly thought.

They had delayed the air-raid warden on the steps of St Paul's so that he hadn't been in time to save someone. Or Theodore's screaming departure had delayed the pantomime a crucial few minutes so that one of the audience hadn't made it home to their Anderson in time. Or her presence on the roofs had altered the actions of the fire watch in some way that would prove fateful later on. Or it might even have been Eileen's taking the bombing victims to hospital or Mike's saving the firemen. In a chaotic system, positive actions could cause negative outcomes. Like losing the war.

Winning it had always been a near thing. 'We are hanging on by our eyelids,' Churchill's chief of staff had said. Events had been balanced on a knife's edge, and they had tipped the balance, and the Germans had won the war.

Oh God, she thought, *Hitler will execute Churchill and the King and Queen and Sir Godfrey, and send Sarah Steinberg and Leonard and Virginia Woolf off to die at Auschwitz, and Mr Dorming and Mr Humphreys and Eileen's vicar off to die at the Russian front. He will breed the blondes, like Marjorie and Mrs Brightford and her daughter Bess, to blue-eyed Aryans, and starve Theodore's mother and Lila and Miss Laburnum. And turn Theodore and Trot into young Nazis.*

But not Alf and Binnie, she thought. *Or Colin, no matter what sort of world he's born into. They'll never go along with it.*

Hitler would have to kill them first. And he would.

'Oh God,' Polly murmured. 'Mike was right. We lost the war. We ruined everything.'

'No,' Mr Dunworthy said. 'I did.'

'I have got to know the worst, and to face it.'

SIR J.M. BARRIE *THE ADMIRABLE CRICHTON*

LONDON – WINTER 1941

'What do you mean, you did it?' Polly said, staring at Mr Dunworthy sitting there by the pub's fire with her coat over his knees. He had stopped shivering, but he still looked chilled to the bone. 'You can't have lost the war. How? By coming to fetch me? Or something you did since you've been here?'

'No,' he said. 'I did it before you and Michael and Merope were even born. When I was seventeen years old.'

'But—'

'It was the third drop we'd done to World War II, and the first to the Blitz. We were still refining the net coordinates, and all I had to do was to verify my temporal-spatial location and go back. I'd come through in the emergency staircase of a tube station, and when I found out I'd come through to the seventeenth of September 1940, instead of the sixteenth, I was frightened I might be in Marble Arch.' He stopped and stared bleakly into the fire. 'Perhaps it would have been better if I had been.'

'Which station were you in?' Polly asked.

'St Paul's,' he said. 'And when I found that out, I thought taking a side-trip to see the cathedral couldn't hurt.' He smiled bitterly. 'I'd been fascinated by it since I first saw the Fire Watch stone as a boy. And here St Paul's still existed. So I ran up the street to look at it, just for a moment.'

He put his hands to his head. 'I wasn't looking where I was going – an apt metaphor for the entire history of time travel. I collided with a young woman, a Wren, and knocked her bag off her shoulder, and all of her belongings spilled out and onto the pavement.' He stared blindly ahead as if he was seeing it happen. 'Coins scattered everywhere, and her lipstick rolled into the gutter. She was carrying several parcels, and those flew out of her hands as well. Two other people – a naval officer and a man in a black suit – stopped to help, but it still took several minutes to gather everything up.'

'And then what?' Polly asked.

'And then the sirens went, and the Wren and the two men hurried off, and I went back to St Paul's Station to my drop and to Oxford.'

'And?'

'And a Wren was killed in Ave Maria Lane that night.'

'And it was the Wren you collided with?'

'I don't know. I never knew her name. I don't even know if she was the one I affected. It might have been the black-suited man. There's no record of a naval officer being killed that night, so I don't think it was him, though my delaying him might have set in motion a sequence of events that killed him the following day, or the following week.'

'But you don't know for certain that you killed any of them, or that the collision altered anything at all.'

'That's true. It may not have been the collision. I gave two children a shilling to tell me the name of the tube station, and had a conversation with a station guard. And I interacted with a number of other people in the station, pushing past them or making them go round me. I might have delayed any of them a critical few moments, and the difference might not have resulted in anything till much later on.'

Mike had said the same thing about the Dunkirk men he'd saved – that the alteration might be invisible for months, even years.

'In which case,' Mr Dunworthy was saying, 'it would be impossible to trace the initial altering event back to its source.'

'But from what you've said, you don't know that there was an altering event at all,' Polly argued. 'There's no proof you did anything.'

'Yes, there is. Up till then there hadn't been any slippage. It began on the very next drop. Unfortunately, that was a drop to the Battle of Trafalgar, and the one after that was to Coventry, and we drew the erroneous conclusion that the slippage made it impossible to alter events.'

'But you said you came through a day later than you were supposed to.'

Mr Dunworthy shook his head. 'I'd made an error in the coordinates. I checked it as soon as I returned. The net was set for the seventeenth.'

'What about locational slippage? You said you thought you'd gone through to Marble Arch.'

'No, I said I *might* have. We couldn't do specific locations back in those days, only a general area.'

'Then there *might* have been locational slippage.'

'But if there had been, it would have prevented me from colliding with the Wren.' He smiled bitterly at her. 'No, I caused the slippage and then misinterpreted that cause. And we proceeded to wander through history,' he said, 'gawking at wars and disasters and cathedrals, with no thought of the consequences of what we were doing.'

Polly looked at Mr Dunworthy sitting there. Mr Humphreys had said he looked like he had the weight of the world on his shoulders. *And he does*, she thought.

'For the past forty years, we've been blundering through the past like bulls through a china shop, fondly imagining that it was possible to do so without bringing about disaster, till it finally came crashing down on us. And on you.'

'But there was no way you could have known,' Polly said, reaching out to pat his arm.

He drew his arm back violently. 'There were dozens of clues,' he said furiously, 'but I didn't *want* to see them. I wanted to go on believing we could insert ourselves into a chaotic system without altering its configuration, even though I knew that was impossible. That our very presence, even if we did nothing more than breathe in and out, had to change the pattern and alter the outcome.'

'But if that's true, then we *all* did it, and every historian who's ever gone to the past is to blame.' She frowned. 'But why weren't there indications up to a few months ago? Why did it take forty years?'

'That I don't know. In a chaotic system, not all actions have significant consequences. Some are damped down by other events or absorbed or cancelled out. It may have taken that long for enough changes to accumulate for a tipping point.'

Like the vases and china and crystal in the china shop, Polly thought. *Each crash of the bull against the table, each pounding step, brings them nearer and nearer to the edge, till one last minor nudge takes them over it. That's what Mike and Eileen and I did, that one last tiny nudge. And it brought the continuum crashing down.*

But Mike had tried to go back through his drop *before* he saved Hardy's life. Why hadn't it let him?

'Why didn't—?' Polly began, and realised Mr Dunworthy was in no condition to answer any more questions. He looked dreadful, and in spite of the fire, he'd begun to shiver again.

'Time to go home,' she said. She put money down for the tea and brandy, removed her coat from his knees and put it on.

When she took his arm, he didn't resist, but let her lead him out of the pub, onto the wet, now-dark street and into a taxi. His hand, as she helped him in, was hot to the touch. 'You've a fever. I think I'd better take you to hospital. Bart's,' she said to the driver.

'*No*,' Mr Dunworthy said, clutching her arm. 'They were very kind to me. They don't … Please, not the hospital.'

'All right, but when we get home I'm telephoning the doctor.'

And I'm going to go in first so I can give Eileen some warning, so she won't think he's the retrieval team and get her hopes up.

But he is the retrieval team, she thought bleakly. He came through to rescue me, and now he's as stuck in this morass as we are.

They pulled up in front of the house. 'I need to run inside and fetch your fare,' she told the driver. 'I'll be back straightaway,' but he was shaking his head.

'I'd best 'elp you take 'im in, miss,' he said. 'You'll never manage 'im by yourself.' And before she could say anything he was out of the taxi and helping Mr Dunworthy out, so she had no opportunity to warn Eileen.

But Eileen seemed to size up the situation instantly. 'Can you help us get him into bed?' she asked the taxi driver.

'Who's *that*?' Alf asked, emerging from the kitchen with a slice of bread in one hand and a spoon in the other.

'Mr D—' Eileen began.

'Mr Hobbe,' Polly said.

'Is 'e soused?' Binnie asked.

'No, he's ill,' Polly said.

Binnie nodded wisely. 'That's what Mum allus—'

'Binnie, go and turn down the bed,' Eileen said.

'Not Binnie. Rapunzel. I've decided my name's Rapunzel.'

I am going to kill that child, Polly thought, but Eileen said calmly, 'Please go and turn down the bed, Rapunzel.'

She did, tossing her perpetually untied hair ribbon as if it were Rapunzel's braid, and Polly helped Mr Dunworthy out of his wet coat and shoes while Eileen ran down to the corner to phone the doctor.

She'd been afraid Alf and Binnie would come in and ask annoying questions, but after a minute of standing in the doorway whispering to each other, they disappeared.

When she came out to hang Mr Dunworthy's wet shirt on the oven door and put the kettle on, Alf asked, "'e ain't a truant officer, is 'e? Or a tube station guard?' which meant they thought they recognised him from somewhere. She hoped they hadn't tried to rob him as he walked to St Paul's.

'No,' she said, 'he's Eileen's old schoolmaster.'

Schoolmasters were apparently as frightening as truant officers. The two of them didn't even attempt to follow her into his room, though by the time the doctor arrived they were back to their old selves.

'It ain't measles, is it?' Binnie asked. 'We ain't going to be quarantined, are we?'

We already are, Polly thought.

'Is 'e going to die?' Alf asked.

Yes. On or before May first.

'He'll be perfectly fine,' the doctor said heartily. 'All he needs is to be kept warm and to rest, and he's not to worry over anything. He needs building up, so he's to have beefsteak and eggs – whole, not dried – every day.'

'But how?' Eileen said. 'The rationing—'

'I'm writing a prescription. Take it to the ration office, and they'll give you the necessary coupons.' He handed her the prescription and a paper packet. 'And he's to take this powder, dissolved in a glass of water, at bedtime.'

'Just like in an Agatha Christie novel,' Eileen said, looking at the packet after the doctor'd gone. 'That's always how the victim's murdered.'

'*Who's* been murdered?' Alf asked eagerly.

'No one. Go and do your lessons,' Eileen said, still examining the packet. 'But I doubt whether there's anything in this powder for a fever. Aspirin's the only thing that will help.'

Nothing will help, Polly thought, but she offered to go to the chemist's for the tablets. 'I need to ring the theatre and tell them I'm not coming in. I can do that while I'm at the chemist's.'

'Oh, I forgot all about your rehearsal,' Eileen said. 'You could still go. I can care for Mr Dunworthy.'

'It's too late. By the time I got there, the performance would be over. And someone's got to go for the aspirin.'

And she needed to get away for a few moments, to think about how she was going to tell Eileen. She would not be upset on her own behalf, but Polly couldn't bear the look she would have on her face when she told her they weren't getting out. And worse, that she wasn't the only one with a deadline. That Mr Dunworthy had one, too.

As soon as she reached the chemist's, she rang up the Alhambra. 'Your luck's in,' Hattie said. 'Canning Town got it last night, so the White Rabbit hasn't made it in either, but he'll be here tomorrow, so *you'd* better be. And if I were you, I'd think of a different excuse in the meantime. He'll never believe the one you just told me.' There was a pause. 'Oh, I've got to go. I'm on. Victory number. Ta.'

But there won't be any Victory numbers, Polly thought, feeling her way back to the house through the darkness of the blackout. *And what will happen to Hattie when we lose the war? And to the other girls in the chorus?*

You know what will happen to them, she thought.

But perhaps it wouldn't come to that. Mr Dunworthy had said he didn't know if the continuum was collapsing or correcting itself. And there were things in his theory that didn't fit. If their actions had been a threat, why had they been allowed to come through at all? Why hadn't they been prevented from coming in the first place, like Gerald?

And once they were here, why hadn't they been allowed to leave? Mr Dunworthy had said it was to contain the infection, but if Polly's drop had opened, she wouldn't have stumbled, shell-shocked and stricken, into Townsend Brothers, and Marjorie wouldn't have ended up in Jermyn Street, wouldn't have become a nurse, and if the people on the beach watching the smoke from Dunkirk hadn't prevented Mike from going to his drop, he wouldn't have fallen asleep on the *Lady Jane* and ended up in Dunkirk and saved Hardy's life. And if Eileen's had opened, she wouldn't have been able to keep the *City of Benares* letter from Mrs Hodbin, she wouldn't have been there to drive the ambulance on the twenty-ninth and save her passengers' lives.

That was the cruelest irony of all, that they had undone the future out of a desire to help – Eileen giving Binnie aspirin to bring her fever down and tearing up the letter to keep the children from drowning, Mike's unfouling the propellor because he couldn't stand the thought of fourteen-year-old Jonathan being killed and pushing the two firemen away from the collapsing wall.

Even the act that had set it all in motion had come not from malice but from a laudable desire to see something beautiful. Eileen was right, it seemed impossible that compassion and kindness should be the weapons of destruction, that just the opposite should be true. It was true that in a chaotic system, good actions could have bad consequences, but why—?

Polly had the sudden feeling that she knew the answer to that, that it lay just out of reach, like a word on the tip of one's tongue. She stopped on the street and stared into the blacked-out darkness, mentally reaching for it. It had something to do with Alf and Binnie blocking Eileen's way, and the shelter at Holborn –

A siren not twenty feet away screamed and she jumped, startled and then annoyed at the interruption of her train of thought. It had had something to do with the shelter at Holborn ... no, that couldn't be right, Alf and Binnie had been at Blackfriars, not Holborn, but it *was* Holborn, she was certain of it. Holborn and Mike's missing the bus and ...

No, it was gone. And this raid wasn't going to be one of those times with twenty minutes from alert to bombs. She could already hear planes, and she should get the aspirin to Mr Dunworthy as soon as possible.

But when she arrived home, he was asleep. Alf was, amazingly, sitting at the kitchen table doing his lessons. Whatever he'd done to the tube station guard or the truant officer must have been something appalling, even for him.

Binnie was reading aloud to Eileen from the book of fairytales. '"You must be home before the clock strikes twelve," the fairy godmother told Cinderella, "or the spell will be broken."'

'Should I wake Mr Dun— Mr Hobbe and give him the aspirin?' Polly interrupted to ask Eileen.

'No, sleep is the best thing for him.'

'What does that mean, the spell will be broken?' Binnie asked. 'What happens when it's midnight?'

'I'll wager Cinderella blows up,' Alf said. *'Boom!'*

'Go on to bed, Polly,' Eileen said. 'You look done in.'

I am, she thought. *We all are. And midnight's coming.*

She went to bed, but sleep was out of the question, and when she heard Mr Dunworthy coughing in the night, she got up quietly, fetched a glass of water and took it and the aspirin in to him.

He was sitting up in bed. 'Oh good, it's you,' he said when she switched on the lamp beside the bed. 'I need to tell you something.' And whatever it was, it was more bad news, because he had the same hopeless look he'd had in St Paul's and in the pub.

'First, you need to take these,' she said, and while he downed them, she felt his forehead. It was still hot. 'You're still feverish. You need to try to sleep. Whatever it is, you can tell me in the morning.'

'No,' he said, 'now.'

'All right,' she said, and sat down on the edge of the bed. He took a deep, ragged breath. 'The continuum will go on attempting to correct itself, whether it can succeed or not.'

Like a vanquished army fighting bravely on, Polly thought.

'And since we're the source of the damage,' he said, 'and since access to the future is no longer available—'

'It will have to kill us to stop us doing any more damage.'

Mr Dunworthy nodded.

'You think that's why Mike – Michael – was killed, to stop him from altering any more events?'

'Yes.'

'And it will do the same to us,' Polly said. 'Including Eileen.'

He nodded.

'When?'

'I don't know. Before the end of the Blitz, I would say. That's its best opportunity. There are a number of large raids between now and the tenth of May.'

'But you know where the raids are and where and when the bombs hit, and we can make certain we're in Notting Hill Gate on those nights. It's safe,' she insisted, but even as she said it, she could hear Mrs Brightford reading *Sleeping Beauty* to Trot, could hear her reading about the king destroying every spinning wheel in the kingdom, vainly attempting to stop the inevitable.

'Isn't there anything that can be done?' she asked.

He was silent, and she thought, appalled, *He still hasn't finished. There's more bad news to come.* And how could anything be worse than a death sentence for Eileen?

'What is it?' she asked, but she already knew. Their actions hadn't just affected the course of the war. They'd affected Theodore and Stephen and Paige and Mr Humphreys. Eileen had kept Alf and Binnie from going on the *City of Benares*, and Mike had kept Hardy from being killed at Dunkirk. Those alterations would have to be corrected, too.

And how many others? Marjorie? Major Denewell? Miss Laburnum and the rest of the troupe? If she hadn't done that reading of *The Tempest* with Sir Godfrey, they wouldn't have formed the troupe. They wouldn't have been safely in Notting Hill Gate every night instead of at home being killed, like they were supposed to be.

'It's not just going to kill us, is it?' Polly asked, her throat dry with fear. 'It's going to kill everyone we've come into contact with, isn't it?'

'Yes,' Mr Dunworthy said.

*'Are these the shadows of the things that will be,
or are they shadows of things that may be, only?'*

CHARLES DICKENS *A CHRISTMAS CAROL*

LONDON – WINTER 1940

For several long minutes after Mr Dunworthy told her, Polly simply sat there next to his bed. In the long nights lying awake on the platform, in the emergency stairway, she'd thought that she'd imagined every possible explanation for their plight, every possible dreadful outcome, but this was unimaginably more terrible. Not only were they going to die, but they would be responsible for the deaths of everyone who'd befriended them, who'd helped them and been kind to them – Marjorie and Eileen's vicar and Daphne and Miss Laburnum and Sir Godfrey. Everyone they cared about.

'So that's that?' she said finally.

'I'm so sorry,' Mr Dunworthy said, and she could only nod, her eyes full of tears for him, for them. And for all the people they had killed.

Would kill. She must have made some sort of sound because Mr Dunworthy reached out a hand to her and said, beseechingly, 'Polly—'

She stood up and took the glass from him. 'Try to rest,' she said, and switched off the lamp. *Put out the light, and then put out the light.*

She took the glass out to the dark kitchen and set it on the table, closed Binnie's fairy-tale book, and then went down to the cellar and sat at the bottom of the stairs, gazing into the darkness.

She had thought she'd given up hoping that they'd somehow be rescued, even before Mike died, even before they'd failed to get a message to John Bartholomew, but she realised now that some part of her *had* gone on hoping, had gone on believing that there was some other, magical explanation that, as Eileen said, accounted for everything. Which fitted all the facts and was right there in front of you all the time, only you couldn't see it. But this wasn't an Agatha Christie murder mystery, with a tidy solution and a happy ending. There was no happy ending. And she was the murderer.

They were all murderers. Mr Dunworthy had killed a Wren, and Mike had killed Commander Harold and Jonathan. Eileen had been responsible for the vicar's joining up, and she had been responsible for Marjorie's enlisting in the Royal Army Nursing Service.

Were they next? Or would it be Private Hardy or Alf and Binnie or Sir Godfrey? Or Mrs Sentry or the FANYs at Woolwich and Croydon whom Polly had wangled supplies from, or the little boy who'd *shhed* her at the pantomime? Or the strangers who had the misfortune of being next to them in Townsend Brothers or the tube station or Trafalgar Square when the continuum – flailing, sparking, melting down like an incendiary and burning through space and time – killed her or Mr Dunworthy or Eileen?

She thought suddenly of Ethel in the book department at Townsend Brothers who had been killed by shrapnel. Had she killed her by talking to her about ABCs and planespotting?

She sat there in the cellar all night, till Alf opened the door and shouted, 'Polly's down 'ere!'

She went upstairs. Eileen was cooking breakfast, and Binnie was setting the table. 'What was you doin' down there?' Alf asked. 'I didn't 'ear no raid.'

'I was thinking,' Polly said.

'*Thinkin'*!' he hooted.

'Hush,' Eileen said, and to Polly, 'You mustn't worry. Mr Dunworthy's going to be all right. His fever's down.'

She sent the children to their room to get dressed. 'You didn't get taken on as an air-raid warden, did you? Or with a rescue crew? Things were so muddled last night, I forgot to ask.'

Muddled.

'No,' she said.

'Are you going to try again today?' Eileen asked.

You don't understand, Polly thought. *I'm the last person anyone would want on a rescue squad, pulling people out of the rubble, administering first aid.*

She thought suddenly of the man in Croydon whose legs she'd tourniqueted. She'd been afraid he'd died, but what if he *should* have died there in the rubble, and her saving him had only doomed him to a worse, lingering death in hospital? And what if the tying of that tourniquet had been the act that had tipped the balance and brought about all their downfalls?

No, it couldn't have been, because her drop had still opened, had still let her go back to Oxford and come through again to finish the deed. But it might have helped, might have jostled the china ever closer to the edge.

'I mean, you've seen with Mr Dunworthy how deadly being out on the streets at night is,' Eileen was saying. 'Working as a warden is far too dangerous.'

'You're right, it is. I'm not going to do it.'

'Oh thank goodness,' Eileen said, and flung her arms around Polly. 'I've been so worried! Now, sit down and have a cup of tea, and I'll take Mr Dun— Mr Hobbe his.'

Polly obeyed.

Eileen was gone several minutes. When she came back out, she whispered, 'I asked him about the Alhambra, and he said it wasn't hit, that only two theatres were damaged during the Blitz, and neither one was during a performance.'

I'm going to have to tell her, Polly thought despairingly. *But not yet. I can't bear it.*

And Alf and Binnie had come back into the kitchen and were arguing over who got to feed the parrot. 'Mind the gap, Binnie!' it squawked.

'My name's *not* Binnie,' Binnie said. 'It's Vera. Like Vera Lynn.'

Alf, his mouth full, said, 'I thought it was Rapunzel.'

'Rapunzel was a noddlehead,' Binnie said. She held out a bit of bread to the parrot. 'Say, "Mind the gap, Vera."'

We'll have to send them away, Polly thought. *It's the only way to keep them safe. They'll have to be evacuated,* and it was almost funny.

'Why'd Rapunzel just sit there in that tower?' Binnie asked. 'Whyn't she cut off 'er hair and climb down it? That's what I'd do. I wouldn't stay in any old tower.'

In the bustle of clearing the table, gathering the children's lessons up, and retying Binnie's hair ribbon, Polly had no chance to speak to Eileen alone.

'Alf, pull your socks up,' Eileen said, putting on her coat. 'Binnie, stop that. Polly, can you go and fetch the meat and eggs for Mr Hobbe?' She handed her the order the doctor had written out. 'And see if the butcher has a soup bone so we can make some broth.'

Polly promised to do that and to go and fetch Mr Dunworthy's things from where he was staying. She dressed, did the washing-up, and then, when she couldn't put it off any longer, went in to see Mr Dunworthy. He looked even frailer in the grey morning light. The skin over his cheekbones and at his temples was nearly translucent, but for the first time since she'd found him, he didn't look like he had more bad news to tell her. 'You look a bit better,' she said. 'How are you feeling?'

'I should be asking *you* that,' he said.

She smiled wryly. 'I'm still standing.'

'Like St Paul's.'

Exactly like St Paul's – battered, damaged, and looking out on a landscape of devastation.

'I had something else to say last night,' he said. 'We don't know for certain that the war was lost. There's a possibility that the continuum may succeed in undoing the damage we've incurred.'

'Though it will have to kill us to do it,' she said.

But it was still better than the alternative. And her dying to stop Hitler from winning the war was no different from what tens of thousands of British soldiers and civilians had done, and they'd had no guarantee that they'd be successful either.

But at least they hadn't had to worry about endangering everyone else in the foxhole or the shelter by their mere presence. 'What about the others?' she asked him. 'The contemps we've interacted with?'

'I don't know,' he said. 'Those factors that protected the continuum for so long – the ability to absorb and diminish and cancel out effects – may be factors in the correction as well.' *Translation: it might only have to kill a few of them.*

'If we separate ourselves from them and don't have any more contact, is there a chance that will keep them from being killed?' she asked him.

'I don't know. Perhaps.' But there was not much hope in his voice. 'It's impossible to know how far the damage has spread and if alterations have already occurred that must be counteracted.'

Were Alf and Binnie supposed to have gone on the *City of Benares* and drowned? Or died along with their mother somewhere near Piccadilly Circus? And was Marjorie supposed to have died in the rubble and Private Hardy at Dunkirk and Stephen Lang on the way to London from Hendon Airfield? Or would Mrs Hodbin have torn up the letter, Private Hardy been picked up by another boat, the others have survived and gone on to do exactly what they did do? There was no possible way to tell.

But if we haven't altered their lives already, Polly thought,

then perhaps our staying away from them from now on can
protect them from being caught within our deadly blast radius.
Thank goodness we're not at Mrs Rickett's anymore, and not
staying at Notting Hill Gate.

And now that she was at ENSA, she had a perfect excuse for quitting Sir Godfrey's troupe. She went and got the ration coupons and then the eggs and a quarter of a pound of beef, but no soupbone. The butcher hadn't any. She had to settle for Oxo cubes.

She took them home, made Mr Dunworthy a soft-boiled egg and then set out again to fetch his things from a dreary, chill room in the only part of Carter Lane that hadn't burned on the twenty-ninth. She'd intended to go and tell Mr Humphreys that she'd got Mr Hobbe safely home, but now she didn't dare risk it. He had been nothing but kind to her. He didn't deserve ...

She stopped short on the pavement. That was what Mr Dunworthy had started to say last night when he'd refused to go to Bart's, that the nurses had been very kind to him and that they didn't deserve to die for it.

She debated leaving a message for Mr Humphreys to the volunteer at the desk, but she wasn't even sure she had any business being in St Paul's. Yet she didn't want Mr Humphreys tracking Mr Dunworthy down out of concern. She settled for giving a note addressed to Mr Humphreys to a woman going inside and asking her to give it to the verger. And what if even that moment-long encounter was enough to require a correction? Or her conversation with Hattie when she went to the Alhambra that afternoon?

'Did you get that rescue job you wanted?' Hattie asked her when she arrived for rehearsal.

'No,' Polly said.

'Then you can rescue the second act. Here,' she said, handing her a bathing suit with a Union Jack emblazoned on it. 'Cheer up. ENSA may not be as heroic as rescue work, but we keep up the soldiers' spirits and make them forget their troubles for a few hours, don't we? Singing and dancing can help win the war, too.'

Mr Tabbitt put her in the show that very night, serving as assistant to a magician. She was very bad at it, but so was the magician, and the main interest of the audience, which consisted almost entirely of soldiers, seemed to be her abbreviated costume.

'Tits and tinsel,' Hattie said, 'that's our motto.'

'I thought it was ENSA: Every Night Sexy Acts,' one of the chorus girls said, flouncing past them in an even skimpier costume as they stood in the wings.

'That's Joyce,' Hattie said. 'Nice, but a bit too fond of the boys.'

A handsome young man dressed as an RAF pilot brushed past them.

'And that's Reggie,' Hattie said, 'also a bit too fond of the boys. That's one thing I like about ENSA. One never has to worry about being fondled. Except by Mutchins, our beloved stage manager. Watch out for him. He's a menace.'

So am I, Polly thought. *Like one of those fiendish delayed-action bombs set to go off when someone comes too close.*

It took her two days to find the courage to tell Eileen. Polly remembered how sick she'd looked when she'd found out about Polly's deadline, remembered her refusal to budge from the foot of the escalator when she found out Mike was dead, and was afraid the same thing would happen, but Eileen took the news with an almost frightening calmness. 'I knew it had to be really bad when you brought him in,' she said. 'He's certain we lost the war?'

'Mr Dunworthy says there's no way to be absolutely certain, and there's a possibility the continuum will be able to correct itself—'

'But it won't help us.'

'No,' Polly said, feeling like a doctor giving a patient a terminal diagnosis.

'And he's certain there's nothing we could do that would change things back?'

'Yes.'

'So we're in an unwinnable situation.'

'Yes.'

An unwinnable situation, with not even a way to get out of it. If Polly killed herself, or even let a convenient HE do it for her, that still wouldn't put an end to the damage she could do, the changes she might effect. She would endanger the rescue crews who had to dig for her, or delay them from digging for someone else, and that someone else would be poisoned by a broken gas main in the meantime. And her death would affect Doreen and Miss Snelgrove and the troupe.

And Sir Godfrey, who last time he thought she was buried in the rubble had moved heaven and earth to find her, who had sent ripples out in all directions.

She'd been wrong – she wasn't a delayed-action bomb. She was a UXB that would blow up if someone didn't defuse it – but that, if someone attempted to, was even more likely to blow up. And once the bomb squad had set it ticking, they didn't dare stop, and the only safe way to dispose of it was to take it out to Barking Marshes, where it could explode without harming anyone.

But the continuum had no Barking Marshes, and short of being dead, there was no way Polly could get out of her service with ENSA and of endangering everyone there, to say nothing of all those soldiers in the audience.

She lay awake nights, thinking of everyone she might have unwittingly endangered – Fairchild and Lady Denewell and Talbot, whose knee she'd wrenched, and Sarah Steinberg and the other shopgirls at Townsend Brothers and the guard at Padgett's who'd chased her up the stairs, the old man with the fringed pink silk cushion who'd caught her when her legs gave way and eased her down to the kerb after she'd seen St George's.

And that was only her. What about Eileen's evacuees and

Agatha Christie and the nurses and doctors and patients at Bart's? And at the hospital in Orpington?

Mr Dunworthy had clearly thought he'd put his nurses and doctors in danger. He'd also said that perhaps not everyone they'd come in contact with had to be part of the correction, but even if only a few of them were ...

She knew now how Theodore's neighbour felt. She wanted to shut herself in the cupboard under the stairs and stay there, even if it offered no protection at all.

But that was impossible. She had to make Mr Dunworthy soft-boiled eggs and tea and keep Alf from asking him how it felt to be blown up and Binnie from sharing her opinions of fairy-tales, had to learn her lines, practise tap routines, rip ruffles off her costumes and sew sequins on them. And face Eileen's unquenchable optimism.

'I don't think Mr Dunworthy's right,' she said the day after Polly told her. 'Saving people's lives is a *good* thing, and, after all, Mr Dunworthy didn't intend to run into the Wren—'

'And the German pilots who got lost didn't *mean* to start the London Blitz,' Polly said. 'The sailor lighting a cigarette on deck didn't *mean* to get his convoy blown up. History's a chaotic system. Cause and effect aren't—'

'Linear. I *know*. But even in a chaotic system, good deeds and good intentions – and courage and kindness and love – must count for *something*, or else history would be even worse than it already is,' Eileen said.

She refused to send Alf and Binnie away. 'When the vicar tried to place them last summer before we left Backbury, no one would take them,' she said. 'And even if we could find someone, they'd only run away to London and begin living on their own again. And collecting UXBs. They'd be in just as much danger as they are with me.'

Except that the continuum wouldn't be after them. 'But by sending them away, you'd be saving their lives,' Polly argued.

'I thought you said saving lives was a bad thing,' Eileen said, 'that that was how we got into this mess in the first place. That if I'd let Alf and Binnie go on the *City of Benares* and drown, if I'd let that man in the back of the ambulance bleed to death, that everything would be fine.'

'Eileen—'

'Don't you see? If I send them away, they may be killed, and if I keep them here, they may be killed. But if I send them away, they'll think I'm abandoning them, and that *will* kill them. They've already been abandoned by everyone they've ever known. They can't survive that again. And I swore I'd take care of them.'

But don't you see? You can't.

But Eileen was right, it was a no-win situation, so it probably made no difference where they were. Eileen had saved both of their lives once and Binnie's twice, and that would clearly have to be corrected. She tried to comfort herself with the knowledge that the Hodbins could take care of themselves. That if anyone could survive a correction – or a war – it was the two of them.

Polly wanted desperately to believe that it was possible for them – and at least some of the others – to survive. And that it was possible to do something even now to protect them, even though she feared it was as useless as Sleeping Beauty's father burning the spinning wheels.

But she kept away from St Paul's and Kensington anyway and took the bus instead of the tube, searching for a seat where she wouldn't have to be next to anyone, taking care to watch where she was going so that she didn't collide with anyone. She stayed strictly away from Oxford Street, and when Mr Tabbitt dispatched her to buy sateen or ribbon for costumes, she went to Regent Street or Harrods and said no more than 'Five yards, please.'

Even that might be enough to seal their fate, but at least she wasn't at Townsend Brothers, where she might endanger Doreen or Miss Snelgrove, or in Notting Hill Gate with the troupe. And the effort of avoiding people kept her mind off the sprawling network of people they'd come into contact with: the bombing victims she'd saved while she was stationed at Dulwich, the bus driver who'd taken her to Backbury, the servants at the manor, the people who'd been on the train with Eileen and her and Mike, and the girls who'd picked Mike up and dusted him off in Bletchley.

And it kept her mind off Mr Dunworthy, who was not improving, in spite of eggs and Eileen's aspirin and a large soup bone that Alf and Binnie had got from somewhere and about which both Eileen and Polly thought it best not to ask questions.

'I'm worried about him,' Eileen said. 'The doctor says it's not the head injury, that that's nearly healed, and that it's not pneumonia. He doesn't know what it is.'

It's thinking about what's going to happen to us and to Charles Bowden, who will still be in Singapore when the Japanese arrive, and to whoever Mr Dunworthy sent off to the storming of the Bastille. And to who knows how many other historians who were in equally dangerous times and places when their drops slammed shut. It's the weight of the world.

'I'm afraid he's not going to recover,' Eileen, who never gave up on anything or anybody said, so Polly wasn't surprised when she found Alf and Binnie waiting for her one night outside the stage door.

'Eileen sent us to fetch you,' Binnie said.

'Is it Mr Hobbe?' she asked.

'Mr *Hobbe*?' Alf said. 'Nothin' like. It's Mrs Rickett's boarding house. It got bombed last night.'

'Direct hit,' Binnie said.

'*Kabloom!*' Alf shouted. 'Ain't it a good thing we was thrown out?'

'The flowers are turning very red. Repeat,
the flowers are turning very red.'

CODED BBC MESSAGE BROADCAST TO THE
FRENCH RESISTANCE BEFORE D-DAY

KENT – APRIL 1944

'**W**orthing!' Cess called and opened the door.

'What is it now?' Ernest asked, typing, 'To the Editor of the *Clarion Call:* I have the misfortune—'

Cess looked offended. 'You asked me to tell you when Lady Bracknell got here,' he said. 'He's here.'

Ernest nodded. '—to reside in—' he typed, and broke off. 'Where's the dummy camp Prism and Gwendolyn are building?' he asked.

'Just north of Coggeshall,' Cess said.

'—in Coggeshall, near the American paratroop base, and I am appalled by the number of beer bottles and—' He paused, fingers poised above the keyboard. 'Will they print the word "condoms" in the newspaper?'

'No,' Cess said. 'He wants to see us.'

Ernest typed, '"—and contraceptive appliances in my lane on Sunday mornings. I have spoken to the camp commander, but to no avail."'

'He wants us in the common room *now.*'

'This is the last one. Listen to this. I need your advice.' He read it aloud to Cess.

'Oh, it'll definitely fool the Germans,' Cess said. 'There's no clearer proof that there's an army in the area than beer bottles and used condoms.'

'No, I need advice on who wrote the letter. Do you think it should be from an irate country squire or a spinster?'

'A vicar,' Cess said promptly. 'Now come along.'

'I'll be right there,' Ernest promised, waving Cess out of the room. He typed two more lines, signed the letter 'The Reverend T. W. Ringolsby', put it and the carbon into the envelope with his articles, hid the envelope in the 'Forms 14C' file and went down to the common room.

Gwendolyn was making his report to Lady Bracknell as Ernest squeezed into a seat next to Cess. 'Camp Omaha has been completed,' Gwendolyn said. 'Fifty barracks, a motor pool, a mess hall and a camp kitchen with smoke coming out of its chimney, but I'm not certain how long that will last, so if a German reconnaissance plane could get through our coastal defences soon, that would be excellent.'

Lady Bracknell nodded. 'I'll arrange it for tomorrow afternoon. The meteorological report is for fair weather till tomorrow evening.' He made a note. 'We'll need soldiers walking between buildings, unloading supplies and drilling in formation.'

'And guess who those soldiers will be,' Cess whispered to Ernest. 'Just my cup of tea – drilling in the pouring rain.'

Lady Bracknell fixed them with a gimlet stare. 'All of you except Chasuble and Worthing will report to Camp Omaha at fourteen hundred hours tomorrow. Chasuble, I need you to arrange a ribbon-cutting ceremony for the airfield in Sissinghurst for Friday next.'

Chasuble frowned. 'Does Sissinghurst have an airfield?'

'It will by Friday next. Worthing, I need you to go to Dover.'

'To the hospital?' Ernest asked warily.

'No, to the harbour. I need you to deliver a parcel to a boat that's docked there.'

'Alone?'

'Yes, alone, Lieutenant Worthing. How many people does it take to deliver a single parcel?'

'Sorry, sir,' Ernest said, trying to look chagrined rather than thrilled. Here was his chance. *Finally*. He'd be on his own *and* with transport. He could finally get to London. And he'd be able to deliver his articles to the Sudbury *Weekly Shopper* and the *Call* without Cess or Prism looking over his shoulder. Especially the *Call*. The editor, Mr Jeppers, always insisted on reading through all of the articles before he okayed them, and on asking all kinds of questions.

He'd be pushed for time if he wanted to do both, but, luckily, Dover was far enough away that a few hours more or less wouldn't look suspicious. Unless Lady Bracknell wasn't sending him right away. 'When do I leave, sir?' he asked.

'As soon as you can. His boat will only be in port a day or two. We need to catch him before he goes out again.'

Better and better. He debated asking when Lady Bracknell expected him back and then decided that was looking for trouble. 'Yes, sir,' he said.

'Report to me when you're ready to leave.'

'Yes, sir.' And as soon as the meeting broke up, he went to borrow Chasuble's peacoat and see who had a suitable shirt. The sooner he left, the less likely it was that Bracknell would change his mind and decide to send someone with him.

No one had a shirt that could pass for a sailor's, but Cess produced a shapeless dingy grey pullover and a pair of canvas plimsolls. 'The jumper's Moncrieff's and the plimsolls are Prism's,' Cess said.

Prism's feet were smaller than his, but it didn't matter. He'd be driving the entire way. 'Perfect. Thanks,' he said, yanking the pullover on. 'You wouldn't have a duffel bag, would you?'

'Yes,' Cess said, and returned immediately with a heavy canvas bag and an umbrella. 'You'll need this as well.'

'Hardy seafaring men don't go about with umbrellas,' Ernest

said, shoving a change of clothes into the bag. 'And why are you so certain it's going to rain? Bracknell said it's supposed to be fair.'

'He also said that pasture hadn't any bulls in it,' Cess said, holding out the umbrella. 'And it always rains when we have to be outside. Remember the oil-depot ribbon-cutting?' He laid the umbrella on the desk and left. As soon as he was gone Ernest opened the file, retrieved the envelope from 'Forms 14C,' and put it into the duffel bag under his clothes.

Cess leaned back in. 'Bracknell wants to see you.'

I knew it was too good to be true, Ernest thought, but Bracknell only wanted to give him the parcel – a flat square package, tied with string – and a letter. 'You're to give both to Captain Doolittle on the *Mlle Jeannette*.'

'The *Mlle Jeannette*?'

'It's a French fishing boat.' He told Ernest where it would be docked. 'You're Seaman Higgins. You're from Cornwall. Can you do a Cornish accent?

He nodded. 'I'm an old hand at accents.'

Bracknell handed him a sheaf of forms. 'These are your papers. You were invalided out of His Majesty's Navy and you're looking for work. You're to say to Captain Doolittle – and *only* to Captain Doolittle—' and he read aloud in his precise upper-class accent, '"Seaman Higgins, sir. Admiral Pickering said as how you was hiring a crew,"' and Captain Doolittle will reply, "Admiral Pickering! How is that old devil?" and then you give him the package.'

'Yes, sir.' He repeated his line back to him in what he hoped was an out-of-work Cornish sailor's accent and then said, 'Am I taking the Austin or the staff car?'

'Neither. You're going on foot.'

I knew it was too good to be true, he thought. 'You want me to walk all the way to *Dover*?'

'No, of course not. I want you to hitchhike. That way you'll be able to discuss the invasion with farmers and other locals.

And you'll be able to stop at pubs along the way and engage the denizens in conversation about the invasion as well.'

But he wouldn't be able to deliver his articles, or get to London.

'The conversations will corroborate the disinformation in our radio transmissions and newspaper articles,' Bracknell said.

'Speaking of which,' Ernest said, 'the *Call*'s and the *Shopper*'s deadlines are both tomorrow, and if I miss them, there won't be anything about FUSAG in either paper till the week after next. There've been planted stories about the American and Canadian troops in every issue of both papers. If they suddenly stop – and in more than one paper – the Germans may notice. And as you're always saying, sir, in an enterprise like this, if any one piece is missing, the entire scheme will collapse.'

'I am well aware of what I've said,' Bracknell snapped. 'Have you written the stories?'

'Yes, but—'

'Then Cecily can deliver them for you.' And before Ernest could stop him, he shouted, 'Cecily!'

'But Cess doesn't know the editors. It would make more sense for *him* to go to Dover and me to stay here. I could deliver them on my way to Camp—'

'No, Algernon specifically requested you make this delivery.'

He did? Why? he wondered.

'Yes, sir?' Cess said, appearing in the doorway.

'Ernest needs you to deliver his planted articles to the newspapers tomorrow morning. Take the Austin,' he said, adding insult to injury, and waved them out of his office.

'Thank you,' Cess said out in the hall.

'For what?'

'For trying to get me out of drilling in the rain. I appreciate the attempt, even though it didn't work.'

'That's the story of my life,' Ernest said, more bitterly than he meant to. And when Cess looked curiously at him, he added, 'Attempts that don't work.'

'Where are the articles you need me to deliver?'

'I'll fetch them,' Ernest said, and to get rid of Cess, he asked, 'You wouldn't have a pair of dungarees I could borrow, would you? These trousers of mine look too good to be a sailor's.'

'What about the ones you wore the day you had that run-in with the bull?' Cess said. 'They surely look bad enough.'

'You're right,' Ernest said, and tried again. 'Ask Prism if he has a knitted cap I can borrow.' And as soon as Cess had gone, he shut the door, dug the envelope out of the duffel bag and pried the sealed edge open. He took the papers halfway out and began pulling out the ones he couldn't let Cess take.

'Did you find your cap?' Cess' voice said outside in the corridor.

'Yes, it's in fairly bad shape, though,' Prism said.

I should have marked the coded articles somehow, Ernest thought, leafing through the papers. *Or written them in red ink that would dissolve when it got wet, like the bigram books.*

There were four of them. Where the hell was the fourth one? There it was. 'Lost, locket inscribed E.O. ....'

He yanked it out, jammed it and the other three sheets of paper into the duffel bag, resealed the envelope and was putting his razor and shaving soap into the bag when Cess came in, carrying a cap even grimier and more ragged than the jumper. 'Perfect,' Ernest said, handing the envelope to Cess. He tried on the cap. 'What do you think?'

'Very seamanlike. All that's wanted is the smell of fish and two days' growth of beard. Which means you won't be needing that razor,' Cess said, reaching for the duffel bag.

Ernest jerked it out of his reach. 'That's what you think,' he said, cinching it shut. 'On my way back I'm supposed to stop at assorted pubs and talk about Calais, and I wouldn't like to frighten the barmaid.'

'Yes, well, stay away from the Bull and Plough,' Cess said. 'Chasuble doesn't want anyone poaching on his time with Daphne.'

'Daphne?' Ernest said sharply.

'The barmaid – you know her. Pretty little blonde, big blue eyes. Chasuble's head over heels about her. Where do I take these articles?'

'The originals go to the *Weekly Shopper* in Sudbury and the carbons to the *Croydon Clarion Call*,' Ernest said, pulling on the canvas plimsolls. His feet hurt already. 'The office is just off the High Street. Mr Jeppers is the editor.' He tied the plimsolls. 'They've got to be there by four tomorrow afternoon.'

He stood up and slung the duffel bag over his shoulder. 'I don't suppose you could run me up to Newenden? I'll have a better chance of catching a ride from there.' *And there's a train I could catch from there to London and then take one to Dover in the morning.*

'Sorry, Chasuble just left,' Cess said, 'and Moncrieff won't be back with the Austin till tonight. Here.' He handed Ernest a tin of pilchards.

'What's this for?'

'I thought you could pour a bit on your trousers for authenticity.'

'I'll wait till I get there,' Ernest said, eager to get away. London was out, but with luck he could catch a ride to Hawkhurst in time to make the bus to Croydon and get his articles in before Cess delivered the others, though how exactly would he explain the necessity of two separate deliveries to Mr Jeppers?

I'll work that out later, he thought, *after I've caught the bus. And a ride.*

But after half an hour of limping along the road in the too-tight plimsolls, no one at all had come along. *It's too bad FUSAG's not really here. I could hitch a ride with one of them.*

He was finally picked up by an elderly clergyman going to the next village to substitute for the local vicar. 'He's volunteered to go over with the troops as a chaplain,' he leaned out of the window to tell Ernest. 'The village is only two miles away. Are you certain you don't want to wait for a better ride?'

Ernest wasn't certain at all, but his feet hurt so badly, he climbed in, only to immediately have a Jeep with a pretty WAC driving it appear out of nowhere and shoot past them. So when the clergyman let him out, he turned down a ride in another lumbering farm truck – a truck that turned out to be the last vehicle on the road for three hours.

He didn't make it to Hawkhurst till nearly ten that night, which, when he reflected on it – and he'd had *hours* to reflect on it – was probably just as well. There was no way to guarantee that Mr Jeppers wouldn't mention his having been there to Cess when he got to Croydon, and if he did, Cess would want to know what was in those articles that was so important. And he was already too interested in what Ernest was typing.

Ernest was too bone-weary to sit in the pub room nursing a watered-down pint and spreading false rumours about the invasion. He hardly had enough energy to wrench the plimsolls off his blistered feet, fall into bed and sleep through his best chance of a ride to Dover. 'You just missed Mr Hollocks,' the barmaid told him when she served him breakfast. 'He was going all the way to Dover.'

The story of my life, he thought, and spent the next day inching towards Dover in lorries filled with chickens, pig muck and a bull he was convinced was the same one he'd faced down in that pasture. He was glad when the farmer turned down a muddy lane and let him out, though he was still 'some way' from Dover and it looked like it was going to rain.

It did. By the time he reached Dover in the mid-afternoon, on the back of an army corporal's Douglas motorcycle, it was pouring, with a blustery wind that drove the rain straight into his face.

Poor Cess, he thought, heading for the docks. On the other hand, Captain Doolittle would still be here. No one would take a boat out in this.

He made his way along the rain-slick dock between wooden crates and coils of rope and tins of petrol, reading the names painted on the boats' bows – the *Valiant*, the *King George*, the *Dreadnought*. *No* Mary Roses, *or* Sea Sprites *here,* he thought. The war had changed all that. They all had either militant or patriotic names, and their decks were hung with camouflage netting. The *Union Jack*, the *Dauntless* ...

The damned *Mlle Jeannette* was going to be the very last one. He'd be drenched by the time he got there. The *Fearless*, the *Britannia* ... Here it was. The *Mlle Jeannette*. But it couldn't be the boat he was looking for. Its hull was covered in barnacles and its paint was peeling. It didn't look like it could stay afloat long enough to make it out of the harbour, let alone do a mission for British Intelligence. It looked almost as unseaworthy as—

'Ahoy, there,' a tough-looking young man called from the bow. 'You got business 'ere?' He was wearing a jersey and worn trousers and had evidently been working on the engine. His face and hands were streaked with black and he was holding an oily wrench as if it was a weapon.

'I'm looking for Captain Doolittle,' Ernest shouted up to him. 'Is this his boat?'

'Aye.' He motioned Ernest aboard. ''e's below. Cap'n!' When there was no response, he went over to the hatch and shouted down it, 'Cap'n Doolittle! Sommun' 'ere t'see you!' and returned to the engine.

Ernest hurried up the gangplank and then stopped, staring around at the unvarnished deck in bewilderment. This couldn't be— She'd been sunk. But the ship's wheel, the lockers, even the hatch looked exactly like it.

Oh my God, he thought, *the* Mlle Jeannette. *I should have recognised the name.*

'What in tarnation are you bellowing about now?' a voice from below shouted, and there was no mistaking that voice, or, as he emerged from the hatch, those bright eyes and that grizzled beard.

You're alive, Ernest thought wonderingly.

'Who are you? And what the bloody hell do you want?'

He doesn't recognise me, Ernest thought, thanking God for the knitted cap and the stubble on his face. 'Are you Captain Doolittle?' he asked.

'I am.'

'I'm Seaman—'

'Come below out of this rain,' he said and motioned Ernest to follow him down the ladder.

Ernest climbed down it after him. The hold looked exactly the same, the littered galley, the bunk with its heap of grey blankets, the same four inches of brackish water on the floor. And the dim, flickering hurricane lamp over the table, which, hopefully, wouldn't illuminate his face too much. If he could deliver the package and get out of here quickly enough ...

He descended the last two rungs and started across the hold, but before he'd waded two steps, the Commander had him in a bear hug. 'You're a sight for sore eyes!' he bellowed, pounding him on the back. 'What the bloody hell are you doing here, Kansas?'

> *'For many years the prince wandered until at last he came to
> the lonely place where the witch had left Rapunzel.'*

RAPUNZEL

IMPERIAL WAR MUSEUM, LONDON – 7 MAY 1995

It was a quarter past nine when he reached the museum. It didn't open till ten, but he'd come through early, hoping they'd arrive early too, and he'd be able to talk to them before they went in.

But there was no one standing outside the doors or on the steps, and no one in the courtyard, where a tank, an anti-aircraft gun and a motorboat were on display. He tried the main doors on the off-chance that the lobby was open, but they were locked, and he couldn't see anyone at the ticket desk yet.

He walked down to the courtyard and looked at the tank, wishing they'd get here. There was a 'St Paul's in the Blitz' exhibit opening at St Paul's Cathedral today as well. He'd debated going to that one instead, then decided his chances were better at this one, since there'd be more attendees here. But he'd hoped that by coming early, he could make it to both. And now there wasn't a soul here.

He wandered over to the boat. It had *Lily Maid* stencilled on its bow. There was an impressive array of machine-gun bullet holes in its stern, and a placard on it reading, 'One of the many small craft manned by civilians who participated in the evacuation of more than 340,000 British and other Allied soldiers from Dunkirk.'

He examined the bullet holes and then retrieved a museum brochure someone had jammed in the windscreen of the boat and went back to sit on the steps and read it. 'FINEST HOURS: A Fiftieth-Anniversary World War II Tribute,' it read, and listed the museum's upcoming special events and exhibitions: *The Battle of Britain; The War in North Africa; Women at War; The Secret That Won the War; The Evacuation of the Children.* If he didn't find anyone here or at St Paul's, he definitely needed to attend that last one.

If he could get here. Badri and Linna hadn't been able to get a drop to open anywhere near *Women at War*'s opening date, even though they'd laboured over it for months, and gone as far afield as Yorkshire. When was *The Evacuation of the Children?* If it was soon, he might be able to stay till its opening. It wasn't till September. He couldn't waste four months on the off-chance that he could find an evacuee who'd had contact with Merope after she went to London. Or who knew which other children had been at Denewell Manor.

The Evacuation Committee's files had been destroyed by the same pinpoint bomb that had vaporised St Paul's, and all he'd learned from local records was that the evacuees hadn't been so much assigned to a particular family or house as dumped on them. A committee head he'd interviewed in 1960 had only been able to name three of the thirty children who'd been at Denewell Manor, and the only reason she'd remembered two of them was that they'd been such hellions.

'Alf and Binnie Hodbin were *dreadful* children. Lady Denewell was an absolute *saint* to have them there,' she'd told him. 'They *stole* things, tormented livestock, damaged people's property. And then they'd stand there and tell you the most outrageous lies.' And when he'd asked her if she'd had any contact with them since the war, she'd said, 'No, thank heavens. I shouldn't be surprised if they were in prison.'

She *had* known where the third evacuee – Edwina Barry, née Driscoll – was, but Mrs Barry had been sent to another home before Eileen had left the manor, and she hadn't known what had happened to the Hodbins either, though she knew they were from Whitechapel. He'd spent the next six months scouring prison rosters and Whitechapel's housing records. He'd found out their address, but their terrace had been destroyed in February of 1941. Their names hadn't been on the casualty list for the bombing, but a list of casualties for the entire Blitz confirmed that their mother had been killed.

Now he wrote down the opening date of the children's evacuation exhibit and perused the rest of the brochure for any other possibly useful exhibitions, then glanced up.

Someone was coming. It was only a pair of tourists. They were in their fifties and, from the look of it, American. They both wore white running shoes and had large cameras round their necks. The wife was wearing sunglasses, even though it looked like it might rain any moment, and the husband was grumbling, 'I told you it wouldn't be open yet.'

'It's better to be too early than too late,' the wife said, and started up the steps. 'Is the museum open?'

'If it was open,' the man growled, 'he wouldn't be sitting out here.'

'I'm Brenda,' she said, extending her hand, 'and this is my husband, Bob.'

He stood up and shook her hand. 'I'm Calvin Knight.'

'Oh, I just love English accents!'

There was no good answer to that, so he asked, 'Are you here for the opening of the *Living through the Blitz* exhibition?'

'No, is that what's on? We didn't know anything about it. Bob just wanted to come because he's interested in World War II. We've already been to the RAF Museum and the Cabinet War Rooms. Did you hear that, honey?' she called down to her husband. 'Calvin says they're opening a thing here on the Blitz today.'

I hope, he thought. Bob and Brenda didn't know about it, and there was no one here yet. Could he have the wrong day? There hadn't been any slippage. This was definitely May seventh, but the article he'd read in the *Times* might have got the date of the opening wrong.

I should have checked it against other historical records, he thought, wondering how he could check it now. With the museum still shut …

'We're from Indianapolis,' Brenda was saying. 'Do you live here in London?'

If he said yes, she was likely to demand tourist information from him, and he had no idea what had been in London in 1995. 'No, I'm from Oxford.'

An Audi was pulling in to the car park. He'd be able to ask whoever was in it about the opening.

'The museum should be opening shortly,' he told Brenda. 'There are some interesting exhibits in the courtyard that you and your husband might like to look at in the meantime.' But she wasn't listening.

'You're from Oxford?' she cried. 'We're going there on Wednesday. You've got to tell us what we should see while we're there.'

He glanced out at the car park. The woman stepping out of the Audi and going round to open the back was too young to be one of the women he was looking for. She couldn't be more than forty, and she was wearing a business suit and high-heeled shoes and was getting an armload of books and papers out of the back. Someone who worked here. She would definitely know whether the opening was today.

'We want to see the university,' Brenda was saying, 'but I couldn't find it on the map, only a lot of colleges.'

He explained that the colleges *were* the university, and told her to go and see Balliol. 'And Magdalen,' he said, trying to think what would have been in Oxford in 1995. 'And the Ashmolean Museum.'

'Is that where they have the dodo?' she asked. 'I'm *dying* to see the dodo and all the other *Alice in Wonderland* stuff.'

'No, the dodo's at the Natural History Museum,' he said. 'Oh, where's that?' she asked, digging in her tote bag. 'Bob!' she called. 'Do you have the guidebook?' But Bob had gone down into the courtyard to look at the anti-aircraft gun and either couldn't hear her or was ignoring her. 'He's got the guidebook,' she said. 'Can you show me where the – what did you say it was? The Nature Museum?'

'The Natural History Museum.' He glanced quickly out towards the car park, but the woman in the business suit was still unloading things from her car, and no one else had pulled in. He went down the stairs and into the courtyard with Brenda.

Bob didn't have the guidebook. 'I thought *you* had it.'

'No, I gave it to *you*, remember? Right before we left the hotel?' she said, but after digging some more, she found it and got it open to the section on Oxford, and he showed her where the museum was and went back to the steps, just in time to see the business-suited woman disappear up them and inside, which meant the doors must be open. But when he tried them, they were still locked, and there were still no cars pulling in to the car park. And it was beginning to rain.

He turned his collar up and ducked under the cover of the doorway, and Brenda came scampering up the steps, holding the guidebook open over her head, her husband behind her, saying, 'I told you we needed to bring an umbrella.'

'I can't get used to how much it *rains* here, Calvin,' Brenda said. 'It said on the sign down by the anti-aircraft gun that it had been in Kensington Gardens. That's not the same Kensington Gardens where they have the Peter Pan statue, is it?'

'Yes, it is,' he said.

'Oh, I want to go there. I love *Peter Pan*,' she said, and began leafing through the guidebook again. 'And to the house where Barrie lived as a child in Scotland.'

'We're only here for ten days,' Bob said, 'not six months.'

'Oh, I know, it's just that there are so many things I'm *dying* to see. There just isn't enough *time*.'

You're right, Calvin thought, looking at the door. *There isn't.*

'Is that the museum schedule?' Bob asked, pointing at the brochure he was holding.

'Yes.' He handed it to him, and he and Brenda pored over it.

'"The Battle of Britain" looks good,' she said. 'Oh dear, it doesn't open till July first. We won't be here. "The Secret That Won the War",' she read aloud. 'What's that one about?'

'I don't know,' Bob said impatiently.

'I believe it's about Ultra and Bletchley Park,' Calvin said.

'Ultra?'

'The secret project to decode the Nazis' coded messages,' he said.

'Oh.' Brenda turned to her husband. 'I thought you said the American forces were what won the war.'

Bob had the good grace to look embarrassed. 'There were all kinds of things that won the war,' he said. 'Radar and the atom bomb and Hitler's deciding to invade Russia—'

'And the evacuation from Dunkirk,' Calvin said, 'and the Battle of Britain, and the way Londoners stood up to the Blitz—'

Brenda beamed at him. 'You're obviously as big a fan of World War II as my husband is.'

A fan. Of World War II. 'Actually, I'm a journalist,' he said. 'I'm here to cover the opening of the Blitz exhibit.'

'Really?' she said. 'Our daughter Stephanie teaches journalism. You'd be perfect for each other. Are you married?'

'Brenda,' her husband said, 'it's none of our business—'

'Oh, don't be silly,' she said. 'Are you?'

He shook his head.

'Girlfriend?'

'Not yet.'

'You see?' she said, turning triumphantly to her husband and then back to him. 'How old are you? Thirty?'

'*Brenda!* This young man is not interested in—'

'Stephanie's twenty-six,' she said. 'She teaches at—'

'Let's go and look at the tank,' Bob said, and took her arm.

'It's raining—' she began.

'It's stopped,' Bob said firmly.

'Oh all right,' she said, starting down the steps, and then said to Calvin, 'Would you mind taking our picture in front of the tank?'

She handed him her camera, and he went down with them and took their picture in front of the anti-aircraft gun and the boat. 'The *Lily Maid*,' she said. 'It's not a very warlike name, is it?'

'They didn't know they were going into a war,' Bob said impatiently. 'Did they, Calvin?'

No, he thought. *They didn't know they were going into a war.*

DOVER – APRIL 1944

'**K**ansas!' Commander Harold bawled in Ernest's ear, hugging him and pounding him on the back. 'I can't believe it's you!' And for the space of perhaps thirty seconds, Ernest wondered if he could convince him he was mistaken – if his two-days stubble and Cornish accent might create just enough doubt that he could look bewildered and say, 'I'm sorry, I'm afraid you've confused me with someone else.'

But it was too late. The Commander had already seen the look on his face when he'd realised this was the *Lady Jane*. And now what the hell was he going to do? If the Commander told Lady Bracknell …

He suddenly remembered Bracknell saying, 'Algernon specifically requested you for this delivery.' *Tensing already knows I know the Commander*, he thought. *That's why he sent me.* But how had he known that? And what was the Commander—?

'What are you doing here, Kansas?' Commander Harold was saying.

'What am *I* doing here? What are *you* doing here? I thought the *Lady Jane* had been sunk at Dunkirk—'

'*Sunk?*' he shouted, outraged. 'The *Lady Jane?*'

Jesus, the sailor up on deck will hear him, he thought 'Shouldn't we—?' he cautioned, pointing at the hatch.

'You're right, lad,' the Commander said, and waded over to the hatch, reached up and pulled the trapdoor shut. 'You should know nothing can sink the *Lady Jane,* not even a Nazi U-boat.'

'But then what happened? Where's Jonathan?' he said, almost afraid to ask. 'Did he make it back?'

'Make it back?' the Commander bellowed, surprised. 'Why, you saw him up there on deck not five minutes ago.' He tipped the hatch again and shouted, 'Jonathan! Get down here!'

'Aye, aye, Captain Doolittle,' a man's voice said, and the sailor came down the ladder, still carrying the wrench, and saying reprovingly, 'Grandfather, you're not supposed to call me Jonathan. My name's Alfred—' He stopped when he saw Ernest, looking uneasily at him. His hand tightened on the wrench.

This can't possibly be Jonathan, Ernest thought, staring at the tall, broad-shouldered sailor. *He's a grown man.*

'Sorry, Captain Doolittle,' Jonathan said uneasily, 'I didn't know you had company.'

'Stop that Captain Doolittle nonsense,' the Commander said. 'Can't you see who this is? It's Mike Davis!'

He may not even remember me, Ernest thought. *It's been four years.*

'*You* know,' the Commander prompted. 'Kansas!'

'Oh my goodness!' Jonathan exclaimed, shifting the wrench to his other fist so he could shake hands. 'Mr Davis!' He was beaming. 'This is wonderful!'

Wonderful was the word, all right. They were alive. His unfouling the propellor hadn't got them killed. Especially Jonathan – the Commander had known what he was getting into when he took off for Dunkirk, but Jonathan hadn't. He'd been just a kid.

Though he wasn't any longer. 'I can't believe it!' he was saying, pumping Ernest's hand vigorously. 'I'm so glad you're here.

I never thanked you for saving our lives. Without you, we'd be at the bottom of Dunkirk harbour. And you nearly got killed yourself, trying to—' He stopped short and looked down at the water Ernest was standing in. 'I mean, your foot and everything. I thought they were going to have to cut it off.'

So did I, he thought.

'We'd never have made it without you,' Jonathan said. 'I should have recognised you, but you look so different!'

'*I* look different? Look at you! You're all grown up!'

'Having German torpedo boats on your tail ages you rather quickly. But what are you *doing* here?'

'That's the same question I've been asking your grandfather. I'd heard you hadn't made it back to Dover after your second trip to Dunkirk.'

'We didn't,' the Commander said. 'We were commandeered.'

'They needed us to go to Ostende to take off an intelligence officer they couldn't afford to let the Germans get hold of,' Jonathan explained. 'So they offloaded our passengers onto the *Greyhoe,* and we went to Belgium instead.'

'And when we got him back to Ramsgate, they asked us if we'd do a few other jobs for Intelligence, like—'

'Grandfather,' Jonathan said warningly. 'That's classified. I'm not certain we're allowed to—'

'Bah! We can tell him, can't we, Kansas?'

'Not Kansas,' he said. 'These days it's Ernest Worthing.'

'What'd I tell you, Jonathan? And I'll wager he's got even more secrets than we do, eh, Kansas?'

'Yes,' he said. *Most of which I can't tell even you.*

'All right, we told you what we've been up to since Dunkirk,' the Commander said. 'Now you tell us what you've been doing these last four years.'

I've been trying to get two of my fellow historians out of this century and back home, he thought. *I've been writing letters to the editor and classified ads and funeral notices with coded messages in them to people who haven't been born yet. And*

I've been trying to find Denys Atherton, who is somewhere in the staging area for the invasion, so he can tell Oxford where Polly and Eileen are and pull them out before Polly's deadline, which passed four months ago. 'I've been delivering parcels,' he said, and when the Commander frowned, he smiled and said, 'I'm Seaman Higgins. Captain Pickering said as how you was hiring a crew.'

'I *knew* it,' the Commander said jubilantly. 'I told Jonathan that Tensing'd put you to work.'

'You're not supposed to call Colonel Tensing that,' Jonathan said. 'You're supposed to call him Algernon.'

'That's only when there might be German spies about.' The Commander turned to Ernest. 'All these made-up names – Captain Doolittle, First Mate Alfred – a lot of nonsense. Wanted me to be Capitaine Myriel,' he said, pronouncing it 'Cap-ee-tayne Meeryell'. 'And what the hell good will that do? If the jerries catch us, they'll know in two minutes we're not Frenchies. Instead of worrying over names, I told 'em, you should be seeing to it we don't get caught.' He turned to Jonathan. 'And Kansas here knows his name's Tensing – he was in hospital with him. Weren't you, Kansas?'

'Yes,' he said, trying to make sense of all this. He'd assumed they'd met Tensing in connection with the assignments they'd done for British Intelligence, and that they'd mentioned him to Tensing, but if they'd known him while he was in hospital …

'How did *you* meet him?' he asked.

'He was the officer we had to fetch from Ostende,' the Commander said.

'He was badly injured,' Jonathan said. 'He'd been shot in the spine.'

'And you told him about me when you were bringing him back?'

'He wasn't in any shape to be told anything,' the Commander said. 'Unconscious the whole way.'

'We didn't think he was going to make it,' Jonathan said.

'And then eight months later up he pops, nearly as good as new and looking for you. Said he'd been in hospital with you and somebody'd told him we'd brought you back from Dunkirk. Said he'd seen you in some town near Oxford and then lost you again, and did we know where you were and what could we tell him about you? Mainly, could you be trusted?'

'And what did you tell him?'

'We told him we didn't know where you were,' Jonathan said, 'but that he should ask in Saltram-on-Sea.'

He knew the rest of it, how Tensing and Ferguson had gone there and given Daphne the address he'd thought was the retrieval team's. He'd wondered how they'd traced him to Daphne, but he'd always assumed one of the nurses at the hospital had mentioned she'd come to see him.

'It looks like he found you,' Jonathan said.

'Yes, he found me.' *Or rather, I found him. I went to the address in Edgebourne Daphne gave me, expecting to find the retrieval team, and there he was. Scared the bejesus out of me. I thought he was going to arrest me as a spy, but he didn't. He offered me a job.*

Which I turned down, till I found out that Polly's deadline was two months before Denys Atherton got here. 'What else did you tell Tensing?' he asked.

'What do you think we told him?' the Commander said. 'That you were as brave as they come, that you'd saved our lives and the life of every soldier on the *Lady Jane* when you unfouled that propellor. And I told him he'd be a blasted fool not to recruit you, in spite of you being a Yank.'

That day in Edgebourne, Tensing had said, 'You come highly recommended,' and he'd assumed Tensing had talked to Hardy, but it had been the Commander and Jonathan. If it hadn't been for them, Tensing wouldn't have found him after losing him at Bletchley. He wouldn't have offered him a job and the possibility of finding Atherton and of telling him where Polly and Eileen were. He wouldn't be working on Fortitude South. And if they hadn't rescued Tensing, would there even have been a Fortitude South? And they couldn't have rescued Tensing if he hadn't unfouled the propellor.

'Tensing *recruited* you?' Jonathan was asking, as excited as when he'd been fourteen, and Ernest was suddenly reminded of Colin Templer. 'You're a *spy*?'

'Nothing so glamorous, I'm afraid,' Ernest said. 'When I'm not delivering parcels I spend most of my time at a desk. And speaking of parcels, I'd better deliver the one I brought and get going.'

He reached for his duffel bag, but the Commander stopped him. 'You can't go yet, not without telling us what all's happened to you since we saw you last.'

I faked amnesia, nearly killed Alan Turing, got knocked unconscious by a collapsing wall, faked my own death, and met the Queen. 'It's a long story,' he said.

'We've plenty of time.' The Commander pulled out a chair for him. 'Sit down. You can't go out in that gale. You want some coffee? Some stew?'

He remembered the Commander's stew. 'Coffee, thanks.'

He sat down. There were things he needed to find out, too.

The Commander sloshed over to light the burner under the coffee pot. 'Jonathan, see if you can find that brandy we were saving for the end of the war,' he said, fished a cup out of the litter of opened cans and charts on the table, poured coffee into it and handed it Ernest.

The mug didn't look like it had been washed since the last time he'd been on the *Lady Jane*. Ernest sipped cautiously. *I should have had the stew*, he thought.

'Here it is,' Jonathan said, bringing the brandy over.

'Are you sure you want to open that?' Ernest asked. 'Won't it be bad luck to drink it before the war's over?'

'It's as good as won already,' the Commander said, 'or it will be a month from now, isn't that right, Kansas?'

And here was the perfect place for his propaganda, the perfect chance to say the invasion couldn't happen till July twentieth at the earliest and mention FUSAG and Patton and Calais. Better than perfect. If they got captured by the Germans and were interrogated, they could help corroborate Intelligence's deception efforts.

But they'd saved his life as much as he'd saved theirs. He owed them the truth, and since he couldn't tell them who he really was, he could at least tell the truth about this. 'That's right,' he said, 'only we need the Germans to think it's mid-July.'

The Commander nodded. 'So Hitler won't bring his tanks up. And you need him to think it's Calais for the same reason.' At Ernest's look of surprise, he said, 'The last two weeks we've been minesweeping in Calais harbour to convince them that's where the invasion's coming. You think it'll fool them, Kansas?'

'If it doesn't, we won't win this war.'

'Then we'd better see to it that it does. Hold out your cup.' He added a dollop of brandy to Ernest's coffee and to Jonathan's and then poured himself a cupful and sat down. 'Now, then,' he said, 'tell us what you've been up to.'

'You first,' Ernest said, and leaned back, sipping his coffee – which even the brandy couldn't improve much – as they told him about their adventures. They'd spirited Jewish refugees and pilots who'd been shot down across the Channel to England and delivered supplies and coded messages to the French Resistance.

And he knew he should be worried that what they'd done – what *he'd* done when he unfouled that propellor and kept them from getting hit by that Stuka – had altered events. He'd been afraid of that ever since Private Hardy. But oddly, he wasn't.

He'd thought he'd got the Commander and Jonathan killed, and he hadn't. Which meant maybe other things he'd feared weren't true either, other things like, that he'd been unable to find Denys Atherton and get Polly and Eileen out before Polly's deadline, things like, that something he'd done that night in Dunkirk, saving Hardy's life or hauling that dog up over the side, had lost the war. If the Commander and Jonathan were alive, then anything was possible.

Or maybe it was just his relief at not being a murderer. Or the brandy.

'These last four months we've been helping map the beaches in Normandy,' the Commander said casually.

Mapping the beaches. Jesus, an incredibly dangerous job. And, if they were caught, one that could undo everything Fortitude South had worked so hard to accomplish in the last few months.

'Your turn,' the Commander was saying. 'What have you been doing? How long were you in hospital?'

'Three and a half months,' he said. 'I tried to get in touch with you. That's why I thought you were dead. After I wrote to you, Daphne—'

'Our Daphne, from the Crown and Anchor?'

'Yes. She came to tell me you hadn't made it back from Dunkirk. Have you sent them word you're alive?'

Jonathan shook his head.

'Not even your mother?'

'No. After we brought Colonel Tensing back, they sent us straight out again to lay mines against the invasion, and by the time we got back, they already thought we were dead.'

'Which we might have been at any time,' the Commander said. 'And then when we started doing missions for Intelligence, everything had to be hush-hush. And we were as good as dead anyway, with the sort of thing they wanted us to do. It was only a matter of our having been killed a bit later than they thought. And if Jonathan's mother had known he was alive, she'd never have let him do it.'

Jonathan nodded. 'So it seemed better all around to let them go on believing we were dead. I suppose that sounds hard to you.'

'No,' Ernest said, thinking of what he'd done to Polly and Eileen, 'I know sometimes things like that are necessary.'

The Commander nodded. 'If it means the difference between winning or losing this war—'

Or getting Polly and Eileen out or not.

'—then it was worth the sacrifice, wasn't it?'

Yes, Ernest thought, *it was worth the sacrifice. And speaking of which* ... 'I need to go,' he said.

'Go? In this weather? Are you daft? Listen to that.' He jabbed his pipe up towards the ceiling. 'It's raining cats and dogs. You'll catch your death, lad. No, you stay. You can sleep in the bunk there.'

It was a tempting offer. *But the last time you did that, you ended up halfway to Dunkirk.*

'Sorry, but I have another delivery I have to make,' he said, and stood up. He waded over to his duffel, took out the parcel and letter and gave them to the Commander, who opened them both immediately. The parcel contained a phonograph record like the one Ernest had played in the field with the bull.

'It says here,' the Commander said, reading the letter, 'that we're to stay here and get fitted with amplifiers, and then when we hear the message that tells us the invasion's on, we're to head for Calais, anchor off-shore, and play this.' He waved the record.

Which would no doubt have the sounds of a landing force debarking on it – the rattle of chains, the scrape of boats being lowered, men shouting – which would hopefully fool some German officer into thinking that what he was hearing was the invasion.

The mission would be a hell of a lot more dangerous than mapping the beaches. 'Good luck,' Ernest said sincerely. He put on his almost-dry coat and shouldered his duffel bag. 'Goodbye, Commander.'

'Not Commander – Captain,' he said proudly.

'Grandfather got his commission,' Jonathan explained.

'Congratulations, Captain,' Ernest said, and saluted. The Commander beamed. 'Good luck to both of you.'

'We don't need luck,' he said. 'Thanks to you, we've got the *Lady Jane*, and she won't let us down. We're going to come out of this all right, you mark my words.'

'I hope you're right,' Ernest said, shook hands with Jonathan, and went up the ladder onto the deck.

And into a veritable hurricane. He had to force his way, bent double, off the boat and back along the dock, hoping he wouldn't be blown into the water. When he heard Jonathan behind him calling, 'Seaman Higgins!' he thought, *If he's coming after me to bring me back, I'll go.*

But Jonathan wanted to give him something – a flat packet wrapped in oilcloth and tied with twine. 'Am I supposed to give this to Tensing?' Ernest shouted, using his real name, since there was no way anyone could possibly overhear them in this gale.

Jonathan shook his head, raindrops flying from his wet hair. 'It's for my mother,' he shouted. 'It's in case we don't make it back. So she'll know what happened.'

'For after the invasion?' Ernest yelled.

'No!' he shouted back. 'For after the war. All these secrets won't matter then.'

No, Ernest thought. *They won't.*

'I'll send it,' he promised, and stuck it inside his shirt, thinking, as he watched Jonathan run back along the dock, *Maybe I could give one to Cess to send.*

But what could it say? 'Dear Eileen, I wasn't really killed that night in Houndsditch. I waited till after Bank Station was bombed and then went to find an incident that the Civil Defence hadn't arrived at yet and left my papers and scarf for them to find, just like a murderer in one of your Agatha Christie mysteries. I'm sorry to have burned the coat, after all the trouble you went to to get it for me ...'

You don't have time for letter-writing, he thought. *You need to get to the railway station.*

He set off through the wind and rain to find it. He knew where it was from when he'd come to Dover that first September, trying to get to his drop, and he could walk/hobble a lot faster now than he could then, but he was so frozen by the time he got there that he had to blow on his numb hands before he had enough feeling in them to be able to get the coins in the telephone's slot so the operator could put him through to British Army headquarters in Portsmouth.

He'd spent the past three months making trips to Army headquarters in London and making calls – under various pretences – to British Army camps all over southwest England, trying to locate Denys Atherton, and he was still only halfway through the list. And God help him if Atherton had had an L-and-A implant and was here as an American GI because there were more than 800,000 American soldiers in England right now.

The operator put him through to Southampton, and he spent what was left of the afternoon and evening being transferred from office to office, officer to officer, to find out there was no Denys Atherton stationed in Southampton or Exeter or Plymouth, and to worm the telephone number of the paymaster at Weymouth out of a reluctant Wren by using his old standby American accent. His implant had long since worn off, but he'd used it so long it was now permanently a part of him.

By the time he got off the phone with the Wren, he was coughing. He couldn't spend the night in the station. It was too cold, and the ticket agent was beginning to eye him suspiciously. He couldn't hope to catch a ride in this weather either, *and* at night, and he couldn't go to an inn anywhere near the docks and risk running into the Commander and Jonathan in the pub room. And he was going to need something hot – and alcoholic – to ward off the chills he was already having.

You can't get sick, he told himself. *You only have a month and a half to find Atherton. And you still haven't done your invasion-propaganda spreading,* to which end he limped out to the edge of town to a pub which catered to the locals, ordered a hot toddy, and prepared to tell all comers that he'd overheard two officers saying the big show was starting on July the eighteenth and it was definitely going to be Calais.

But there were no comers, in spite of the pub actually having beer *and* whisky – a rarity at this point in the war. The weather was apparently too much even for hardy English seafarers. Ernest spent the evening drinking one hot toddy after another and composing imaginary letters:

'Dear Eileen, I know I said we shouldn't split up, but Denys Atherton didn't come through till after Polly's deadline, and it was the only way I could think of to get a message through to him. Remember me telling you about how Shackleton had to leave his crew behind and go off to get help because if he didn't, no one would have had any way of knowing where they were and they'd all have died? And how he made it to the island and found help and came back to rescue them? Well, I didn't tell you the whole story. When Shackleton got to the island, he was on the wrong side and had to walk over the mountains to get where he needed to be, and the same thing happened to me ...'

And after two more drinks: 'Dear Polly, I lied to you when I came back from Manchester. The person who came to Saltram-on-Sea asking about me wasn't Fordham. It was Tensing. He'd been tracking me down since Bletchley Park, but you were wrong. He didn't want to hire me for Ultra. He wanted to recruit me for a Special Means unit, and I thought it would mean I'd be able to get to Denys Atherton, but as it turned out ...'

But he couldn't write to Polly because her deadline had passed, and she was already dead. She'd been dead since December.

He'd got drunk that night, too, and tried to call her in Dulwich to warn her, and then remembered she wasn't there until after D-Day and hung up. And when Cess had asked him what he was doing, he'd said, 'She's not here yet. She's dead.'

And if he had any more toddies tonight, he might blurt out the whole story to the barman, or worse, write it all down, and there was no point. A letter wouldn't reach Polly in Dulwich because it *hadn't* reached her. And if Eileen was here to send it to, then his plan hadn't worked – he hadn't found Atherton or got a message through and Polly had died – and if that was the case, then Eileen was better off not knowing that he was alive, that he'd gone off and left them for nothing. It wasn't like Jonathan, whose mother would at least have the comfort that he and his great-grandfather had died heroes.

He stood up unsteadily, set down his mug, which was *much* cleaner than the one the Commander had given him, and prepared to stagger off to bed, but before he made it to the stairs, a pig farmer came in, shaking water everywhere, announced it was 'a fit night out for nowt' – a sentiment Ernest agreed with wholeheartedly – and demanded a pint.

'And make it quick,' he said. 'I've got to take a load of shoats all t'way down to Hawkhurst.'

Ernest promptly begged a ride, crawled into his truck, and was rewarded by the farmer's asking where he thought the invasion would be and then, without waiting for an answer, saying, 'Mark my words, it's going to be Calais,' and regaling him for the remainder of the trip with how he'd come to that conclusion.

Ernest didn't have to say a word, which was just as well because the minute he got back to Cardew Castle, Chasuble said, 'Oh, excellent, you're here – good Lord, what's that smell?'

'Pigs.'

'I thought you were going to sea. Well, never mind. You need to shave and bathe, *particularly* bathe, and get into this.' He tossed a dinner jacket and Bracknell's too-small shoes at him, told him he had ten minutes, and hauled him and Cess off to another reception, this one for General Montgomery.

'Only it won't be Monty,' he said after they were in the staff car.

'What do you mean, it won't be Monty?' Ernest asked, attempting to tie his tie in the rearview mirror.

'It's a double,' Cess said. 'An actor.'

Oh God, out of the frying pan into the fire. 'It's not Sir Godfrey Kingsman, is it?'

'It can't be,' Cess said. 'He's dead. He was shot down.'

'No, that's Leslie Howard you're thinking of,' Chasuble said.

'It is *not*. He was on his way to entertain the troops—'

'And *that's* Jane Froman,' Chasuble said. 'What does Kingsman look like? Whoever this actor is, he's supposed to be the spitting image of Monty.'

Which ruled out Sir Godfrey. Actors could work wonders with make-up and wigs, but not with height. Montgomery was a good eight inches shorter than Sir Godfrey. And Cess was right. The general at the reception was a dead ringer for Monty, right down to the high cheekbones, toothbrush moustache and imperious manner. 'Are you *certain* he's not Montgomery?' Chasuble whispered after they'd all been introduced to him as assorted officers and aides to General Patton. 'He sounds exactly like the old boy.'

'I'm certain,' Cess said. 'And it's your job to see to it that he stays in character. Monty's a teetotaller, and he's not, so keep at his elbow and make certain he doesn't get hold of anything but lemonade. This is a dry run – quite literally – to see if he can pull it off.'

'And if he does?' Ernest said, watching the dapper general chatting with the guests, who all seemed completely taken in.

'They're sending him off to Gibraltar to convince the Germans the invasion's going to be in the Mediterranean, or, if they won't believe that, to convince them it's not coming till July.'

And I suppose I'll end up having to accompany him and see to it that he stays sober, Ernest thought, cursing his luck. Why couldn't Monty's double have been sent to the invasion's staging area instead and *Monty* sent off to Gibraltar?

He was right about being assigned to accompany him, but 'Monty' wasn't scheduled to leave yet, so Ernest spent the next week dragging motor-car headlights along a fake runway in the rain while the phonograph played engines-revving-up sounds,

by the end of which the cold he'd caught in Dover had blos-
somed into full-blown influenza, and he realised he'd never
really appreciated antivirals. Or paper tissues.

On the other hand, he didn't have to go to Gibraltar, and the
doctor prescribed bed rest for a week, during which time he was
able to get nearly caught up on his articles and his own coded
messages, writing in bed with a typewriter on his knees:

'For sale, hothouse poinsettias, hibiscus, pearl hyacinth cut-
tings. Contact E. O. Riley, Harbour House', with Mrs Rickett's
address, and 'Lost in Notting Hill Gate Underground Station, gold
monogrammed compact, inscribed "To Polly from Sebastian".'
Also, a review of a production of *The Tempest* put on by the
Townsend Players, which listed as cast members Eileen Hill and
Mary Knottinge, and commented, 'The shipwreck which begins
the action was well done, but the ending is rather doubtful,
though this reviewer hopes that will improve with time.'

And the day after he was allowed to get up, Lady Bracknell
sent him and Chasuble to the Bull and Plough to spread invasion
propaganda, and he had a chance to put a call through to the
paymaster in Taunton while Chasuble flirted with the barmaid.
But there was no Denys Atherton listed on the payrolls there or
at Poole, and time was running out.

Even sooner than he'd thought. A pilot he'd talked to in the
pub said, 'Whenever it is, it's soon. Three weeks from now
they're locking down the entire staging area. No one in, no one
out, not even the post.'

'That's to fool the Germans into *thinking* it's in June,' Ernest
told him. 'There'll be an attack then, but it's only a feint, to
draw the Germans off. The *real* invasion won't come till mid-
July.' But he was thinking, *If I don't find him by next week, I'm
going to have to steal the Austin and take off for Wiltshire to
track him down.*

But he didn't have to. The next morning Cess leaned in the
door and told him Lady Bracknell wanted the two of them to go
and make a pick-up.

'I can't,' he said. 'I need to finish these and get them to the *Call* by five tomorrow, and I've barely started on them.'

'What vital news is it this time?' Cess asked, leaning over his shoulder as he typed, and thank goodness this wasn't one of *his* articles. 'Another garden party?'

Ernest shook his head. 'Friendship Dance.' He read, '"The Welcome Club of Bedgebury will host a Friendship Dance for the newly-arrived American troops—"'

'We're officers,' Cess said, 'and we'll be driving Bracknell's Rolls, not walking. There won't be any mud. Or bulls.'

'No. I told you, I've got a deadline. Can't Chasuble go with you?'

'No, he has a date to take Daphne to dinner.'

'Can't he do that tomorrow night? Or the night after?'

'It *is* the night after, but Chasuble's afraid we won't be back by then, and he's already in her bad graces for having had to cancel when we went to the Savoy to meet Monty.'

Tomorrow night? 'Where is this pick-up we need to make?'

'I don't know exactly,' Cess said. 'Lady Bracknell gave me a map. And he said something about Portsmouth.'

Which was right in the centre of the invasion area where Atherton was. 'All right. Are we going as civilians?'

Cess shook his head. 'Army officers.' Which meant they'd be picking up whatever it was at an army camp, and no one would consider it odd if an officer asked where a Denys Atherton was stationed. He could even order an enlisted man to check the records and find him. He'd have to get away from Cess, but over the course of a two-day journey, there should be ample opportunities, and if they weren't leaving till tomorrow morning, he might be able to drop his articles by the *Call* on the way. 'When do we have to make this pick-up?'

'Tomorrow morning at nine. Does that mean you'll go?'

'Yes,' he said, and as soon as Cess left, he typed, 'Music will be provided by the 48th Infantry Division Band', yanked the sheet of paper out of the typewriter, rolled a new one in, and typed,

'Mr and Mrs James Townsend of Upper Notting announce the engagement of their daughter Polly to Flight Officer Colin Templer of the 21st Airborne Division, currently stationed in Kent. A late June wedding is planned.'

Cess opened the door and leaned in. He was dressed in his officer's uniform. 'Why aren't you ready?'

'I thought we were leaving tomorrow morning.'

'*No*,' Cess said. 'Lady Bracknell wants us to leave now.'

Which made no sense – Portsmouth was only a few hours away. But Ernest didn't object. The sooner they got there the better, and if they stopped for the night along the way, he'd have even more opportunities to ask about Atherton.

'Give me twenty minutes,' he said.

'Ten. You don't know where our map got to, do you?'

'I thought you said Bracknell gave one to you.'

'No, a map of this area.'

'Prism had it, I think,' Ernest lied, and as soon as Cess had gone off to look for it, he dug the map out of the pile on his desk, stuck it in his pocket, and bolted down to the mess to hide it in the silverware drawer. Then he ran to throw his razor and soap into a bag, answer Cess' 'Are you *certain* you didn't have it after Prism?' and take the bag and his officer's uniform back to the office. He put it on and began typing madly again.

He managed to finish another message—'Schoolgirl Mary P. Cardle won the war saving-stamp competition at St Sebastian School last week. Fourteen-year-old Mary, known to her friends as Polly, earned the money to buy the stamps by running errands. Said headmaster Dunworthy Townsend, "Let's hope we can all do as much for the war effort as Mary has."' – before Cess reappeared with the map, saying, 'You won't *believe* where I found this,' and demanding to know why Ernest still wasn't ready.

Ernest stuffed the articles into an envelope, sealed it and hurried out to where Cess had already started up the Rolls. He pulled out onto the road before Ernest even had his door shut.

'We need to run these articles by the *Call* office,' Ernest said, showing the envelope to Cess.

'We'll have to do it on the way back.'

'But Croydon's right on the way.'

Cess shook his head. 'We have to go up to Gravesend and then back down to Dover and Folkestone first.'

'*What?*' If Cess had lied about Portsmouth, he'd kill him. 'Why?'

'We need to write down the names of all the roads and all the villages we go through,' Cess said.

'Why? Can't Bracknell get those off the map?'

'Yes, but not the landmarks. And the distances have to be right, in case a member of the German High Command happened to spend a holiday hiking through Kent before the war.'

'The German High ... what exactly are we picking up?'

'A German prisoner of war,' Cess said. 'We're picking him up at his prison camp and driving him to London. He's extremely ill, and the Swedish Red Cross has arranged to have him sent home to Germany. But first we're driving him to Dover through the staging area in Kent so he can see our invasion preparations firsthand.'

'A few rubber tanks, wooden planes and a sewer-pipe oil refinery? Those were meant to fool a reconnaissance plane from twenty thousand feet up, not a—'

'No, we're going to show him the real thing,' Cess said, 'ships, aeroplanes, everything. He's only going to *think* he's in Kent. That's why we have to drive to Gravesend this afternoon. We've got to map out a false route so he can accidentally overhear us talking about where we are.'

It was a clever plan. With signposts down all over England, the colonel would only have their word for where they were, and if they could convince him he was in Kent, and he went home and told the German High Command, it could help convince them the Allied attack would come at Calais.

But it played hell with his plan to find Atherton. He could

hardly ask a soldier where Denys was with the colonel listening. He'd have to get away from him and Cess.

'You said we'll be gone two days,' he said. 'Where are we spending the night? At an Army camp or in Portsmouth?'

'Neither. We're bringing him straight to London.'

'But I thought you said we wouldn't be back in time for Chasuble's date?'

'*Chasuble* said that. He's convinced something will go wrong and we'll blow the gaff,' Cess said. 'No, we're not to stop for anything, except to go the loo. And we're not to let the colonel out of our sight for a moment. Lady Bracknell wants both of us with him at all times.'

*When peace breaks out again (as it will, do you know) and
the lights come on again, we shall look back on these days
and remember gratefully the things that brought us
cheer and gave us heart even in the glummest hours.*

NEWSPAPER ADVERTISEMENT, 1941

IMPERIAL WAR MUSEUM, LONDON – 7 MAY 1995

By five to ten, the group he was waiting for still hadn't arrived
at the museum, and it was pouring with rain. The American
woman had given up trying to set him up with their daughter
and gone off to find 'someplace dry' to have 'a decent cup of coffee, if there *is* such a thing in this country, Calvin', which was
a blessing, but there was no sign of any other visitors. *What if
they all went to the exhibition at St Paul's instead?* he thought.
*Or what if this isn't the right day? What if the exhibition
doesn't begin till tomorrow? Or began yesterday?*

At one minute to, an elderly museum guard appeared, unlocked
the doors and let him come inside the lobby to wait. 'Today *is*
the first day of the "Living Through the Blitz" exhibition, isn't
it?' he asked the guard.

'Yes, sir.'

'And it's a special Free Day for civilians who were involved
in war work?'

'Yes, sir,' the guard said warily, as if he suspected him of
attempting to pass himself off as one of those survivors. 'You

purchase your exhibition ticket over there.' He nodded stiffly towards the still-unoccupied ticket desk. 'Admission to the museum and the permanent collections is free. The museum will be open shortly. Till then you're welcome to go into the gift shop.' The guard pointed to where it stood just past the ticket desk.

'Thank you. I'll just look around the lobby,' he said, pointing up at the high ceiling where a Spitfire and a V-1 and a V-2 rocket all hung suspended. As soon as the guard had gone, he went back over to the window to see if anyone was coming.

No one was. He read the 'Upcoming Lecture and Events' poster. 'June 18 – *So Few: The Battle of Britain*', it said. 'June 29 – *Unsung Heroes of World War II. A slide presentation of the civilians who gave their lives to win the war, from bandleader Glenn Miller to decoding genius Dilly Knox and Shakespearean actor Sir Godfrey Kingsman*'.

The car park was still deserted. He looked at the clock behind the ticket desk. Ten past. *They're all at St Paul's,* he thought, and wondered if he should give up and go there, but it would take him at least half an hour to get there by tube, and in the process he might miss them at both places. He decided to give it ten more minutes.

At a quarter past, they all arrived at once. Two large vans pulled up and began disgorging a score of elderly women. They were too far away for him to be able to see their faces clearly, and as they started for the steps, they opened out umbrellas and ducked under them so he couldn't see them till they were nearly at the top of the steps.

And what if one of them was Merope? He hadn't thought of that possibility till this moment, he'd been so intent on finding someone who'd known Polly, who would have a clue to where she'd gone after she left Mrs Rickett's. *If* she'd left Mrs Rickett's. If she and Merope hadn't been killed as well that night.

But their names hadn't been in the casualties lists, and even if they had, it wouldn't necessarily mean anything.

They weren't at Mrs Rickett's that morning, he told himself, had been telling himself every single day since he'd stood in front of the gaping hole that had been the boarding house. *They were safely in a shelter, and after they were bombed out, they moved to another boarding house. Or, if Polly joined an ambulance crew, into quarters at their post, and one of these women here today will know where.*

His first impulse when he'd seen the wreck of timbers and plaster that had been Mrs Rickett's had been to stay there in 1941 and find them – correction, his *first* impulse had been to start digging through the rubble for Polly with his bare hands – but the bomb had hit days or possibly even weeks before, and every day he spent looking for them then was one he wouldn't be able to come to again. And one of those days might be the day he had to pull her out because if he didn't, she'd be killed.

And he knew too well from being at Notting Hill Gate, in Lampden Road and Oxford Street, that being in the same general temporal-spatial location wasn't enough. He had to know exactly where she was before he went to get her.

And one of these women can tell me that. They'll have been on the same ambulance crew as Polly or shared the same air-raid shelter or the same flat.

But what if Merope walked through those museum doors? What if he hadn't rescued Polly and her and she was still here, fifty years later?

If she is, there's no way she'd come to something like this, he told himself. *The war's the last thing she'd want to be reminded of.* But he posted himself next to the doors so he could get a good look at each woman as she came in, bracing himself as they reached the top of the steps and paused to lower their umbrellas and shake the water out of them and he could see their faces.

The first ones through were all discussing the weather. 'What a pity it had to rain today!' one of them said, and the other replied, 'But it will be good for my roses. Poor things, they've been absolutely parched.' He wondered if they were here for the exhibition after all. They were the correct age – in their seventies and eighties – and they were all dressed as for a special occasion in frocks and hats – including one enormous one with an entire herbaceous border on it. And one very elderly, very frail-looking lady was wearing white gloves. But they looked as though they were going to a garden party, not a World War II reunion. And it was impossible to imagine them ever having done anything less genteel than pour tea, let alone put out incendiaries, dig bodies out of the rubble or man aircraft guns.

This isn't them, he thought. *They're all at St Paul's, and this is the Women's Institute of Upper Matchings on their monthly outing.* He was about to turn away when the frail-looking one pointed a white-gloved finger up at the V-1 and said, 'Oh my God, look at that! It's a doodlebug. One of those chased me all the way down Piccadilly.'

'I do hope it isn't armed,' the woman who'd come in with her said, and then squealed, 'Whitlaw!' and flung her arms around a grim-looking woman. 'It's me! Bridget Flannigan – we were in the same WAAF brigade!'

'Flanners! Oh my God! I don't believe it!' And the grim-looking woman broke into a broad smile.

They *were* the women he was looking for after all. But another van had arrived, and they were pouring into the lobby too quickly for him now, shaking out their umbrellas, shedding raincoats, talking excitedly. He stood by the door till they were all inside and then made a circuit of the noisy lobby, scanning the faces of the ones he'd missed as they called to one other across the room and greeted each other with cries of delight, oblivious to him as he worked his way through the crowd, searching their faces, looking for Merope.

He caught snatches of their conversations as he moved among them.

'No, she couldn't come, poor dear. Her rheumatism, you know ...'

'Are you still married to your American – what was his name? Jack?'

'Jack? Lord, no, I've had two husbands since then—'

'—were not, you were a dreadful driver. Remember that poor American admiral you ran over?'

'He wasn't an admiral! He was only a commander, and he had no business looking the wrong way like that. If Americans drove on the proper side of the road, they'd *know* which way to look when they were crossing—'

'Ladies!' shouted a large, florid-faced woman with iron-grey hair in front of the door to the museum. She was holding name badges and a sheet of gold stars. 'Ladies! Attention please!' she shouted, to no avail. The women were intent on locating old friends, finding familiar faces.

Like I am, he thought, working his way past the name-badge woman and over to the corner where the four women he hadn't got a close look at yet were passing around snapshots, he assumed of children and grandchildren. He pulled out his notebook and pretended to take notes on the V-1 and the Spitfire while he scanned their faces.

Don't let any of them be Merope, he prayed.

They were all huddled over the snapshots, their faces hidden, and it took several moments before they raised them again and he was able to see their faces.

Merope wasn't here. That meant he hadn't failed, at least not yet, that there was still time to find someone who could tell him where Polly was after March 1941, and he could find her and Merope and pull them both out. And this was the place to find that someone. These women had all done war work, and most of them would have been in London during the Blitz. One of them was bound to have known Polly.

Beginning with the group he'd just been watching. They'd finished looking at the snapshots and were discussing the war.

He edged nearer to hear what they were saying and to find a way to insinuate himself into the conversation.

'Do you remember when we went to that dance at Biggin Hill?' the one who'd been passing around the snapshots was asking the woman next to her. 'And that RAF pilot – what was his name?'

'Flight Officer Boyd. I certainly do. He kept begging me to go out to see his plane,' she said, even though it was difficult to believe any man had ever begged her to go anywhere. She was a stout, washed-out-looking woman and her face was a railway map of wrinkles. 'And *I* said good girls didn't go out alone in the dark with men they'd only just met, and *he* said there was a war on and we might both be dead by tomorrow—'

'Original,' the woman next to her said.

'My particular favourite was "It's your patriotic duty,"' a third woman said, and the others nodded. 'Think of it as doing your bit.'

Somehow I don't think this is the right moment to break in, he thought, and looked studiously up at the Spitfire.

'So did you go with him?' one of the women was asking.

The first woman looked offended. 'No. I told him I wasn't about to fall for an antiquated line of chat like that, and I didn't intend to go anywhere with him, and a good thing I refused, too. A few moments later his plane took a direct hit. Blown to bits. They couldn't even make out where it had been. It had vanished without a trace.

'I saved his life,' she said. 'I told him that. "You should be grateful I'm a good girl," I told him. "If I weren't, we'd both be dead."'

'And was he?' the second woman asked dryly. 'Grateful?'

'I knew a girl who vanished without a trace,' the woman next to her said.

So do I, he thought. And it was clear he wasn't going to find out whether these women had known Polly just by eavesdropping. He approached them, notebook in hand. 'What was her name?' the woman was saying. 'It began with an S. You remember, Lowry, she was hit by an HE. Totally vaporised—'

'I'm sorry to interrupt, ladies,' he said. 'I'm Calvin Knight. I'm here to do a story on the opening of the exhibition, and I was wondering if I might interview you. You all did war work during World War II, is that right? Were you all in London?'

'She was,' the white-haired one with the lace collar said, pointing at the one who'd spoken of the girl vanishing without a trace, 'and these two' – she pointed at the crone and the one with the photographs – 'were WAACs.'

'Women's Auxiliary Army Corps,' the crone said. 'We were radio operators.'

'And what did you do?' he asked the lace-collared one.

'*Well*,' she said, dimpling, 'until just a few years ago I couldn't tell you. I was in Intelligence.'

'She was a *spy*,' the crone said. 'But I had an even more exciting job. I drove a mortuary van.'

'During the Blitz?'

'No, I'm younger than this lot. I was still at school in Surrey during the Blitz. I didn't join up till July of 'forty-four.'

Which was too late. Polly would already have been driving an ambulance near Croydon by then. And her deadline would already have passed. 'Were the two of you in London during the Blitz?' he asked the WAACs.

'No, we were stationed at Bagshot Park,' the first one said, and the second handed him the snapshot he'd supposed was of her grandchildren. It wasn't. It was a black-and-white photograph of two slim, pretty girls in uniform, one fair, one dark, perched, laughing, on a tank. 'I'm the blonde,' she said, 'and that's Louise.' She pointed at the curly-haired girl perched next to her in the picture and then at her friend.

'That's *you*?' he said, staring at the snapshot. The faded, stout old woman in front of him bore no resemblance at all to the vivid, laughing girl in the photograph.

'Yes,' Louise said, coming round to look at it. 'I was a brunette in those days.'

He had assumed he'd recognise Merope if he saw her, even

though he hadn't seen her in nearly eight years and she'd be far older than she'd been then, but now that he saw this snapshot ... There was no resemblance at all between the curly-haired girl in the photo and the dumpy, faded woman in front of him. Too much time had gone by.

Too much time. Merope could be here, right now, in this lobby, perhaps only a few feet away, and he simply hadn't recognised her. And if she recognised him, would she come up to him and say, 'Where *were* you? Why didn't you *come*?'

He was still staring blindly at the snapshot. 'Are you all right?' Louise asked him.

'He's stunned by how little we've changed,' her friend said, and the women all laughed good-naturedly.

'She's quite right. Neither of you've changed a bit,' he said, recovering himself. He handed the snapshot back to them and asked the four their names, 'so I can quote you in the article.'

Thankfully, none of them was named Merope, or Eileen O'Reilly, which had been her cover name. But he couldn't ask every woman here her name. He remembered the woman with the name tags and went looking to see if she'd managed to pass them out, but he couldn't find her.

No, there she was, over by the ticket desk, conferring with the woman he'd seen earlier out in the car park. She was probably asking for a microphone.

She'd need it. The noise had risen to a din, and several women had their hands cupped to their ears in an effort to hear, though when he attempted to ask one of them who was wearing an ARP armband whether she'd been in London during the Blitz, she said, 'I beg your pardon, I couldn't hear you. I'm deaf in that ear.'

And in the other one as well. When he shouted, 'Were you in London during the Blitz?' she said, 'List? What list?'

He bellowed at her for a bit longer till he got her maiden name out of her – Violet Rumford – then moved on through the crowd, eavesdropping on their conversations, attempting to catch their names, but a large number seemed to be calling one another by nicknames—'Stodders' and 'B-1' and 'Foxtrot', and the rest by their last names.

The name-badge woman had apparently given up on attempting to get either a microphone or the entire group's attention and was moving among the crowd, passing them out. Good.

He worked his way over to her. 'Print your name on the badge and fix this gold star in the corner,' she was saying, handing the women badges and pens, 'and then go through that door.'

But not until I've had a chance to read your names, he thought.

'Which names should we put?' a woman in a pink feathered hat asked. 'Our name now or our name during the war?'

'Both,' the organiser said. 'And write the name of the service you were with below it.'

Thank you, he thought, and followed in her wake, reading the women's names as they printed them. Pauline, Deborah, Jean. Netterton, Herley, York. No Eileen, no O'Reilly, though the woman in charge evidently hadn't given all of the women the same instructions. Several had printed only one name, and only a few had listed the service they'd been in. ARP, WAAF, WVS.

They were beginning to drift out of the lobby into the museum. He needed to purchase his ticket, but there were still several ladies who hadn't put their tags on yet. Walters, Redding ...

The third woman's hand shook with palsy when she wrote her name, and when she pinned it to her breast, he couldn't decipher it, though the first letter might be an O. He'd have to corner her once they got inside and find out.

The fourth woman, a tiny creature who looked like she might break in two, still hadn't finished printing her name, though he didn't see how she could possibly be Merope, whom he remembered as being taller. But he'd grown since then, and people had still shrunk with age in this era, hadn't they? 'Did she say we were supposed to put what unit we were in?' the woman asked.

'Yes,' Walters and the one with the unreadable name tag said in unison and then laughed, and Unreadable Name Tag said, 'Walters? Is that you?'

Walters gaped at her. 'Oh my goodness!' she cried. 'I can't believe this!' She flung her arms around her. 'Geddes!'

Geddes. Good. It had been a G, not an O.

'We were stationed at Eastleigh together,' Geddes was telling Redding. 'We were Atta Girls.'

'Air Transport Auxiliary,' Walters explained. 'We ferried new planes to their airfields for the RAF.' And if they'd been stationed at Eastleigh, they hadn't been anywhere near London and couldn't have known Polly.

'What did you do in the war?' Walters was asking Redding.

'Nothing so romantic, I'm afraid,' she said. 'I was a land girl. I spent the war shovelling pig muck in Shropshire.'

Which eliminated her too. That left the tiny woman who'd finally finished printing her name and pinned her badge on. Mrs Donald Davenport,' it read, and below it, 'Lt Cynthia Camberley.'

He let out a breath he hadn't realised he'd been holding. Merope wasn't here. Thank God.

But he still had no idea where Polly was, and he still hadn't found anyone who might know. And Camberley, who hadn't said if she'd been in London during the Blitz, was already going in with the others. He started after her, remembered he hadn't bought a ticket and raced over to the desk, but by the time he got it and went in, they'd vanished.

Directly inside the door was a bright red signpost with arrows pointing to various exhibits: *The Battle of the North Atlantic, The Holocaust, Living through the Blitz.* He followed the last arrow down a corridor to a doorway piled high with sandbags. A bucket of water stood in front of the sandbags with a stirrup pump in it. Above the door was written, '"This was their finest hour." Winston Churchill', and, as he passed through the doorway, an air-raid siren began to warble.

He was in a short corridor lined with framed black-and-white photographs: a burnt-out church, rows and rows of barrage balloons floating over London, a street of bombed houses, the dome of St Paul's floating above a sea of smoke and flames. At the end of it was another doorway, across which hung a heavy black curtain. From somewhere beyond it, he could hear a drone of planes and the *crump* of bombs. He went through the curtain.

Into total blackness. 'Look out in the blackout,' a recorded voice said. He peered into the darkness, searching for Lt Cynthia Camberley. He couldn't see her, but as his eyes adjusted, he could make out two round white lights with black bars across them that must be a motor car's headlamps, and on the floor, a white-lined pathway leading to another curtained door, dimly illuminated by the headlamps. And just going through it, Lt Camberley. He started towards her.

'Connor?' a woman's voice called from behind him. He turned round and then remembered his name wasn't Connor here and stopped, hoping the darkness had hidden his involuntary reaction.

That was how the Nazis caught British spies, he thought, *by suddenly calling them by their real name.*

He continued following Camberley. 'Connor?' the woman's voice said again and he felt a hand on his arm. 'I *thought* that was you. What a lucky coincidence! What are you doing here?'

'Nothing could be seen but the tops of the towers of the palace, and even those only from a good way off.'

SLEEPING BEAUTY

WALES – MAY 1944

The prison camp wasn't near Portsmouth. It was in Gloucester-shire, and Ernest and Cess ended up driving all night to get there. They got lost twice, once because of their inability to see anything in the blackout, and the second time because of the lack of signposts. 'Which is a good thing, really,' Cess said, struggling with the map. 'If there were signposts, we wouldn't be able to pull this off.'

If we can't find the Colonel, we won't be able to pull it off either, Ernest thought irritably. He hadn't felt this tired since that endless day in Saltram-on-Sea. If the *Lady Jane* were available, he'd have gladly curled up in her hold, but they were nowhere near water. Or anything else. 'Have you any idea at all where we are?' he asked Cess.

'No. I can't find— Oh bloody hell, I've got the wrong map.' Cess unfolded the other one, peered at it, and then looked out at the road. 'Go back to that last crossroads,' he said, and as Ernest backed the car around, he added, 'I've just had an idea. I think we should get lost.'

'We *are* lost.'

'No, I mean after we pick up Colonel von Sprecht. We should pretend we don't know where we are.'

'We may not have to pretend,' Ernest said as they reached the crossroads. 'Which of these roads do I take?'

Cess ignored him. 'You could say, "Where are we?" and I could say, "Here, at Canterbury," and you could say, "Give me the map," and we could hold the map so he can see it and then argue over where we are. People always say things they shouldn't when they're arguing, and it would be far more believable than my saying, "Here we are at Canterbury," for no reason. What do you think?'

'I think you need to tell me which road to take.'

'Bear left. Oh, and we're going to need a code, in case I need to tell you something we don't want him to hear. Suppose I say, "I believe we have a puncture?" Then you'll know to stop the car, and we can get out and talk.'

'No, a puncture's something he'd be able to feel. How about, "I believe I hear a knock in the engine?"'

'Yes, that's good. It will mean putting the bonnet up, which will keep him from reading our lips. If I tell you I hear a knock, you pull over— No, I don't mean now. Why are you stopping?'

'Because left was obviously the wrong way to turn,' Ernest said, indicating the lane, which had ended in the middle of a sheep-filled meadow.

'Oh, sorry,' Cess said, consulting the map again. 'Go back to the crossroads again and bear right.'

'You have no idea where we are, do you?' Ernest asked, backing.

'No,' Cess admitted cheerfully, 'but it's growing light. That should make it easier to find our way.'

If he'd known they were going to spend hours and hours wandering around Wales like this, he'd have insisted on delivering his articles to the *Call* on the way. It would only have meant half an hour's detour, and he'd at least have something to show for this damned trip. He obviously wasn't going to have any chance to ask where Denys Atherton was. There wasn't even anyone they could ask where the camp was.

'Now which way do I turn?' he asked.

'Left ... no, right ...' Cess said doubtfully. 'No, go straight ahead.' He pointed. 'There's the camp.'

Ernest drove up to the gate. 'Who are we again?'

Cess checked their papers. 'I'm Lieutenant Wilkerson and you're Lieutenant Abbott.'

'Lieutenants Abbott and Wilkerson here to pick up Colonel von Sprecht,' Ernest told the guard. The guard glanced at their papers, handed them back and waved them towards the camp commander's office.

'I'll inform the commander you're here,' the sergeant there said. 'Please wait here.' He disappeared into the commander's office.

An hour later they were still waiting. 'What's taking so long?' Cess asked anxiously. He stood up and went over to the window to look out. 'What if the weather clears up?'

'The forecast said it would be cloudy all day, with rain after noon,' Ernest said, looking at the route they were going to be taking. It led straight through the centre of the invasion build-up. And Denys Atherton was there somewhere, if he could just find him.

'What if the forecast's wrong? The one for the dedication of that dummy oil depot in Dover was wrong. It said the weather would be fair that day, and we nearly drowned. If it's fair today, the colonel will be able to tell by the sun what direction we're going, and it won't matter what we tell him.'

'It won't turn fair. Stop worrying,' Ernest said, still thinking about Atherton. How was he supposed to look for him with a German prisoner-of-war in the car? Even if he could think of a reason for asking which would satisfy Cess, anyone he asked might mention their real location, and he couldn't risk jeopardising the mission they were on.

He wished for the thousandth time he knew whether historians could affect events. And which of Fortitude South's deceptions had worked. Had the Germans believed what von Sprecht told them? Had they even questioned him? And had they believed the faked photo ops and the carefully planted articles in the *Call* and the *Shopper* and the *Banner*? Which ones? The ones he was supposed to have turned in to the *Call* yesterday?

'It's definitely clearing up,' Cess said. 'I'm certain I saw a patch of blue. What if he tries to escape?'

'Who?'

'The *prisoner*. What if he tries to run off? Or kill us? He might be dangerous—'

'He's ill,' Ernest said, frowning at the map. 'That's why they're repatriating him. If he was dangerous, they'd scarcely have sent *us*.'

'A lot you know. Remember that farmer's bull?'

'He'll be handcuffed. Colonel von Sprecht, not the bull. Come here and show me the route we take.'

Cess traced the route on the map for him. 'We go through Winchester – that's Canterbury – then south to Portsmouth so he can see the invasion armada and then—'

'We can't go through Winchester,' Ernest said. 'Its cathedral doesn't look anything like Canterbury's. We'll need to go around.' Cess nodded and made a note on the other map. 'And we'd best steer clear of Salisbury. He's likely to recognise the spire.'

'Which can be seen for miles,' Cess said, frustrated. 'I'll need to completely redo the route.'

Good, Ernest thought, *it will keep you from constantly looking out of the window.* Cess was making him nervous. What *was* taking them so long? They could have repatriated the entire German Army by now.

Cess calculated a new route, wrote it out for Ernest, and went over to the window again to check the sky. 'What if the Americans have put new signposts up? If the colonel finds out where he is—'

'He won't. Stop worrying. And stop talking. I need to finish memorising this route before they bring him in,' Ernest said.

Which got him five full minutes of silence, and then Cess said, 'How long can it take to sign a few papers? You don't suppose they're checking up on us, do you? What if Algernon didn't tell the camp commander what he's up to, and when they find out we're not who we say we are, they decide we're spies?'

'We *are* spies.'

'You know what I mean.'

'They won't think we're spies. And the weather's not clearing. Stop fretting. Haven't you ever been to the films? Spies are supposed to possess an icy calm.'

'But what if—?' The door opened and the sergeant came in again, followed by the camp commander, two guards and – between them – the prisoner in a German officer's uniform.

Ernest had been wrong, he wasn't handcuffed. But there was obviously no need for him to be. He leaned heavily on the arms of his guards, and his face was grey.

'Lieutenants,' the commander said, nodding at them, and then turned to the prisoner. 'Colonel von Sprecht, you are being repatriated to Germany through a programme instituted by the Swedish Red Cross. These two officers will drive you to London, where you'll be handed over to the Red Cross and taken back to Germany.'

Colonel von Sprecht gave no indication of understanding what the commander was saying. What if Tensing was wrong and he didn't speak English? But when the commander asked, 'Do you understand, Colonel?' he said, with only a trace of a German accent, 'I understand very well.' He drew himself up as he spoke, but the guards nearly had to carry him out to the car. He didn't look strong enough to survive the journey by car, let alone the sea voyage, and apparently Cess was thinking the same thing.

'What if he dies along the way?' he whispered as the guards put the colonel into the backseat.

They climbed in. Ernest started the car and then adjusted the rear-view mirror so he could see the colonel. He had leaned back against the rear seat, and his eyes were shut.

And if he stays like that the whole way, this whole scheme will have been for nothing, Ernest thought, driving south to Swindon, glancing occasionally in the mirror at the colonel. His eyes were still closed. Ernest drove into the town, feeling suddenly nervous. If there was even one signboard saying this was Swindon …

But Cess' fears about the Americans having put up signs were unfounded, and the Home Guard or whoever had been in charge of taking down the signposts at the beginning of the war had done a thorough job. There was no name on the railway station and not even an arrow pointing to 'Town Centre'.

'This is Brede, right?' Cess asked, looking at the map. When Ernest nodded, 'At the next turning, you go north to Horns Cross and take the Oxney Road to Beckley.'

'Shh. What if the colonel hears you?' Ernest said in a stage whisper.

'Don't worry, he's asleep,' Cess said, glancing back at him. 'I don't suppose we can stop in Nounsley, can we?'

'Why?'

'I know a girl there. A Wren. Name of Betty. She's General Patton's driver.'

'I thought Patton's headquarters were in Essex. In Chelmsford.'

'They are, but she's billeted in Nounsley, and she has a very understanding landlady. What do you say?'

'No,' Ernest said, 'we can't stop in Nounsley. Or Dover. You know our orders are to take the prisoner straight to London and hand him over to the War Ministry—'

'Shh,' Cess said, jabbing a thumb towards the backseat. 'He's awake.'

Ernest glanced over his shoulder and then called back to him, 'Colonel von Sprecht, are you comfortable back there?'

'Yes. Thank you,' the colonel said.

'If you need anything, sir, just ask. Our orders are to take good care of you.'

'Would you like some tea?' Cess held up their Thermos.

'No, thank you.'

'A cigarette?'

'No,' he said curtly, but at least he was awake and looking at what they'd brought him this way to see: fields full of tents and vehicles and equipment. Ernest had been worried about their being able to stay on the prescribed route without the aid of signposts, but it wouldn't matter which road they took. Every one they passed, even if it was a narrow country lane, was lined with Quonset huts or jeeps parked bumper to bumper or mobile anti-aircraft guns. One of the fields was crisscrossed with tank tracks, just like the ones they'd so carefully made in that pasture, only the tanks half-hidden under the trees at the far end weren't inflated rubber – they were the real thing. And so were the huge pyramids of oil drums and stacks of ammunition boxes further on.

But when Ernest glanced in the mirror, the colonel's eyes were closed again. They shouldn't have brought such a comfortable car. 'Colonel von Sprecht,' he called, 'are you warm enough back there? Would you like a rug?'

'No,' he said without opening his eyes.

'It's rather cold for May,' Ernest said, and when the colonel didn't answer, Cess asked, 'Do you have this sort of weather in Germany?'

Still no answer.

'What part of Germany do you come from?' Ernest asked, and the colonel began to snore.

You can't fall asleep, Ernest thought. *We're doing this for your benefit.* He drove into a large mud hole, but even the jolt didn't wake the colonel. Stopping would, but every field they passed was full of soldiers – drilling in formation, doing calisthenics, loading supplies, standing in line outside mess tents. One of them was bound to come over and ask them if they needed directions, so Ernest had no choice but to keep driving, straight past everything the sleeping colonel was supposed to be seeing.

There was a village up ahead. Good. *If there's a garage there, I'll stop for petrol,* he thought, but there wasn't one on the village's single street, and just ahead was, Oh Christ, a signpost. He wasn't close enough to read it, but he could make out letters and arrows pointing in opposite directions. And there was no side lane he could turn off onto.

He glanced in the rear-view mirror, hoping to God the colonel was still asleep. He wasn't. And in a minute, he'd see the sign-post. 'Look!' Ernest said, pointing off to the other side of the road. 'Parachutists!'

'Where?' Cess said. He leaned across him to look, and the colonel followed his gaze.

'There,' Ernest said, pointing at nothing. 'I hear the Americans are planning to land twenty thousand parachutists in the Pas de Calais area the night before they invade.' While Cess and the colonel were gawking at the sky, he shot past the signpost.

He needn't have panicked. Next to one arrow it read, 'Berlin' and next to the other, 'Good Old USA'. He almost wished the colonel had seen it, but when he glanced back, his eyes were closed again.

Ernest drove on another mile and then pulled the car to a jolting stop opposite an aeroplane-filled field. 'I don't think this is the right road,' he said. 'We passed these planes before.'

'No, these are Hurricanes,' Cess said. 'The ones before were Tempests.'

'No, they weren't. I think we should have turned left at that last crossroads.' When Cess still didn't catch on, he said, 'We're *lost.*'

'Oh,' Cess said, the light dawning, 'no, this is the right road.' He opened the map out. 'Look, here's where we are. We came through Newchurch, and Hawkinge's that way.'

'Here, let me see the map,' Ernest said, snatching it away from him and holding it so the colonel could see it. 'Where did you say we are?'

'Here, just north of Newchurch,' Cess said, pointing. 'See,

here's Gravesend, where we picked the colonel up. We came across to Beckley and then took the Oxney Road.'

Ernest sneaked a glance in the mirror. The colonel was looking intently at the map as Cess traced their route.

'And this is the road we're on now. It takes us through Dover, and then we take the Old Kent Road to London.'

'You're right,' Ernest said. He started the car and yanked on the gearstick. The gears ground. He jiggled the knob back and forth, trying to get it to shift, and it finally slid into reverse. He backed the car out onto the road and went on, past more camps and storage dumps and so many airfields he lost count, full of P-51s and DC-3s, parked wingtip to wingtip.

'Good Lord, will you look at all this?' Cess said, sounding awed, and Ernest wasn't sure that was just for the colonel's benefit. He'd known the D-Day invasion had been a massive project, but the sheer magnitude of the undertaking was impossible to get one's mind around – thousands upon thousands of planes, tanks and trucks, and tons of equipment.

As they drove, the colonel seemed to grow more and more ashen and to sink into himself, deflating like one of their dummy tanks.

He knows there's no way they can win against this, Ernest thought. He wondered if that was part of the plan, if the purpose of this trip was not only to fool von Sprecht into believing they were invading at Calais, but also to show him the overwhelming might of the Allied invasion force and convince him of the hopelessness of the Germans' resistance. If so, the plan was succeeding. He looked more defeated with every passing mile.

But he wasn't the only one being affected by the sprawling tent cities, the squads and companies and battalions drilling in the fields and crammed into the trucks that passed them. *I'll never be able to find Atherton among all these camps and all these men,* Ernest thought. Atherton could be anywhere, in any one of the fifty fields they'd passed or the hundreds of transit camps. There was no way Ernest could find him in the next five weeks – correction, *three* weeks – even if he dumped Cess and the colonel out of the car right now and started asking for Atherton at every army HQ from now straight through to the fifth of June.

'A chap I met said there are a million men in this corner of England,' Cess said. 'Do you think that could be right?'

No, Ernest thought bitterly, *it's two million.*

'I mean, one would think Kent would sink under the weight. Perhaps that's what the barrage balloons are for,' Cess said, pointing to hundreds of silver specks in the sky ahead. 'To hold England up.' He grinned. 'We should be coming to Dover soon,' he added, consulting the map.

Which meant Portsmouth. That meant they were on schedule, in spite of their late start. At least something was going right. At this rate they should be in London by three and he might still be able to deliver his articles to Mr Jeppers before the *Call's* deadline.

He'd spoken too soon. Half a mile on, they ran into a convoy of very slow trucks. They were behind a canvas-covered four-by-four that he couldn't see around at all, and it was slowing down till it was scarcely crawling. 'Can you see what's causing the problem?' Ernest asked Cess.

'No,' Cess said, rolling down his window and leaning out. 'We're coming into a village. Burmarsh, I think.' The behemoth ahead slowed to a stop between a church and a pub, with no room to squeeze past on either side.

Cess leaned out again and then got out and walked past the truck to see. 'It looks rather bad,' he reported, getting back in the car. 'There are vehicles and tanks and artillery as far as one can see, and it doesn't look as though they'll move any time soon. Some of them are sitting on the bonnets of their lorries, drinking tea and eating sandwiches.'

'We'll have to go back the way we came,' Ernest said. Cess reached for the map. Ernest put in the clutch and tried to shift it into reverse. It ground and then jammed.

A movement from in front of the car made him glance up. An MP was walking towards them.

Jesus. He was bound to ask them where they were going. Ernest jiggled the gearstick, trying to work it back into gear, but it wouldn't budge. 'Cess,' Ernest said, glancing quickly in the mirror. Hopefully the colonel had fallen asleep again. No, he was awake and watching interestedly.

'Cess, roll up your window before the colonel catches a chill,' Ernest said. 'Cess!'

'Hmm?' Cess said from behind the map.

The MP was nearly even with the car. Ernest yanked on the gearstick, trying to force it into gear, any gear. 'Roll up the bloody window. *Cess!*'

'What?' Cess said and finally looked up, but too late. The MP was even with the window. Cess shot Ernest a look of panic. 'There's a soldier—'

'I see him,' Ernest said grimly and gave the gearstick one last desperate yank. It slid into reverse, and he let out the clutch. And killed the motor.

The MP leaned in. 'You can't get through this way, sir. The road ahead's full of troops and equipment. You'll have to go back the way you came.'

'Right,' Ernest said, restarting the car. 'Sorry.'

'Where were you trying to go, sir?'

Don't say Portsmouth, Ernest ordered Cess silently. *Or Dover.* 'Bunbury,' Cess said.

'We'll be out of your way in a moment, Corporal,' Ernest said, and put the car in gear. He laid his arm on the back of the seat and looked back to see a half-track pull up behind them.

'Bunbury, sir?' the MP repeated. 'Do you mean Banbury?'

Which was close to Bletchley Park. Ernest leaned across Cess. 'We're blocked in, I'm afraid. Can you ask the vehicle behind us to move?'

The MP nodded, but the half-track's driver had already taken matters into his own hands and pulled up beside them on the driver's side, with inches to spare.

Good, Ernest thought, and started to back. In time to see a jeep driven by a Wren pull up behind the two of them.

'Bunbury's near Bracknell,' Cess was saying to the MP, who'd leaned in the window again. 'West of Upper Tensing.'

'Upper Tensing? Is that near P—?'

'It's near Lower Tensing,' Cess said desperately.

Disaster was seconds away. Ernest had to somehow get the MP away from the car and out of earshot so he could explain their mission. He snatched up their papers and opened his car door, but there were only inches between it and the half-track, and while he was in the process of squeezing out and making it to the other side, the MP would say something fatal, and he wouldn't be there to stop it.

The MP was already saying it. 'Never heard of any of them. Are they on the road to Por—?'

'We're looking for Captain Atherton,' Ernest cut in, leaning across Cess. 'Can you tell us where to find him?' and Cess shot him a look of relief he hoped the MP didn't see.

He didn't. He'd pushed back his helmet and was scratching his head. 'Captain Atherton?'

'Yes, we were told he was up ahead. Go and tell him—'

'What's the hold-up?' the Wren who'd been driving the jeep demanded, walking up to the MP. 'Why are we stopped?'

'You can't get through this way,' the MP said to her, and Ernest grabbed the opportunity to squeeze out of the door – snatching up their papers as he went – and dart around to the passenger side of the car, where the MP was explaining to the Wren that the jeep would have to turn around. 'This whole division's being moved to their transit camp,' he was saying. 'There's no way you can get through.'

The Wren looked annoyed. 'But I must get through to Por—'

'I need to speak to Captain Atherton immediately,' Ernest barked. 'Take me to a field-telephone. *Now*, soldier.'

575

'Yes, sir,' the MP said.

'Wait!' the Wren said. 'What about—?'

'And move that jeep, Lieutenant!' Ernest ordered her.

'This way, sir,' the MP said, and led Ernest past the lorry. 'I'll take you to Captain Atherton right away, sir.'

If only that were true, Ernest thought, following him. It was unbelievably tempting to make the MP get on the field-telephone and try to locate Atherton, but he didn't dare, not in the middle of hundreds of soldiers, any of whom might blurt out 'Portsmouth' at any second. Finding Denys wouldn't mean a thing if von Sprecht told Hitler troops were massing in south-western England. He had to get them out of here. Fast.

So, as soon as they were out of earshot – Cess still hadn't rolled the damned window up – Ernest stepped ahead of the MP and said in a low voice, 'We're on special assignment from British Intelligence. It's imperative that we reach Portsmouth by fourteen hundred hours.' He pulled the papers out of his pocket and flashed them at him so the MP could see the 'PRIORITY' and 'ULTRA-TOP-TOP SECRET' stamped at the top. 'Invasion business.'

The MP's eyes widened. 'Yes, sir,' he said, looking ahead at the traffic jam. 'I'll see to it that these vehicles are moved out of your way—'

Ernest shook his head. 'There's no time for that. Just move those that are blocking us in.'

'Yes, sir.' He started back towards the car.

The Wren was coming towards them, looking determined. 'Have you moved your vehicle?' the MP demanded.

'No,' the Wren said. 'Officer, you don't understand, it's imperative I get to Portsmouth.'

Ernest shot a look at the car. Cess had finally rolled up the window, thank God.

'I have an important dispatch to deliver,' the Wren said.

The MP ignored her. 'Do you still want me to locate Captain Atherton, sir?'

Ernest shook his head. 'There's no time for that.'

'Atherton?' the Wren said. 'Do you mean *Major* Atherton?'

Ernest stared at her.

'No,' the MP said. 'The lieutenant wanted *Captain* Atherton.'

Ernest cut him off. 'Major Denys Atherton?' he asked her.

'Yes,' she said.

Jesus. 'Do you know where he is?'

'Yes. At the holding camp at Fordingbridge.'

'How far is that from here?' Ernest demanded.

'Thirty miles,' she said, and the MP added, 'It's just outside Salisbury.'

Which meant going there today was out, but it didn't matter. He had the name of the camp – if Atherton didn't move to a transit camp in the next few days, like this division.

The Wren was rummaging in her shoulder bag. 'I've got his number,' she said, produced it and handed it to him.

And that was that. After over three years of plotting and searching, it had been handed to him, just like that. *It can't be this easy*, he thought. *Something will go wrong at the last minute.* But it didn't. The Wren, smiling and waving, moved her jeep, Ernest got into the car and said, 'The whole division's moving to their transit camps. Patton's orders. He said we'll have to go all the way back to Aylesham and take the other road to Dover.' The MP held up traffic till they were turned around, and the Winchester Road was not only empty of traffic but lined with B-17s and Flying Fortresses.

'That was brilliant,' Cess said when they stopped to check on a fictional knocking sound in the engine. 'I thought we were for it back there, but you saved the day. How did you know Atherton was there?'

'I didn't,' he said, keeping his voice low so the colonel wouldn't hear. 'It was a lucky shot. I used a name from one of my letters to the editor.'

'Well, it was a *very* lucky shot. And lucky we went past those bombers. Did you see the colonel's face? He's utterly demoralised. We've fooled him completely.'

'If nothing happens between here and London,' Ernest said grimly. 'We've still got to get through Portsmouth—'

'You mean Dover,' Cess corrected.

'Through Dover, and the next roadblock we run up against, we may not be so lucky. And there's still London. If he sees St Paul's in the wrong spot—'

'I suppose you're right,' Cess agreed. 'The moment you think you're in the clear is when something disastrous always happens.'

He was right. They were no sooner back in the car than the cloud cover began to break up and patches of blue began to show. Ernest jammed his foot down on the accelerator, praying it would be cloudier near the coast.

It was. By the time they reached Portsmouth, wisps of fog were beginning to drift across the road.

I hope it doesn't get too foggy, Ernest thought. *We won't be able to see the ships*, but they were clearly visible, troop transports and destroyers and battleships riding at anchor as far out as they could see. The fog actually helped, obscuring the surrounding coast so that when Cess asked, 'Which way are the White Cliffs of Dover?' he was able to point confidently off towards an invisible shore and say, 'Over there.'

Cess sang, 'There'll be bluebirds over the white cliffs of Dover,' and then said, 'How long do you think it'll be before the—?' He glanced back at the colonel, who promptly closed his eyes, then Cess dropped his voice. 'Before ... you know?'

'Not before mid-July at the earliest,' Ernest said. The fog looked like it was beginning to thin. He started inland from the docks before the colonel could see there weren't any cliffs, white or otherwise. 'One can't count on good weather before that. And the American troops haven't all arrived.'

Cess said, 'My brother – he's in the Second Corps in Essex – says it'll be August, but he says they'– another surreptitious glance at the 'sleeping' colonel – 'may launch an attack somewhere before that to fool the Germans. Turn here.' He consulted the map. 'And then at the next street, right again, and that will be the road to Kingston.' And they were safely out of Portsmouth and on the road to London.

'I don't care what you say about not getting over-confident,' Cess said jubilantly when they stopped at the border of the staging area to show their papers. '*I* say we've pulled it off.'

Yes, Ernest thought, *and so have I*. In spite of impossible odds and obstacles, he'd found out where Atherton was, and with over a month to spare. And even if he couldn't get to him in that time, he could phone him and tell him where Polly and Eileen were.

I need to do it as soon as possible, though, he thought, driving through Haslemere, *in case his drop's somewhere outside the staging area or is on a once-a-week schedule like Eileen's was.* But how? He couldn't phone him from the post. If Cess or Prism saw him making unauthorised calls …

I'll have to get to a phone somehow, he thought. *I'll tell Cess it's too late to deliver my write-ups to Mr Jeppers tonight, that the* Call's *office will be shut, and find a way to take them over alone tomorrow.*

But that'll mean my messages won't get in till at least the week after next, he thought, and realised it no longer mattered. *You don't need to send any more messages,* he thought jubilantly. *You've found Atherton! All you've got to do is get to London without von Sprecht realising he's been duped and hand him over to the War Ministry.*

And even that proved simple. The colonel's feigned slumber turned into the real thing, and Ernest took advantage of his sleeping and Cess' – he'd fallen asleep against the door, his mouth open – to speed through Kingston and Guildford and across the southern edge of London so they could approach the city the way they would have if they'd really been coming from Dover. That way they wouldn't have to worry about a glimpse of St Paul's in the wrong spot ruining the entire illusion.

They were both still asleep when he turned north onto the Old Kent Road. *Home free*, he thought. *Now all we have to do is deliver the colonel to the authorities and—*

Cess woke up. 'Where are we?' he asked sleepily, and then said, 'I think I hear a knock in the engine.'

Oh God, what now? He glanced back at the colonel, but he was still asleep, and Ernest could see his chest moving, so he hadn't died.

'There's a garage ahead,' Cess said, pointing.

Ernest pulled in to it and stopped the car, and they both got out. 'What's wrong?' he whispered as soon as he had the bonnet up.

'Nothing. I need to look at the map. Where are we?'

'On the Old Kent Road. What do you need the map for? This'll take us straight to Whitehall and the War Ministry.'

'We're not taking him to the War Ministry,' Cess said. 'They're having a state dinner for him. With General Patton. To put the finishing touches on.' And after a minute, he added, 'Oh good, we can take the same route in as I do when I deliver my press releases. Look.' Cess showed Ernest the map. 'We take this to the Holborn Viaduct and then the Bayswater Road to Kensington—'

Kensington? Jesus. 'Where's this dinner being held?'

'Kensington Palace. It's at the western end of Kensington Gardens. Just before Notting Hill Gate.'

LONDON – SPRING 1941

Two of Mrs Rickett's other boarders who'd decided to stay at home that night had been killed along with her. The bomb, a five-hundred-pound HE, had hit several minutes before three. The raids had been fairly heavy early in the evening (as Polly knew – she'd had to shout over the bombs during ENSA's evening performance) and then tapered off. By midnight, it had looked like the Germans were done for the night, and at half past two, Mrs Rickett had announced she was going home to sleep in her own bed, but she hadn't made it. She'd been killed on her doorstep, by flying glass.

Luckily Miss Laburnum and Miss Hibbard hadn't gone with her – they were arguing with Mr Dorming and the rest of the troupe over whether to do a dramatic reading from *The Little Minister* or from *Dear Brutus*.

But Polly had spent far more time with them than with Mrs Rickett, and yet the wounded, flailing continuum had still killed her. So what chance did the troupe or Marjorie or Mr Humphreys have? Or Hattie and the rest of the ENSA cast, with whom she had to be in contact every day and who were all friendly and eager to show her the ropes?

You don't want to have anything to do with me, Polly wanted to scream at them. *The continuum's going to vainly keep on trying to correct itself, and next time, it will get me and all of you.*

But there was no avoiding them. The entire cast and crew were onstage together every afternoon rehearsing and in the crowded wings every night, and the girls shared a single dressing room.

Polly did the best she could. She came in early to do her make-up, turned down all offers to go out for a drink or supper afterward, and spent most of her time backstage 'with her nose in a book', which she'd borrowed from the shelter library at Leicester Square – not Holborn, where the ginger-haired librarian who'd been so kind to her worked.

The book was a mystery by Agatha Christie. 'You'll never guess the ending,' Hattie said, and she didn't. She stared blindly at the pages and thought about losing the war and Mr Dunworthy's deadline and all the innocent people she might be responsible for killing – the ones Stephen Lang's tipped V-1s had landed on, the customers who'd had to wait till she'd fumbled to wrap their purchases and consequently been late getting to the shelter, the soldiers, many of them no older than Colin, who hung about the stage door waiting for her to come out and were caught by their commanding officer sneaking in late and punished by being shipped off to North Africa or the North Atlantic.

But making the soldiers late back to camp was safer for them than going out with them, and she was far more worried about the cast, with whom she still had far too much contact. ENSA mounted a new production every fortnight, so they were perpetually in rehearsal.

When Polly arrived they'd been doing 'ENSA Stirs the Pudding'. The following week, 'ENSA Pulls the Crackers' opened, and a fortnight later, 'ENSA Springs Towards Victory', though Polly had difficulty telling them apart. They all consisted of patriotic songs, chorus lines, comedians and assorted war-related skits.

Polly played, in rapid succession and very short skirts, an anti-aircraft gunner, a gum-chewing American WAC, a debutante in a munitions factory (complete with tiara, ball gown and spanner), and a girl saying goodbye to a soldier in a railway station.

'But I'm being shipped out,' Reggie, in a BEF uniform, said, attempting to put his arm around her. 'Can't you give me just one tiny kiss?'

Polly shook her head coyly, and he stuck his hand out for her to shake. She looked at it, then at the audience (who were shouting, 'Aw, come on, give him a kiss!' and making loud smooching noises), then grabbed his hand, swung him into a dip, and planted a torrid kiss on him.

'Zowee!' he said, doing a double-take. 'I thought you said you wouldn't kiss me goodbye.'

'I did, but then I remembered Mr Churchill said we must do everything we can for the war effort.'

'And that was what you were doing?'

'No,' she said, and batted her eyes. 'But it's everything I can do in a railway station.'

It was also her job to come out on the stage in a very short skirt when the sirens sounded, turn her back to the audience, bend over and flip up the back of her skirt to reveal satin bloomers on which were sewn red flannel letters spelling out, 'Air Raid in Progress'.

That bit was wildly popular, and by the end of her fifth week with ENSA, Mr Tabbitt had put her photograph (smiling, hands on hips, *not* bent over) with the caption 'Air-Raid Adelaide' up on the display board at the lobby entrance and told her glumly that ENSA's head wanted her to go on tour to the RAF's airfields, starting the third week of April.

'It's more money,' he said. 'And you'll have top billing.' And it would get her away from Eileen and Alf and Binnie, who she still held out hope might survive.

But Hattie, who had never done her any harm, had already agreed to the tour, and they would have to share a room and spend hours on crowded buses together, so Polly turned it down.

'Oh, marvellous,' Mr Tabbitt said, and the next night had her put on her Air-Raid Adelaide costume and went out in front of the curtain. 'I have an official announcement,' he said. 'If the Luftwaffe attacks tonight, the "Air Raid in Progress" notice will be displayed.'

Whistles, applause.

'I *repeat*, if the Luftwaffe attacks tonight, and *only* if the Luftwaffe attacks tonight—'

Cheers, applause, and a long, low 'woo-oo-ooh' from the second row, rising to the up-and-down wail of the alert as several others and finally the entire audience joined in.

Mr Tabbitt cupped his hand to his ear. 'Hark, is that an air-raid alert I hear?' he said, and Polly walked out (cheers, whistles, hoots), turned to face the curtain, and bent over.

He was so pleased he decided to make the bit a regular feature of the show, and by the end of the week Polly was doing it up to six times a show and getting bouquets and boxes of chocolates addressed to 'My Favourite Siren'.

Don't notice me, Polly thought in despair, and asked Mr Tabbitt to let Hattie do it instead, but he refused. 'You're bringing them in in droves,' he said.

I am so *sorry*, she thought, looking out at the soldiers' eager faces. But at least here she wasn't endangering Alf and Binnie or the girls at Townsend Brothers or Sir Godfrey and the troupe.

The next night at intermission, the stage manager, Mutchins, stuck his head into the dressing room.

'You were told to knock!' Cora said, outraged, and Hattie clutched a towel to her front.

He knocked on the open door. 'Visitor to see you, Adelaide,' he said. 'Gentleman.'

'What happened to no men allowed backstage?' Cora demanded.

Mutchins shrugged. 'Talk to Tabbitt. He said to come and

ask was you decent and if you was, to send him up,' he said, addressing Polly. 'Are you?'

'Yes.' She abandoned her effort to fasten the stiff strap on her gilt shoe and pulled on a dressing gown. 'Who is it?'

'Never saw him before. Some old gent.' He turned to the other girls. 'Tabbitt said to tell the lot of you to clear out—'

'Clear out?' Cora said. 'Well, I like that! And where are we supposed to go?'

'He didn't say. Just that you was to leave and give Adelaide here some privacy.'

Oh God, Polly thought. *Something's happened, and Mr Dunworthy's here to tell me—*

But it was Sir Godfrey. 'Ah, Viola,' he said, coming into the dressing room. '"Thus she sleeping here is found, on the dank and dirty ground."'

You weren't supposed to find me, she thought frightenedly. 'Sir Godfrey, what are you doing here?' she said, and from down the corridor heard excited whispers.

'Sir Godfrey Kingsman?'

'Yes!'

'Not *the* Sir Godfrey! The actor?'

And the last thing she needed was for the cast to gather around him and insist he stay and see the show. She led him quickly into the dressing room, shut the door and set a chair against it.

'Let me take your hat and coat,' she said, hanging them on the screen. 'Sit down. What are you doing here?'

'I came to find you,' he said, 'a task which has proved somewhat daunting. Your previous employers at Townsend Brothers were under the impression you'd left London, and no one in the troupe has had any news of you for weeks. And to make it yet more difficult, you are performing under a stage name that is, alas, not Viola nor Lady Mary. Luckily, your photograph is displayed outside.'

I knew I should have made Mr Tabbitt take my picture with my bloomers showing instead of my face.

'Miss Laburnum said she'd heard you had become an ARP warden,' Sir Godfrey was saying, 'so I went to any number of ARP posts and St John's units and incidents—'

Incidents? 'Oh, you shouldn't have,' Polly said, looking at him in dismay. Even her disappearing had put him in danger.

'But I had need of you, and it was a chance to play the Great Detective again – a role I had not acted in years. My search led me to the Works Board and a Mrs Sentry, who, alas, had been killed by an oil bomb the week before I arrived, and your file there did not indicate the theatre to which you were assigned. But, as I said, I was able to track you here through your photograph and to confirm that it was you during the performance last night. An impressive theatrical endeavour.'

'I know it's not Shakespeare.'

'But it's not Barrie either, which is a point in its favour, and some parts were very amusing. I quite liked your air-raid alerts, and apparently I was not alone. I'd hoped to catch you afterward at the stage door, but there was such a throng I realised I could not possibly compete, and decided to wait and take a more direct approach.'

He smiled at her, and she realised how much she'd missed him, how much she'd longed to tell him about ENSA and the shows.

But she couldn't. She shouldn't even be sitting here chatting with him.

'Did you have a reason for coming, Sir Godfrey?' she asked briskly. 'I'm afraid I haven't much time, I need to change—'

'Of course. I shall come directly to the point. I am here to ask your assistance with a theatrical endeavour Mrs Wyvern and I are currently putting together.'

'Mrs Wyvern?'

'Yes. You may remember her determination to rebuild St George's and to aid the children of the East End who have lost their parents in the Blitz, or as she refers to them, "our poor, sad, helpless war orphans". To that end, she has determined on a benefit to aid both her ends. A theatrical production—'

'Oh dear,' Polly said. 'Not *Peter Pan*, I hope?'

'Worse. A pantomime.'

She couldn't help smiling. 'But aren't pantomimes usually only at Christmastime?'

'They are – a point I made several times in attempting to dissuade her, but Mrs Wyvern is an extremely formidable woman. An amalgam of Lady Macbeth and—'

'Julius Caesar?'

'A German Panzer,' he said grimly. 'She is impossible to stand against. It's a pity she's not in command of the Army. We'd have defeated Hitler already. In any case, I find myself forced to play the Bad Fairy in *Sleeping Beauty*. Which is why I have come. I wish to enlist you in our enterprise. The others of our little band have already agreed to participate. The rector and Mrs Brightford are to be Sleeping Beauty's parents, Miss Laburnum the Good Fairy, and Nelson the Good Fairy's dog. I want you for the lead.'

'Sleeping Beauty?'

'Great God, no! All she does is lie there for three acts, waiting to be rescued. A *bolster* could play the role. Or a film actress. Mrs Wyvern is attempting to recruit one as we speak.'

'A bolster?'

He smiled. 'No. A film actress. Madeleine Carroll, perhaps, or Vivien Leigh. I want *you* to be the principal boy.'

'Principal boy?'

He nodded. 'Sleeping Beauty's prince. The male lead in pantomime is always played by a girl, and the prince is quite the best role in the play – except for mine, which is rife with Teutonic shouting and violet smoke. You will get to wave a sword about and wear a plumed hat and substantially more clothes than you do as Air-Raid Adelaide. Come, say you'll do it.'

'But surely there are lots of other people you could get, like Lila—'

'She's joined the ATA.'

'Oh. Well, Mrs Brightford, then. Or Vivien Leigh. I'm certain she'd rather play the prince than a bolster.'

'I do not *want* Vivien Leigh. My heart is set on you. You're the only thing that can make dealing with Mrs Wyvern for the next month at all bearable. And you were born to play the part. Viola, dressed as a boy. What could be more perfect?'

Nothing, Polly thought. Being with Sir Godfrey again, and acting with the troupe would be heaven. But it was too dangerous. Even having him here ...

'I can't,' she said. 'ENSA—'

'Can easily spare you for four weeks. I'll gladly arrange for someone to take your place. I know a number of actresses who would jump at the chance to show their knickers to an enthusiastic audience,' he said. 'Or to anyone, for that matter.'

And he would clearly be able to persuade Mr Tabbitt to go along with the plan. The fact that he'd allowed Sir Godfrey backstage proved that.

'If you refuse, there will be no one there to avert the inevitable disaster I foresee,' he said. 'Say yes. You would be saving my life.'

No, Polly thought bitterly, *I would be sealing your doom. And I have no intention of letting you be part of the correction if I can help it.*

'I'm sorry, Sir Godfrey. I can't.'

'The head of ENSA's an old friend of mine. We acted in *Henry V* together. I'm certain he'd be willing to release you from your National Service duty for the duration of the rehearsals and performances.'

Polly looked at him in despair. He did not intend to take no for an answer. He would come back tomorrow and the next night. He would send Mrs Wyvern to convince her. Or worse, Miss Laburnum, or Trot, exposing them all to danger. *And I can't bear that, to see any of them made to pay the price for my sins. Especially not you. I couldn't have survived without you.*

And knew what she had to do. There was only one sure way

to send him away for good, to make certain he wouldn't come back. 'It's not my being in the show,' she said. 'It's ... I didn't want to tell you this, because I was afraid you might ... but I've met a young man. We've been seeing a good deal of each other, and—'

'A young man,' he said slowly. 'Exactly how young?'

'Much younger than—' She stopped and bit her lip as if she had only just realised how cruel that sounded, and then rushed on. 'I only just met him a few weeks ago, here, and his regiment's due to be shipped out any week now, so we haven't much time left—' and that at least was true. There was almost no time left.

'You do understand, don't you? You've been in love, haven't you?'

'Yes,' he said quietly. 'I have.'

He sat there for a long minute, looking at her, his face unreadable. *I did it*, she thought. *I've succeeded in sending him away for good.*

And in hurting him cruelly. I am so sorry, Sir Godfrey, but it's for your own good.

'I *am* sorry,' she said carelessly. 'I'm afraid I've got to go on in a moment.' She bent down and began fastening the gilt strap on her shoe. 'I've got a costume change.'

'Of course,' he said. 'I understand. You mustn't miss your entrance.' He watched her struggle with the stiff strap for a moment, then stood up and, with great care, took his coat down from the screen and turned to go.

I'll never see you again, she thought, keeping her eyes firmly on her shoe.

'Goodbye,' she said without looking up.

He moved the chair aside, put his hand to the doorknob, stood there a moment, and then turned back to face her. 'Have I ever told you what a wretched actress you are, Viola?'

Her heart began to pound. 'I thought you said I was born to be on the stage,' she said, her chin in the air.

'And so I did,' he said, 'but not because you could act. Your acting wouldn't convince Trot. Or Nelson.'

'Well, then it's a good thing I turned down your offer, isn't it?' she said angrily. 'Luckily, ENSA audiences aren't quite so critical.' She reached past him for her railway station costume. 'Now, if you'll forgive me—'

'There is nothing to forgive,' he said, 'except perhaps that unnecessarily unkind reference to my age. But then again, you *were* attempting to send me away—'

And I didn't succeed, Polly thought despairingly.

'—so you may be excused for employing extreme measures. You *are* meant for the stage,' he said, 'but not for your ability to dissemble. Quite the opposite. It is because everything you feel is there in your face – your thoughts, your hopes—'

He looked hard at her. 'Your fears. It's a rare gift – Ellen Terry had it, and, on rare occasions, Sarah Bernhardt – though it is not an unmixed blessing. It makes it quite impossible to lie, as you have so obviously been attempting to do to me for the last quarter of an hour. It is equally obvious you are in some sort of trouble—'

'That's ridiculous,' she said. 'I told you, I've met a young man. We're in love—'

He shook his head. 'Whatever your reason for turning down my offer, it is not some green and callow youth you met outside a stage door. It's also clear this trouble is something you think you must face alone, else why would you hide yourself away from your friends?'

He cocked his head inquisitively at her. 'Perhaps you are right to do so. Illyria is a dangerous place. But silence is not always the best defence.' He looked at her steadily. 'Are you quite certain I can't help?'

No one can help, Polly thought, *and I'm putting you in danger just by standing here talking to you. Please go away. If you love me, please …*

'Two minutes,' Reggie said, sticking his head in the door, and she had never been so glad to see anyone in her life.

'Coming,' she called. 'It was ever so nice to have seen you, Sir Godfrey, but as you can see, I have a show to do—'

'Very well. We shall act the scene as you have written it. You have found young love and have no time for an old man with a foolish fondness for you. And I, heartbroken, shall retire from the field and set about finding another principal boy. Miss Laburnum might look well in tights,' he mused.

'I'm sorry you had to come all this way for nothing,' Polly said, taking her costume off its hanger.

'Oh, but it wasn't for nothing,' he said. 'I learned a good deal. And I found a theatre to house our pantomime. On my way here last night as I came down Shaftesbury Avenue, I saw that the Forrest was standing empty, and I arranged with the owner – an old friend of mine, we did *Lear* together – to let us use it for *Sleeping Beauty*. If you should change your mind ...'

'I won't.'

'If you should change your mind,' he repeated firmly, 'I shall be there both tonight and tomorrow. I will be backstage looking at possible sets and attempting to forestall the disaster that I know is to come. So if your young man should turn out to be a cad and a bounder, and you should reconsider—'

'I'll know where to find you,' she said lightly, stepping behind the screen. 'Now, I'm afraid I really *must* change. Goodbye.' She shrugged off her dressing gown and flung it carelessly over the screen. 'Tell everyone hullo for me, won't you?'

'Yes,' he said, and after a pause, 'my lady.'

And it was a good thing she was behind the screen, that he couldn't see her face, because that was the line from Lady Mary's final scene with Crichton. She had to clutch her costume to her chest to keep from holding her hand impulsively out to him, as Lady Mary had done, to keep from saying, 'I will never give you up.'

She swallowed hard. 'Tell them to break a leg,' she said lightly.

There was no answer, and when she peeked around the screen a long minute later, he was gone. For good. Because that was what that last scene of *The Admirable Crichton* was all about, lovers parting forever. And that was what she'd wanted, wasn't it? What she'd—

The girls came tumbling through the door, grabbing up costumes, plunking down to touch up their make-up. 'No wonder you wouldn't go out with the stage-door hangers-on,' Cora said. 'Clever girl. You had your eyes on something *much* better, didn't you?'

Polly didn't answer. She stepped into her costume and turned to have Hattie do her up.

'What I don't understand is, what are you doing at ENSA?' Hattie asked. 'He could get you a part in a *real* show.'

Reggie leaned in again. 'Curtain.'

Polly hurried onstage, glad to have something to take her mind off Sir Godfrey. When she came off, Mr Tabbitt told her to go and change into her Air-Raid Adelaide costume.

'But what about the barrage balloon skit?'

'Cora can do it,' he said. 'I have a feeling the raids are going to be bad tonight.'

He was right. She'd scarcely had time to get into her bloomers before the sirens went, and it was a bad raid – nearly all HEs. Polly, changing into her nurse's costume for the hospital skit, felt her heart jerk with each one. What if she hadn't sent Sir Godfrey away soon enough?

I shouldn't have talked to him at all, she thought. *I should have shut the door in his face.*

Mr Tabbitt knocked and then leaned in. 'The bombs are making the audience nervy. I need you to do another air-raid bit,' and he sent her out to show her knickers again.

'I don't like this,' Hattie said nervously as Polly came off. 'That last one sounded like it was next door.'

'It was two streets over,' Reggie said, pulling on his general's uniform. 'On Shaftesbury Avenue.'

'How do you know?' Hattie demanded.

'I was outside, smoking a fag, and the warden told me. The Forrest got hit.'

LONDON – MAY 1944

Ernest stared stupidly at Cess across the raised bonnet of the car. 'We're to take Colonel von Sprecht to Kensington Palace?'

'Yes,' Cess said, looking from him to the colonel, still asleep inside the car. 'What's wrong, Worthing?'

Kensington Palace is only two streets away from Notting Hill Gate Station, that's what's wrong. It's only a few streets away from Mrs Rickett's.

'You don't think the colonel will die before we get him there, do you?' Cess asked nervously.

'No,' Ernest said, pulling himself together. 'I thought we were done with him, that's all. Every mile we're in that car with him, there's a chance he'll tumble to what we're doing.'

'Not if we keep our mouths shut,' Cess said. 'There's nothing he can see now to give it away. It was brilliant, your driving while he was asleep so we'd come in from the east. And Kensington Palace isn't far.'

'Where is it exactly? Show me on the map,' Ernest said, hoping it wasn't as close to Notting Hill Gate as Cess had said, but it was. There was a road that went directly to the palace, though. He wouldn't have to drive past the tube station, and with dignitaries like Patton there, civilians wouldn't be allowed anywhere near the palace.

And there wouldn't be any more air raids till after the invasion, so Eileen wouldn't be going to the tube shelter, and the chances of running into her, even in Notting Hill or Kensington, were tiny. *You looked for her and Polly for* weeks *during the Blitz and couldn't find them.*

Right, and you managed to collide with Alan Turing not ten minutes after you'd arrived in Bletchley. And this was the time of day when she could be arriving home from work.

But she wouldn't still be working on Oxford Street. When the National Service Act had gone into effect, she'd have been assigned to some kind of war work. She might not even still be in London.

And if you didn't get them out, you didn't get them out, and seeing Eileen – or not seeing her – doesn't change whether she's here or not, whether you're going to be able to reach Atherton or not. It's already happened.

But he couldn't rid himself of the idea that now, at the very last minute, *this close* to contacting Atherton, he'd ruin things by catching sight of her stepping off a bus or coming down the street in her green coat, and it was a huge relief to turn down the road to the palace, to pull up to the gates.

The guard looked at their papers and said, 'If you'll just pull in there, sir, behind that staff car.' He indicated the last car in a long line stretching all the way to the palace.

'Our passenger's ill. He can't possibly walk that far,' Ernest said. 'We need to take him to the door.'

After examining their papers again and looking in the back seat at the colonel, the guard waved them on, but Ernest wasn't sure they'd make it through the already-parked staff cars and Rolls-Royces. It was like threading a needle. *This is where Churchill or Patton steps out suddenly in front of me and I run over him,* he thought, but they made it safely up to the palace.

He pulled the car up to the foot of the stairs, got out and came around to help the colonel out of the car. It took both of them. Ernest had to hold him up, while Cess got his suitcase out and shut the car door.

'I'm sorry to cause so much trouble,' the colonel said to Ernest, and he felt a sudden pang of pity for him.

You're going to cause them to lose the war, he thought, *and not even know it.*

'Sorry, sir, but you can't park there,' a regimental guard said, hurrying up. 'You'll have to move your car.'

'It's only till we can get the colonel inside,' he said.

'This is Colonel von Sprecht,' Cess said, holding out their papers. 'We've just brought him all the way from Dover. We have orders to deliver him directly to General Moreland.'

But the guard was shaking his head. 'Sorry, sir. You can't leave your car here.'

'Well, then, at least let me run inside and fetch someone to assist Lieutenant Wilkerson,' Ernest said. 'The colonel can't make it up those stairs without assistance.'

'I can't let you do that, sir. Captain's orders. You must move it now.'

'I want to speak to the captain—' Ernest began, but Cess shook his head.

'We can't stand here arguing,' he said. 'I can manage the colonel.' He draped the colonel's arm around his shoulder. 'You go and park the car, Lieutenant Abbott.'

'But—' Ernest began, and Cess nodded towards the top of the steps, where two officers were hurrying down to help. Good. 'Where do you want me to park?' he asked the guard.

'At the end of this road,' he said, pointing, but that end of the narrow lane was packed with cars, too, some with young women in FANY and ATS uniforms at the wheel, waiting for the generals they'd delivered.

Oh Christ, what if one of the drivers was Eileen? She'd talked about trying to get the National Service to assign her to be one.

He glanced in the rear-view mirror. Two more staff cars were pulling in to the lane behind him. It was more dangerous here than out on the streets of Kensington.

He pulled his visored cap down over his forehead and drove as fast as he dared to the end of the lane. Another guard stood there. He came over to the car. 'Sir, you can't stop here.'

'I know. Tell Lieutenant Wilkerson that Lieutenant Abbott's taken the car round the corner to park it.' Then he drove out onto Kensington Road and back along the edge of Kensington Gardens, where they'd been when Polly told them she had a deadline.

Polly. She might be one of the drivers, too, only that wouldn't be her name. It would be Mary Kent, and right now she was at an ambulance post in Oxford, waiting to be transferred to Dulwich, but he knew from the FANYs he'd run into that they were often assigned to driving officers, and it looked like every officer in England was here tonight. What if she was, too?

She can't be, he told himself, *because if she was, you could rap on her window and warn her, and if you warn her, she'll go back to Oxford and tell Mr Dunworthy what happened, and he'd never have let them come through.* Just like with Bartholomew.

It's Atherton you need to concentrate on finding, he thought. *And there's a telephone box. And Cess isn't here.* And Lady Bracknell had sent along a purse full of money in case something went wrong while they had the colonel and they had to phone the castle. He pulled over to the kerb, took the purse out of the glove compartment and got out of the car. He went into the telephone box, dialled the operator and gave her the number the Wren had told him. 'Just one moment, please,' the operator said.

Let it go through, let it go through, he repeated silently.

'I have that number for you, sir,' she said.

'Yes, hullo, is Major Atherton there?' he said.

Too quickly. It was still the operator. 'I have your number for you, sir,' she repeated. 'I'll connect you.'

He waited, thinking, *Any second now I'll see Cess turning that corner, wondering where the hell I've got to.* 'You're through, sir,' the operator said, and in the next instant, an American woman's voice said, 'Major Atherton's office.'

Thank God. 'Hullo,' he said, trying to keep the excitement out of his voice, 'I need to speak to Major Atherton.'

'I'm sorry, sir, he's not here right now.'

Of course not. 'When will he be back? It's urgent.'

'I don't know, sir. I can have him ring you as soon as he returns. Is there a number where he can reach you?'

'No,' he said, 'I'm in transit. Will he be back tonight?'

'Yes, sir. Do you wish to try again later?'

No. I need to talk to him now.

'Yes,' he said. 'And tell him I called. Tell him Michael Da—'

'I *never*,' a boy's voice said, and he looked up sharply. A boy and a girl were coming down the street towards the telephone box. The boy was nine or ten, and the girl older. They were arguing loudly.

'You did *so*,' the girl said.

'I didn't nick it,' the boy said. 'She give it me.'

Oh God, he thought, *it's Alf and Binnie Hodbin.*

They hadn't seen him yet, they were so busy arguing. He had to get out of here. He hung up and was out of the telephone box and back in the car in a flash. He snatched up the map Cess had left on the seat and opened it out to shield him from them.

'I *seen* you,' Binnie said.

Oh Jesus.

'You did *not*,' Alf said.

They weren't talking about him. They were talking about whatever it was that Alf had nicked. But his relief was short-lived. Because there was only one reason they'd be here, this far from the East End. They were on their way to see Eileen, or on their way home from seeing her. Which meant she was still here. And if he didn't get out of here, Alf and Binnie would see him, they'd tell Eileen he was alive, that he'd gone off and abandoned them.

He reached to turn the key in the ignition, but they were already even with the car. They'd hear the engine start and look over and see him. He'd have to wait till they were past.

'I'm going to tell,' Binnie said.

'You better not!' Alf said, and then, 'Look!'

Oh Christ. They were running right at the car. He'd have to convince them he was Lieutenant Abbott and that he had no idea who this Mike Davis was. But when had anybody ever been able to put anything over on the Hodbins?

They ran straight past the car into the road. He peeked cautiously over the map. A staff car pulled up and stopped. The children ran up to the car window.

Oh Christ, he'd been right about Eileen being a driver.

'Where's Mum?' Alf asked.

Mum?

'She's going to be late,' a woman's voice – not Eileen's – said. Ernest slid up on the seat to where he could see the children leaning in to talk to a blonde in an ATS cap and uniform. And now that his adrenalin wasn't raging, he saw what he hadn't before, that both children were wearing school uniforms and carrying satchels, and that their hair, or at least the girl's, was neatly combed. They looked much too well cared for to be Alf and Binnie, in spite of the similarity in looks, in their voices.

'Your mother had to drive General Bates to Chartwell for a meeting,' the blonde said, and from what Eileen had told him about Mrs Hodbin, he couldn't imagine her driving anyone anywhere, and certainly not a general. 'She told me to pick you two up and give you some supper.'

'Can we go to Lyons' Corner House?' the boy asked.

'We'll see,' the blonde said. 'She also said to see that you did your lessons.'

'We haven't any,' the boy said. 'We done 'em all at school.' He turned to the girl. 'Didn't we?'

'Don't be a noddlehead,' the girl said. "'e's got spelling, and I've got maths. But I've done my 'istory lesson.' She pulled a paper out of her book bag to show the blonde.

The Alf and Binnie he'd seen that morning at St Paul's would never have done lessons in their life. Or have voluntarily gone to school.

It wasn't them. He'd jumped to that conclusion because he'd been thinking about Eileen. He'd broken off his call to Denys Atherton for nothing, damn it. He watched the children, whoever they were, pile into the car, waiting for it to drive away so he could go and telephone again. He'd have to tell the woman he'd talked to that he'd been cut off. Maybe the interruption would turn out to be a good thing, and Atherton might be back by now; he'd be able to talk to him instead of leaving a message.

The car rounded the corner and was gone. Ernest got out of the car and started over to the telephone box. And there was Cess, trotting towards him, waving. 'They told me you'd come over here to park,' he said, coming up to him.

'Did you hand the colonel over?'

'Yes,' Cess said, 'now all I have to do is report in to Lady Bracknell, and we're free to go home.'

If only that were true, Ernest thought, watching Cess as he went into the telephone box to call Bracknell. How was he going to call Atherton now? He might not have a chance to get away on his own for days, and he was running out of time.

'No luck,' Cess said, coming out. 'I couldn't get through.'

'We can try again on the way home,' Ernest said. *And next time I'll see to it I'm the one who makes the call.* 'An hour or two won't make any difference now that the colonel's been safely handed over.' He got into the car.

'Right,' Cess said. 'It was a near thing, though.'

'A near thing? What do you mean?'

'After I'd handed him over and was leaving, who should I run into but Old Blood and Guts—'

'General Patton?'

'None other,' Cess said. 'He looked straight at me, and I could tell he was trying to place me, and I was afraid he was about to remember he'd seen me at the reception and shout out "Holt!" in that carrying voice of his. But luckily his aide came up just then and dragged him off, and I was able to get away with the colonel none the wiser.'

'And Patton didn't see you with him?'

'No, and I'm fairly certain he didn't remember where he'd seen me. But the sooner we're out of here, the safer I'll feel,' he said.

'My sentiments exactly.' Ernest started the car and pulled away from the kerb.

'Besides, I'm starving,' Cess said. 'Turn right. I know a little place on Lampden Road that has— Where are you going? That's the wrong way.'

'I know,' Ernest said, racing through Notting Hill. 'I just thought of something. If we hurry, we can make it to Croydon before the *Call* closes and I can turn in my pieces.'

'Croydon?' Cess yelped. 'That's *miles*, and I'm starved!'

'There's a good pub there. Excellent shepherd's pie,' he said, even though he'd never set foot in the place. 'And a very pretty barmaid.' *And a telephone box down the road from the* Call *where I can call Atherton from while you're in the pub.*

'I thought you said the *Call*'s deadline was at five.'

'It is, but the editor's sometimes there late, and if he hasn't finished setting the type, I may be able to persuade him to put my articles in.'

He shot through Notting Hill and turned onto the road south.

'What about Lady Bracknell?' Cess asked. 'We were to report in.'

'We can do it from Croydon. After we eat. If we phone him now, he'll tell us to come straight home, and then you'll really be starving.'

'All right,' Cess said, 'but if he loses his temper, you have to tell him this was your idea.'

'I will. Thanks. It's important I not miss this deadline.'

Cess nodded, and then, after a minute, said, 'Do you really think the German High Command reads the Croydon *Fish and Chips Wrapper* or whatever it is?'

'The *Clarion Call*,' he said. 'I don't know. But we don't know that they're listening to our wireless messages either, or taking aerial photos of our cardboard camps and rubber tanks. *Or* that Colonel von Sprecht actually bought our little charade. Or even if he did, that he'll tell the German High Command. Or that they'll believe him.'

Cess nodded. 'The poor devil might not even live long enough to make it to Berlin.' He sighed. 'That's the hell of doing this sort of thing. We never know whether anything we've done has had any effect at all.'

And perhaps we're better off not *knowing,* Ernest thought, speeding through Fulham.

'Will we find out after the war, do you think?' Cess asked. 'Whether it worked or not?'

'If it didn't work, we won't have to wait that long. We'll know next month. If the entire German Army's waiting for us in Normandy, then it didn't.'

'True,' Cess said, and after a minute, he added, 'History will sort it all out, I suppose. Will we make it into the history books, do you think? Von Sprecht and our encounter with that bull and all your letters to the editor of the *Bumpkin Weekly Banner*?'

If I can't get through to Atherton, those letters to the editor had better, Ernest thought, driving into Croydon. He turned off the High Street so Cess wouldn't spot the telephone box and drove past the *Call*'s office.

Mr Jeppers' bicycle stood outside it. Ernest had been lying to Cess about being able to make it to Croydon before the *Call* closed. He hadn't expected the office to be open this late, but the printing press must have jammed again. Which meant he really *might* be able to get his articles in this week's paper.

'I'll drop you at the pub,' he told Cess, stopping in front of it, 'and I'll go and deliver my articles. It may take some time. Mr Jeppers likes to talk. Order for me,' he said, and drove back to the telephone box.

The operator put him through immediately, and the same young woman answered. 'This is Lieutenant Davies,' Ernest said, 'General Dunworthy's aide. I telephoned earlier this afternoon, but we were cut off.'

'Oh yes,' she said.

'I need to speak with Major Atherton.'

'Oh dear, he came back, but he's gone out again.'

Damn.

'Is it a medical emergency? This is his nurse. If it's an emergency, I can try to contact Dr Atherton.'

Dr Atherton. He was a doctor. Which meant he wasn't Denys. Historians posed as lots of things, but there were no subliminals for medicine. Even Polly's driving an ambulance had been unusual, and all she'd had was emergency first-aid training. Which she'd done here. There was no way Atherton could have got a medical degree here since February.

'Sir?' she said. 'Are you still there?'

'Yes. I think I may have the wrong Major Atherton. I'm trying to contact Major *Denys* Atherton.'

'Yes, sir. That's Major Atherton's name.'

'Tall man, dark curly hair, mid-twenties?'

'Oh no, sir. Major Atherton's fifty and has scarcely any hair at all. Is your Major Atherton an Army surgeon, too?'

No, he thought grimly. *He's a historian, and he's not here under his own name.* Dunworthy would have insisted Research run a check on the names of everyone involved in the invasion build-up. Two soldiers with the same name would automatically attract attention, and historians were supposed to blend in, to avoid being noticed.

There's no way you'll be able to find him if he's here under another name, Ernest thought. He'd always known it was a long shot, but the knowledge still hit him with the force of a punch to the gut. He hung up the receiver and then just stood there.

I should go and deliver the messages to Mr Jeppers, he thought. *It's even more important now that I get them into the* Call. But he continued to stand there, staring blindly at the telephone.

Cess was knocking on the telephone-box door.

Oh Christ, he hadn't just messed up rescuing Polly and Eileen, he'd been caught by Cess. He'd demand to know who he was phoning and why he'd lied about delivering the articles. He'd tell Lady Bracknell, and Bracknell would tell Tensing, and they'd have to cancel Fortitude South. They couldn't take a chance that a German agent had infiltrated Special Means. And Eisenhower would postpone the invasion and try to come up with a new plan. And they'd lose the war.

Cess was still banging on the glass. Ernest opened the door. 'Oh good,' Cess said. 'You remembered to phone Bracknell. I was going to tell you to, and then I forgot, so I came after you. You were right about their barmaid. *Very* pretty. What did Bracknell say? Were you able to reach him?'

'No,' Ernest said. 'I wasn't able to get through.'

LONDON – SPRING 1941

Polly ran out of the Alhambra and through the firelit streets to Shaftesbury Avenue, and into dense fog.

No, not fog. Dust from the explosion. It smelled of sulphur and cordite and was completely impenetrable. *I'll never find the Forrest in this*, she thought, but as she felt her way forward, it began to thin and she could see the theatre's marquee. Reggie must have been wrong – it was still standing.

But the street in front of it was roped off. And as she came closer, she saw that half of the theatre's front was missing, exposing the lobby and the gold-carpeted staircase. An officer in a white helmet was standing next to the blue incident light, peering at a clipboard. Polly ducked under the rope and ran over to him. 'Officer—'

'This is an incident,' he said brusquely, 'no civilians allowed.'

'But I'm looking for—'

He cut her off. 'The theatre was standing empty. I must ask you to leave. Warden!' He beckoned to an ARP warden. 'Escort this young lady—'

'But there's someone inside,' she said. 'Sir God—'

'Officer Murdoch!' another warden called from up the street. 'Quick!' and the incident officer hurried off.

Polly started after him, but so did the warden he'd called to have her thrown out, and she was afraid he'd do it before she could explain. And even if he'd listen, they obviously had their hands full.

She darted across the street and climbed over the heap of wood and plaster that had been the front of the theatre and into the lobby. Scarcely any damage had been done to it. The bomb must only have been a hundred-pounder, in spite of its loudness. She tried to open the double doors to the theatre proper, but they were locked.

The mezzanine doors weren't. She slipped through them.

Into chaos. The balcony and boxes had collapsed onto the rows of red-plush seats below, and the seats themselves were piled atop one another as though tossed there by a wave. The walls still stood, and there was still a ceiling except for a large, jagged hole on one side. Through it, the fiery sky lit this part of the theatre with a pinkish-orange light. The front part of the theatre and the stage lay in shadow.

'Sir Godfrey! Are you in here?' Polly called and started carefully across the sea of openwork metal supports and cushions spilling out stuffing and splintered mahogany from the balcony. Some of the rows of seats were still intact and upright, discarded theatre programmes still on the red plush seats. But they were unstable, threatening to topple as Polly walked across them, grabbing for seat backs as she worked her way forward, and her shoes made it worse.

I have no business trying to do this in high-heeled shoes, she thought, stepping carefully over a curved panel which had been part of one of the theatre boxes.

Sir Godfrey had said he'd be backstage, looking at sets. She looked out across the jumble of upended seats, seeking something that would tell her when she'd reached the stage – a footlight or a curtain or a fallen catwalk – but there was nothing beyond the rows of tangled seats except what looked like a huge blanket, as if the rescue squad had covered the site with a tarpaulin to hide the wreckage.

As if it were a dead body, Polly thought, and realised what the tarpaulin was. The asbestos safety curtain. It had collapsed backwards, draping the entire stage. *At least it can't catch fire*, she thought, but if Sir Godfrey was under it, there was no way she'd be able to lift it off him. The one at the Alhambra weighed a ton.

She started towards the shrouded stage, calling, 'Sir Godfrey! Where are you?', and stepping gingerly from seat to seat as if onto stepping-stones. She remembered the governess at the pantomime telling her charges, 'No, no, you mustn't stand on the seats. You'll tear the cloth,' and even as she thought it, her gilt heel went through the plush upholstery, her ankle twisted and she fell sideways.

She grabbed for the back of the chair, which threatened to go over, steadied herself, and attempted to free her foot. The heel was caught on something, one of the springs. She jerked her leg sharply upward, but it wouldn't budge.

'Blast these heels,' she said, and tried to tear the upholstery further so she could see what she was caught on, but it was much stronger than it looked. She would have to take off the shoe. She tried to slide her foot out of it. No good. She bent awkwardly over to unstrap it. The stiff buckle wouldn't budge either, and she bent over further, struggling with it.

And heard a faint sound from the direction of the balcony. 'Sir Godfrey?' she called, and thought she heard an answering groan. 'I'm coming!' she said, 'My shoe—' She yanked viciously up on the end of the gilt strap. It came away in her hand, and she pulled her foot out of the shoe and reached back into the seat's stuffing for it, wrenching the shoe from side to side to free it. It wouldn't come.

'Hang on! I'm coming!' she called, abandoning the shoe, and

scrambled back towards where the sound had come from. 'Sir Godfrey?'

'Here,' a man's voice answered so faintly she couldn't tell if it was Sir Godfrey's.

'Are you injured?' she called, moving in its direction. 'Keep talking so I can find you!'

'"Here I lie and thus I bear my point. Four rogues in buckram let drive at me,"' he said. And it was most certainly Sir Godfrey. Who else would quote Shakespeare at a time like this?

He was only four rows back, under a tumble of seats. She could see his arm in the space between them. 'Sir Godfrey,' she said, squatting down, but it was too dark under there to see him. 'Is that you?'

'Yes. As you can see, my attempt to avert disaster was unsuccessful.'

'What are you doing out here in the theatre? I thought you'd be backstage.' She was babbling in her relief that he was alive. 'If I hadn't caught my shoe, I'd never have heard you.' And as she said it, something echoed in the back of her brain: Eileen saying at Padgett's, 'If Marjorie hadn't told you where I was,' saying, 'If Alf and Binnie hadn't delayed me, I'd have caught Mr Bartholomew.'

Polly stopped, struck by the sudden sense that this was important, that it held the key to something if she could—

'I heard the bombs,' Sir Godfrey said, 'and was on my way to find you.'

And if you hadn't done that, she thought with that same sense of being on the verge of something vital, *you'd have been underneath that asbestos fire curtain when it came crashing down.*

'I was worried that you ...' Sir Godfrey began.

'You mustn't worry. Everything's going to be all right. Can you move?'

'No. There's something on my legs. All the world's a stage, and at the moment it seems to be on top of me.'

'Can you feel your legs? Are they injured?'

'No.'

Thank goodness. 'Are you injured anywhere else?'

'No.' The pause again. '"Who would have thought the old man to have had so much blood in him?"'

Oh God.

'I'll have you out of there in a minute.' She raised her head and shouted, 'There's an injured man in here! We need a stretcher!' She stood up and began pulling the seats off him. The row of seats had broken apart, which was a good thing. If they'd still been connected, she'd never have been able to shift them.

Sir Godfrey murmured something. 'What is it?' she asked, crouching down to hear.

'Leave me,' he said. 'Go and find Viola. She's at the Alhambra. The bombs—'

'I'm here, Sir Godfrey. It's me, Polly— Viola.'

'No,' he said. '"Thou art a soul in bliss. You do me wrong to take me out o' the grave."'

He's only quoting Lear, she told herself fiercely. *It doesn't mean anything.*

'Don't try to move,' she said, looking back towards the doors. 'Help's coming.' But it wasn't; there was no sign of the incident officer or rescue workers.

They didn't hear me, she thought, and cupped her hands around her mouth. 'There's an injured man in here! We need a stretcher and a jack! Hurry!' She went back to shifting the seats, and then a piece of the balcony.

Oh God, it was too heavy to lift. She put both hands against the end and gave a mighty shove, and there he was, a foot below her in a narrow hole, lying on his back across a row of upended seat backs, his legs under a piece of the balcony that she could see at a glance was far too heavy for her to lift.

'" She lives",' he said, smiling up at her. '"If it be so, it is a chance which does redeem all sorrows that ever I have felt."'

Polly bit back tears. 'Where are you hurt?' she asked, but

she could already see. A black stain covered the top half of his shirt.

She stretched out over the edge of the hole so she could reach down to the wound. He didn't flinch, but her hand came away wet. She tore open his shirt. The wound was an inch wide and above his heart, but it was bleeding badly, and there was no way to put a tourniquet on it. And no time to go for help. By the time she clambered back over the wreckage to the front of the theatre, he'd have bled to death. She needed to stop the bleeding now.

Direct pressure. She replaced the torn shirt over the wound and pressed down with the palm of her hand while she looked about for something better. His coat – no, it was twisted under him so she couldn't get at it. The upholstery from the seat cushions might work, but she knew from trying to free her foot that it was too tough to tear.

If that woman at the Works Bureau had let me become a rescue worker, she thought, *I'd have had a medical kit and bandages with me.*

She hoisted herself to her knees and wrenched off her skirt. 'Help! Casualty over here!' she shouted, folding it into a not-nearly-thick-enough compress.

ENSA's costumes are much too skimpy, she thought, wriggling out of her bolero and bloomers and folding all three into a thick square. She stretched out flat again, clad only in the bathing suit, laid the pad against the wound, and pressed down as hard as she could with the heel of her hand. Sir Godfrey grimaced. 'Did you come to tell me you've decided to do the pantomime after all?' he asked.

'Shh,' Polly said, 'you mustn't try to talk.'

'Nonsense. How else shall I do my death scene?'

Her heart twisted. 'You're not dying,' she said firmly. 'It's only a flesh wound.'

'You always were a wretched actress, Viola,' he said, shaking his head against the timbers he lay on. 'This isn't quite the farewell I'd imagined. I'd always hoped to die onstage. Halfway through the second act of a Barrie play so I would be spared from doing Act Three.'

He could always make her laugh, even here in the rubble with him bleeding to death and no sign of a rescue squad. *What's taking them so long?* she thought. *They're as bad as the retrieval team.*

Blood was soaking through the compress. She wasn't applying enough pressure. She inched forward, trying to get into a better position, and pushed down as hard as she could on it.

'Which speech will you have?' Sir Godfrey asked. 'Hamlet? "There's a divinity that shapes our ends, rough-hew them how we will."'

No, it isn't a divinity. I caused this. But he's not going to die if I can help it, she thought, pressing down with all the force she could muster. The continuum was going to have to correct itself some other way.

She raised her head and shouted for help again, trying to remember everything Sir Godfrey had taught her about projecting to the very back of the stalls. 'In here! Help!' And, as if in answer there was the sound of planes in the distance.

'They're coming round again,' Sir Godfrey said, looking up at the ceiling, 'You must get to a shelter—'

'I'm not leaving without you.'

'You must, Viola. Your young man would never forgive me if I got you killed.'

Her young man. 'I lied to you back there at the theatre,' she said. 'There's no young man.'

'Of course there is. He's why I never had the ghost of a chance with you,' he said, and after a minute, he asked, 'Was he killed?'

'I think he must have been, or he'd have come by now.'

'He may yet come,' Sir Godfrey said gently. 'Which is why you must go, Miranda. "Fly, Fleance, fly".'

She shook her head. '"If it be not now, yet it will come. The readiness is all."'

'Shakespeare!' he said contemptuously. 'I have always *loathed* actors who quote the Bard. "Go, get you gone, foul varlet." I *will not* have your death on my hands.'

'You have it the wrong way round,' she said bitterly. 'This is *my* fault. I did this to you.'

'I fail to see how, unless you abandoned your air-raid duties with ENSA and enlisted in the Luftwaffe within the last hour. I fear the guilt is mine. I shouldn't have come to ask you to be in the pantomime,' he said, and then murmured, as if to himself, 'I should have told Greenberg yes. I should have gone to Bristol.'

He closed his eyes in pain. '"We are not the first who with best meaning have incurred the worst."'

'No, we're not,' she said. 'None of us meant to do any harm.'

But Sir Godfrey wasn't listening to her. 'What's that?' he asked, moving his head slightly as if trying to catch a sound. 'I thought I heard something.'

'The planes seem to be moving away,' she said, but he shook his head, still with that attentive look. She raised her head, straining to catch the clang of ambulance bells, of voices.

The raiders' drone faded away, but she still couldn't hear anything except a creak as a piece of the wreckage gave. And the faint hiss of escaping gas.

And why had she ever thought she stood a chance against the entire space-time continuum? Why had she ever believed she could save Sir Godfrey's life, could stop history in its blind attempt to correct itself?

I am so sorry, Sir Godfrey, she thought. *I am so sorry, Colin*, and she must be crying. Hot drops were splashing on the back of her hand, onto the compress, onto Sir Godfrey's already soaked chest.

'"Boy, why are you crying?"' he said, and at any other time that line from the play he most despised would have made her laugh, but not now. Not now.

'Because I couldn't save' – her voice broke – 'your life.'

'What?' he said, and his voice held some of its old strength. '"You lie! Thrice now hast thou plucked me from the jaws of death. And in repayment of that solemn debt, would I save your life now."'

She no longer knew what play he was quoting from, but it didn't matter. *You can't save it*, she thought. *We're both done for.* And she remembered the man looking up at the incendiary halfway up St Paul's dome saying, 'She's done for.'

But it hadn't been, The fire watch had saved it. And it might look as though they were done for, but she didn't have to put out twenty-eight incendiaries, didn't have to *keep* putting them out night after night. All she had to do was keep Sir Godfrey alive and conscious till help came.

'We shall never give in,' she murmured, 'never surrender,' and bent over the hole to see if she could do something to stop the gas.

The hiss was louder from the left. She told Sir Godfrey to turn his head to the right and to breathe shallowly, wishing she'd obeyed all those government directives to 'Carry your gas mask with you at all times,' and tried to pinpoint the source of the gas. It was coming from a narrow gap between two of the seats. If she could block the gap with something ...

All that was left of her costume was the bathing suit. It wouldn't be enough to fill the space, and at any rate, she didn't think she could wriggle out of it with only one hand free. And she couldn't go and fetch something. He'd begin bleeding again. But she had to block the space up somehow, and quickly, before the gas rendered him unconscious.

If it hadn't already. 'Sir Godfrey?'

'What is it?' His voice was already drowsy, blurred.

You need to keep him talking, she thought.

'Sir Godfrey, you asked me which speech I wanted. Do the one from that first night we acted together – Prospero's speech. "Our revels now are ended—"' she prompted.

'My dear, our revels now *are* ended,' he said.

'I still want to hear it. "These our actors—"'

'"These our actors,"' he said, '"as I foretold you, were all spirits ..."'

Good, that should keep him going for a bit, she thought, looking around for something to fill the gap with. The stuffing from a seat would do it, but all of the seats within her reach were intact, with the playbills still lying on them.

The playbills. Keeping her right hand clamped down on Sir Godfrey's chest, she shimmied carefully backwards and reached behind and around for them with her free hand.

They weren't booklets. They were only single sheets. *The bloody paper shortage,* she thought, wadding them up and pushing them into the space one after the other. She could smell the gas now.

'"Are melted into air, into thin air,"' Sir Godfrey said, '"and like ..."' His voice trailed off.

'"And like the baseless fabric,"' she prompted, stretching her arm out again, this time in front of her.

'"And like the baseless fabric of this vision,"' Sir Godfrey said. '"the cloud-capp't towers, the gorgeous palaces ..."'

The tips of her fingers touched something wide and flat. A piece of wood, or plaster. She leaned further forward, stretching her arm out till it hurt, but it wasn't enough to do more than touch it.

Of course not, she thought, trying from another angle. *This is the correction,* and felt something shift under her hand. It was a snapped-off piece of one of the openwork chair supports, too small to cover the space, even if it had been solid. But large enough that it might bring the chunk of wood within reach.

She jabbed the end awkwardly into the wood, like a fork, and dragged it towards her till it was close enough to grasp. She let go of the support so she could grab the wood and then thought better of it and laid the support on Sir Godfrey's chest while she picked it up.

'"And like this unsubstantial pageant faded,"' he murmured, '"leave not a wrack behind."'

She shoved the wood up tight against the space the gas was issuing from. It wasn't a perfect fit, but it should stop most of it.

I hope, she thought. When she leaned down to jam it more tightly against the space, she could still smell gas. Which meant they *must* get out of here.

But at least she had bought them a bit of time. She resumed feeling about the space next to the hole, this time for another chair support, or something else metal.

A piece of pipe, sticking out of the debris. *The gas line?* she wondered. She picked the openwork support up off Sir Godfrey's chest.

He was still reciting Prospero's speech. '"We are such stuff as dreams are made on,"' he said, '"and our little life is rounded with a sleep."'

She began banging on the pipe with the support as hard as she could. The metal made an unholy racket, loud even over the drone of the planes, which seemed to be coming round again. In between clangs she shouted, 'Help!' and 'In here!'

'Someone *must* have heard that,' she said, pausing to rest a moment to make certain she was still pressing down on the compress hard enough. 'Don't you think, Sir Godfrey?'

He didn't answer.

'Sir Godfrey!' she said urgently.

'Cheer up, my lady. Things ...' His voice trailed into silence.

'Sir *Godfrey*!' she cried, casting desperately around for something, anything, to keep him talking, 'you quoted a line about my saving your life. Which play was that?'

'Tell you after the all-clear ... ,' he said drowsily.

'*No!* Now. Which play was it?' She couldn't reach his shoulder to shake it, didn't dare move her hand from the compress. 'One of Barrie's?'

'*Barrie's?* It was *Twelfth Night*. A knock on the door and there you were ... shipwrecked ... the letter ...' His voice trailed away.

'What letter?' she said, even though there was no letter, he was making no sense, but she had to keep him talking. 'Who was the letter from? Sir Godfrey?'

'An old friend ... we'd played together in *A Midsummer Night's Dream* when we were young ...'

'Do Oberon's speech,' she urged him. '"I know a bank where the wild thyme grows,"' but he went on as if he hadn't heard her.

'He wrote ... to offer me the lead in a touring company,' he said after a minute, his voice drowsy and slow again, ' ... Bath ... and Bristol ... but then you came ...'

'And you didn't go.'

'And leave fair Viola?' he murmured, and then, barely audible, '... you knew all your lines ...'

She realised now that, even now – digging him out, trying to stop the blood, she had still harboured a secret hope that this was not part of the continuum's attempts to correct the damage they'd done, that it was, as he'd said, the Luftwaffe's fault and not hers. But he was supposed to have gone with the touring company, he was supposed to have left London. He'd stayed because of her.

'I am so sorry,' she said.

The stench of gas was growing stronger. She should see if she could find something else to stuff into the gap, a playbill or a newspaper. There were some in the lending library at Holborn. No, that was too far away.

'... killed ...' Sir Godfrey said from a long way away. Her seat must be at the very back of the stalls, but that couldn't be right, because he was saying, 'Viola! Awake, fair maid! I hear our rescuers at hand.'

'"It is the nightingale,"' she murmured. '"We shall sing like two birds i' the cage ..."'

'*No*,' Sir Godfrey said furiously, 'it is the *lark*. The rescue team is coming—'

'They didn't come in time,' she said, and laid her head on the rubble and composed herself to sleep, though her hand still pressed down firmly on the compress. 'Not in time.'

IMPERIAL WAR MUSEUM, LONDON – 7 MAY 1995

'W hat on earth are you doing here, Connor?' the woman said. He couldn't see more than her outline in the pitch-darkness of the blackout exhibit, but it must be the fortyish-something woman whom he'd seen unloading things from her car and then going into the museum when he first arrived, though she was far too young to be Merope.

And Merope wouldn't have called you Connor, he thought, *so this woman's clearly mistaken you for someone else.* 'I'm afraid you've—' he began, but she was plunging eagerly on.

'I saw you going into the exhibit, and I thought, that *has* to be Connor Cross.'

Oh God, he thought, *it's Ann*. 'I'm sorry, you've mistaken me for someone else,' he said firmly, thanking God the room was dark. 'I'm not—'

'You don't remember me, do you?' she said. 'Ann Perry? We met at the British Library, years ago. We were both doing research on British Intelligence in World War II. It was in 1980, just after they'd released all the classified documents. You were looking for an agent who'd rescued downed fliers – I don't re-member his name, Commander Something—'

Commander Harold.

'—and I was researching the false articles they'd put in the newspapers to convince Hitler the invasion was going to be at Calais,' she said.

And you showed me an announcement in the Croydon Clarion Call *of May 1944,* he thought, *which read, 'Mr and Mrs James Townsend of Upper Notting announce the engagement of their daughter Polly to Flight Officer Colin Templer of the 21st Airborne Division, currently stationed in Kent. A late June wedding is planned.'*

It's because of you that I found Michael Davies, he thought, *that I'm here looking for someone who worked with Polly.*

But he couldn't say that. 'I—' he began, but she was still talking.

'I designed this exhibition for the museum,' she said, putting her arm in his. 'I came this morning to make certain there weren't any last-minute muck-ups, and I'm so glad I did. It gives me the chance to tell you that you were responsible for my deciding to specialise in the history of World War II,' she went on, leading him along the white arrows towards the exit curtain. 'I had the most awful crush on you, but you were completely oblivious.'

No, I wasn't.

'I was convinced you must already have a girlfriend—'

I did.

'—or that you had some sort of tragic secret.' She pushed the curtain aside, and the light beyond spilled into the room where they were standing, revealing the chopped-off bonnet of a bus with shuttered headlamps. And Ann.

She was as pretty as ever, even though it had been fifteen years, but he couldn't say that either.

'And I was determined to find out what your secret was—' She smiled up at him and then stopped, appalled, and jerked her hand away from his arm. 'Oh, I'm terribly sorry,' she said, blushing. 'I thought you were someone I knew. You must think me a complete fool.'

'Not at all,' he said. 'I've done the same thing myself.'

'It's only that you look exactly like—' she said, frowning bewilderedly at him. 'You're certain you're not Connor Cross? No, of course you're not. Fifteen years ago you'd have been, what, eight years old?'

'Ten,' he said. But it hadn't been fifteen years ago. It had been five, and they'd both been twenty. He extended his hand. 'Calvin Knight. I'm a reporter for *Time Out*. I'm here to write an article on the exhibition.'

'How do you do, Mr Knight,' she said, turning pink again. 'You haven't a much older brother who looks just like you, have you? Or an uncle?'

'No, sorry.'

'Or a portrait of yourself stashed away somewhere, like Dorian Grey?'

'No. You designed this blackout exhibit?' he asked to change the subject.

'Yes, the entire Blitz exhibition, actually,' and he was afraid she'd offer to give him a tour, but she said, 'I'd show you round, but I have a meeting at the British Museum. I'm doing an intelligence-war exhibition for them in August which you'd be interested in, about Fortitude South and the deception campaign—' She stopped, looking embarrassed all over again. 'No, you wouldn't. I am *so* sorry. I keep forgetting you're not Connor. You look *exactly* like him.'

'I'm sure it will be a very interesting exhibition. I'll certainly come,' he lied. He couldn't run the risk of running into her again. Ann had been a very bright girl. He might not be able to fool her twice.

'You're very kind,' she said. 'I hope my idiotic behaviour won't influence your review of the Blitz exhibition.'

'It won't, I promise.'

'Good. Again, I *am* sorry,' she apologised and hurried off before he could say anything, which was probably just as well – though he wished there was some way he could thank her for having given him the clue he'd spent the previous five years looking for. And for producing this exhibition so he could, hopefully, find the next one.

Which he needed to get on with. But he stood there in the dark for several minutes, looking at blackness, remembering those long months spent in the reading room searching for some clue as to where Michael Davies and Merope were, for some hope that Polly wasn't dead. Ann had talked to him, asked him about his research, commiserated with him over the clumsy microfilm readers and the faulty heaters. She'd brought him sandwiches and contraband cups of tea and cheered him up, especially after he'd found the notice of an unidentified man who'd been killed by an HE on September tenth, the day Mr Dunworthy had attempted to go through to.

That had been a black day, and Ann, seeing him sitting there, staring blindly at the microfilm screen, had insisted he come out with her for supper and 'a stiff drink' and then had held his head when he vomited in the pub's loo. *I couldn't have done it without you,* he called silently after her.

And you still haven't done it, he thought. *You still haven't found Polly, or anyone who knew her, and it's already half past ten.* And Cynthia Camberley and the rest were probably already halfway through the exhibition by now.

He hurried into the next room. There were sandbags piled along the walls, a door with an air-raid-shelter symbol on it, and next to it a mannequin in an ARP helmet and overalls holding a stirrup pump. The muffled sounds of sirens and bombs came from inside the shut door. The other three walls of the room were lined with display cases. Lt Camberley was looking at one filled with ration books and wartime recipes. 'Do you remember those dreadful powdered eggs?' she was asking the woman in the flowered hat.

'Yes, and Spam. I haven't been able to look at a tin since.'

He went over to them, pretending to look at the display. 'What's that?' he asked, pointing at a loaf of mouldy-looking grey bread.

'Lord Woolton's National Wheatmeal Bread,' Camberley said, making a face. 'It tasted of ashes. It's my personal opinion that Hitler was behind the recipe.'

'Can I quote you on that?' he asked, pulling out his notebook. He introduced himself, then asked them their impressions of the exhibit and what they'd done in the war.

'I drove an ambulance,' Camberley said. It was difficult to imagine her being tall enough to see over the steering wheel.

'In the Blitz?' he asked.

'No, during the V-rocket attacks. I was stationed at Dulwich.'

Dulwich. That was near Croydon, which meant she might have known Polly, but that was no help. He needed someone who'd known her later, or rather, earlier, after she went to the Blitz. 'Did you drive an ambulance as well?' he asked Herbaceous Border, whose name tag read, 'Margaret Fortis'.

'No, nothing so glamorous, I'm afraid. I spent the Blitz cutting sandwiches and pouring tea. I worked in a WVS canteen in one of the Underground shelters,' she explained. 'They're supposed to have a replica here.' She looked vaguely about.

'Which station?' he asked, trying not to sound too eager. If it was the one Polly had used as a shelter, there was a chance she might have known her.

'Marble Arch,' she said. Marble Arch had been hit, so that didn't help.

'You're interested in the Blitz?' Camberley asked.

'Yes, my grandmother was in London during the Blitz.' *Forgive me, Polly*, he thought. 'And I was hoping to find some-one who knew her.'

'What did she do?'

'I don't know. She died before I was born. I know she worked at Townsend Brothers during the first part of the Blitz and then did some sort of war work, and an uncle of mine said he thought she might have driven an ambulance.'

'Oh, then Talbot might know her.'

622

'Talbot?'

'Yes. Talbot – I mean, Mrs Vernon. During the war we got in the habit of calling one another by our last names, and we still do it, even though most of us have married, and those aren't our names any longer. Mrs Vernon was at Dulwich with me. She drove an ambulance in the East End during the Blitz.'

If Polly'd known Mrs Vernon, or rather Talbot, during the rocket attacks, she'd have taken care to keep out of her way during the Blitz, but he went with Camberley to find her in case she knew of other ambulance drivers he could contact.

Talbot, a formidable woman three times Camberley's size, was listening to a BBC recording with headphones on. Camberley had to tap her on the back to get her to turn around. 'This is Mr Knight. He's looking for someone who knew his grandmother. She was an ambulance driver.'

'What was her name?' Talbot asked.

'Polly. Polly Sebastian.'

'Sebastian ...' she said, shaking her head. 'No, I don't remember anyone by that name in the FANYs. But I know who you should ask. Goody. Mrs Lambert,' she explained. 'She's our group's historian, and she knows everyone who worked in the Blitz.'

'Which one is she?'

'I don't see her,' Talbot said, looking round the room. 'She's medium height, grey hair, rather stout.' Which described three-quarters of the women he'd seen this morning. 'I know she's here somewhere. Browne will know.'

She dragged him over to a grey-haired woman peering through her spectacles at a parachute-mine. 'Browne, where's Goody Two-Shoes, do you know?'

'She's not here. She had to do something in the City this morning, I don't know what, but she said she'd come as soon as she'd finished with whatever it was.'

'Oh dear,' Talbot said. 'This young man is looking for someone who might have known his grandmother.'

'Oh. What did your grandmother do in the war?' Browne asked, and he went through the entire rigmarole again.

'Were you an ambulance driver?' he asked her.

'No, an RAF plotter. So I was only in London for the first two months of the Blitz. You said your grandmother worked at Townsend Brothers. So did Pudge. That's her over there in the green dress,' she said, pointing at a thin, birdlike woman looking at a display of clothing ration books.

But Pudge, whose name tag read 'Pauline Rainsford', had worked at Padgett's, not Townsend Brothers. 'Till it was hit,' she said matter-of-factly, 'at which point I decided I might as well be in the armed services, and I volunteered to be a Wren.'

'Do you know of anyone who *did* work at Townsend Brothers?' he asked.

'No, but I know who you should ask. Mrs Lambert. She's our group's historian.'

'I was told she wasn't here.'

'She's not,' Pudge said, 'but she's coming. In fact, I expected her here already. I'll let you know as soon as she arrives, and in the meantime, you can ask the others. Hatcher!' she called to an elegant elderly woman in tweeds and pearls. 'You were in London during the Blitz, weren't you?'

'No. Bletchley Park,' she said, coming over, 'which was not nearly as romantic as the historians make it sound. It was mostly drudgery, sorting through thousands upon thousands of combinations, looking for one that might work.'

Like the last eight years of my life, he thought, calculating coordinate after coordinate, searching for clues, trying to find a drop that would open.

'Do you know of anyone who was in London during the Blitz?' Pudge was asking Hatcher.

'Yes,' she said, pointing at two women looking at a display of war posters. 'York and Chedders were.'

But neither York nor Chedders – Barbara Chedwick, according

to her name tag – remembered a Polly Sebastian, and neither did any of the other women they passed him on to.

'There was a Polly in our troop,' a large woman whose name tag read 'Cora Holland' said.

'In your troop?' he asked. 'You were in the WAACs?'

'No, not troop, *troupe*.' She spelled the word out. 'We were in an ENSA show together. We were both chorus girls.' He must not have succeeded in hiding his astonishment because she snapped, 'I realise you may find that difficult to believe, but I had quite a good figure in those days. What did you say her last name was?'

'Sebastian.'

'Sebastian,' Cora repeated. 'No, that doesn't ring a bell, I'm afraid, though that doesn't necessarily mean anything. I might not have ever heard her last name. The White Rabbit – I mean, Mr Tabbitt – called us all by our stage names. Polly's was Air-Raid Adelaide. If her name *was* Polly. It might have been Peggy.'

Well, and Polly wouldn't have been a chorus girl in any case. But he couldn't afford to leave any stone unturned. 'Do you know what happened to her?'

'I'm afraid not,' she said apologetically. 'It's so easy to lose track of people in a war, you know.'

Yes.

'I seem to remember having heard that she'd been assigned to one of the groups touring airfields and army camps.'

So, definitely not his Polly. And neither was the girl who'd worked with Miss Dennehy on a barrage-balloon crew, even though Miss Dennehy was certain her last name had been Sebastian. 'She was killed in August of '40,' Miss Dennehy said.

By half past eleven he'd interviewed the entire group except for another white-haired woman too deaf to understand anything he'd said to her, and Mrs Lambert still wasn't there. And if he waited any longer, he'd miss the ones at St Paul's.

He went to find Pudge to ask for Mrs Lambert's address and telephone number, but she'd disappeared. He checked the black-out room, holding the curtain aside so he could see, and then the mockup of a tube shelter.

Pudge wasn't in there, but Talbot was, looking at a 'Report Suspicious Behaviour' poster on the tiled tunnel wall. 'Did you find Lambert?' she asked. 'Did she know what your grandmother did during the Blitz?'

'No,' he said, 'she's not here yet, and I'm afraid I must go. I was wondering if you—'

'She's not here yet? I can't imagine what's keeping her,' she said, and dragged him off to find the woman who'd been too deaf to interview.

'Rumford,' Talbot said, 'did Goody Two-Shoes tell you what she had to do before she came here?'

'What?' Rumford said, cupping her hand to her ear.

'I *said*,' Talbot shouted, 'did Goody Two-Shoes – Mrs Lambert – tell you what she had to do before she came here? *Mrs Lambert!*'

'Lantern?'

'No. *Lambert*. Do you know where she was going this morning before she came here?'

Rumford looked round vaguely. 'Isn't she here yet?'

'*No*. And this young man wants to speak to her. Do you know where she went?'

'Yes,' she said. 'To St Paul's.'

St Paul's, where he could already be if he hadn't waited here for her.

'St Paul's?' Talbot said. 'Why did she need to go there?'

'What?' Rumford cupped her hand to her ear again.

'I said, why did— Oh good, she's here,' Talbot said, pointing at the far side of the exhibit where a plump, friendly-looking woman was rummaging in her handbag. 'Goody Two-Shoes!' Talbot called, and when she didn't look up, 'Lambert! Over here. Eileen!'

'Do you know why they're waving as we come along?
We're all bloody heroes.'

SERGEANT LESLIE TEARE ON ARRIVING IN ENGLAND
AFTER BEING EVACUATED FROM DUNKIRK

KENT – JUNE 1944

'28 June 1944,' Ernest typed. 'Dear Editor, I live in Sellindge, near Folkestone, and our little village has always been a charming, tranquil place. For the past fortnight, however, that tranquillity has been destroyed by a constant stream of troop transports. I have been forced to hang my washing inside because of the dust, and my cat, Polly Flinders, has nearly been run over twice. How long will this continue? When I spoke to Captain Davies, he said it might last until—'

He paused, wondering what date he was supposed to use for the invasion. Immediately after they'd invaded at Normandy, they'd discussed July first as an invasion date, but that was when the most they were hoping for as to the deception holding was D-Day-plus-five. It was already D-plus-twenty-two, and there was still no sign the Germans had caught on.

'They've got to tumble to it soon,' Cess had said disgustedly the night before in the mess. 'There are more than five hundred thousand Allied forces in France. What do the jerries think they're doing there? Picking flowers?'

'You're only annoyed because you lost the pool,' Prism had said.

Ernest had lost the pool, too. *It's too bad I didn't study the post-invasion period,* he thought. *I could have won fifty pounds.* He'd guessed the eighteenth of June – D-plus-twelve – even though he'd privately believed the whole deception would collapse the moment the troops hit the beaches of Normandy. But here he was, in the last week of June, still typing phony wedding announcements and irate letters to the editor.

He went to find Chasuble, but he wasn't in his office, and Prism didn't know where he was.

'Gwendolyn might,' Prism said, and Ernest went out to the garage to find him.

Gwen was underneath the staff car. Ernest leaned under and asked, 'Do you know where Chasuble is?'

'He went to Station X to drop off the radio messages,' Gwen said.

Damn. 'Do you know—' he began, then stopped and looked up, listening. There was a faint *putt-putting* off to the east. It sounded like a motorbike approaching.

'That's odd,' Gwen said, sliding out from under the car. 'I didn't hear the siren.'

'Perhaps they've stopped bothering with them.'

Gwen nodded. 'Or worn them out.'

It's possible, Ernest thought, listening to the *putt-putt* grow louder. In the two weeks since the V-1s had started, the sirens had sounded at least five hundred times.

'What did you ask me before?' Gwen asked.

'I asked you,' Ernest said, raising his voice over the chugging of the V-1, 'if you knew when we were invading France.'

Gwen waited till the rocket had passed safely overhead and headed loudly off to the northeast and then shouted, 'Invading France? I thought we already had!'

'Very amusing!' Ernest yelled back. 'Not the real one. I'm talking about the one we've been working on for the last five months!' He was suddenly shouting into silence as the V-1's motor cut out.

Gwen held up his hand, signalling him to wait. There was a brief silence and then a muffled boom off to the northwest.

'That's the eighth flying bomb today,' Gwen said. 'You'd think Hitler would be growing bored with his new toy by now.' He slid back under the car.

'You still haven't told me when we're invading Calais.'

'I think they decided on the eighteenth, but I'm not certain. Cess will know.'

But Cess would follow him back to the office and stand there watching him type.

'Whenever it is, I hope it's soon,' Gwen said from under the car. 'I can't wait to get out of this bloody place.'

They'd all be out of this bloody place as soon as the Germans caught on to the deception.

And then what? Ernest thought. Where would he be assigned? He had to see to it he wasn't sent to France. He hadn't realised deception units had operated over there after D-Day till last week, when an officer from Dover had arrived and requisitioned all their dummy tanks. They apparently planned to set up dummy tank battalions in France to confuse the Germans, and the officer'd said the units manning them would be drawn from Fortitude South. 'We need people who've had experience with these bloody unwieldy inflatables,' he'd said, which meant everyone in the unit was vulnerable.

Hopefully, Ernest's bad foot would keep him from being sent, but he couldn't count on it – the officer had asked him how much experience he'd had with tanks, and Cess had told him the entire story of the bull. Ernest wished he knew what other deception missions they'd done after D-Day so he'd know what to avoid and what to ask for. He needed an assignment that would keep him in England, and one that involved sending messages that a historian might have an interest in. It was his only hope, now that D-Day was over and Denys Atherton had gone back to Oxford.

It also had to be an assignment where he wouldn't have to

undergo a background check, and where he wouldn't be likely to get caught.

He'd had a close call last week. He'd been typing one of his messages when Cess came in, and before he could get the paper out of the typewriter, Cess had begun reading over his shoulder. 'I say, haven't you already used the name Polly?' he'd asked. 'It's a common-enough name, but you don't want to do anything to make the Germans suspicious.'

Or you, he thought. *Or Tensing*. And he had dutifully Xed out the name and typed 'Alice' above it.

Maybe the safest thing to do would be to try to get invalided out and land a job on a newspaper. Whatever he did, he had to do it soon, before they were shut down and he was assigned elsewhere. Once he'd been assigned, it would be almost impossible to get it changed.

And in the meantime he needed to finish his news story and get it put away before Cess caught him using 'Polly' again and got suspicious. He went back to the office and changed the sentence to, 'When I spoke to Captain Davies, he said it was scheduled to last another full month. I realise Sellindge is located on the direct route to Dover, but is it necessary for the *entire* First United States Army Group to parade past my door? At my wits' end, Miss Euphemia Hill, Rose Gate Cottage—'

'You may as well stop typing,' Cess said from the doorway. 'The jig's up.'

Ernest looked up at him, startled. Cess was leaning lazily against the doorjamb, his arms folded. 'What?'

'I said, the jig's up. It's American slang. It means we've been found out. Hitler's finally tumbled to the fact that there's no FUSAG. And no second invasion.'

Ernest waited a moment to give his heart time to stop thudding and then said, 'Hitler's caught on to the deception?'

'Yes, and about time. I'd begun to think he'd only realise he'd been tricked when he saw Monty rolling into Berlin.'

Patton, Ernest thought. *And Hitler won't be there. He'll already have killed himself in his bunker.* 'Who told you he's caught on?'

'No one,' he said. 'I'm in Intelligence, remember? I've deduced it from the clues.'

'What clues?'

'One, Algernon's here. And two, Lady Bracknell's called a general meeting in the mess.'

Cess was right. It looked like the jig was up. In more ways than one. *I should have talked to him earlier about being re-assigned,* he thought. Or perhaps there was still time. 'When's this meeting scheduled for?'

'Now,' Cess said, showing no sign of leaving.

And Ernest couldn't leave either, not with a story with the name Polly in it still in the typewriter. 'Coming,' he said, putting a cover over the machine and standing up. 'You need to go and tell Gwen. He's in the garage underneath the staff car.'

'Oh right,' Cess said, and left. Ernest yanked the cover off and the letter out of the typewriter, hid it in the file cabinet and was at the door when Cess returned.

'Gwen wasn't there,' he reported. 'He must already be in the meeting.'

He was, and so was everyone else except Chasuble. Lady Bracknell, in full-dress uniform – another bad sign – was saying, 'Colonel Algernon has something to say to you.'

'Thank you,' Tensing said, standing up. 'First of all, I want to thank all of you for your hard work during these past months and to tell you how handsomely it's paid off. Our efforts to deceive the Germans as to the time and place of the invasion have been successful beyond our greatest hopes. Even after receiving news of the Normandy invasion, the German High Command continued to believe that was a diversion and that the main invasion was still to come at the Pas de Calais.'

He was talking in the past tense. Cess was right. The jig was up.

'As a result of this belief,' Tensing went on, 'they held

significant numbers of troops and tanks in readiness for that invasion, numbers which, if sent to Normandy, would have significantly altered the outcome. Fortitude South's work was decisive in the outcome of the invasion, and you're to be congratulated.'

The men began to clap and cheer. 'We did it!' Cess shouted. 'We beat them.'

'Right,' Prism said wryly. 'Singlehandedly. I'm certain all those destroyers and planes and paratroopers and landing forces had nothing to do with it.'

'Lieutenant Prism makes an excellent point,' Tensing said. 'The invasion was a combined effort, and there are countless others who deserve credit for its success. But they'll receive medals, and there will be speeches praising what they did. And newspaper accounts.' He nodded briefly at Ernest. 'You won't. Your part in all this must unfortunately remain secret. My thanks and the knowledge of a job well done are all the reward you are likely to get. *And*' – he paused dramatically – 'a bottle of Scotch with which to toast your accomplishment!' He held it up, and there was more clapping and cheering.

'That's not dummy Scotch, is it?' Cess asked suspiciously.

'It's an inflatable rubber bottle,' Prism said.

'No, it's glass,' Tensing said, tapping it with his finger. 'I'm quite certain it's authentic. The label says, "Aged at Shepperton Film Studios".'

Everyone laughed. 'Can we open it now?' Gwen shouted.

'Not just yet,' Tensing said.

'Watch out,' Cess whispered to Ernest.

'I said the Germans were deceived into thinking there would be a second invasion,' Tensing went on. 'That isn't quite correct. The German High Command continues to believe that, and it's essential that we perpetuate that deception for as long as possible.'

'I was wrong,' Cess whispered to Ernest. 'Apparently the jig isn't up.'

'To that end, you'll continue with your current deception and disinformation campaigns. In addition, you'll increase the number of radio messages to the Pas de Calais' Resistance Underground cells, and you'll disseminate disinformation regarding the location of the Third Army, which is currently in the process of embarking for France under the tightest possible security. Your job will be to keep its presence in France – and General Patton's – secret until General Patton takes official command of it.'

'Oh Lord,' Moncrieff muttered.

'With him swaggering about in that star-studded uniform of his and making incendiary statements?' Cess whispered. 'He must be joking.'

'*But*,' Tensing said, glaring at Cess, 'in the event that his presence *is* detected, we will obviously need an explanation for what the commander of the army poised to attack Calais is doing in France. We've developed a cover story in which General Patton made a controversial statement and has been demoted to the command of a single army under Omar Bradley.'

'Who's supposed to have been put in command of FUSAG in place of Patton?' Gwen asked.

'General McNair,' Tensing said. 'We're putting out the story that he is being leashed until the German High Command sends the Fifteenth Army to Normandy, and then he'll strike. That way we needn't commit to a particular invasion date.'

So it's a good thing I didn't put one in Euphemia Hill's letter to the editor, Ernest thought.

'I've given Lady Bracknell the script,' Tensing said. 'Your job will be to work up an array of supporting materials – wireless traffic, dispatches, doubles if necessary, photographs, newspaper articles.'

Good, Ernest thought in relief, *that means I can go on sending messages*. And articles referring to Patton were something historians were even more likely to look for than the planted Fortitude stories.

'It's rather a rush job, I'm afraid,' Tensing said. 'It all needs to be in place before Patton leaves.'

'Which is when?' Moncrieff asked.

'July the sixth.' Tensing ignored the groans. 'Moncrieff, I also want your report on the convoy activities before I leave. And again, my hearty congratulations on a successful job. And let's hope the next one is as successful as the last. That will be all.' He stood up. 'Cess, Worthing, I want to see you in Bracknell's office in five minutes.'

He walked out.

'Sounds like you two are for it,' Prism whispered, and Cess nodded, looking worried.

'You don't suppose we're being sent on one of those secret missions no one comes back from, do you?' Cess asked Ernest anxiously. 'What do you think?'

I think I waited too long to speak to Tensing, Ernest thought.

They went into the office. Tensing was sitting behind Bracknell's desk. 'You wanted to see us, sir?' Cess said.

'Yes,' Tensing said. 'Shut the door.'

Oh God, it is something big. We're being sent to Germany. Or Burma.

Cess shut the door. Tensing walked stiffly over to Lady Bracknell's chair and sat down. 'Don't look like you're about to be court-martialled,' he said, and smiled. 'I called the two of you in here so I could congratulate you.'

'For what?' Cess asked suspiciously.

'For the success of the Normandy invasion. We've received word – I'm not at liberty to say through what channels—'

Ultra, Ernest thought.

'—that the decisive element in the High Command's refusal to release General Rommel's tanks for use in Normandy was the eyewitness account of the massive numbers of troops and materiel in the Dover area from a repatriated high-ranking German officer.'

'And not all those letters to the editor Worthing wrote?' Cess said, sounding disappointed. 'Or all those dummy tanks we inflated? Worthing here risked life and limb for those tanks.'

'I've no doubt the tanks *and* the letters to the editor both played their part,' Tensing said wryly, 'though even if they didn't, they still had to be done. That's unfortunately the nature of intelligence work. One does a number of things in the hope that at least one of them will work.'

Like going off to Biggin Hill and Bletchley Park and Manchester, Ernest thought, *and putting messages to the retrieval team in the classified ads.*

'One rarely ever knows which schemes succeeded and which failed.'

It was true. He would never know which, if any, of his messages had got through, never know whether Polly had been pulled out in time.

'It's unfair, but there it is,' Tensing said. 'We were lucky in this case to have found out, though I'm certain we don't know the full story, and I doubt we ever shall. That will be for the historians to sort out long after we're dead.'

'I wonder what they'll make of the Reverend T.W. Ringolsby and the condoms,' Cess said. 'Do you suppose that will merit a chapter of its own?'

I hope so, Ernest thought.

'With footnotes,' Cess said. 'And—'

'*As I was saying*,' Tensing interrupted, 'what we do know is that you two were responsible for keeping the Fifteenth Army tied down in the Pas de Calais during a critical time. You've saved countless lives. The original casualty estimate for D-Day was thirty thousand. We had ten thousand, and every day those tanks have stayed in Calais, even more lives have been saved.'

He and Cess had saved more than twenty thousand lives. And he'd been worried when Hardy'd told him about saving five hundred and nineteen.

'Congratulations,' Tensing said, standing up and coming

around the desk to shake hands with them. 'I can't overstate the importance of what you've done. We had only sixteen divisions. If Hitler had brought those tanks up, we'd have been going up against twenty-one. It's my personal opinion that you may very well have won the war.'

Not lost it. Won it. He'd been afraid every single day since he'd unfouled that propellor, since he'd saved Hardy's life, that he had somehow irrevocably altered the course of history, the course of the war, and that Hitler would win. And now—

'Does that mean we can go home and rest on our laurels now?' Cess was asking, grinning.

'Not just yet, I'm afraid,' Tensing said.

Oh no, here it comes, Ernest thought.

'I've asked Bracknell to assign the writing of newspaper articles about Patton to someone else, Worthing,' Tensing said. 'I have another job for the two of you.'

Oh God, they *were* being sent to Burma.

Tensing leaned across the desk and folded his hands. 'The Germans have contacted their agents – or rather, our double-agents – and ordered them to report the times and places of V-1 incidents.'

'Why?' Cess asked. 'Don't they already know that? I thought the V-1s were remote-controlled.'

Tensing shook his head. 'The Germans know where they intended them to go, not where they went. They're aimed at the target, Tower Bridge – which, by the way, they have thus far not hit – and a mechanism is set to make a certain number of revolutions and then cut off the fuel supply, at which point the engine switches off and the rocket goes into its dive. But whether they reach the target depends on whether that mechanism was correctly set.'

'So they need the times and locations of the incidents to see whether the rockets are reaching their target so they can make the necessary course corrections?' Ernest asked.

'Yes,' Tensing said, 'which puts us in a rather nasty situation.

If we provide accurate information to protect our agents' credibility, we're providing aid to the enemy, and a particularly deadly form of aid at that – obviously an unacceptable situation. If, on the other hand, we give the enemy false information, and it's disproved by German aircraft reconnaissance, it will—'

'Blow our agents' cover,' Cess said.

Tensing nodded. 'And jeopardise any future deception plans. Which is equally unacceptable.'

'So we need to deceive the Germans into thinking their rockets fell where they didn't,' Cess said. 'How do we do that? Create dummy bomb sites?'

Ernest had a sudden vision of an inflatable heap of rubble. He suppressed a smile.

'We did consider that,' Tensing said. 'Already-existing rubble moved to another site was used effectively in North Africa. But one of our science chaps has come up with a better plan.'

He unrolled a map of southeastern England on the table. It was marked with a number of red dots, which Ernest assumed were V-1 incidents. 'We know from our intelligence that in the trials at Peenemünde, the V-1 tended to fall short of the target, and, as you can see from the map, that problem has continued, with the largest number of bombs falling here,' he pointed at an area southeast of London, 'rather than in the centre of the city.'

'Which is what the Germans are worried about,' Ernest said, 'and why they're demanding the information.'

'Yes, but it's in our interest to keep them from correcting the trajectory, to see to it that the V-1s continue to fall short.'

'So you switch the bombs that fall short for the ones that reach their target,' Ernest said.

'Exactly.'

'*What?*' Cess said, looking thoroughly confused. 'How can you switch bombs?'

'Bomb A falls in Stepney at nine o'clock at night,' Ernest explained. 'Bomb B falls on Hampstead Heath at half past two in the morning. Our agent tells the Germans bomb A was the one that fell at half past two.'

'In Hampstead,' Tensing said. 'And the Germans think it overshot its target, and they shorten its trajectory.'

'Which makes the next one fall short,' Cess said, catching on. 'But how do we ensure it falls somewhere where it won't do any damage?'

'Unfortunately, we can't, but we *can* increase the chances of a rocket falling in woods or a field—'

'Or a pasture,' Cess said. 'Worthing, this is your chance to eliminate that bull that caused you so much trouble.'

Tensing went on as if Cess hadn't spoken. 'We *can* increase the chances of their landing in a less populated area than central London.'

That's why you were so eager to point out the thousands of lives we saved, Ernest thought. *Because now we're going to start killing people.*

'The retargeting will allow us to provide false information without arousing suspicions of our double-agents,' Tensing said. 'And to significantly lower the number of casualties.'

And kill people who wouldn't otherwise have died, Ernest thought. 'So what's our job?' Cess asked. 'We're to match up the bombs?'

'No, I need you two to provide corroboration,' Tensing said, and handed Ernest a photograph of a pile of rubble. It was impossible to tell what it had been from the tangle of bricks and lengths of wood.

'This happened in Fleet Street Tuesday afternoon at 4:32 p.m., but we're telling the Germans it's Finchley. The high level of destruction makes substitutions comparatively easy. We've told the newspapers they're not to print any photographs or information about rocket attacks without our authorisation.'

'What about the casualty lists in the papers?' Ernest asked. 'Won't the addresses of the people killed give the location away?'

'We've thought of that,' Tensing said. 'You'll need to write false death notices to go with the incidents, and we've requested the newspapers hold theirs for several days and list only the name of the deceased. In instances where several members of the same family are killed, we've asked them to publish them on separate days, and you'll do false corroborating stories.'

'What a bloody business,' Ernest said bitterly.

'Yes,' Tensing said. 'I'll need captions and news stories to go with the photographs, and anything else you can come up with – eyewitness accounts, classified ads, letters to the editor – the same sort of thing you were doing before. No direct mention of location, of course. We want the Germans to work that out on their own, and our double-agents will be verifying it.'

'When do we begin?' Cess asked.

'Now,' Tensing said, pulling a sheaf of black-and-white photographs from his briefcase and handing them to Cess. 'These need to be checked for identifying landmarks or signboards that may need to be cropped out.'

He handed a second sheaf to Ernest. Each one had a memo pinned to it with the actual time and location, and the falsified one. 'A basic news story for the London dailies,' Tensing said, 'and a local connection for the village papers – local resident visiting someone in the town when it hit. You know the sort of thing, Worthing.'

He knew exactly, and he couldn't have asked for a better job. Not only did he not have to worry about being sent to Burma, but he'd be able to send his own coded messages in the articles.

'Cess, you'll do the London dailies,' Tensing said. 'Worthing, you'll do the village papers. Chasuble will be in on this, too.' He shut up his briefcase. 'I'd like to speak to him before I leave.'

'I'll go and see if he's back,' Cess said, and went out.

'Shut the door,' Tensing said to Ernest, and after he did, added, 'It *is* a bloody business. That's why I chose you. I know I can count on you.'

'What do the higher-ups say about this scheme?' Ernest asked.

'They don't know yet. We have a meeting to discuss the deception plan with them the week after next.'

'And if they vote not to approve it?' Ernest asked, looking at Tensing closely.

'Then I suppose we shall have to think of something else,' he said. 'But I can't imagine them doing anything so irresponsible. It would mean jeopardising hundreds, perhaps thousands of lives – so many that if I was told they'd voted the idea down, I'd be forced to conclude that the person who told me had got the story wrong.'

In other words, he intended to ignore the order and continue deceiving the Germans till he got caught and then plead ignorance. Like Lord Nelson had done at one of his battles. Tensing was risking his career, and his future. He could be court-martialled, or worse, for disobeying orders, but he'd do it anyway. In order to save lives.

I didn't get to observe Chaplain Howell Forgey at Pearl Harbor, Ernest thought, *or the firemen at the World Trade Center, but I've done what I set out to do. I've gotten to observe heroes.* Not just Tensing, but the Commander and Jonathan. And Cess and Prism and Chasuble, fighting recalcitrant inflatables and angry bulls. And Turing and Dilly Knox, patiently deciphering code.

And Eileen, driving an ambulance through burning streets and coping with the Hodbins. And Polly, dealing daily with the threat of certain death.

If I ever get back to Oxford, I won't need to go to the Pandemic and the Battle of the Bulge, he thought. *I've collected more than enough material for my work on heroes right here.*

'So I take it you won't be at this meeting where the policy's to be discussed?' Ernest asked.

'Of course I'll be there.' Tensing drew himself up indignantly. 'Unless, of course, my back is acting up. Old war injury, you know.' He allowed himself a smile. 'Lord Nelson's not the only one who has a blind eye he can turn.'

Cess opened the door and came in. 'Chasuble just rang from Tenterden. He says the Austin's acting up again.'

Right outside the Plough and Bull, no doubt, Ernest thought, *where his barmaid Daphne works.*

'You two will need to bring him up to date, then,' Tensing said. He picked up his briefcase and started out. 'Those photographs need to be in the dailies by tomorrow and the village papers by their next deadline.' He opened the door.

'Wait,' Cess said. 'I've only just thought of something. These rockets, we wouldn't be sending any of them down on our own heads, would we?'

Tensing shook his head. 'You're too far east. If this works as planned, the bulk of the bombs will fall on Bethnal Green, Croydon and Dulwich.'

'Time, which was once said to be on the side of the Allies,
has turned out to be, after all, Hitler's man.'

MOLLIE PANTER-DOWNES 15 JUNE 1940

IMPERIAL WAR MUSEUM, LONDON – 7 MAY 1995

'Here she is, Mr Knight,' Talbot said. 'Eileen!' she shouted, waving across the room at the woman who'd just come into the Blitz exhibit.

She was just as Talbot had described her: grey hair, medium height, rather stout. 'Lambert! Over here!' Talbot called, and then turned to Calvin, beaming. 'I told you she'd be here soon, Mr Knight.'

'Her name's Eileen?' he asked, hoping to God he'd misheard her.

'Yes. Eileen! Goody Two-Shoes!' Talbot called, waving again. Mrs Lambert still hadn't looked up. She was fumbling in her handbag, apparently looking for a pen to write on the name tag she held in the other hand.

There were lots of Eileens in the war, he told himself over the sickening thud of his heart. That's why Merope chose the name, because it had been so common. And this Eileen looked nothing like the slim, pretty, green-eyed redhead he'd seen in Oxford eight years ago.

But she would have aged fifty-five years since then, and the curly-haired brunette WAAC in the photo had looked nothing

642

like the elderly woman he'd talked to either. And Mrs Lambert's grey hair as she bent over a display case, writing her name on the name tag, bore hints of what might be faded red.

Now she was struggling to put on her name tag. And what if, when she finally managed to pin it on, it read, *Eileen O'Reilly*?

'What did Mrs Lambert do in the war?' he asked Talbot. *Let her say she was a Wren*, he prayed. *Or a chorus girl.*

'She drove an ambulance,' Talbot said. 'Oh dear, she still doesn't see us. Come along.' And Talbot dragged him across the room to Mrs Lambert. She didn't look as old as Talbot, but that was no doubt due to her plumpness, and Merope had been younger than Polly. The evacuation of the children had been her first assignment. And, if this was her, her only one.

'Eileen,' Talbot said. 'Here's someone who wants to meet you.'

Eileen had finally got her name tag attached, but it was no help. It merely read, *Eileen Lambert*, and below the name, *Women's World War II Alumni Association*, and when she looked up, her eyes were a pale aqua, which might or might not have been green when she was younger.

'I'm sorry,' Talbot was saying. 'I've forgotten what your name was, Mr—?'

'Knight. Calvin Knight. It's a pleasure to meet you, Mrs Lambert,' he said, watching her closely as he shook her hand. 'I'm from Oxford,' he added, and thought he saw a flicker of recognition. Oh God, it *was* her.

'Mr Knight is looking for someone who might have known his grandmother,' Talbot said. 'Where were you, Goody? Browne said you had to run some sort of errand?'

'Yes. At St Paul's. I'd asked my brother to go for me, but he couldn't. He's down at the Old Bailey this morning, so I had to go.'

Brother. She had a brother. It wasn't Eileen after all. The relief hit him with the force of a punch to the stomach.

'And the traffic was *wretched*,' Mrs Lambert was saying.

Talbot nodded. 'They simply *must* do something about that area near Bart's. It's impossible.'

Pudge came up. 'Oh, you two have found each other. Excellent. Did Lambert know your grandmother?' she asked him.

'I haven't asked her yet.'

'His grandmother was in London during the Blitz,' Talbot explained to Eileen. 'Her name was Polly – what did you say her last name was, Mr Knight?'

'Sebastian. Polly Sebastian.' Both ladies looked expectantly at Eileen Lambert, but she was already shaking her head.

'No, there isn't anyone by that name in the organisation,' she said. 'Was Polly a nickname for Mary?'

'Yes.'

'We had a Mary in our ambulance unit,' Talbot said, 'but her last name was Kent.'

Mrs Lambert ignored her. 'What was your grandmother's maiden name, Mr Knight?'

'Sebastian. Her married name was O'Reilly,' he said, just in case, but he couldn't detect any reaction from her.

'No, sorry,' she said. 'We haven't any Mary O'Reillys either. Have you tried the museum's archives?'

Yes, he thought. *And the British Museum's. And the Public Record Office's. And the morgues of the* Times *and the* Daily Herald *and the* Express.

'That's a good idea,' he said. 'I'm afraid I haven't time today, but I'll certainly come back. Thank you for your help. And for yours, Mrs Vernon,' he said to Talbot, 'and yours.' He shook hands with each of them in turn. 'I don't want to keep you from the exhibition.'

'Yes. Oh, Eileen, you must see the *Beauty in the Blitz* display,' Talbot said. 'They have nylons from the American PX and that dreadful face powder made from chalk. And there's a lipstick just like the one I lost when Kent pushed me into the gutter that time. It may even be the same one. I'll never forget that lipstick. "Crimson Caress", it was called.' She and Pudge dragged Mrs Lambert off, and Calvin headed for the exit, winding his way through the displays to the VE Day exhibit, which was complete with cheers and simulated fireworks.

It was already after eleven, but if he hurried, he might be able to reach St Paul's by noon and catch some of the visitors having lunch in the cathedral's café. He walked swiftly towards the exit.

'Mr Knight!' someone called from behind him. He stopped and looked back. Mrs Lambert was bustling along the corridor after him. He stopped and waited for her to catch up. 'Oh good,' she panted, 'you're still here. I was afraid you'd already gone.' She hurried up to where he was standing.

'What is it?' he said. 'Did you remember something?'

She shook her head, attempting to catch her breath, her hand to her bosom.

'Are you all right?' he asked. 'Can I get you a glass of water or something? We could go into the cafeteria.'

'No, they'll all be coming in for lunch shortly. I'm sorry about that just now. I couldn't say anything with Talbot and Pudge there.' She took his arm and led him past the gift shop and into the main hall, looking around – presumably for somewhere they could talk. 'I'd hoped to catch you when you first arrived, but I wasn't certain where you'd be. St Paul's is opening their exhibition today as well, and I thought you were more likely to go there to look.'

Oh God, it *was* Eileen, and the story about the brother was a fabrication, part of the identity she'd had to adopt after Polly died and she'd been left to fend for herself. She'd had to cope all alone with the duration of the war and all the long years after. *And how could she stand there smiling,* he wondered. *Knowing what I did to her, to them?*

She couldn't, he thought. *It isn't her. She's talking about something else, a reporter she was supposed to meet or a—*

'... and they had exhibits all over the cathedral, in the crypt and both transepts, so it took *forever* to make certain you

weren't there, and then another *hour* to drive out here, and—'
She stopped, frowning at him. 'You *are* Colin, aren't you?'

And there went any doubt. It *was* her.

'Oh dear, I'm afraid I've made a dreadful mistake,' she said,
just as Anne had. 'I thought—'

'You didn't make a mistake,' he said. 'I'm Colin.'

'Colin Templer?'

He nodded.

'Oh good,' Eileen said. 'I was afraid for a moment I'd got
the wrong man. It's been so many years since I saw you.' She
glanced towards the gift shop. Three chattering women were
headed their way from it with bags full of parcels. 'Come, let's
go and find somewhere quiet where we can talk.' She led him
back into the Blitz exhibit and over to the door marked 'Air-
Raid Shelter'.

She opened the door, took a swift look around, and pushed
him through it. Inside was a replica of an Underground station
platform. Mannequins sat along the curved tile walls and lay on
the floor wrapped in blankets.

Eileen shut the door. 'This is perfect,' she said over the muffled sound of a bomb. She sat down on a bench and patted the
seat beside her.

He sat down.

'Now, then,' she said and beamed at him.

And how can she? he thought. *Knowing how I failed her?*
'Eileen,' he said helplessly, 'Merope, I am so sorry ...'

She looked up at him in surprise. 'Oh, Colin, I *am* sorry. I
recognised you, so I suppose I thought you'd recognise me, but
I was forgetting you haven't met me yet.'

Haven't met—?

'And even if you had, it's been more than fifty years. I should
have told you straightaway.' There was another explosion and
a flash of red light. 'I'm not Eileen— I mean, I am, but I'm not
Eileen O'Reilly.'

Hope leaped in Colin. This wasn't Eileen, which meant there

was still a chance he could get them out. And if this Eileen knew where they were—

'I should have started at the beginning,' she said. 'I'm Binnie Hodbin. My brother, Alf, and I were evacuees. We were sent to the manor where M— where Eileen worked as a maid.'

Alf and Binnie Hodbin, the children everyone had remembered because they were such terrors. And apparently Alf still was, since he was 'detained' at the Old Bailey. Was that merely a polite way of saying he was under arrest? Or worse?

But this made no sense. Binnie had been a child during the war. 'But the women said you drove an ambulance,' he said.

'I did. During the V-1 and V-2 attacks.'

'But you'd only have been—'

'Fifteen,' she said. 'I lied about my age.'

And that certainly went with what he'd been told about the Hodbins. And now that he looked more closely at her, she was obviously younger than the other women. 'But you said your name was Eileen—'

'It is. Binnie wasn't a real name – it was short for Hodbin. So, since I hadn't any name of my own, Eileen said I could choose any name I wanted, and that's the name I chose. And then after the war, when Mum – I mean, Eileen – and Dad legally adopted us, that was the name that was put down.'

After the war. Oh God. 'You called her Mum.'

'I'm sorry. I keep forgetting you don't know any of this yet. After we went back to London at the beginning of the Blitz, Eileen took us in and raised us. Our mother had died, and we were living in the Underground, and Eileen found us and ...'

He wasn't listening. *Eileen* had raised them. He hadn't got them out. That was why Binnie was here. Eileen had sent her to tell him he'd failed, that she'd spent the last fifty-five years waiting for him to come and rescue her. To no avail. 'She doesn't want to see me, does she?' he asked. 'I don't blame her.'

'No, you don't understand,' Binnie said. She took a deep breath. 'Mum died eight years ago.'

KENT – OCTOBER 1944

'**D**unworthy, James,' Ernest typed. 'Died suddenly. At his home in Notting Hill. Of injuries incurred in a V-2 rocket attack.'

Cess leaned in the door. 'Have you seen Chasuble?'

'No,' Ernest said, typing, 'Mr Dunworthy, originally of Oxford—' 'Did you check the mess?'

'No, I'll do that,' he said, and, amazingly, left.

Ernest went back to typing. '—is survived by his children Sebastian Dunworthy and Eileen Ward—'

'Hullo,' Chasuble said, coming in with several photographs. 'Is that the caption for the church in Hampstead you're typing?'

'No, here it is.' Ernest handed it to him. 'Check the time, will you? I couldn't decipher your handwriting,' and while Chasuble was reading it, he typed hastily, 'The funeral will be held at St Mary-at-the-Gate in Cardle on October 28 at ten o'clock,' ripped it out of the typewriter and laid it face-down on the desk. 'Is that the right time?'

'No,' Chasuble said. 'It should be 3:19 p.m., not 2:19.' He handed it back to Ernest, who rolled the sheet in, Xed out the time and typed 3:19 above it.

'Where did it actually hit?'

'Charing Cross Road,' Chasuble said, and handed Ernest several photographs. 'Here are last week's incidents, but I don't think there's anything we can use. Only one church and one shopping street, and they were both totally demolished. Nothing identifiable. The V-2's simply too good at what it does.'

Ernest leafed through the photos. 'What about this one?' He held up a photo of a demolished school with a dozen uniformed students clambering happily over the wreckage.

Chasuble shook his head. 'Photo's already been in the *Daily Express*.'

'I thought they'd been told they had to run it by us first.'

'They were, but they failed to tell the reporter that and it slipped through.' He shuffled through the photos and handed Ernest one of a tangle of timbers. 'See that?' he said, pointing to a broken sign in one corner.

Ernest squinted at the tiny letters. 'Dentist?' he guessed.

'Dental surgeon,' Chasuble said. 'Or, rather, "dental surg—" I know it's small, but I thought perhaps a personal-interest story – "Extreme Cure for Toothache", or something, about a man who was on his way to the dentist when the V-2 hit, and the blast knocking the offending tooth out.'

Ernest nodded. 'Where's this supposed to be?'

'Brixton,' he said. 'It's actually a street in Walworth, but I was able to crop out the village hall. The bomb fell at—' He consulted his list, '4:05 a.m. on Monday the twenty-fourth.'

'4:05? That won't work. The dentist wouldn't be open at that hour, not even for an emergency root canal.'

'Oh, right,' Chasuble said, taking the picture back. 'I'll see what else I've got.' But he still didn't leave.

'Cess was here earlier looking for you. He said it was urgent,' Ernest said, and Chasuble finally departed so he could get back to his typing. He'd had more and more difficulty finding time to write his messages since D-Day. Now that Moncrieff and Gwendolyn were in France, Cess had no one else to pester and was always coming in to sit on the edge of his desk. And when he wasn't there, Chasuble was, talking about Daphne the barmaid and reading over his shoulder, and that meant he had to snatch odd moments in which to compose his messages.

And the disinformation articles he was writing now gave him fewer opportunities to work in Polly's and Eileen's names and information, since the locations had to be the false ones they'd agreed on, and since Chasuble and Cess frequently ended up delivering the stories to the papers. But he did the best he could, writing an assortment of announcements, letters to the editor and human interest pieces, and sticking them in with the captioned V-1 and V-2 photographs whenever he was the delivery boy.

'Christmas is still two months off,' he typed, 'but two Nottingham girls are already hard at work on a festive project: sending a bit of Advent cheer in the form of homemade crackers to our brave lads in uniform. Misses Mary O'Reilly and Eileen Sebastian of Cardle Hill are making the—'

'I couldn't find Cess,' Chasuble said, coming back in.

'Try the mess,' Ernest suggested.

But it was too late. 'There you are, Chasuble' Cess said, appearing in the doorway. 'I've been looking everywhere for you. Remember how Daphne told you she wouldn't go out with you?'

'I've been trying to forget it,' Chasuble said glumly.

'Well, you needn't. I've got good news. I'm taking her to a harvest fête in Goddard's Green this afternoon. Wait!' he said, backing away from Chasuble's raised fists and putting his hands up to protect himself. 'Hold on till you've heard the whole thing.'

'Go ahead,' Chasuble said grimly. 'How exactly is this good news?'

'Because she's bringing her friend Jean with her, and I told her I'd bring along a friend for her. Wait!' He circled around behind the desk.

Ernest draped a concealing arm over the paper in the type-writer.

'Don't you see?' Cess said. 'While you're impressing Daphne with your prowess at the coconut shy, I lure Jean off to the tea tent, and by the time you find us, I'll have worked my fatal charm on Jean, you'll have worked your fatal charm on Daphne, and we swap. We're leaving at ten.' He started out of the door.

'Wait,' Chasuble said, 'isn't it a bit late in the year for a harvest fête? And why on a Wednesday?'

'Yes,' Cess said. 'The fête had to be delayed when a V-2 hit the Women's Institute.' He started out again and then leaned back in. 'Oh, I nearly forgot,' he said to Chasuble. 'Lady Bracknell wants to see you.'

'What about? You don't think he's found out about the Austin, do you?'

'I do hope not,' Cess said. 'You're no use to me dead,'

And the two of them finally left.

And hopefully, whatever it was Lady Bracknell wanted, it would take at least half an hour, Cess would be curious enough to listen at the door the entire time, and he'd have time to finish his article. 'The Christmas crackers are made of cardboard tubes and wrapping paper donated by Townsend Brothers Department Store and contain tissue-paper crowns. As for the traditional "pop" of a cracker, Miss O'Reilly, known to her friends as Polly, said, "No, our soldiers have had enough 'bangs' for the year and should like peace and quiet for the holidays."'

Not that they'd get it. Christmas week was the Battle of the Bulge. *Another event I'll never be able to observe,* he thought, remembering the attack on Pearl Harbor, which he'd spent decoding intercepts. *And during the Battle of the Bulge, I'll be typing articles about Christmas on the Home Front and sending V-2s down on innocent people's heads.*

'The Christmas crackers will also contain a sweet,' he typed, 'and a handwritten motto, such as "A stitch in time saves nine" and "Seek and you shall find".'

Chasuble stomped in. 'Well, that's that,' he said disgustedly.

Cess leaned in the door. 'What happened?'

Damn it, Ernest thought, stopping typing. At this rate, Christmas would be over before he finished the story.

'The boiler at St Anselm's in Cricklewood blew up,' Chasuble said angrily.

'Cricklewood?' Ernest said, frowning. 'I thought you were taking the girls to Goddard's Green.'

'Not now. I'm not taking them anywhere. It seems the bell tower is still standing.'

'What?'

'It's Norman. And famous. Bracknell wants photographs, captions and accompanying stories delivered to all the London papers for the evening-edition deadline.'

Oh, now he understood: the damage from the boiler explosion looked like that from a V-2 attack, and the famous Norman tower would have been in travel guides, which would make the identification of the church by the German Abwehr not only possible but likely. And it was northwest of London, where they were trying to convince the Germans their V-2s were landing.

'It's not fair,' Chasuble said dejectedly. 'I'll never get another chance at Daphne.'

'You're quite right,' Cess said. 'You go to Goddard's Green with the girls, and *I'll* go to Cricklewood.'

'No, I will,' Ernest said. *And deliver my pieces to the village weeklies on the way back.*

'You will?'

'Yes. But before you go, get me the time of the V-2 we're going to say this is. And I'll need directions to St Anselm's. Oh, and ring up the *Herald* and tell them not to print anything about St Anselm's till we say so.'

'I will,' Chasuble said and rushed out.

'Thanks, old man,' Cess said. 'I'm in your debt.'

'Get me directions to St Anselm's and we'll consider it even,' he said.

Cess nodded and left. Ernest only had a few minutes. 'Quartermaster Colin T. Worth will see that the crackers reach their destination,' he typed, 'and several hundred lucky soldiers will have a happy Christmas, thanks to two resourceful girls doing their bit, just as the Prime Minister has asked of all of us.'

He rolled the sheet out, retrieved the funeral notice, stuck both of them inside his jacket then sat back down at the desk, fed in a blank sheet and three carbons and typed in caps, 'GERMAN TERROR ROCKET DESTROYS HISTORIC CHURCH.'

'It fell in Bloomsbury, last Wednesday,' Chasuble said, coming in. He'd changed into a jacket and tie. 'At 7:20 p.m.'

Wednesday evening. Perfect. Wednesday was choir-practice night. 'Any casualties?'

'Yes, four – all fatalities, but there was a second V-1 in the same area at 10:56, so that's not a problem.'

Except to the four people who died, Ernest thought. *And the people who'll be killed in Dulwich or Bethnal Green when the Germans alter their trajectories because of this photograph.*

Cess came in. 'Here are the directions to St Anselm's.' He handed Ernest a hand-drawn map.

'Good,' Ernest said. 'Did you telephone the *Herald*, Chasuble?'

'Yes. The editor said they'll hold the story till they hear from you.'

'Come along,' Cess said. 'The fête starts at ten.'

'Coming,' Chasuble said. 'I'll never forget your doing this for me, Worthing.'

'It's nothing. Go and knock over milk bottles and win Daphne's heart,' Ernest said, waving him out.

He wrote up the St Anselm's stories, grabbed the copies, the camera and several rolls of film and took off for Cricklewood.

It was easy to see why Lady Bracknell had been excited about St Anselm's. Not only was the distinctive Norman tower intact, but the wrought-iron arch saying St Anselm's, Cricklewood was as well, and the rubble behind it looked exactly like the wreckage from a V-2.

'That's what I thought it was at first,' the talkative verger said, 'there not being any warning noise beforehand, you know. So did the reporter from the *Mirror* when he came out, but while he was photographing it, I noticed the stones were wet, and, as it hadn't rained, that made me think of the boiler. And that was what it was.'

'You said the reporter was from the *Daily Mirror*?' Ernest asked. 'Did he say they were going to run a story?'

He nodded. 'Tomorrow morning. Odd, isn't it, how St Anselm's came all through the Blitz and this last year without so much as a mark on her, only to be done in by a faulty boiler?' He shook his head sadly.

'Did the reporter tell you his name?' Ernest asked.

'Yes, but I can't remember now what it was. Miller, I believe. Or Matthews.'

'Have reporters from any other papers been here?'

'Only from the local paper. Oh, and the *Daily Express*. But when I told him it was the boiler, he lost all interest. He didn't even take any photographs.'

Ernest asked if he could use the telephone in the rectory and put a call through to Lady Bracknell.

'I'll try to intercept the articles,' Bracknell said, 'or at least the photographs in the dailies from this end. You stop the one in the local paper, and then ring me back. You're certain it's only the *Mirror* and the *Express*?'

'Yes,' Ernest said, but after he'd rung off he questioned the verger again, who insisted that only the two journalists had been there. Ernest told him to ring him if any other newspaper showed up, and gave him Lady Bracknell's number. 'And if any other reporters arrive, you're *not* to let them take any photographs,' he said, and went to see the local paper's editor, hoping he wouldn't ask too many questions.

A vain hope. 'But I don't see how printing the story can be

654

giving the enemy information when it's nothing at all to do with the war,' the editor said. 'This was a boiler explosion, not a bomb.'

'Yes,' Ernest said, 'but giving the enemy accurate information about *any* destruction aids them in their propaganda efforts.'

'But you've put that it was destroyed by a V-2,' he said, frowning. 'Don't the Germans know where their V-2 rockets hit?'

They will if I don't pull this off, he thought.

'And won't saying the church was destroyed by a V-2 *assist* them in their propaganda efforts?'

'No, because we'll be able to discredit it later, you see,' Ernest explained, and that actually seemed to satisfy him. To make sure, Ernest offered to set the type himself and then stayed to see the front page printed, which took forever. The paper's printing press was even more prone to breakdowns than the *Call*'s. It was after noon by the time he reported in.

'I had to threaten them,' Lady Bracknell said, 'but I've managed to kill the stories at both the *Mirror* and the *Express*. But I couldn't give them the new version, so I need you to run it in to Fleet Street.'

In to Fleet Street? That would take all afternoon. 'Can't I phone it in? I was hoping to get the photo into some of the village weeklies today as well.'

'No, I want you to go to the *Mirror* and the *Express* in person to oversee things. I don't want any muck-ups. It takes only a single story slipping through to ruin the whole scheme.'

Or for Home Secretary Morrison to realise what they were up to and order them to stop, and then he'd have no reason to be planting stories in the village papers. And it was entirely possible that the editor at the *Mirror* or the *Express* had agreed to hold the story but forgotten to tell the reporter. Or the typesetter. Which meant he'd better get in to Fleet Street as soon as possible. He hoped they didn't prove as difficult as the Cricklewood paper.

They didn't. The *Mirror* was holding page three, and the *Express* had bumped the story to the next morning's edition. Both papers allowed him to check the galleys, and the printer gave him a plate of the photo to use in the village weeklies and the name of the stringer who'd written the story.

Ernest tracked him down – at a pub near St Paul's – to make certain he hadn't sold the picture and the story to anyone else. He hadn't, but as Ernest was leaving, he mentioned having seen a reporter from the *Daily Graphic* leaving St Anselm's as he arrived, so Ernest had to go and talk to him, and then make the rounds of the remaining newspapers, just to make certain.

By the time he was satisfied that the only version that would be appearing in the papers was his, it was nine o'clock, which eliminated the local papers, except possibly the *Call*. If Mr Jeppers' printing press had broken down, he might still be printing the edition at midnight.

If he could get there by then. It was pitch-black, and foggy out. He had to creep along, and when he reached Croydon, the door of the *Call*'s office was locked.

But Mr Jeppers' bicycle was there. Ernest pounded on the door, rattling the taped glass. 'Mr Jeppers!' he shouted, hoping the printing press wasn't running. If it was, he'd never hear him. 'Let me in!'

'We're closed!' Mr Jeppers shouted through the door. 'Come back in the morning.'

'It's Ernest Worthing!' he shouted back.

'I know who it is! Who else would it be this time of night?' He opened the door. 'Well, what's so important it can't wait till morning? Has Hitler surrendered then?'

'Not yet,' he said, handing Mr Jeppers the articles.

He refused to take them. 'You're too late. I've already put the front page to bed.'

'They needn't go on the front page,' Ernest said. 'At least put this one in.' He handed him the St Anselm's story. Next week would have to do for the others.

Mr Jeppers took it from him. 'It says, "accompanying photo-graph",' he said, shaking his head. 'I haven't time to set a photo-graphic plate.'

'You needn't. I've got it right here.' He held it up. 'All that needs to be set is the story. I'll set it myself,' he said, and before Mr Jeppers could object, he peeled off his jacket, threw it on top of a roll of newsprint and grabbed a tray of type.

'All right, have it your way.' Mr Jeppers kicked the lever. The printing press started up. 'But if it's not set by the time I'm done with the front page, it goes in next week!' he shouted over the rumble of the press.

Ernest began setting up the sticks of type, searching the trays for the letters he needed and sliding them into place. This could work out even better than he'd planned. The classifieds at the bottom of the page had already been set and proofed. If he could get the caption set quickly enough, he could substitute his own pieces, and Mr Jeppers would be none the wiser.

If. The printing press was shooting out pages at a steady clip, with no sign of jamming. Why, tonight of all nights, had it decided to run properly? And why had he thought using phrases such as 'historic architecture' was a good idea?

Where were the Us? He slotted the finished stick of type into place and grabbed an empty one.

His ears pricked up at the sound of a rattle. Good, the printing press was up to its old tricks. Where the bloody hell were the Cs?

The rattle grew louder and more clanking. It sounded like a wrench had got caught in the gears. 'Shut it off!' he shouted, though in another minute, he wouldn't need to. The press would rattle itself apart.

'*What?*' Mr Jeppers cupped his hand behind his ear.

'Something's wrong with the printing press!' Ernest shouted, jabbing his finger at it. 'That rattle. It's—!'

The noise cut off abruptly. 'Rattle?' Mr Jeppers shouted over the sound of the smoothly running press. 'I can't hear anything!'

That's because it's stopped, Ernest thought. And then, *What if that was a doodle—?*

But there was no time to complete the thought or shout to Mr Jeppers or run. No time.

'Our little life is rounded with a sleep.'

WILLIAM SHAKESPEARE *THE TEMPEST*

LONDON – APRIL 1941

Someone was calling her. *The all-clear must have gone*, she thought, but it was Sir Godfrey. 'Wake up,' he said sternly. 'Can you hear me, miss?'

Her head ached. *I must have nodded off during rehearsal. He'll be furious.* And then, *It can't be Sir Godfrey, he always calls me Viola*, and she remembered where they were.

They were still in the bombed theatre, and she was lying on top of Sir Godfrey, her full weight pressing down on him. 'I'm sorry, Sir Godfrey,' she said. 'I must have fallen on you when I passed out.'

He didn't answer. 'Sir Godfrey? Wake up,' she said, and attempted to shift herself off him, but the effort made her head ache worse.

'Don't try to move, miss, we're coming,' the voice said from somewhere above them. 'Careful. I can smell gas.'

'Sir Godfrey,' she said, but he didn't respond.

And she should have known she couldn't save him, that they would come too late. 'Oh, Sir Godfrey, I am so sorry,' she murmured, and laid her head against his shoulder.

'Miss!' the voice said imperatively. 'Are you trapped?'

Yes, she thought, and then hands were reaching down, lifting her off Sir Godfrey.

'No, you mustn't, he's bleeding,' she protested, but they had already pulled her out of the hole and sat her down, and now they were lifting the theatre seats from Sir Godfrey's legs, placing a jack under a pillar, jumping down into the hole, bending over him.

'Was there anyone else in the theatre when the bomb hit, miss?' the one who'd pulled her out asked.

'I don't know. I wasn't here. When I saw the theatre'd been hit, I came to find Sir Godfrey, and I caught my heel,' she said, trying to explain, 'and while I was trying to free it, I heard his voice—'

'Well, it's no wonder your heel got caught. This isn't the sort of shoe to be clambering about an incident in,' he said, looking down at her gilt shoe, at her other, bare foot, and then at her costume, or what was left of it.

'I had to take off my skirt to make a compress,' she began, but he wasn't listening.

'She's injured,' he called to someone else, and when she looked down, she saw that her bathing suit and her hands were both covered in blood.

'That isn't mine. It's Paige's,' she said, and even though it was too late and he was already dead, she told them, 'Sir Godfrey has a chest wound. You need to apply direct pressure.'

'We'll see to him, don't you worry,' he said, examining her hands. 'You're certain you're not hurt?'

I have blood on my hands, she thought, watching him dully as he turned them over, looking for cuts. *Like Lady Macbeth.* '"What, will these hands ne'er be clean?"' she murmured.

'Miss—'

'You don't understand. I killed him. I altered events—'

'She's in shock,' he said to someone.

'No,' she said. Not shock. Shock was when one didn't see it coming, like that day at what was left of St George's when she realised something terrible had happened, that no one was coming for her. This was different. She had known all along it would end this way.

'Bring a stretcher!' he called.

It's no use. You can't save me either, she thought, and wondered dimly why she hadn't died from the gas, too. *That way I wouldn't be able to do any more damage. I wouldn't be able to kill anyone else.*

'I need to get you over to the ambulance,' he said. 'Can you walk, do you think?'

'Yes,' she said, thinking, *They must not have had a stretcher. Major Denewell must have borrowed all of them.*

'That's a good girl,' he said, and put his hand under her arm and helped her to her feet. 'Here we go.'

But when she tried to walk, she swayed and fell against him.

He grabbed her arm. 'Is your leg injured?'

'No, it's my shoe,' she said. 'I'm all right,' but when she tried again, her head spun and she nearly pitched forward. 'My head—'

'You've breathed in a bit of gas, miss, that's why you're dizzy,' he said, easing her down onto the toppled back of a theatre seat. 'You need to take deep breaths … that's it.'

He raised his head and called over her to the men gathered round the hole, 'Sit here a minute, miss – what's your name?'

'Mary,' she said, but that wasn't right. This was the Blitz, not the V-1s. 'Viola.'

'Viola, listen, my name's Hunter. I want you to stay here a moment while I go and fetch some oxygen to help you breathe, all right?'

She nodded.

'I'll be back straightaway,' he said, and went to meet two men coming across the wreckage with a stretcher. He said something and took the stretcher from them, and they clambered back across the rubble. He took it over to the hole, where they were lifting out the section of balcony wall.

So they can remove Sir Godfrey's body, she thought, watching them. *You should wait till the gas is shut off.*

'Fetch me a plasma drip,' someone called from the hole, and

one of the men bounded off like a deer across the tangle of wreckage.

Why is he hurrying? Polly thought, bewildered. *Sir Godfrey's already dead.*

She limped over to the hole. They were lifting him out and onto the stretcher. His chest was bandaged, a pad of white gauze taped to the wound, and there was a bandage on his wrist and a line of tubing running up his arm to a glass bottle full of plasma one of them was holding.

'Easy, don't jar him,' the man holding the bottle said as they lifted the stretcher. 'You'll set him bleeding again.'

He isn't dead, she thought wonderingly.

But that didn't mean she'd saved his life. She'd only delayed his death. He'd die on the way to hospital. Or on the way to the ambulance, as they carried him across the wreckage on the stretcher. 'I'm *so* sorry,' she said, and the men looked over at her.

'What the bloody hell's she still doing here?' the one holding the plasma said. 'She needs medical attention.'

Hunter hastened over to her. 'Viola, I'm going to take you to the ambulance now,' he said. 'Put your arm round my neck.'

'Careful,' one of the stretcher-bearers warned as they started across the wreckage with it. 'If you strike a spark, you'll send us all up.'

'We must go, Viola,' Hunter said urgently. 'The theatre could go up any moment.'

Of course, the gas. *One of the stretcher bearers' hobnailed boots will scrape against the iron leg of a seat, and the gas will explode in a fireball and envelop us all. Including Hunter, who stayed behind to try to help me.*

She had to get away from him. Perhaps if he wasn't near her or the stretcher when the theatre went up, he'd only be injured. 'I'm all right. I can walk on my own,' she said, and struck out away from him across the tangle of seats, going as quickly as she could with one shoe and one bare foot.

'Careful, slow down!' Hunter called behind her. 'You'll fall.'

She clambered across a row of seats and over a mahogany railing. The men carrying the stretcher were halfway across the theatre, the bottle of plasma held aloft like a lantern.

Polly stepped down onto what had been a wall, painted with masks of Comedy and Tragedy. She glanced back at Hunter. He was only a few steps behind her. *Go away*, she thought frantically, hobbling across Tragedy, across Comedy, *I'm deadly*, and her single heel went through the plaster, all the way up to her ankle. She fell forward onto her hands and knees.

'What happened?' Hunter said, and before she could warn him to keep away, he jumped down beside her and helped her to standing. 'Are you hurt?'

'No, my foot—'

'I need some help here,' Hunter called after the stretcher bearers. 'She's—'

'*No*,' Polly said. 'You need to leave me here and go and fetch a crowbar.' But he was already on one knee beside her, pulling on her ankle.

'The heel's caught,' he said. 'Can you pull your foot out of the shoe?'

No, she thought, twisting around to look at the stretcher. The rescue crew nearly had it to the opening. The explosion would come any moment. Hunter wouldn't have time to make it out, even if he left her now.

'I'm so sorry,' she said.

And he must have thought she was talking about the shoe because he said, 'No matter. We'll just have to get you out, shoe and all. He reached his hand down through the ragged-edged plaster and fumbled with her foot. 'I told you you'd get into trouble clambering about an incident in high heels, though all in all, it's a very good thing you did.'

No, it isn't, she thought bitterly. *I got you all killed.* She turned to take one last look at Sir Godfrey and the men carrying the stretcher, but they weren't there.

'Where ... ?' she said, and heard voices shouting, doors slamming, a motor starting up.

The ambulance, she thought. *They're transporting him to hospital.* The ambulance roared off, bells ringing. Which meant he was still alive. And the rescue crew was still alive. The theatre hadn't gone up.

'They made it out,' she murmured, unable to take it in.

Hunter looked up briefly from struggling with her foot. 'Good. He should be right as rain once they get him to hospital and get him stitched up. You should be proud. You saved his life.'

Like Mike saved Hardy's life, she thought. *And like Eileen kept Alf and Binnie from going on the* City of Benares.

'It was clever, you stopping up that hole with your clothes,' Hunter was saying. 'If you hadn't found him and known what to do, he'd have been for it.'

It's true, she thought. If she hadn't caught her heel and bent down to free it, she'd never have heard him calling. And if she hadn't been wearing these shoes, her heel wouldn't have caught.

'For want of a shoe,' she murmured, and had a sudden vision of Mike saying, 'If I hadn't come through when I did, I wouldn't have missed the bus and been stuck in Saltram-on-Sea, I wouldn't have fallen asleep on the Commander's boat ...'

And if I hadn't gone to the Works Board to volunteer to be an ambulance driver, I wouldn't have been assigned to ENSA, I wouldn't have been performing at the Alhambra—

'Try to move your foot back and forth,' Hunter said. 'That's it.' He reached his arm down deeper. 'Keep moving it. I've nearly got it free.'

She nodded absently, thinking, *If Mrs Sentry hadn't seen me in* A Christmas Carol, *she wouldn't have assigned me to ENSA.*

But why, if the continuum was trying to repair itself, hadn't it kept her from being here the way it had kept Mike from getting to Dover, the way it had kept her and Eileen and Mike from reaching Mr Bartholomew on the night of the twenty-ninth?

Mike pushed two firemen out of the way of a collapsing wall that night, Polly thought suddenly. *And Eileen saved someone's life, too. The man in the ambulance.* And Binnie had been driving. Binnie, whom Eileen had nursed through pneumonia.

Why, if the past had sealed itself off to repair the damage Mike had caused, hadn't it stopped Eileen from saving that bombing victim's life? A hundred and sixty people had been killed the night of the twenty-ninth. It would have been easy to kill Mike and Eileen, and her, too. Or to let them find John Bartholomew and go back to Oxford.

If they'd gone back, they wouldn't have been here to further complicate things. She wouldn't have been able to save Sir Godfrey, and Eileen wouldn't have been able to save the man in the ambulance. And Eileen had had John Bartholomew in her sights. She'd run after him.

And Alf and Binnie had kept her from catching him. Alf and Binnie, whom Eileen had kept from going on the *City of Benares*.

'Got it,' Hunter said, and her heel, and foot, came abruptly loose.

She nearly fell. 'Are you all right?' he asked, steadying her.

'Yes,' she said, righting herself and pulling her foot up out of the broken plaster, annoyed that he had interrupted her train of thought. What had she … ? Alf and Binnie. They'd kept Eileen from catching John Bartholomew—

'Is your ankle injured?'

'No.' She set out across the wreckage again so he'd stop talking, so he wouldn't break the fragile thread of thought she was following. If Alf and Binnie hadn't kept Eileen from catching John Bartholomew …

They kept her from going back to Oxford the last day of her assignment, too, Polly thought, *by getting the measles.* If Alf hadn't fallen ill, Eileen wouldn't have been caught by the quarantine, and she wouldn't have been there to take them back to London and keep the letter from Mrs Hodbin. And if the net had sent Mike through on the right day, he would have been able to catch the bus to Dover, and he would never have ended up in Dunkirk and saved Hardy.

And if the net had sent me through at six in the morning instead of the evening, I wouldn't have been caught out during a raid and ended up at St George's. I wouldn't have met Sir Godfrey.

But the slippage was supposed to *prevent* historians from altering events. It was supposed to—

'Wrong way,' Hunter said, taking her arm.

'What?'

'You can't get out that way. It's blocked. Through here,' he said, leading her over a fallen pillar and down a broken staircase. 'That's it, only a few more steps.'

'What did you say?' Polly asked him, pulling back against his hand on her arm, trying to make him stop.

'I said, "only a few more steps". We're nearly there.'

'No, before that,' she said. 'You said—' But they were down the stairs and out of the theatre and he was handing her over to two FANYs.

'She needs to be taken to hospital,' Hunter said. 'Possible internal injuries and exposure to gas. She's a bit muddled.'

'Over here!' a man in a helmet called from across the street, and Hunter started towards him.

'Wait!' Polly called after him.

She had nearly had it, the knowledge which had been hovering just out of reach since he'd told her she'd saved Sir Godfrey's life. 'I need to speak to him,' she said to the FANYs, but he was already gone, she was already being wrapped in a blanket, being bundled into the back of an ambulance. 'I need to ask him—'

'The man you saved has already been taken to hospital. You can speak to him there,' the FANY said, putting a mask over her nose and mouth. 'Take a deep breath.'

'*No*,' Polly said, pushing it violently away, '*not* Sir Godfrey.

Hunter, the man who brought me out.' But the doors were already shut, the ambulance was already moving. 'Driver, you've got to go back. He said something when we were coming out of the theatre. I must ask him what it was!'

'She's confused,' the attendant called up to the driver. 'It's the effects of the gas.'

No, it's not, Polly thought, *it's a clue.*

Hunter had said ... something, and when she'd heard the words, they'd set up an echo of someone else, saying the same words ... and for an instant it had all made sense – Alf and Binnie blocking Eileen's way, and Mike unfouling the propellor, and the measles and the slippage and *A Christmas Carol.* If she could only remember ...

Hunter had said, 'You can't get out that way. It's blocked.' Like their drops. Hers had been bombed, and Mike's had a gun emplacement on it, and Eileen's had been fenced off and turned into a riflery range, blocking their way back. Like Alf and Binnie had blocked Eileen's way, like the station guard had kept Polly from leaving Notting Hill Gate and going to the drop the night St George's was destroyed—

It has something to do with that night, Polly thought. *The guard wouldn't let me leave, and I went to Holborn—*

'This won't hurt,' the attendant said, clamping the oxygen mask down over her nose and mouth and holding it there. 'It's only oxygen. It will help clear your head.'

I don't want *it cleared,* Polly thought. Not till she remembered what he said, not until she'd worked it out. It was a puzzle, like one of Mike's crosswords. It had something to do with Holborn and Mike's bus and ENSA and her shoe.

No, not her shoe – the shoe the horse had lost. 'For want of a horse, the battle was lost. For want of a battle, the war was ...'

The ambulance jolted to a stop and they were opening the doors, carrying her inside the hospital past a woman at a desk.

Like Agatha Christie that night at Bart's, Polly thought, and for an instant she nearly had it. It was something to do with

Agatha Christie, and that night she'd gone to Holborn. The sirens had gone early, and the guard wouldn't let her go to the drop, and so she hadn't been there when the parachute-mine exploded, she had thought they were all dead and had staggered into Townsend Brothers, and Marjorie had seen her and decided to elope with her airman—

'Let's get you out of those clothes,' the nurse said, and they were taking her bloody swimsuit off, putting her into a hospital gown and a bed, bombarding her with questions so that she couldn't concentrate. She had to keep explaining that her name wasn't Viola, it was Polly Sebastian, that she wasn't a chorus girl at the Windmill, that she wasn't injured.

'It's not my blood,' she insisted. 'It's Sir Godfrey's.'

She'd nearly forgotten about Sir Godfrey, she had been so fixed on remembering what Hunter had said, but if he'd died on the way to hospital, it didn't matter. If she hadn't saved his life …

'Is he here?' she asked. 'Is he all right?'

'I'll send someone to see,' the nurse promised, taking her pulse, pulling the blankets up over her. 'This will help you sleep.'

'I don't want to sleep,' Polly said, but it was too late. The needle was already in her arm.

'Marjorie,' she murmured, determined not to lose her train of thought. Marjorie had decided to elope with her airman, and she'd been in Jermyn Street when it was hit and so she'd …

But the sedative was already working, her thoughts already breaking up like fog into wisps of thought, already drifting from her grasp. She couldn't remember what Marjorie … no, not Marjorie. Agatha Christie. And the measles and a horse and that night at Holborn. There hadn't been anywhere to sit, so she'd queued up at the canteen waiting for the escalators to stop, and Alf and Binnie had run by, had stolen the woman's picnic basket. Alf and Binnie, who'd kept Eileen from going to St Paul's … no, that wasn't Eileen, it was Mr Dunworthy. They'd kept Mr Dunworthy from going to St Paul's, and he'd collided with Alan Turing. No, *Mike* had collided with Alan Turing. Mr Dunworthy had collided with Talbot, and her lipstick had rolled into the street, and Sir Godfrey …

Polly must have called out his name because the nurse hurried over. 'He's resting comfortably. Now try to sleep.'

I can't, Polly thought groggily. *I have to be there.*

'If you aren't, there will be no one there to avert the inevitable disaster,' Hunter had said. No, that was Sir Godfrey, talking about Mrs Wyvern and the pantomime. Hunter had said, 'It was lucky you knew what to do.'

I learned it in Oxford, she thought, *so I could pose as an ambulance driver and observe the V-1s and V-2s. But the Major sent us to Croydon to find John Bartholomew. No, not to Croydon, to St Paul's. But the streets were roped off because of the UXB, and I sneaked past the barrier and up the hill, but it was a cul-de-sac. I'd gone the wrong way—*

Wrong way. That was what Hunter had said.

'Wrong way,' Polly murmured, and saw the ginger-haired librarian at Holborn holding an Agatha Christie paperback, heard her saying, 'I'm convinced I know who the murderer is, and then, when I'm nearly to the end, I realise I've been looking at the entire situation the wrong way round, that something else entirely is going on.'

No, the librarian hadn't said that, Eileen had, that day in Oxford. No, that wasn't right either. But it didn't matter. Because Polly had it – the idea she'd been pursuing all the way across the wrecked theatre. And it all – Talbot and Marjorie and St Paul's and the measles and the stiff strap on her gilt shoe – fitted together. It all made sense, and she knew it was vital to hold on to it, not to let it drift away, but it was impossible, the sedative was already closing in like fog, obliterating everything.

'Like the spell in *Sleeping Beauty*,' she tried to say, but she couldn't. She was already asleep.

CROYDON – OCTOBER 1944

'We weren't killed,' Ernest tried to say to Mr Jeppers. 'The V-1 didn't kill us,' but he couldn't find the editor in the smoke. It billowed up blackly around him.

They must have hit the Arizona, he thought, coughing, trying to see out across the deck of the *New Orleans*.

But that couldn't be right. *I never got to Pearl Harbor*, he thought. *Dunworthy changed the order of my assignments. Oh God, I'm still at Dunkirk. My foot ...*

But that wasn't right either, because he was lying down. There hadn't been room on the boat to lie down. He'd had to stand up, squashed against the rail the whole way. And the smoke was too thick for it to be Dunkirk.

He couldn't see anything. It was completely dark. He must be belowdecks. He could see flames through the smoke and hear fire bells. *They're going to an incident*, he thought, and remembered the V-1. *I hope it didn't damage the printing press. I've got to get that picture of St Anselm's in. And take a photo of this incident.*

He looked around, trying to see if the name on the newspaper office was still there. If it was, Cess could crop off the word 'Croydon', and they could say it was the Cricklewood *Clarion Call*

But the fire wasn't bright enough to light more than the few feet beyond it, and there were no landmarks there, only bricks and broken timbers shrouded by orangish dust. It hadn't been smoke. It was plaster dust. That was why it was so choking, why he couldn't stop coughing. He had to try several times before he managed to say, 'Mr Jeppers! I need a torch so I can look at your sign!'

Mr Jeppers didn't answer. *He can't hear me for the fire bells*, Ernest thought. They got very loud and then stopped, and he could hear doors slamming and voices.

Perhaps they had a torch. 'Hullo!' he called to them, and stopped to cough. 'Do you have a torch?'

But they must not have heard him because they were walking away from him. 'No, over here!' he shouted. A mistake. It caused him to suck in a huge amount of plaster dust and choke.

'I thought I heard something,' one of the girls said, and he could hear the crack of wood and the slither of dirt as they came towards him. 'Where are you?'

'Here,' he said. 'Jeppers, it's all right. Someone's coming.'

'Where are you?' the second girl called after a moment, but he didn't answer her. He was listening to her voice. It sounded somehow familiar.

'Here he is!' the first one shouted from what seemed like far away. He heard a scrabbling sound, and then, 'I found him,' and he could tell from the tone of her voice that he was dead.

But I'm not, he thought. *We survived the V-1—*

'There's another one here somewhere,' the second voice said and something else – he couldn't make out what. More scrabbling. 'Over here!' she called, closer. Then she was there, bending over him. 'Are you all right?'

He looked up at her, but the light from the fires wasn't bright enough for him to see her face. All he caught was a glimpse of fair hair under the tin helmet. 'You mustn't worry,' she said. 'We'll get you out of here straightaway. Fairchild!' she called sharply, 'Over here!' and moved down to his legs and began tossing aside bricks and pieces of wood. 'I need a light!'

The girl she'd called Fairchild arrived. 'Is he alive?' she asked, stooping down next to him, and the fire must be growing brighter. He could see *her* face clearly. She looked very young. 'How bad is he?'

'His foot—'

'That wasn't the V-1,' he said. 'It happened at Dunkirk.' But they didn't hear him.

'I've tied a tourniquet. Go and get the medical kit,' the first girl said to Fairchild. 'And a stretcher. Is Croydon here yet?' she asked, and her voice sounded just like Polly's.

'No,' Fairchild said. 'Are you certain we should move him?'

'He'll bleed to death if we don't,' the girl who sounded like Polly said, and he could hear Fairchild run off across the rubble. 'Telephone Croydon. And Woodside,' she called after her. 'Tell them we need help.'

It can't be Polly, he thought as she tried to free him. *The deadline's passed.*

'Don't worry, we'll have you out of here in no time,' she said, bending so close he could see her face in the light of the fire, and it *was* Polly. He would know her anywhere.

No, Oh no, no. She was still here, and it was too late. Her deadline was already past. He hadn't got her out. 'I'm so sorry,' he croaked.

'It's not your fault,' she said.

But it *was* his fault. He hadn't been able to find Denys Atherton, and none of his messages had got through to Oxford. If they had, she wouldn't be here. 'I am *so* sorry,' he tried to say, choking on dust, on despair. It had all been useless – all those personal ads and wedding announcements and letters to the editor. His messages hadn't got through. No one had come. She'd still been here when her deadline arrived.

'I thought if I left, I could get you and Eileen out,' he said, looking up at her, but the fire must have burned out, he couldn't see her face, though he knew she was still there. He could hear her scrabbling at the bricks and wood, pushing them off his chest, freeing his arm.

'I didn't think you'd be here—'

'Don't try to talk.' She crawled over him to reach his other arm.

'You were not supposed to be here,' he tried to say. 'You were supposed to be in Dulwich.' But the only part that came out must have been 'Dulwich' because she said, 'We'll take you to Norbury. It's quicker. You mustn't worry about that. That's our job.'

He could hear her raise her head suddenly, as if she had heard something, and then he heard Fairchild call from a long way off, 'I can't get the stretcher out! It's stuck!'

'Leave it. Just bring the medical kit,' Polly called back.

But Fairchild must not have heard her because she shouted, 'What? I can't hear you, Mary!'

Mary? 'Mary?' he said.

'Yes,' she said, so softly he could scarcely hear her, and relief broke over him in a great wave. She wasn't here after her deadline. She wasn't Polly. She was Mary, and this was her rocket-attacks assignment, and he wasn't too late. None of it had happened yet – she hadn't even gone to the Blitz – and there was still time to save her, to already have saved her, and he must be weeping with relief and the tears must be running down his cheeks into his mouth because he could feel wetness on his tongue, in the back of his throat.

'Fairchild!' she shouted. 'Bring the kit! Hurry!'

He had to tell her the drops wouldn't open, had to warn her. 'You mustn't go! There's something wrong with the net. The drops won't open. Don't go!'

But she didn't understand. 'I need to,' she said. 'I'm going,' and started to leave.

'*No!*' he shouted, and grabbed hold of her wrist. 'You can't go! You'll be trapped there!'

673

'I won't leave you trapped here. I promise.'

'No! You don't understand. You can't go to the Blitz!' he cried, but he couldn't get the words out, the tears and dust in his mouth had mixed into a choking mud. 'Your drop, it won't open—' and there was a sudden, shattering noise and a blast so powerful it knocked them both down.

No, that wasn't right. He was already down. *The* Arizona, he thought. *It took a bomb right down its stack, and the concussion knocked her off her feet.*

She was getting back to her feet, running towards him. 'No!' he tried to call to her, 'Get down! The Zero's coming around again!'

She hadn't heard him, she was still running. 'Hit the deck!' he called, but it was too late. The Zero had already strafed her. She fell across him.

'Where are you hit?' he asked her, afraid she was dead, but she wasn't. She was getting to her knees, fumbling with his collar.

'It was a V-2,' she said, but it couldn't be. He'd made the Germans shorten their trajectories so they'd fall on Croydon.

'I need to go,' Polly said, bending over him, or had he said that? He couldn't tell.

'I have to leave,' he said again in case it hadn't been him who'd said it. 'It's the only way I can get you out before your deadline.' But she wasn't listening. She'd stood up and was running across the deck.

And he had been wrong about its being a Zero. It was a Stuka. It had dropped a stick of bombs and sunk the *Grafton*. And the *Lady Jane* was pulling away from the mole, leaving without him. 'Don't go!' he shouted. 'The Germans will be here any minute.'

Then, miraculously, she was back, bending over him again, and he had to tell her something, only he couldn't remember what. Something important. 'Tell Eileen Padgett's was hit,' he said, but that wasn't it.

What *was* it? He couldn't think for coughing. 'Tell her to take the stairs,' he said, thinking of the stuck elevator, and remembered. He had to warn Polly not to go through to the Blitz.

'It's a trap,' he said again. 'You won't be able to get out!' but it wasn't her, it was a soldier wearing a helmet.

Oh God, it's the Germans. I didn't get off Dunkirk in time.

The German shone a torch full in his face, and he flinched away from it. *They've captured me, and they're interrogating me. If they find out about Fortitude South, they'll know we're going to invade at Normandy.*

But it was an English soldier. 'How badly are you hurt?' he was asking, bending over Ernest, and his helmet was the tin hat of an ARP warden. 'What's your name?'

He thinks I'm Cess, Ernest thought. *Thank goodness he's not here*, and tried to tell the warden about Cess' having traded duties with Chasuble, and *his* having traded with Cess, and about the harvest fête, and Daphne at the Crown and Anchor.

No, that wasn't right. That was the other Daphne, and she wasn't there. She was in Manchester, and she was married …

The warden was shaking him. 'Davies?' he asked, wiping the plaster dust from his face. 'Michael?'

Yes, he thought. But he wasn't sure, it had been so long since he'd heard his real name, and he'd had so many names since he was killed …

The warden was shaking him and saying urgently, 'Can you hear me, Davies? Michael?'

'Yes.'

'Oh, thank God. Michael, listen, I'm here to take you back to Oxford. I'm Colin Templer.' But he couldn't be. Colin was only a boy.

'You're too old,' he murmured.

'I've been looking for you for a long time.'

'You got my messages,' Ernest said, feeling sick with relief. They were here, they could warn Polly not to go to the Blitz. And they could …

'You have to get Charles out,' he said, trying to raise himself by his elbows. 'He's in Singapore. You have to get him out before the Japanese—'

'We did,' he said. 'He's safe. He's waiting for you in the lab. Do you think you can stand up?'

He shook his head. 'You have to tell Polly—'

'She's alive? She was alive when you left her?'

Ernest nodded.

'Oh thank God,' Colin breathed. It *was* Colin after all.

'You have to tell her—'

'I'll find her and get her out,' Colin said, 'but first I've got to get *you* out of here.'

'No, she's here,' he tried to say, but he was coughing too hard.

'Can you tell me where you're hurt?'

'My foot,' he said. 'I was unfouling the propellor,' but Colin wasn't listening. He was digging someone out of the rubble.

It must be Mr Jeppers, he thought. 'Is he all right?' he asked and heard a siren. 'We need to get to a shelter,' he said.

'That's the ambulance. I've got to get you out of here before they arrive,' Colin said, stooping to lift him. 'We can't let them see us.'

'No, wait, you have to tell Polly not to go,' he tried to say, but he was overcome with a spasm of coughing. It was all the plaster Colin had stirred up digging out Mr Jeppers. It was making him choke, and all he could get out was her name.

'I'll go and fetch Polly, I promise, as soon as I get you back to Oxford.'

Oxford, Ernest thought, and could see the spires of Christ Church and St Mary's, and Magdalen Tower, and Balliol's quad green in the April sunshine.

'This'll hurt,' Colin said, reaching his arms around him. 'Sorry.' And the V-2 hit, ripping the world apart.

No, that wasn't right, the V-2 had already hit, and he wasn't in the wreckage, he was on a cot and an orderly was covering him with a blanket. 'Am I in hospital?' he asked.

'Not yet,' the orderly said. 'I'm taking you there now.'

'You can't,' Ernest said, struggling. He had passed out on the way to hospital. He had been unconscious for more than a month, and when he'd come to, nobody had known who he was. 'I can't go to Orpington. The retrieval team won't know where I am.'

'I'm the retrieval team, old man,' the orderly said. 'It's Colin. Colin Templer. You're in Croydon, in an ambulance. I'm taking you back to Oxford.'

Ernest clutched Colin's arm. 'But I have to tell you about Polly,' and some of his desperation must have got through because Colin nodded.

'All right. When did you see her last, Michael?'

Had it been a few minutes or longer than that? 'I don't know. She—' He tried to raise his hand to show Colin where she'd gone. '—left.'

'When did you leave?' Colin asked. 'On January eleventh? That's when the *Times* said you died.'

No, he thought, *it's September.* But Colin meant when he'd been in London. 'Yes, on the eleventh.'

'Where was Polly working when you left? Was she still working in Oxford Street?'

He nodded. 'At Townsend Brothers. On the third floor. But she and Eileen—'

'Eileen? Merope's there?' Colin said eagerly. 'She and Polly are together? Do you know where they're living?'

'Fourteen,' he said, swallowing. There was an odd metallic taste in his mouth. He swallowed, trying to get rid of it. 'Cardle Street,' he attempted to say, but he couldn't for coughing – and he must have coughed so hard he vomited because Colin was wiping at his mouth with a corner of the blanket. 'Mrs—'

'Don't try to talk,' Colin said, dabbing at his chin. 'They're living at Mrs Rickett's in Cardle Street. Number fourteen.'

Ernest nodded. 'In Kensington,' he tried to say, but more coughing overtook him.

But it was all right, Colin understood. 'In Kensington, right? We worked that out from your messages. And the shelter they're using is Notting Hill Gate?'

Ernest nodded, grateful he didn't have to try to say all that because there was something else he needed to tell him, something important. 'She didn't come through in June. She came through in December of '43. You have to get her out before the twenty-ninth.'

'I will. But first I've got to get you back.' He stooped over him. 'Can you put your arms round my neck?'

'Don't,' Ernest said, afraid the V-2 would hit again when he lifted him. 'Get Polly to help you. Tell her to bring the stretcher.'

'She's not here,' Colin said gently. 'She's in 1941. Remember? You told me where to find her.'

'No. Here. At the incident.' But Colin wouldn't know that word. He wasn't a historian. He was just a boy. 'She was the one who found me in the wreckage,' he tried to say. 'She rescued me. She's an ambulance driver at Dulwich.'

But that must not have been what he said because Colin asked, 'She wasn't working at Townsend Brothers when you left? She was driving an ambulance?'

'No. Here. In the wreckage ...' He swallowed. '... after the V-1 hit—'

'Polly was here just now?' Colin cut in.

'No, Mary. She hasn't gone to the Blitz yet. But it's all right. She didn't recognise me. I didn't ruin it,' he said between coughs. 'You've got to warn her. You've got to tell her not to go.'

'If I'd known—' Colin said, looking off into the distance, and Ernest knew they weren't at the incident, that Colin had taken him somewhere else.

'Are we in the ambulance?' he asked.

'No, we're at the drop. If I'd known Polly was there ...' he said, and he sounded full of despair and longing.

Like that night I left London, Ernest thought, *when I knew I could never see her or Eileen again*. But he had to see her. 'You have to stop her. Go back—'

'I've got to get you home first. The drop'll open any second now. There's an emergency medical team waiting for us in the lab. We'll have you fixed up in no time, old man.'

'There's no time. She'll be gone,' he opened his mouth to say. 'You have to go and find her,' but without any warning he was vomiting again, all down Colin's overall, only it wasn't vomit, it was blood.

'I'll find them, I promise,' Colin said, and put his arms around him.

Good, he thought. *I won't have to die alone*. 'Why the bloody hell doesn't the drop open?' Colin said angrily.

'It's broken. We're all trapped here in the Blitz ...'

'Stay with me, Davies. We'll be there any second. We'll get you to hospital, and they'll get you all fixed up, they'll get you a new leg, and I'll go and fetch Eileen and Polly. They'll be there before you come out of surgery. They'll be so glad to see you. You're a hero, you know.'

'I know,' he said. 'I saved Cess' life.' *And Chasuble's. And Jonathan's and the Commander's. And that dog's*. He wondered what had happened to it, and whether it had helped to win the war.

'Don't quit on me, Davies,' Colin said. 'You can do this.'

Ernest shook his head. 'Kiss me, Hardy,' he murmured.

'What?'

He bent nearer, and Ernest saw it *was* Hardy. 'I'm glad I saved your life,' he said. 'No matter what.'

'Finally!' Hardy said, 'Thank God!' and scooped him up in his arms.

Just like at St Paul's, Ernest thought, *the captain dying in Honour's arms*, though he'd never seen it – the sandbags had hidden it. And the captain hadn't seen it either. He'd died the moment after he'd tied the boats together. He'd never known whether they'd won or not.

'Did we?' he asked Colin.

And he must only be a boy after all because he was crying. 'Don't do this, Davies,' he pleaded. 'Not now. Michael!'

No, not Michael. Or Mike Davis. Or Ernest Worthing. And not Shackleton. 'That's not my name,' he said, and tried to tell him what it was, but the blood was everywhere, in his mouth, his ears, his eyes, so he couldn't hear Colin, he couldn't see the drop opening. 'It's Faulknor.'

LONDON – APRIL 1941

The sedative the nurse gave Polly must have been morphine because her sleep was filled with muddy, mazelike dreams. She was trying to get to the drop, which lay just on the other side of the peeling black door, but it had already shut, the train was already pulling out, and this was the wrong platform. She had to get to Paddington in time for the 11:19 to Backbury, and the troupe was blocking her way. She had to step over them – Marjorie and the woman at the Works Board and the ARP warden who had caught her that first night and taken her to St George's. And Fairchild and the librarian at Holborn and Mrs Brightford, sitting against the wall reading to Trot. '"And the bad fairy said to Sleeping Beauty",' Mrs Brightford read, '"You will prick your finger on a spindle and die."'

'No, she won't,' Trot said. 'The good fairy will fix it.'

'She can't fix it,' Alf said contemptuously. 'They got here too late.'

'She can *so*,' Trot retorted, going very red in the face. 'It says so in the *story*. Can't she, Polly?'

'I don't know,' Polly said. 'I fear they'll only make things worse.'

'Hush,' Mrs Brightford said. '"And then the good fairy said, 'The spell is already cast, and I cannot undo it, but I will do what I can'."' And Polly wanted to stay and listen to the end of the story, but she was late, she had to get to Dulwich before the twenty-ninth. She ran through tunnels and corridors and up stairs that were sometimes in Holborn and sometimes in Padgett's, and she couldn't run very fast because she was carrying the answer that she had puzzled out, clenched in her fist like a penny.

She didn't dare let go of it. She had to hold it tight against her stomach till she had the string wrapped around it, till she had all the ends tucked in. She had been late getting to Dulwich and missed hearing the first V-1s, so she hadn't known what they sounded like, so she had knocked Talbot into the gutter and wrenched her knee and had had to drive Stephen, and if she hadn't, he and Talbot would have been killed in Tottenham Court Road, and he wouldn't have come up with the idea of tipping the V-1s ...

But it wasn't a V-1, it was a siren, and Polly had to go onstage and bend over and flip up her skirt, but her knickers didn't say, 'Air Raid in Progress', they said 'Wrong Way Round', and when she tried to look over her shoulder to read the message, a V-1 came over, rattling like a motorcycle, and she had to run downstairs to the shelter in Padgett's basement, holding the answer tight in her hand, the answer that made it all make sense – Eileen's driving lessons and Stephen and the Wren and Alf and Binnie's parrot and the library at Holborn.

But she wasn't in Holborn, she was in St Paul's, trying to find a way up to the roofs. But she couldn't. It was too dark. She needed a torch.

Mike had it, he was swinging it back and forth, trying to see what was fouling the propellor. 'Shine it over here,' she said, but Mike said, 'I can't. There's no time. The U-boats will be here any minute.' And when she looked up at the boat looming above them, she saw it wasn't the *Lady Jane*, it was the *City of Benares*.

'Get the lantern!' Mike shouted.

'What lantern?'

'In the painting,' he said, and she ran back down the curving staircase, past the masks of Comedy and Tragedy, her hands cupped protectively around the answer, through the north transept and under the dome to the south aisle …

And full tilt into Alf and Binnie, colliding with them, her hands reaching out instinctively to break her fall, opening, spilling all of it – the slippage and Agatha Christie and the *Lady Jane* and the air-raid warden and her bloomers – like pennies, like Crimson Caress lipstick onto the pavement and into the road. 'Oh no,' she said, bending to pick it up. 'Oh no.'

'Shh, it's all right,' someone said, and she opened her eyes. A nurse in a white starched apron was bending over her, taking her pulse. 'You're in hospital.'

'I lost—' Polly murmured.

'Whatever it is, you can find it later,' the nurse said. 'You must try to sleep.'

'No,' Polly said, thinking, *It had something to do with detective novels. And* Sleeping Beauty. *And a horse. 'A horse, a horse, my kingdom for a horse—'*

'I must see Sir Godfrey,' she said.

'Sir Godfrey?' the nurse said blankly, and Polly thought, *They've taken him to some other hospital, like the man I tied the tourniquet on in Croydon. Or to the morgue.*

He died on the way to hospital, Polly thought. *I didn't save his life after all.*

But the nurse was saying, 'It was lucky you found him in time. And lucky you knew what to do.'

But we weren't lucky, Polly thought. *I was late getting to Dulwich. Mike missed the bus to Dover. He missed Daphne in Saltram-on-Sea and had to follow her all the way to Manchester, and Eileen came to Townsend Brothers the one day I was gone.* And the night of the twenty-ninth, everything had conspired against them – the air-raid warden who stopped them just as they were going into St Paul's and the doctor who hijacked Eileen, and the fires and falling walls and blocked-off streets. And Alf and Binnie.

'Why is it everywhere I go there are horrible children?' Eileen had asked, but it if hadn't been for the Hodbins, Eileen wouldn't have survived after Mike died. And if she hadn't insisted on taking them in, if they hadn't insisted on bringing their parrot, Alf and Binnie wouldn't have got them thrown out of the boarding house. They all might have died along with Mrs Rickett.

'It's lucky we got thrown out, ain't it?' Alf had said, and Mr Humphreys had said, 'What luck you came to Saint Paul's today. He's here, the man I told you about.' And Mike had said, 'It's lucky that was the only available room in Bletchley, or I'd never have found out what happened to Gerald Phipps.'

'It was lucky the warden heard me in the rubble,' Marjorie had said, and that night in Padgett's, Eileen had said, 'It's lucky I heard you calling.'

And at some point Polly must have fallen asleep, must have murmured Eileen's name, because Eileen said, 'I'm here,' and when Polly opened her eyes, she *was* there, and it was morning. A nurse was pulling back the blackout curtains from the tall windows, and sunlight was streaming into the ward.

Polly held her hands up in the light and looked at them. They were open, empty of anything, but it didn't matter. She hadn't lost the answer she'd been holding carefully cupped in them. It had been there all along. She had just been looking at it the wrong way round.

'Are you all right?' Eileen asked.

'Yes,' she said wonderingly. 'I am.' *If I'm right. If Alf and Binnie—*

'Oh, thank goodness,' Eileen said, and Polly saw that she had been crying. 'Mr Dunworthy and I have been so worried …

When you didn't come home last night … The warden told us there'd been bombs all over the West End, and then when I rang the theatre and the stage manager said you'd run out during the performance into the middle of a raid and hadn't come back, I …'

Eileen broke off, blew her nose, and attempted to smile. 'Matron said they found you inside the Forrest Theatre. What on earth were you doing there?'

'Saving Sir Godfrey's life,' Polly said. 'Eileen, how ill was Binnie?'

'How ill? What—?'

'With the measles. Would she have died if you hadn't been there?'

'I don't know. Her fever was dreadfully high. But you're not going to die, Polly. The nurse said you'd be fine—'

'What happened to the firewatcher?'

'The fire—?'

'The one who was injured who John Bartholomew took to Barts? Did Mr Bartholomew save his life?'

'Polly, you're not making any sense. The doctor said you breathed in a good deal of gas. I think you may still—'

'On the last day of your assignment, why didn't you go back to Oxford?'

'I told you, the quarantine.'

'No, I need to know exactly what happened,' Polly said, clutching Eileen's hand. 'Please. It's important.'

Eileen looked at her as if trying to decide whether to call the nurse, and then said, 'I was leaving to go to the drop when some new evacuees arrived. Theodore was one of them.'

Theodore, who had prevented them from going straight to St Paul's to find John Bartholomew. They had had to take him home to Stepney, and by the time they reached St Paul's, the sirens had gone and the ARP warden—

'I had to get the evacuees settled,' Eileen was saying, 'and then as I was leaving, the vicar asked me to help him get out of giving Una her driving lesson, and when I drove round the curve, Alf and Binnie were standing in the middle of the lane.'

Blocking the way. Delaying her. As they had delayed her on the twenty-ninth, as the troop trains had delayed Polly reaching the manor in Backbury till after Captain Chase had left for London, as the slippage had delayed Mike till after the bus had left for Dover, as she was almost certain the Hodbins had delayed ...

'Are Alf and Binnie here at the hospital?' she asked.

'Yes, downstairs in the waiting room. Children aren't allowed in the wards.'

'Is Mr Dunworthy here?'

'No, I thought it best not to tell him what had happened till I found out for certain ...'

That's what I'm trying to do, Polly thought. *Find out for certain.*

'Go and ask Alf and Binnie—' she said, and then stopped. They wouldn't tell Eileen the truth. If they even remembered the incident. Alf and Binnie had clearly thought they knew Mr Dunworthy from somewhere that night she brought him home from St Paul's – they'd asked her if he was a truant officer – but they hadn't been able to place him. And if Eileen asked them, they'd assume the guard – or the authorities – were involved.

Polly would have to ask them herself and then ask Mr Dunworthy. If *he* remembered. And even if he did, it wouldn't prove anything. The proof lay with Sir Godfrey. He had said she'd saved his life, but he'd been shocky from loss of blood and confused from the gas ...

'Eileen,' Polly said, 'I must see Sir Godfrey. I need you to go and find out what room he's in. And fetch me my clothes,' she added and then remembered they consisted of a bloodied bathing suit and one gilt high-heeled shoe. 'Where's your coat?'

'I ran out without it when I found out you—'

'See if there's a dressing gown in the cabinet there.'

Eileen opened the cabinet and the drawers of the nightstand.

'There's no dressing gown. I can bring you one when I come back this afternoon.'

'That's not soon enough,' Polly said. 'I must ask Sir Godfrey something. It's urgent. You must go and find me a dressing gown and find out what room he's in, and then we need a diversion.'

'A *diversion*? I can't—'

'Not you. Alf and Binnie,' Polly said. 'And if I'm right, it's only fitting that they do this.'

'Fitting?'

'Yes. Do you remember when you said Alf and Binnie could defeat Hitler all on their own?'

Eileen nodded.

'Well, you may have been right.'

'But how can they create a diversion if children aren't allowed in the wards?' Eileen began, and then sighed. 'You're right. They're the ones for the job. What do you want them to do?'

'I'll leave that to them,' Polly said. 'They're the experts. Tell them I'll need a clear shot at the stairwell and the corridor outside Sir Godfrey's room. And don't forget the dressing gown.'

'I won't, if you'll promise to rest till I come back.'

'I will,' Polly lied.

There wasn't time to rest. There were too many pieces to fit into the puzzle, too many clues to decipher. Mike had saved Hardy, and Hardy had rescued two hundred and nineteen soldiers, and the patient with gangrene that she and the other FANYs had driven to Orpington from Dover had said he'd been rescued from Dunkirk by someone who'd been rescued himself. 'You saved my life,' he'd told Polly. 'I'd have been a goner without you.' And Hardy had told Mike the same thing.

Mike had thought the slippage had been trying to keep him from affecting the evacuation of Dunkirk and had somehow failed. But what if he'd been sent through at Saltram-on-Sea *because* the *Lady Jane* was there? What if it had purposely sent him there after the bus and Mr Powney had gone so he—?

Binnie ran in carrying a scarlet kimono. ''ere.' She dumped it unceremoniously on the bed. ''e's one flight up.'

'In which ward?'

''e ain't *in* a ward, 'e's got a private room. Last one on the right,' Binnie said and raced out again.

The kimono had a large golden dragon embroidered on the back. *I should have specified an* inconspicuous *dressing gown*, Polly thought, hastily putting the kimono on. She pulled the bedclothes up to her neck and then lay still, listening.

There was a shriek and a clatter, and then the sound of hurrying feet. Polly flung the covers off, hurried over to the doors and peeked out in time to see two nurses and an attendant disappearing through the doors to the other ward.

Polly padded quickly along the corridor to the stairs. There was another shriek, and a woman's voice shouted, 'Catch him!'

Polly ducked into the stairwell and up the steps, braced for the sound of the ward doors opening, of running feet.

More shrieks. 'You wretched little—' the woman's voice said, and then cut off.

Oh Lord, I hope they haven't killed anyone, Polly thought, reaching the landing and starting up the next set of stairs, wincing at the sounds drifting up from below – a horrible thumping, followed by feet pounding down some other flight of stairs and a sound of something (or someone) falling – trying not to think of the effects of the chaos she had just set in motion.

'I think they went that way!' someone shouted. More shrieks.

Polly reached the top of the stairs. The floor was deserted. A flurry of papers lay on the linoleum in front of the Matron's desk, and halfway down the corridor a wheelchair lay on its side, fortunately with no one in it.

Polly ran down to Sir Godfrey's room. His door was shut. *Oh God*, she thought, *don't let him be dead*. She took a deep, ragged breath and opened the door.

Sir Godfrey was lying propped up against pillows, a grey

pyjama top open over his bandaged chest. His eyes were closed, and his face and hands were nearly as white as the bandages. A tube ran from his arm to a bottle of dark red blood hanging next to the bed. Polly went over to the bed and looked down at him, watching his almost indiscernible breathing. '"Time hath not yet dried this red blood of mine",' he murmured, and opened his eyes.

'You're all right,' Polly said thankfully.

'Yes, though imprisoned here and set about with foul fiends who refuse to let me up. How did you succeed in escaping their iron grip?'

'I had assistance,' Polly said, shutting the door. 'Sir Godfrey, last night you told me—'

'Oh dear, I do hope I didn't say anything I shouldn't have. I didn't confess undying love to some girl fifty years my junior, did I? Or quote *Peter Pan?*'

'No, of course not. You said last night that I'd saved your life—'

'And so you have, as you can see.' He spread his arms wide. 'I am made new, brought back to life again, like Claudio's Hero. "I do live, and surely as I live—"'

'No, I don't mean what happened last night. I mean before. When we were there in the theatre, I told you I was sorry I couldn't save your life, and you said I already had.'

'And so you had, thrice over. You saved me from having to act the part of Captain Hook—'

'Sir Godfrey, I'm serious—'

'And so am I. If you had not dissuaded the troupe from doing that odious play, I should have had to fling myself under one of the District Line trains.'

'Sir Godfrey, please don't joke. I must know.'

'Very well, then, I shall tell you. But first, I demand a forfeit.'

'A forfeit?'

'As Beauty was forced to pay a forfeit for straying into the

Beast's garden, so must you. My current plight is, after all, your fault. If I had died last night, I should have escaped doing the pantomime. Now I must put up with Mrs Wyvern for a full month. I hold you entirely responsible.'

And I might be, Polly thought. *I might be.*

'I feel the least you can do,' Sir Godfrey went on, 'for consigning me to what is, quite literally, a fate worse than death, is to keep me company during my ordeal.

'Yes, all right. I promise. I'll do the pantomime, if you'll only tell me—'

'Excellent. "We shall sing like two birds i' the cage," as soon as I've located another theatre. I wonder if the Windmill would lend us their stage for a month. We could send you to ask them, in your eloquent bloomers—'

'You promised you'd tell me if I paid the forfeit,' Polly said. 'How did I save your life, if I did save it?'

'You did, you have, sweet Viola, every day and every night since first you entered my life. And what an entrance! Worthy of the divine Sarah – a knock upon the door, and there you stood in the doorway – frightened, beautiful, lost. A creature from another country, washed up on the shores of St George's. And the embodiment of everything I thought the war had destroyed.'

He smiled at her. 'During those first nights of the Blitz, it seemed to me that not only the theatres, but the theatre itself, *and* the Bard, had become casualties of war. That Shakespeare's quaint notions of honour and courage and virtue were all dead, murdered by Hitler and his Luftwaffe. And I felt I had been murdered along with them.

'And then you came,' he said, 'looking like all of Shakespeare's lovely heroines and loving daughters – Miranda and Rosalind and Cordelia and Viola combined into one – and restored my faith.'

She had been wrong. When he'd said she'd saved his life, he had been speaking figuratively, not literally, and her theory hadn't been right after all.

'What is it?' Sir Godfrey said, frowning at her with concern. 'Why do you look so disappointed? Do you regret saving an old man from despair?'

'No,' she said, 'no, of course not. I only thought you meant I'd really saved your life.'

'But you had. There are a hundred ways a man can bleed to death. And he can be pulled from the rubble of bitterness, of despair, as well as from the wreckage of the Forrest. And which rescue is the more real? Which mattered more at Agincourt, the longbows or Henry's St Crispin's Day speech? Which matters more in *this* war, Panzers or courage? HEs or love? Nothing you could have done for me, dear child, was more important than the restoration of my hope.'

She tried to smile through her disappointment.

'But you were the salvation of my corporeal being as well. That night when first I saw you—'

'*There* you are,' the nurse said to Polly, flinging the door open. 'I've been looking for you everywhere. You're supposed to be in bed.'

'This young lady saved my life,' Sir Godfrey said. 'I was thanking her for—'

Another nurse appeared, looking fierce. 'Sir Godfrey is *not* to have visitors,' she said to Polly's nurse.

'Please, I only need another moment,' Polly said.

'Who's this?' Sir Godfrey's nurse demanded of Polly's nurse. 'A *patient*? What's she doing out of bed? Why weren't you watching her?'

Polly's nurse looked defensive. 'She got out of bed without my permission, and—'

'Silence!' Sir Godfrey shouted. 'Begone, varlets. I would speak with this lady.' But Sir Godfrey's nurse wasn't impressed.

'Take this patient back down to her ward immediately,' she said to Polly's nurse.

'Please,' Polly said. 'You don't understand—'

'Help!' a voice called from the end of the ward. 'Oh, help!'

Binnie, Polly thought. *Thank heavens.*

'Come quick!' Binnie sobbed. 'My mum's bleedin'. Hurry!'

Both nurses took off at a run.

'Quick,' Polly said, gripping the railing at the foot of the bed with both hands. 'Tell me how I saved your life.'

'That night you stumbled into St George's, I had received a letter from an old friend of mine, offering me a role in a repertory company. It was to tour the provinces – Salisbury, Bristol, Plymouth. It was a dreadful programme, no Shakespeare at all, Barrie, Galsworthy, *Charley's Aunt*' – he grimaced – 'and rep is even *worse* than pantomime. But all the theatres in the West End were shut, and it would have been a chance to get away from London and the bombs. And it scarcely mattered which play I did, or where. It was all for naught, "full of sound and fury, signifying nothing".'

We haven't got time for you to do Macbeth, Polly thought desperately. *They'll be back any minute.*

'And then you came, and I knew that was a lie. That beauty, courage, meaning still lived.'

'What's the meaning of this?' Polly heard Sir Godfrey's nurse shout from the end of the corridor. 'Children aren't allowed up here.'

'And then,' he said, 'when you knew your lines, I realised I could not possibly leave.'

'Come back here, you wretched child!' the nurse shouted, but Polly scarcely heard her.

'The next morning,' Sir Godfrey said, 'I wrote to him, turning his offer down.'

Polly waited, afraid to speak, afraid to breathe.

'The theatre in Bristol was bombed during the second act of *Sentimental Tommy*, a direct hit. The entire company was killed.'

> MIRANDA: 'What foul play had we that we came from thence?
> Or blessèd was't we did?
> PROSPERO: 'Both, both, my girl.'

WILLIAM SHAKESPEARE *THE TEMPEST*

LONDON – APRIL 1941

It took the staff of the hospital another quarter of an hour to apprehend Alf and Binnie, during which time Polly was able to assure Sir Godfrey again that yes, she'd do the pantomime *if* he could find another theatre to put it on in, hurry back down to the ward, divest herself of the Chinese robe, climb in bed and be lying there looking nearly as innocent as Alf and Binnie did when they were dragged in by the scruff of their necks.

'Do you know these children?' Matron demanded.

'They're my foster-children,' Eileen said, coming in. 'I told them to stay in the waiting room while I visited Polly. They've been very worried about their aunt,' she explained.

Alf nodded. 'We was scared she was dead.'

'We was orphaned before, you see,' Binnie said, sniffling.

Alf patted his sister kindly. 'We ain't got nobody to take care of us 'cept Aunt Eileen and Aunt Polly.'

'I'm sorry if they attempted to come up to the ward to see me,' Polly said. 'They meant well—'

'Attempted to come up to the *ward*?' Matron said. 'They've turned this entire hospital upside down. They've been racketing through the corridors, terrorising patients, wreaking—'

'We was only trying to catch Alf's snake,' Binnie said, ''afore it frightened anyone.'

'*Snake*?' the Matron said. 'You two let a snake loose in hospital?'

''course not,' Binnie said, her eyes wide and innocent. ''e got away on 'is own, didn't 'e?'

'But don't worry, we caught 'im,' Alf said, pulling a snake out of his pocket and dangling it in front of Matron.

Matron blanched. 'I want these two children – *and* their reptile – out of this hospital *immediately*.'

'Yes, Matron,' Eileen said, and hustled the children out.

'I'm afraid they'll only come back,' Polly said. 'They're very much attached to me.' And within a quarter of an hour she was pronounced fully recovered, discharged and allowed to telephone someone – but not Eileen – to bring her her clothes and handbag.

Polly rang up Hattie, and spent the time till she got there from the Alhambra thinking of everything that had happened, trying to fit it into the puzzle.

Because she'd driven Stephen, Paige Fairchild had gone with her to Croydon and had stopped the car to confront Polly. If she hadn't, they wouldn't have been there when the V-1 hit, they wouldn't have found the man with the severed foot. Had she saved his life, too?

I hope so, Polly thought, remembering how he'd clutched her hand, how he'd told her he was sorry.

Just as I told Sir Godfrey I was sorry for getting him killed. But the man at Croydon hadn't got either of them killed. It was just the opposite. If Paige hadn't been bringing the medical kit, she'd have been in the ambulance when the V-2 hit and been killed. So why had he said he was sorry—?

'Oh thank goodness you're all right!' Hattie said, bursting into the ward. 'I was so afraid – I kept telling the Incident Officer Reggie'd seen you run into the Forrest, but it took me an *age* to convince him.' She handed Polly her clothes. 'Tabbitt says you're not to come in tonight or tomorrow night.'

Good, Polly thought, *that will give me time to go to Bart's.* But when she arrived home, Eileen wouldn't hear of it. 'You're going to bed,' she said. 'You've only just got out of hospital. I'll go. What is it you want me to find out?'

'The names of the people you took to Bart's on the night of the twenty-ninth, especially the officer you kept from bleeding to death. And any information you can find out about them and about what happened to them after they got out of hospital if they did get out of hospital.'

'You think I did something to lose the war, don't you?' Eileen said, anguished.

'No,' Polly said, 'I think you may have done just the opposite, but I need proof. Where are Alf and Binnie?'

'At school.'

'What about Mr Dunworthy?'

'He's sleeping, finally, and you're not to wake him. He's been so worried.'

'But there's something I must ask him.'

'You can do it after I come back,' Eileen said firmly, and made Polly get into bed.

'Wait, before you go, you said Alf did the navigating that night. How did he know the streets?'

'From his planespotting,' she said. 'He pored over his maps of England and London for hours.'

'Where did he get them? Did you give them to him?'

'No, the vicar did. During the quarantine. Alf was driving me mad, and I asked Mr Goode to *please* send over something to keep him occupied, and he sent the maps.'

And if Eileen hadn't been there, none of it would have been able to happen. Alf wouldn't have known the streets, and Binnie wouldn't have known how to drive, wouldn't even have been alive. It all fitted perfectly, as if it had been planned: Steps for Saving Bombing Victim During an Air Raid.

'You're to rest till I get back,' Eileen said.

Polly promised, and Eileen left. Polly waited five minutes, in case she came back to check on her, and then dressed and went to Alf and Binnie's school and told the headmistress she needed to take them home. 'It's an emergency,' she said, which was true.

The headmistress sent a pupil to fetch them.

'Where's Eileen?' Binnie asked when she saw Polly.

'At Bart's,' Polly said, and Binnie went ashen.

'She's dead, ain't she?' Alf said hoarsely.

'*No*,' Polly said, 'she's perfectly fine. I sent her there to find out something for me.'

'You swear?'

'I swear,' Polly said, and Binnie's colour began to come back.

'Then what are you doin' here?' Alf asked.

'I came to take you out for a treat to thank you for helping me at the hospital.'

'What sort of treat?' Alf asked suspiciously.

She hadn't thought that far ahead, but the Hodbins knew exactly where to go. Polly bought them both ices and then asked, 'This autumn did you ever go to St Paul's Station?'

Binnie, her mouth full, began to say no, but Alf was already blurting out, 'That guard was *lyin'*. We didn't do nuffink. 'e *give* me that shilling, for tellin' 'im wot station it was, and then the guard come along and said we picked 'is pocket, but we never. 'e isn't goin' to put us in gaol, is he?'

'I don't know,' Polly said consideringly. 'If the guard says you did ... Do you remember what the gentleman looked like who gave you the shilling? Perhaps if we could find him, he'd be willing to speak to the police—'

'It weren't no gent,' Alf said, ''e was a boy.'

'How old?'

Alf shrugged. 'I dunno.'

'Older 'n' us,' Binnie said. 'Maybe sixteen.'

'And where were you when he gave you the shilling?'

'By the map,' Binnie said. ''e was standin' there, and we come up to look at it. There's no law says we can't look at a map, is there? 'ow else do you find out which line to take?'

'And then what happened?'

'The guard come up,' Binnie said, sounding outraged, 'and told 'im 'e'd better check 'is money and papers.'

'We didn't do *nuffink*,' Alf said.

Except delay him in the tunnel for a critical few minutes. If it *was* him.

Binnie was frowning at her thoughtfully.

I need to change the subject before she puzzles it out, Polly thought. 'It was very clever of you to think of the snake at the hospital, Binnie,' she said.

'It was *my* idea,' Alf said, offended.

'It was *not*, you slowcoach.'

'Well, it was my *snake*. D'you want to see 'im?' He reached for his pocket.

'No,' Polly said, bought them both a lollipop, delivered them back to the headmistress, and hurried home. Eileen wasn't there yet, and Mr Dunworthy's door was still shut. Polly rapped softly on it and went in.

Mr Dunworthy wasn't in bed. He was sitting by the window, looking out, and she was struck all over again by how weary and defeated he seemed. 'Mr Dunworthy,' she said gently.

'Polly!' he cried and held out his hands to her. 'Last night when you didn't come home, I was afraid—' He stopped and gave her a searching look. 'What is it? Has something happened to Eileen?'

'No,' Polly said. She pulled a stool over in front of his chair and sat down facing him. 'I need to ask you some questions. Mike said on the night of the twenty-ninth, Mr Bartholomew saved the life of the firewatcher who was injured. Is that right?'

'You think he contributed to what's happened, too?'

'Yes, but not in the way you think. *Did* he? Save his life?'

'I don't know. He said Langby had fallen on an incendiary and was badly burned. He might have.'

'I thought so,' Polly said. 'Now, I need you to tell me exactly what happened that first time you came through to the Blitz, when you collided with the Wren. You came through into the emergency staircase and went out into the station—'

'Yes, to ascertain my temporal-spatial location, and when I found I was near St Paul's, I ran up to see—'

'No, before that. In the station.'

'I went to look at the Underground map, but there was nothing on it to indicate where I was, so I asked these two children who'd come over, and the boy – it was a boy and a girl – said they'd only tell me if I paid them.'

Of course, Polly thought.

'So I gave them a shilling,' Mr Dunworthy went on, 'and they told me I was at St Paul's. And then a station guard came up and asked if they were causing me any trouble. He told me to check to make certain they hadn't picked my pocket. And then he hauled them off, I think, or they ran off – I can't remember. It was so long ago.'

'Do you remember what they looked like?'

'No, aside from their being extremely grubby.' He squinted, attempting to call up a picture. 'The boy might have been seven and the girl—'

He stopped and looked at Polly. 'You believe it was Alf and Binnie, don't you?'

'No, I *know* it was. They told me,' she said, and at Mr Dunworthy's sceptical look, 'You forget, it only happened six months ago as far as they're concerned, not fifty years. They don't know it was you they ran into, though. How long did you stand there, speaking to them and the guard?'

'Five minutes, perhaps. Not long.'

'But long enough that if they'd told you straight out where you were instead of trying to get money out of you, you wouldn't have collided with the Wren.' She leaned forward. 'On the night we were looking for John Bartholomew, Eileen saw him and ran after him, but she wasn't able to catch him because Alf and Binnie jumped in front of her. And they were what kept her from going back to Oxford on the last day of her assignment.'

'I don't understand. You think Alf and Binnie are somehow responsible for that, and for what I did? That it's their fault and not mine? But if I hadn't come through, if I hadn't decided to go and see St Paul's, it wouldn't have happened.'

'Exactly,' Polly said. 'Listen, because they kept Eileen from going back through to Oxford, she was there to save their lives at least once and possibly more than that.' She told him about the measles and the *City of Benares*.

'And they repaid her by keeping her from catching John Bartholomew?'

'Yes,' Polly said eagerly. 'And because they delayed her, when she did go after him she was waylaid by a fireman and forced into driving a bombing victim to Bart's. She saved that bombing victim's life, and Mike saved Hardy's life, and last night I saved Sir Godfrey's.'

'And you think those people went on to do something important in the war?' Mr Dunworthy asked. 'What?'

'I don't know. Perhaps someone went to see the pantomime Sir Godfrey's going to put on, and their house was bombed while they were at the theatre. Or your Wren's RAF plotting saved some pilot's life, and he went on to do bombing runs over Berlin. Or the naval officer who stopped to help your Wren torpedoed a U-boat or captured the Enigma codebooks or sank the *Bismarck*. Or one of them affected someone else who did something. We know Hardy brought back five hundred and nineteen soldiers from Dunkirk. And those soldiers could each have—'

'And you think this is all part of some grand plan?'

'Yes— No, not a plan, but ... the thing is, it wasn't an accident that I was performing at the Alhambra, and it wasn't an accident that Sir Godfrey was at the Forrest.' She told him about her shoe and ENSA and Mrs Sentry at the Works Board seeing her in *A Christmas Carol* and what Sir Godfrey had told her about his decision not to join the touring company and go to Bristol.

'I was able to save his life because I was here, because none of our drops would open. I think we may have been wrong about why they're not opening, and about the slippage. What if it's not to prevent us from altering the course of history? What if it's to put us where we can? To keep us here until we do?'

She reached forward and took his hands in hers. 'What if by colliding with the Wren you saved her life instead of causing her death? What if she was on the way to meet the Wren who was killed, and because you delayed her, she wasn't there when the bomb hit? Or what if you saved the life of the naval officer? Or the man in the black suit? Was he going towards St Paul's or coming from it?'

'Towards St Paul's.'

'Then he might have been a member of the fire watch going on duty, and on the twenty-ninth he found one of the incendiaries and put it out, and if you hadn't run into him, St Paul's would have burned down. And Alf and Binnie were what made you run into him.'

'But—'

'Mike saved Private Hardy's life because the slippage caused him to arrive in Saltram-on-Sea too late for the bus. And I met Sir Godfrey because the net sent me through in the evening instead of the morning.' She told him about being grabbed by the warden and taken to St George's. 'And because of the slippage, that first time you came through, you ended up at St Paul's Station. Where you needed to be to run into the Wren.'

'So you're saying slippage's function is to *bring about* alterations, not prevent them? That it kept us here intentionally?'

'I know what you're going to say, that a chaotic system isn't a conscious entity—'

'That's exactly what I'm going to say.'

'But it wouldn't have to be. You thought the shutting of our drops was a defence mechanism. Perhaps it is, only not to shut off interference from the future, but to enlist it when the continuum's threatened. If Hitler'd won the war, he'd have had time to develop the atomic bomb, and he wouldn't have hesitated to use it against the United States and all the other non-Aryan peoples. He already had a plan in place for wiping out Africa's "mud people", and he wouldn't have stopped there. He could have ended up wiping out—'

'—everything,' Mr Dunworthy finished her sentence. '*Götterdämmerung*, the twilight of the Gods. But if that's the case, and the continuum wanted to protect itself, why didn't it simply let us come through and shoot Hitler?'

'I don't know. Perhaps the system only allows minor changes. Or unintentional ones. Or perhaps something else is going on in those divergence points which makes it impossible to alter them. Or perhaps we came into the picture too late. Like the Good Fairy in *Sleeping Beauty*—'

'The Good *Fairy*?'

'Yes,' she said earnestly, 'she couldn't undo the spell, she could only make it less terrible. Time travel wasn't invented till long after the start of the continuum. Perhaps we're too late to completely repair it, but we can still—'

'But even if that's true, and even if you saved Sir Godfrey's life and Mike saved Hardy's and I saved the Wren's, we still altered events, and history's a chaotic system where a good action, done with the best intentions, can have the opposite effect. How can you be certain even if the continuum intended us to make repairs that we did? That we didn't make things worse instead?'

'Because they were already worse.'

'Worse? What do you mean?'

'I mean, what if we've been looking at the war the wrong way round? What if the disaster had already occurred, and the outcome we were altering was a *bad* outcome?'

'A bad outcome?' Mr Dunworthy said bewilderedly.

'*Yes*. What if the Allies *lost* the war? You said there were dozens of times when the outcome balanced on a knife's edge, like in that old saying, "For want of a nail, the shoe was lost, for want of a shoe—"'

'"—the horse was lost".'

'Yes, and because of that, the rider and the battle and the war were lost. There were scores of times in World War II like that, when if things had gone even slightly differently, we'd have lost. Well, what if we did lose?' she asked. 'What if your Wren was killed in Ave Maria Lane and Sir Godfrey was killed in Bristol and Eileen's bombing victim died in the back of the ambulance because they couldn't find a driver and Hardy ended up in a German POW camp and they lost the war?'

'But then time travel would never have been invented. Ira Feldman—'

'No, because the continuum's a chaotic system, which means time travel was already a part of it, and they *hadn't* lost it. Because you'd come and run into a Wren and set a cascade of events in motion. And Mike was part of that cascade, and our being stranded here.'

'We're the horseshoe, in other words.'

'*Yes*—'

'And you're saying we waltzed in, tightened a few nuts and bolts, and won the war?' Mr Dunworthy said. 'Historians as Little Miss Fix-its? My dear, history's a chaotic system. It's far more complicated than—'

'I *know* it's complicated. I'm not saying we won it. And I'm not saying your Wren or Hardy or Sir Godfrey or Alf and Binnie or whoever it is they and Eileen treated on the twenty-ninth was who won it either. Or even that saving them was what tipped the balance. It may have been something else altogether – Marjorie's deciding to become a nurse or one of the FANYs I worked with borrowing my dance frock or Mike's nearly colliding with Alan Turing. Or something we don't even know we did – stepping ahead of someone onto an escalator or hailing a taxi or asking for directions. Mike might have done something in hospital, or Eileen might have affected one of her evacuees.

Or I might have taken too long to wrap a customer's parcel and delayed *her* five minutes, so that she missed her bus, or got caught in the tube when the sirens went.'

'But you think whatever that action was, one of us did it,' Mr Dunworthy said. 'And it was one of us who won the war.'

'No,' she said, frustrated, 'I'm not saying that either. No one person or thing won the war. People argue over whether it was Ultra or the evacuation from Dunkirk or Churchill's leadership or fooling Hitler into thinking we were invading at Calais that won the war, but it wasn't any one of them. It was *all* of them and a thousand, a million, other things and people. And not just soldiers and pilots and Wrens, but air-raid wardens and planespotters and debutantes and mathematicians and weekend sailors and vicars.'

'All doing their bit,' Mr Dunworthy murmured.

'Yes. Canteen workers and ambulance drivers and ENSA showgirls. And historians. You said no one can be in a chaotic system and not affect events. What if your – *our* – coming to the past added another weapon to the war, a secret weapon, like the French Resistance or Fortitude South?'

'Or Ultra.'

'Yes,' Polly said, 'like Ultra. Something which operated behind the scenes and which, combined with everything else, was enough to avert disaster, to tip the balance.'

'And win the war,' Mr Dunworthy said softly.

There was a long silence, and then he said, almost longingly, 'But there's no proof …'

No, she thought, *except that so many lives saved and so many sacrificed – so much courage, kindness, endurance, love – must count for something even in a chaotic system.*

'No,' she said. 'I haven't any proof.'

There was a knock, and Eileen leaned in the door, her red hair windblown and her cheeks rosy. 'What are you two doing sitting here in the dark?' she said, and switched on the light.

'You look as if you could both do with some tea. I'll put the kettle on.'

'No, wait,' Polly said, 'did you find out who the man you saved was?'

'Yes.' She took off her hat. 'The admitting nurse wouldn't tell me anything, and neither would the Matron, so then I hit on the idea of going to the men's ward and telling the nurse that Mrs Mallowan had sent me to find out.'

'Mrs Mallowan?' Mr Dunworthy said.

'That's Agatha Christie's married name.' She unbuttoned her green coat. 'The nurse and I chatted a bit about *Murder in the Calais Coach*, and I told her about Agatha Christie's new book, which hasn't come out yet – it's all right, Polly, I told her I had an editor friend who'd let me look at it. And as a result, she let me look at the ambulance log.'

'And the man you saved was—?'

'There were three people, actually, or at any rate the nurse said she doubted they'd have survived if they hadn't got to hospital immediately. I wrote them down,' Eileen said, taking a sheet of paper out of her handbag and reading from it. 'Sergeant Thomas Brantley, Mrs Jean Cuttle – that was the ambulance driver – and Captain David Westbrook.'

Mr Dunworthy made an involuntary sound.

'Do you know who Captain Westbrook is?' Polly asked him.

Mr Dunworthy nodded. 'He was killed on D-Day, after singlehandedly holding a critical crossroads till reinforcements arrived.'

'For there is nothing lost that may not be found, if sought.'

EDMUND SPENSER *THE FAERIE QUEENE*

LONDON – SPRING 1941

'So you're telling me Alf and Binnie are *war heroes*?' Eileen said after Polly and Mr Dunworthy had explained Polly's theory to her.

'Yes,' Polly said. 'You were right about their being a secret weapon. Only they're on our side. Their jumping out in front of you when you were chasing John Bartholomew and delaying you was what was responsible for your being forced into driving the ambulance that night, so that you were able to save Captain Westbrook's life—'

'And they delayed the train.'

'Train?' Polly said.

'When we came to London. They chased a headmistress out of our compartment, and she tried to have us thrown off the train, and it made us late leaving the station. And later we found out the railway bridge ahead of us had been bombed, and Alf said, "It was a good thing we was late."'

She looked up at Polly wonderingly. 'They saved my life. *And* the headmistress'.'

'And you saved Captain Westbrook's.'

'And you two and Mike and I won the war?' Eileen said.

'*Helped* to win the war,' Mr Dunworthy said. 'Tipped the balance.'

'But I don't understand. If they'd lost the war before we came, then how could you have been at VE Day? There wouldn't have *been* a VE Day, would there?'

'Yes,' Polly said, 'because by 1945, you'd already saved Captain Westbrook's life and I'd already saved Sir Godfrey—'

'But you hadn't done that when you were at VE Day,' Eileen said, hopelessly confused. 'You hadn't even come to the Blitz yet.'

'Yes, I had,' Polly said patiently. 'I came to the Blitz in 1940, and I went to Trafalgar Square on VE Day five years later, in 1945.'

'But what about all those years before any of us came here, before time travel was even invented? The war was lost then, wasn't it?'

'No,' Polly said, 'it was always won because we had always come. We were always here. We were always a part of it.'

'The past and the future are both part of a single continuum,' Mr Dunworthy said, and launched into a long and involved explanation of chaos theory.

'But I still don't understand—'

'Don't understand what?' Binnie asked, coming in and announcing that from now on that she wished to be called Florence – 'like Florence Nightingale' – and become a nurse, which put an end to the conversation.

But the next morning after Alf and Binnie had gone to school, Eileen brought up the subject again. 'So because Mr Dunworthy ran into the Wren and Mike untangled the propellor and you saved Sir Godfrey, it changed things just enough that we won the war, is that right?'

'Yes,' Polly said.

'Then there's no reason to keep us here,' she said, 'and we can go home.'

'Eileen—'

'Mr Dunworthy said every historian who's come here has altered events, and *they* all went back to Oxford. And after you ran into the Wren, Mr Dunworthy, *you* went back to Oxford. So now that we've done what we were supposed to do, they should be able to come and fetch us, shouldn't they? Or our drops should begin working again.' She looked expectantly from Polly to Mr Dunworthy and back again. 'We need to go and check them.'

'I'll go to the drop in St Paul's this morning,' Mr Dunworthy promised. But after Eileen had elicited a promise that Polly would check her drop on her way to the theatre and had left to drive General Flynn, he said to Polly, 'She may, of course, be right about the drops—'

'But if she were, Colin would already be here.'

'Yes,' he said, 'and the fact that he isn't very likely means our part in this is not over.'

'I know,' Polly said, thinking of how Major Denewell had told her and the other FANYs the war could still be lost, even during that last year.

'More may be required of us before the end,' Mr Dunworthy told her.

Including our lives, Polly thought.

She had nearly died rescuing Sir Godfrey. The next time she might not make it. Like the countless rescue workers and ARP wardens and firemen who'd died digging people out of the rubble or taking people to shelter or defusing bombs. Or she might simply be killed outright by an HE, as Mike had been, and all the other people who'd died in the Blitz and in hospitals and prison camps and newspaper offices. Casualties of war.

But still part of it. Still, even in death, doing their bit. Like Mike. It was his death that had made her go to the Works Board and volunteer to be an ambulance driver and be assigned to ENSA and save Sir Godfrey.

'I know there's a good chance we won't make it back,' she told

Mr Dunworthy, and as she did, it struck her that that was what soldiers said when they were leaving for the front.

'But it doesn't matter,' she said, and meant it. 'All that matters is that Sir Godfrey didn't die, and that I'm not responsible for losing the war, and that I can see Miss Laburnum and Doreen and Trot without getting them killed. And if I'm killed, I won't be the only one to die in World War II. I'm only sorry I got you into this.'

'We got each other into it. And we may yet get out.'

'And if not, we still stopped Hitler in his tracks.' She smiled at him.

'We did indeed,' he said, and looked suddenly years younger. 'And we, like St Paul's, are still standing, at least for the moment. Speaking of which, when I go there, I intend to ask to be taken on as a volunteer. I have always wanted to serve on the fire watch and help save St Paul's—'

He stopped, an odd look on his face.

'What is it?' Polly asked. 'Are you feeling ill?'

'No,' he said. 'It's just occurred to me ... I think I may already have saved it. The night I came through, I crashed into a stirrup pump, and two of the fire watch came down to investigate it and found an incendiary that had burned through the roof. If I hadn't been there—'

'They might not have discovered it till too late, and the fire—' Polly said and stopped as well, thinking of the fire on the desk which she had put out the night they'd been trying to find John Bartholomew.

'And if my being there *did* save it, then it may do so again,' Mr Dunworthy was saying, 'even if I can only be at St Paul's for two weeks. But you will need to help me persuade them. And convince Eileen.'

Convincing Eileen proved to be the more difficult of the two. 'But it's dangerous,' she said. 'The north transept—'

'Won't be bombed till the sixteenth,' Mr Dunworthy said. 'I'll phone in and tell them I'm ill that night.'

'What about the big raids on May tenth and eleventh? You said the entire city—'

'St Paul's wasn't hit either of those nights,' he reassured her.

And it doesn't matter, Polly wanted to shout at her. *He won't be here. His deadline will already have passed. And the chances are I'll only have two weeks after that.* If she had another task, it almost certainly lay between now and the end of the Blitz. There would be only occasional raids after that, but they'd had far fewer casualties, and her death in one of them would be much more likely to alter events. Which meant her deadline wasn't the end of 1943. It was May eleventh.

But she couldn't tell Eileen that. In the first place, she wouldn't believe her. And in the second place, the task at hand was to convince her to allow Mr Dunworthy to join the fire watch. So instead Polly said, 'St Paul's won't suffer any more damage till 1944 and the V-1 and V-2 attacks.'

'But if there won't be any more damage, then why do you need to be in the fire watch, Mr Dunworthy?' Eileen persisted.

'Because *I* may be the reason there wasn't,' Mr Dunworthy said, which didn't help his case.

'No,' Eileen said firmly, 'it's too dangerous. The incendiaries and the roofs … you might fall.'

'None of the fire watch was injured or killed in 1941,' Mr Dunworthy told her, and Polly wondered if that was a lie, if Mr Dunworthy was hoping to die at St Paul's as well as work there.

'And being in the cathedral will give me opportunities to check the drop when no one's around,' Mr Dunworthy said, and Eileen eventually relented, though she insisted on walking him to the cathedral every night he was on duty.

'St Paul's may be safe,' she said, 'but there's still the journey there and back again. I have no intention of letting either of you get killed five minutes before the retrieval team arrives.'

'All right,' he agreed, and let her walk him there every night, except for the seventeenth, when he sent Eileen on an errand and had Polly accompany him instead so Eileen wouldn't see the damage from the raids the night before.

'It left a huge crater in the middle of the floor,' he told Polly. 'If Eileen sees it, I fear she'll never let me go on working with the fire watch.'

'And she'll see you can't get to your drop,' Polly said, guessing the real reason.

'True. I can't.'

When they reached St Paul's, Mr Humphreys was delighted to see Polly. 'Miss Sebastian, you must be an excellent nurse. Mr Hobbe looks quite recovered.'

He insisted on showing them the north transept, or rather, the mountain of plaster and splintered timbers and broken marble that blocked access to it. 'Still, though, the damage could have been worse,' he said.

Far, far worse, Polly thought, going to the Alhambra that night, thinking of Hitler unvanquished, unstoppable, marauding and murdering his way through England and the rest of the world. And the future.

But we stopped him, she thought, her heart lifting.

'You look like the cat that swallowed the canary,' Mr Tabbitt said. 'Did you meet a handsome doctor in hospital?'

Hattie said, 'You're in awfully good spirits for someone who nearly bought it.'

The troupe had noted her lightness of mood as well. 'You're too cheery by half,' Viv had said when she went to the theatre for the first pantomime rehearsal.

'It's just that I'm so happy to see all of you,' she said. Sir Godfrey and Mrs Wyvern had not only found another theatre – the Regent – for them to stage the pantomime in, but had managed to talk Mr Tabbitt into shifting Polly to matinees for the duration and had bullied the entire troupe to be in the play. Miss Laburnum was to be the narrator, Mrs Brightford Sleeping Beauty's mother and the queen, and the rector the king and one-half of the prince's horse. Viv was the other half, Nelson was the prince's dog, and Miss Hibbard was helping with costumes.

'We're happy to see you, too, my dear,' she said.

'And delighted to see you looking so well after your ordeal,' the rector added.

'It's the spring weather,' Miss Laburnum said. 'I find the coming of spring always lifts one spirits.'

'*I* say it's a man,' Viv said.

'Well, whatever it is, it suits you,' Mrs Brightford said. 'You look positively radiant.'

But when she went backstage with Sir Godfrey, he said, 'What is this fey mood which has come now upon you? Such moods are dangerous. Are you certain you're fully recovered from your exertions on my behalf? Perhaps we should postpone the play.'

'No, better not,' she said, and when he looked up alertly, added, 'I only meant the theatre may not be available for an additional week. And ENSA may be sending me to the provinces in May.

'*Not* to Bristol,' she added hastily. 'There's no need to postpone. I'm all right.'

Which was true. She was only sorry she wouldn't get to see Colin again, and anguished over what his failure to rescue her and Mr Dunworthy would do to him.

It wasn't your fault, she wished she could tell him. *I know you would have come to rescue me if you could.*

Sir Godfrey was looking worriedly at her. 'Simply because you've cheated Death once,' he said, 'doesn't mean he will not try again. I could not bear to lose you.'

'Only because you'd have to find another principal boy,' she said, smiling.

And she seemed to have allayed his fears because he became his old tyrannical directing self again, bellowing at everyone and shouting orders at Mr Dorming, who'd been recruited into painting sets. Mrs Brightford's three little girls had been enlisted, too, and by the time rehearsals began – and over Polly's protests – Alf and Binnie.

'Oh, I don't think that's a good idea,' Polly said when Mrs Wyvern suggested it.

'It's an *excellent* idea,' Mrs Wyvern said. 'The pantomime is being given to benefit the orphans of the East End. What could be better than having actual children from the East End in it? They can be in the christening scene.'

'We're fairies,' Binnie told Mr Dunworthy proudly.

'*I* ain't,' Alf said. '*Girls* are fairies. I'm a goblin. And a bramble-bush. *First* Bramblebush.'

'Liar,' Binnie said. 'All the bramblebushes are the same. I'm goin' to wear a beautiful glittery dress and wings.'

If Sir Godfrey doesn't throttle you first, Polly thought, which seemed highly likely. They teased Nelson, trod in paint, bounced on Sleeping Beauty's bed, and hit each other with the fairies' wands and the prop swords.

'Those swords were borrowed from the Covent Garden!' Sir Godfrey bellowed at them. 'The next miscreant I catch with one will be strung up by his heels.'

Which had no effect on them at all. Polly had to talk Eileen into coming to rehearsals with her to keep them from destroy-ing the theatre, and Mrs Wyvern promptly latched onto her and made her prompter.

'At least when the retrieval team comes, we'll all be in one place,' Eileen said cheerfully.

She'd refused to give up hope, even though it was obvious by this time that no one had been able to get through. 'The bombing of St Paul's must be a divergence point,' she said, 'and the retrieval team can't come through till it's over.'

Nothing happened on the sixteenth or the seventeenth. On the eighteenth, Eileen said, 'With us not on Oxford Street anymore and Mrs Rickett's house gone and the vicar not in Backbury, they've no way to find us. We need to go to Townsend Brothers and give them our new address. Do you think I should write to

Lieutenant Heffernan at the training school at the manor?

It doesn't matter, Polly thought, *if they were able to come, they'd have done it long before this. They know Mr Dunworthy's deadline is the first.* And the weather was supposed to be clear for the next three nights. Perfect bombing weather.

'I'll write to Lieutenant Heffernan tonight when we get home,' Eileen said. 'Perhaps they moved the training school, and we can go to Backbury and use my drop.'

It won't open either, Polly thought, and wished she could tell Eileen, *You mustn't blame yourself that we weren't able to get out in time. It's not your fault.*

But Eileen would only say, 'They'll get us out. You'll see. At this very moment, there are all sorts of things happening, all sorts of people working to rescue us,' and Polly didn't think she could bear it. So instead, after Eileen left to walk Mr Dunworthy to St Paul's, she wrote what she wanted to say in a note and added a list of the dates, times and locations of every V-1 and V-2 in her implant.

She copied it out in case the original was destroyed when she got killed and hid the copy in Eileen's *Murder in the Calais Coach.* The original she sealed in an envelope addressed to Eileen, sealed it and the half-charred lithograph of *The Light of the World* in a second envelope, which she put in her coat pocket.

Nothing happened on the eighteenth either. On the nineteenth, Eileen said, 'Tomorrow I want you to show me the drop in Hampstead Heath. If the sixteenth *was* a divergence point, it might be far enough outside London to be working.' She pulled on her coat. 'I'll meet you at the theatre. I need to walk Mr Dunworthy to St Paul's – he's on duty tonight. Tell Mrs Wyvern I hid the magic wands and the bramblebush branches on top of the costume cupboard so the children can't get at them.'

'Are Alf and Binnie going with you?'

'No,' Eileen said, but they set up such a clamour that she gave in and took them along. Polly was relieved, even though it would make them late for rehearsal and bring Sir Godfrey's wrath down on her. But so long as they were with Eileen, they'd be safe – or at any rate, safer than with her. And Mr Dunworthy would be safe in St Paul's. The cathedral hadn't been hit again after the sixteenth.

Which meant he would be killed on the way back from there, or at home. It seemed to her likely that she would be killed at the same time, but she hoped not. She would like to be able to do the pantomime for Sir Godfrey.

She loved doing it – in spite of Sir Godfrey's loathing of panto-mime, perhaps because it was the last thing she would ever do. And inside the theatre she forgot the days remorselessly ticking down – forgot the war and parting and death, and thought only of lines and costumes and attempting to keep Alf and Binnie from destroying everything they touched.

The two of them had managed not only to wreak havoc back-stage every night since they joined the cast but to corrupt every other child in the pantomime. Especially Trot. After a week of being with the Hodbins, her hair ribbons were untied, her rosy cheeks were streaked and dirty, and when Polly arrived at the Regent, she was shouting, 'I *ain't* a dunderhead!' and whaling away at her sisters with her magic wand while Nelson barked wildly.

'I gave the wand to her,' an unhappy Miss Laburnum admit-ted, 'so she could become used to using it, but perhaps that wasn't a good idea.'

She had also given Mrs Brightford (the Queen) her royal robes for the same reason and had forced Sir Godfrey (the Bad Fairy) to put on his Hitler-style moustache 'in case it shows a tendency to fall off'.

'Madam, I have had more than fifty years' experience putting on false moustaches with spirit gum! I have *never* had one *fall off*!' he was shouting, and didn't even note Alf and Binnie's absence.

Half an hour later, Polly saw them come in through the

doorway at the back of the house. They were alone. 'Where's Eileen?' Polly called to them, squinting out across the footlights. 'Didn't she come back with you?'

'Hunh-unh,' Alf said, slouching down the centre aisle.

'Why not?'

'She said she had to do something,' Binnie said, 'and for us to come here so we wouldn't be late.'

'And not to follow her,' Alf put in.

'And did you?'

'*No*,' Alf said with his best outraged innocence air.

'We tried,' Binnie said, 'but she was too quick for us, so we come here.'

She's gone to my drop again, Polly thought, wishing Eileen hadn't. The sirens had gone while Polly was on her way to the Regent, and she could hear the drone of planes and the thud of distant bombs. Logic told her nothing could happen to Eileen, that she'd survived all the way to VE Day, but she couldn't help listening anxiously to the buzzing planes, trying to gauge whether they were over Kensington.

They seemed to be over the East End thus far. She went backstage, where Miss Laburnum gave Polly her principal-boy costume, belt and scabbard, 'so you can become used to wearing your sword.' And when Polly protested that she needed to get onstage, she said, 'There's more than enough time. The safety curtain's stuck. They've been attempting to get it up for half an hour. Sir Godfrey's absolutely livid.'

He was. When Polly came onstage in her doublet and hose, he was yelling at the rector – a scene made worse by the fact that Miss Laburnum had insisted Sir Godfrey try on his costume. In his Führer's uniform and Hitler moustache he looked positively dangerous.

'Vivien Leigh will be here at ten o'clock tonight to rehearse her scenes, and not only will they not be ready, but she will not even be able to get *onstage*!' he shouted. 'Alf and Binnie had better not be behind this.'

'They only just got here,' Polly said, though that was hardly proof of their innocence. They could easily have booby-trapped the safety curtain last night.

They're a force for good, she told herself. *They saved Captain Westbrook's life. And Eileen's. They won the war.* But she had difficulty persuading herself of it, particularly when she found them duelling backstage with her sword and one of Mr Dorming's wet paintbrushes.

The rector and Mr Dorming finally got the safety curtain to work, but when they tried to raise the painted scrim with the forest and the castle on it for the transformation scene, *it* stuck. 'Perhaps we should send for a carpenter,' Miss Laburnum suggested timidly.

'And where exactly will we find one this time of night, *and* in the middle of a raid?' Sir Godfrey said, gesturing with his riding crop at the ceiling. 'We might just as well send for the walrus!' His moustache quivered. 'Or the March Hare, who would be entirely appropriate in this madhouse.

'Well, what are you waiting for?' he said to the cowering Miss Laburnum. '"Go and catch a falling star! Get with child a mandrake root!"'

Miss Laburnum scurried off to find a carpenter, and Sir Godfrey turned to Polly. 'I knew I should never have agreed to do pantomime, Viola.'

'*I* think we should've done *Rapunzel*,' Trot piped up. '*It's* got a tower.'

Sir Godfrey, his Hitler moustache quivering, raised his riding crop threateningly.

'And a witch,' Trot said.

'Trot, go and fetch the other children, there's a good girl,' Polly said, shooing her out of Sir Godfrey's reach. And to him, 'We can do the prologue and most of the first act in front of the scrim, and then, when the carpenter comes, we can do the transformation scene.'

'Very well. Prologue!' he called. 'Places, every—' There was a terrific clatter of metal from the wings. 'Alf!' Sir Godfrey roared.

Alf came onstage, holding one of the prop swords, slightly bent. 'I didn't touch nuffink. They just fell over. I *swear*.'

They won the war, Polly repeated silently. *They won the war*.

'If any of you foul fiends touch anything else, *anything*,' Sir Godfrey said, looking apoplectic, 'I will cut off your head and nail it to the theatre door as a warning to all other children!' and even Alf looked impressed. '*Give* me that sword and go and sit down out front. Close the curtain! Places!'

Polly stepped out in front of the curtain and delivered her prologue to the audience, which consisted of Alf, Binnie, a sceptical Trot with her arms folded belligerently across her little chest, and Nelson in the front row. Polly welcomed them to the pantomime, telling them they were about to see miraculous things, and assuring them that, in spite of appearances, it would have a happy ending. '"His evil will not triumph. In the end,"' she said, '"it is the Führer who'll be round the bend."'

The audience clapped and cheered, except for Trot, who apparently was still annoyed they weren't doing *Rapunzel*.

'"And now, to our tale,"' Polly said, sweeping her arm out towards the curtain. '"Its beginning lies in a royal castle, with a king, a queen, and their infant daughter."'

The curtain, thankfully, opened, revealing Mrs Brightford wearing a crown and holding a doll in her arms.

'*Where* is the king?' Sir Godfrey demanded, roaring out onstage.

'You mean the rector?' Binnie said. 'He went with Miss Laburnum to fetch the carpenter.'

'"My kingdom for a horse",' Sir Godfrey muttered. 'Mr Dorming!'

Mr Dorming appeared in the wings, paintbrush and bucket in hand.

'You'll play the king.'

'I don't know his lines,' Mr Dorming said.

'Prompter!' Sir Godfrey roared.

'Eileen's not here yet,' Polly said.

'*I'll* play the king,' Binnie said, racing on stage. 'I know *all* the lines.'

She went over to Mrs Brightford. '"My queen, we must have a great christening and invite all the fairies in the land."' She turned to Sir Godfrey. 'See?'

Sir Godfrey rolled his eyes and waved at her to proceed, and they made it safely through that scene, and the next, which involved, for some reason, a song and dance by the Three Bears, but they needed Miss Laburnum and the rector, neither of whom had come back yet, for the christening scene.

Eileen hadn't arrived either, and Polly listened nervously to the bombs. It sounded like they were over Chelsea and moving west. Towards Kensington and Polly's drop.

'I *said*, we'll rehearse the prince's scene,' Sir Godfrey was saying. 'If the bramblebushes haven't deserted us as well.'

'Sorry,' Polly said, and went to find the children.

They were backstage, standing on Sleeping Beauty's bed. Alf and Binnie were teaching Trot and the rest of the bramblebushes to thrust and parry with their branches.

'Onstage. Now,' Polly ordered, and they jumped off the bed, scrambled under the scrim and formed a more or less straight line, their branches crossed in front of their chests.

'Where's Nelson?' Alf said, and started off to find him.

'*Stop!*' Sir Godfrey roared. 'Do it without Nelson.'

'But—'

'*Now*,' he ordered.

Polly hastily said, '"Long years have I searched for this fair princess of whom I have heard,"' and thought suddenly of Colin. '"Long weary miles have I ridden ..."'

'Prince Dauntless,' Sir Godfrey interrupted, 'this is a comedy, not a tragedy.'

'Sorry,' Polly said, putting what she hoped was a hopeful and undaunted look on her face. '"Long years have I searched for this fair princess—"'

'Wait,' Alf said, 'that's s'posed to be Sleeping Beauty, ain't it? And we're s'posed to be guardin' 'er, ain't we?'

'Yes,' Sir Godfrey said, glaring.

'Well, where is she?'

'She will be here at ten o'clock,' Sir Godfrey said. 'If I live that long.'

'*I'll* play Sleeping Beauty,' Binnie said. 'I know all the lines.'

'She ain't *got* no lines,' Alf said. 'She's asleep.'

But Binnie was already dragging the prop bed under the scrim. She flung herself onto it and lay down, crossed her arms decorously over her chest and closed her eyes.

Polly was afraid Sir Godfrey would explode, but he only nodded wearily at her to begin.

'"Long, weary miles have I ridden,"' she said, and put her hand to her scabbard. '"What evil, dark forest is this? And what trees are these?"'

'"Bramblebushes!"' Alf said. '"We let no man pass!"'

Trot stepped forward. '"Our thorns will tear you limb from limb!"'

'"I do not fear a few brambles,"' Polly said.

'"We are no ordinary brambles!"' Bess shouted.

'"We're *Nazi* brambles!"' Alf said. '"I'm Goebbels!"' and opened his branchy arms to reveal a picture on his chest of the Nazi propaganda minister.

'"I'm Goering!"' Bess said.

'"I'm …"' Trot shifted from one foot to the other, frowning, and then looked at Polly. '"I'm …"'

'Himmler,' Polly whispered, but it didn't help.

'Who *am* I?' Trot asked plaintively.

'You're Himmler, you noddlehead,' Binnie said, sitting up on the bed.

'I'm *not* a noddlehead!' Trot cried, and hit Alf, who was nearer, with her branch.

719

'Why isn't that prompter here yet?' Sir Godfrey said, stomping onstage.

'I don't know,' Polly said. 'I'm worried that she—'

'You want me to go and look for 'er?' Alf volunteered.

'*No,*' Sir Godfrey said, 'Mr Dorming! I need you on prompt-book.'

Mr Dorming nodded, stuck his paintbrush in his bucket, set them down where Alf was almost certain to knock them over and went in search of the promptbook.

'Stop that,' Sir Godfrey said to Trot, who was still whaling away at Alf. 'By God, it was easier to get Birnam Wood to Dunsinane than to get you six to do a five-minute scene. 'Line up,' he ordered the children, and looked over at Binnie. 'Lie down. Take it again, from "We're *Nazi* brambles!"'

And Sir Godfrey must have put the fear of God into Trot because she got her line and the ensuing 'Song of the Brambles' – including their line about Fortress Europe and the ending, which involved their lunging forward and thrusting their branches at Polly – word-perfect.

'"You shan't stop me from getting through!"' Polly said, drawing her sword. '"I'll cut you down with my trusty sword, Churchill. *En garde!*"'

'Oh no!' the children cried, and collapsed in a heap.

'No, no, *no!*' Sir Godfrey said, striding out onstage. 'Not all at once.'

The children scrambled to their feet.

'You go down one after the other, like dominoes.' He put his hand on Bess' head. 'You first, then you, and you, on down the line.'

'They didn't stick their branches up like they were s'posed to, neither,' Binnie said, sitting up on the bed.

'I did *so*—' Alf began.

Sir Godfrey silenced him with a look. 'And hold your branches up.' He turned to Binnie and roared, 'Go back to sleep. Don't *move* until you're kissed.' To Polly, he muttered as he passed,

'There is a reason Shakespeare never put children in his plays.'

'You're forgetting the little princes.'

'Whom he had the good sense to murder in the second act. Again!'

Polly nodded, drew her sword, and stepped forward. '"And my trusty shield—"'

There was a horrific crash somewhere backstage. Polly looked instantly at Alf, who was wearing his innocent expression.

'Can anything *else* happen tonight?' Sir Godfrey said, and stormed backstage, shouting, 'And *don't* follow me! When I come back, I expect you to be all the way through this scene and the next! And tell me the instant that carpenter arrives.'

The children looked interestedly after Sir Godfrey.

'Get back in line,' Polly said. 'Cross your branches.' She raised her sword. '"And my trusty—"'

There was a sound at the rear of the theatre, and a man appeared in the doorway at the back.

Thank goodness, Polly thought, walking out to the edge of the stage, still holding her sword. *It's the carpenter.*

But it wasn't. It was Mr Dunworthy. His coat was open, his scarf dangled unevenly to one side, and he was bareheaded.

'Mr Dun— Mr Hobbe,' Polly called to him, shading her eyes with her free hand, trying to see out into the darkened theatre. 'What are you doing here? What's happened?'

He didn't answer. He took a stumbling step down the aisle. *Oh God, he's injured*, Polly thought.

Alf appeared beside her. 'Did somefink 'appen to Eileen?' he asked.

Mr Dunworthy made an effort to speak, but nothing came out. He took another step forward, where Polly could see his face. He looked stunned, his face ashen.

No, she thought, *not Eileen. It can't be. Mr Dunworthy and I are the ones with the deadlines. Eileen survived the war. She—*

Binnie, trailing bedclothes, pushed past Polly. 'Where's

Eileen?' she demanded, her voice rising. 'Did somefink 'appen to 'er?'

Mr Dunworthy shook his head.

Thank God.

'Are you all right?' Polly called to him.

'I was at St Paul's …' he said, looking up at her and then back towards the doorway he'd come through.

A young man was standing in it. He started down the aisle, and Polly saw he had an ARP warden's armband and a helmet, which he'd taken off and was holding in both hands. *Oh God,* she thought, *it's Stephen.*

But it couldn't be. Stephen hadn't even met her yet. He wouldn't meet her till 1944. And the warden's hair was reddish-blond, not dark. 'Polly—' he said.

'Sir Godfrey!' Trot shouted into the wings. 'The carpenter's here!'

'It ain't the carpenter, you noddlehead!' Alf shouted at her. 'It's an air-raid warden.'

No, it isn't, Polly thought.

It wasn't Stephen either, and the sword that Polly had been holding all this time, that she hadn't realised she was still holding, fell from her fingers with a loud clatter.

It was Colin.

*'Trying to unweave, unwind, unravel, and piece
together the past and the future ...'*

T.S. ELIOT *FOUR QUARTETS*

IMPERIAL WAR MUSEUM, LONDON – 7 MAY 1995

Colin sat there in the shelter replica with Binnie, not hearing the siren sound effects, not seeing the red flashes, not doing anything but attempting to take in what Binnie had just told him. Eileen was dead. She'd died eight years ago. Which meant Polly had died in December of 1943.

There was a poster on the wall behind Binnie with a picture of a housewife, a nurse and an ARP warden on it. *You Can Win the Battle*, it read.

I didn't win it, he thought numbly. *I was too late. Eileen's been dead nearly a decade. I wasn't able to rescue her. Or Michael. Or Polly.*

'I'm so sorry,' Binnie said, 'I should have told you about Mum first thing. It was a cancer.'

A cancer that could have been cured easily if Eileen had been home in Oxford where she belonged. Which they still might be able to cure if he could go back and get her out in time. If she had been alone when she died, he might still be able to ...

'Did she die in hospital?' he asked urgently. 'Was anyone with her?'

Binnie looked at him, frowning. 'Of course. All of us were.'

Which meant there was no way to rescue her at the last moment, no way to whisk her off in a stolen ambulance and send her back through. He sank back down on the bench beside Binnie and put his head in his hands.

'We all got to tell her goodbye,' Binnie said. 'The end was very peaceful.'

Peaceful, he thought bitterly. *Dying stranded in the past like Polly before her, waiting in vain for rescue. Only Eileen must surely have given up waiting, given up hoping, years before.* 'I'm so sorry.'

'It's a pity,' she said, 'she would have loved to see you again. But at least we found you.' She beamed at him. 'When you didn't find Mum, we were afraid something had gone wrong. Or at least I was. But Alf said we *had* to have found you, because if we hadn't, you couldn't have come to fetch Polly and—'

'Fetch—?' He grabbed her by the shoulders. 'What are you talking about?'

'Your coming to take them back through the drop.'

'But you just said I wasn't able to find Eileen.'

'I didn't say that,' she replied, surprised. 'I meant you didn't find her *now*, not then.'

'I found Eileen and Polly?'

She nodded. 'And Mr Dunworthy.'

'Mr *Dunworthy*? He's *alive*?'

Binnie nodded. 'Polly found him at St Paul's.'

'He's alive,' Colin murmured, unable to take it all in. 'I thought he was dead. His death notice was in the newspapers.'

'No, he was only injured. By a parachute-mine.'

'And I was able to come through to get them out?' he asked. She nodded.

But if he had succeeded, Eileen wouldn't still have been here. She wouldn't have died still trying to find him. 'What happened?' he asked, but he already knew the answer. 'I came too late to be able to get them out, didn't I?'

'Journeys end in lovers meeting.'

WILLIAM SHAKESPEARE *TWELFTH NIGHT*

LONDON – 19 APRIL 1941

Polly's sword hit the stage with a clatter. 'You're gonna catch it now!' Alf told her, but she didn't hear him.

'Colin,' she tried to say, but no sound came out. She glanced over at Mr Dunworthy, still standing there gripping the theatre-seat back for support, and then back at Colin.

Though it wasn't the Colin she'd known. There was nothing of the eager, high-spirited boy who'd followed her around Oxford like a puppy, who'd told her he intended to marry her when he grew up, in the man standing there in the aisle before her with his ARP helmet in his hands.

But it didn't matter. Polly had known the moment she saw him standing there in the aisle that it was Colin. And that he had come, just as he had promised he would, to rescue her. But at what cost? He looked not only older but sadder, grimmer, his face lined with suffering and fatigue.

Oh Colin, she thought, *what's happened to you since I saw you seven months ago?*

But she knew that, too. He had spent weeks, months, *years,* frantically trying to get to them – trying to get the drops, *any* drop, to open. And then, when he'd failed, trying to puzzle out what had happened, trying to follow a trail which had gone cold.

I have ridden long, weary miles, she thought. *I have searched long, hopeless years.* And fought battles and spells and brambles and time. And found her.

Found all of them. She looked at Mr Dunworthy, still hanging on to the back of the theatre seat for dear life, as though he still couldn't believe what had happened. He looked like the Admirable Crichton and Lady Mary must have looked when the ship had finally arrived.

'They've reconciled themselves to living out their remaining lives and dying on the island,' Sir Godfrey had said when they were rehearsing the rescue scene. 'And now rescue is at hand. No, no, no! No smiles! I want staggered, stunned, unable to believe they have been saved. Joyous and sad and afraid, all at once.'

And silent, Polly thought, *as if we're under a spell.*

And Colin was under it, too. He hadn't moved, hadn't spoken. He stood there perfectly still, with his ARP helmet in his hands, looking at her, waiting.

For me to break the spell, she thought.

'Oh Colin,' she said, and smiled. 'You said you'd come and rescue me if I got into trouble. And here you are!'

'Here I am,' he said, and his voice was changed, too. It was both rougher and gentler than the boy Colin's – a man's voice. 'Rather late, I'm afraid, and somewhat the worse for wear.' He grinned at her, and she had been wrong. It was exactly the same Colin who had followed her into the Bodleian that day. He hadn't changed at all.

Her heart lifted. 'You're not late. You're exactly on time.'

He started towards her, and she was suddenly breathing hard, as if she had been running. 'Colin—'

'Polly!' Alf shouted from the stage. 'Is the warden 'ere to 'vacuate us?' He pointed at Colin, who had stopped only a step away from her.

''course 'e ain't, you puddinghead,' Binnie said, coming out to the edge of the stage beside Alf. 'Air-raid wardens don't 'vacuate people.'

'They do if there's a UXB,' Alf retorted. 'Is 'e 'ere with the bomb squad, Polly?'

'*I* know who he is,' Trot said, joining Alf and Binnie. 'He's the prince. He's come to rescue Sleeping Beauty.'

'Don't be daft,' Binnie said, while Alf collapsed in laughter. 'There ain't no such thing as Prince Dauntless.'

Oh yes, there is, Polly thought, *and he's here. In the very nick of time.*

'He is *so* the prince,' Trot said, and started down the steps on the side of the stage. 'I'll show you.'

'No, you won't,' Polly said. That was all they needed, the children down here asking questions. 'Go and change into your christening-scene costumes this instant.'

Trot headed immediately for the wings, followed by Nelson, but Polly should have known better than to think Alf and Binnie would obey her.

'Sir Godfrey told us we was s'posed to go on from where we was,' Binnie said.

'I don't care what he said, Binnie. Go and put on your fairy costumes.'

Next to her Colin murmured, 'That's Binnie?'

Even he's *heard of the notorious Hodbins*, Polly thought.

'Yes,' she said. 'Go and change for the christening scene *now*.'

'I can't,' Binnie said. 'Eileen ain't back yet.'

Eileen. She'll be overjoyed at the thought of going home.

'Eileen isn't here?' Mr Dunworthy asked.

'No, I think she went to check my drop first,' Polly said. He and Colin exchanged glances.

'Why?' she asked worriedly. 'The raids aren't over Kensington tonight, are they?'

'No, they're largely over the docks,' Colin said.

'We can't do the christening scene without me wearin' my costume,' Binnie said. 'And Eileen said not to put it on till she

727

fixed the wing. It's broke. Alf was the one wot broke it,' she added unnecessarily.

'Put on the costume *without* the wings,' Polly ordered.

Eileen will be even more overjoyed at not having to cope with the Hodbins than she will be at going home, she thought and then felt guilty. Alf and Binnie had already lost their mother, and now they were going to lose Eileen. Poor little—

'Eileen said *not* to,' Binnie said belligerently. 'And Sir Godfrey said we was s'posed to go straight through to the end and no stoppin'.'

'And *I* said go and put on your costume,' Polly ordered. 'And when Eileen gets here, tell her I need to speak to her.'

'All right, but you're goin' to be in trouble,' Binnie muttered darkly.

You're wrong, Polly thought, *we were in trouble, but now Colin's here.*

'Do as I say this instant,' she said, and Alf and Binnie trudged off the stage into the wings.

Polly turned back to Mr Dunworthy and Colin. 'I still can't believe you're here, Colin.'

'I can't either. I had the very devil of a time finding you. *Far* worse than looking for a needle in a haystack.'

She could imagine. No one at Townsend Brothers would have known where they were, and even if he'd managed to find out they'd lived at Mrs Rickett's—

He must have seen the announcement of the pantomime in the newspapers, she thought. Mike had said they'd be reading the newspapers, looking for clues to where—

Oh God, Mike. 'Mr Dunworthy,' she said, 'did you tell him about Mike?'

'He already knew.'

Of course, she thought, *he read that in the newspapers as well. Mike Davis, American war correspondent for the* Omaha Observer. *Died suddenly.* 'What about Charles Bowden?' she asked Colin. 'He's in Singapore. He needs to be pulled out before the Japanese Army—'

'His drop was still working,' Colin said. 'We pulled him out as soon as we realised something was wrong.'

Oh thank God. 'What about Denys Atherton?'

'He never came through, and neither did Gerald Phipps. Nor Jack Sorkin. Nothing would open. Except your drop, Mr Dunworthy,' Colin said, 'and it stopped working the moment you'd gone through. Till last year we thought the entire war was permanently shut to us.'

Last year, Polly thought. And how many years before that had he kept searching, had he refused to give up, even though he'd believed they were permanently lost?

'Merope was right, Polly,' Mr Dunworthy was saying. 'She said our drops would open now that you'd saved Sir Godfrey. I went in to check mine, and there Colin was. I thought at first he was an air-raid warden and he'd seen an incendiary fall on the transept roof and come in to check on it, and then he said, "I've got to get you out of here, Mr Dunworthy," and I realised it was Colin.'

'I've got to get you both out of here,' Colin said. 'We need to get back to St Paul's.'

Polly nodded, wondering why Colin hadn't sent Mr Dunworthy on through. He must not have known where the theatre was and needed Mr Dunworthy to show him the way.

'Colin, you need to take Mr Dunworthy there right now and send him through,' she said. 'His deadline's only two days off, which means he's in far more danger than I am. I'll stay here and wait for Eileen. I've got to notify everyone I'm leaving, at any rate. I can't just go off without telling them. And they'll have to find someone else to play my part. The pantomime's in two weeks. I owe it to them ...'

She faltered to a stop. *I'll have to tell them all goodbye,* she thought sickly. *Miss Laburnum and Trot and, oh God, Sir Godfrey. How can I bear—?*

'Polly?' Colin said. 'Are you all right?'

'Yes,' she said. 'Yes.' She managed a smile. 'I'll stay here and tell them, and then when Eileen arrives, we'll come and meet you at St Paul's.'

But Mr Dunworthy was shaking his head. 'I want to wait till she comes,' he said, looking at Colin.

Colin nodded. 'There's time.'

There was something here Polly didn't understand, something they weren't telling her. 'Why is Eileen late?' she asked, remembering Mr Dunworthy's ashen look when he first came in and the unhappiness in Colin's face. 'Tell me. Has something happened to her?'

Mr Dunworthy and Colin exchanged glances.

'*Tell* me,' she demanded.

'Polly?' Eileen's voice called from the front of the theatre. 'Where are you?'

Oh thank God, Polly thought, whirling to look at the stage.

Eileen came out in front of the safety curtain from the wings in her hat and coat. She must have come in through the stage door. She shaded her eyes, squinting out past the footlights.

'I'm here,' Polly called to her, and before she could tell her, Eileen pattered down the side steps and started up the aisle, asking, 'Why aren't you rehearsing? And where's the rest of the cast? I hope you haven't been waiting for me to— Mr Dunworthy,' she said, spotting him, 'what are you doing here? Did something happen at St Paul's?'

'No,' Polly said, 'yes— oh, Eileen, it's Colin, and he's here to take us home.'

'Colin?' she said joyfully and turned to look at him, and as she did, her expression changed to one of – what? Shock? Dismay?

Polly looked questioningly at Colin, but he was staring at Eileen, and all the weariness had returned to his face.

What—? Polly thought, but the next instant she decided she must have been mistaken, that what she'd seen as dismay was only astonishment because Eileen ran forward to embrace Colin.

'I knew you'd come!' she cried happily. 'I told Polly things were happening behind the scenes.' She stood back to take a long, searching look at him, and then smiled. 'And here you are! I told them they mustn't give up hope, that you wouldn't let—' Her voice broke. 'I knew you'd pull them out in time.'

'*And* you, you noddlehead,' Polly said. 'Just think, you'll never have to eat Victory Stew again.'

But Eileen didn't laugh. She was looking at Mr Dunworthy, her eyes full of tears.

'You mustn't cry. This is a happy occasion. The drops are working again, and Charles is all right. He wasn't in Singapore when the Japanese arrived. They were able to rescue him.'

'But not Mike,' Eileen said, looking at Colin.

'No.'

Eileen nodded slowly. 'When I saw you, I thought perhaps he was all right, that he'd somehow told you where— How did you know where we were? There was no one left in Backbury or at Townsend Brothers who knew, and Mrs Rickett's ...'

She looked intently at him, as if the answer was of immense importance. 'How did you find us?'

'We can talk about that in Oxford,' Polly said. 'We need to go before the raids get any worse.'

'You're right,' Eileen said. 'Of course.'

But neither Colin nor Mr Dunworthy moved. All three of them stood there looking at one another, as if waiting for something.

'What—?' Polly asked, bewildered.

'You said you needed to tell them you're leaving, Polly,' Colin said.

'Yes, and change out of my costume. Do the three of you want to go on ahead, and I'll meet you at St Paul's?'

'No.' Colin was looking at Eileen. 'We'll wait for you.'

'I'll be back straightaway,' Polly said, and ran down the aisle, up onto the stage, and into the wings.

Mrs Brightford was there, attempting to repair the damage

Alf and Binnie had inflicted on the bramble branches. 'Have you seen Sir Godfrey?' Polly asked.

Mrs Brightford shook her head. 'I think he went to find a carpenter.'

Oh no. She couldn't leave without telling him goodbye. 'You don't know *where*, do you?'

Mrs Brightford shook her head again.

'If he comes back, tell him I need to speak with him,' Polly said, and ran down to the dressing room. She'd change and then, if he still wasn't back, see if anyone knew where he'd gone and go and look for him.

And when (and if) she found him, what could she say? *I'm a time traveller? I was trapped here, but now my retrieval team's come, and I must go home? I don't have a choice – I'll die if I stay?*

Perhaps it would be just as well if she couldn't find him. She stepped out of her leggings and pulled on her stockings, but in her haste she snagged one of them.

It doesn't matter, she thought, yanking her doublet off and putting on her frock. *I never need to worry about ladders again, or ration books, or bombs.*

She buttoned her frock. 'I won't ever have to wrap another parcel,' she said, and found herself suddenly, inexplicably, in tears.

Which is ridiculous, she thought, *you* hate *wrapping parcels. And this is a happy ending, exactly like in Trot's fairy-tales.*

She pulled on her shoes, caught up her coat and hat and went out, putting them on as she went, and then hesitated. In another six months, Mrs Brightford or Viv would be desperate for those stockings, even with a ladder in them. She went back into the dressing room, took off her shoes, stripped off the stockings and draped them over the make-up mirror. Then she grabbed up her bag and opened the door.

Sir Godfrey was standing there in his Hitler uniform and moustache. He took in Polly's clothes, her coat. 'There's no need for that, the carpenter's on his way,' he told her, and then stopped.

'You're leaving us,' he said, and it wasn't a question. 'It's your young man. He's come.'

'Yes. I thought he couldn't, that he—'

'—was dead,' Sir Godfrey said. 'But he's arrived "despite all obstacles, true love triumphant".'

'Yes,' she said, 'but I—'

He shook his head to silence her. 'The times were out of joint,' he said. 'It would not have been suitable, Lady Mary.'

'No,' she said, wishing she could tell him why it wouldn't have been, that she could tell him who she really was.

Like Viola, she thought. Sir Godfrey had named her well. She couldn't tell him why she'd been here or why she had to leave, couldn't tell him how he'd saved her life as much as she'd saved his, couldn't tell him how much he meant to her. She had to let him think she was abandoning him for a wartime romance. 'I'd stay till after the pantomime if I could—' she began.

'And spoil the ending? Don't be a fool. Half of acting is knowing when to make one's exit. And no tears,' he said sternly. 'This is a comedy, not a tragedy.'

She nodded, wiping at her cheeks.

'Good,' he said and smiled at her. 'Fair Viola—'

'Polly!' Binnie called from the top of the stairs. 'Eileen says to hurry!'

'Coming!' she said. 'Sir Godfrey, I—'

'*Polly!*' Binnie bellowed.

She darted forward, kissed Sir Godfrey on the cheek and ran for the stairs, calling to Binnie, who was leaning over the railing, looking down at her, 'Go and tell Eileen I'm coming now!'

Binnie raced off, and she ran up the stairs. 'Viola!' Sir Godfrey called to her as she reached the top. 'Three questions more before we part.'

She turned to look back down over the railing at him. '"What is your will, my lord?"'

'Did we win the war?'

She had thought she couldn't be amazed by anything after Colin, but she had been wrong. *He knows*, she thought wonderingly. *He's known since that first night in St George's.* 'Yes,' she said. 'We won it.'

'And did I play a part?'

'Yes,' she said with absolute certainty.

'I didn't have to do Barrie, did I? No, don't tell me, or my courage will fail me altogether.'

Polly's laugh caught. 'Was that your third question?' she managed to ask.

'No, Polly,' he said. 'Something of more import.'

And she knew it must be. He had never, except for that one scene in *The Admirable Crichton*, called her by her real name.

'What is it?' she asked. *Will I ever see you again?*

No.

Do I love you?

Yes, for all time.

He stepped forward and grasped the staircase's railing, looked up at her earnestly. 'Is it a comedy or a tragedy?'

He doesn't mean the war, she thought. *He's talking about all of it – our lives and history and Shakespeare. And the continuum.*

She smiled down at him. 'A comedy, my lord.'

There was an ungodly crash from the stage. 'Alf! I *told* you not to touch nothing!' Binnie shouted.

'I never! The scrim just fell down.'

'The *scrim*!' Sir Godfrey bellowed. 'Alf Hodbin, I told you not to mess about with those ropes!'

'Don't try to pick it up,' Binnie's voice warned. 'You'll tear it!'

'Touch *nothing*!' Sir Godfrey roared, galloping up the stairs past Polly and out onto the stage, where she could hear Alf and Binnie both insisting, 'I didn't do nuffink! I *swear*!'

'"They have all rushed down to the beach ..."' Polly murmured, looking after him, and then turned and ran down into the theatre and up the aisle to where Eileen and Mr Dunworthy and Colin stood.

The three of them were standing very near one another, their heads bent, talking, and Polly thought of that first night when she and Mike and Eileen had sat in the emergency stairwell, catching one another up, making plans. 'I'm going to get you both out of this, I promise,' Mike had said, and he had.

He'd died, and because he had, she'd wanted to do something, anything, to make her life matter and had gone to St Paul's to ask Mr Humphreys to help her get a job as an ambulance driver. And because she'd done that, she'd found Mr Dunworthy and despaired. And if she hadn't despaired, she would never have been at the Alhambra when the Forrest was hit, would never have rescued Sir Godfrey, and the drop would never have opened.

You did save us, Mike, she thought. *Just as you promised.*

She reached the group.

Eileen had been crying. She wiped clumsily at her cheeks as Polly joined them, and then smiled at her. 'Are you ready?' Eileen asked.

No, Polly thought. 'Yes.'

'Are you certain?' Colin said. 'I know how hard this must be for you. We haven't a lot of time, but we've enough for you to say goodbye, if there's anyone else you need to—'

I love you, Polly thought.

'No, I'm ready.' She looked back at the stage, where the children, Sir Godfrey, Mr Dorming and Nelson were struggling with the collapsed scrim.

'Should we help them?' Colin asked her.

'No, we'll never get away if we do. Let's go,' she said and turned to start up the aisle, and oh no, here came Miss Laburnum.

'It's all right, you needn't go for the carpenter, Polly,' she said. 'I found him at last, and he'll be here shortly. Is the scrim still stuck?'

'No,' Polly said dryly.

'No, no, no!' Sir Godfrey bellowed and Miss Laburnum looked down at the stage.

'Oh good heavens! What happened?' She started down the aisle.

'We need to go,' Colin said quietly to Polly. 'We haven't got much time.'

She nodded. 'I'm ready,' she said.

'Go?' Binnie, who'd been on the stage only a moment ago, said at Polly's elbow. 'Where are you all going?' and Miss Laburnum immediately turned and hurried back up the aisle towards them.

Alf jumped off the stage and tore up the aisle after her, with Trot – and Nelson, barking wildly – in his wake. 'Are you goin' someplace?' he called.

And now how are we going to get out of here? Polly thought.

'Has something happened?' Miss Laburnum asked, seeming to take in Colin's ARP uniform for the first time.

'Yes,' Polly said. I'm sorry to let you all down, but—'

'This is Polly's fiancé,' Eileen cut in.

'Are you going to marry Polly?' Trot asked him.

'Yes,' he said, 'if she hasn't fallen in love with someone else in the meantime.'

'He's unexpectedly come home on leave,' Eileen was explaining.

And has gone to work for the ARP? Polly thought, but Miss Laburnum apparently hadn't noticed the oddness of that, or the sudden appearance of a fiancé Polly had never mentioned before.

'Oh my, it's a pleasure to meet you, Mr—' She looked expectantly at Polly.

'Lieutenant Templer,' Eileen volunteered.

'It's a pleasure to finally meet you, Miss Laburnum,' Colin said. 'Polly's told me about all your kindnesses to her.'

'Don't we get to meet 'im?' Alf demanded.

'This is Alf, Trot and Binnie,' Polly said, indicating each in turn.

'Vivien,' Binnie corrected, 'like Vivien Leigh.'

'Alf, Trot and Vivien,' Polly said resignedly, and Colin shook hands with Alf and then Trot.

'Did you look for Polly for a hundred years?' Trot asked.

'Nearly,' he replied and turned to Binnie. 'It's an honour to meet you, Vivien,' he said solemnly, and Binnie shot Polly a triumphant glance.

'Why *can't* you be in the pantomime?' Alf asked Polly.

'Can't be in the pantomime?' Miss Laburnum said, alarmed. 'Oh, but Miss Sebastian, you can't desert us now. Whom shall we find to play the part of principal boy?'

'I'll do it,' Binnie said. 'I know all the lines.'

'Don't be a noddlehead,' Alf said. 'You ain't old enough.'

'I am *so*.'

'You're already a fairy,' Eileen said, 'and a bramblebush. You're too important to the pantomime to play any other parts,' and before Alf could put in his penny's worth, she added, 'Alf, go and tell Sir Godfrey that the carpenter will be here in just a moment. And help him put the scrim back up in the meantime. Take Trot with you. And Nelson.'

Which was a cruel thing to do to poor Sir Godfrey, but at least it got rid of Alf for the moment. Now if they could only get rid of Miss Laburnum, who was saying, 'But we shall never be able to find another principal boy at this late date. I entreat you, Miss Sebastian – think of how disappointed the children will be.'

'I *ain't* a child,' Binnie said, 'and I am *so* old enough to play the prince. Listen.' She flung her bramble-covered arms out dramatically. '"Long years 'ave I searched—"'

'Hush,' Eileen said. 'Go and fetch Polly's costume and bring it to me.'

Binnie took off at a run towards the stage and Eileen turned to Miss Laburnum. 'I'll substitute for her.'

'But you can't,' Polly blurted out, 'you're going with us,' and then she could have kicked herself because Binnie was tearing back up the aisle, demanding, 'What does she mean, you're goin' with them, Eileen? You ain't goin' away, are you?'

'No. She was talking about my going to her wedding,' Eileen said glibly. 'She and Lieutenant Templer are going to be married, and I should love to go, but someone has to stay behind to do the pantomime.' She turned to Polly and Colin. 'You must promise to write to me all about the wedding.'

'Wedding?' Miss Laburnum said to Polly. 'You're being married? Oh, well then, of course you must go! But couldn't the wedding wait till after the performance? Sir Godfrey had his heart set on—'

Eileen shook her head. 'She hasn't time. There are licences to get and arrangements and things—'

Colin nodded. 'We're going to see Dean Matthews now.'

'And Lieutenant Templer only has a twenty-four-hour leave,' Eileen said smoothly, 'but it's all right. I can play the prince. Binnie will help me with my lines, won't you, Binnie?'

What are you doing? Don't lie to Binnie, Polly thought, *even if we do need to get out of here. She's already had too many betrayals, too many abandonments.*

'Eileen—' she said warningly.

'Binnie,' Eileen said, ignoring her, 'go and fetch Polly's costume and bring it to me. You'd best go with her, Miss Laburnum. The doublet will need to be taken up. I'm shorter than Polly.'

Miss Laburnum nodded and started down the aisle. 'Come, Binnie.'

Binnie stayed where she was. 'When I had the measles, you said you wouldn't leave,' she said. 'You *promised*.'

'I know,' Eileen said.

'The vicar says breaking a promise is a *sin*.'

Tell her sometimes it's not possible to keep your promise, Polly willed her. *Tell her—*

'The vicar's right,' Eileen said. 'It is a sin. I'm not leaving, Binnie.'

'You swear you're stayin'?' Binnie said.

'I swear,' Eileen said, and smiled at her. 'Who'd take care of you and Alf if I left? Now, go with Miss Laburnum.'

And Binnie ran off after her.

This time Polly waited until she was certain they were out of earshot and then said, 'You shouldn't have lied to her. It isn't fair. You owe it to her to tell her that you're leaving.'

'I can't tell her that,' Eileen said.

'What do you mean?'

'I'm not going back with you.'

'Parting is such sweet sorrow.'

WILLIAM SHAKESPEARE *ROMEO AND JULIET*

LONDON – 19 APRIL 1941

'What do you mean you're not going back?' Polly said, staring at Eileen standing calmly there in the theatre aisle. She looked from Colin to Mr Dunworthy. 'What does she mean?'

'I've decided to stay,' Eileen said.

'Because they need a *principal boy*?' Polly burst out. 'They can get Mrs Brightford to play the prince. Or Binnie. She knows all the lines. And how do we know the drop will open again after the pantomime's over? You can't—'

'I'm not staying till after the pantomime, Polly,' Eileen said. 'I'm staying for good.' She looked at Colin and Mr Dunworthy. 'It's already settled.'

'*Settled?* What are you talking about?'

'Remember how you saw me in Trafalgar Square on VE Day? I wasn't there because we hadn't been rescued. I was there because I stayed behind.'

'No, you weren't – there could be a dozen other reasons why you were there that day. You could have been there on some other assignment, or—'

Eileen laughed, a clear, happy laugh. 'Oh, Polly, you know Mr Dunworthy would never let me go anywhere again after this. If I want to go to VE Day, I'm going to need to do it from here. Isn't that right, Mr Dunworthy?' she asked, smiling at him.

He was looking solemnly at her.

He's going to let her stay, Polly thought incredulously. *But he can't.*

'This is ridiculous, Eileen,' she said. 'I don't even know for certain it was you. I was halfway across Trafalgar Square. It might have been someone else entirely—'

'In my green coat,' Eileen said.

'Someone could have bought it at an applecart upset,' Polly said. 'You said yourself it was perfect for a redhead.'

Eileen shook her head. 'It was me. I have to be there so everything else can happen.'

'But there *must* be some other way,' Polly said, appealing to Colin. 'You can't let her—'

'That isn't the only reason I'm staying,' Eileen said. 'There's Alf and Binnie. I promised the vicar, Mr Goode, that I'd look after them, and I can't let him down.'

'But there must be someone else who could take them, the rector or Mrs Wyvern or someone,' Polly said, knowing even as she said it that it was impossible. They had already had this argument when Eileen took them in.

'There isn't,' Eileen said. 'Binnie's growing up far too fast as it is, and by next year England will be overrun with American soldiers. I can't abandon her – or Alf – in the middle of a war.'

Which they might not live through even if you do stay, Polly thought.

Neither Alf nor Binnie had been with Eileen on VE Day in Trafalgar Square. But if she told her that, it would only make her more determined to stay and try to protect them.

'And if Alf's left on his own,' Eileen was saying, 'he's likely to end up destroying the entire space-time continuum.' She smiled. 'Don't you see? I can't leave them. There's still a war on. And they saved my life.'

And mine, Polly thought. *And England's.* She knew there was no way to talk Eileen out of this.

'But you *hate* it here,' she said tearfully. 'The raids and the rationing and the dreadful food. You said believing you'd be able to go home someday was the only thing that kept you going.'

'I know, but wars require sacrifices. And this spot in history's not so bad. It is, after all, England's finest hour. And I'll get to see VE Day, which I always wanted to go to.'

'But—'

'Please try to understand,' Eileen said, taking Polly's hands. 'You've done your job by saving Sir Godfrey. My job's not finished yet, and I can't do it unless I stay here.'

'That isn't true. Colin, tell her she has to—'

'He can't,' Eileen said. 'He knows I stayed.' She looked at him again. 'Don't you?'

Colin didn't answer.

'Mr Dunworthy knows it, too,' Eileen said, turning to him. 'That's why you risked your life coming back here to the theatre with Colin instead of staying at St Paul's and going through to Oxford, isn't it? To say goodbye to me?'

'Yes.'

'But ... I don't understand,' Polly said, looking helplessly from one to the other. 'What's she talking about?'

'I was the one who told Colin where we were,' Eileen said. 'Didn't I?'

And when he didn't answer, 'He found me after the war, and I told him where you were. He'd never have been able to find us otherwise. So you see, I've got to stay. I've got to be here when he comes to look for me.'

'Is that true, Colin?' Polly said. 'Did Eileen tell you where we were?'

He still didn't answer.

'*Did* she?' Polly demanded. 'Tell me. Did she stay here in the past to tell you we were here?'

'Yes,' he said. 'She did.'

She turned on Eileen. 'You sacrificed yourself to save Mr Dunworthy and me?' she said angrily. 'How could you *do* that? How could you think I—?'

'It wasn't a sacrifice. Polly, you have no idea how much I've despised being helpless, how much I've *hated* knowing you and Mr Dunworthy were going to die and not being able to stop it. You saved my life that night at Padgett's and, oh, dozens of times since then – especially after Mike died – but I couldn't do *anything* to save yours.'

She clasped Polly's hands. 'But it wasn't true. There was something I could – I *can* – do. I can stay here. I can find Colin and tell him where you are,' she said, her face radiant. 'And I'm so *glad*!'

That's what they were telling her while I was gone, Polly thought, remembering Eileen wiping away tears as she came up the aisle.

'You shouldn't have told her,' she said bitterly to them. 'It's not fair to put a burden like that on her—'

'No one told me,' Eileen said. 'I knew it the moment I saw Colin.'

Just as I knew it was him, Polly thought, *that he'd come to rescue us.*

And that was why he had looked so sad, so careworn. Because he knew Eileen wasn't coming with them. Because he'd already seen her, years from now. She had already told him where they were.

It's already happened, she thought, *all of it, Eileen's staying here and VE Day and Colin's asking her where we were. It's all already happened, and there's nothing I can do to stop it.*

But she had to try. 'I'm not going without you, Eileen,' she said.

'You're right, you're not. I'll always be there with you,' Eileen said briskly, as if she were sending her off to school like Alf and Binnie. 'Now go. I'll take care of everything.'

'Oh my goodness, what about ENSA? Mr Tabbitt—'

'I'll tell him you were transferred to a touring troupe or something. Go.'

There was a whistling screech and then a *crump*, and the theatre shook slightly.

Eileen looked up at the ceiling. 'The raids sound like they're growing worse, and I won't have you blown up now after all the work I've done – will do – to get you out of here. And if I know Alf and Binnie, they'll be banned from the stage at any moment and come tearing up here to ask all sorts of questions, and you'll never get away in time.'

She hugged Mr Dunworthy. 'Goodbye. You take care to rest and get well.'

'I will, my dear.'

'Polly, eat lots of eggs and bacon for me, and *heaps* of sugar.' She hugged her tightly. 'And be *happy*.'

'"This is a comedy, not a tragedy,"' Polly murmured.

'*Yes*,' Eileen said joyfully. 'Only just think, you're going *home*!'

'But I can't bear the thought of leaving you here all alone—'

'I'm not alone. I have my children. And Sir Godfrey and Miss Laburnum and Winston Churchill. And Agatha Christie. And who knows what may happen? I may get to meet her properly next time and tell her how much I owe to her. She taught me to solve mysteries,' she said, and turned to smile at Colin. 'My dear boy,' she said, embracing him and then holding him out at arm's length to look at him again, 'take care of her for me.'

'I will,' he said solemnly.

'Now, go,' she ordered, propelling them up the aisle towards the exit.

'Wait,' Polly said, and fished in her pocket for the letter. 'Here. It's a list of the V-1s and V-2s in London and the southeastern suburbs, but not Kent or Sussex, so stay out of them if you can.'

'I'll be perfectly fine,' Eileen said. 'You saw me on VE Day, remember?'

I saw you, not Binnie and not Alf, Polly thought, and, as if she'd said his name aloud, Alf came pelting up the aisle towards them, pulling on his coat and cap as he ran.

'Why aren't you helping Sir Godfrey?' Eileen said sternly.

''e sent me to look for the carpenter,' he said, starting past them.

'You can't go outside in this,' Eileen said, blocking his way. 'There's a raid on.'

'I won't get killed,' Alf said, trying to get past Eileen. 'I been out in lots of raids.'

'Not this one,' Eileen said, putting her hands on his shoulders and turning him firmly around. 'Go and tell Sir Godfrey I'll let him know as soon as the carpenter arrives.'

She gave him a push to start him down the aisle, but instead he went over to Colin and said, 'Are you *sure* you ain't 'im?'

'Perfectly sure,' Eileen said. 'I told you, he's Polly's fiancé. He's home on leave.'

'On leave from *where*?' Alf said suspiciously.

'He's a pilot,' Polly said hastily because Colin clearly wouldn't have had time to research troop movements *and* raids. 'In the RAF.'

'What sort of plane did you fly?' Alf asked.

Out of the frying pan into the fire, Polly thought, but she had underestimated Colin.

'A Spitfire now,' he said. 'A Blenheim before I was shot down.'

'You were shot *down*?' Alf said, awed.

'Twice. I had to ditch in the Channel the second time.'

'Are you a hero, then?'

Yes, Polly thought.

'Course 'e's a hero, you dunderhead,' Binnie said, coming up the aisle in her spangled fairy gown and wings, one of which dangled broken behind her. She was carrying Polly's costume, green hose trailing, the scabbard dragging behind on the aisle carpet. 'All RAF pilots are heroes. Mr Churchill said so.'

'You're the dunderhead!' Alf shouted, and charged head down at her midsection like a bull. Binnie began flailing at him with the scabbard.

'You're certain you don't want to change your mind and come with us?' Polly whispered.

Eileen grinned. 'It's a tempting offer,' she whispered back, and grabbed Alf by the scruff of the neck. 'Alf, Binnie, stop that.' She snatched the scabbard from Binnie.

'She started it,' Alf said.

'I don't care who started it. Look what you've done to Binnie's wings. Binnie, go to the dressing room and take them off before you do any more damage. Alf, fetch the glue.'

Binnie shook her head vehemently. 'Miss Laburnum said I was to make *you* come and try on your doublet for 'er so's she can shorten it.'

'Tell her I will, as soon as I've said goodbye to Polly. Now go along,' she said, and gave them a push to get them moving, but Binnie resisted.

'I want to say goodbye to them, too,' Binnie said.

And make absolutely certain we don't take Eileen with us, Polly thought, looking at her standing there like a determined angel, broken wings dangling, arms folded belligerently across her chest, as if she would prevent them with brute force if necessary.

'That's right,' Alf said, planting himself firmly beside his sister. 'We got a right to say goodbye to 'em same as you.'

They had definitely earned that right, driving ambulances and providing maps and a place to meet in secret, preventing Eileen from reaching her drop, from catching John Bartholomew, from giving way to despair. Delaying Mr Dunworthy so he could collide with a Wren, delaying the nurses so she could speak to Sir Godfrey, obstructing, interfering, stopping things. As they were stopping Eileen from going now. She wondered if her rescue and Mr Dunworthy's were part of the continuum's plan, or if there was some other reason Eileen had to stay here, some other part she had to play in winning the war or the larger war that was history. Or if they did.

Even if it was critical to the continuum, it didn't make parting any easier, and Sir Godfrey's beloved Bard didn't know what he was talking about. There was nothing sweet about it.

'Oh, Eileen,' Polly said, embracing her, 'I don't want to leave.'

'And I don't want you to,' Eileen said.

'This is just like that day at the station,' Alf said contemptuously, 'when we put Theodore on the train. 'e didn't want to go neither. This 'ere's just like that, ain't it, Binnie?'

'Except Theodore kicked 'er,' Binnie said, 'and the vicar ain't 'ere.'

No, Polly thought, seeing the pain that flickered across Eileen's face, *the vicar's not here, and Mike's dead.*

And there were still four years of war and deprivation and loss to be got through. 'You two take care of Eileen,' she said fiercely.

'We will,' Binnie said.

'We won't let nuffink 'appen to her,' Alf promised.

'And both of you be good.'

''im good?' Binnie hooted, looking at Alf, and he promptly proved her point by kicking her in the shins. Binnie began whaling away at him.

'Alf, Binnie,' Eileen said, and moved to intervene, but before she could there was an outraged shout from the stage.

'Alf Hodbin!' Sir Godfrey bellowed. 'Binnie!'

'We didn't do nuffink!' Alf said. 'We was—'

'Bramblebushes, onstage!' Sir Godfrey shouted, and Alf and Binnie said, 'G'bye!' and tore off down the aisle.

Thank goodness, Polly thought. *Now we can—*

A deafening thud shook the theatre. The chandeliers rattled. 'We really do need to go, Polly,' Colin said, looking up at the ceiling.

'I know,' Polly said, pressing the list of raids into Eileen's hand.

'I told you, we'll be fine—'

'How do you know the reason you were fine wasn't that you'd memorised the list?' Polly folded Eileen's fingers over it. 'You've got to make certain you're all down in the tube both the nights of the ninth and the tenth. Fifteen hundred people were killed and eighteen hundred were injured. Those will be the last big raids till the V-1s, but you still need to heed the air-raid alerts—'

'Prince Dauntless!' Sir Godfrey shouted from the stage, and Polly looked up automatically, but he wasn't calling her. He was calling Eileen. 'Miss O'Reilly! Onstage! Now!'

'Coming!' Eileen said.

'Keep away from Croydon,' Polly said, still not letting go of her hand, 'and Bethnal Green and—'

'I must go,' Eileen said gently.

'I know,' Polly said, her voice breaking. 'I'll miss you terribly.'

'I'll miss you, too.' She leaned forward and kissed Polly on the cheek. 'Don't cry. We'll see each other again. In Trafalgar Square, remember?' she said.

'Prince *Dauntless*!' Sir Godfrey roared.

'Here!' she called and ran lightly down the aisle. 'Goodbye, Mr Dunworthy!' she called back over her shoulder. 'Colin, take care of Polly! I'll see you at the end of the war.' She pattered up the steps and onto the stage and vanished behind the safety curtain.

'*Finally*,' Polly heard Sir Godfrey thunder from behind it. '*Miss* O'Reilly, you seem to be labouring under the notion that we are putting on a *Christmas* pantomime. It is not. It is only two weeks till opening night. Time is of the essence!'

And that's my cue, Polly thought. *Half of acting is knowing when to make one's exit.*

But she still stood there, looking at the curtained stage.

Behind her, Colin said, 'Polly, we need—'

'I know,' Polly said.

'I'm sorry,' he said. 'It's just that there's not much time. Mr Dunworthy?'

Mr Dunworthy nodded and started up the aisle towards the exit.

'Polly?' Colin said gently. 'Ready?'

'Yes,' she said. 'Let's go home,' and started up the aisle with him.

'Wait!' Sir Godfrey called, 'I would speak with thee ere you go.'

Polly and Colin turned in the doorway and looked down at the stage. Sir Godfrey stood in front of the curtain, still in his Hitler uniform, his ridiculous moustache.

'My lord?' she said, but he wasn't looking at her. He was looking at Colin, and he wasn't Duke Orsino or even Crichton. He was Prospero, just as he had been that first night they had acted together in St George's cellar.

'"I have given you here a third of mine own life,"' he said, '"or that for which I live."'

Colin nodded.

'"I promise you calm seas,"' Sir Godfrey called, and raised his hands in benediction, '"auspicious gales, and sail so expeditious that shall catch your royal fleet far off."'

*'She lives. If it be so, it is a chance which does
redeem all sorrows that ever I have felt.'*

WILLIAM SHAKESPEARE *KING LEAR*

IMPERIAL WAR MUSEUM, LONDON – 7 MAY 1995

I *managed to come through and find Polly and Merope,* Colin
thought, *but I came too late to rescue them. Too late.* 'I was
too late, wasn't I?' he asked Binnie, and, as if on cue, the sound
effects of the bombs started again.

'No,' Binnie said when they'd diminished to where she could
be heard.

'What? I got Polly and Mr Dunworthy out before their deadlines?'

'I don't know. I know you left with them for the drop,
and Mum – I mean Eileen – said you must have got through
because—'

'But if I left to take them to the drop, why didn't Merope – I
mean Eileen – go with us?'

'Because of us,' Binnie said. 'Alf and me. She'd promised she
wouldn't leave us. And she needed to be here to tell you where
Polly and Mr Dunworthy were.'

And so she'd sacrificed herself and stayed behind. But there
must be some other way, especially since she wasn't the one
who'd told him; Binnie was. But he could deal with that later.
Just now, he needed to find out where they were.

'Binnie,' he said eagerly, 'we've got to come up with times when they were together in one place. You said Eileen made the decision to stay – which means she must have been there as well – so it has to be a time when all three of them were together. Before the first of May. That's when Mr Dunworthy's deadline is. I'm assuming the best time for them to be together is during a raid. Did they go to a tube shelter during the raids?'

'Yes, but—'

'And you need to tell me where they're living and what times they're likely to all be at home. I know about Mrs Rickett's. Are they still in Kensington? If they are, then that may mean the drop Polly used will open …'

Binnie was frowning at him.

'I know this was a long time ago,' he said, 'and it's difficult to remember exactly where they were at any given time, but this is critical. If you can't remember an exact date, then if you can just tell me which tube shelter, I can look up the dates when there were raids and—'

She shook her head, still frowning.

'Why won't that work?' he said. 'Did they not always go to the tube station when there were raids?'

'It doesn't matter whether they did or not,' Binnie said. 'That isn't where they were.'

'Where they—?'

'When you came.' She smiled at his uncomprehending look. 'You're forgetting, this all happened already. More than fifty years ago. Mum stayed behind so she could be here to *make* it happen, to tell you where they were.' She smiled ruefully. 'And when she couldn't be—'

'She sent you.'

'Yes.'

'She told you who she was?' he said, trying to process all this.

'Yes, but we'd worked it out on our own ages before that. When we were at the manor, we followed her out to the drop.'

'You saw her go through?' The drop wasn't supposed to have opened if anyone was nearby.

'No, but we saw her just after she'd come back, and there were lots of other clues, mistakes and things, and then when you came and took Polly and Mr Dunworthy, we were dead certain. Only there's still lots we don't know. Like why it took you so long to get here.'

'None of the drops in England in 1940 would open,' he said. 'After Mr Dunworthy went through, we tried every possible temporal and spatial location, and nothing would work. At first, we thought it was *every* drop, but the ones in other places and times weren't affected, just those in England and Scotland, and the first three months of 1941. We could get a few drops to open after mid-March, but by then we had no idea where they were. Polly'd left Townsend Brothers, and they weren't at Notting Hill Gate.'

'So you came here to find someone who might have known her so they could tell you where she was,' Binnie said.

'Yes.' He didn't mention all the months he'd spent searching National Service and Civil Defence records looking for their names after Michael had told him Polly and Eileen had been planning to sign up, or all the years before that he'd spent sitting in libraries and newspaper morgues trying to find out if they were still alive, and calculating coordinates for drop after failed drop, and attempting to convince Badri and Linna that rescue was possible, and meeting with Dr Ishiwaka and every other time-travel theorist he could corner, trying to find out what the bloody hell had gone wrong.

'Alf said he was certain it had happened at one of the anniversary celebrations,' Binnie was saying.

'Wait,' Colin said, 'didn't Eileen tell you I'd be here today?'

'No.'

'I don't understand,' Colin said. 'Why not?'

'Because she didn't know where you'd be. All she knew was

that at some point she'd told you where they were, and that that was how you'd known where to come.'

'But—'

'She said she didn't need to know, that she'd be able to find you because she *had* found you,' Binnie said, and smiled. 'Mum was always rather an optimist. Even when she found out about the cancer, she told us, "You mustn't worry. It will all come right in the end." When she died I was afraid something had gone wrong, but Alf said it couldn't have because then you couldn't have come, so it was up to us to *make* it happen.' She beamed at him. 'And we did.'

'But I still don't understand. How did you and your brother know I'd be here on this particular date?'

'We didn't. We've been looking for you ever since Mum died.'

'Ever since—?'

She nodded. 'At first we concentrated on Notting Hill Gate Underground Station and Oxford Street and of course Denewell Manor – it's a school now – but it was too much territory to cover, even with Michael and Mary—'

'Who?' he cut in.

'Michael's my son and Mary's my sister – half-sister really, though I never think of her that way.'

'She's Eileen's *daughter*?'

'I'm sorry, I keep thinking you know all this. Mum – Eileen – married the—'

There was a loud screaming *swish* and the sound of an explosion. The shelter walls shook, and a bright white light flashed on, simulating the flash from the bomb. It went to yellow and then red, bathing the shelter and Binnie's face in an orange light.

'Eileen married—?' Colin prompted her, shouting over the noise.

Binnie didn't answer. She was staring at him with an odd look on her face, as if she'd just realised something.

'What is it? What's wrong?' he said, wondering if the sounds had triggered some traumatic memory. 'Are you all right?'

'How strange,' she murmured. 'I wonder if she ... that would explain ...'

'You wonder if she what? Who? Eileen? What is it?'

She shook her head, as if to clear it. 'Nothing. I keep forgetting you don't know anything that's happened. Eileen married shortly after the war, and they had two children. Besides Alf and me, I mean. Godfrey, that's her son, assisted us as well, but even with all of us looking, we hadn't any luck, and then Alf said, "We've got to think about this from Colin's point of view. Where would *he* look?" And that was when it occurred to us that you'd go where people who were in the Blitz were likely to be, and luckily that was just before the fiftieth anniversary of the war's beginning, and—'

'You've been doing this since 1990?'

'No. 1989. The war actually began in '39, you know, though there weren't any battles for nearly a year. But there were several evacuated children's reunions, and then in the spring there were all the Battle of Britain exhibitions, and of course every year the VE Day parades. Those were the most difficult. So many cities had their own, and all on the same day—'

'Do you mean to tell me you've been going to parades and anniversary celebrations and museum exhibitions for *six* years?' There must have been scores, even hundreds. 'How many have you gone to?'

'All of them,' she said simply.

All of them.

'It's not so bad as it might have been,' Binnie said. 'It's only May. Since it's the fiftieth anniversary of the war's end, there will be celebrations all year, including a special memorial service for the fire watch at St Paul's on December the twenty-ninth.' She grinned mischievously at him. 'At least you didn't go to that.'

No, but I was planning to, he thought, *and the Dunkirk*

Commemoration at Dover and the Eagle Day Air Show at Biggin Hill and the 'Life in the Tube Shelters' exhibit at the London Transport Museum. And if he had, Binnie or Alf or one of Eileen's other children would have been there as well. They'd spent nearly as much time and effort searching for him as he had for Polly. 'Binnie—' he said.

'My, will you look at that,' a woman's voice said from only a few feet away, 'a gas mask! Do you remember having to carry them everywhere with us? And having those tiresome gas drills?'

'Oh dear, they're coming back from lunch,' Binnie whispered. She stood up.

'Wait,' Colin said. 'You still haven't told me where they are.'

She sat back down. 'I'm not sure I *did* tell you. I think Mr Dunworthy may have—'

'Mr Dunworthy? I thought you said they were all in one place.'

'They were, but Mr Dunworthy was the one who found you, or you found him – I don't know that bit of it – and brought you there.'

'But where did I find *him*?'

'In St Paul's.'

St Paul's? That meant he'd used Mr Dunworthy's drop. But it hadn't opened once since Mr Dunworthy had gone through, despite thousands of attempts. 'Did I use the drop in St Paul's?' he asked.

'I don't know that either. Why?'

'Because it's not working.'

'Oh. Then you must have found him – or he found you – somewhere else. All I know is that we left him at St Paul's that night—'

'Which night? You still haven't told me the date.'

'I'm afraid I don't know that either. It was so long ago, and we were only children. It was sometime in late—'

'Have you been in the air-raid shelter yet?' a woman's voice said, and the door opened on Talbot, Camberley and Pudge. 'So here you are, Goody,' Talbot said, looking from Binnie, who'd shot to her feet, to Colin. 'What are you two up to?'

'I was showing him the shelter,' Binnie said.

'We can see that,' Pudge said dryly. She looked around at the shelter. 'My, this is cosy.'

'And much nicer than I remember shelters being,' Talbot said. 'We were looking for you, Goody. You must come and see the ambulance display. You drove an ambulance.'

'I'll come in a moment,' Binnie said. 'Mr Knight and I weren't quite done—'

'Obviously,' Talbot said.

'I only have one or two more questions,' Colin said, belatedly pulling out his notebook. 'Would you mind if I borrow Mrs Lambert for a bit longer?'

'Of course not,' Talbot said. 'We shouldn't want to stand in the way of true love.'

'Don't be a noddlehead, Talbot,' Binnie said. 'Mr Knight's a reporter – and young enough to be my grandson.'

'Impossible,' Colin said gallantly. 'And at any rate, I've always liked older women.'

'In that case,' Talbot said, taking his arm, 'you *must* come with us to see the ambulance display.'

'Yes,' Camberley said, 'it looks exactly like the ones we drove.'

'You can ask her your questions on the way there,' Talbot said, leading him, her arm still firmly linked in his, towards the ambulance exhibit, but he had no chance to ask Binnie anything. Half a dozen women latched onto her before they reached it, asking her questions, and when they reached the ambulance, half a dozen others were waiting for her. They insisted she climb into the back and then into the driver's seat.

He pushed through the crowd to her and leaned in the window. 'If you could just clear up a few details, Mrs Lambert,' he said.

'You mentioned the bombing of Westminster Abbey. When did that happen?'

'May the tenth,' Camberley said before Binnie could answer.

And so much for that clever idea, Colin thought.

'I remember,' Camberley said, 'because I was supposed to go to dinner and a show that night with a simply gorgeous flight officer, and instead I spent the entire night ferrying casualties. I'll never forgive Hitler for ruining my evening.'

'What show was he taking you to?' Binnie asked.

This is no time to be discussing 'Theatre During the Blitz', Colin thought in annoyance.

'Was it the naughty revue at the Windmill?' Talbot suggested.

'"We never closed",' Pudge quoted.

'Nor wore any clothes,' Talbot said.

'*No,*' Camberley said, 'he took me to a play! And I wore—'

'What sort of play?' Binnie asked. 'A pantomime?'

'Pantomimes are for children.'

'I saw a pantomime once during the Blitz,' Binnie said as if she hadn't heard her. '*Sleeping Beauty.* At the *Regent.* Sir Godfrey Kingsman was the Bad Fairy.'

'Oh, speaking of sleeping,' the woman who'd passed out the name badges said, 'you all *must* see the display on "Sleeping Through the Blitz". Do you remember Horlicks? And those siren suits? It's this way,' she said, and they all started through the doorway and down the corridor, taking Binnie with them.

Colin followed, but before he reached the door, a new group of women with Union Jacks on their name badges swept in, and by the time he made it into the corridor, he expected her to have vanished. But Binnie was only halfway down it, stopped in front of a black-and-white photograph of a church, its tower in flames.

'Isn't that St Bride's?' Binnie asked, pointing at it. 'I remember the night it burned. The raids were so terrible that night. It was sometime at the end of April—'

'No, it wasn't,' Pudge said. 'St Bride's burned in December.'

'Oh, that's right,' Binnie said, 'the same night St Paul's nearly did.' She looked down the corridor at Colin. 'I must have got it confused. I know something happened at the end of April.'

I found Polly and Eileen and Mr Dunworthy, Colin thought. *Thank you*, he mouthed silently at Binnie, but she'd already turned back to look at the photograph. Camberley said something to her and the other women closed in about her, blocking her from his view. The Union Jack women surged into the corridor, chattering and exclaiming.

'Harris!' someone in a bright green hat called, '*there* you are. I thought I'd never find you. It's time to go.'

Time to go. Colin squeezed out of the corridor and walked back through the exhibition towards the exit. *And now all I have to do is get Mr Dunworthy's drop to open. If that's the drop I used. And not get caught by the fire watch. Or if it won't open, find another drop. And then find Mr Dunworthy. And the theatre.*

But he had the name of it. And the knowledge that he hadn't been too late, that Polly was still alive.

He reached the exit. It was flanked by a photograph of the King and Queen, waving to the jubilant VE Day crowds from a balcony of Buckingham Palace, and a life-sized cutout of Winston Churchill making the V-for-Victory sign. As he walked through the doorway, the triumphant note of the all-clear sounded.

He made his way quickly through the lobby to the ticket desk. 'Can you give Ann Perry a message for me?' he asked the ticket seller. 'Would you tell her thank you and that the exhibition was extremely informative? And tell her I'm genuinely sorry I wasn't who she thought I was.'

'Yes, sir.' The ticket seller wrote the message down, and Colin went outside, thinking about what he had to do. Find out the address of the Regent and how to get there from St Paul's, and decipher what 'the end of April' meant. The twentieth? The thirtieth? He hoped it wasn't the thirtieth. Mr Dunworthy's deadline was the first of May. The thirtieth would be cutting it a bit fine.

Binnie had said the raids were bad the night he came. That should narrow it down a bit, unless there'd been raids every night in April. He went down the steps. If he could find out what dates *Sleeping Beauty* had been performed, that would—

Binnie was standing down by the *Lily Maid*. 'How did you get out here?' Colin asked.

'I used a trick I learned from Alf,' she said.

He looked back at the building. 'You set the Imperial War Museum on fire?'

'No, of course not. I told them I'd dropped my contact lens,' and when he looked at her blankly, 'Contacts are eyeglass lenses that fit directly on the eye. Breakable lenses. They're all crawling about on the floor looking for it. But I haven't much time. I wanted to make certain you understood everything.'

'Yes. The Regent Theatre. During a performance of the pantomime *Sleeping Beauty*.'

'No, a rehearsal,' she said.

'And you don't know the date?'

'No, Alf and I tried to work that out. It was after the north transept of St Paul's was hit—'

Which had been on April sixteenth. 'And there were raids that night?'

'Yes – at any rate I think so. It's difficult to remember. There were so many raids. I'm sorry I can't be of more help.' She put her hand on his arm. 'You mustn't grow discouraged if you're not able to find the right date straightaway.'

'Did Eileen tell you that happened?'

'No, and I'm not certain it did, but you seem younger today than you did the night you came through.'

'Is that why you gave me that odd look in the mock-up of the air-raid shelter?'

'The air-raid shelter?' she said, looking suddenly cornered, caught out.

'Yes,' he said. 'We were talking about Eileen, and then the bomb sound effect went off and the shelter lit up, and you gave me an odd look and said, "I wonder if she ... that would explain ..." Was that what you meant? That I looked older?'

'It must have been. That's the worst thing about growing old. One can't remember what one was talking about five minutes afterward.' She laughed. 'I can't think what else it could have been. Oh, I know – it wasn't about you at all. Mrs Netterton said she didn't remember there being red lights in the shelters, and I had no idea what she was talking about. She's rather scattered, poor dear. And then when the bomb went off, and there was that red light to simulate the explosion, I realised that must have been it.'

It sounded plausible, and he'd have no doubt believed it if it hadn't been for the head of the Evacuation Committee telling him, 'They'd stand there looking all wide-eyed and innocent and tell you the most outrageous fibs.'

But what possible reason could she have for lying to him? She had spent the last six years trudging from one place to another to find him and tell him the truth, not hold it back.

Unless it was something terrible. But she had looked bemused, not distressed. Perhaps something had occurred that night at the theatre that she hadn't fully understood till now.

Whatever it was, it was clear she had no intention of telling him. 'I *must* get back before they miss me,' she was saying, looking up at the museum. 'They'll think we've run off together.'

'I wish we could,' he said. '*Thank* you. For everything you've done.' He leaned forward and kissed her on her cheek, in spite of what it was likely to do to her reputation. 'It was above and beyond the call of duty.'

She shook her head. 'It was the least we could do for her after all she did for us. She took us in, fed us, clothed us, sent us to school. She was "the only one wot was nice to us", as my brother would say.' She smiled at him. 'I doubt if we'd have survived

760

the war without her. And even if we had, I'd have ended up on the streets, and Alf – I hate to think where he'd be.'

'But I thought – You said he was down at the Old Bailey.'

'He is – oh, you thought because I said he'd been detained that he was the *defendant*.' She laughed. 'Oh dear, I must tell Alf that. No, he's had an important case on this week, and the jury stayed out longer than expected.'

'He's a *barrister*?' Colin said, astonished.

'*No*,' she said, and laughed again. 'He's a *judge*.'

LONDON – 7 MAY 1945

At three, Eileen picked up Colonel Abrams from the Savoy in the staff car. 'To the War Office, Lieutenant,' he said.

'Yes, sir,' she said. She pulled out of the drive onto the Strand and then jammed on the brakes as a man ran straight in front of the car and across the road, shouting, 'It's here!'

'It's not a V-2, is it?' Colonel Abrams, who was newly arrived from the States, said, peering anxiously out of the window.

'No,' she said. *It's the end of the war.*

And as soon as she'd delivered him to the War Office and he'd gone inside, she drove straight to Alf and Binnie's school.

'I've come for Alf and Binnie,' she told the headmistress. 'I need to take them home with me at once.'

'Have you heard something, then?' the headmistress asked.

And what should she answer? The surrender wouldn't be officially announced till tomorrow, even though it had been signed at three this morning. And the newsagents' billboards she'd seen on the way had said only, 'Surrender Soon?'

'I haven't heard anything official,' she said, 'but everyone's been saying they expect the announcement at any moment.'

The headmistress beamed. 'I'll fetch them,' she said, and bustled off down the corridor.

She was gone for what seemed like forever. *They'd better not have chosen today to play truant*, Eileen thought anxiously. She leaned out of the door to look down the corridor and caught a glimpse of a teenage girl at the end of it, taking her coat out of the cupboard. The girl was tall and graceful, with shining blonde hair. *What a pretty girl*, Eileen thought.

The girl shut the cupboard and turned, and Eileen realised with a shock that it was Binnie. *Oh my, she's nearly grown up*, Eileen thought, and then saw the stunned look on Binnie's face. She'd seen that look before – on Mike's face, when she told him Polly had already been here, on Polly's face, when the warden told them Mike was dead.

Binnie thinks something dreadful's happened, Eileen thought, and hurried down the corridor to reassure her. 'It's not bad news. The war's over. Aren't you excited?'

'Yes,' Binnie said, but she didn't sound excited.

She'd been very moody lately. *Don't be difficult tonight*, Eileen thought. *I haven't time for this.* 'Where's your brother?' she asked.

Alf came tearing down the corridor, shirttail out, socks down, tie askew, followed by the headmistress.

'The war's over, ain't it?' he said, skidding to a stop inches from Eileen. 'I knew it was going to be today. When'd you hear? We been listenin' to the wireless in class all day—' He glanced guiltily at the headmistress, but she was still beaming. '—but they haven't said anything at all!'

'Come along,' Eileen said, 'we need to go. Alf, where's your coat?'

'Oh, I forgot it! It's in my classroom. I'll fetch it.' He tore off down the corridor.

'Don't tell—' Eileen said, but she wasn't quick enough. There was a loud whoop from the end of the corridor, followed by the sound of cheering and doors banging open. The headmistress scurried off to deal with it.

Alf came tearing back with his coat clutched to his chest. 'Alf,' Eileen said reprovingly.

'It was just on the wireless!' he shouted. 'The war's over! Come on, let's go. They're gonna turn on the lights in Piccadilly Circus.'

He caught sight of Binnie's face, and his grin faded. 'You're lettin' us go, ain't you, Mum?' he said to Eileen. 'Everybody'll be there. The King and Queen and Churchill.'

And Polly, Eileen thought.

'The whole *city's* goin'. The war's over!' He appealed to Binnie. 'Tell Eileen we must go!'

'Are we going?' Binnie asked.

'Yes, of course,' Eileen said, wondering if Binnie had somehow picked up on her anxiety. 'We must be there. Come along, Alf, Binnie.'

Alf shot through the door, but Binnie still stood there, looking resentful.

'Binnie?' Eileen said, taking her arm, and when she still didn't move, 'I'm sorry, I forgot you wanted to be called Roxie.' She'd insisted on the name ever since seeing Ginger Rogers play an unrepentant murderess in *Roxie Hart*, which wasn't surprising.

Binnie wrested free of her grasp. 'I don't care a jot what you call me,' she said, and flounced out of the school.

Alf was waiting for them at the bottom of the steps, but Binnie marched past him and started up the street towards the tube station. 'We're not going by tube,' Eileen said. 'I've got Colonel Abrams' car.'

'Can I drive?' Alf said, clambering into the front.

Binnie was still standing there, looking at the car. 'Don't you have to take this back to headquarters?'

'They won't miss it,' Eileen said. 'Get in.'

Binnie did, slamming the door.

'And I'm not certain I could get it there. The crowds were already starting to gather in front of the palace when I drove past,' she lied.

'Is that where *we're* goin', Mum?' Alf asked. 'To Buckingham Palace?'

'No, we must go home first so I can change out of my uniform,' Eileen said.

'Good. I need to fetch my Union Jack.'

'I think you should take the car back,' Binnie said from the back seat. 'If you get in trouble, you might lose your job.'

'She can't lose 'er job, 'cause she won't '*ave* a job,' Alf said jubilantly. 'And you ain't got a job drivin' ambulances no more neither, Binnie. The war's over. I think we should go to Piccadilly Circus and *then* Buckingham Palace.' He leaned out of the window, waving. 'The war's over! Hurrah!'

Her lie about the crowds turned out to be the truth. People clogged the streets, shouting and waving flags. It took forever to reach Bloomsbury.

I'll never be able to get the car to Trafalgar Square through this, Eileen thought, parking outside the flat.

'I still think you should take it back to headquarters,' Binnie said.

'There isn't time,' Eileen said, and ran upstairs to change out of her uniform. She put on a summer frock and her green coat and then rang up Mrs Owens and told her the good news.

'We've only just heard,' Mrs Owens said. 'Theodore's mother just telephoned,' and Eileen could hear Theodore in the background saying, 'I don't *want* the war to be over!'

Of course not, Eileen thought.

Binnie came out wearing her white dress.

The Union Jack wasn't the only thing Alf had wanted to come home for. 'Can Mrs Bascombe go with us?' he asked, coming out of his room with the parrot in its cage.

'Of course not, you noddlehead,' Binnie said.

'She's really glad about us winning. She '*ated* the war.'

'No, she can't go with us,' Eileen said, and sent Alf back to his room.

When he came out again, he had his Union Jack and three Roman candles and a long string of squibs.

'Where did you get those?' Eileen demanded.

'I been savin' 'em up for the victory celebration,' he said, which wasn't an answer, but it was growing late and they still had to get to Trafalgar Square.

'You can take the squibs and one Roman candle,' she said, trying to ignore Binnie's look of disapproval. 'And no setting them off when there are people nearby. Come along.'

She hurried them out of the door and down to Russell Square – another ordeal. The streets and the station were jammed, and they had to wait through several trains for one there was room enough to squeeze onto.

At Leicester Square she ordered Alf and Binnie off the tube.

'Why're we gettin' off 'ere?' Alf asked. 'We ain't at Piccadilly Circus yet.'

'We're not going to Piccadilly Circus,' Eileen said, leading them through the crowd to the Northern Line platform. 'We're going to Trafalgar Square.' She herded them onto the train, which, fortunately, was too crammed to permit further conversation.

The station at Trafalgar Square was even worse, a wall-to-wall mass of shouting, jostling people and noisemakers and paper streamers. 'You could nick lots of stuff 'ere,' Alf said.

'*No one* is nicking anything,' Eileen said, grabbing his and Binnie's arms and propelling them up the escalator and the stairs and out onto the street.

There were people everywhere – cheering and singing and waving Union Jacks. Church bells were ringing wildly. A BEF soldier was moving through the crowd kissing every woman he saw, and none of the women – including two elderly ladies in flowered hats and white gloves – seemed to mind at all.

A double-decker bus with a hand-lettered banner reading, 'Hitler Missed the Bus!' crept past, honking its horn nonstop and parting the crowds in front of it, and Eileen and the children were able to cross the street before the mob closed in again.

But the moment they reached the other side, they were engulfed. 'We should've gone to Piccadilly Circus instead,' Alf said.

'We're going to Trafalgar Square,' Eileen said firmly. 'We'll be fine. We just need to keep together.'

'Keep together,' Binnie echoed coldly. She had that stunned look again.

What is *the matter with her?* Eileen wondered, grabbing her by the arm and Alf by the sleeve and pushing them determinedly through the crowd to the square. It was filled to bursting with sailors, soldiers, Wrens, waitresses still wearing their aprons, all waving Union Jacks. They had climbed up onto the base of the monument and the sandbagged sentry points, and one American Marine was trying to shin up the monument itself while a policeman below him shouted at him to get down.

Eileen forced her way into the square, dragging Alf and Binnie with her. Polly had said she'd seen her standing by one of the lions, but getting there was easier said than done, and holding on to the children even more difficult. She'd lost Alf before they'd gone ten feet, and had had to grab him by the collar and haul him back.

She twisted her arm around to look at her watch. Oh no, it was already past nine, and they were nowhere near the lions. She couldn't even *see* them in this mêlée. She stretched herself on tiptoe, trying to spot the lion which had had its nose knocked off above the heads and hats and flags.

There it was, but she couldn't get to it. The crowd was surging away from it, towards the fountains. She needed to use her hands to force her way through, but she didn't dare let go of Alf and Binnie, and the crowd between her and the monument was rapidly becoming a solid wall of people.

What if I can't get there? she thought, and felt a flutter of panic.

Of course you can, she told herself. *You already did. And you won't have to do it on your own. You've got troops at your disposal.*

She pulled Alf back beside her. 'I need you to get us to that lion,' she said, pointing. 'Can you do it?'

"course,' he said, and pulled a GI lighter from his pocket. Eileen resisted the impulse to demand to know where he'd got it and watched instead as he took a large firecracker from his other pocket and held it up in front of him.

'Fire one!' he shouted, struck a flame in the lighter, held it an inch from the firecracker, and marched them through the crowd, who scattered, shrieking, out of their way on either side. Even so, they were nearly separated twice before they reached the lion's pedestal, and as soon as Alf clicked his lighter shut, the crowd closed back in.

Eileen turned to look for Polly on the National Gallery steps and Alf and Binnie were both caught by the surging crowd and had to shove their way back to her.

'If we get separated,' she told them, struggling in the crowd to get her bag off her shoulder and open, 'go to the base of the monument and wait for me.' She took out two half-crowns. 'And if you can't find me at all, here's money for you to take the tube home.'

She handed one half-crown to Alf and held out the other to Binnie.

Binnie didn't take it. She stood there, looking steadily at Eileen. She was very pale.

'I'll take it,' Alf said, reaching to grab it.

Eileen automatically closed her fist over the coin, her eyes on Binnie's white face. 'What's wrong, Binnie? Are you ill?'

'No,' she said belligerently. 'I know why you brought us here today. Polly's here, isn't she?'

'Polly?' Alf said. 'I thought you said she got married to that ARP warden and went to Canada. Where is she?' He began scrambling up the side of the lion's base.

'That's why you wore that coat,' Binnie said, ignoring him,

her eyes never leaving Eileen's face, 'so she could spot you in the crowd. She's here, isn't she?'

'Yes,' Eileen said.

'Where?' Alf called down to them. He had climbed up onto the pedestal and was clinging to the lion's nose. 'I can't see her anywhere.'

'You're leaving, aren't you?' Binnie asked. 'That's why you let Alf bring fireworks and why you didn't care if you got in trouble over the car. Because you're leaving. You came here to find Polly so you can go back with her.'

'Back?'

Binnie nodded. 'To where you came from. I 'eard you talkin' in the theatre. And I seen you. In the woods at the manor,' she said, reverting to her old Cockney speech. 'Alf said you was meetin' somebody in the woods. 'e thought you was a spy. So I followed you. And me and Alf 'eard you talkin' in the emergency staircase.'

They had always been two steps ahead of her. 'Binnie—'

'You were goin' to lose us on purpose in the crowd, weren't you?' Binnie said accusingly. 'Like in *Hansel and Gretel*—'

'No. Binnie, I'm not going anywhere.' She reached her hand out to the girl.

Binnie flinched away from her. 'Then why did you bring us 'ere?' she said, nearly crying with rage. 'Why'd you wear that coat?'

'Because Polly has to see us standing here.'

'So she can come over and get you.'

'No.'

She glanced around at the surrounding crowd. They had no business discussing this here, but no one was paying any attention to them. They were all cheering, laughing, waving flags. 'Polly has to see us so everything that's happened *can* happen. Because where I come from, this night has *already* happened, and when it did, Polly saw me in the crowd wearing my green coat. And she saw you, too.'

769

'And then what?'

And then she went back to Oxford, Eileen thought, *and we stood in the quad and talked to Mike and he went to Dunkirk and lost his foot and you got the measles and we went to London and your mother was killed and Mike was killed and Polly and I took you in and we found Mr Dunworthy and you saved our lives.*

'Then what?' Binnie repeated angrily.

'Then nothing. Polly didn't speak to me. She didn't take me back with her. She wasn't even certain it was me she'd seen. And all of that already happened so you see, I couldn't go back with her even if I wanted to. Which I don't, because I want to stay here with you and Alf.'

And because if I did go back, Mr Dunworthy would have pulled me out and cancelled all our drops, and none of this would have happened. Including this VE Day celebration.

There'd have been no cheering crowds, no church bells, no victory. Binnie would have died of pneumonia and Alf on the *City of Benares,* and Colonel Westlake would have died waiting for an ambulance, and they would have lost the war.

'*When* did Polly see you?' Binnie demanded.

'I'm not certain,' Eileen said. 'She told me she got to Trafalgar Square around half past nine, and she was only in the square an hour.'

'Then why'd you come and get us out of school? Why'd you make us hurry?'

If she lied to her now, Binnie would never trust her again. 'Because I hoped that Colin – the man who came to fetch Polly and Mr Dunworthy that night – might be here.'

'And *he'd* take you back.'

'No. I told Colin – will tell Colin – where to find us, and I thought tonight might have been when I told him. I thought he might be here, but I don't know that for certain. I don't know when I told him. It might be tonight, or years from now.'

'And when you tell him, he'll go back and find everyone at the theatre,' Binnie said.

'Yes.'

Binnie frowned at her. 'You should have asked him when it was you told him,' she said practically. 'And where, so you wouldn't have to go running about looking for him.'

'That's true,' Eileen said, 'but it doesn't matter. We'll find each other in time, and I'll tell him.'

'Because he had to have found you or he wouldn't have known where you were, so he couldn't have come to the theatre,' Binnie said.

And why did I assume she wouldn't be able to understand time travel? Eileen wondered. 'Exactly.'

'And that's why you had to stay here. To tell him.'

'No, I stayed because I couldn't leave you and Alf.' She smiled at Binnie. 'Who'd take care of me if I left—?'

But she didn't get it out. Binnie had flung herself at her, her arms around her neck, clinging so tightly Eileen could scarcely breathe.

'Binnie—' Eileen said gently, enfolding her in her arms.

'I can't see Polly nowhere,' Alf said, jumping down from the lion. 'Are you sure she's 'ere?'

'Yes,' Eileen said.

'What part of the square was she in?' Binnie asked.

'I don't know. She said she saw me from a long way off.'

'Well, I can't see nuffink. She must've climbed up on Nelson's statue or somefink,' he said, elbowing his way over to a lamp-post.

'She would *not* have climbed a lamppost,' Eileen said.

'I *know*,' Alf said. 'I'm only climbing up so's I can see.' He stuck the staff of his Union Jack between his teeth, like a pirate's cutlass, and shinned up it.

'Can you see her?' Eileen called up to him.

'No,' Alf said, taking the flag out of his teeth. 'Are you sure she's – there she is!' He pointed towards the National Gallery with his Union Jack. 'She's got on a red hat.'

Eileen craned her neck, standing on tiptoe and hanging onto the lamppost for balance. *Red hat, red hat ...*

'I see her!' Binnie said excitedly.

'Where? Show me where she's standing.'

'There,' Binnie said, pointing. Eileen sighted along her outstretched arm. 'On the porch.'

'No, she ain't!' Alf shouted from halfway up the lamppost. 'She's comin' down the steps.'

'Where?' Eileen still couldn't see her, and if she'd started down the stairs already ...'*Where?*'

'*There.* At the foot of the stairs.'

If Polly had already gone down the stairs, she had already seen her standing by the lion, was already leaving for her drop in Hampstead Heath.

'Did you see her?' Binnie asked.

'No,' Eileen said, 'but it doesn't matter. It wasn't necessary for me to see her.' But she'd hoped so much that she would catch a glimpse of her. All these last four years, she'd held to that hope, that she'd see her again, if only from a distance.

'I'm sorry, Mum,' Binnie said.

'It's all right.'

She gave Binnie a hug. 'Let's go and get some supper.' She looked for Alf, but he was no longer on the lamppost. 'Where's Alf?' she asked. 'Can you see him anywhere?'

'No,' Binnie said, scanning the crowd.

She darted off suddenly into the middle of the Square. 'Binnie, wait! No!' Eileen said, grabbing for her, but she was already out of reach.

And out of sight. The crowd closed about her as if it was water, leaving no trace. 'Binnie! Come back!' she called, starting after her through the crush.

And saw Polly. She was only a few yards away, working her way against the current towards Charing Cross Station. She looked younger than Eileen remembered, nearly as young as Binnie, her face without the worry and sorrow it would have. And without the transcendent joy it had had that night when Colin came.

Because none of it's happened yet, Eileen thought.

She had hoped for one final look, but this wasn't the end, it was the beginning. Everything – the escape from Padgett's and the race to St Paul's the night of the twenty-ninth and Christmas dinner with Miss Laburnum and Miss Hibbard and Mr Dorming – was all still yet to come. Standing in line together at the canteen and walking home from Notting Hill Gate in the foggy dawn after the all-clear and sitting on the platform after everyone else was asleep, talking of Mrs Rickett's appalling meals and the trials of wrapping parcels and mending stockings.

'Oh, Polly,' she murmured, 'we're going to be such good friends!'

And though she couldn't possibly have heard her, Polly turned as if she had and looked straight at her. But only for an instant, and then a group of GIs pushed in front of Eileen, blowing on noisemakers, hiding Polly from sight.

Eileen had thought she'd lost her, but she hadn't. Polly was still there, moving steadily towards the tube station and her drop and Oxford. *Where she'll see me walking to Oriel and she'll tell me I must get a driving authorisation first and I'll tell her Colin's in love with her and we'll go to Balliol and stand talking to Michael Davies in the sunlit quad.*

'Goodbye!' she called after Polly, over the sound of a brass band that had struck up, 'Show Me the Way to Go Home'. 'Don't be frightened. Everything will work out all right in the end,' and then stood there, looking after her, oblivious to the music, the noise, the people shoving and jostling against her, till Polly was out of sight.

Then she turned to go and look for Alf and Binnie, though she had no idea at all how to find them in this solid mass of people.

There was a *whoosh* and a *boom* from over by the National Gallery, followed by screams.

Alf's fireworks. She started towards the fountains, hoping to climb up on the rim and get a better look, pushing her way through the crowd past several tipsy soldiers and a man enthusiastically selling Churchill buttonhole badges, towards an elderly man in a black suit who was attempting to go in the same direction she was. If she could follow in the opening he made, she might be able to—

'Mr Humphreys!' she called, recognising him. She caught hold of his sleeve and he turned to see who had grabbed him.

'Hello!' she said, shouting over the din.

'Miss O'Reilly!' he shouted back, and then, as if he was greeting her at the door of St Paul's, 'How nice to see you!' He looked around at the swirling, shoving mob. 'I'm attempting to get to St Paul's. Dean Matthews rang me up and said there are hundreds gathering at the cathedral already, and I thought I'd best go and see if I could assist.'

He beamed at her. 'This is a wonderful night, isn't it?'

'Yes,' she said, looking around at the crowd. She had wanted to come here, to see this, ever since she was a first-year student. She'd been furious when she'd found out Mr Dunworthy had assigned it to someone else.

But if she'd come then, she would never have properly appreciated it. She'd have seen the happy crowds and the Union Jacks and the bonfires, but she'd have had no idea of what it meant to see the lights on after years of navigating in the dark, what it meant to look up at an approaching plane without fear, to hear church bells after years of air-raid sirens. She'd have had no idea of the years of rationing and shabby clothes and fear that lay behind the smiles and the cheering, no idea of what it had cost to bring this day to pass – the lives of all those soldiers and sailors and airmen and civilians. And of Mike and Mr Simms and Mrs Rickett and Sir Godfrey, who'd been killed two years ago on his way home from entertaining the troops. She'd have had no idea what this meant to Lady Denewell, who'd lost her husband and her only son, or to Mr Humphreys and the rest of the fire watch who'd worked so hard to save St Paul's and who, hopefully, would never know what had eventually happened to it.

'I feared this day would never come,' Mr Humphreys was saying.

'I know,' she said, thinking of all those dark days after Mike died, when she'd thought that no one was coming for them and that Polly was going to be killed, of the even darker days when she'd thought she and Alf and Binnie had lost the war.

'But it has all come right in the end,' Mr Humphreys said, and there was a *whoosh* and a *boom* over by the bonfire. Pigeons wheeled frantically up over the square.

'I think I'd best go and look for Alf and Binnie,' she said. *Before they kill someone.*

'And I'd best get to St Paul's,' he said, and in his best verger manner, 'we're having a service of thanksgiving tomorrow. I do hope you and your children will come.'

'We will,' she promised. *If Alf's not at the Old Bailey.*

Mr Humphreys pushed off through the crowd towards the Strand, and she started for the National Gallery, guided by further booms, an outraged 'You hooligan!' and a shower of sparks. A harried-looking mother with three little girls, all eating ice creams, went by. A conga line snaked past her, kicking.

She waited for it to pass, craning her neck, looking for the flare of fireworks, for Binnie's blonde head. 'Alf!' she called. 'Binnie!' She would never find them in this crowd.

'Were these what you were looking for, madam?' a man's voice said behind her, and she turned to find an Army chaplain with both children in tow, one hand on Binnie's shoulder and the other firmly gripping Alf's collar.

'Look who we found!' Alf said happily. 'The vicar!'

He had a two-day stubble of beard and looked exhausted. His

chaplain's uniform was covered in mud, and he was terribly thin.

'Mr Goode,' Eileen said, unable to take in the fact that he was here and well and safe. 'What are you doing here?'

'The *war's* over,' Alf said.

'They flew us over this afternoon,' the vicar said. 'Thank you for your letters. I wouldn't have made it without them.'

And I wouldn't have made it without yours, she thought.

'Aren't you going to tell him welcome home?' Binnie prompted.

'Welcome home,' Eileen said softly.

'What sort of welcome's that?' Binnie hooted, and Alf said, 'Ain't you gonna kiss him or nuffink? The *war's* over!'

'Alf!' Eileen said reprovingly. 'Mr Goode—'

'No, he's right. Kissing's definitely in order,' he said, and took her in his arms and kissed her.

'I *told* you,' Binnie said to Alf.

'I didn't think I had a hope of finding you in this crush,' the vicar said after he'd released her, 'and then I spotted Guy Fawkes here.' He gave Alf's shoulder a shake. 'Though it's a miracle I recognised either of them, they've changed so much. Alf's a foot taller, and Binnie's nearly grown.'

'Do you want to come with us?' Alf asked him. 'We're goin' to Piccadilly Circus.'

'We are *not*,' Binnie said. 'Mum said we're goin' to supper.'

'I think you'll find they haven't changed all that much,' Eileen said dryly.

'Good. I got through many a bad period by thinking of the time they painted blackout stripes on Farmer Brown's cattle.'

'Remember the time you come to the station and helped Mum get Theodore on the train?' Binnie asked.

'I do,' Eileen said. She looked at the vicar. 'You came to rescue me just in the nick of time.'

'If we don't go to Piccadilly Circus now,' Alf whined, 'they'll have turned off the lights!'

'How about supper in Piccadilly Circus?' the vicar said.

'Are you certain you want to go with us?' Eileen asked him. He looked ready to drop. 'Perhaps Mr Goode would like to go home and get some rest.'

'And miss VE Day?' He smiled at Eileen. 'Absolutely not.'

'This ain't the real VE Day,' Alf said. 'The real one's tomorrow.'

'Then we'll have to do that, as well,' the vicar said, and took Eileen's arm. 'So what's happening tomorrow, do you know?'

Continued rationing, she thought, *and such serious food shortages the Americans will have to send us care packages, and then Hiroshima and the Cold War and the oil wars and Denver and pinpoint bombs and the Pandemic. And the Beatles and time travel and colonies on the Moon. And nearly fifty more Agatha Christie novels.*

Alf tugged at her sleeve. 'The vicar said, "What's 'appenin' tomorrow?"' he shouted over the cheering crowd.

'I have no idea,' Eileen said, and smiled up at the vicar.

'Well, come on. Let's see if there's still a war going on.'

GENERAL GEORGE S. PATTON 6 JULY 1944

LONDON – 19 APRIL 1941

Colin wanted to take the tube to St Paul's, but Polly, remembering the guard who'd prevented her from leaving during a raid, said, 'We can't risk getting trapped in the station. We need to walk there.'

'Is there a chance we can find a taxi?' Colin asked.

'In this? I doubt it. Where did you say the raids are tonight?'

'Over the docks,' he said, looking down the street, trying to work out which way to go.

She watched him as he stood there against the backdrop of fires and searchlights, intent on finding a way to get them to St Paul's. Like Stephen Lang, trying to think of a way to bring V-1s down. He looked so much like Stephen. Was that because their jobs had required the same determination and resourcefulness? Or might Stephen and Paige Fairchild have been two of his – what would they have been? – great-grandparents?

'Since most of the bombing will be near the Thames,' Colin said, 'I think the best plan is to take the Strand to Fleet Street.'

Mr Dunworthy shook his head. 'It's too easy to get lost in the maze of streets in the City.'

'He's right,' Polly said, remembering the night they'd tried to find Mr Bartholomew.

'The Embankment's the most direct route,' Mr Dunworthy said.

'But that's where the bombing is,' Polly objected.

'No, he's right,' Colin said, 'the majority of the bombs were east of Tower Bridge, and most of the raids occurred after midnight. So we need to hurry.'

'And we need to be as quiet as we can,' Polly said. 'We don't want a warden to catch us and drag us into a shelter.'

'You forget, *I'm* a warden,' Colin said, tapping his helmet. 'If he – or she – stops us, I'll simply tell them that I'm taking you somewhere safe. Which, as a matter of fact, I am.'

He led the way, supporting Mr Dunworthy and keeping close to the buildings. It had rained. The pavement shone with wetness, and, even though there were still clouds, the sky directly overhead was clear. In the wake of the searchlights, she could see stars.

As they neared Trafalgar Square, Colin said, 'I hope it's less crowded than the last time I was here.'

'You came to VE Day to find me?'

He nodded. 'I knew I wouldn't be able to find you because I *hadn't* found you, but at that point I was willing to try anything. And I wanted to see you.'

'And did you?' she asked, thinking of Colin somewhere in that crowd, searching for her.

'No, some wretched child tossed a firecracker at me and nearly blew my foot off. But it wasn't a total loss. I got kissed by a large number of pretty girls.' He grinned his crooked grin at her.

'Ah, not *quite* as crowded, I see,' he said as they came into the deserted square. The fountains had been shut off, and the lions slumbered in the grey and silver silence. Even the pigeons were asleep.

Sleeping Beauty's palace, Polly thought, and its spell seemed to fall on them. They passed silently through the square and down to the Strand, moving like wraiths through the darkened, deserted streets.

They ran into several diversion barricades and had to go around, till Polly was thoroughly lost, but Colin seemed to know exactly which way to go. Twice, at crossings, Colin took Polly's arm to keep her from pitching off the kerb, and once, on an uneven brick pavement, he took her hand. Otherwise he didn't touch her, though even in the blackest lanes, when she couldn't see him at all, she was intensely aware of his presence.

It grew lighter as they neared the Thames. The searchlights were blunted against the overcast sky, and the fires from the docks stained the clouds pink, so they were able to see their way more easily. The diversions had forced them further west than their original plan. The twin spires of Westminster Abbey lay directly ahead of them, and beyond the Abbey, the tower of Big Ben.

'It's half past eleven,' Colin said as they went down the steps to the Embankment. 'We need to hurry,' and they set off quickly along the walled walk, following the curve of the river. The air should have smelled of mud and fish, but it didn't. It was cool and clean and smelled of rain. And once, lilacs. They walked quickly, silently, past the Houses of Parliament and Westminster Bridge and Cleopatra's Needle. *I'm seeing all this for the last time*, Polly thought.

Mr Dunworthy halted for a moment to look at the House of Commons, which would be gutted in May, and she wondered if he felt the same way. She had worried the long journey would be too much for him, but he showed no signs of tiring, though he still leaned on Colin's arm, so she was concerned when Colin said, 'We need to stop for a moment,' and led Mr Dunworthy over to an iron bench set against the Embankment's wall.

'I can go on,' Mr Dunworthy protested.

Colin shook his head. 'You sit down, too, Polly. Before we go through, I need to tell you something.'

And she knew that look. She had seen it before on Miss Laburnum's face the night Mike died, on Mr Dunworthy's when he told her he'd destroyed the future.

You'll only be able to get one of us out, she thought. *Or you won't be able to go with us.* She held on to the ironwork arm of the bench, bracing herself.

'I didn't save you by myself,' Colin said. 'I had help. From Michael Davies.'

'One of the messages he put in the paper got through,' Polly said.

'Yes. It was a message he wrote in 1944—'

'1944?' Polly said. 'But—'

'He wrote it while working with British Intelligence on Fortitude South. He wasn't killed that night in Houndsditch. He faked his death so he could try to find Denys Atherton and get word to Oxford.'

Mike's not dead – but that's good news, she thought, and looked over at Mr Dunworthy, but the expression on his face was the same as on Colin's. Whatever the bad news was, Colin had already told him, and she thought suddenly of them standing there in the theatre's aisle when she came back from changing her clothes, and of Eileen's wiping away tears.

'Tell me,' she said.

'It was a newspaper engagement notice.' He smiled wryly. 'Announcing the engagement of Polly Townsend to Flight Officer Colin Templer. His job was writing false newspaper articles and classified advertisements and letters to the editor for the local newspapers, but some of them were also coded messages to us.'

Eileen was right, she thought, *there were things going on behind the scenes that we knew nothing about.*

'So I began looking for other messages,' Colin said. He told them about finding out everything he could about Fortitude South, finding out what name Davies had been using and where he'd been stationed.

'And you went through to get him,' Polly said. 'But you weren't in time.'

He nodded. 'We tried, but we couldn't get the drop to open

till after—' He didn't finish what he'd been going to say. 'We were too late to save him,' he said instead.

But, as on that day in the pub with Mr Dunworthy, that wasn't all. There was still bad news to come.

And then she knew what it was – had on some level always known. 'He was killed by a V-1,' she said, and didn't need to see Colin's face to confirm it. 'In a newspaper office in Croydon.'

'Yes.'

'I should have stayed with him,' she murmured. 'I shouldn't have gone off to help Paige. If I'd stayed with him, I could have—'

Colin shook his head. 'Even we couldn't save him. He was too badly injured. But the tourniquets you tied kept him alive long enough to tell us that you'd still been alive when he left in January of 1941 and that Eileen was with you.'

So Colin had gone to find Eileen after the war, and she'd told him where they were. Mike had got them out, just as he'd promised he would. But at what a cost!

'I should have known it was him,' she said.

Colin shook his head. 'He was doing his best to keep you from finding out. His one thought was rescuing you. And if you hadn't gone, I couldn't have got him out of there and back to Oxford.'

You were the person in the ambulance from Brixton, Polly thought, looking at Colin. There was nothing of the impetuous, impossible boy she'd known in the man standing in front of her now, and nothing of the careless, charming Stephen Lang.

Colin sacrificed himself, too, she thought despairingly. How much of his youth, how many years, had he given up to come and find her, to fetch her home? *I am so sorry. So sorry.*

'Michael insisted on telling me everything he knew about where you were before he'd let me take him through to Oxford,' Colin said. 'He was afraid once he got to hospital, he wouldn't have the chance. He would have been so glad to know he got you out.' He smiled at her. 'And if I'm going to do that, we'd better go.'

She nodded wearily. Colin helped Mr Dunworthy get slowly to his feet and they set off again, following the rose-coloured river, guided by the drone of planes and the *crump* of bombs and the deadly, starry sparkle of incendiaries, till they came at last to Ludgate Hill. And there above them at the end of the street stood St Paul's, silver against the dark sky, the ruins all around it hidden by the darkness or transformed to enchanted gardens.

'It's beautiful,' Colin breathed. 'When I was here in the seventies, it was totally hidden by concrete buildings and car parks.'

'The seventies?'

'1975, actually,' he said. 'The year they declassified the Fortitude South papers. I'd been here earlier – I mean, later – earlier *and* later – in the eighties. We couldn't get anything before 1960 to open or anything after 1995 when we could have gone online, so I had to do it the hard way. I came here to search the newspaper archives and the war records for clues to what might have happened.'

Colin, who had wanted to go to the Crusades, spending – how long? – in archives and libraries and dusty newspaper morgues.

'And you found the engagement announcement,' Mr Dunworthy said.

'Yes. I also found your death notice, Polly.'

'Mine?' Polly said. 'But I checked the *Times* and the *Herald*. It wasn't—'

'It was in the *Daily Express*. It said you'd been killed at St George's, Kensington.'

How must Colin have felt, reading that, all alone and eighty years from home? And how many years had he sat there in archives, hunched over volumes of yellowing newspapers, over a microfiche reader?

'But you didn't stop looking,' Polly said.

'No. I refused to believe it.'

Like Eileen, Polly thought.

'I had a bit more trouble hanging onto the belief that you were alive after Michael Davies told me you and Eileen were at Mrs Rickett's, and it had been bombed.' He smiled at her.

'But you didn't stop looking.'

'No, and you weren't dead. And neither was Mr Dunworthy. At least for the moment. But the sooner I get you both back to Oxford, the better I'll feel. Let's go,' he said, and hurried them towards St Paul's.

Halfway there, Mr Dunworthy stopped and stood there on the pavement, his head down.

Oh no, Polly thought. *Not now, not this close.* 'Are you all right?' she asked.

'I ran into her here,' Mr Dunworthy said, pointing down at the pavement. 'The Wren.'

'Lieutenant Wendy Armitage,' Colin said, 'currently working at Bletchley Park. One of Dilly's girls. She helped crack Ultra's naval code. Come along. It's nearly midnight.'

They hurried on up the hill. 'We need to go in the north door,' Colin said, and started across the courtyard.

Mr Dunworthy pulled him back. 'The watch'll see you. They're still up on the roofs. This way,' he whispered, and led the way around the perimeter of the courtyard, keeping to the shadows, till they were even with the porch.

'We still have to cross that open space,' Colin whispered, pointing to the thirty feet between them and the steps.

'We wait for the next bomber,' Mr Dunworthy said. 'They'll look up at the sky, and we can make a dash for it. Here comes a bomber.' And he was right, Colin and Polly both instinctively looked up at the drone of its engines.

'Now,' Mr Dunworthy said, his voice scarcely audible above the Dornier's roar, and started off across the open space.

Colin grabbed Polly's hand and they shot across it after him and up the steps, past the star-shaped burn mark where the incendiary had been, past the place where she and Mike and

Eileen had sat on the morning of the thirtieth, up to the porch she had darted across that first day when the rescue squad was defusing the UXB and under the porch's concealing shadows to the north door. He pulled the heavy handle.

It wouldn't open. 'It's locked,' Colin said. 'What about the Great West Door?'

'It's only open on important occasions,' Mr Dunworthy said, as if this wasn't the most important occasion of his life.

'The side door to the Crypt should be unlocked,' Colin said, and started back towards the steps.

'No, wait,' Polly said, 'some of the fire watch may be down there. We need to try the south door first.' She ran lightly along the porch and yanked on the handle. It wouldn't open either. But it was only stuck, as it had been on the night of the twenty-ninth. When Colin gripped the handle too, the door opened easily. 'Mr Dunworthy,' he whispered, beckoning, and pushed him and then Polly through into the dark vestibule.

The cathedral, in spite of the spring weather and the nearby fires, was as cold as winter and very dark.

'Hear anything?' Colin whispered, pulling the door silently shut behind them.

'No,' Polly whispered back. Only the audible hush St Paul's always had. The sound of space and time. 'I know the way,' she said softly and led them up the south aisle. There was enough light from the fire-lit clouds and the searchlights to navigate by, but only just.

The long walk, and that last sprint across to the porch, had taken its toll on Mr Dunworthy. He was badly winded, and leaned heavily on Colin's arm. Polly led them past the spiral staircase she'd fled up the night of the twenty-ninth, the chapel where they'd held Mike's funeral. Only he hadn't really been dead.

No, that was wrong – he'd died that night in Croydon, before she ever came to the Blitz.

Up the aisle, past the blown-out windows to the bay where

she'd found Mr Dunworthy. She looked towards the niche where *The Light of the World* hung, as if she expected the golden-orange lantern to be glowing in the darkness, but it was too dark to see it, or the painting.

No, there it was. She could just make out the white robe, insubstantial as a ghost, and the pale gold of the flame within the lantern. And then, as if the flame were growing brighter, lighting the air around it, she began to be able to see the door and Christ's crown of thorns, and finally his face.

He looked resigned, as though he knew that wretched door – to where? Home? Heaven? Peace? – would never open, and at the same time he seemed resolved, ready to do his bit even though he couldn't possibly know what sacrifices that would require. Had he been kept here, too – in a place He didn't belong, serving in a war in which he hadn't enlisted – to rescue sparrows and soldiers and shopgirls and Shakespeare? To tip the balance?

'What's that light?' Mr Dunworthy whispered as the aisle grew brighter, and after a moment's tense waiting, 'It's someone with a torch.'

'No, it's not,' Colin said. 'It's the drop. It's opening.' He hurried them up the aisle to the dome.

We should have more than enough time, Polly thought. The shimmer was just beginning to brighten.

But she'd forgotten about the damage from the bomb. The huge crater in the centre of the transept was still there, and piled around it, heaps of splintered wood, broken columns and smashed masonry. Which they would have to climb over to reach the drop.

An attempt had been made to begin the clean-up, but that had only made it worse. They'd taken the sandbags that had protected the statues and piled them and stacks of wooden folding chairs across the entrance to the transept as a barricade and tossed the broken timbers and splintered rafters to the sides of the crater, in just the place where they needed to cross.

And the shimmer was beginning to grow and spread, filling

the transept. None of the fire watch must still be down in the Crypt, or they'd have seen the shimmer. When Polly leaned over the edge of the hole, she could see all the way down to the Crypt's floor.

Colin climbed up on the wreckage and turned to reach for Polly's hand.

'No, Mr Dunworthy needs to go first,' she said. 'His deadline's sooner than mine.'

Colin nodded. 'Sir?' he said, but Mr Dunworthy wasn't listening. He'd turned and was looking back out at the dome, now golden in the growing light of the shimmer, and at the shadowy reaches of St Paul's beyond.

He can't bear to leave it, Polly thought, *knowing he'll never see it again. Like I can't bear to leave Eileen and Sir Godfrey and Miss Laburnum and all the rest of them.*

But when Colin said, 'Mr Dunworthy, we need to hurry,' and he turned back to them, he was smiling fondly. Like Mr Humphreys, leading her around the cathedral, showing her all the treasures which had been removed for safekeeping.

Perhaps that's how I should think of them, Polly thought, *the troupe and Miss Snelgrove and Trot. And Sir Godfrey*. Not as lost to her, but as removed to this moment in time for safe-keeping.

Which was fine for Mr Humphreys and Hattie and Nelson, who belonged here. But not for Eileen, who'd only stayed here to save her. *I can't bear to think of her sacrificing her life for me.*

'Mr Dunworthy?' Colin said. 'Polly? It's time.'

'I know,' Mr Dunworthy said, and let Colin help him over the barricade and across the rubble, Polly clambering after them in case Mr Dunworthy slipped, in case something went wrong.

'Be careful,' Colin called back to her as they climbed over the wreckage. 'I nearly killed myself on this when I came through. It's unstable.'

Like history, she thought, *balanced always on a knife's edge, threatening always to come tumbling down at the slightest misstep, to pitch them into the abyss.*

They had only a few yards to go, but it seemed to take forever. The rubble slanted down towards the hole and they had to grab for the statues and use them as handholds as they went. Polly clutched at a statue of an Army officer and then at the memorial to Captain Faulknor that Mr Humphreys had talked so much about. The ships Faulknor had bound together stood in bas-relief behind him as he slumped forward into the arms of Honour, dying. Unaware that he'd won the battle.

Like Mike.

The shimmer was growing rapidly brighter, filling the entire end of the transept, illuminating the smashed doors, the broken columns, the shattered glass as Colin helped Mr Dunworthy over the last few feet of rubble. It began to flare.

We'll never make it in time, Polly thought, stepping quickly onto a rafter. It broke, and she lurched forward, hands out, and her other foot plunged through the stacked, splintered wood. And caught.

No. Not now.

She leaned against the dying Faulknor, grabbed onto Honour's arm and twisted her ankle, trying to free her foot. Her shoe was stuck fast. *It's the Forrest all over again*, she thought.

Colin had leapt lightly down off a chunk of broken stone and had helped Mr Dunworthy – who looked like he might not make it – down off the pile of rubble, and was leading him over to the brightness in front of the door. He glanced back at Polly, saw her and started back towards her.

'Go with him!' Polly called softly across the rubble. 'I'll come next time. Go!'

He shook his head, said something to Mr Dunworthy and stepped back away from the shimmer, out of its reach.

'Colin, go—'

'I'm not going anywhere without you,' he said, and the shimmer brightened to a white-hot flame.

It looks exactly like an incendiary, Polly thought. It lit Mr Dunworthy's face and then hid it, obliterating it, and the light began to fade, to shrink. Mr Dunworthy was no longer there.

He made it, Polly thought. *He's safely home.* A weight seemed to lift off her. *But Mike didn't make it. Eileen didn't. They both sacrificed themselves for you. And so did Colin.*

He was already clambering back over the wreckage to her. 'Stay there,' he whispered.

'I haven't any choice,' she said. 'My foot's stuck.'

'And you'd have let me go through and leave you here?' he said angrily. 'Is your foot injured?'

'No, it's my shoe. It's caught. Careful,' she warned as he hurried to her.

He knelt beside her and began shifting timbers aside.

'Take care *you* don't get stuck,' Polly said.

'You're a fine one to talk.' He broke off the end of a wooden slat, pried another rafter up with it, reached down into the hole, and took hold of her ankle. 'Do you care about your shoe, Cinderella?'

'No.'

'Good.' She could feel him yanking on her foot and then pulling up on whatever was holding it down, and her bare foot came suddenly free.

He straightened. 'All right now, let's go before anything else—' he said, and the rafter he'd pushed aside went clattering suddenly down the pile of rubble with an unholy crash and into the crater.

'Oh Christ! Hurry! No, not that way.' He pushed her back across the rubble in the direction of the transept's entrance. 'If someone comes, there's nowhere to hide in there.'

They clambered quickly across the wood and broken stone. *And please don't let one of us get caught again*, she thought.

The shimmer was fading rapidly. By the time they were safely back down on the floor – which, thankfully, wasn't as strewn with glass on this side – and over the barricade, it was nearly gone.

'What's the best place to hide?' Colin whispered. 'The choir?'

'No,' she said. 'There's no way out.' She grabbed his hand, and they darted across the nave and down the south aisle. They could hide in the Chapel of St Michael and St George, behind the prayer stalls—

Colin grabbed her around the waist and thrust her behind a pillar. 'Shh,' he whispered against her ear. 'I hear footsteps.'

She listened. 'I don't—' she began, and then did hear them. Footsteps from inside the main stairway. And a flash from a torch.

They ducked further behind the pilaster and pressed against it, listening. The sound of footsteps came out onto the floor, into the north transept, and there was another flash of light. *He's looking at the wreckage*, Polly thought.

More footsteps, and a wide sweep of light as he shone the torch slowly around the transept.

'How much longer till the drop opens again?' Polly whispered to Colin.

'Twelve or thirteen minutes.' It wouldn't open if the fire-watcher was still there, of course, but they were running out of time. When the all-clear went, the men would come down from the roofs, and from then on there'd be men in the Crypt and going off-duty. She remembered the firewatchers on the morning after the twenty-ninth walking out through the nave, standing on the steps talking. And Mr Dunworthy had said they made morning rounds, checking for incendiaries and damage.

Now the firewatcher was shining the torch up at the ceiling to see if something had fallen.

Leave, Polly said silently, but it was forever before the torch finally switched off and the footsteps went back upstairs.

They faded away, but Colin still didn't move. He went on standing there, pressing her against the stone, his arm still around her, waiting. She could feel his breath against her cheek, feel his heart beating.

'I think he's gone,' he whispered finally, his mouth against her hair, 'more's the pity.'

And she felt her heart lift.

But how could even love repay him for the years, the youth he'd sacrificed for her?

'I wish we could stand here forever,' he said, pulling away from her, 'but we'd better—' There was a flicker of light. 'He's back.'

Colin pushed her behind the pillar. And a moment later he said, 'That's not a torch. It's the shimmer. The drop's already opening again.'

'No, it isn't,' Polly said, 'it's outside. A flare, I think.' But it must have been an incendiary, because a yellow-orange light began to fill the aisle.

She hadn't realised they were in the bay that held *The Light of the World*. As the light grew, as orange as the light inside the lantern, she could see the painting more clearly than she ever had. And Mr Humphreys was right. There was something new to see every time you looked at it.

She had been wrong in thinking Christ had been called up against his will to fight in a war. He didn't look – in spite of the crown of thorns – like someone making a sacrifice. Or even like someone determined to 'do his bit'. He looked instead like Marjorie had looked telling Polly she'd joined the Nursing Service, like Mr Humphreys had looked filling buckets with water and sand to save St Paul's, like Miss Laburnum had looked that day she came to Townsend Brothers with the coats. He looked like Captain Faulknor must have looked, lashing the ships together. Like Ernest Shackleton, setting out in that tiny boat across icy seas. Like Colin had looked helping Mr Dunworthy across the wreckage.

He looked … contented. As if he was where he wanted to be, doing what he wanted to do.

Like Eileen had looked, telling Polly she'd decided to stay. Like Mike must have looked in Kent, composing engagement announcements and letters to the editor. *Like I must have looked there in the rubble with Sir Godfrey, my hand pressed against his heart. Exalted. Happy.*

To do something for someone or something you loved, England or Shakespeare or a dog or justice or the Hodbins or history – wasn't a sacrifice at all. Even if it cost you your freedom, your life, your youth.

She turned to look at Colin. He was looking uncertainly at her, and his soot-smudged face was as open to her as hers had been to Sir Godfrey. 'Colin, I—' she said and stopped, amazed.

She hadn't seen him clearly either. She'd been so intent on finding in his face echoes of the seventeen-year-old boy she'd known, so entranced by his resemblance to Stephen Lang, that she hadn't seen what was so obviously there. Though Eileen clearly had.

No wonder Eileen had said, 'You know I didn't go back.' And no wonder Colin had looked at her after she'd said, 'Colin knows I stayed, don't you?' for that long, silent moment before he'd said, 'Yes, I know.'

How could Polly not have seen the resemblance before? It was right there. No wonder, at the last, that Eileen had hugged Polly and said, 'It's all right. I'll always be with you.' No wonder she'd called Colin, 'My dear boy.'

Oh, my dear friend, Polly thought, and the light in Christ's face seemed to deepen, to grow more bright—

'The shimmer's starting,' he said gently. 'We need to go.'

Polly nodded and turned back to *The Light of the World* for one last look. She kissed her fingers and pressed them gently against the picture, and then she and Colin ran hand in hand like children up the aisle and across the nave.

Colin helped her over the barricade, and then they clambered onto the wreckage and across the precarious timbers, holding on to Faulknor, on to Honour and each other, picking their way